CHILD OF FORTUNE

Norman Spinrad

BANTAM BOOKS
TORONTO · NEW YORK · LONDON · SYDNEY · AUCKLAND

CHILD OF FORTUNE
A Bantam Book / August 1985

Library of Congress Cataloging in Publication Data

Spinrad, Norman.
    Child of fortune.

    I. Title.
PS3569.P55C47   1985   813'.54   84-91728
ISBN 0-553-05089-3

Published simultaneously in the United States and Canada

PRINTED IN THE UNITED STATES OF AMERICA

MV   0 9 8 7 6 5 4 3 2 1

For
PHILIP K. DICK

Some stand on the shoulders of giants
Some peer through the heart of a friend
Some lives have stories
Whose spirit never ends

CHILD OF FORTUNE

A Histoire of the Second Starfaring Age
by Wendi Shasta Leonardo

INTRODUCTION

And so, after half a lifetime and some score histoires telling the eternal tale in all its timebound incarnations, I venture herein at last to speak my own wanderjahr's story from the memories of the heart.

Wandering tinker and masterless samurai, troubadour and hippie, Rom and Arkie, Zen hermit and cowboy—uncounted avatars of the archetypal wanderkind have followed the Yellow Brick Road which wanders eternally through space and time from the villages and forests of prehistoric Earth to the San Franciscos and Samarkands of myth and history, via the first arkologies to brave the starry seas at a sublight crawl, and thence to the celestial cities of the far-flung worlds of men.

The singers and the avatars pass, but the song goes on, for the story is always the same: that of the wanderjahr, the eternal journey from childhood to maturity through the wondrous and terrible chaos of the region between.

This too is a histoire of that archetype as it is incarnated in our own era: the Child of Fortune whom we have all been or will become. But herein will the detached observer shed all pretense of objectivity, for this is *my* name tale's story, this is *my* wanderjahr's song.

So in this modern version of the timeless histoire, our ingenue begins the tale as the little Moussa on Glade, and the Yellow Brick Road she follows leads from planet to planet, and she travels not by horse or motorad but by Void Ship. In this histoire as in all my others, you will meet the avatars of the great and eternal journey of youth into maturity, of spirit into culture, of the comrades of the passage from what we dream into what we are destined to become.

But here you will meet them as did this Child of our Second Starfaring Age: as friends and lovers, freeservants and ruespielers, Charge Addicts, Honored Passengers, domos and mages, and the wandering children of all the worlds of men who were ourselves.

So this, my own wanderjahr's story, is also the tale of that journey which goes on above and below the historical annals. In the Second Starfaring Age we call that journey, as in another era deep in the past, the wanderjahr, though for some it is measured in weeks and for others in lifetimes. By whatever name that passage has been called—wanderjahr, summer of love, grailquest, voyage d'ark—until I took the freenom Wendi and began writing my histoires, it was a tale that what we have called "history" had ignored.

For "history" is the story of deeds done by those who have shaped the evolution of the species humaine, from the nameless hominid who crafted the first tool to the inventors of fire and the wheel, to the organizations that put the first humans into orbit and onto Earth's moon, to the builders of the arkologies that first brought men to the stars, to those who developed the Jump Drive out of the mysterious artifacts left by We Who Have Gone Before and thereby inaugurated our Second Starfaring Age. Those whose names are known to "history" have been scientists and explorers and politicians and generals and creative artists. They have elucidated the laws of nature, invented wondrous devices, established nations, waged wars, found new habitable worlds, created lasting works of art, and indeed have been those who recorded "history" itself. For "history" is the timebound story of the evolution of specific human societies.

But outside of history there is another story just as ancient, the story of that which has always existed outside, within, and as often as not in opposition to "society," yet which in another and deeper sense has carried the true esprit humaine forward to this day.

It has been called many things by many cultures. The

Romany Road. Bohemia. Counterculture. The Floating World. The Underground. Arkie Sparkie. Demimonde. Its denizens too have been known by many names, most of them pejorative. Ronin. Gypsies. Freaks. Wayfarers. Tinkers. Arkies.

Until the Second Starfaring Age, this eternal demimonde could be defined only by what it was not. A "culture" in essence consisted of the social, political, economic, cuisinary, linguistic, technological, and esthetic patterns shared in common by its citizens; on a deeper level, it was the consensus reality, the consciousness style which *defined* a "people." The demimonde, then, was the psychic heimat of those, who, through choice or fortune, existed within the spacial bounds of a culture but outside its consensus reality. Hence outside both "the law" and "history."

Here were to be found the criminals and social pariahs, the madmen and ethnic outcasts, the devotees of socially proscribed vices and the followers of gods other than those of the local tribe. But here too were the visionaries born outside their proper time, the artists who *created* new styles of consciousness, the seekers and the dreamers—in essence all those whose spirits could not be contained by the parameters of the consensus reality of their given social realm. Here was the heimat of Chaos in its eternal dialectic with Order, the Chaos out of which all new culture, hence history itself, has always evolved. Here, in other words, was the psychic heimat of the adventurous spirit of youth.

To the demimonde was drawn both the best and the worst of a culture's youth—the dreamers and the rebels, the idealists and the psychopaths, the artistic and the indolent, the seekers after vice and the seekers after Enlightenment.

Some sojourned a while in the realm of Chaos and emerged once more as history's movers and shapers. Some passed through their wanderjahr and grew only old. Some were lost forever. A few remained young forever until the day they died.

But all too many adolescents in all too many cultures never passed through Chaos at all. They were born, they were acculturated, they were schooled, they took up their adult stations in life, passed through an ill-defined period of mid-life angst, resigned themselves to old age, and died, without ever walking the Yellow Brick Road, indeed without ever understanding what it was that they had missed in their lives.

Unwritten though it was until I began creating my histoires, this too is now a kind of history, in the sense that it is a story of humanity past.

Today, in our Second Starfaring Age, that ancient concept of "culture" as the prison of individual consciousness is happily gone. As each of us speaks our own sprach of Lingo, so is each human consciousness its own self-created style of reality, unique to itself, yet part of the infinitely complex vie humaine.

For each of us passes through our wanderjahr as a Child of Fortune; rare indeed is the child of our age who becomes a man or woman without having passed through the region between.

What is the greatest glory and proudest achievement of the Second Starfaring Age? The Jump Drive which enables our Void Ships to traverse the great and empty distances between the stars and enables us thereby to spread our species to hundreds of worlds? That humanity has finally put war and chauvinism far behind it? Our total knowledge of mass-energy phenomena?

I say that the greatest achievement of the Second Starfaring Age, that which sets us above and apart from all previous human civilizations in spirit and not merely in artifact, is that *our* civilization alone has had the wisdom to decree the wanderjahr for all. For while some of us create histoires and some of us are Void Captains or mages or political leaders, und so weiter, *all of us* have been *Children of Fortune.*

Indeed, is not the choosing of one's freenom the declaration of the lifeswork to come, and is the freenom not chosen at the end of the wanderjahr, and is not the wanderjahr the very process by which we, as Children of Fortune, find our destiny and ourselves?

Moreover, since each of us has tasted the freedom and the peril of the Child of Fortune, indeed since each of us remains a Child of Fortune until we have surfeited ourselves with the vie, unlike parents of previous ages, we seek not to chain the child to the cradle, the eaglet to the nest, we envy not our children the Golden Summer we ourselves have known and relinquished only voluntarily when we have found our own true names. And here is the story of mine, of how the little Moussa became the very Wendi Shasta Leonardo who now tells this, her wanderjahr's tale.

Once within our time, on a planet not so very far away . . .

1 I was born on Glade, a planet, like most of the far-flung worlds of men, of no particular fame in starfaring lore, and no economic significance in the transstellar scheme of things. Like most of the worlds of men, Glade is an almost entirely self-contained economic unit, which is to say that its plains, rivers and seas provide sufficient nutriment to support a healthy human population of about 300 million without the need to import significant amounts of trace elements from other stellar systems, and its mineral wealth, supplemented by the occasional asteroid, provides a sufficient raw materials base for its industrial economy.

Verdad, through hindsight's eye I can thus dryly state that I was born and grew up on a world ordinaire, not unlike hundreds of such worlds warmed by G-type suns. But my girlhood perception of my heimat's centrality to the larger scheme of things was quite a grander matter, for I was also born and raised as a child of Nouvelle Orlean, considered by all on Glade to be the jewel of our planet, and no more so than by the citizens of the city itself.

Like its legendary Terrestrial namesake, Nouvelle Orlean was built upon the ocean-mouth delta of a great continent-draining river system, but naturellement, in an age of primarily aerial transport, the original settlers had not chosen the site for its

1

geographic significance as an ideal nexus of river and ocean commerce. Rather had the settlers of Glade chosen the venue for our planet's metropole along esthetic—and indeed perhaps spiritual—parameters from the outset.

Glade, by the standards of human genetic parameters, is a somewhat cool world, capped by mountains of glacial ice at either pole, and dominated by less than simpatico semitundra in its middle latitudes, so that the most favorable zone of human habitation is the tropics, where the bulk of the populace is therefore to be found. Portions of three continents lie within this optimal climatic zone. Of these lands, southern Arbolique is clearly the geographic heimat of the human spirit on the planet.

Arbolique is the mightiest continent of Glade in more ways than one. It extends from the northern ice cap to just short of the equator at its southernmost point at the tip of the Culebra Peninsula, and the Grand Massif begins beneath the polar ice, rises into a towering longitudinal cordillera of snow-capped and moss-crusted rock, then splits into eastern and western chains as it marches down the continent nearly to the shores of the tropical sea.

Between these two mountain chains lies the Great Vale, a broad and fertile central valley veined and subdivided by chains of lesser mountains and hills, the whole more of an enormous mountain meadow than a peneplain, beginning in the north at an elevation of some three thousand meters and reaching sea level only at the delta mouth of the Rio Royale, the mighty central river whose headwaters begin as myriad lesser streams draining the ice cap runoff, and which foams and roars over great falls and wild rapids through the passes of the high cordillera, finally debouching into the sea via its delta as a broad stream of clear blue fresh water visible from the air against the contrasting greener ocean waters many miles from the shoreline.

Nouvelle Orlean lies somewhat upstream from the lowland marshes of the true alluvial delta of the Rio Royale, at a point where the wide and placid river flows through a mild canyon cut through the low coastal mountains. Here there are narrow river flats on both sides of the Royale, and immediately behind them loom hills and river cliffs crusted with the gnarly and intergrown trees of the Bittersweet Jungle and dripping with lianafungi, crawlervines, and saphroflors, like brilliant and varicolored molds

2

festooning huge green mounds of ancient bread. Here, too, there are islands in the stream, most mere sand and mud bars held together by their crowns of jungle growth, but some large enough to hold whole arrondissements of the city.

Nouvelle Orlean spreads itself on both banks of the river, on the islands, both natural and crafted, inbetween, and some folk have chosen to build manses on the jungled heights above. Beneath the palisades on both banks of the river, tall buildings rise, sheathed for the most part in numerous subtle tints of mirror-glass, and between them and the river on either side are tree-shrouded esplanades lined with kiosks, restaurants, and pavilions. Above and behind the east and west bas-corniches, haute-corniches wind among the jungle-shaded manses of the Hightowns.

But the heart, and indeed the soul, of the city, for all who style themselves true Orleaners, is Rioville, the magical archipelago spreading across the Royale and uniting what would otherwise be twin cities into one. Here the buildings have been kept low and rambling, in harmony with the jungle and wooded parklands which have been allowed to occupy most of the terrain, both for esthetic effect, and in order to bind the islands together so that the river will not sweep them away. Rioville architecture relies upon wood, brick, and stone, or at least on excellent ersatzes of natural materials, though not to the point of excluding wide expanses of windowglass overlooking every vista. Porches, breezeways, gazebos, open pavilions, and interior rooms that fling open whole walls to the natural realm while inviting vegetation inside are also very much in the Rioville mode. As are the hundreds of foot-bridges which span the smaller channels and the thousands of small boats of every type and fancy which give the city the ambiance of fabled Venice of ancient lore, and not without deliberate homage to the spirit of the Doges.

By custom with greater moral force than law, the arrondissements of Rioville are given over entirely to the realms of art, leisure, cultural endeavor, pleasure, and tantra, while most of the plyers of these trades have residences within these precincts, as well as those of more prosaic callings who have the desire and wherewithal to live within its ambiance of perpetual fiesta.

My parents had built a rambling house on the low crown of a small island near the north end of Rioville close by the center of the river, and for the first eighteen years of my life, I spent many late afternoons and early evenings on the second story porch, watching the sun set behind the western Hightown, the lights of the manses winking on from between the folds of the deeply shadowed jungle as the stars slowly emerged in the purpling sky above and the mirrored buildings of the eastern bank flashed deep orange as they reflected the sunset like a sheath of flame across the island-studded waters.

From my little aerie, I could look north up the river as it poured through the gorge that reached up into the icebound crown of the continent, and sometimes a fragrant wind, redolent of jungle vegetation and oncoming night, would blow down from what seemed to me at the time the very roof and mystery of the world, and I could inhale deeply and imagine that I was breathing in the very spirit of the planet. On other evenings, a tongue of fog might blow in from the sea, enveloping Rioville in perfumed billows of dream stuff, turning the lights of the city into the faerie fires of a Brigadoon rising ghostly and triumphant from the mists.

And at all times, after night had finally fallen, and the full panoply of stars had come out, and one could scarcely tell where the stellar concourse ended and the lights of the Hightown began, I would walk to the other end of the porch and gaze out over the islands of Rioville itself, a carpet of multicolored jewels flung across the waters, a brilliant spiderwork of illuminated bridges, the running lights of thousands of boats bobbing in the currents, and wafting up on the sea breeze towards me, the faint, far-off music of the magical city, compounded of laughter, and sighs, and myriad voices, and the sounds of instruments, fiestas, and entertainments. At such times, I would grow giddy with the intoxicating aroma of Nouvelle Orlean itself, a heady brew compounded of dozens of cuisinary styles offered up by hundreds of restaurants, the perfumes of lovers, intoxicants, incenses, wood shavings, oil paints, leather, and the overwhelming nighttime effluvia of tropical flowers.

May the young girl that I then was therefore not be forgiven for supposing that she was favored by fate and blessed by fortune, a citizen of Xanadu and destiny's darling?

Moreover, as I grew from relatively innocent young girlhood into early pubescent flower, as the social relativities of Nouvelle Orlean society began to impinge upon my consciousness, my

4

sense of humility was hardly enhanced by the knowledge that my parents, far from being mere ordinary burghers of this extraordinary city, were figures of some local fame, if not quite the leading luminaries of the haut monde that I portrayed them as to my schoolmates.

My mother, Shasta Suki Davide, had herself been born in Nouvelle Orlean, and after spending her wanderjahr exploring the vie of an erotic adventurer, had studied for two years at the Academie Tantrique on Dravida, where she became an adept of the tantric arts both erotic and healing. Her freenom, Shasta, she had chosen upon completion of her studies homage à Nicole Shasta, a figure of considerable controversy in her day, who had first elucidated the mass-energy phenomena underlying the ancient metaphorical and metaphysical tantric principles and had thus founded the science my mother followed.

My father, Leonardo Vanya Hana, had been born on Flor del Cielo, and had spent only a rather brief period as a wandering Child of Fortune, for he was one of those rare people who seem to have known what they wish to become almost from birth, namely an inventor and fabricator of personal enhancement devices, several of which he had already created as a schoolboy.

Naturellement, the conclusion of his wanderjahr found him on Diana, perhaps the planet most famed for the production of just such personal amplifiers, where he secured employment in one of the leading fabriks as an artisan and sometime designer of same. His freenom, Leonardo, he had chosen somewhat grandly upon beginning this career homage à Leonardo Da Vinci, artist and inventor of the ancient Terrestrial Age, and legendary archetype of the fusion of esthetics and technology to which our Second Starfaring Age in general and my father in particular have always aspired.

My parents met on Diana, where my mother had gone as an itinerant tantric artiste and sometime healer, after having sojourned as same on several other planets. Already beginning to think more fondly of home and Nouvelle Orlean at the time, smitten by a pheromonic attraction to Leonardo whose mutuality was mightily enhanced by the puissance of her erotic artistry, and realizing that a marriage of tantric science and electronic personal enhancement might have as much to offer in the way of deepening and enhanc-

5

ing the practice of their respective arts as union in the personal sphere seemed to offer to their spirits, she had little trouble convincing Leonardo that the opportunity to live up to the grandeur of his freenom would be much greater on Glade than on Diana. And most particularly in Nouvelle Orlean, a city whose true charm was exceeded only by its own highly exaggerated sense of its own sophistication, where a personal enhancement mage from Diana would have considerable cachet no matter his modest former position on that planet, and where the relative state of the art would certainly insure his primacy.

So it is written, so it shall be done. Soon after arriving in Nouvelle Orlean, Leonardo was able to display for potential investors three personal enhancement devices entirely novel to Glade, if somewhat reminiscent of theoretical musings that had been current in the designers' workshops on Diana.

One was called the Voice, and established an electrophysiological loop between relevant cerebral centers and the larynx so that the wearer could by conscious craft and act of will impart subliminal sonics to song or speech that acted directly on the listeners' consciousness via the auditory apparatus, greatly enhancing the artistic puissance of singer or thespic artist, and not without value to salespersons either. Another was the Eye of Argus, tiny lenses of complexed gels worn over the pupils and electrolinked to the vision centers, so that the wearer could vary their optical properties through a wide range of focuses and wavelengths, and thus view directly microscopic realms, astronomical phenomena, the infrared and utraviolet spectrum, not to mention the interiors of distant boudoirs of amorous interest. Not the least arcane if perhaps the most fanciful and disreputable of the three was that which Leonardo dubbed the Gourmand's Delight, whereby glutton or exorbitant imbiber could willfully adjust his metabolism of an evening so that he might feast and drink to enormous excess and pay no consequence in girth or malaise the morning after.

Not only were these devices of immediate obvious marketability, they established the reputation of Leonardo Vanya Hana as an artificer from whom further wonders could be expected, and so my father found no lack of investors willing to finance the establishment of his boutique on favorable terms. Indeed, he would have been easily able to finance the establishment of a fabrik able to flood the planet with replicated wares at modest prices. This he eschewed for reasons of personal esthetics, preferring to remain a craftsman and artist modeling each device to the whim and fancy of individual clients rather than become a magnate of manufacture. Moreover, by maintaining the individuality of his wares and the mystique of personal craft in their production, he was able to keep their prices elevated into the realm of artistic pieces, just as a painter or sculptor who refuses to license reproduction maintains gallery prices for his originals.

My mother, meanwhile, gave occasional tantric performances at palaces of pleasure, but for the most part concentrated her attentions and energies on developing her skills and repute as a tantric healer, aided in this endeavor by my father's science and his intimate knowledge of the bioelectronics of the human nervous system.

After a time and the accumulation of sufficient funds, my parents decided to consolidate their professional venues and domestic menage by purchasing a small island and erecting upon it the house in which I was to grow up. The first story of this building was given over to Leonardo's boutique and Shasta's tantric salon, each presenting a public facade to an opposite side of the little island, but connected within via intermediary storerooms, common service areas, and a hallway. The second story, with its grand viewing porch, was given over to our living quarters, and was entered by a separate stairway which debouched into a garden entirely secluded from the commercial venues by a hedge of Purple Cloud trimmed into different topiary designs according to the mode of the season. On the occasion of my fifth birthday, when the possibility of retreating into my own private realm was deemed necessary to my development, a fanciful playhouse was built for me deep in a patch of Bittersweet Jungle in the nethermost reaches of the garden.

Here as a young girl would I spend many hours with young playmates, and many more with no other companionship than that of the moussas I soon learned to entice from the trees with bits and morsels from the breakfast table. Of all the native creatures of Glade, these cunning little mammals, small enough to fit in a child's cupped hands, and willing enough to remain there for the pettiest of bribes, have cozened themselves closer to the human heart than any other, for they are the common pets of childhood.

Though in truth, perhaps, it is as much the little human children of Glade who are the pets of the moussas, for these golden-furred, emerald-eyed, monkey-tailed, leaf-eared, primatelike rodents never survive in a cage or as domesticated house pets, sullenly fasting unto death in any form of captivity. Nor, although they abound throughout Nouvelle Orlean and the surrounding environs, thriving amidst the habitats of men, will they ever deign to descend from their trees to frolic with gross and clumsy adults, even to accept the choicest dainty. But put a child in a garden with a few scraps of bread or a berry or two, and the moussas will soon enough come a-calling. Indeed often, when through negligence I appeared empty-handed, the moussas of the garden, though they might chide me in their piping whistles for my thoughtless lack of hospitality, would nonetheless come down to play.

And like a little moussa myself, I would often, in the late afternoon or early evening, emerge from my garden retreat to play the pampered and cunning pet of the clients and friends of my parents. As the children of Glade imagine that the moussas chattered and capered for their amusement, so, no doubt, did the adults of my parents' salons imagine that the fey creature, whom everyone soon began to call kleine Moussa, herself frequented their precincts to amuse *them.*

But from the moment their kleine Moussa knew anything of significance at all, I, like the moussas of the garden, knew full well that these huge and marvelous beings, with their extravagant clothes, incomprehensible stories, strange and mysterious perfumes, and secret pockets of sweets, existed, like the garden, and the river, and the myriad wonderous sights and sounds and smells of Nouvelle Orlean, and indeed the world itself, to amuse *me.*

2 Thus did the little Moussa frolic through young girlhood with the creatures of the garden and the clients of her parents' trades and the favored children of these denizens of Nouvelle Orlean's haut monde. Though naturellement I was not yet capable of appreciating the rarefied and elite ambiance of my parents' salon until my basic schooling was well under way and I was deemed old enough to travel to the academy on my own and venture forth into the city with my playmates.

Then, of course, my awareness of my favored place in the scheme of things became somewhat keener than the reality itself. As I became interested in the wider world around me, and began first to listen to word crystals and then learned to read them for greater speed, as I was taught the rudiments of esthetics, acquainted with the history of our city and our planet and our species, as my teachers introduced me to the sciences, the mutational sprachs of human Lingo, the basic principles of mathematics, und so weiter, I began to perceive that the discourse that had swirled about my little head like so much moussas' babble chez mama and papa was in fact in good part an elevated and rarefied version of my various teachers' discourse at the academy.

This was a somewhat heady satori for a young girl of eight or nine, and not exactly conducive to humility in the schoolroom. While my teachers lectured on various subjects on a level deemed suitable for children by the maestros of developmental theory and commended simple texts thereon to my attention, at home, true maestros of the arts and sciences of which they were mere pedagogs were forever discussing the most esoteric aspects of these very same schoolroom subjects while awaiting my mother's ministrations or being fitted by my father or taking their ease with my parents and myself over wine and delicacies.

Moreover, as I began to wander the fabulous precincts of Rioville at leisure, alone or with my schoolmates, the concept of fame and renown began to impinge on my hitherto naive and entirely egalitarian weltanschauung. Sauntering into a gallery to idly peruse paintings or holos or worldbubbles, I would often discover that the creator of *this* one had bounced me on her knee, that Ari Baum Gondor, who had crafted the tiny ecospheres that set all these tongues wagging, was the very same Ari who had always been the source of my favorite sweets, that I had feasted only the night before with the artist whose paintings were deemed the finest of the season. Attending a concert or a songfest or a dance, I would often find myself enjoying performances by artists who had sung and capered for my private amusement since before I could remember. Libraires were well stocked with word crystals written by my tios and tantes, and I could easily enough dine in cuisinary salons presided over by chef maestros who sat at my own parents' table.

In short, I grew aware that humanity was divided into two subspecies: the famous and the anonymous, the creators of art, music, literature and science, and the mere consumers of same, the elite of the haut monde, and the generality of the vie ordinaire. And I, as my own eyes and ears so amply demonstrated, was a child of the former, one of destiny's special creatures by right of birth.

Which is not to say I became any more a monster of ego than the average ten-year-old, for the circle of playmates with which I traveled were children of the same ambiance, indeed many of their parents were the very maestros and celebrities whose easy intimacy fed my secret pride, and naturellement within the adult sphere of this haut monde, I was still indulged as a child rather than accepted as an equal power.

Even in the educational realm, this inner perception of my true place in the world was not without both its negative and positive consequences. On the one hand, my respect for the authority of my teachers was eroded by my free and easy congress with their intellectual and social superiors, and I was not above hectoring them from time to time with what I imagined was superior knowledge gleaned from bits and pieces of table talk. On the other hand, I had almost from birth dined on intellectual haute cuisine, and much true learning had actually been absorbed as it were by osmosis; further, what little ambition I then had lay in the direction of acceptance as an equal by the denizens of my parents' salon, and so I was at least motivated to avoid the public intellectual embarrassment of the unprepared student.

The overall result was that I was a skilled if shallowly motivated and not excessively diligent student, lacking any true passion for scholarly pursuits, content to breeze through my studies with a parsimony of effort, and quite innocent of any perception of the educational process as connected to spiritual, intellectual, or karmic goals.

As such, though at the time I would have been mightily offended at the generalization, I was typical of the preadolescent stage of our species, for the biochemical matrix of passion—whether intellectual, artistic, political, spiritual, or sexual—simply cannot be generated by the prepubescent human metabolism. Thus does the wisdom of passing through the wanderjahr before contemplating that deeper education which must be informed by passionate dedication to some true life's work extend from the social and spiritual clear down into the molecular realm.

Which is also why the onset of puberty effects a tumultuous series of psychic transformations quite literally akin to the effects of ingesting powerful psychoactive drugs. While the earliest and most obvious social and psychological manifestation of this biochemical revolution is the awakening of that most presentient of human passions, sexual lust, once the biochemical matrix of passion itself has evolved in a young girl's physiology, that molecular hunger for novelty, somatic excitation, and adventure of the spirit seeks its polymorphous fulfillment in every realm.

Biochemically speaking, adolescence is a loss of endocrine innocence in that it opens the human spirit to all the possibilities and dangers of passionate motivation denied to the juvenile metabolism. Yet at the same time, there is no more perfect naif than the newly

11

pubescent creature, who all at once perceives the world through eyes, ears, nostrils, and spirit radically heightened and transformed by this psychochemical amplification of the childhood mind.

In many primitive Terrestrial cultures, before psychesomics was a developed science or the bioelectronic basis of tantra elucidated, all sorts of bizarre and entirely counterproductive social mechanisms evolved, aimed at either "managing" these adolescent passions from the point of view of adults, suppressing their outward manifestations, or worse still, capturing, channeling, and perverting their energies in the service of theocratic dogmas, territorial aggressions, or the convenience of the adult body politic. Since the earliest, simplest, and somatically strongest of the nascent adolescent passions is of course sexual lust, most of these disastrous social control mechanisms revolved around delaying, transposing, or even entirely suppressing its natural amatory expression.

The results, of course, were exactly what modern psychesomics would predict—polymorphous adolescent rebellion against adult authority, violently separatist adolescent subcultures, excessive random indulgence in psychoactive substances without proper prior study of their effects, neurosis, depression, hysteria, the romanticization of suicide, militarism, cruelty to animals, and a scornful attitude towards scholarly pursuits.

Mercifully our Second Starfaring Age has long since put this torture of the innocent far behind it, and so my earliest experiments with satisfying this new somatic hunger were conducted, as was natural, convenient, and esthetically pleasing, in the playhouse of my parents' garden.

Of course I hardly considered myself a clumsy young experimenter in the amatory arts even on the occasion of my first passe de deux in that bucolic boudoir. Was I not, after all, the daughter of Shasta Suki Davide, tantric maestra? Had I not grown up steeped in the ambiance of her science? Had I not, out of childish curiosity, ofttimes perused the catalogs of positions long before the illustrations therein were capable of arousing any but theoretical interest?

Indeed I was. Indeed I had. Moreover, I was not so unmindful of the benefits of motivated study that I neglected to delve deeper into the texts when the motivation for such studies grew deliciously immediate. Nor did I neglect to interrogate my mother for anecdotal expertise or to persuade my father to offer up both his lore on human nervous physiology and his more general knowledge of how men might be blissfully transported.

Verdad, I must confess that I had determined to gain the enviable reputation of a fabled femme fetale while still a virgin, for not only would such a mystique among my peers enhance my perception of my own centrality, it would also insure me the amatory services of most any boy who piqued my interest.

For my first granting of favors, I made the perhaps somewhat calculating choice of a handsome boy of fourteen known as Robi; not only did his slim and nearly hairless body and wide blue eyes arouse the proper spirit within my loins, though a year older than I, he was still charmingly tentative with girls, albeit something of a braggart among his male friends by way of compensation.

I was not unaware that a truly impressive tantric performance for Robi—especially, if, as I suspected, he was still a virgin—would speedily become common lore among the boys of our mutual acquaintance, thereby establishing my mystique as a lover of puissance from my premiere performance.

Enticing Robi into my bower was a simple matter of issuing an unambiguous invitation in the presence of his fellows, though once we retired to my garden playhouse, his tentativeness was all too limply apparent despite his attempts at verbal bravado.

Undaunted by this phenomenon, which was well reported in the word crystals I had purused in preparation, I applied a simple sequence of digital and oral remedies which at first seemed to further discombobulate the pauvre petit with their no-doubt-unexpected level of tantric sophistication, but which soon enough transferred his attention from the uncertainties of the virgin psyche to the naturally firm resolve of the youthful lingam.

Once the natural man in Robi had been properly aroused, he became an enthusiastic if rather hasty and clumsy participant, achieving his own satisfaction in the most basic of tantric configurations with all too much ease, and then satedly supposing that the performance had reached an esthetically satisfying resolution.

When of course it had hardly properly begun, for I was determined to essay certainly no less than a dozen basic positions with several variations of each, to enjoy several tantric cusps of my own in the process, and not to relent until I was entirely

13

satisfied that he was thoroughly, totally, and finally exhausted beyond any hope of further arousal.

Though I lost count somewhere after the first four or five movements of the tantric symphony and probably did not achieve the first of my artistic goals, and though my still barely pubescent physiology left me far short of anything approaching platform orgasm, there was no doubt that the poor boy had been properly exhausted, for I was only persuaded to relent after his moans of pleasure had long since become pleas for surcease and his manhood openly confessed its surrender to the protoplasmic impossibility of rising to further challenge.

To say that Robi was constrained to crawl from our erotic encounter would be to descend to hyperbole, but in truth he staggered from the garden in something less than a triumphant strut, though to judge from subsequent events, his version of the affair would seemed to have gained considerably more machismo in the telling.

For I was soon the smug recipient of numerous displays of male courting behavior, from which smorgasbord of possible swains I chose carefully, venturing not to offer up my tantric performances to older, more experienced, and hence more critically acute connoisseurs of the art until my mystique was well established and my store of experience sufficient to insure that it would survive congress with boys whose dedication to the mastery of the tantric arts was no less serious and diligent than my own.

Then, at last, I was able to enter into liaisons in which the pleasure I sought and ofttimes received was equal to that which I offered up in the service of my continued lofty self-appraisal, and genuine mutual affection was thereby enabled to bloom on the tree of passion, though I was still far too enamored of my reputation as a tantric adept and still far too hungry for new experience to even contemplate entering into any compacts of undying love or sexual exclusivity.

Thus through the sexual realm did the dimension of male companionship enter my life and with it the dyadic explorations of the possibilities of adventures and passions beyond those of the boudoir, for just as even the most avid and athletic of lovers can scarcely pass more than a few hours daily in actual embrace, so the passionate adolescent spirit cannot confine its sphere of attention and its hunger for novelty and adventure to the erotic realm alone.

In this manner did the boudoir door also open into the wide world around me, for each lover was also a person entire, possessed of interests, passions, and even obsessions beyond the object of his amorous desire, and more than willing to share them with a venturesome friend.

And so did the kleine Moussa, without noticing the transition, cease to be a child content to frolic in a child's world and become a true adolescent whose garden was no longer that of the parental menage but Nouvelle Orlean itself and the countryside beyond.

With Genji did I begin to appreciate the variety of cuisinary styles to be found in Rioville and learn to distinguish the masterworks of the true chef maestro from mere cuisine ordinaire; so too did I gain some modest sophistication in the products of the vintner's art. Pallo was fairly obsessed with music, and with him I must have visited a hundred or more concert halls, tavernas, al fresco performances, and the like. My passage with Cort was a stormy and brooding one and my parents were not at all displeased when I grew tired of his company, for he was an afficionado of psychoactive chemicals with much more enthusiasm and reckless courage than accurate lore or tasteful discrimination. Ali flew Eagles—great helium-filled gliding wings of gossamer, which took us over land, sea, and river with the magical exhilaration of unpowered flight, but not without a certain peril to life and limb. Perhaps the swain that my parents regarded with the most dubious eyes of all was Franco, who took me on expeditions, sometimes for three and four days at a time, into the Bittersweet Jungle, with only our feet for locomotion, stunners for protection against the more bellicose fauna, and simple covers over piled mosswort for a bed.

Let it not be said that I became merely the mirror of my lovers' passions, for I too had interests of my own which I shared with them, though none of them reached the heights of overweening obsession. To be my companion was to frequent galleries of the graphic arts and become conversant with the styles of world-bubbles, to power-ski the Rio Royale for a hundred kilometers and more upstream and become something of a jesting pest to

15

the boat traffic thereon, and to play endless games of rather inexpert chess.

Moreover, there was much cross-fertilization of adolescent passions and interests in the circles in which I moved, which is to say Pallo gained cuisinary sophistication from dining with me, Franco was introduced to new psychochemicals, and even Cort was constrained to try his hand at gliding through the skies beneath an Eagle. In short, by the time I was seventeen I was a member of a society of my own, a circle of friends, lovers, rivals, former and future swains, which modestly mirrored the social coherence, shifting interests and relationships, and independent life of my parents' salon society, if hardly the seriousness of purpose, artistic and scientific attainment, or depth of scholarship to be found therein.

If I have given the impression that eroticism, intoxicants, athletics, adventure, and entertainment were far more central to our lives than were our academic studies, it is also true that the requirements of same, both in time and effort, were quite deliberately loosened by the mavens of the academy after one's sixteenth birthday. For the natural inclination of the adolescent spirit is to seek out just such pleasures as dominated our attentions, and to tie its wings to the nest of arduous study would be to teach only the entirely counterproductive lesson that scholarship is a grim and bitter task imposed by one's parents and one's society, rather than a joy and intellectual adventure to be avidly pursued as a heart's desire.

Indeed, by the age of sixteen one's childhood education is all but drawing to a close; having learned to read, compose word crystals, comprehend basic mathematics, having gained some facility in shifting fluidly among the infinitely varied sprachs of human Lingo, having been acquainted with the history of the species and the various sciences, having been at least exposed to the variety of possible spiritual disciplines and physical arts available for individual development, und so weiter, there is really little else of lasting value for the nonself-motivated student to learn. One has been given the tools with which to develop the mind, body, and spirit, but until one finds one's own inner light, one's own self-generated image of what one wishes to become as an adult of the species, one's own true intellectual passions, more serious and specialized learning thrust upon the still immature mind is as pearls cast before swine.

Which is not to say that my friends and I were not slowly learning an important lesson as our schooling trailed off into an endless summer of ease and self-indulgence. Though some learned it more rapidly than others, and I was not to achieve this satori until I was eighteen, the lesson that our parents, teachers, and society were so wisely allowing us to teach ourselves at our own leisure was that the young adolescent's ideal existence of entertainment, intoxication, eroticism, sport, and easy adventure, unhampered by work, arduous study, or hardship, eventually becomes as cloying as an exclusive diet of the pastry chef's art. Through a surfeit of this endless frolic, one finally learns *boredom*, and once this karmic state is attained entirely by one's own efforts, one is ready to contemplate the next quantum leap of spiritual development, the wanderjahr.

Naturellement, I had learned something of the history of the wanderjahr in the academy, and had known from early girlhood onward that some day I too would take my turn at the vie of the Child of Fortune.

The first clear records of the wanderjahr as a conscious stage in human development come from medieval Europa, where students—alas, in those days only the male of the species—were set to wandering afoot along the highways and byways, either as subsidized Children of Fortune or as mendicants, before embarking on their studies at the universities, though some authorities claim more ancient and universal origins, such as the wandering monks of Hind and Han, the name-quests of would-be Indian braves, the years that Masai boys spent as tribal wanderers before their puberty rites, the Walkabouts of the Abos, und so weiter.

Be that as it may, the wanderjahr seemed to disappear for a time with the coming of the industrial phase of the Terrestrial Age, when the spiritual education of the young came to be regarded as an indolent frivolity in the light of what was seen as the practical economic necessity of processing idle youth into productive members of the workforce via an uninterrupted passage from the schoolroom through the university and into gainful employment as rapidly as possible.

Nevertheless, the wanderjahr, long-suppressed, reemerged at the dawn of the Age of Space in the rather chaotic form of youthful rebellion against this very concept. Alas, *these* Children of Fortune, far from being wisely granted a period of wandering freedom between schooling and serious study by their society in which to discover their adult callings and true names, fled from their parental venues ofttimes at a far too tender age, or on the other hand had already embarked on serious university study before realizing that they knew not who they were, and broke off in media res in a state of karmic crisis and confusion.

The unfortunate result was turmoil, angry conflict between youth and maturity, the spiritual and the social realm, between the universal quest for spiritual identity and the restraints of formal education, and between endocrine imperatives and the body politic. Many educations, having been interrupted in midstream, were never properly completed, others were never fairly begun, and those who had been restrained from ever following the vie of the Child of Fortune often awoke as if from a trance in their middle years to find themselves strangers to their own beings.

Once more the wanderjahr fell into social disrepute, for precisely the wrong lesson was learned by the unfortunate results of forcing the youthful spirit into chaotic rebellion rather than nurturing the Child of Fortune from whom the spiritually self-motivated adult of the species must emerge. Only the Arkies carried the torch forward into the First Starfaring Age.

But when the development of the Jump Drive reduced the duration of interstellar voyages from decades and generations to weeks, the wanderjahr reemerged again as the rite de passage of youth into maturity.

Naturellement, in our Second Starfaring Age, the Children of Fortune wander not afoot from town to town nor across the continents and seas of a single planet, but throughout the far-flung worlds of men, in the timeless sleep of the dormodules of the Void Ships, or as Honored Passengers in the floating cultura if parental fortune permits.

For the Children of Fortune of *our* age do not flee from home in rebellious defiance of parents and body politic; rather do they depart with the blessings, not to say necessary largesse, of same, since those who bid bon voyage have themselves lived out their wanderjahr's tales before choosing their freenoms in homage to the adults they have become.

18

To learn this sociohistorical lore as a young student in the academy is an abstraction of the mind, but the moment when you realize that the time has come to set your own feet upon the wanderjahr's path is a satori of the spirit, which can be neither arbitrarily determined by the passage of time nor forced upon the spirit from without.

Nevertheless, the decision is almost always made between the sixteenth and nineteenth year of life, and it cannot be denied that society plows and fertilizes the ground in which this flowering of the young spirit blooms. For it is the policy of society to ease off serious studies after the sixteenth year, and it is the endless idle summer resulting therefrom which teaches the lesson that this child's dream of perfect paradise is not the ultima Thule of the human spirit, that the time must come when of our own free will we must move on.

My first dim perception of this last lesson that we are taught, which is also the first we learn on our own, came as a certain sense of pique, a petulant feeling of betrayal as, one by one, the older members of my circle of friends and lovers first announced their intent to leave our garden of juvenile delights and then departed for other worlds. When those whose faces were no longer to be seen among us were a year and more my senior, the lofty airs and moues of condescension with which they said good-bye could be laid to the arrogance of peers who suddenly conceived themselves to be older and wiser beings than their comrades of the week before.

But when at last some who left began to be no more mature in years than I, when I began to see myself as no longer quite the precocious femme fatale sought after by older boys and instead found myself forever repulsing the unwanted attentions of what I perceived as callower and callower youth, my unease by slow degrees began to focus less and less on the decaying social life without and more and more on the growing mal d'esprit within.

As the esthetics of karma would have it, the moment when this spiritual malaise crystallized itself into satoric resolve came with the clarity and definition of a classic koan.

I was lying in my garden playhouse boudoir with Davi, a boy some several months my junior to whom I had begun to grant my puissant favors not three weeks before, more out of ennui and a sense of charity than any grand passion.

19

As we lay in each other's arms during what I then supposed to be a brief recumbent interlude between the acts, I could sense him becoming somewhat distant, withdrawing into himself. At length, he prised himself from my embrace and sat some small but significant distance apart from me on the cushioned floor, eyes downcast, shoulders hunched, as if nerving himself up to inform me of a rival for his affections.

"Qué pasa?" I asked, with no more than a careful petulance of tone, for on the one hand my primacy in his affections was a matter to which all save my pride was indifferent, and on the other, this would obviously best be served by the assumption of an air of superior calm.

"Verdad, you're the finest lover I've ever had," he muttered fatuously.

"Verdad," I agreed dryly, for given the modesty of his mystique in this regard among our peers and his no more than ordinary skill in the tantric arts, this was a pleasantry that left my girlish heart less than overwhelmed.

"Don't make what I have to say more difficult . . ." he fairly whined, meeting my gaze with a pout, obviously all too relieved to exchange his shy discomfort for a facade of pique with me.

"Relax, klein Davi," I said with quite the opposite intent, "if you're afraid to wound me with a confession of some other amour, rest assured, my pauvre petit, that I myself have a surfeit of lovers, past, present, and future, and will therefore hardly be crushed to learn of any peccadilloes of yours."

But instead of flinching at the planting of this barb, he smiled at me most foolishly, or so it seemed. "Ah, Moussa, I *knew* you'd understand . . ." he fairly moaned in relief.

"Who is it then—Andrea, Flor, Belinda?" I inquired, with a nonchalance that was both feigned and sincere. For while the undying loyalty of this lover whom I was already regarding in the past tense would in fact have been a tiresome burden to my indifferent heart, the outré notion that this lout could possibly prefer the favors of some other to my own, while the ultimate proof of his callow unsuitability as a swain, was still an outrage of lèse majesté, which, nevertheless, I could hardly acknowledge with less than lofty amusement, even to myself. *Especially* to myself.

Once again, however, my perception of the situation proved

to be at variance with the reality. "There isn't anyone else, Moussa," he said. "How could there be? Of all the women that I know, you're the only one who tempts me to stay."

"Tempts you to stay?"

"Verdad, you *do* tempt me to stay, but . . ."

"But *what*, cher dumkopf? What are you blathering and babbling about?"

He regarded me as if *I* were the one who could not find the sprach to make the Lingo of my meaning plain. "But I leave to begin my wanderjahr next week," he blurted. "Next week, the *Ardent Eagle* leaves for Nova Roma, and I'll be aboard. My parents have already bought my passage."

He beamed at me. He fairly glowed. "Fantastique, nē?" he exclaimed. "The Grand Palais of the *Ardent Eagle* is presided over by Domo Athene Weng Sharon! My mother once voyaged with her, and she says that the decor is marvelous, the entertainments superb, the ambiance exhilarating, and the chef maestro, Tai Don Angelica, one of the half-dozen finest in the entire floating cultura!"

"You're . . . you're off on your wanderjahr next week. . . ?" I stammered. "As an Honored Passenger?" Why did this entirely unexpected revelation cut me to the quick as no confession of human rival could have done? From whence this sudden pang of loss? What was Davi to me but a casual lover whose season had already passed? Why the desire to hold him here with me which I could not deny but which I could still less understand?

"Naturellement," he said gaily, answering my words with total obliviousness of the import of their tone. "My parents, as you are certainly well aware, can afford to pay my way from world to world in proper style with ease. Why would they have me stacked like so much meat in electrocoma when they can afford to buy me access to the floating cultura without even noticing the debit in their accounts? Surely your own mother and father will do no less for you?"

"Of course!" I told him, though the subject had never been broached between us. "But why such haste? Has life on Glade become such a bore? Will you not be sad to leave Nouvelle Orlean behind?"

"*Haste?* But soon I will be *eighteen standards*. Many are our friends who became Children of Fortune long before reaching such an advanced age...."

Such an advanced age? But this silly boy was younger than I! All my young life I had wished to be, or at least wished to appear to be, older and more mature than my years, and now, all at once, this ... this imbecile was making me feel like some sort of eighteen-year-old crone! For the first time in my life, I wished, at least for the moment, to be *younger* than my years; there are those who would contend, nicht wahr, that that is precisely the moment when a woman ceases to be a girl.

"And as for Nouvelle Orlean ..." Davi blathered on, entirely oblivious to my mood, entirely blind to the havoc his prattle was working on my spirit.

"And as for Nouvelle Orlean?" I demanded sharply.

Al fin, Davi began to dimly perceive that his discourse was being met with something other than avid enthusiasm, though the concept that he was being the cause of no little dolor d'esprit never seemed to penetrate his primitive masculine brain. He touched his palm to my cheek as one would console a child.

"As for Nouvelle Orlean," he said, "I'll miss you, Moussa, most of all. Indeed for nearly a year, I dreamed of nothing but being your lover. If not for that, I probably would long since have gone. Verdad, if we had not yet had our time together, I might tarry still. But as for the rest ..."

He smiled, he shrugged, he cupped my cheeks and kissed me like a proper man, and for that moment at least, I saw once more the sincere and naive charm that once had won some small portion of my heart.

"Have we not tasted what there is to taste, seen what there is to see, been what there is to be, as children of Nouvelle Orlean, Moussa, you and I?" he said. "Nouvelle Orlean is the most marvelous city on our entire world, and we both know and love it well. But having tasted it to the full and come to know it as well as we know our parents' gardens or each other's spirits, is it not therefore time to travel on?"

I regarded him in silence, glimpsing for the first time the sweet and noble man that this lightly regarded lover of mine might one day grow to become, and in this moment of farewell I do believe I was touched to depths that never before had been stirred within my heart.

22

"Next week I depart for my wanderjahr, and soon enough you'll be a Child of Fortune too, mi Moussa, nē. Could I have remained here with you forever and never lived to learn my true name tale? Would you have stayed here with me until we both grew old and never walked the lands of another world?"

"No," I said softly.

"Then may we part as friends? For truly of all that Glade has meant to me, the finest of it all has been my time with you. Should not the best memory of home be the last?"

"Truly and nobly spoken, cher Davi," I told him, with more sincere affection than had ever before filled my callow young heart. "Friends forever, Davi. May your road rise up to meet you. Bon voyage."

And I kissed him one last time, as much to hide my tears as to bid him good-bye. Verdad, my best memory of all the lovers that I had on the planet of my birth was my final sight of the very last.

After Davi left, I went out into the garden and sat for a time under the overhanging trees, deep in formless thought. The sky was cloudless, the air was still, and the sun was warm, and soon I became aware of the piping whistles of the little moussas in the treetops.

For a long time I sat there, staring up into the trees, catching quick glimpses of little golden shapes frolicking high in the branches. Now and again, or so it seemed, tiny bright emerald eyes looked down as if through the billowing green mists of the innocent past. Foolishly, I hoped that the playmates of my young girlhood would descend one final time to nestle in my hands, if only to bid a final farewell to the Moussa that had been.

Naturellement, they never came, not even after I took some crumbs of cake from the playhouse and sat there offering them on my open palms as I had not done for many years.

And as the sky began to deepen towards sunset over my parents' garden and still my little lost friends deigned not to call, I tried to remember when last it had been that the little Moussa had held one of her namesakes in her childish hands. Verdad, when last I had even spared the moussas of the garden a passing loving thought.

And failed. And in that failing understood that it had not been the moussas who had forsaken me but I who had forsaken them, as that little girl grew into the creature who short hours before had bidden the final lover of her childhood a fond and tender bon voyage.

At the moment of this wistful satori, a golden shape chanced to pause in a small bare spot among the branches; tail wrapped around a twig for balance, the moussa stood half erect, as if dubiously testing the posture of a little man.

Or was it chance? For a long moment, the moussa's wide green eyes seemed to lock on my own as if remembering back across time to my childhood years. As if to say, bon voyage, old friend, may your road rise up to meet you. As if to say, mourn not what has been but greet what is to come with a happy heart, and know that we of your childhood's garden wish you no less than your heart's desire. No blame, little Moussa that was, remember us sometimes out there among the stars, and hold our memory in the palm of a child's hand.

Then, with a little chirp of farewell, he was gone, and with him the little girl that longed to stay in her parents' garden, for in that moment, that wanderjahr of my spirit had begun.

3 That evening, my mother, my father, and I dined en famille out on the second-story porch overlooking Rioville, and the river, and the mirrored towers of the western bank, and the Hightown looming high above the shore. Of the viands and vegetables and pastas, of the wines and sauces and desserts, I remember nothing, for I was full of myself, engorged with sudden resolve, trepidatious at the thought of leaving all I had known behind, and, if truth be told, not quite so certain of the lavishness of my parents' largesse as to Davi I had pretended. So I spent the opening courses contemplating various strategies for the maximization of same and silently rehearsing the declaration that must come before the sweets were served, which put me sufficiently off my feed to be the object of some bemused regard.

Sin embargo, I do remember the sight of the sun setting into a nest of purple clouds behind the lights of the Hightown, the stars peeping in and out of the half-overcast sky as it deepened to black, the tongue of seafog enrobing the flash and dazzle of Rioville in the softening mists of legend, the bobbing boats plowing upstream through the foaming little crests of the river, the twice-reflected flame of the sunset on the waters, all as if a holo of the setting for my pronouncement of my intent were lased into the cells of my brain.

So too, even now, will the smell of jungle musk, or the

overrich fragrance of a river bank, or the perfume of any great city arising at night to some peripheral venue upon a bank of fog recall to my sensorium the internal climate, the precise sensual memory of what it felt to be inside the body of that girl on that very night, the languor in my sated loins, the tension in my viscera, the adrenal storms roiling within my being as I finally found the courage to give my new spirit voice.

"I have a matter of some import which I . . . that is, I think it is time . . . something is on my mind . . ."

"So much we have gathered from the way you've been picking at your food," my mother said, exchanging somewhat arch glances with my father.

"Come, out with it, Moussa," my father demanded. "Such reticence has hardly been your usual style."

"I am already in my eighteenth year. . . ."

"We too can mark the passage of time," Leonardo said in an ironic tone belied by the amusement in his eyes.

"Many of my friends have already begun their wander-jahrs. . . ."

"And Davi leaves on the *Ardent Eagle* next week," my mother said to my wide-eyed astonishment.

Leonardo laughed. "We dine at his parents' table often enough," he pointed out. "At the very least, such a matter of cosmic import is suitable table talk among us, nē."

"Davi is three months younger than I am. . . ."

"Quite so."

"So. . . ."

"So. . . ?"

All at once I found my ire at this foolish game overriding any further reticence between my unease at the import of what I was about to announce and the desire to make my meaning plain. "So it's time I began my wanderjahr too!" I exclaimed with no little pique. "Both of you knew what I wanted to say all along!"

Shasta laughed. "We had a certain inkling surmise," she owned. "But naturellement such a declaration is one we must all make on our own. It's hardly a confession to be prised from uncertain lips like an admission from the guilty conscience of a child."

"I'm *not* a child!"

"Indeed, kleine Moussa?" my father said, smiling paternally, or so it seemed, to mask a certain sense of loss.

"I'm not your kleine Moussa anymore!" I declared, all at once coming to detest this innocent term of endearment which I had always accepted in the loving spirit with which it was intended. "I've completed my schooling. I've had many lovers. I can power-ski with the best. I can fly an Eagle. I'm conversant with cuisinary styles and vintages. I have survived many a night in the Bittersweet Jungle. I can compose word crystals and play chess. What more is there for me to learn in Nouvelle Orlean before I'm ready to become a Child of Fortune?"

At this my parents burst into such laughter that even I was constrained to hear the foolishness of my own words.

"Voilà, our kleine Moussa has become a woman of the worlds, skilled in all the means whereby one may survive as an independent human among indifferent strangers," Leonardo ironically declared.

"So now that you have mastered the rudiments of the tantric arts and hedonic sciences, you consider yourself a sophisticated daughter of Nouvelle Orlean, more than ready to conquer the wider worlds of men?" my mother asked, and though this was said with no little reflexive jocularity, still I could not but perceive its serious intent, nor could I fail to wonder whether in truth I might not be entirely unequipped to survive without parental largesse.

But on the other hand, I told myself as this unpleasant thought passed like a cloud across the bright blue sky of my young spirit, the absence of parental largesse was hardly what I had in mind.

Thus did it finally dawn upon me that the leave to travel as a Child of Fortune was already a foregone grant in my parents' hearts and that without exactly knowing when the transition had occurred, we had now entered into negotiations vis-à-vis the financial arrangements.

In which case it would be better to remain their kleine Moussa a while longer, the little girl whom mother and father would fear to loose upon the seas of fate without the protective might of beaucoup d'argent.

"Certainly not to conquer, mama," I said in quite a more childish tone. "And no doubt you are right, papa, I've not yet

27

learned the skills required to earn my way as a full independent adult among strangers. But how am I to learn to make my own way among the worlds unless I try? Surely you would not contend that *Davi* is better equipped for the vie of a Child of Fortune than I?"

Leonardo laughed. "You have me there, Moussa," he said. "But on the other hand, Davi's parents have weighed the freedom of his spirit down with a chip of credit sufficient to finance a life of indolent ease in the floating cultura and the grand hotels of even the most extravagant of worlds for several years."

I liked not the drift of my father's words, I liked them not at all. "Naturellement, papa," I said in a daddy's darling voice I hadn't used in years. "As you yourself have said and I in all humility must agree, I've yet to learn the skills required to earn my own way on distant worlds far away from home. Fear not, papa, though I must often seem a creature of foolish and overweening pride, I am not such a monster of ego that I will out of any exaggerated sense of my own economic puissance refuse funds sufficient to travel in a safe and proper style and ease thereby your fears for my survival."

Mother giggled. Father frowned. "Nobly spoken, my kleine Moussa," he said dryly. "But rest assured, we will not allow any foolish fears of ours to rob you of the wanderjahr's true essence, as Davi's tremulous parents have robbed him. Not for *our* daughter the empty ersatz wanderjahr of a haut turista *playing* at being a Child of Fortune!"

"The wanderjahr's true essence. . . ?"

"Indeed," Shasta said. "We will grant you the *vrai* wanderjahr, the vie of the *true* Child of Fortune that we ourselves have known, without selfish regard for our own misgivings."

"The *vrai* wanderjahr? The vie of the *true* Child of Fortune?" Somehow I was beginning to suspect that the magnanimity of these professions was something other than what it seemed.

"Just so!" Leonardo enthused. "We cannot allow you to throw away your wanderjahr as a subsidized haut turista out of your tender regard for us. For what is there for the spirit to learn indolently voyaging in the floating cultura and flitting weightlessly from world to world insulated and pampered inside a voidbubble of parental gelt except sloth and ennui?"

"Verdad!" Shasta agreed. "Instead we grant you the freedom to live the life of the true Child of Fortune, which is to say, surviving by your wits and your own travail, earning your own passage from planet to planet by sweat or guile, entering intimately thereby into the life of every planet you touch, rather than skimming along the gelt-paved surface. For *you,* mi Moussa, the true adventure of the spirit, the wanderjahr as it was meant to be, the vie of the Child of Fortune, with all its dangers, hardships, and fairly won delights!"

My mouth fell open. My stomach dropped in gross dismay. My gorge, not to say my ire, began to rise. "You . . . you would have me *starve?* You would have me wander the streets of some far-off city on an entirely hostile world without the chip to rent a room in which to sleep? You would leave me to wear the same clothes for *years?* You would allow me to expire of hunger or exposure scores of light-years from home? You would see your own daughter reduced to begging in alien streets for scraps of bread?"

"Fear not, kleine Moussa," my father said. "Our hearts are not quite so hard as that. Before you rage, hear the traveling gifts we propose. First, we will purchase your passage in electrocoma to any world you choose. Second, we will give you a chip of credit good for similar passage back to Glade from any world of men, so that if hunger or privation pushes you to the brink, you can always return safely home. Finally, we will give you a second chip sufficient to subsidize two standard months' sojourn in decent ease if not luxury on a planet of mean galactic cost of living."

I sprang to my feet shouting, overturning a wineglass in the process. "Merde! Caga! What minge! Electrocoma passage! A mere two months' funds! What have I done to deserve this outrage? How can you do this to your own daughter?"

"With wisdom and a higher regard for the development of your spirit than for your indolent ease," my mother said loftily.

"Pah!" I spat. "With a higher regard for hoarding your treasure than for your own flesh and blood, you mean!" I spread my arms as if to enfold their luxurious manse, their lucrative boutiques, all the fine furnishings and works of art within, the boats moored at our dock, the fulsome hoard of credit behind the chips they carried. "Is this house any less grand than Davi's? Are your chips backed by any less credit than his parent possess? Yet *they* have given *him* a chip backed by sufficient credit to voyage as

29

an *Honored Passenger* to as many worlds as suits his fancy, there to dwell in a style suitable to a true child of Nouvelle Orlean!"

Neither my foul-mouthed rage, which should have earned me the severest of reprimands, nor my accusations of selfish minge, which should at least have wounded their pride, swayed my mother and my father from their calm, measured certitude.

"You have said it yourself, Moussa, in a style suitable to a true child of *Nouvelle Orlean,* not to a true Child of *Fortune,*" my father said, taking no little amusement in pouncing on my words and turning them back on me.

"If you simply wish to continue a never-ending round of divertissements with never the need to face hardship, true danger, or responsibility for your own destiny, we will continue to subsidize you in a style suitable to a true child of Nouvelle Orlean, cher Moussa, until you have had your fill," my mother chimed in, as if all this had long since been rehearsed between them. "But here, on Glade."

"Contrawise, if it is the life of a true Child of Fortune that you seek, this you shall have on the terms we offer," Leonardo said. "We would rather now have a young daughter think us cheap and cruel than be chided later by a more mature avatar for ruining her wanderjahr with an excess of indulgence."

I sank back into my seat, my anger simmering down from a boil into a sullen silent pout, for I had to own, at least to myself, that my accusation of mean-spirited miserliness was probably unjust, for even the disappointed child that I in that moment was could dimly comprehend the philosophy behind what seemed like minge, though I liked it not. I was reduced to silent attempts to project my state of wounded funk with twist of lips, hunch of shoulders, and frown of brow, and when, after consuming the salad course without extracting another word from their kleine Moussa's lips, my parents fell to discussing the subtle merits of the dessert between them, I gave it up for the night, retiring to my room to plot and scheme and brood, the rejection of the sweet my final, futile, parting shot.

Of my efforts to extract a greater largesse over the next few days, there is little of significance to relate, except to say that they were entirely futile until the very end, when my father relented to the extent of granting a further boon unlike any of my requests.

I alternately pouted behind a sullen wounded mask and minced about attempting to play the role of daddy's little girl. Could I not at least travel as an Honored Passenger, or failing that, be granted a chip good for electrocoma passage to a succession of worlds instead of only one? No, I could not.

I stayed out all night and reeled home at noon of the next day in a state of toxicated dishabille. Surely my subsidy could at least be extended to a full year without damaging the philosophic purity of their wise intent? Nein.

In short, over these several days, the single firm result of my campaign of wheedling, pouting, arguing, and thespic fits of pique was to convince me, increment by increment, that their terms were set in stone.

As this slow and unpleasant satori forced its way upon my spirit against my hope and will, so too did I begin at length to accept the fact that I was going to have to select a single planet out of nearly three hundred on which to begin my wanderjahr, which is to say that by the time I began my listless and alas somewhat perfunctory study of the catalog of worlds, I knew in my heart of hearts that they had won.

Only when I studied the entry for Edoku did my spirit rise and some spring return to my step and my soul resolve that I would now give up my futile and sullen quest and accept electrocoma passage thereto on the next Void Ship that would take me there.

Edoku, from one perspective, was the largest city in all the worlds of men, from another it was a small planet, and from both, it was certainly the ultimate example of the planetmolder's art. This much, naturellement, was common lore, which is to say that even as indifferent a scholar as I knew Edoku as a Xanadu among the worlds of men, but upon delving deeper, I soon enough became quite entranced.

In the middle of the First Starfaring Age, a terminally damaged arkology had managed to transfer its citizens to the surface of a fairly large satellite of a gas giant. Rich in mineral resources but devoid of atmosphere or biosphere, this moon was a tabula rasa upon which generations of planetmolders, landscape architects, genetic designers, und so weiter, had created a totally ersatz geography, ecosphere, and cityscape, a planetary metropolis and garden, in which every hill and stream, every plant and creature, indeed clime, gravity, and the quality of light itself, was a conscious work of human craft, and Edoku entire, so some said, our species' highest work of art.

Naturellement, over the centuries, such a celestial city became one of the cultural, artistic, scientific, and commercial centers of the worlds of men—an El Dorado of riches and extravagance, a Rome to which all roads led.

Including, I determined, my own, for it is not in the nature of the naive and inexperienced to wish to begin their adventures in a venue any less exalted than the brightest jewel to catch their eye, and if I was to be limited to the choice of free passage to a single world, where better to go than such a world of wonder and opportunity, where certain streets, it was said, were quite literally paved with gold, and where, therefore, a girl of spirit, resource, and wit might best and most easily win a fortune with which to travel on.

While my parents were openly cheered at the transformation in my spirit when at breakfast I informed them of my decision to accept the terms for my wanderjahr that they had laid down and commence to make my preparations for departure at once, my choice of worlds was greeted with something less than unbridled joy.

"*Edoku?*" my mother fairly moaned. "Could you not choose some less exalted world to conquer?"

"With ease," I drawled. "For is it not the general lore that Edoku is a jewel among the worlds of men, a planet rich in knowledge, beauty, wisdom, and art, and dripping, moreover, with wealth?"

"All that and more, or so I have heard," Leonardo agreed sourly. "And as such, a magnet for Children of Fortune seeking a portion of same, as well as merchants, mountebanks, and thieves from all the worlds of men far better equipped than my kleine Moussa to survive, let alone prosper, in such a realm."

"I think it best you choose a more modest venue in which to begin your journey far from home," my mother said. "Some world where a young girl on her own would have a better chance to earn credits toward—"

"Where better to accumulate gelt than on a world where it is as common as dirt on Glade?" I demanded. "Is it not yourselves, dear parents, who have limited your largesse to passage to a single world? And passage to *any world I choose,* by your own words! Have you not commended to me the true vie of the Child of Fortune, with, as I remember the quote, 'all its dangers, hardships, and fairly-won delights'?"

I could scarcely contain my glee as they glanced at each other in bemused and discomforted silence, for now, at last, it was *I* who had turned their words back on *them,* it was *my* turn to rest easy on the very philosophic ground upon which they had so adamantly stood, and *their* turn to be reduced to impotent silence in a logical cul-de-sac.

"Perusing the Void Ship schedules, I have learned that the *Bird of Night* departs Glade ten days from now on a course which will eventually take it to Edoku," I informed them. "It is my intention to be on it, unless . . ."

"*Unless?*" they said in unison, grasping at the straw I could not forbear from offering in a teasing spirit.

"Unless, of course, you choose instead to modify your terms for my wanderjahr to include, mayhap, passage to five planets of my own choosing as an Honored Passenger, and a living subsidy which, with reasonable prudence, will last me for a full year. In which case, in loving deference to your trepidations, I will reluctantly forgo the Edoku of my heart's desire. . . ."

At this suggestion, naturellement, their discomfort took on a certain glowering tone. "We will speak of this again shortly," my father said unhappily, rising from the breakfast table. "I have clients to attend to at the moment."

Before he could entirely depart, my mother, with a worried look, touched his arm. "*You and I* must speak of this, Leonardo," she said firmly.

So, in the succeeding days they did, and so too did they apply their own versions of the charm, and wheedling, and pouting with which I had so unsuccessfully attempted to sway their wills when the shoe, as it were, had been on the other foot, though unlike me, they were above resorting to fits of pique or thespic appearances in a toxicated state.

The gist of their campaign was to convince me that a naif

such as myself from a planet such as Glade—which they now attempted to portray as little more than a frontier world inhabited entirely by bumpkins—would have little chance of amassing credits against the sophisticated competition I would encounter for same on a world like Edoku. To which I inevitably replied that I was a sophisticated child of mighty Nouvelle Orlean, which was hardly to be likened to the society of a peasantry living in rude log huts, and that I was merely determined to follow their own sage advice and brave the vie of the true Child of Fortune to the utmost.

To their credit, honor forbade them to either deny me the passage to the single planet of my choice that they had promised or bribe me away from my chosen path by relenting on their financial terms for my wanderjahr. Indeed mayhap to *my* credit, by the time it became necessary to purchase my passage on the *Bird of Night* three days before departure, I doubt whether such a bribe would have any longer swayed my resolve to brave the golden streets of Great Edoku, for necessity had proven the mother of desire, and by then I was all but convinced that I had chosen this course entirely of my own free will.

And so the die of my fortune was finally cast, passage booked, and my parents, so the events of the next morning were to prove, reconciled to the inevitable, at least to the point of providing, in perhaps somewhat desperate aid of my survival on Edoku, and inspired by my father's protective desires, the latest miracle of Leonardo's art.

After breakfast, and before opening his boutique to the public, Leonardo, with Shasta in train, ushered me into the workshop area and extracted from a cubby a simple and in fact tawdry-looking ring such as might be purchased in the most modest of street bazaars on the poorest of planets. A simple golden band—in fact upon second glance a not-very-cunning job of gold plating over synthetic—adorned, if that is the word, by a single over-large glob of ersatz which might conceivably have convinced a three-year-old that it was a sapphire.

This ugly and patently worthless bijou my father slipped upon my right ringfinger as portentously and proudly as if it were the priceless relic of some ancient emperor's crown jewels, while I curled my lip in open distaste.

"After much discussion, your mother and I have decided

34

that, since you cannot be swayed from your desire, you should at least have some means of survival on Edoku beyond mere wit or sweat," he said.

I glanced from him to the ring on my finger, to my mother, and back again, thinking they had both gone mad. "This ring might secure me a glass of wine and a piece of bread in some low taverna, I suppose. . . ."

Leonardo laughed. "I have crafted the casing to create just this illusion so as to discourage the attention of thieves," he told me. "In point of fact, it is the latest and some might say most puissant product of my art, designed, moreover, with the aid of your mother's science as well. . . ."

The Touch, he called it, invented just for me, and not to be duplicated for his trade until I gave my leave. Within the stone was a power-pil and the band itself contained circuitries which, activated by a press of my thumb, could send a pulse therefrom directly into my nervous system, amplifying my kundalinic energies so as to greatly enhance my abilities to manipulate chakras and nerve plexes, said power to be directed by the fingers of my right hand.

When I professed continued incomprehension as to how the ring could aid in my practical survival, Shasta donned the device herself, activated it with her thumb, and, with a wry grin, barely touched the tip of her finger to the nipple of my breast beneath my blouse's cloth.

Instantly, such a flash of kundalinic fire seared through my breast and straight down into my loins at my own mother's touch that I flushed what must have been a brilliant scarlet and nearly fainted from mortification. Unrelenting, Shasta put a finger to the chakra where the spine emerges from the derriere's pelvic crown and I was fairly rocked off my feet by an orgasmic blast.

Laughing uproariously, Shasta dropped the ring into my quivering palm. "Naturellement, the effect upon a lingam itself will be dramatic indeed, while more subtle effects may be obtained in the natural act by playing the spine as it were a flute," she said. "Minimal, the Touch will give you the possibility of emergency employment as a tantric performer of supernormal power, if not of the true artistry to be gained only by diligent study. Moreover, in conjunction with the serious study of the inner lore in which you have alas thusfar shown little interest, the

35

Touch can amplify the healing aspects of the tantric sciences as well."

"Finally," Leonardo said, "there is the inverse effect, which prudence dictates not be demonstrated unless the necessity arises, for the opposite of pleasure is an equally exquisite paralytic pain." From another cubby, he withdrew a simple schematic chart of the corpus humain, of the sort given to students of the martial arts, veined with a nervous diagram, and spotted with plexes marked in red.

"A simple Touch to any of the standard plexes will render the most powerful attacker entirely helpless," he said, "adept of the martial arts or not."

Thus was I provided on the eve of my wanderjahr, if not with pecuniary largesse, at least with a practical token of the most puissant yin and yang arising from the true marriage of my parents' arts.

And so, having bidden farewell to parents and friends, with a pack of clothing, two modest chips of credit, and a ring upon my finger, I found myself at last in the sky ferry rising into orbit to rendezvous with the Void Ship that would bear me away from all I had known and been on the first leg of the journey to whom the teller of this tale has become.

Beyond the port and below the ferry, Nouvelle Orlean quickly dwindled to a splash of tiny buildings flung across the mouth of the mighty Rio Royale, and just as quickly the river itself became a twisting vein of blue meandering down the center of the piebald greens and browns of the Great Vale, and then the great valley itself became merely an addendum to the Grand Massif, in turn reduced to a pile of dull rocks at the base of a gleaming shield of white ice. Then even this lost its grandeur of scale as the horizon curved, and the sky became black, and I beheld the continent of Arbolique entire, an island feathered by clouds in the brilliant green sea.

At which point, certain conventions literaires would have me wax nostalgic, would require a soliloquy in a tone of sweet tristesse, would have the young Moussa cast a last, loving regretful look backwards, would portray her deep philosophic musings engendered by the sight of the planet that gave her birth and the only world she had ever known dwindling away to a beautiful abstraction in the endless void of the interstellar night.

Indeed such emotions may have flickered for an augenblick across my mind's sky like a wisp of cloud punctuating a brilliant blue summer's day, but I would be untrue to the essence of the moment if I herein paid them significant heed, for as soon as the future became visible in the form of myriad bright stars displayed like jewels for my consideration across the black velvet cloth of space, I became a true Child of Fortune, gazing forward into my wanderjahr among those unknown star-flung worlds with scarcely a thought in my mind or a place in my spirit for looking philosophically back.

And then, as the ferry curved into orbit a quarter way around the circumference of the planet below, I caught sight of what from this vantage seemed a tube of silver filigree set off against the blackness in which it floated like a webmoth's nest reflecting starlight on the edge of visibility against a jungle night.

A frisson of excitement went through me as knowledge supplied a sense of scale that vision could not, for I knew that this must be Glade's Flinger, and far from being a little webmoth's nest seen close at hand, it was a huge framework of cryowire half a kilometer in diameter, a hundred kilometers long, and orbiting, therefore, very far away.

I was impressed by far more than the overwhelming grandeur of its scale, for a planet's Flinger is its gateway to the wider worlds of men. While the Jump Drive enables a Void Ship to traverse light-years in an augenblick, it must make its final approach to orbit via more conventional means. To achieve the needed relativistic velocity from a dead rest in space would require either immense onboard reaction mass or many weeks, or both. Fortunately, a Void Ship emerges from its Jumps with the velocity with which it entered, and thus the construction of its Flinger marks a frontier world's mature emergence into easy commerce with the worlds of men.

The cryowire gridwork is electrified, the Void Ship, resting at the bottom of the tube like a seed in a blowpipe, is encapsulated in a magnetic bubble of opposite charge, at which moment, voilà, it is accelerated electromagnetically by the Flinger field, flung down the hundred-kilometer tunnel and into the void at near-light speed.

My excitement at first beholding this device, which would

soon propel the *Bird of Night* out of Glade's solar system on its way to distant stars, was darkened only by the knowledge that the experience of this magic moment would be one which I would be denied. While the Honored Passengers celebrated and toasted the beginning of the voyage at the departure fete in the grand salon, I would be lying insensate as one more item of human cargo in a dormodule.

But even this resentment, which had been simmering inside of me ever since I had been told that the experience of traveling as an Honored Passenger in the floating cultura would not be mine, faded away into no more than a faint regret as the sky ferry rounded the limb of the planet and I at last beheld the *Bird of Night* herself, silvery and magnificent against the star-flecked dark.

She hung there, a vision of baroque complexity, glowing and glittering in the light of our sun as it peeked around the edge of Glade. The *Bird of Night*, like all Void Ships, was a modular construct assembled around a long central spine depending from the ellipsoid capsule of the bow, which contained the bridge and Jump Drive machineries, so that its essential core appeared like an enormous flagellate microbe, or, I thought with some bemusement at the workings of my own mind, like a giant silvery sperm. Slung along this rigid spermatozoon's tail, like literary clutter designed to obscure the metaphor, were assorted cylinders of various sizes seemingly affixed there at asymmetrical random like so many silvery sausages and salamis.

Yet somehow the whole retained a grandeur and even beauty not entirely implicit in the seemingly haphazard assembly of its parts. Indeed even the imagery which the artifact evoked seemed appropriate to its true essence if not without a certain obscene humor. For was not the Void Ship the vrai ubersperm of our species, and were not the dormodules for the human cargo, fastened as they were to this ultimate symbol of the fertilizing propulsive principle of the all-penetrating yang, the containers of the varied genes of our kind, cross-fertilizing the worlds of men that were and the worlds of men that were to come?

Be such florid musings as they may, once the sky ferry had docked with the *Bird of Night,* I found myself in a far more prosaic venue, to wit, the long, plainly-functional spinal corridor down which I was hustled by the Med Crew Maestro without so much as a glimpse of the country of the Honored Passengers, though I was allowed to be tantalized by the sight of several of these lordly and extravagantly accoutred birds of paradise making their ways between their staterooms and the entrance to the Grand Palais, a simple door like all the others which lined the corridor from my plebian vantage, but one from within which drifted the sounds of music, discourse, and laughter, and the odors of haute cuisine, exotic incenses, and intoxicating vapors which once more made me long to gain entrance to the endless fete.

And so yet again was a somewhat sullen and pouting mood thrust upon me as, with singular lack of ceremony, I was escorted not into the gay milieu of the floating cultura but into a grim and cheerless chamber indeed, entirely suitable to my state of spirit, though hardly calculated to ease my sense of deprived outrage.

Vraiment, my spirit sank even further as I beheld the dismaying venue in which I was to travel from world to world. Long tiers of coffin-sized glass cubicles were stacked on either side of the dormodule's central corridor from floor to ceiling, those above floor level to be reached by metal ladders set at regular intervals. Perhaps half of these chambers lay idle, but the others displayed human figures lying fully clothed and entirely inert like the corpses of ancient commissars displayed in state, or like the fare offered up in automatic refectories.

A chill entered my bones, as if this were in fact one of the ancient cryogenic facilities of the First Starfaring Age, in which the life processes were slowed by the bitter cold of space itself rather than, in the modern mode, by the far safer means of electrobionic control. I knew the theory well enough in the higher cerebral centers of my mind, but the ancient reptilian backbrain was gibbering its endocrine dread of an impending state that could be distinguished from death only by instruments of considerable sophistication.

The Med Crew Maestro touched a stud and a cubicle door slid open three rows up the lefthand tier. I stood there transfixed with terror, gaping at this invitation to brave a sleep beyond sleep, a coma but a hairsbreadth away from death, a dreamless nothingness that would endure for the seven weeks it would take the *Bird of Night* to voyage from Glade to Edoku, a leap of faith, a trusting to the machineries of—

"Well what are you waiting for, child?" the Med Crew Maestro demanded. "Do you imagine that I have no other tasks to perform? Schnell, schnell!"

I looked into his indifferent gray eyes, seeking some human contact, some warm assurance against the metaphorical cold. What I perceived was nothing more than the owlish expression of a harried functionary to whom this was nothing more than another quantum of an endless routine.

"I've never . . . this is my first. . . ."

"Ah," he sighed, and in that moment, a human spirit seemed to emerge from behind the mask. "Fear not," he said more softly. "No harm comes. Never have I lost a passenger yet. You sleep, and then you awake, c'est tout, and this you have braved every night of your life, nē. Up, up, up meine kleine! In a moment, your fears will all dissolve in sleep."

I shuddered. I smiled wanly. I took a long deep breath and within my mind chanted a silent mantra against my fear. Then, step by step, each footfall as portentous as the ringing of some solemn chime of doom, each metal rung sounding a note in a symphony of courage that only I could hear, I ascended the ladder and eased myself into the cubicle as if I were entering my grave.

I lay upon a padded pallet with a spiderwork helmet behind my head. "Sleep well," a voice called out from what seemed like far below.

Then with an all-but-inaudible whine, the cubicle door slid shut and I was alone with a claustrophobic dread that brought a silent scream of terror to my throat which I choked back by a last heroic act of will.

Another hum of hidden machineries, and then a cold metallic caress as if the icy hand of death had been laid upon my skull, and then—

4 —I awoke.

That was the extent of the subjective experience of my first voyage from world to world: I lost consciousness in a state of terror in a sealed cubicle and then awoke from a dreamless sleep into an enormous sense of relief, for the first sight that greeted my eyes was that of the cubicle door already sliding open to release me from my tomb.

Needless to say, I scrambled out of the cubicle and down the ladder without delay, and only when my feet were firmly planted on the deck did my spirit come fully awake and perceive, somehow, that I had truly crossed the void.

There were no physical symptoms to tell me that my life processes had been suspended for some seven weeks, nor did so much as a molecule of the dormodule seem altered, but there was an electricity in the air, an alteration of the music of the spheres, that somehow convinced my skeptical instincts that the *Bird of Night* now orbited another world. Sleepers were clambering down from the cubicles, floaters appeared bearing our luggage, and a ship's annunciator was chanting a marvelous mantra of anticipation: "Passengers departing for Edoku please proceed to the sky ferry dock. . . . *Passengers* departing for *Edoku* please proceed to the sky ferry dock. . . ."

There was no need for more detailed instructions, for a

41

stream of passengers was already bustling up the ship's spinal corridor, ordinary folk such as myself carrying packs or accompanied by a floater or two, and what were obviously Honored Passengers surrounded by whole convoys of floaters, and all one had to do was find a clear place in the melee and be borne along by the current.

Soon I found myself seated in one of the sky ferries into which we were all unceremoniously ushered without apparent regard for our previous statuses, and a moment later I was gazing out of the port at my first sight of Edoku.

My mouth fell open. I gasped. It must have taken several minutes for my mind to even begin to form a coherent set of images out of the data impinging upon my retinas, for the sky ferry was already under way before I could even vaguely comprehend what it was moving toward, and even then—

Rather than the starry blackness of space, I beheld an endless curtain of gaseous turmoil, swirls within swirls, whorls within whorls, magenta, orange, brown, red, purple, these seething eddies and whirlpools in turn organized into bandlike higher patterns, and the whole seeming to be frozen in midmotion like a still image abstracted from a holocine.

As the attitude of the sky ferry shifted, the curve of a planet drifted into view from below, and sprinkled liberally above it, hundreds, indeed thousands, of brilliant discs of light from which beams descended, moving, shifting, changing colors, as if a cast of thousands were performing a pavane on an immense stage below, each performer tracked and illumined by a private spotlight.

Then the sky ferry, still descending, performed a slight roll, and a slice of black space appeared at the periphery of my visual sphere, forming a subtly curved edge to the chaotic maelstrom of colors, and at last I began to make sense out of what I saw, finally relating the raw sensory data to my prior astronomical knowledge.

Edoku was not a true planet but a satellite of a large gas giant, and it was the surface of *that* huge world, or rather the roil of its atmosphere, seen from so close on that the eye could not encompass it as a whole, which was the backdrop against which Edoku appeared. The discs of light, then, must be the orbiting luz redefusers, each illumining a small portion of Edoku's surface.

And indeed the onrushing surface of the planet was faceted like the jeweled eye of an insect or a mosaic window of colored bits of glass; each facet, each glass tile, each domain, illumined from on high by its own chosen quality, tint, and even hour of "daylight"—noon, twilight, sunrise, pale lunar glow, und so weiter—and the whole shimmering and rippling as the luz redefusers slowly cycled through their changes like a forest floor dappled in a thousand colors beneath a windblown jungle canopy.

As the sky ferry descended swiftly from orbit, the view became more dazzling and disorienting still, as we flew through sunrises, sunsets, blazes of noon, islands of night, with the speed of a stroboscopic flicker. Mountains, plazas, buildings great and small, rivers, deserts, all blurred into each other to form a pointillistic landscape where the organic tints of the natural realm and the starker and more varied hues of the obvious works of men so intermingled, overlapped, and underlaid, that the whole appeared en passant as a single formless and colorless sprawl, within which were contained, nevertheless, all conceivable permutations of color and form, all conceivable transmutations of the organic and the crafted.

Thus I first beheld Great Edoku, gaping out the port in an overload of the visual senses and a rapture of the spirit, like a toxicate beholding the universe entire within the formless chaos of a single flame!

Moreover, my first vision of Edoku's surface proved to be more of the same, and if my description of it herein should lack a certain coherence and form, vraiment, the rendering thereof through hindsight's cooler and more mature eye still achieves more in the telling than the young girl I then was could encompass in the moment of quite literally overwhelming confrontation with the spectacle of the reality itself.

Our sky ferry landed and debarked its passengers on a noonday meadow nestled near the summit of a small wooded mountain, or so at least at the moment it seemed, and half a dozen similar craft also rested on this alpine lawn, three of them also disgorging travelers. From this vantage, Edoku lay spread before me, stretching away to dissolve into the horizon along an arc of nearly three hundred degrees.

What I beheld from this tranquil meadow was a chaos that not only took my psychic breath away but failed to resolve its baroque piling of detail upon detail into any coherent overall reality no matter how long I gaped and blinked.

For what I saw seemed not so much a vista on any planet I could have imagined but an immense holo crafted by an artist dedicated to the surreal or to the inner vision of the subconscious mind.

Half the sky and more was filled with the mighty sphere of Edoku's gas giant primary, and the rest was the star-studded black of deepest space. Yet the illuminated air above the landscape below me seemed entirely disconnected from the sky above, as if what I was seeing was a diorama highlighted and brightened by beams of filtered light shining down through holes in a painted ceiling. From horizon to horizon, the landscape glowed and shimmered, brightened and darkened, beneath a complexly interwoven tapestry of light; noonday, sunset, darkness, sunrise, winter, spring, summer, and fall lay in slowly shifting patterns upon the land as if dancing to the unheard music of thoroughly toxicated gods.

Further, to speak of what lay illumined beneath this kaleidoscope of the hours and the seasons as a *landscape* in any quotidian sense is to play the reality false, for mountains, buildings, lakes, pavilions, streams, flora, statuary, deserts, und so weiter, were all jumbled and tossed together in a manner which destroyed any sense of the natural and the urban, indeed even any sense of scale.

Picture if you will an entire planet manicured, formed, bonsaied, and tended like a formal abstract garden in the nihonjin mode, replete with snowcapped mountains, roaring rivers, desert wastes, green forests, mirror lakes, massifs of naked stone, but with no single detail of the geography forced into the pattern of any overall scale, and no geologic sense imposed on the succession of the terrain. Thus here might be a forest whose canopy overtops a nearby mountain peak, there a river circling an island of desert dunes, in another place a jungle marsh atop a sere butte from which falls a great cataract entirely dwarfed by the tranquil lily pool at its base.

Now superimpose upon this whimsically crafted garden an endless city built in a mélange of every conceivable architectural style and in a scale completely indifferent to that of any part of the garden from which its buildings grow like so many bizarre

44

fungal blooms. Thus a mountain peak may serve as the centerpiece of a public square, trees may grow taller than a neighboring pagoda tower, while in another arrondissement a forest seemingly of the same species serves as the hedge of a lakeside promenade. A waterfall in one venue roars and foams behind a street of wooden houses, while somewhere else a cascade that seems no less grand is a mere trickle off the side of a low building.

Neither a planetwide city liberally landscaped nor a worldwide garden dotted with buildings, the surface of Edoku combined elements of both sans any separation of realm or any overall concept of scale, save that the geological elements which should have dwarfed the works of man—mountains and rivers, deserts and lakes—tended to rather be dwarfed thereby, and contrawise, such floral features as trees or even single blooms might like as not be huger than towers of silver or glass. To further meld the urban and the bucolic and surrealize the nonexistent interface between, great trees might display the windows of a dwelling, spiral stairways rise circling to a snowcapped peak, or forests grow atop a pavilion's roof.

And all spread out before me not under the light of a single foreign sun but illumined in a crazy quilt of day and night, sunrise and noon, wan winter light and blazing summer, the whole beneath an incongruous sky of star-spangled black dominated by the immensity of the mighty gas giant's slow surface boil.

What is more, or mayhap less, this vertiginous vista, alas, is more of an overview of Edoku than one may achieve from most any other vantage, for, as I was to learn, the debarkation site is crafted to afford a relatively easy psychic access to the auslander, whereas the esthetic of the planet as a whole is designed entirely to please the Edojin themselves, and these are of the firm philosphic opinion that *any* overview is both false and hopelessly jejune, that "reality" itself is no more than a local artistic style, that perpetual immersion in the ever-changing fine detail of chaos is the only proper mode of civilized existence, and that to apprehend Edoku entire would be to achieve both a boredom terminal and an existentially daunting vision of the entirely unnatural and artificial nature of their vie and their world, which the best minds of the species humaine, to wit their own exalted selves, have spent a thousand years and more of history and craft in an effort to transcend.

45

Naturellement, such an appreciation of the weltanschauung and esprit de vie of the Edojin was entirely foreign to the girl who stood there gaping and entirely overwhelmed by her very first sight of their venue. Nor was her composure exactly enhanced when the ground fell away beneath her feet.

In truth, not quite literally beneath my feet, though the psychic import was not at all dissimilar as a large round hole suddenly appeared in what I had supposed was the solid ground of a mountaintop meadow, and my fellow travelers from the *Bird of Night,* followed by their luggage-bearing floaters, began to quite blithely step over the edge and disappear into the bowels of the mountain.

"Quelle chose!" I exclaimed, as one by one the people around me leapt off into the abyss as if it were the most natural thing in the world, as indeed, as I was to learn, on *this* world, it was.

A tall dark man dressed all in red velvet took a moment's pity on me as I stood there afraid to even peer over the lip. "C'est nada," he said, grasping my hand. "Droptube des'. Null-g, like a feather to float. Geronimo!"

So saying, he leapt over the edge, dragging me screaming by the hand.

I found myself not plummeting like a stone down a dark tunnel into the depths of the earth, but floating nearly weightlessly downward through a great light and airy atrium inside this mountain which was not a mountain.

What a profusion of sound and color and people! The great hollow space, through which I and countless others drifted like motes of dust through a golden sunbeam shaft that seemed to rise from the distant floor, was circled round by tier after tier of balconies. Some were garden promenades dripping greenery, others strogats lined with restaurants, tavernas, and boutiques, still others the venues of what might have been impromptu carnivals, thespic displays, concerts, and other entertainments which seemed entirely incomprehensible. A dozen modes of music merged in a not unpleasant discord, the air hummed with the babble of countless voices, and my mouth began to water as I slowly drifted downward through various zones of cuisinary aromas.

As for the Edojin who thronged this inverted tower, a generalization as to their modes of dress, accoutrement, or genetic style can hardly be attempted, for they seemed as dedicated to the outré, idiosyncratic, and surreal in their personal adornment and cosmetic stylizations as in their planet-molding arts. While none seemed to vary significantly from the general range of size and mass of our species, and they all possessed the number and arrangements of limbs and external sense organs appropriate thereto, any finer details seemed entirely a matter of personal whim. Skin hues encompassed the entire visual spectrum, hair colors también, coiffures both male and female might be anything from close-cropped fuzz to huge bouffants trimmed and shaped into abstract or even representational topiary hedges of hair, clothing might be no more than body paint or all-encompassing recomplicated robes of a dozen colors and anything and everything between, and ears, noses, limbs, and torsos might be richly bejeweled in any conceivable mode, or just as likely be left entirely unadorned.

I drifted slowly down through this wonderland in the state of ecstatic befuddlement that seemed to have become the basic mode of my consciousness since first I set eyes on Edoku, scarcely aware that my knight in red velvet armor had long since let go my hand and alighted birdlike on one of the intervening balconies, and only became aware that the giddy ride was over when at length I felt the true surface of Edoku gently kiss the soles of my feet.

That is, if anything that lay beneath the soles of one's feet on Edoku could be said to be vrai terra firma, for the floor I alighted upon appeared to the eyes as golden, shining, transparent sand, to the kinesthetic senses as thick-pile carpeting, and the gravity gradient thereof as that of a minor asteroid.

What had appeared to be a solid mountain from its meadowed crest and a substantial building as I drifted down its hollow core now seemed to be a floating confection from my present vantage, for the building ended a good twenty meters from the floor, held aloft by the same sort of gravitic machineries which had enabled me to drift down like a speck of dust and which now informed my motor senses that I weighed no more than the moussas which as a babe I had held in the palm of my hand.

I stood there with the enormous mountain of a building floating above my head like an immense parasol while a three hundred sixty-degree panorama of the immediate environs surrounded me, each few points of the compass, moreover, offering their own hour and season, tempting me with the illusion that I stood at the fulcrum of space and time, though in my present psychic circumstances I knew full well that, here in Edoku, nothing could be further from the truth.

On my right hand, I was offered what might have been an arrondissement of small residences piled up the sides of low hills with only a few folk to be seen abroad to welcome the dawn. Some degrees further, an afternoon parkland with a lakeful of small boats, sunbathers on the lawn, more athletic Edojin engaged in arcane sport and al fresco amour. Or I could venture down the narrow midnight streets of some sort of pleasure district, thronged with revelers crowding between tall and garishly lit emporiums. I might wander among the enormous succulents and little gazebos set in sunset desert sands or ascend to the ridgeline of a miniature range of mountains circled by what might have been manses or just as easily fabriks.

In truth, I knew not where to begin, nor what to begin, nor did I have guide or knowledge or the foggiest notion of how to orient myself in this chaotic terrain. Giddy and toxicated already, and growing discomforted by both my indecision and the psychic weight of the mountain floating above my head, I resolved to let fortune decide, and so, closing my eyes, I spun around until I was truly dizzy, then ceased whirling and bounced airily off towards the pleasure streets of midnight, which were the next sight to greet my eyes.

How long did I wander through Edoku in a toxicated fog? How may duration be measured where midnight is a few steps from dawn and one may stroll in a minute or two from spring into fall? Naturellement, one may consult one's timepiece, but what sort of spirit resorts to such digital measurement in elf hill? Certainement not the spirit of the virgin Child of Fortune that I was, enraptured by an endless succession of marvelous, chaotic, and upon occasion daunting realities, such as Cort and I had never succeeded in conjuring from quotidian Nouvelle Orlean or our own psyches even during our most prolonged and eclectic séances with the psychoactive pharmacopoeia.

Though in truth, of all the knowledge, skills, and lore that

I had acquired in my previous incarnation on Glade, it was precisely my experiences with a plethora of psychochemically altered reality states which stood me in best stead on my initial wanderings in Edoku. While with Cort the perception of an entirely fragmented and disconnected succession of bizarre and unpredictable realities was entirely the result of alteration in the biochemical matrix of the consciousness perceiving them, and on Edoku it was the environment itself which rang the changes, the psychic state induced thereby was subjectively the same, to wit an entirely fractured consciousness wandering through them totally immersed in the immediate moment-to-moment flow of the fine details of chaos sans any overview integrated over space and time.

There were cafe tables of living wood arising from the gilded pavement of midnight streets, mighty towers of glass and stone set in avenues among miniature mountain ranges bustling with urban commerce in the earnest early morning light, a twilit dance pavilion beside a cooling waterfall where naked figures performed an erotic pavane weightlessly in the air, a desert garden under the blaze of noon and the gravity of a massive world, promenades lined with tavernas and cuisinary emporiums on arching bridgeways spanning wild rapids, cafes set high in the boughs of trees, al fresco carnivals on emerald meadows in the centers of public platzes, buildings in the form of mountains, on rocky islands in clear blue lakes, incised into canyon cliffs, and all manner and scale of trees, rivers, waterfalls, und so weiter, festooning towers and pavilions. . . .

Through all this I wandered like a random animalcule in brownian movement, and vraiment, there was randomness in more than the geographical realm, for noon and midnight, sunrise and sunset, the round of the seasons, were as much a matter of neighborhood caprice as the weight of my body, which, from moment to moment, venue to venue, might be dragged down by heavy mass, light as a moussa in the treetops of home, entirely weightless, or any gradient in between. So too the odors, perfumes, scents and, vraiment, stenches, which alternately tempted, tantalized, seduced, and befouled my nostrils seemed to bear no causal connection to their apparent sources. A floral bouquet might drift from a refectory, blooms might give off the aroma of roasting meat, a beautiful garden might reek of rot, or buildings of glass and steel smell of a mountain dell.

49

As for the activities, civilized or otherwise, which played themselves out in this chaotic matrix, they were so recomplicated and arcane as to remain largely incomprehensible to a onetime sophisticate from Nouvelle Orlean. I could hardly tell a restaurant from a palace of pleasure, for all manner of emporiums in every sort of architectural mode seemed to purvey both cuisine and tantric performances, as well, for that matter, as vestments, bijoux, machineries and objets d'art. Was the extravagantly gesticulating crowd inside that glass dome engaged in a theatrical performance, was it a mental retreat, or did the tote board signify a commercial bourse?

Each and every Edojin composing en masse the roiling and colorful throngs of the planetary city seemed determined to outdo every other in outrageousness of clothing, artificiality of skin tint and coiffure, floridity of gesticulation, and general aura of breathtaking and self-important sophistication, the Lingo of the Edojin seemed to be a mélange of the most exotic and nearly incomprehensible sprachs I had ever encountered, and everyone save myself, or so it appeared to me, seemed to be intently engaged in affairs of cosmic import or baroque decadence or both, far beyond my auslander comprehension.

Vraiment was the state of consciousness in which I wandered in those first few hours all but indistinguishable from that induced by the ingestion of a smorgasbord of psychoactive chemicals. So too, at last, the dissolving of sequential expectation and linear logic as the organizing principle of my psyche's passage through space and time to release that higher yet también more primitive being which egolessly merges with the flow of that which is, becoming no more and no less than the moment-to-moment passage of its spirit through realities, as the perfect singer becomes the song.

From this perspective, or rather in truth from this annihilation of separate perspective, I began to dimly apprehend, if not the individual import of the chaotic sights, sounds, smells, and feelings of Edoku, then at least, in a vague and ill-formed manner, the essential spirit of the place, the esthetic weltanschauung of the Edojin, the higher logic behind the random chaos in which they chose to live.

Consider the history of this planet. Millennia ago, after a voyage of generations in the simple, bounded, and entirely artificial reality of their arkology, the original settlers of Edoku found themselves stranded not on a planet teeming with the open-ended complexity of an evolved ecosphere, but on a bleak and lifeless tabula rasa of dead stone and perfect vacuum. Thus they were faced with the esthetic challenge and spiritual necessity of crafting a world, indeed for all practical purposes a total reality, out of nothing more than mass, energy, and their own inner landscapes, which is to say devoid of any surprise, chaos, or animating spirit not created by their own conscious hand.

So, over the centuries, did they create a world in which ersatz recomplicated upon ersatz, in which artificial order recomplicated upon artificial order, in which the parts were deliberately crafted to bear no unified relationship to any whole, in which the "natural" and the "man-made" were terms without meaning, in which day and night, winter, summer, spring, and fall, gravity and terrain, flora and fauna, being of necessity arbitrary human creations to begin with, were allowed to follow the random dictates of human caprice and the surreal esthetic of the imagination unbounded by the natural laws of geography, meteorology, biology, or time. Thus, as if by magic, did human craft itself rescue their spirits from the dead and soulless determinism of a reality crafted entirely by the rational mind, thus by a transcendent act of will was chaos reconjured out of order.

In essence, then, Edoku was a quicksilver environment created to induce and perpetually maintain in the spirits of its inhabitants precisely that state of permanent surprise, that eternal flow of one unpredictable into another, that ongoing illusion of an organically complex and unencompassable chaos which I found so disorienting and daunting.

Naturellement, the foregoing is informed by hindsight's more mature wisdom as well as a perusal of the relevant texts; at the time, all that I began to finally perceive was that an orienting overview might very well be something that Edoku was in fact designed to avoid, certainement at the least it was something no amount of random wanderings were likely to allow me to attain, and therefore, rather than continue my intellectual attempts to crystallize order out of this chaos, my only course was to embrace it, and seek to impose upon it only the structure of my own desires.

Upon achieving this satoric state, a certain clarity of percep-

51

tion and purpose began to coalesce out of the mists. While I had no clue to or concept of the absolute passage of time, I knew with certainty that the soles of my feet were growing sore, that the muscles of my legs had long since lost their spring, that the weight of the pack on my back was bowing my shoulders, that my stomach was beginning to demand nourishment, and that my bladder was filling to the point of some urgency.

In short, biological imperatives and ultimate surrender to the knowledge that further aimless wanderings would be productive of nothing more than further confusion had finally combined to produce a motivational vector, which is to say that I realized that it was time to find what in this strange land at least served the practical purpose of a hotel.

In Nouvelle Orlean I knew the repute of every hotel in the city and in any other human habitation that I had previously heard of or imagined, one simply located the typical sort of arrondissement where hotels were to be found, and selected one on the basis of general ambiance. But here on Edoku, I had not the faintest notion of where such an arrondissement might be found, might not have recognized same were I standing at its center, and could hardly have distinguished a hotel from a palace of pleasure or a hospital on the basis of architectural style.

I was therefore reduced to screwing up my courage and accosting total strangers.

"Pardon, good sir, but I've just arrived on Edoku, and I'm looking for a good hotel—"

"Good hotel, jai nai ici by my lights, and I agree it is a disgrace to our ciudad grande, but there you have it, bonne chance and buena suerte!"

"Excuse me, but would you—"

"Certainly not! Ruegelt for Children of Fortune arimasen!"

"Pardon me, but I'm new on Edoku—"

"Y yo, I appear old, nē? Vraiment, I *knew* this skin tint suited me not, but to hear it from a rank auslander!"

"Would you know the location of a good hotel?"

"Would I know the location of a good hotel? C'est possible. Aber primero, define *good* and *location* kudasai, since these are locutions subjective, whereas *hotel* is a noun objective in most sprachs of Lingo—"

52

Et cetera, et cetera, und so weiter.

Finally, near tears with frustration, and shaking with fatigue and no little outrage at what seemed to pass for street manners in Edoku, I cornered three Edojin lying on a lawn close by a waterfall in a garden strewn with cafe tables, who seemed sufficiently toxicated from the contents of a flagon of wine they were passing around to be incapable of flight, and essayed what I fancied was my own version of the local conversational style.

"Merde! Caga! Why do you imagine that Edoku has totally disgraced itself?"

The three of them—a silver-skinned woman in a chemise of black and white harlequinade, an orange fellow wearing only tight green breeches, and an entirely nude man with rainbow body paint and a crest of hair in the same style—exchanged arch glances of amusement.

"Porqué Edoku hast keine acceptable restaurant in the Magyar mode?" the woman ventured.

"Weil Edoku nikulturi des'?" said the nude man.

"I imagine Edoku disgraces itself because no one has a clever answer to your koan, babaji!" the orange fellow declared triumphantly. "Ken sie the one about Diogenes and the Honest Man?"

"Wrong, wrong, wrong!" I told them. "Edoku has disgraced itself because nowhere in its precincts is a good hotel to be found!"

At this there was general consternation. Then the clever orange one clapped his hands and laughed. "Ach, I comprend!" he cried. "Nowhere within Edoku is *a* good hotel to be found because everywhere good hotels abound!"

"Indeed? Then why can you not direct me to one nearby?"

"Très facile! We cannot direct you to *one* nearby because there are *several* close at hand!"

"Then which of them is the *best* hotel?"

"Mit more precision, kudasai," the woman said. "*Best* a subjective adjective of comparison desu, nē, signifying maximization of an adjective of *quality*. Best extravagant? Best outré? Best bucolic? Best large? Best small?"

"How about the cheapest?" I asked. "Or to be more precise, the *best* value?"

"So," said the orange man, "du bist no wandering guru of

53

the zen koan after all. Merely green auslander with a chip of credit of modest amount seeking a bargain hotel?"

"I am overwhelmed by your perceptivity," I admitted.

"Then why didn't you simply say so?"

"Because I surmised that such a straightforward request on Great Edoku might mark me as a bumpkin and a bore. . . ?" I suggested.

At this, the three of them broke into delighted laughter. "Well spoken!" the orange man exclaimed. "Bienvenidos a Edoku! Such regard for the niceties of civilized discourse deserves its reward. I commend therefore the Yggdrasil. Direct through midnight, links at the cliffs of sunset, circle round the noonday fountain, and there in the petit wald, voilà!"

"You cannot miss it," the woman said. "It's the only building in the vecino fashioned in the likeness of a tree."

I could not. It was.

Rather pleased with myself for having successfully negotiated my first more or less coherent conversation on Edoku, I followed the directions I had been given with little difficulty. Indeed I began to appreciate the manner in which Edoku's bizarre mélange of architecture and landscaping provided starkly unmistakable landmarks at every hand. Vraiment, every conceivable vista consisted of little else *but* an endless succession of unmistakable images!

The hotel Yggdrasil was hardly an exception to this rule.

In the center of the small forest to which I had been directed was a clear blue lake which was little more than a decorative moat surrounding a central island, which indeed may have existed solely to esthetically justify the rainbow bridge which soared airily above it. Rising from the island, indeed all but overgrowing it with the enormous maze of shaded porchways formed by its system of unburied "roots," was a gigantic silver tree.

A good two hundred meters tall at its leafy crown and perhaps forty meters thick through its trunk, to this day I cannot say precisely to what extent the Yggdrasil was a building and to what extent a gene-tailored floral artifact. Vraiment, the trunk and the overarching branches were unmistakably metallic, though their surfaces were worked in the most cunning simulation of natural bark, but the profusion of greenery festooning the whole and growing directly therefrom was just as unmistakably organic. The upper surfaces of the main branches were shaded walkways equipped with railings, along which I could see hotel guests gamboling as lightly as the moussas of Glade. Depending from the branches were several score "fruits" of various colors and generally ovoid shapes, the least of them the size of a small bungalow.

Enchanted, overawed, I danced across the rainbow bridge, which had scarcely any gravity gradient at all, through the maze of porches formed by the roots, where people sat sipping drinks at table or lounging in garden bowers, and into the main lobby. Here the gravity gradient was set to give the kinesthetic senses a heavy, almost oppressive, sense of solidity and weight, in keeping with the decor, for the lobby gave the appearance of a vast subterranean grotto beneath the tree; earthen walls veined with the traceries of great gnarled wooden roots, blazing torches set high in brazen sconces, seats in the form of brightly colored giant mushrooms, cool, somewhat dank air redolent with the smell of wet loam.

Against the far wall, behind a counter of rough-hewn gray stone, sat a prim-looking man whose skin had been painted, or mayhap actually bioformed, to simulate the color and texture of rich old wood, dressed in the somewhat ludicrous green garb of an elf of ancient lore.

I approached this worthy and somewhat tremulously announced my desire to secure a room. He seemed to eye me dubiously, as if "auslander" and "indigent" were blazoned on my brow.

"Indeed," he said rather haughtily for someone dressed as if for a masquerade. "Weil the Yggdrasil a hotel desu, and you bearing luggage are, I had little difficulty deducing your intent, nē, aber the operative questions sind, primero, what class of chambre might suit your fancy, segundo, for how long, tercero, can you afford it?"

Such lofty churlishness, far from intimidating me further, only served to remind me that I was a child of Nouvelle Orlean, entirely unaccustomed to such boorish manners from one whose establishment I was favoring with my custom.

"*First*, I require a chambre ordinaire in your median price range, *second*, the duration of my stay will depend upon the extent to which your hotel meets with my approval, and *third*, voilà!"

I said in a tone to match his hauteur, handing over my chip, which I knew full well was backed by enough credit to finance two full months of all my expenses at mean galactic living standard.

The domo of the Yggdrasil fingered the plastic wafer thoughtfully for a moment, as if he fancied he could read the current balance stored in its circuitry by touch alone. Then he relented, popped it into his credit slot, scanned the readout, raised an eyebrow, shrugged, deducted a sum, and returned it to me.

"First day's rent debited ist," he said in what seemed a somewhat more respectful tone. "Since you plan a stay of indefinite duration, crediting in advance on a day-to-day basis mandates itself." He came close to favoring me with a smile. "Unless, naturellement, you prefer to give over a week or two's rent in advance at this time. . . ?"

"Quelle chose! Since I have not yet inspected your accommodations, I hardly think it prudent to commit myself to a week's stay in advance."

"As you will," he said with a diffident shrug. "A hopper now to your room conveys yourself, which in order I'm sure you will find. Gravity control knob on right bedstand desu, transparency control on the left."

A chime sounded. From somewhere behind the counter, mayhap from a hidden access hole, the most outré little creature appeared. About a meter tall, and the best part of that devoted to an enormous derriere and a pair of haunchy legs, the hopper sported a coat of bright scarlet fur bibbed with white, two enormous stylized humanoid eyes, and a mouth which the gene-crafters had fashioned in the bizarre simulacrum of a permanent human grin.

Loading my pack onto a floater with its long springy arms and executing a little bow, the hopper bounded across the lobby, and led me through a cavelike opening into a brightly illumined shaft whose negative gravity gradient carried us high up the trunk of the hotel to a landing stage which debouched directly onto a branch high in the boughs of the Yggdrasil. Although the height should have been dizzying, the light gravity gradient, the sturdy railings, and the profusion of overgrowing foliage which screened and softened the direct sight of the drop to the ground, all cunningly combined to set me at my ease as I followed the hopper along the treetop walkways.

The creature came to a halt where a bright yellow "fruit" hung from the branch directly beneath us. Taking my comparatively gross paw in its delicate little hands, it pressed my palm against a yellow spot on the silver bough, and a hole opened up directly before me.

I descended a ladderlike stair of dark wood—or rather drifted down it, since the gravity gradient was set at near zero—into a marvelous bower of a chamber. Brightly dappled sunlight poured into the room through the lacy network of green vines which covered its transparent walls and ceiling. The floor was a deep bed of some brown mosslike material, the bed was a gel-filled affair formed in the shape of an enormous all-embracing lavender flower, the twin bedstands, the chests, the tables, the armoire, were of a whitish wood painted and carved in floral motifs, there were three soft chairs and a couch also done up as enormous flowers, and through an open connecting door I saw a toilette done in rough-grained gray stone polished to the sheen of marble and richly appointed with golden fixtures.

The vines papering the wall were judiciously speckled with simple little white blossoms, and among these flitted perhaps a dozen brightly hued and softly singing little birds, each no bigger than my thumb.

As I stood there utterly enchanted, the hopper bounded down the stairs and over to the right-hand bedstand, where it demonstrated the full range of gravity control at some small discomfort to my stomach, and then, twirling the knob on the other bedstand, treated me to the pièce de résistance.

This knob controlled the light level, but the illumination varied not merely in quantity but quality. A full turn of the control put the room through a full day's cycle, from the brightness of vine-shaded noon, through subtly muted afternoon light, on into rich orange sunset, thence to pale moonlight, utter blackness, dawn's early light, and straight on into morning. To perfect the wonder, by some arcane means which to this day I still cannot fathom, the birds fell instantly silent as soon as the knob was set to late evening, and burst into song to greet the ersatz dawn.

The hopper cocked an inquisitive glance at me as if to inquire whether the accommodations met with my approval. I nodded my assent and added a little salute to express my true pleasure, and the creature departed, leaving me to enjoy the end of my first day on Edoku in solitude.

After relieving and refreshing myself in the toilette, I realized that I was far too exhausted to seek nourishment, too exhausted in fact to even contemplate leaving the tranquility of my cozy magical nest for the daunting chaos that teemed without.

So, setting the gravity gradient a shade above zero to keep my body from drifting, and opting for early evening, I luxuriated on my flower and in my sense of accomplishment at having secured this safe harbor, and drifted quickly off to sleep to the lullaby of birdsong.

5 For the next two weeks, the Yggdrasil served as a secure and comforting home base for my still tentative explorations of Edoku; here I had shelter and toilet facilities at hand, and cuisine could be ordered up in the hotel refectory or even for delivery to my room without requiring knowledge of the locations or menus of the city's numerous but outré and more often than not well-camouflaged restaurants.

I say the *city's* restaurants rather than the *planet's,* for after only a few days' sojourn, even a jejune auslander such as I began to adopt the perceptual mode of the Edojin and regard Edoku as an enormous city rather than a small planet.

For the fact was that Edoku had few of the attributes of a planet. There were no continents, no seas, no characteristic gravity gradient, no coherent weather systems, no regular procession of night and day, and no real sense of geographical distance. Within a day or two, I began to realize that the horizon was always much closer at hand than it seemed, for the ersatz geographical features, while betraying no overall relationship of scale taken one to another, were as a generality crafted as miniatures so as to create the illusion of a far larger planetary surface. The totally arbitrary crazy quilt of gravity gradients was also a necessary part of this legerdemain of perspective, for in point of astronomical fact, Edoku was a modest-sized moon whose natural gravity would have been only about .2 standard g, a kinesthetic clue which would have immediately destroyed the visual illusion of a far distant horizon on a much larger world.

Somehow, my penetration of this trick of scale made Edoku slightly less daunting—at least in terms of locomotion if not location—and once I began to learn something of the arcana of the public transportation system, the perceptual transformation was complete.

On a planet where gravity varied abruptly and dramatically every kilometer or so, low-level aerial transport was far too risky to life and limb for even the Edojin to contemplate, and so this mode was confined to suborbital ballistic shuttles, and these horrendous craft, perversely propelled as they were by primeval rockets belching flame, smoke, and earsplitting thunder, seemed to exist more for thespic effect than any semblance of practicality. So too the boats, punts, barques, canoes, und so weiter, available for hire on every body of even marginally navigable water.

The occasional small vehicles—wheeled, legged, or gravity floated—which were to be seen in arrondissements where a system of streets was in evidence might be practical for locomotion within their precincts, but were useless for travel of any real distance. As for those Edojin who rode about on a bewildering assortment of steeds, no two of which seemed to betray a genetic commonality, these folk, as far as I was concerned, were prime candidates for a mental retreat.

Indeed, for the first few days my modest wanderings were constrained, first by the distance I could cover afoot, and second by the necessity of keeping the hotel Yggdrasil either constantly within my visual sphere or, at most, no further from my sight than a short trail of memorizable landmarks away.

Only when I screwed up my courage and inquired of the domo of the hotel as to how an auslander entirely unfamiliar with the city might explore beyond walking distance from the hotel without becoming hopelessly lost, was I somewhat patronizingly informed of the existence of the Rapide.

Unbeknowst to me, there was a network of tunnels under the entire surface of Edoku, with stations in almost every building of significance as well as cunningly concealed in a plethora of geographic features, though for esthetic reasons, these were unmarked and had to be either memorized or inquired after locally.

Once access to the Rapide was achieved, however, the system was such that it could be utilized with relative ease even by a naif such as myself. In each Rapide station was a goodly supply of Bubbles. These were simple seats mounted on floaters and enclosed in the same sort of voidbubble field used for inspecting the exteriors of Void Ships. Each Bubble was equipped with a chip slot and a display screen.

There were two modes of command. If the cognomen of a specific destination was spoken, the Rapide would forthwith deduct the proper debit from your chip and convey you thither. If one requested a class of destination such as "hotels," "restaurants," "mountains," "palaces of pleasure," und so weiter, a complete alphabetized list of same would scroll across the display screen until a choice was announced.

Distance was not a relevant parameter, for the tunnels of the Rapide were maintained in hard vacuum within an inertial nullifier field, permitting enormous accelerations without discomfort, and so once the destination was announced, you were whisked down the mercifully featureless tunnel at tremendous if entirely imperceptible velocity; via the Rapide, no point on Edoku was more than twenty minutes from any other.

Thus, once I became conversant with the Rapide, Edoku became, in practical effect as well as psychic perspective, an endless and randomly accessible succession of possible venues discontinuously distributed by name or category and bearing no geographical or temporal relationship one to the other. The restaurant in which I chose to dine might be a few minutes' walk from the mountain on which I took a postprandial stroll or it might be halfway around the planet. Moreover, no matter where I chanced to find myself when fatigue set in, I had only to insert my chip, speak its name, and be safely returned to the hotel Yggdrasil in a matter of minutes.

While the Rapide gave me random access on a hit or miss basis, and while it reduced the Edoku of my perception from a chaotic planetary vastness to an infinite succession of wonders and bizarrities, each in effect a close neighbor of every other, it can hardly be said that such a mode of transport served to enhance my sense of psychic orientation.

Au contraire, while I was now at liberty to wander Edoku

entire, my perception of its realities was now, if anything, more fragmented, and so too, therefore, the consciousness informed by same, which went through the rounds of the arbitrary hours and days not merely disconnected from any sequence of time save that of hunger, fatigue, and sleep, but disconnected as well from any topographical map of the territory.

Moreover, my selections of restaurants, palaces of pleasure, entertainments, scenic vistas, and the like, were determined entirely by arbitrary choices from the categorical lists offered up by the data bank of the Rapide, and these listings, or so it seemed, were compiled with no little arbitrary caprice themselves.

Vraiment, I could rest assured that any establishment filed under "restaurants" would supply me with nourishment, but the cuisinary style and venue of same might be anything and everything.

I was delighted at a banquet in the Han mode consumed on a barge floating down a river in a twilit canyon, bemused to find myself supping entirely on pastries circulating on platters affixed to the heads of birdlike creatures high in a treetop, appalled to be offered a breakfast consisting entirely of tidbits of raw meats and fishes in the midst of an extravagant tantric performance, disgusted to find myself in a firelit cave where the diners, required to doff their clothing for the occasion, were constrained to rip small roasted animals and fowl apart with their fingers, entirely outraged by the establishment in which the cuisine consisted of bizarre living gene-crafted birds and beasts which burbled and chittered as they were consumed, and nauseated by the pungent and acrid savors of abstract cubes of many colors served up in an emporium constructed entirely of gleaming white tile.

Similarly, a random selection of "palaces of pleasure" might present me with emporiums offering more or less quotidian assortments of sexual scenarios, if often conducted in venues of bizarre decor.

But as often as not, I would find myself presented with a selection of gross and mindless creatures whose phallic, oral, digital, and tentacular endowments and sexual tropisms had been gene-crafted for the performance of tantric figures that would have astounded even my mother. And while I essayed a few of these grotesque figures with creatures who were all lingam or indeed were equipped with multiple phalluses of superhuman puissance, and while I had certainly never considered myself an archreactionary in matters of sexual esthetics, I nevertheless found these experiences universally appalling in a psychic sense even while enjoying, if that is the word, a multiplicity of orgasms.

"Theaters" and "holocines" could be relied upon to offer up more or less what the categories implied throughout the worlds of men, namely live performances of dramas on the one hand and hologramic renderings of same on the other, but on Edoku, "entertainments" covered a broad spectrum of the sublime, bizarre, boring, incomprehensible, and vile indeed! Even now, my memories remain a kaleidoscopic blur of images, sounds, odors, experiences, and feelings whose fragmentation owes far more to the nature of the realities themselves than to the intoxicants I consumed to enhance, or in some cases mitigate, my perception thereof.

There were soaring dances in zero-gravity in which the groundlings of the audience were invited to join clumsily with the performers, and slow-motion dances performed by mixed troupes of humans and gene-crafted saurian behemoths under crushing gravity in a setting which simulated the imagined surface of some gas giant planet.

There were displays of hopefully ersatz tortures and executions performed in grim stone dungeons and public squares, and a plethora of mock battles between human warriors of various historical periods and creatures gene-crafted to simulate nonhuman sapients of fanciful imagining as well as monsters out of literature and myth.

In a vast amphitheater under pale moonlight several hours' worth of assorted colorful and earsplitting explosions were set off for the delectation of the audience. Another "symphony" consisted entirely of fugal sequences of odors—sublime, outré, and disgusting—experienced in perfect, soundless, weightless blackness.

And of course more quotidian music of every conceivable style, mode, and period, intermixed and interwoven with much of the foregoing, but also performed in solemn isolation on mountaintops, amidst desert dunes, on floating barges, even in simulacra of ancient Terrestrial concert halls, where the audience was outfitted with stiff and uncomfortable vestments of white and black and constrained to endure a stifling humidity.

If I give the impression that I passed these first two weeks on Edoku as little more in a psychic sense than a wide-eyed indiscriminate viewpoint, soaking up and recording sensory images with no more self-awareness or analytical attempt at integrating same into the timestream of my spirit than a word crystal mindlessly storing everything spoken into the scriber, vraiment the state of my consciousness was, if anything, even more trancelike than that might imply.

Strange to say, or mayhap not so strange at all, I made no friends, or indeed acquaintances, during this period, for I had no psychic energy left over for even quotidian human interaction, let alone attempts to touch the spirits of the arcane and enigmatic Edojin. Not with every waking moment, every quantum of my attention, given over to coping with the overloading of all my senses and perceptions by a veritable torrent of fragmented, novel, and entirely disorienting experiences.

Which is not to say that this totally experiential state of consciousness was unpleasant, even during those moments when the surreal landscape through which it wandered appeared disorienting, distasteful, or even daunting. Au contraire, to the spirit of that young child of Nouvelle Orlean who had spent the last two years in the pursuit of precisely the ecstatic state of consciousness induced by satoric moments of the transcendently novel, this state of perpetual and all-but-permanent intimacy with wonder was the blissful perfection of all that I in my wildest imaginings had hoped the vie of a Child of Fortune would be.

It is therefore, upon reflection, not so surprising, nē, that my mind had no place for thoughts of exploring means of securing ongoing wherewithal, nor that a young girl in such a state of ecstatic intoxication with wonder itself, and a girl, moreover, who had never had to pay much attention to value given for value received in the bargain, was hardly in a frame of mind to give much thought to the price of wine in Xanadu.

Out of this trance I was at last inevitably awoken by a rude karmic satori.

One day upon awakening and completing my toilette, I paused by the counter in the lobby of the Yggdrasil as had become routine to have the next day's rent debited from my chip. As always, the domo of the hotel inserted it into his credit slot.

But now a garish sound issued forth, something like a loud mechanical buzz, and something like a lip-vibrating brak of chastisement.

I leaped backward at this boorish and insulting noise, but the domo, far from being startled by this event, assumed an air of prim and knowing disapproval, directed not at his obviously malfunctioning equipment but at my own person.

"Quelle chose?" I demanded.

"*Quelle chose?* Voilà, meine kleine urchin, your credit balance the mathematical perfection of absolute zero has now achieved."

"Impossible!" I cried. "My father assured me that chip was good for *two months'* living expenses on a planet of mean galactic cost of living!"

"Indeed?" said the domo, presenting me with a printed readout of all my debits, a scroll of daunting length. "And you imagine *Edoku* a planet dedicated to providing bargains ist? Mayhap largesse chez papa did not calculate ninety-seven trips via Rapide, four dozen meals of the hautest cuisine, not please to mention this truly impressive plethora of palaces of pleasure, theatrical performances, holocines, concerts, and assorted spectacles and entertainments? Moreover, the Yggdrasil be not some rude country inn on a frontier planet. You may verify the figures by your own calculation, naturellement, though this might consume several hours. . . ."

I ran a quick scan of the horrendous and lengthy document. This was more than enough to fill me with a dreadful dismay, a certain sense of outrage and no little chagrin at my own profligacy, as well as to convince me that verifying the mathematics of several hundred deductions would avail me nothing. It was all there, and no doubt I had taken all these Rapide trips, eaten all these meals, attended all these entertainments, und so weiter. The galling truth was that I had never inquired as to the cost of any of these items at the time, and as I now retrospectively learned just how extravagantly expensive everything on Edoku truly was, I had no doubt that I had managed to squander two months' worth of ordinary living expenses in two short weeks.

"But . . . but what am I to do now?" I stammered.

"Vacate forthwith," I was told. "A hopper now fetches your baggage."

"But . . . but I'm entirely without funds! Where will I sleep? How will I eat?"

"By your wits, nē, assuming you possess them. Any venue of commerce will credit your chip in return for ruegelt."

"*Ruegelt?*"

"Ruegelt," the domo affirmed, displaying for my enlightenment three small discs of silvery metal. "Each 'coin,' so-called, represents a unit of credit."

"But how do I secure this *ruegelt?*"

The domo shrugged. "Usual means," he said.

"The usual means?"

"Hai," he said more crossly. "Gainful employment, mendicancy, or theft. I am aware of no others."

As I stood there shaking in a state of absolute despair and terror, a hopper arrived and presented me with my pack. Such was my state of chagrin and helplessness that I imagined that this little creature too was regarding me with contemptuous amusement.

Desperately, and without regard for the folly of the attempt, I presented my other chip to the domo. "I can pay with this," I told him.

"So?" he inserted the chip into his slot, perused the readout, and returned it to me with a moue of contempt. "Valid only for passage to Glade for one Moussa Shasta Leonardo. Sans value on the surface of any planet." His expression softened somewhat. "Naturellement, you can use it now to return home forthwith without having to brave the vie of the indigent Child of Fortune, nē. . . ." he suggested.

At this, my spirit was sufficiently roused from the timidity induced by its state of helpless despair to vow "Never!"

"*Never?*"

"Well at least not without trying. . . ." I said in a much tinier voice.

"Well spoken, child," the domo replied. "Bonne chance, buena suerte, vaya con glück, und so weiter. But now you must leave the premises tout suite."

And so I was constrained to shoulder my pack and slink

out of the lobby of the Yggdrasil, through the porchways where guests more fortunate than I were taking their ease, and across the rainbow bridge which led, as it were, from the safety and security of lost Eden into the harsh and unknown world of trial and toil, and while there were no angels with flaming swords to bar my return, I knew that from here on in it would be a road of my own making that I must travel.

6 I know not how long I wandered in a state of numb dread and formless sullen anger, nor even whether I traversed any great distance from the Yggdrasil or staggered in rough circles, for this was *Edoku,* where the hour of the day in any given locus gave no clue to time's passage, and the random landscape gave no clue as to vector. Moreover, if Edoku had daunted my spirit entirely before I had found the Yggdrasil, and had seemed impossible to encompass in any coherent fashion before I had discovered the Rapide, now I was reduced to an even more discombobulated state than that of the naif who had first set foot on the planet, for I was cursed with the knowledge of what I had lost, and while the little girl I had been might rail against the outrageous prices which had been her downfall, the nascent Child of Fortune could not entirely escape the perception that she really had no one to blame for this disaster but herself.

Vraiment, what a catastrophe it was! Immediately upon being expelled from the Yggdrasil, the fact that I no longer had funds to secure food and shelter, horrendous though it was to a girl who had never been forced to miss a meal in her life, had seemed to be the full extent of the dilemma. But when I reflexively started for the nearest familiar Rapide station and then suddenly realized that I had no funds even for transport, I began to perceive that the vie of a total pauper in a venue such as Edoku was likely to present difficulties beyond even starvation and exposure.

For one thing, my sphere of operations was now limited to the range of my feet, and what was worse, I had no idea of how to reach any familiar locus by the tedious process of laying one down after the other, for all my explorations of the city had been conducted via Rapide, and I had therefore learned exactly nothing of the quotidian topology.

My only consolation from this perception was that a mental map of the territory would in any case have been useless knowledge, for I had no means of securing food from any of the emporiums I had previously patronized even if I could find them.

Nor would even the magical power to transport myself to anywhere I wished by act of will have enabled me to even begin to seek remunerative employment. For when it came to the ebb and flow of credit, I had been entirely occupied with exploring the manifold possibilities of expenditure, and had not given so much as a passing thought to the process of accumulation.

Indeed, as I wandered aimlessly through the streets and parklands, the public squares and arrondissements of what seemed like commercial activity in a slowly escalating state of agitated depression sharpened by the apprehension of the empty space in my stomach where breakfast should have been, as I regarded the extravagantly dressed Edojin sipping wine, inhaling intoxicants, and languidly picking at haute cuisine, I realized that while everyone in the city seemed lavishly wealthy, I had never given the slightest thought as to how all these riches were acquired.

Or rather how *I* might insinuate myself into the economic bourse. I knew that Edoku was a center of the arts and sciences and commerce, and that this, no doubt, was the foundation of the general wealth of the populace, but in these areas of endeavor my only skill, at best, was that of the appreciative connoisseur. Vraiment, I could perceive within my own repertoire not even some skill that might earn me credits in some humbler occupation; I could not prepare even rude cuisine, I knew nothing of the art of waiting on table, and my lack of knowledge of the rudiments of commerce had been more than amply demonstrated. Humbling myself to the point of begging for alms I might eventually consider if only I had some notion of the graces and techniques of the mendicant's trade, and theft, if not precluded by moral

69

niceties, seemed entirely beyond my powers, for I could hardly imagine myself overpowering a victim and absconding with what ruegelt his purse might contain.

Naturellement, I was still in possession of the ring of Touch which my father had given me, and in some venue far less sophisticated than Edoku, its amplification of my tantric puissance combined with what I had once regarded as my considerable amatory skills might very well have allowed me to secure funds as a tantric performer according to parental plan. But *here,* where creatures were gene-crafted for performances in palaces of pleasure and the sensual arts were refined to levels beyond my comprehension for the delectation of the most jaded connoisseurs of same, even augmented by my father's art, it seemed to me that I had about as much chance of succeeding as a tantric performer as a tantrically unschooled rube from a frontier world would have had in Nouvelle Orlean.

At length, these weighty considerations of economic survival, and even the gnawing hunger in my belly, were superseded by an even more overwhelming matter of immediate urgency which I had thusfar not even considered but which nevertheless had proceeded stealthily beneath my conscious attention to the point where it now intruded into my awareness to a level of entirely alarming dominance. Which is to say that after many hours of wandering, my bladder had finally filled to the point of bursting, and I would now *have* to rouse myself from my funk and take my first practical survival step. I had to find a toilet at once.

Far easier said than done. Toilets, I knew, were to be found in every hotel, restaurant, taverna, and entertainment emporium in Edoku, and naturellement I had used them often enough. Alas, all of these establishments required the presentation of valid chip of credit as a bone fide in order to even gain admittance, and it was made clear to me in terms of considerable outrage that their sanitary facilities were not available gratuit to other than paying customers.

By the time I had screwed up my courage for a sixth attempt to gain access to toilet facilities after five curt and altogether belligerent rebuffs, this time in a modest taverna carved into a miniature desert butte, I was fairly squirming in agony, to the point where the upholding of dignity was no longer even a

70

passing consideration, and I accosted the domo of the taverna in a forthright whine.

"Please! Bitte! Por favor! Your toilet, kudasai! I have no funds, but I am bursting with need! I beg of you—"

"The grossity!" exclaimed this worthy, a thin green man in a saffron robe. "Taverna desu! Public jai nai!"

"What?"

"The Public Service Station over the stream and in the woods desu! Ici, nein! The insult!"

"What are you *talking about?*" I cried.

"What do I talk about? What do *you* talk about? Surely even Children of Fortune comprend the difference subtle between a taverna and a Public!"

"Kudasai, bitte, mercy upon my ignorance, good sir," I begged. "I'm entirely new at this. I have no idea what you mean by a Public Service Station!"

The domo's expression softened somewhat, at least to the point of regarding me as an ignorant bumpkin in some distress rather than a deliberately insulting churl. "Nouvelle Child of Fortune desu, auslander, nê? Wakaru. Attends, kind: Edoku a magnet for indigent Children of Fortune desu, nê, therefore wir wollen nicht a great display of public munificence to render to same, nê, lest what is already a flood become a tsunami. But Edoku a civilized planet desu, and we cannot therefore allow even such as yourself to starve or suffer disease, and certainly not to be forced to relieve yourself al fresco, nê. Voila, the Public Service Stations, where you will find the necessities of survival and no more, pared to the edge of physical discomfort, but not beyond."

Thanking him far more profusely than his modest aid justly required, I hastened, indeed fairly ran, to the venue he had suggested, and there in the little wood, screened from casual sight by tall hedges, was the first truly unesthetic construct I had seen on Edoku. Vraiment, as if in contrast to every other building in the city, the Public Service Station—or rather Stations, for, as I was to learn only too well, the hundreds of them secreted all over the city were entirely identical—seemed designed to negate all concepts of esthetics. It was a single-story windowless cube constructed of some textureless gray material, the perfect nullity of its design marred only by an oblong doorless portal.

Inside, the Public was only marginally less unappetizing.

All of the interior surfaces were of the same gray substance, entirely unadorned, and the lighting was an unwholesome bluish-white harshness emanating from naked overhead fixtures. The central area of the single room was given over to benches and tables seamlessly extruded from the gray material of the floor; at these sat about a dozen people more or less the same age as myself. The far end of the room was given over to shower stalls, for the doors supplied only a modicum of privacy, and I could see the shanks of bathers abluting themselves within. To the right as I entered was a counter with a bored-looking elder functionary lounging behind it, a long rack holding several dozen gray garments, a series of water fountains, and then a long narrow table piled with strange rubbery-looking gray blocks.

All these accoutrements I perceived, as it were, en pissant, for the left-hand wall was given over entirely to toilet stalls, and to the nearest unoccupied stall I scurried, with only the briefest nod of my head to a young boy in a singularly unappealing gray smock who had lifted his arm and pointed his finger thereto in an entirely superfluous gesture of friendly, if jocular direction.

After relieving myself of both catabolic waste products and the chagrin of my not exactly graceful entry, I emerged from the toilet stall to essay my debut into the society of the Public Service Stations and apprise myself of the nature of the facilities and services which Edoku in its magnanimity provided gratuit to indigent Children of Fortune such as myself.

Now that I had dealt with the most pressing matter, I could more exquisitely appreciate the extent of my thirst and hunger, and so I first repaired to one of the fountains, where I surfeited myself on water so perfectly tepid and tasteless as to be remarkable for the very perfection of its blandness.

Food, however, seemed nowhere in evidence, and so I next introduced myself to a group of two young boys and a young girl lounging at the nearest table. "Hello, I am Moussa Shasta Leonardo. My mother, Shasta Suki Davide—"

The younger of the two boys, dressed, like the girl, in a singularly unappealing gray smock, held up his hand to stay the telling of my name tale. "Greener, nē?" he said. "We don't exchange name tales, since we've just started to live the tales of our own freenoms, right, so all we have is the kindernoms someone

72

else gave us, and paternoms and maternoms mean nothing to the *vrai* Child of Fortune, nē. So in the Publics, you're just Moussa, I'm just Dan, she's just Jooni, and he's just Mart."

While this bizarre mode of introduction seemed entirely uncivilized to me, I felt in no position to deliver a lecture on manners; they seemed friendly enough, and, moreover, I had more pressing needs than the desire to hear their name tales. "Bien," I said amiably, "as you surmised, I'm entirely innocent of the ways of the Public Service Stations. I was given to understand that food was available gratuit, but I see no refectory, nor even a cold buffet. . . ."

For reasons which I was about to learn, the three of them seemed to regard this as high comedy, breaking into raucous and ironic laughter. There were half a dozen gray oblong blocks on the table before them; Dan handed me one of them with an exaggerated courtly flourish.

"Voilà, your very first fressen bar, Moussa," he said. "You are about to enjoy a unique culinary experience."

I fingered the unappetizing-looking gray thing dubiously. It felt like soap. I sniffed at it. It was almost odorless, save for a subtle odor of something chemical, perhaps formaldehyde. It seemed to me that I was being set up as the victim of some juvenile prank. . . .

Seeing my reluctance, Jooni took up another fressen bar, bit off a large chunk, and rapidly chewed it down with an entirely neutral expression. "Mangia, Moussa," she said. "Not only perfectly safe, but each fressen bar is perfectly compounded to provide optimum nutriment for one human for one standard day."

"But we may eat as many as we want," Mart added.

"Though we may not want as many as we eat," Dan muttered enigmatically.

Properly famished, and at least assured that I wasn't about to poison myself, I bit off a sizable chunk of my fressen bar and masticated it appraisingly.

It had the nontexture of a bland fromage made of cellulose dust. It had no taste at all, or rather, perhaps, the perfectly neutral savor of a wad of wet paper. I chewed it down swiftly and mechanically, if only to clear my palate of this wretched substance, while my companions, seeing my expression, burst once more into laughter.

73

"It's vile!" I cried. "It's disgusting!"

"Try again and reconsider," Mart said. "You will find it neither vile nor disgusting, but something both easier to consume and more boring."

"Perhaps you have sampled the art of some great chef maestro and marvelled at its culinary perfection?" Jooni said. "Such art is a triumph of cuisinary esthetics, nē?"

"Well you should also appreciate the art behind the creation of the fressen bar," Dan said. "Somewhere on Edoku there is a chef maestro who has achieved, through the exercise of daunting skill, total culinary *anti*perfection. The fressen bar is not the result of cuisinary incompetence; au contraire, it is a triumph, a perfectly nutritious meal perfectly shorn of the slightest hint of cuisinary esthetics!"

"Entirely in keeping with the Edojin's general regard for Children of Fortune," Jooni added, and then, as ravenous hunger overcame esthetic reluctance and I glumly gobbled down the rest of my fressen bar, the three of them delivered up a communal lecture which admirably served to apprise me of my current true status in Edoku's scheme of things and induct me into the demimonde of the Public Service Stations.

Indeed the latter were the perfect practical incarnation of the former, for the Publics were designed with demonic perfection to supply us with precisely the absolute essentials of animal existence and exactly nothing more. Toilets and bathing facilities. A medical dispensary and other minimal healing services. The strictly functional and esthetically dismal gray smocks for those of us without serviceable clothing on our backs. Entirely tasteless distilled water. And of course the unspeakable but perfectly nutritious fressen bars.

As for sleeping accommodations, did not Edoku abound in every sort of public parkland to suit any conceivable taste for temperature, climate, hour of the day, season, and even gravity gradient?

Edoku, according to the social philosophy of the Edojin, was morally obligated to safeguard our protoplasmic existence, but our esthetic and spiritual requirements were the responsibility not of the body politic but of ourselves.

Moreover, we were assured at every opportunity, the people of Edoku would accuse us not of ingratitude on the basis of wounded civic pride should any of us choose to desert their planet for a venue of more lavish public munificence. Au contraire, as a bona fide of their good will in this regard, Children of Fortune leaving Edoku were gifted with a subsidized 25% discount on electrocoma passage in any and all Void Ships departing the planet.

Thus did the Publics serve as the salons, restaurants, and bazaars of the Children of Fortune of Edoku, and thus did I become a citizen of the demimonde which existed in the interstices of Great Edoku, if not exactly out of sight of the educated eye, then at least discreetly tucked away in the nooks and crannies.

When I had been a haut turista with a valid chip of credit and quarters in the hotel Yggdrasil, I had never noticed the small gray buildings screened by shrubbery or built in the obscured bottoms of ravines or hidden in rarely-frequented copses or secreted in alleyways between tall towers. Nor had I regarded the occasional figure dressed in a gray smock as anything but an Edojin with a peculiarly outré sense of style; in fact, among the colorful throngs of birds of paradise, such dull plumage faded into effective invisibility, unless, of course, you were a bird of the same species.

Similarly, who was to notice that the parks and gardens and woodlands served as regular dormitories for a considerable population of indigents when these same venues were also frequented by the Edojin themselves, who were much given over to lounging on lawns, postprandial al fresco naps, and amatory exercises conducted in dells and bowers?

Now, however, being barred by pecuniary circumstances from the restaurants, hotels, and entertainment emporiums, and being limited in the range of my wanderings to the ground I could cover afoot, I experienced a perceptual reversal of figure and ground. The extravagant buildings of the urban arrondissements, the pavilions and palaces of pleasure, the hotels and entertainment emporiums, all hardly impinged on the forefront of my conscious attention, for they had now become facets of a society, indeed a reality, from which I was exiled; these now assumed the perceptual role of a background blur, an extravagant kaleidoscopic ground against which I perceived with a vividness and detail sharpened by practical imperatives the quotidian realm of

75

the Children of Fortune which all along had been cunningly hidden in plain sight.

I might not know which fanciful building contained a restaurant or taverna nor the modes of cuisine and drink to be found within as I wandered aimlessly about a relatively circumscribed territory, but within a few days I knew the precise location of every Public therein. The entertainments to be had for a price within this vecino might be a matter of complete indifference, but soon enough I became a knowledgeable connoisseur of the gardens, woods, and parklands. I knew where one might find a luxuriant lawn under warm midnight skies with just enough gravity to keep a sleeping body from drifting, or where one might nap on a forest floor at twilight, or bake one's bones on a noonday beach beside a lake, or secure a bower by a cooling stream in a land where dawn remained perpetually imminent.

In short, I was a typical Child of Fortune of Edoku: fresh from home, out of funds, on the planet only a short time, subsisting on fressen bars, sleeping al fresco, and frequenting the Publics as much to pass the time as to utilize the practical facilities.

For in truth, most of us had little to do with ourselves in this stage of our evolution as Children of Fortune but wander aimlessly about the landscape and public venues, sleep, engage in desultory amorous dalliance, or gather in the Public Service Stations to exchange tales, lore, and gossip.

Most of which involved stratagems whereby we might somehow obtain sufficient ruegelt to either regain access to the restaurants, hotels, entertainment emporiums, and particularly to the Rapide, or to quit Edoku for a less financially demanding planet. That, and methods whereby we might gain entré to the elite circles of Public Service Station Society—those wiser, older, and more experienced Children of Fortune who had neither gone home in surrender nor chosen to work their way off the planet, but who had carved out their niches in the social ecology of Edoku itself by organizing themselves into small tribes for the communal purpose of securing ruegelt from the throngs of the city.

While these lordly urchins consumed fressen bars only when they were down on their luck, the ruegelt in their pockets could not purchase freedom from the need to void their bowels and bladders, and so they too were required to pay regular visits to

76

the Publics, though by and large they deigned not to mingle with the likes of us.

But we saw them often enough, and for the most part they were quite distinguishable from greeners like ourselves. For one thing, they were *never* seen to take a fressen bar; even when the necessity did arise, so it was said, they would patiently seek out a Public that was empty for a moment and then scoop up as many as they could carry to consume secretly in their hidden burrows. Nor was this tale difficult to credit in light of the general hauteur with which they carried themselves in our lowly presence. Then too they were generally older and wore either cheapjack versions of extravagant Edojin modes or Public smocks painted with grandiose tribal ensigns, and carried out their necessary business among us with a swiftness and indifference to social niceties that led us to declare that they would have given up excretion entirely in order to preserve their dignity in our eyes if only they could.

Among the *true* elite of Edoku, however, dignity was not exactly their stock in trade. There were four tribes working the parklands and streets of the vecino for ruegelt and it was easy enough to observe their techniques, though any attempt to ape them by someone not formally inducted into the guild, we were obliquely given to understand, would result in a sound thrashing.

The largest of these local tribes was the Sparkies, some fifteen or twenty strong, who frequented the busy streets and particularly the parklands, peddling tidbits of finger food. While the Edojin could easily purchase more artful fare at any of a hundred restaurants, the Sparkies catered to their immediate whims on the spot, and, moreover, many of the Edojin found it drôle to grant their custom to these urchins upon occasion. Similarly did the Tinkers depend upon the aura of quaintness clinging to the repute of the crafts of Children of Fortune in the eyes of the Edojin, for the quality and design of the rude jewelry, paintings, items of personal adornment, and assorted geegaws that they hawked was such that they could hardly have had much trade on the basis of intrinsic worth alone.

As for the Buccaneers, who numbered no more than a dozen, their commerce depended upon certain peculiarities of the ambiguous Edojin legal philosophy which even to this day I find difficult to comprehend. While certain items of trade—mainly psychochemicals with unpleasant or even dangerous side effects—

were legally proscribed to the extent that no transaction involving same could be recorded on a chip, Edoku was entirely indifferent to what changed hands outside the electronic bourse for ruegelt.

Indeed, even the legal attitude towards the smallest of the local tribes, the Wayfaring Strangers, who were straightforward pickpockets and pilferers, was difficult for an auslander to fathom. Any miscreant caught in the act of a simple theft would be deprived of everything in his possession including the clothes on his back by an impromptu posse, but no further sanction would be taken. On the other hand, anyone apprehended for applying violence of any sort in the commission of a theft would be subject to a session of physiologically benign but nevertheless temporarily agonizing torture.

While it was only too obvious that the only feasible means of escaping indigency was to gain entry to one of these tribes, the truth is that I had little desire to do so, for I did not relish the thought of spending my time cooking or peddling, I had absolutely no skill when it came to crafting trinkets, and I had too much pride, not to say moral scruples, to descend to thievery.

To the endless scheming and theorizing on means and methods of gaining entre to a tribe and critical discussions of the comparative merits of the Tinkers, Buccaneers, Sparkies, and Wayfaring Strangers which were current in the society of the local Publics, I was therefore rather loftily indifferent.

Until, that is, I learned of the Gypsy Jokers.

I was lounging about the Public in the bottom of the miniature canyon which marked the border between noonday woods and desert night, nibbling absently on a fressen bar, when two of these legendary creatures made their appearance.

Two boys entered the Public, and without a glance or word to anyone, made straight for the toilets. The one wearing yellow and green divided blouson from trousers with a strange sash I thought must have been quite ancient, for it was so thoroughly patched with scores, or even hundreds, of irregular scraps of wildly assorted cloths that none of the original material was visible. The one dressed in red and blue striping wore a beret of the same sort of patchwork.

But as soon as the toilet doors were closed behind them, the whole place began to buzz with bemused if not astonished excitement.

78

"Gypsy Jokers, nē?" exclaimed Jooni, who was sitting at table beside me but directed her remark across the table at Rand, a boy known for his devotion to the lore of the tribes, and in truth for a certain pedantry on the subject.

Rand nodded solemnly. "You can tell by the Cloth of Many Colors; all the Gypsy Jokers are said to wear some item made of it. It is said that Pater Pan wears a great cloak of it, though some say a coat, and other versions have him dressed in a whole suit of patchwork, the so-called Traje de Luces."

"But isn't their camp a long way from here—"

"What are the Gypsy Jokers, bitte, who is this Pater Pan, and what is this excitement?" I demanded of Rand.

He gave me a somewhat patronizing look, but of course was only too willing to enlighten my abysmal ignorance out of his vast store of knowledge. "The Gypsy Jokers are a tribe, naturellement, it is said one of the largest on Edoku, and surely the richest, for they ply many trades, all of them with great success."

At this, my interest was definitely piqued. "What sorts of trades?"

"Crafts, cuisine, all the ordinaire, but also, most lucratively, ruespieling, street theater, circus, tantric performance, the various arts of entertainment. It is said that they have their own village somewhere, an Edoku for Children of Fortune, as it were. Or more precisely, for those fortunates they deign to admit to their tribe."

"*Indeed?*" I said with no little enthusiasm. For the first time, I considered using my wiles to gain admission to a tribe, for the vie of a Gypsy Joker seemed far more promising than that of a Tinker or a Sparkie. "And this Pater Pan?"

"You have not heard the tales of Pater Pan?" Rand exclaimed in what seemed like sincere astonishment. "He is their domo, it is said. The wisest, oldest, and most outré Child of Fortune in all Edoku, it is said, if not in the worlds of men. A mage of all possible arts of accumulating ruegelt, it is said. . . ."

He paused and shrugged, as if for once he could not entirely credit the veracity of the lore he was about to convey. "Other things are said . . . that Pater Pan is a thousand years old . . . that Pater Pan was once an Arkie . . . that he was born on Earth before the Age of Space began . . . that he has been a Rom and a

79

Hippie and a Ronin . . . that he is the eternal spirit of the Child of Fortune of which the present incarnation is merely an avatar. . . ."

At this extravagance, I curled my lips and snorted. For as everyone knew, the Arkies passed with the First Starfaring Age, no human has ever lived to be four hundred, and reincarnation is nothing more than a literary metaphor.

On the other hand, the *real* Pater Pan, if such in fact existed, must be a fellow of no little puissance to inspire such a mythos, the Gypsy Jokers were real enough for two of them to be relieving themselves in these very premises, and I might be willing to credit Rand's tale of the tribe's riches.

"And where might the encampment of the Gypsy Jokers be found?" I inquired, already beginning to consider practical steps to become one of their number.

Rand shrugged. "Quién sabe? Certainly not nearby enough for me to have ever spoken with someone apprised of the location."

Jooni laughed. "You are thinking of becoming a Gypsy Joker, Moussa?" she said japingly.

"I thought I might explore the true nature of the vie and allow this Pater Pan to recruit me if I deemed it suitable," I japed back. But as soon as the words passed my lips, I realized that I might not be joking. Legend or not, this Pater Pan, if he existed, was a male animal, nē, almost certainly possessed of the usual phallic equipment, and just as certainly not uninterested in the pleasurable employment of same. And while I had little confidence in the puissance of either my wiles as an erstwhile femme fatale of Nouvelle Orlean or the as-yet-untested pouvoir of the ring of tantric amplification I wore on my finger when it came to persuading the sophisticated Edojin to part with ruegelt in exchange for my amatory services, surely I possessed at least a certain unsporting advantage when it came to winning the favor of some egoistic tribal guru by the gratis granting of same.

Moreover, while this chain of logic might lack a certain mathematical inevitability in terms of proceeding remorselessly from initial premise to desired conclusion, the fact that at present I had no other quest to pursue or avenue of escape from indigency was suddenly all too apparent. In short, why not? I had nothing to lose in the venture save the present sequence of idle hours and of that I had certainly had a surfeit.

"Come, come, Rand," I demanded. "Surely, with your vast

80

store of knowledge, you must have some clue as to the vicinity of the Gypsy Jokers' territory?"

But for once Rand fell silent.

"Why not merely inquire of *them?*" Jooni said archly, nodding her head in the direction of the two Gypsy Jokers who had now emerged from the toilet stalls and were making their way past us to the egress.

"Indeed, porqué no?" I shot back, rising to my feet, flush with a certain indignation, courageous with rediscovered pride. Vraiment, I knew full well that it was considered gross lèse majesté for such as myself to approach even members of a lowly tribe such as the Wayfaring Strangers, but when all was said and done, was I not still Moussa Shasta Leonardo of Nouvelle Orlean, and were not even these lordly Gypsy Jokers no more than puffed-up street urchins?

"A moment, bitte," I said, stepping into their path and effectively blocking them. I was favored with a matched pair of sneers and a lofty cocking of eyebrows.

"I wish to inquire as to the location of your tribe's encampment . . ." I continued in a tone far more polite than their boorish manners justified.

"Porqué?" the one in the beret at last deigned to utter.

"For the purpose of traveling thither."

This was greeted with snorts of derision and an attempt to sidle by me. For a moment I was tempted to Touch one or the other in the solar plexus so as to remove some of the excess wind from their sails, but I had not yet used the ring, and besides, such a public embarrassment of these Gypsy Jokers would not be exactly politic. Any riposte must be confined to the verbal level.

"I can see from your churlishness that you are entirely unaware of my identity," I told them haughtily. This at least had the desired effect of stopping them in their tracks. "Fear not," I went on, "this innocent ignorance will to some extent stand in mitigation when I relate this incident to Pater Pan." I now had them exchanging glances of some uncertainty.

"You be an intimate of Pater Pan?" said the one with the patchwork sash.

"Precisely spoken!" I told him. "I am his favored inamorata, having wandered from his embrace in a fit of pique, but now willing to relent and grant him my favors once more." Since this

81

was exactly my intent, the only falsehood lay in a certain bending of the temporal sequence, and was this not Edoku, where the procession of days and hours occurred with just such a relativistic nonlinearity?

The Gypsy Jokers, alas, broke into braying laughter. "In that case," said the beret, "we *do* know your identity. Vraiment, your name is Legion!"

Even louder laughter at my expense. "Still," said the sash, "such outrageousness is at least the right spirit, and deserves its reward, nē?"

"Porqué no?" said the beret. "Let's try her wit, eh?"

"Bon," said the sash. "Attends, muchacha! Where are the Gypsy Jokers to be found. . . ?"

"Over the river and through the woods. . . ."

"Where the sun never sets and the moon never shines. . . ."

"First star on the left, and straight on till morning. . . ."

"Somewhere under the rainbow. . . ."

"The circus is in town!"

And having performed this duet of doggerel, they pushed past me, fairly doubled over with merriment, and made their exit, leaving me standing there like a fool, with the laughter of the entire Public Service Station ringing in my burning ears.

Chagrined, outraged, fairly shaking with fury, I stood there transfixed with embarrassment for an endless moment, and then, not quite knowing what I was going to do, but determined that she who laughed last would laugh hardest, I shouldered my pack and followed.

7 As I dashed from the Public, my intellect was far too occluded by storm clouds of rage and embarrassment to lay any rational plan; I sought nothing more cunning than to keep the two Gypsy Jokers within range of my sight. Indeed, I did not even think this thought with any clarity until I realized that I *was* in fact tracking them, up out of the little canyon, through the woods, around the margin of a lake, and then into the narrow streets of a residential arrondissement of rambling wooden houses. This vecino, though not exactly bustling, still was crowded enough to screen the tracker from the sight of the prey, especially since the two Gypsy Jokers simply ambled along with never a look backwards, entirely unaware that I was following.

The practical task of following the two miscreants at a more or less constant distance of some fifty meters soon assumed a mantric quality which began to calm my spirit and clarify my mind. These two archurchins were, after all, not quite so clever as they thought, for there they were, no doubt, making their way back to their lair, and I need do nothing more arcane than follow them home to reach my goal.

Alas, even as I was beginning to congratulate myself on my acumen, my simple plan was laid low by an equally simple flaw that I had entirely failed to consider, a false assumption generated by my own indigency, to wit, that my quarries, like myself, lacked the wherewithal to travel by Rapide.

But after no more than half an hour of this stealthy pursuit, my quarries, as if they had been tantalizing me all along, strolled quite cavalierly into a Rapide station whose entrance was crafted in the form of a tree, and by the time I had followed them within, were long since gone, somewhere, no doubt, under the rainbow, leaving me once more to play the fool.

For want of any further course of action, I stood there in the empty Rapide station trying to gather my wits about me. For want of any other coherent cerebral content, my mind's ear began to cycle through the taunting doggerel with which the Gypsy Jokers had answered my entirely straightforward inquiries. "Where are the Gypsy Jokers to be found? Over the river and through the woods, where the sun never sets and the moon never shines, first star on the left and straight on till morning, somewhere under the rainbow. . . ."

Could this be something more than meaningless blather? Indeed was this not *Edoku,* where the only practical means of reciting the lay of the land was just such a skein of imagery? Vraiment, there were as many venues as not where the sun never set and the moon never shone, and as for rivers, woods, ersatz stars, and places of perpetual morning, they were all as common on this planet as Bittersweet Jungle on Glade. . . .

But the rainbow. . . . Since Edoku was entirely lacking in natural meteorology, such an effect, if it existed here, would be the result of artifice, and, given the penchant of the Edojin for abolishing the natural cycle of the elements, would like as not be a permanent rather than a transient phenomenon. Moreover, given the penchant of the Edojin for novelty, there might be only one such feature on the entire planet. . . .

It would be easy enough to find out. Merely insert my chip into the slot of the nearest Bubble, order up the list of "Scenic Meteorology," and—

Merde!

For want of the smallest quantum of credit on my chip, or even a few coins of ruegelt to exchange for same, my brilliant chain of deduction led only to the most exquisite state of frustration!

At this karmic nexus, fate, or mayhap mere random chance, chose to cross my path with a catalytic agent sufficient unto transmuting my state of forlorn impotence into a reckless, not to say courageous, determination to at long last become an active agent of my own destiny with the single practical means at my disposal, the ring of tantric power that I wore upon my finger.

A man with skin tinted pale white and dressed all in green velvet had entered the station and was in the process of seating himself in a nearby Bubble. The specificity of his person, however, was entirely without relevance, for it was the generality of his gender which impelled my action—was this not a male of the species, and had not the time finally come to test the power over same of the ring that my father had placed upon my finger, to see if Moussa was the true daughter of Shasta and Leonardo?

Thumbing the Touch ring on and screwing up my courage, I accosted the fellow, who greeted the approach of a rather obvious mendicant with a moue of distaste. "Pardon me, good sir, if I may have a—"

"Ruegelt for Children of Fortune arimasen! Raus, urchin!"

This reaction had not been exactly unanticipated; au contraire, it allowed me to lay a gentle hand on the juncture of neck and clavicle in the form of a polite gesture of restraint, as I laughed goodnaturedly and said: "You mistake my intent. I seek not alms, only your aid in settling a wager, and it will cost you not a single credit."

"A . . . wager. . . ?" he stammered, gazing up at me with an altered expression, which seemed not to be entirely the result of my words, seeing as how a red flush was now clearly visible under his alabaster skin.

"Just so," I said, now allowing my thumb to brush upwards and contact a more sensitive point near the juncture of jaw and throat, "the object of the wager is whether or not a rainbow exists in Great Edoku."

"Je . . . je . . . wakarimasen . . . know not . . ." he blithered, not taking his eyes from mine, and beginning to gape somewhat foolishly. I, on the other hand, took a quick sidelong glance at the crotch of his pantaloons, and verified in the firmest terms possible that this first test of my father's cunning invention was thusfar proceeding nominally.

"Ah, but *this* knows, nē?" I said, leaning over his seated figure, removing my hand from his shoulder, and chancing to brush the back of it against his thigh in the process of laying the palm of it on the screen of the Bubble; en passant, I could feel his whole body twitch. "It would cost you nothing to insert your chip and inquire, and I, alas, am suffering, shall we say, a temporary embarrassment of funds. . . ."

He regarded me with a face upon which I could clearly read the conflict between the cynical intellect and the natural man. On the one hand, he must now realize that he *had* been accosted by a mendicant of some kind after all, but on the other hand, his lingam was informing him that he had been smitten by an instant and primal lust for same, which, as far as he knew, this innocent young creature had done nothing to provoke. It but required a slight act of boldness to consolidate my position; Leonardo's puissance as a mage of personal enhancement devices was about to be confirmed.

I put on the best expression of innocent childish implorement that I could muster under the circumstances. "Oh, please!" I cooed like a babe, touching an imploring palm to his cheek as a child might do in the act of begging a sweet from a favorite uncle.

I could feel him breaking into a light sweat. He squirmed on the seat of the Bubble. Was it my imagining that he stifled an incipient moan? "P-p-porqué no?" he sighed throatily, in a voice entirely inappropriate to converse with a favorite niece. With a somewhat trembling hand, as if all too cognizant of the imagery of the gesture, he inserted his chip into the slot. "Scenic M-meteorology. . . ." he commanded.

The screen began to scroll. "Alpine mist . . . blue clouds . . . fog banks . . . hurricane . . . neige . . . rainbow. . . ."

Voilà!

Elated by the tentative confirmation of my deductions, emboldened further by the fruit of my first act of courage, flush with the success of my first employment of the Touch, determined to see how far I could push my luck, and not without a certain honest girlish pleasure, I cried "I win!" and threw my arms around his neck in a hug.

When he moaned aloud and returned the embrace with a force and passion that had nothing to do with childish glee, the die was cast.

Much later in life, perusal of certain obscure historical texts revealed to my bemusement that certain ancient Terrestrial cultures held bizarre beliefs concerning the granting of sexual favors which the modern mind must find entirely outré, if not mentally diseased. In these cultures, it was actually held that amatory pleasures were to be withheld by the femme of the species as a commodity to be traded for a contract of marriage under which the homme was required to provide economic sustenance. Naturellement, such artificially created scarcity provided a strong sellers' market for tantric performance such as present practitioners of the art could not imagine in their wildest dreams. But the paradoxical result was that the tantric performer was held in low esteem, for by and large, these "putains" enjoyed a clientele of such uncritical avidity for simple sexual release that the mere granting of crude sexual favors was sufficient, by and large, to command a living wage, and diligent study and true artistry were almost entirely unnecessary to the successful "whore."

While the young girl who then proceeded to finger the vertebrae of the fellow's neck like a flute, eliciting a music of sighs, groans, and mutters, lacked the benefits of this historical perspective, I did have the instinctual understanding that the electronic enhancement of my tantric energies, combined with the immediacy of his desire, would be sufficient to overcome my lack of serious study and artistic accomplishment relative to what was available in the palaces of pleasure of Edoku, much as the rude finger food of the Sparkies, available on the spot at the moment of impulse, was sufficient to satisfy the whim of sophisticated Edojin, who, under circumstances of more formal and critical consideration, would have eschewed it for haute cuisine.

"I would love to see the rainbow," I told him forthrightly to his panting face. "It is, in fact, at present my heart's desire. A few credits of your largesse would be sufficient to grant it, nē?"

Under the circumstances, the inquiring cock of his eyebrow was a mere nicety, a formality which I answered in kind. "In return for which, I would be most willing to grant *your* present heart's desire," I said. "Not to say that of your lingam," I added, lightly Touching the organ in question.

When, bewitched and bedazzled, and cognizant of same, he still managed a certain expression of niggardly uncertainty, I told him, "I sense that you are a man of honor. Should you look me in the eye afterward and declare in honesty that the experience was not worth the few coins of ruegelt I require, I will cheerfully forgo my fee."

With that, mingy uncertainty was reconciled with the natural man. "Well spoken!" he declared. "A secluded bower desu, only short walk away. Vamanos!"

To this bucolic boudoir we forthwith repaired, doffed only the minimum necessary garments to effect the union of lingam and yoni, and forthrightly consummated our transaction. Once I had him in my full embrace so that I was easily and openly able to finger the full range of his spinal chakras and even more intimate plexes of his kundalinic neuroanatomy, he was speedily transported to and held at such sustained and heightened levels of bliss that I was confident that I would secure the credits I sought unless I was in the arms of an utter villain and churl.

Moreover, I found myself experiencing pleasures entirely divorced from anticipated pecuniary gain. For one thing, a man who has been granted the ecstasy of such full kundalinic arousal becomes a more tireless and unselfish lover, for another, the premiere performance always has a certain spiritual piquancy for a tantric artist, and perhaps best of all, for the first time in my young life, I could bask in the moral satisfaction of providing fair value given for value received, of doing an actual job of work, and doing it well.

Vraiment, such sincerity and powerful if not entirely polished craft did not go without its just reward, which is to say that after I had pleasured him to the sweet razor-edge of exhaustion, he readily and in good faith agreed to return to the Rapide station and send me on my way via his largesse.

And so, thanks to my father's providence, my own pluck, and the first piece of honest labor I had performed in my life, a few minutes later I emerged from a Rapide station concealed within a large stone statue aping a piece of rude primitive art to stand beneath the rainbow's grand and palely shining spectral arch.

The immediate vecino in which I found myself was an arrondissement of fanciful towers set in an alpine meadow between two entirely contrasting ranges of mountains. On my right hand, jagged desert buttes broiled and flashed in the noonday sun while a mighty cataract poured over the edge of the highest cliff to crash against a rocky riverbed in immense billows of mist and foam. On my left hand were green, wooded, rolling hills sprinkled with manses and houses, reminding me, somehow, of the Hightowns of Nouvelle Orlean at early twilight, with the lights of men outshining the sparse stars, and even a bank of fog hovering over the distant ridgeline.

Overarching the intervening afternoon valley was the immense preternaturally brilliant rainbow, which seemed to arise from the mists at the foot of the cataract and bridge the sky to the fogbank behind the wooded hills.

The architecture of the large urbanized area beneath the rainbow was in its way no less extravagant than the style of the landscape in which it had been set. The cityscape was dominated by scores of tall, flowing, indeed somehow organically shaped, towers of multicolored glasses, all fusing and melting and whirling into each other, as if the rainbow itself were mirrored in a slick of oil poured over mounds of gelati. The ground floors of these buildings were given over to all manner of restaurants, tavernas, boutiques, cafes, and the like, all open to the vie of the streets, which were paved not with stone nor yet gold, but a mosslike grass that was an arabesque of intermingled greens, reds, blues, and yellows.

These streets, moreover, were fairly choked with pedestrian traffic, the usual Edojin throngs in their tinted skins, bizarre coiffures, and extravagant garments, but more to the point, a liberal sprinkling of finger-food hawkers, wandering musicians, trinket peddlers, und so weiter, accoutred with items of the Cloth of Many Colors of the Gypsy Jokers.

Having come this far on impulse and boldness, I was now impelled towards a certain caution, or at any rate it seemed most politic not to call undue attention to myself until I had reconnoitered the territory and formulated a plan of action. Judging from my single experience with the manners of the tribe towards Children of Fortune of my lowly station, it would avail me nothing to simply accost the nearest Gypsy Joker and demand an audience with Pater Pan, nor would I likely gain anything but the rudest rejection if I managed to locate their encampment and grandly announce my availability as a member of the tribe and paramour of its domo. Even fresh from my triumph at the Rapide station, and basking in not-undeserved self-congratulation at my own cleverness, I knew I needed a strategem somewhat more subtle than that.

Fortunately, it was not long before the need to visit a Public arose, and upon being reminded of this biological imperative operating with inevitable regularity in my own quotidian existence even when my attention was focused on far weightier and loftier matters, I realized that this Pater Pan, incarnation of the eternal Child of Fortune and perfect master of the Gypsy Jokers or not, would also sooner or later need to relieve himself even as mortal men.

My next step, therefore, was first to locate the nearest Public and deal with the biological necessities, and then to utilize the lore and gossip current in the society thereof to locate those Public Service Stations most commonly frequented by the Gypsy Jokers.

The former required nothing more arcane than inquiring of the first person in a gray smock that I saw, who straightaway directed me to the usual blockhouse, which had been concealed in plain sight all along behind a tall hedge of brilliant blue flowers screening off an alcove set between two nearby buildings. The latter was merely a matter of informing the denizens thereof that I was new to the vecino, planned to tarry awhile, and therefore would be pleased to be informed of the various locations of the Publics therein.

Vraiment, the matter proved even easier than I had hoped, for the greeners of this vecino, having for the most part been drawn thither by the mystique of the Gypsy Jokers, spoke of little else, for indeed there was little else to speak of.

For one thing, the Gypsy Jokers were the only organized tribe in the area, a monopoly they enforced not so much by threats of force implied or otherwise as by their puissant mastery of all the arts of gathering ruegelt save thievery; they were simply too good at all they did for competing tribes to survive.

As for tribes of pickpockets and pilferers such as the Wayfaring Strangers, these avoided the vecino entirely, for the cunning Pater Pan had endeared the Gypsy Jokers to the local Edojin by a lucrative stratagem. Whether engaged in the peddling of food or crafts, street theater, ruespieling, or any of the other main Gypsy Joker enterprises, all members of the tribe kept a sharp watch for thieves and pickpockets at work, and upon spying same, used secret voice and hand signals to form up a posse of apprehension out of their own numbers. Since such a posse was empowered to confiscate everything in the possession of a thief

90

caught in the act down to his clothing, it was the Gypsy Jokers, famed among the locals for honesty, who paradoxically reaped the only gain from what isolated acts of pilferage might occur within their sphere of operation.

Naturellement, the local greeners could think of little else but gaining entrée to the Gypsy Jokers, and in the matter of recruitment as well, Pater Pan had evolved a method which combined moral justice with financial gain. A Gypsy Joker was required to be a person of pluck, resource, and wit, nē, and what required more of these qualities than the securing of ruegelt by a lone Child of Fortune in a vecino where the competition for same was the Gypsy Jokers themselves? Therefore, anyone might gain membership in the Gypsy Jokers by the simple expedient of appearing before Pater Pan and donating one hundred coins of ruegelt to the tribe as a fee of admission.

Verdad, the accumulation of such a vast fortune was far easier said than done, and, moreover, the bizarre notion of forking over same to a fellow who clearly felt no pecuniary pain struck me as an outrageous imposition, and one with which I certainly had no intention of trafficking.

Nevertheless, one aspect of this dastardly ploy fell in quite neatly with my own chosen strategy: Pater Pan made fairly regular appearances at a Public located behind the waterfall, ostensibly for the purpose of bathing his worthy person, but in point of practical fact in order to make himself readily available to the fortunate and foolish few able and willing to cross his palm with ruegelt.

The Public behind the waterfall proved, naturellement, no different from the many others that I had previously frequented, save that it remained continually crowded with greeners who seemed to throng it for no more practical purpose than to catch a glimpse of the Great One or at least members of his entourage. For in the four days that I lounged therein awaiting his advent with an impatience that stepwise transmuted itself into an entirely unjustified personal pique against him for his tardiness, I encountered no one possessed of any sum remotely approaching the required entrance fee, and, I learned, even as I had surmised, the acceptance of one of our lowly number into the Gypsy Jokers was an event of such rarity that each such occurrence assumed the aura of legend.

Nevertheless, while patience had never been my dominant virtue, if there was one art in which Nouvelle Orlean had provided me with a useful education it was that of lying in ambush for the masculine prey of my choosing to cross my path, for all he knew at random, and so I persevered in my stalk.

Eventually, inevitably, my quarry approached the water hole, accompanied, as I was to learn was his custom, by several female members of his pride, accoutred with items of the Cloth of Many Colors and mooning expressions continually cast in his direction.

This comparatively drab entourage, however, scarcely impinged upon the sphere of my attention, for Pater Pan himself lit up my sky the moment I laid eyes on him, a phenomenon which I was to learn was hardly uncommon to the sisters of my gender, and one which he himself did nothing to discourage.

Strange to say under the circumstances, it was his garb which first drew my attention, for Pater Pan affected a costume which even on Edoku drew the eye in amazement, and which on a lesser being would have made him a ludicrous figure.

This was the Traje de Luces of Public Service Station lore, and upon actually seeing it worn by this noble creature, I could understand why no words could describe the effect justly. Pater Pan wore a loose blouson of the Cloth of Many Colors, open like a sleeved cloak over his bare chest, and crowned with a thespic high collar, a garment composed of hundreds of assorted patches of old cloth, yet somehow a royal robe rather than a ragamuffin's rags when worn by this lordly specimen. Similarly, the tight breeches which seemed expertly tailored to hug every curve and bulge of his lower anatomy were the same random patchwork of colors and textures.

Naturellement, only a noble and daunting visage could rescue such an apparition from the realm of farce; this Pater Pan possessed, and just as clearly, he knew it. His hair was golden yellow and worn in a carefully groomed shoulder-length mane, and he affected a beard of the same color and style to complete the haloing nimbus. All that was visible of his facial features was an aquiline nose, full sensuous lips, high forehead, noble brow, and piercing yet merry blue eyes; artfully outlined by the golden mane and partially concealed by the beard, this face seemed at once youthful and ancient, in truth quite literally ageless.

Ah, he was perfect, a persona artfully self-crafted to express a proud perfection of the masculine spirit within, and oh, did every step and gesture declare that this work of art was his own most avid aficionado!

Indeed it was this very air of utterly self-assured narcissism which both caused my knees to tremble and rescued me from mere paralyzed gaping; he was beautiful, he was king of this particular little world, and I wanted him. On the other hand, he also seemed a paragon of ego, a challenge to every female within range of his charisma, the fellow all-too-obviously knew it, and therefore *I* must have *him* as *my* conquest.

Only some time later did I learn that the projection of precisely this determination into the spirit of the generality of my gender was his most puissant erotic tactic.

Be that as it may, while every other female in the Public was foolishly engaged in watching this brilliant cock parade and preen, Moussa Shasta Leonardo retained the wit to consider strategy.

In this regard, my experience in the Rapide station admirably served to engorge my confidence, for I now had proven by practical application of same that the claims made by my father for the tantric puissance of the ring on my finger owed little to hyperbole; all I had to do was get my hands on him and science would put even such a man as this in my power.

Pater Pan, so it was said, customarily abluted himself as part of these visitations; this Public being so habitually crowded, the ten shower stalls at the far end of the room were usually well occupied, and queuing was common, though no doubt lesser beings would vacate at the pleasure of the monarch.

However, fate, or destiny, or mere random chance, once more favored me with a minor smile of patronage. Perusing the bare shanks visible below the doors of the shower stalls, I saw that two of them, side by side, were now empty.

Seizing this opportunity, I entered the one on the right, doffed all my clothing, hung it on the hooks provided, turned on the overhead shower, took up the bar of soap from its alcove, and waited. If my luck held, and my quarry was not so haughty as to eject a bather from an occupied stall for sake of status when another was empty, Pater Pan would soon be naked in the stall beside me. The partitions between the stalls ended at knee height; it would be a simple matter to drop my soap so that it slithered into the adjacent stall, and then, in the innocent act of groping . . .

So it is written, so it was done. Within less than ten minutes, I heard the adjacent shower stall door open, then swing shut, and by perusing the patchwork-clad legs below the partition, I knew that it was he. A moment later I was presented with the sight of trim shanks lightly dusted with golden hair, a delightful sight to my eyes, though the feet depending therefrom were no more objects of esthetic refinement than those of any other male of my previous or future acquaintance.

I waited for the sounds of his ablutions and was treated as well to the wordless off-key singing so common to the bathing male of our species when he believes no critical ear is at hand. Then I activated the Touch, lathered my bar of soap to the required degree of slickness, reached down below the partition, shouted "Merde!" and shot the soap beneath it and into his stall with a squeeze of my hand.

Forthwith, I squatted down for sake of clear vision of my target, but began groping about at arm's length in the manner of someone trying to retrieve the errant soap by blind touch alone.

While neither the foot nor the calf is exactly an erogenous zone rich in surface connections to the kundalinic neurology, there is a nerve trunk running behind the tendon of the heel up the leg and into the groin, and this I "chanced" to grasp quite firmly in the act of attempting to recover my soap.

I could feel a tremor ripple up his leg as I did so and heard a grunt of surprise with certain subtle undertones which led me to believe that the stimulus had indeed penetrated to the target area.

"Pardon," I said, not removing my hand, "I was looking for my soap."

"*That's* no soap, muchacha," said a rich masculine voice with the considerable savoir faire necessary under the circumstances to affect a certain jocular tone, but not enough to suppress a husky quaver. Nor did he pull his foot from my grasp.

"Vraiment?" I said archly, running my hand gropingly up the inner surface of his calf, past his knee, and a few inches up his thigh, which was as far as my arm would reach. "I know it's in there somewhere."

At this, he let forth an honest sensual moan, and forthwith contrived to bend his knees, leaning forward and downward into my Touch, so that my hand slid up his thigh to brush against his cojones and lingam.

94

"Quelle chose!" I squealed in great mock consternation while feeling the slickly hard object as if to verify my perception. "*That's* not a piece of soap either!"

At this, he fairly shouted in ecstasy, and I released my grip and withdrew my arm, sensing that further such ministrations might bring matters to a premature conclusion.

There was a long moment of silence as we both stood there separated by the partition with only our calves and feet visible to each other.

"A saucy wench indeed!" the male voice said in a tone that seemed to convey a somewhat false composure. "Who are you?"

"Cabeza de caga!" I shouted in equally insincere outrage and wounded innocence. "Who am *I?* Who are *you* to take such liberties with a fresh young virgin?"

From the other side of the partition came a strangled gurgling sound halfway between a cough and a laugh. "You really don't know the who of the what you just grabbed?" he said somewhat guardedly.

"Do you imagine me to be possessed of such arcane powers that I can deduce your identity from the sight of your feet and the size of your lingam?"

"To judge from certain other powers you seem to possess, it wouldn't surprise me, lady fair. . . ." he mused. "Well, know then that you've just had the high honor of giving the goose to *Pater Pan,* my ah, fresh young virgin!" he added grandly.

"Who?" I replied, as if the name had not quite registered.

"*Pater Pan!*" he replied with some vexation.

"Bien," I said diffidently. "And you have been favored however inadvertently with the touch of Moussa Shasta Leonardo."

"You speak as if that makes it a fair trade," he complained.

"Is it not?"

"*Merde!*" he muttered. "I am *Pater Pan,* girl."

"You speak as if that statement bore some cosmic significance."

"You put me not on? You really don't know who I am?" he said, the tone of his voice betraying a mélange of outraged ego and charmed bemusement at such unaccustomed ignorance.

"Should I?"

"For sure!" he said much more genially. "But perhaps we should continue this séance face to face and belly to belly. . . ."

95

"Porqué no?" I said after some hesitation. "I have no pressing affairs for the next hour or so, and if your company amuses me half so much as it does yourself, the time will be well spent."

With that, the discourse temporarily ended, as we toweled ourselves dry, donned our clothing, exited our respective shower stalls, and then met face to face. He looked me up and down appraisingly for a moment and then favored me with a lordly smile of measured approval.

I for my part ran my eyes up and down his patchwork-clad body while contriving to fix an expression of suppressed mirth on my face. "Drôle," I finally said dryly.

"*Drôle?*" he exclaimed. "Is that all you have to say upon first confrontation with the full magnificence of my being?"

"Surely you are not unaware of the jocular effect of your . . . ah, costume!"

He eyed me narrowly. I regarded him in kind. Then we both laughed and the congruent expressions, while hardly changing in content, became something shared, as if our spirits had touched and at any rate found each other equally outrageous.

"Perhaps this duet should continue without an audience?" he suggested, discovering via sidelong glances that in fact everyone in the Public, and in particular the feminine entourage with which he had entered, was now regarding this scene with avid, though in the case of the female Gypsy Jokers, not quite amused, attention.

"Indeed," I agreed, clasping his hand and causing his eyes to widen in lustful amazement. "I find such shyness in a man not without a certain boyish charm."

Thus did we make our exit, hand in hand, and his beginning to grow quite sweaty, to a certain buzz and mutter which I for my part could not refrain from taking as applause for what under the circumstances I considered my own masterly performance.

The Public was hidden behind the great cataract which tumbled from the lip of the desert butte high above, and close by was a cave in the face of the cliff into which Pater Pan led me. This proved to be the entrance to a lift tube which took us to the top of the butte. The landscape above bore no sane geographical relationship to the appearance of the plateau as seen from below.

Indeed the top of the butte was not a plateau at all but a great shallow bowl or "natural" amphitheater hidden from below by a ringwall of rock so as not to spoil the effect of a stark desert landscape when viewed from afar. For in fact here was a lush green garden, a landscape of tiny rolling green hills and secluded dimpled little dells, many with small ponds at their bottoms interconnected by a tracery of burbling brooks that flowed in winding paths around the hills and through the valleys. The hillcrests, moreover, were planted with copses of low trees heavy with a profuse variety of colorful and fragrant blooms, so that each little valley was a secluded perfumed boudoir, complete with private bathing pool. What lay underfoot was not so much lawn as something green with more the texture of a deep-pile animal pelt than vegetation, the air was the temperature of the body's heat, though gentled by breezes, and the gravity gradient was such that we fairly drifted along on the tips of our toes.

There was no mistaking the nature of the pleasures for which such a garden had been crafted, nor, therefore, was there any mistaking the forthright purpose of the man who had brought me there.

Nevertheless, I was determined to retain the initiative, and so, as soon as we had secluded ourselves in a dell by one of the crystal pools, I straightaway made my own bold suggestion. "Since our baths were interrupted, let us now continue our ablutions." And so saying, without waiting for his assent, I removed my clothes and displayed my nakedness for his delectation.

He stood there fully clothed for a moment as I regarded him with an impatient expression, hands on hips. "Well?" I demanded. "What is it that you see which has turned you to stone?"

"Yo no se," he said with a shake of his head, "but somehow I doubt it is any fresh young virgin."

So saying, he began to remove his clothing, and then followed me into the pool, into which I had leapt before he could complete his disrobing.

The water too proved to be heated to hot blood's temperature, and in this frank and heady brew, there was a minimum of coy thrashing and splashing before we found each other embracing. Once our lips had met in a kiss and our bodies had touched, the niceties of the chase were fairly concluded, and when I searched out his lingam and treated it to an open and electronically en-

97

hanced caress of lingering duration, he trembled, and moaned, and writhed in my grasp, and then snatched me up in his arms, carried me out of the water in a headlong stumble, threw me on the spongy ground, and proceeded to essay a mighty proof indeed of his considerable manly virtues.

Vraiment, he was tender and indefatigable, surely as schooled in the finer points of the tantric arts and the chakras of sensual pleasure as my mother herself, and never before or since have I known such a demon lover.

Yet even while given over entirely to the pleasures his puissance afforded, I was never transported so far beyond guile as to eschew my determination to display for him the unique ecstasies available to him via the graces of Moussa Shasta Leonardo and to be found in the arms of no other lover.

I ran my fingers up and down the cordillera of his spine, flashing tantric lightning from peak to peak. I Touched secret places in the root of him, I felt him lingering on the knife edge of ecstasy as I did so, as if by act of will or the iron control of a perfect master, he might remain there forever. This hubric self-control I allowed him to exercise for a goodly while to my own considerable pleasure, and then, as if to demonstrate who was the mistress of tantric power and who the acolyte, I suddenly thrust my preternaturally puissant finger into the very seat of kundalinic intimacy, and he uttered an orgasmic howl fit to rouse the dead if such might be sleeping in a nearby bower.

Nor were our exercises then at all concluded, for, aroused to an egoless state of tantric communion on the one hand, and a contest of loverly wills which had everything to do with ego on the other, we proceeded through countless tantric configurations, half a dozen cusps at the least, each determined to master the other via the giving of a surfeit of pleasure, not to say outlasting the rival in a contest of sheer endurance.

Pater for his part seemed possessed of a stamina and skill far beyond anything I had previously imagined possible to the masculine anatomy, and at length I was fairly trembling with a surfeit of ecstasy and panting with fatigue. Nevertheless, mighty though he was far beyond my fleshly power to outlast, I was possessed of an entirely unsporting advantage which no mother's son could in the end overmaster; utterly spent physically, I needed move no more than my finger to have him crying out once more.

And so at length, at great length, vraiment at entirely admirable length, it was the great Pater Pan who rolled over on his back, heaving and puffing, and cried: "Enough! What are you *doing* to me, girl?"

"Surrendering my virginity," I giggled. "Has anything out of the ordinary happened?" I said archly. "I am entirely inexperienced in these matters. Is it not always thus for a virile fellow like yourself with all the lovers you are so obviously accustomed to having throw themselves at your feet?"

"If you are an inexperienced virgin, then I am the Queen of the May," Pater said, raising the upper half of his body into a seated position, hunching forward, and regarding me with a certain post-coital skepticism which his hormonal metabolism had not previously permitted. "Jive me not, Moussa Shasta Leonardo, who are you, what is the nature of your game, and what sparks this strange power?"

Still playing the naif as closely as possible, I took this as a mere suggestion to exchange name tales, a natural nicety under the circumstances, and presented him with a somewhat edited version, which is to say that I styled Leonardo in a general way as a mage of electronic arts, without feeling the need to mention the subject of personal enhancement devices.

After I had finished, Pater Pan seemed to chew it over in silence for a moment, as if sensing that I had not been entirely forthcoming. "So your mother is a tantric healer and performer?" he finally said. "Then you admit that your profession of naïveté in these matters was less than the whole and nothing but truth?"

I laughed. I shrugged. "Naturellement, I was jesting," I owned. "As you have had occasion to experience, I have actually had no little schooling in my mother's science."

"For sure," said Pater Pan appraisingly, "for a girl of your age and relative unsophistication, you seem to have a decent enough knowledge of the lay of the man."

"*A decent enough knowledge!*" I exclaimed in outrage. "Is that the best you have to say for my tantric performance after what you have just experienced?"

He laughed, but only briefly. Then he fixed me with those piercing blue eyes and spoke in a tone of voice that somehow convinced me of his veracity despite the absolutely outrageous import of his words.

99

"While I am not the sort of creepy-crawlie who scribes a running tally, by conservative estimate, I have granted my favors to some several thousand women on at least a hundred planets over a span of several centuries. Sure, and these have ranged from babes admittedly snatched from their cradles to veritable hagdom, and have included courtesans of great renown, tantric maestras and low putains, bumbling virgins, and every form of feminine life between, and on worlds of every level of sensual sophistication from crabbed puritanism to a hedonic excess that would make Edoku seem like a rest home for celibates. Therefore, while my overwhelming modesty may forbid me to judge my own prowess as a cocksman, when it comes to judging *feminine* performance, I am The Man, the greatest living connoisseur in all the worlds of men."

At this grossly overblown yet somehow sincere and almost believable boast, I was entirely at a loss for words. Pater Pan, au contraire, as I was to learn, never suffered this affliction, and was always more than willing and able to step into a conversational breach.

"Therefore," he went on, "I put you not down when I declare that in my expert critical opinion, while your actual level of tantric artistry is comfortably above the mean, your chops and moves can *in no way* adequately account for what I just experienced, which was probably the numero uno erotic experience of my entire long life."

Well how was a girl to take *that*? On the one hand, this puffed-up creature was relegating my personal performance to a level little above mediocrity, and on the other hand he was declaring that I had pleased him like no other lover! In truth, of course, it was the artistry of *Leonardo* to which he paid his extravagant homage, but I was hardly in a position or mood to admit to that!

Once more, however, Pater Pan's loquacity was more than equal to the task of discounting my silence. "So what I want to know is how in the flaming heart of a million suns such a thing can be possible!" he exclaimed. "What is this magic? How *did* you do it? And more to the point, perhaps, can you do it again?"

At this, I found my tongue and regained the composure of a certain mastery of the strategic situation. "As to the latter," I said slyly, "that is for you to discover if you can charm or bargain me into the attempt. As for the former, surely an innocent naif

100

such as myself, possessed, as you declare, of no overwhelming erotic artistry, is entitled to retain her one poor little secret in the presence of such a puissant mythic personage as the great Pater Pan."

"So now you admit that you knew who I was all along!"

I shrugged. "I have heard some ridiculous and hyperbolic tales which only a fool would credit," I admitted. "But I would rather hear your name tale from your own noble mouth. Have I not told you mine?"

Pater Pan smiled, gave a lofty toss of his golden-maned head. "The full tale of my name would take years to recount," he said grandly.

"No doubt," I replied dryly, "but surely a fellow who by his own admission has had congress with several thousand women has in the course of time and necessity evolved a suitably condensed version for just such occasions as this."

"Vraiment," Pater admitted. "If you are willing to content yourself with a pale shadow of the full magnificence. . . ."

"This I am grudgingly willing to endure," I told him. "Proceed, kudasai."

"I am Pater Pan, famed throughout the worlds of men, or at least wherever Children of Fortune walk the Yellow Brick Road of freedom," he declared grandly, "and this is both my chosen freenom and my identity entire, for long ago, before the Second Starfaring Age was born, before the Ark's first Spark, before the Age of Space itself, truth be told before the memory of this avatar who now speaks began, my paternom and maternom I tossed into the void with all the maya-bound ties chaining my eternal spirit to the Great Wheel.

"So say that my mother was an Arkie and a Rom, a Hippie Queen and a Princess of the Night, and say that my father was an Indian brave or Bodhidharma or Chaka Zulu or the Fliegende Hollander himself, maya, maya, for the spirit of Pater Pan was born before yours truly crawled blinking from some mortal mother's womb and will live on when this Second Starfaring Age is nothing but a dim legend of the prehistoric past.

"Vraiment, I chose not the freenom Pater Pan in homage to the name of the spirit, rather did the *spirit of the name* choose *me* to carry its torch forward into our Age, for Pater Pan was born before the first ape climbed down from our ancestral trees to wander the plains of Earth. I was the very song which drew that dim creature out of the forest of ignorance to take his first halting steps on the Yellow Brick Road to sapience, and thus was born the Child of our species' Fortune, who from that day unto this has danced the camino real to the Pied Pipes of Pater Pan.

"Yes, before the singer was the song, to which we wandered from apes into men, and I was the horny billy-goat music leading us onward by the compass of our desires, and the Pied Piper urging the Children onward from the dusty streets of Hamelin town into the Magic Mountain of eternal Oz, and so too was I the Minstrel of Aquarius who slew the timebound rule of chairmen of the board and kings.

"When the Children's Crusade of the Ages of the Night set forth in quest of Jerusalem's Holy Grail, they marched to my spirit's song. And I was the Piper of Pan in the garden of the Flower Children that bloomed to my music in a golden Summer of Love.

"When the Arkies embarked upon their wanderings in the endless stellar night, Pater Pan was the Spark that rode their great slow arkologies with them, holding aloft the torch in the darkness of the long light-years and frozen centuries between the stars.

"And when the mages of our species wrested the secret of the Jump from the forgotten lore of We Who Have Gone Before and our Second Starfaring Age began, then did the King of the Gypsies and the Prince of the Jokers sally forth from his long sleep under the Magic Mountain to carry the Spark of the Ark forward wherever Children of Fortune wander the Yellow Brick Road out among the far-flung worlds of men!"

Golden, godlike, blue eyes mirroring the azure depths of the sky, declaiming in a mighty voice that seemed to speak not *from* him but *through* him, this marvelous creature seized up his patchwork blouson, whirled it over his head, and draped it grandly about his naked shoulders.

"Voilà, the mystery of the Cloth of Many Colors, the Traje de Luces, the Pied banner of the eternal Piper!" he shouted in a leonine roar. "Each ragged patch is a piece of transient cloth! Each fragment of the whole is a moment, a face, a piece of time, a smile, a laugh, a companion along the Way! Each in its turn frays and unravels and is replaced by another! Each single patch adorns the banner which has cloaked the spirit of Pater Pan for a million years for a time and then is gone! Not one single thread of the original garment which never was remains! Yet that which is the Traje de Luces itself lives on and on and on!"

He crouched down and regarded me face-to-face, and in that moment I knew not whether I regarded a creature out of legend or a man. "C'est moi," he said in a voice that suddenly seemed a good deal less grand. "This Cloth of Many Colors is *me*, girl. The eternal spirit and the natural man. An old patch of cloth, and the glorious whole entire, the singer who passes, and the song which goes forever on."

He shrugged, he smiled, he seemed to shrink back into himself like a great flower subsiding backwards in time into the modest bud from which it was born.

"Thus," he said quite conversationally, "the name tale of Pater Pan."

Needless to say, I had never before heard a name tale like *that*! And certainly not one declaimed in such a thespic manner, as if the quotidian man of flesh and blood whom I had shortly before held in my arms had become an actor upon a stage assuming the mantle of a character far greater than himself, vraiment greater than any mortal man, speaking words that another and at the very least more literarily puissant spirit declaimed through him.

On the other hand, even in my state of charisma-drunken awe, I could perceive that Pater Pan had told me nothing about the man of flesh and blood at all and had cloaked the nakedness of this obfuscation in a tapestry of grandiose rhetoric and extravagant poetry no less devoted to confusion and flash than the blouson of Cloth of Many Colors now draped around his lordly corpus like a royal robe. Blarney indeed, but what wonderful blarney it was, how grander than whatever the unadorned truth of any merely human pedigree could be!

Moreover, even then it seemed to me that some spirit great and true did in fact speak through this marvelous mountebank of a man, for while I could hardly credit the *words* which boasted of a millennial lifespan at the eternal center of history humain entire, my heart was filled with the higher and less coherent truth of the *music* of the song.

103

For as Pater Pan had declared, before the singer was the song, and if the man who sat beside me had long since chosen to subsume his mere pedigree into the higher truth of metaphor, to become the legend of which he sang, who was I to say that mundane veracity was truer to the spirit thereof than literature's noble lies?

Mayhap I speak thusly not as the young girl who was, but as the teller of tales who is, possessed of both the will to declaim the supremacy of my own chosen fictional art over the truth of mere accuracy, and the mature theoretical basis to put such wisdom into the mind of the girl I then was.

But if this is so, it only serves to speak my meaning the stronger, for the inner truth of the matter is that this was the moment when the heroine of the story took the first step on the road to the becoming of the teller of the tale, which is to say that for the first time in her young life, Moussa Shasta Leonardo had heard the music of a spirit that transported her ambitions beyond the song of self.

Not that I was any less determined to make this man my patron and my lover, to rescue myself from indigence by gaining entry to his tribe; but now pecuniary calculations had merged with the ding an sich, for now my desire was to truly partake of the spirit of what now seemed a noble and glorious enterprise, to become a true Gypsy Joker with the song of the tribe in my heart.

As if possessed of the power to read my spirit, or in more likely point of fact, possessed of the long experience to fully comprehend the effect on such as myself of the performance of his name tale, Pater Pan reverted to his earlier, less daunting, and at the same time more practically minded persona.

"And so," he said, "now that you have impressed me with your secret powers as a lover, and I have impressed you with my noble name tale, what be the down and dirty, girl, what is it that you really want?"

"Why to be with you as you surely must know by now!" I declared with an innocent openness of spirit. "To become a Gypsy Joker! With all my heart!"

Pater laughed. "When it comes to my phallic favors, pas problem, since this much I grant gratuit to all who please me, as *you* surely must know by now you have," he said. "When it comes to becoming a Gypsy Joker, this you can achieve by crossing my palm with one hundred pieces of ruegelt."

104

"*What?*" I shouted, brought crashing down from the clouds of the spirit into the muck of mendacious maya by the outrage of such a demand. "Quelle chose! What kind of man are you to speak thusly to a lover? How dare you—"

"Peace!" Pater Pan declared, holding up his hand and smiling the entirely inappropriate smile of sweet reason. "Surely for a woman such as yourself, possessed of secret tantric powers sufficient to win the exhausted admiration of even the mighty Pater Pan, a mere hundred pieces of ruegelt is nada, a mere token, the earnings of a lazy afternoon. . . ."

The thrust, as it were, of this discourse brought back all my previous guile. If he insisted on bringing down our congress to the level of the marketplace, then I too could descend to the logic thereof, and we would see which of us would prevail.

"It is your considered expert opinion that I could easily enough earn one hundred pieces of ruegelt in the performance of the tantric arts?" I said in a wondering and innocent tone that, au contraire, emanated in this moment from anything but a guileless naif.

"For sure!" my victim declared. "You need only summon up half the pluck you've already shown, and offer up your services on the bourse of the streets. A few discreet caresses gratuit to establish your bona fides and hook the mark, then set your price, and voilà!"

"Perhaps you are right," I allowed. "But I am a complete naif in matters of value given for value received. How much ruegelt do you believe I could demand?"

Pater Pan shrugged. "Quién sabe?" he said. "The horniness of the patron, the fullness of his purse, the generosity of his spirit, these are all as relevant as the absolute value of the wares, nē. But always set an initial price of some extravagance, for never will you receive an offer higher than your own best boast."

"Might I ask two hundred?" I inquired.

"Two hundred!" Pater exclaimed. "You will do no volume trade at such a price. Of course, there are always a few who will be willing to meet it, since your performance is somewhat extraordinaire, as I have just had occasion to learn. . . ."

"Indeed you have," I said slyly, coiling for the pounce. "I bow to your wisdom, oh Great Spirit of the Bourse. Henceforth I shall set a price of two hundred pieces of ruegelt. . . ." I paused as if considering the matter. *"Henceforth . . . ?"* I mused. "Vraiment, why not *right now?*"

I held out a demanding palm. "Two hundred pieces of ruegelt, bitte, for the services you have just enjoyed and praised so highly, mon cher!"

Pater Pan's eyes widened in astonishment, his jaw fell open. *"What?"* he exclaimed. "Pay? *Me?* You demand two hundred pieces of ruegelt for enjoying the embraces of *Pater Pan?* Which you yourself have schemed to obtain? What kind of woman are you to speak thusly to a lover?"

And then, hearing his own words mirroring my previous protest of outrage, he broke into raucous and not disapproving laughter.

"A true Gypsy Joker, nē?" I giggled.

He regarded me in arch silence for a moment. Then he shook his head ruefully, but not without the warmest of smiles. "A true Gypsy Joker for sure!" he said. "But surely you will not demand *two hundred* from the domo of your own tribe?"

"From the domo of my own tribe, I would demand nothing at all," I told him. "Vraiment, it was not *I* who intruded pecuniary considerations into any transaction between us, nē. So let not our love be sullied by the passage of filthy lucre from hand to hand. Consider that my price, even as yours, is one hundred pieces of ruegelt."

I cupped my hands as if to receive just such a sum. "Imagine that you are now counting out the coins. . . ."

With a laugh, he pantomimed the donation that I required, and with a laugh, I returned the phantom coins to his own outstretched hands.

We giggled. We kissed. We embraced.

Thus by this phantom commerce of the bourse and true commerce of kindred spirits was our bargain sealed. Thus did my life as a Gypsy Joker justly and triumphantly begin.

It was indeed somewhere under the rainbow, Pater Pan did lead me over the river at the base of the waterfall and through some woods, one could spot an ersatz evening star from its precincts, and if the part about straight on till morning proved to be poetic hyperbole, the circus truly was in town.

Which is to say that despite the prohibition of Child of Fortune favelas on Edoku for understandable esthetic reasons, the Gypsy Jokers had managed to erect and maintain a carnival caravanserei in a choice piece of parkland which lay in perpetual high noon between the arrondissement of glass towers and the rolling residential hills of twilight.

I will never forget my first sight of the encampment from afar as Pater led me toward it along one of the avenues lined with glass towers, an angle of approach he had chosen, as I was soon to learn, for pedagogic as well as esthetic reasons.

A few hundred meters before us, afternoon and the arrondissement of bustling streets ended, and in the far distance the twilit hills formed a dark backdrop sprinkled with the lights of men which entirely outshone the few stars visible in the blackish purpling sky above their crestline. Glowing on the margin of lawn between in the bright light of noon as if purposely highlighted by a celestial spotlight (as in point of fact it of course was) flashed what first appeared to be an immense display of multicolored pennants.

107

A few moments later, I realized that what I saw was a veritable city of tents whose fabric roofs and walls were flapping gently in a light breeze, a wonderful chaos of colors and stripes flung across the parkland like a giant Cloth of Many Colors. As we approached closer, I saw that the tents displayed as great a profusion of forms as hues; there were small closed tents such as might shelter a small camping party, large ones with extravagantly striped sides such as might enclose performers and audience alike, tents that were no more than awnings against the sun, round tents, square tents, oblong tents, tents in a pyramidal shape, und so weiter.

Soon I could make out tiny figures thronging the impromptu streets of the tent city, hear the faint strains of music, catch the aromas of cuisine and incense and intoxicants drifting invitingly towards me on the breeze.

"So, Moussa," Pater Pan said, "what do you see?"

"Xanadu. . . ?" I suggested breathlessly.

Pater laughed. "So should it appear to the rubes," he said, "and so it does. But now that you are a Gypsy Joker, you must learn to see through streetwise eyes."

I cocked an inquisitive eyebrow at him.

"First, you will notice that the location of the carnival is straight athwart the natural route between this busy commercial district and the houses of the hills. So that those Edojin who stroll between the two rather than use the Rapide must pass within its spell. Conversely, the existence of our carnival along the route between bourse and home *encourages* such a lazy stroll. One must always grant the rubes the maximum opportunity to discover their whim to part with ruegelt. Now why did I choose noon rather than evening or night?"

I shrugged and held out my hands in a confession of ignorance.

"Because on Edoku, as on most of the worlds of men, evening is the chosen hour for dining on haute cuisine in grand restaurants, and night is the chosen hour of elaborate and expensive spectacles and entertainments, and our quaint shows and simple fare can go mano á mano with neither," he told me. "The clever Child of Fortune caters to immediate whim and caprice, tidbits of food, not haute cuisine, impromptu music, ruespiels, and busking, not formal theater or spectacle, trinkets and geegaws, not noble craft or high art—all thrust under the noses of the rubes before they even recognize the desire for same, and all available at prices which prevent the decision to part with ruegelt from causing significant reflection."

"You make us sound little more than mendicants. . . ."

"Right on!" Pater exclaimed approvingly. "Sure, and we *are* little more than mendicants. The mendicant plays upon the pity and empathy of his mark to secure alms but offers nothing of value in return save a certain pompous sense of self-satisfaction, nē. The Child of Fortune offers *a little* more. We amuse. A laugh, a smile, a savor, a few moments of pleasure, a nostalgic remembrance of a youth when the customer was free and weightless as the breeze, a Child of Fortune even as you and I."

"But that is no *little* difference at all!" I declared. "For the mendicant plays upon a confrontation with misfortune and makes the donor feel smugly superior, whereas *we* play upon a confrontation with lost freedom and return a memory of joy, nē. To me, that is all the difference in the worlds." And why, I realized, that come what may, I could never reduce myself to begging for alms.

Pater gave me a strange and narrow look, compounded, or so it seemed, of amazement, approval, satori, perhaps even a certain sense of awe. "Well spoken indeed, my little guru," he said. "The spirit moves through your words, and in retrospect, I now congratulate myself for having the wisdom to know it all along."

And so, basking in the approval of the domo of the tribe, in thrall, in love, pledging my spirit to him and his enterprise in the depths of my loyal young heart, and quite erroneously convinced that I had captured his soul and made him my own as surely as he had made me his, I entered the carnival of the Gypsy Jokers hand in hand with the noble Pater Pan, quite confident that I would be its queen as surely as my man was king.

While the former supposition was one of which I was soon to be disabused, the latter was reconfirmed as soon as we entered the camp, for Pater Pan could go nowhere within its precincts without being the center of attention of Gypsy Jokers and Edojin alike, though the mode of homage differed in tone between the two.

As Pater made the rounds of the carnival with myself in train, ostensibly for the benefit of my orientation, but in truth, as

I was to learn in the next few days, as part of his regular preening ritual, the Edojin patronizing the divertissements honored the presence of the living legend with sidelong glances, whispered comments to each other, the occasional frank stare, though these burghers of Great Edoku never seemed to favor the Gypsy King with a word or gesture of direct salutation. Nor, for his part, did Pater stoop to acknowledge the groundlings with banter or even direct eye contact, any more than an actor upon a stage would betray cognizance of their existence to the audience.

Vis-à-vis our fellow Gypsy Jokers, it was entirely another matter.

The caravanserei of the Gypsy Jokers encompassed a bewildering profusion of enterprises, and as Pater commended each of them to my attention, he held impromptu court with the maestros and journeymen thereof, questioning and advising, bantering and suggesting, collecting a portion of the take for the common purse or mayhap his own, and contriving to introduce the latest member of the tribe casually en passant.

That Pater was in truth the ultimate maestro of each and every art as he pretended was difficult for even the smitten Moussa to credit, but certainement he was deferred to, or at least humored, as such by the practitioners thereof. At food kiosks, he nibbled at tidbits and suggested alterations in the recipes. The wares of jewelers, potters, sculptors, leatherworkers, und so weiter, were eyed, fingered, even sniffed at; many were praised, but certain items were ordered removed from the market for lack of sufficient craft, and the subject of the proper price for everything was discussed in some detail.

Pater would try his hand against his own minions at the varied games of chance and skill to be found within the camp, and more often than not would win a small pile of ruegelt which he would pocket with wry admonitions and homilies of gambling lore, praising extravagantly those few who managed to wrest coin from him.

The grounds were also full of buskers of every sort—musicians, singers, ruespielers, dancers, jugglers, artistes of sleight of hand, und so weiter—performing gratis or for whatever coins passing Edojin might be moved to toss their way. Pater would take in their performances, and then during an intermission in same, take them aside and offer his advice. Jugglers had roughnesses in their performances pointed out, musicians and singers were referred to colleagues for the enhancement of their repertoires, sleight of hand artistes were shown new tricks, ruespielers were given new variations on old tales.

There were many tents within which tantric tableaus were enacted before audiences, and many more within which the clientele took part in the erotic choreography or enjoyed solo performances in a mode of their own choosing.

Pater not only was quite free with his critiques, not only advised male tantric performers in the niceties of their art (a subject in which I would be the last to declare him less than a master), but saw fit not only to advise tantric artists of my own gender in the means of pleasing his own, but offered to supply private lessons in same more than once under my very nose!

In truth—which is to say sans self-serving dissembling—if I have conveyed a certain less than enthusiastic attitude on the part of the young Moussa towards Pater Pan's performance of his royal rounds, if I have portrayed him as intruding into every art and enterprise with the self-importance of the kibbitzing dilettante and withheld my wholehearted appreciation of his puissance as a maestro of them all, verisimilitude would also have me own that it was neither the tone of his discourse nor the generality of its reception which soured the edges of my delight at this grand tour of Xanadu, or to be even more painfully forthright about the source of my discomfort, I could find little fault with his conversational congress with the *males* of our tribe.

These were all younger than my great lover, indisputably callow in my eyes by comparison, and I could only approve of the open-spirited manner in which they all deferred to him in matters great and small, sought his favor, desired to emulate his noble model, and accepted his advice and teachings even in the subtleties of their own arts with the intellectual avidity of the sincere student.

His behavior vis-à-vis the *female* of the species and their frank and mooning attentions to him, however, were entirely beyond the scope of my selfless admiration and approval. Vraiment, in my brief career as a femme fatale of Nouvelle Orlean, I had never been subject to such treatment by a swain, and would have eschewed the further company of any such boor the first time I caught him exchanging fey glances with a lesser female being, though admittedly the techniques of covert theft of amatory attention with which these creatures constantly sought to poach on my preserve were not exactly foreign to my own repertoire.

All the more reason to resent the cooing words with which he was constantly laved, the light chance touches of numerous feminine hands to various portions of his anatomy, the inquiring glances, the intrusion of their corpuses into the intimate aura of his body space, all as if I were not present, or worse, was too much the fool to comprehend the import of this sub rosa mating dance. Pater, moreover, played *his* part to the hilt, returning amatory banter, playing quite free and easy with his little intimate touches of hand upon flesh, eschewing not the contact of eye with eye, and in short, openly reveling in his status as cock of the walk.

Most galling, not to say most amazing, of all, the fact that I was forthrightly introduced to one and all as both the newest member of the tribe and a lover fresh from his embrace did absolutely nothing to dissuade his legion of feminine admirers from paying him court in my presence, indeed my rivals for his attentions welcomed me with what even I in my outraged state could not distinguish from sincere friendliness, even while they were clearly offering themselves up to my man!

At length, vraiment at what seemed like interminable length, this disjunctive combination of delightful introduction to the wonders of the carnival and torturous display of universal flirtation, or worse, concluded and Pater ushered me into the sanctuary of his own tent.

Without, this pavilion could not have been mistaken for the dwelling of any other, for the entire tent was constructed of the same Cloth of Many Colors which cloaked the much-sought-after body of Pater Pan, but within, it was a venue of humble simplicity entirely out of keeping with what seemed to me to be his elevated opinion of his own grandeur. Indeed, there was nothing inside the small tent save a large bed constructed of a red velvet cloth flung over a deep nest of branches, a few plain wooden chests, some low tables, and a varied assortment of lighting fixtures which were capable of casting whatever hue and intensity of illumination might suit his mood.

While it was a definite improvement over the parklands and gardens which had been my most recent habitations, it was a far cry from the luxury and charm of my chamber at the Yggdrasil, and I immediately resolved to utilize my own more refined tastes and the plentiful resources so obviously at his command to improve matters at once, for such spartan bachelor quarters were hardly suitable to the conjugal arrangements I so erroneously assumed we would now share.

Pater, flopping on his bed with his hands clasped behind his head in the self-satisfied manner of a sated pasha, nevertheless had the wit to read from my demeanor that something was amiss. "Qué pasa, Moussa?" he asked appraisingly.

"I expected a domicile of somewhat higher style from a man who professes to be the perfect master of so many arts. . . ."

"Au contraire," he said, "possessions are anchors to the spirit, and simplicity is the highest style of all. In the encampment of the Gypsy Jokers I am surrounded by all manner of *communal* delights. Why hoard treasures like a miser of the spirit? All I really require is this pallet on the floor and light to meet my fancy." He laughed. "Besides, I sleep elsewhere more often than not."

The latter I could well imagine. "All very well for the wandering cocksman," I told him, "but now that we are a ménage à deux, we shall require furnishings more appropriate to genteel domesticity, nē. You can hardly expect me to share a bed of branches in an empty tent."

At this, Pater sat upright and regarded me first with surprise, then with consternation, and finally with a certain knowing ruefulness. "Whoa, lady, you seem to be laboring under a whole series of misapprehensions," he said not unkindly. He patted the bed beside him. "Setzen sie sich, girl, and receive enlightenment."

I liked the sound of it not at all; nevertheless I did as he asked, though not without a tremor of trepidation, and not without the maintenance of a certain physical distance congruent with my sudden unease.

"You cannot be more than twenty standard years old, nē?" he said. "Whereas I have traveled the worlds of men for millennia. . . ."

"Such hyperbole is all very well for poetic boastings for the mystification of rubes," I snapped, "but hardly suitable to a serious discussion of matters of the heart en boudoir! No human may attain the age of four hundred, and the scientific reasons therefor have been known for centuries."

"Ah, but I speak of *time,* not *age,* Moussa, and in our Second Starfaring Age, these are not bound so tightly together, nē. Greater mysteries aside, we do not slowly decay into dotage as men once did, but all at once, when our nervous systems wear out. So, for all you know, in span of my body's years, I could be three hundred as easily as thirty. . . ."

"Thirty, three hundred, three thousand, je ne sais pas!" I declared. "What has all this talk of age and time to do with *us?*"

"*All,*" he said flatly. "Believe it or not, believe at least that *I* believe that I've been around the worlds of men longer than even I can remember. Knowing me as you already do, for sure you can believe that the last several thousands of years were not quite passed in monkish celibacy, which is to say I am far more experienced in affairs of the heart than you, or at least I have known as many women as you have days."

"Now at least I surmise that you speak sans hyperbole," I admitted dryly.

"Bien. And I tell you true, their spirits were as precious to me in their time as yours is now."

"*Spirits?*" I sniffed. "You would have me believe you have cherished several thousand lovers for their *spirits?*"

Pater shrugged. "Am I not a man of great charisma?" he said. "Am I not the cocksman supreme? Do you imagine I am anything less than a perfect master of seduction? Is it not the fact that I am a universal object of feminine desire precisely the cause of your present pique?"

"And modest to a fault as well," I said, hardly able to believe that I had in fact heard such incredible boasting from the lips of mortal man. But unable to deny the obnoxious truth either.

But Pater Pan did not laugh. Instead, his face became a visage of such intense sincerity, he regarded me with a look of such caritas and tenderness, that somehow he managed to make himself seem like a hero for having the spiritual courage to utter the very words which the previous moment had marked him as a boor and a braggart. Never had a man looked at me thusly. Never had a spirit touched mine so deeply or inspired such totally irrational trust. Never had I felt such love.

"Do you imagine that such a man need grant his favors to any who has not touched his heart?" he said.

"It was not precisely your *heart* that I touched in the shower stall. . . ." I reminded him.

Once again, Pater did not so much as smile at my jape, indeed he came as close as I had ever seen to an impatient frown. "Merde, muchacha, be *real!*" he said. "Do you imagine that I have not been the object of more such ploys than I could count? Do you imagine that my lingam rules my heart? Do you really believe I knew not your true intention, namely to achieve exactly what you have?"

My ears burned. My eyes began to tear. "What a silly little fool you must have thought I was. . . ." I whispered forlornly. Yet still I could not avert my gaze from the depths of his bright blue eyes.

Nor his from mine. "*Fool?*" he exclaimed. "Your courage and your guile won my heart!"

"They did?"

Now Pater broke into a boyish grin that made me want to laugh, though I knew not why. "It takes one to know one, n'est-ce pas?" he said. "Have I not lived by just such courage and guile for all these centuries? How could an ego as massive as that of the great Pater Pan fail to love a spirit in which he sees to his delight the mirror of his own?"

Now I *did* laugh as I felt a great weight lifted from my spirit by his words. Pater sprang from the bed and began pacing as he spoke, or rather declaimed in the thespic style of his name tale, and now as then, a mighty spirit seemed to be speaking through him, but now, via his bright blue eyes which never broke contact with my own, I felt it moving through me as well, as if we were two singers who had become the music of a single song.

"Ah, Moussa, we are two avatars of a single spirit, you and I, sister and brother, and equal lovers, no matter that you have hardly begun to walk the Yellow Brick Road, and I have been the Piper of the dance time out of mind on a hundred worlds and more. Are we not true Gypsies and true Jokers, Children of the same Fortune? *That* is why you are now in this encampment, not because you knotted my lingam around your finger, but because you out-Joked the Joker, and out-Gypsied the Gypsy, and proved thereby that you belonged to the tribe by droit d'esprit, a Gypsy Joker of the true spirit before you even knew the name!"

Then all at once he collapsed back onto the bed and became the mere man and trickster once more. "And that is why I am not about to let you live with me in this tent or delude your-

115

self that you or any other woman can be my one and only, girl," he said. "Could I be so heartless as to deprive the women of the worlds of the full glory of my being? Could I be such a jealous churl as to deprive the *men* of the worlds of the full glory of *yours*?"

"What a farrago of self-serving merde!" I exclaimed in wounded anger. "What high-sounding rhetoric to justify what low-minded lust!"

Pater only smiled at me warmly in a superior manner that further inflamed my rage against him. "Would not such a low-minded swine of selfish lust play a lower-minded game? Would he not *encourage* the delusion that, given time and patience and a casual enough disregard for his peccadilloes, you could make him your own?"

"You believe that I would watch you play the stud to the entire barnyard and loyally await my turn at your favors in hope thereby of cozening you into mending your ways?" I snapped.

Pater Pan seemed to stare right into my soul. He placed a gentle hand upon my knee. "Can you look me in the eye and honestly declare that if I had never spoken this truth you would not?" he said all-too-knowingly.

I could not reply. Indeed, I could no longer even meet his gaze.

"How long before such a love turned to hate?" Pater persisted. "Vraiment, even if you caponized the cock, would you not lose as much as I?"

"May I not at least be permitted to be the judge of that?" I muttered bleakly.

Pater cupped my chin in his hands and raised my eyes to meet his own. "So be it, girl," he said. "Suffer one more long-winded koan, after which you have only to say so, and I will be forever yours."

Once more that preternatural spirit seemed to emerge from manly flesh to speak to its own avatar within my heart, but now my lover spoke as well, or so it seemed, with a human warmth even I in such a moment could not deny.

"I have known thousands of women on hundreds of worlds and you mayhap a few score fellows on a world or two. Yet tell me true if you can that you in your short span have been any more addicted to pacts of eternal monogamy than I!"

At this, I was constrained to merely curl my lips, for of course no such vows had ever passed through them, nor indeed had such thoughts previously even trammeled my admittedly somewhat fickle heart.

"We are Children of the same spirit, nē, you and I," Pater went on relentlessly. "What sort of man, what a false Child of Fortune, would I be to allow a lover to tie herself to me and lose thereby that very spirit which she loves in me, which has made me what I am? Vraiment, to turn her back on the Yellow Brick Road after her first few steps thereon?"

He smiled. He took my hand in his. "Instead, why not a treaty of equal spirits, one Gypsy Joker to another? Take from a lover's hand this carnival, and Edoku, and all the worlds of men beyond. Let me be your lover, and you be mine, but live the life that I have lived, be true to the spirit that we share. Eat, drink, toxicate yourself, wander, learn, adventure, dare all, have ten lovers, a hundred, a thousand, vie with the great Pater Pan in running up the score, and become thereby not my spouse but a true consort of my heart! For what do I lose thereby? What substance is depleted? And you have worlds to gain that I already know. So allow me to give a greater gift than what you seek, chère Moussa, the gift of freedom as my lover and an equal spirit. And in return, only seek not to diminish mine."

I trembled at the touch of his hand, I knew not how to reply, for the greater part of me wished to gather up this wise and noble creature in my arms, while the worm of intellect whispered in my ear that I was somehow only the latest victim of this perfect master of the truthful lie.

"Well?" said Pater. "Which do you choose? Sister and brother of the same free spirit? Or dour misers of the heart?"

Put thusly, was not the question its own answer? Even now, with hindsight's wisdom long years and many lovers after the fact, *still* I cannot find the flaw in his irrefutable logic d'amour. Nor, on the other hand, can I escape from the entirely illogical conviction that it was there.

I shook my head ruefully, acknowledging that I was in the presence of a perfect master, though of *what* I was not quite sure. "You have the tongue of an angel and the guile of a serpent," I told him. "Why then, knowing this, do I now trust such a monster with my heart?"

Pater laughed. He hugged me to him and kissed me on the lips. With a great relenting sigh, I snuggled into his embrace. "Because," he said, "beneath the mythos and blarney of the great Pater Pan, there is nothing more sinister than the soul of a little boy."

I slept that night in the arms of Pater Pan, or rather he allowed himself to innocently repose in mine after a somewhat briefer passage d'amour than our first mighty duet, which served, nevertheless, to reaffirm my arcane tantric mastery over his flesh and to reaffirm his primacy, despite all, in my heart, and thus to fairly seal our bizarre "treaty of equal spirits."

Vraiment, in the days and weeks to come we slept together thusly often enough, and if I had given up all hope of becoming the exclusive consort of the cock of the walk, I could content myself with the admission, wrested from his panting lips by the magic of the Touch, that I could, whenever the spirit moved me, not merely please him like no other lover, but overmaster, outlast, and outpleasure this most puissant of cocksmen, and leave him gasping limply and crying "Enough!"

Indeed having established myself in my own mind and his as the secret mistress of the ultimate object of feminine desire in open competition, I began to appreciate the wisdom of the pact he had forced upon me. Though at first I sulked and pouted when I spied Pater engaged in intimacies with others, soon enough I began to take a certain satisfaction in this erotic competition, in which, courtesy of the art of Leonardo, I was assured of certain, if not exactly sporting, victory.

Moreover, once my full confidence in my own erotic puissance had thereby been restored, I regained once more the spirit of that Moussa Shasta Leonardo who had been in her own small way no mean femme fatale of Nouvelle Orlean. I took to denying my favors to Pater from time to time for my own amusement. I dallied with lesser males of the tribe and soon developed a reputation as a tantric performer of preternatural power and some artistry.

Soon enough I was invited to take minor parts in tantric group performances in which the audience participated actively and met with the general approval of same via the raw power of the Touch, though the featured performers would often chide me for upstaging their more demanding roles.

When it came to performing in tantric tableaus in which the audience remained passive spectators, however, I was a good deal less successful, since the employment of the Touch therein did nothing for the audience and tended to disrupt the concentration of the ensemble with ill-timed orgasms, and when I therefore confined myself to ordinary performance of my modest roles, my relative lack of studied artistry was all too apparent.

Nevertheless, the cachet derived from being even a minor and occasional public performer, combined with the electronically enhanced certainty of providing fair value, allowed me to earn some ruegelt as solo tantric artist, though I never summoned up the hubris or courage to demand more than twenty pieces of ruegelt from a customer.

True to his word in letter and spirit, Pater never displayed a moment of jealousy, or indeed anything less than openhearted enthusiasm for my enterprises and amours, though truth be told my initial motivation had been the eliciting of same. And once I had quite convinced myself that his dedication to the spirit of our mutual freedom was quite genuine and unconstrained, I had to admit to myself that I would have been a fool to have had it any other way.

For it was a grand and glorious time. Having known nothing of life but an existence based on parental largesse and then a period of utter penury resulting from the exhaustion of same, the vie of the Gypsy Jokers was more to me than a garden of delights, it was my very first experience of a world in which I was neither the darling daughter nor the helpless waif but a free, equal, and independent agent. The strip of Cloth of Many Colors that I wore sometimes as scarf, sometimes as sash, sometimes as headband, was purchased with ruegelt earned by my own efforts, as were the simple meals I bought in the camp in lieu of fressen bars. While the former was hardly an item of haute couture and the latter could not pretend to haute cuisine, I was adorned with the ensign of my own enterprise and dined on the fruits thereof.

I was Moussa Shasta Leonardo, Gypsy Joker, true avatar of the spirit of the Child of Fortune, a free and equal lover of Pater Pan, and indeed he had seen my future self truly, for having attained this station, never would I have then willingly traded it for being the mere consort of even the noblest of men.

119

9 While at first I was more than content to find myself earning my way as a Gypsy Joker via the various modes available to a tantric performer of modest artistry and secret power, after a time I became gradually seized by the somewhat incoherent desire to expand my sphere of interest and enhance my possibilities, for I could not forever deny that my sole means of earning ruegelt consisted of a smattering of my mother's noble art and the electronic enhancement of my modest attainments in the disciplines of same which was mine courtesy of my father's craft.

Moreover, the more I took minor parts in tantric tableaus whose feature players displayed a diligent and indeed obsessive dedication to the true mastery of the high art of which I was no more than a feckless dilettante, the more I realized that I lacked the inner drive to endure the long hours of study and exercise required to achieve the status of a tantric maestra.

Indeed, the atmosphere of the carnival was not exactly conducive to dedicated diligence in the pursuit of any single craft or art, at least not for a youthful spirit new to the life of a true Child of Fortune, for every waking hour offered up a smorgasbord of possible pursuits, not to say a plethora of diversions to distract me from any thought of gainful employ whatever. There were jugglers, sleight of hand artistes, singers, musicians, und so weiter wandering the grounds, and to a Gypsy Joker, admission to the shows and performances taking place within tented walls was gratuit. Not to mention endless possibilities for idle hours of amorous dalliance, though this began to lose a certain piquancy for a laborer in the vineyards of the tantric trades.

Then too I had the example of the polymathic Pater Pan, by the definition of our tribe the ideal Child of Fortune incarnate, far more interested in playing jack-of-all-trades than in becoming a true maestro of any of them, whom, naturellement, I desired to please with the ultimate homage of successful emulation.

Moreover, the Gypsy Jokers did not confine their trades to the environs of the camp; the buskers who thronged our caravanserei also roamed the nearby vecinos giving impromptu performances on the streets thereof for contributions. So too did other members of the tribe hawk finger food, geegaws, and our simple crafts beyond the confines of our bidonville of tents. The street trade served to spread the repute of our carnival; contrawise, the mythos of the permanent fete enhanced the street trade.

Indeed, as Pater Pan would often enough declare, the true venue of the Child of Fortune *was* out in the streets among the bustling throngs of the quotidian worlds of men, for here we had performed our highest public roles when we were Troubadours and Tinkers, Romany and Hippies, for by playing the part of the Free Spirits of the worlds, we did our part to keep the spirit of the people free. In this, he told us, pecuniary profit was happily at one with a sense of noblesse oblige.

Be such grandiosity as it may, it began to seem to me that it was time to venture forth from the cozy confines of the encampment I had come to call home into the streets of Edoku where once I had been a helpless waif but where I now might carry the piebald banner of the Gypsy Jokers forth as a soldier of a Children's Crusade whose Holy Grail was the ruegelt to be gained therein.

While the spirit was willing, my skills were, to say the least, somewhat circumscribed. I could not sing, dance, juggle, do sleight of hand, or play a musical instrument, and the opportunities for tantric performances on crowded thoroughfares were few and far between. Yet such was my desire to venture forth as a true Child of Fortune of the streets that at length I swallowed my pride and deigned to try my hand at the street hawkers' trade.

Exerting my erotic charms to gain the good graces of Dani

121

Ben Bama, a youth who, while he could in no way be mistaken for a chef maestro, was generally regarded as our premiere artiste of finger food, I spent several days wandering the vecino of glass towers with trays of his dainties. These were a cunning assortment of steamed dim sum of variously flavored doughs filled with all sorts of viands, legumes, sweet curries, and flavored creams, liberally spiced with assorted mild intoxicants, and I knew full well that I could find no more promising fare to hawk than this.

But truth be told, though I sallied forth each day with high hopes, more often than not I would return with but a few coins and a great heap of stale buns. For once on the street, I lacked the chutzpah and enthusiasm to continually proclaim the virtues of my wares at the top of my voice or to accost strangers; instead, my technique consisted of wandering aimlessly about in a daze with the haughty expression of one performing a task she clearly considered below her natural station.

At length even Dani, avid though he was for my continued tantric ministrations, was reluctantly moved to suggest that I favor another enterprise with my services.

I met with little more success hawking such items of adornment as embroidered sashes, netsuke of wood and metal, belts woven of silver wire, mirror-berets, und so weiter, though at least the craftsmen of same could afford to be more tolerant of my failures, since these items were not perishable and could be sent back to market with a peddler of more puissant skills.

Finally, I did somewhat better with jewelry crafted by Ali Kazan Bella. Ali was a lusty young man whose good humor and considerable tantric skills I quite enjoyed, and his jewelry, while crude by Edojin standards, manifested a skill and somewhat demented energy for which I could generate a sincere enthusiasm. With cunning little knives he had fashioned himself and under the influence of central nervous system enhancers, Ali carved necklaces, bracelets, earrings, and brooches out of single blocks of wood; filigree bijoux of such intricate fineness that at first glance they appeared to be twisted together out of wire.

This jewelry epitomized precisely those qualities which charmed the Edojin when it came to quaint Child of Fortune crafts: rude materials mimicking those of a higher technological level, clear evidence of long hours of tedious hand labor, and what they called "the wu of blood, sweat, and tears."

122

Adorned, indeed bedecked, with several rings on every finger, bracelets up and down each arm, a dozen or more necklaces, several pairs of earrings, and brooches pinned all over my tunic to the point where I was fairly armored in wooden filigree, I cut a figure of sufficient bizarrité to attract considerable attention even on the streets of Edoku, and even I, the least forward of street hawkers, was able to do a reasonable trade.

Still, even this modest success as a peddler left me discontent with my place in the life of the streets, or rather, perhaps, such success at the expense of my own dignity after a series of failures resulting at least in part from the disdainful husbanding of same, forced upon me the perception that I was really quite indifferent to success or failure as a mere merchant of the wares of others. Indeed, if I had desired such a vie, I would have been much better advised to remain on Glade and become an agent for the wares of my own father in the haut monde of the wealthy rather than a peddler of snacks and trinkets in the streets.

No, though I continued to hawk his jewelry upon occasion out of affection for Ali, and though I continued to supplement my modest share of this trade with tantric performances in the camp, at length I admitted to myself that I had developed a genuine personal ambition that went beyond mere membership in the Gypsy Joker tribe or even becoming a free spirit of the streets.

It seemed to me, then as now, that it was the Gypsy Joker buskers who wandered Great Edoku performing for what fortune and the impromptu audiences tossed their way who were the *true* Children of Fortune, the spiritual raison d'être of our very existence in the wider scheme of things. For it was *they* who were in truth both living out and extolling the ancient and noble legends of the Gypsies and Hippies, the Troubadours and the Arkies, and, by serving as avatars incarnate of the spirit of the Child of Fortune's millennial romance, keeping it alive in the Second Starfaring Age.

With hindsight's vision, I perceive that this was my first dim inkling of my own future calling, the formless desire to live a life where the spirit meets the mind, to share the vie of the tale-teller or performer, to immerse myself in some higher enterprise for the ding an sich, to present the product of my own inner being for the titillation and edification of an audience of kindred spirits.

Vraiment, at the time I desired nothing more than the egoistic pleasure of the vie itself, for I had no tale to tell or song to sing, nor the craft to do so if I had. Indeed, that was the precise nature of my dilemma: I had fixed my heart's desire upon the life of a street performer, yet I lacked even a passing acquaintance with any entertainer's art.

Naturellement, it was to Pater Pan that I turned for wisdom in the sated afterglow of an evening's erotic exercises in his tent.

"Pas problem, girl!" he told me airily after a less than cogent recitation of my desires. "For sure *you* will have little difficulty extracting free instruction from some male maestro of your chosen art!"

Curled in his sheltering arms, I nodded my assent. "But what art may that be?" I said.

"You know not?" he said in some perplexity.

I shrugged. "I am less than pleased by the sound of my own voice in song, when it comes to musical instruments, I seem to have several thumbs, I have no interest in sleight of hand, juggling, or dance. . . ."

Pater laughed. "Apprentice yourself to a street theater group then," he told me. "You can hardly converse for ten minutes without betraying thespic talent!"

I rolled this conceit around the palate of my mind; while it seemed to me that my life on Glade and my small successes on Edoku gave a certain evidence of my talent for playing roles, these had always been of my own crafting, and something about a life of mouthing other people's words left a taste for which I did not entirely care.

I shook my head. "Something about it pleases me not. . . ."

"Qué?"

"Je ne sais pas. . . ."

"If not you, then who?" Pater demanded. "Speak, girl, I command you, the free sprach of your heart of hearts!"

Something in the tone of his voice, some arcane magic of personal puissance, did indeed impel me to give free verbal rein to the glossolalia of my unformed thoughts.

"I wish to do what you do, Pater, which is to say, I wish to be like you, or rather my own version of the spirit you say we share, which is to say, I wish to live the life of that which I speak, or speak the life of what I am, I mean, you speak, vraiment to become, as you say, both the singer and the song, metaphorically of course, since even I lack the hubris to attempt to subject an audience to my cracked warblings, I mean, that is. . . . *Merde!*"

I threw up my hands and snorted in frustration, unable to encompass with any precision that mystery for whose clear image I was searching.

But Pater Pan understood more than what I was saying, or perhaps was able to see the unoccluded vision behind my fog of words. "Aha!" he cried. "It is a ruespieler you wish to become, though perhaps you know it not."

"Ruespieler? *Me?*"

On the one hand, his declaration rang a chime in my spirit which immediately harmonized with its vibration, but on the other hand, the notion was one which I had never consciously considered. Certainement, ruespieling required not the least bit of musical ability or physical dexterity. Nor was one constrained to play out a role crafted by another or mouth someone else's words. Au contraire, a ruespieler needed only stories to tell, the loquacity to tell them, and the chutzpah to stand in the street and begin spieling in the confident hope that passersby would be moved by her art to listen and then be moved by her tale to contribute to the cause.

"Ruespieler. . . ?" I repeated much more thoughtfully. "Me. . . ?"

"Surely you have noticed your own gift of gab?" Pater said dryly. "It was your tantric powers which gained you access to my arms, but for sure it was the power of your blarney which made you a Gypsy Joker without having to pay the fee!"

I was not burdened with false modesty to the point where I need deny this obvious truth. Having accepted this satori from my guru, I could then easily enough perceive that I had always used words and the twists I could put on their meanings to achieve certain practical ends. While my career as a femme fatale of Nouvelle Orlean could not have flourished in the face of tantric ineptitude, surely I had known full well as far back as my initiation with Robi that words were a necessary part of the armamentarium d'amour. Indeed, had I not fought my parents to a standstill

125

by artfully turning their own words to my devices? Had I not at length enticed the incomprehensible Edojin to direct me to a hotel by besting them at their own verbal sport?

As for chutzpah, while I had to admit that I fell short of the necessary amount when it came to hawking the wares of cooks or craftsmen, I was not entirely unforthcoming when it came to peddling my *own* goods.

But alas, it was precisely this in which I found myself lacking, for while my mystique was what I was hawking in Nouvelle Orlean and my electronically enhanced tantric services thusfar in Edoku, the goods of the ruespieler were *stories,* and of these I had none.

"I do believe you are right when it comes to ambition," I told Pater, "and I perceive that I may have both the talent to play with words and mayhap the courage to stand naked on the street and declaim, but what story can I tell?"

"There is only *one* story to tell, and we all tell it," Pater said. "Like the Cloth of Many Colors, each patch has its own tale, but the true story is the whole."

"And what story is that?" I demanded dubiously.

"The story you must learn to tell, of course. What else?"

"Merde! And how do you expect me to learn it if you won't tell it to me?"

"But I've *been* telling it to you since the first ape climbed down from the trees!"

"May we descend from the lofty heights of the zen koan to the realm of quotidian knowledge?" I suggested dryly. "Just how am I to trap this mythical unicorn of a story?"

"Fortunately, virginity is not required," Pater said archly. "In the realm of maya, it is simply a matter of listening to enough versions until you are sufficiently moved to sew your own patch into the fabric. In even grittier terms, ruespieling, like any art, is a matter of applying the will of the spirit to the diligent study of the craft."

"Quelle chose!" I said with less than enthusiasm. "Do my ears deceive me, or have I truly heard an endorsement of *diligent study* from the lips of *Pater Pan?*"

"For sure!" Pater exclaimed grandly. "It has taken me several millennia of diligent study to create that ultimate triumph of the ruespieler's art, my own magnificent legendary self!"

*   *   *

I was only to perceive the inner truth of this extravagance much karma later in the depths of the Bloomenveldt, when it was to lead me out of the forest of flowers and back into the worlds of men, but even then, as soon as I began to take practical steps to learn the ruespieler's art, I started to see a certain bizarre veracity behind Pater Pan's modest and outrageous boast.

Having no story to tell to earn myself ruegelt, I continued to vend both my own tantric services and Ali's jewelry in order to maintain a small supply of same while I spent more and more of my time listening to the ruespielers who worked the carnival and following them forth when they took their tales into the street.

Indeed it was the very self-created legend of which Pater Pan had boasted which was the cloak of mythos onto which the tales of the Gypsy Joker ruespielers were sewn. Or mayhap, just as likely, it was Pater Pan who had sewn his own mythic persona together out of swatches of tales snipped from cycles of stories that may indeed have begun as odes sung by bards of the preliterate primeval past, or at any rate certainly seemed to have antecedents that predated the Age of Space. Whether the ruespielers of the Gypsy Jokers unraveled the fabric of the legend of Pater Pan to craft their own tales, or whether Pater had assembled his cloak of personal mythos out of tales told by generations of ruespielers, or whether indeed the truth of the matter was both, the eternal Child of Fortune was the hero of all the most popular tales, and the domo of the Gypsy Jokers was clearly enough the main avatar thereof in the lore of the tribe.

Indeed, each ruespieler had a rather limited repertoire of tales, or so it seemed to me, many of them shared in common, though the more successful ruespielers all had a tale or two that they had made entirely their own, and all would style the tales they held communally somewhat differently, turning what in one version might be romance into another version's farce.

Lance Della Imre told the best version of the most oft-told tale, *Spark of the Ark*, the story of the Eternal Arkie, who chose to span the entire history of the First Starfaring Age by the expedient, outré even to the Arkies, of passing all but the peak moments thereof in cryogenic slumber.

"And where did he go when the Jump Drive rang down the final curtain on the great slow centuries of the First Starfaring

127

Age?" Lance would demand in his peroration, the most perfect segue from a tale into a plea for donations that any of the ruespielers had contrived.

"Everywhere! Nowhere! Into the space between which lies within our human hearts! There, in that urchin in a Public Service Station smock, here, within this simple teller of the tale, and best of all within the Arkie Sparkie hearts of all you poor quotidian creatures who still retain the nobility of spirit to honor the Arkie Spark within yourselves by showering the teller of the tale with ruegelt!"

Shella Jin Omar's favorite tale, *The Pied Piper of Pan*, was perhaps closest to the immediate personal inspiration of the source, since, like myself, she enjoyed certain intimacies with same, and well do I remember her artful declamation thereof, if not without a certain jealous pique.

"Hola, was the Age of Space the wondrous time when our species first pecked its way free of the natal egg of Earth and ventured forth into the starry realms beyond. Mighty for those bygone days in argent and spacefaring science was the land called from afar the Gold Mountain, and all-powerful was its board of directors, the Pentagon, who dreamed of building a new *Gold Mountain,* an arkology in which generations of their minions might travel to conquer worlds circling distant stars.

"But alas, the Pentagon was utterly mean-spirited and ruthless in the service of this mighty and noble task, and so those who should have had their wanderjahrs as Children of Fortune were constrained thereby to expend their youth as wage slaves in durance vile.

"Cependant, energy, as the mages even then declared, can be neither created nor destroyed, only channeled or transformed, and no more certainly than when it comes to the kundalinic fires of youth, for to seek to destroy them in the name of obedient servitude is only to arouse and inflame the Serpent's ire.

"Thus did the Serpent Kundalini arise in outrage, and smite the land of the Gold Mountain as Circe had the minions of Odysseus, for behold, the army of young wage slaves was now nowhere to be found, and the fabriks and streets were overrun with a plague of rutting, savage, evil-smelling, hairy, ordure-smeared pigs.

128

"The pigs were everywhere, soiling the cities, spreading loathsome diseases, smearing the very name of their land with excrement, so that the land of the Gold Mountain came also to be known as the Belly of the Beast. Desperately did the Pentagon strive to complete the arkology *Gold Mountain* so that they might flee themselves in a simulacrum of their lost golden age from the swinishness and chaos they had themselves unwittingly released.

"Ah, but then did the Pied Piper of Pan appear in the city of the Pentagon, playing that eternal priapic music which has power over both man and beast, and lo, in his passage, the pigs gave over their rootings and ruttings and danced along gaily in his train.

"I will aid you in the nobility of your enterprise," the Pied Piper told the Pentagon, and he declared that he would pipe all the swine out of the Belly of the Beast and into the *Gold Mountain*, after which it would be a simple matter to let in the void.

"To this the Pentagon readily enough agreed, with scarcely an honest thought as to how the Piper would be paid.

"And so did the Pied Piper of Pan lead the pig people from the Belly of the Beast, but so too did he lead the wage slaves of the Pentagon into the *Gold Mountain*, for naturellement, the former were only the manifestation in the realm of maya of the thwarted youthful spirits of the latter.

"True to his word, once all were aboard the arkology, the Piper let in the void, but true to his spirit, the void to which his charges were exposed was the one which only the song of the Yellow Brick Road can fill.

"Vraiment, as the tune was changed from the music of unreason to the song that our species had long ago followed from apes into men, so did the wage slaves of the Pentagon follow it out of the Belly of the Beast and into their true selves as Children of Fortune, as the first spacefaring generation of our tribe, as wanderkinder on the first arkology to brave the long light years between the stars, as the first bright flickering of the Arkie Spark. Thus at the very dawning of the First Starfaring Age was the Child of Fortune in glory from the Belly of the Beast reborn."

Thus was the conclusion of one ruespiel the beginning of another, thus did the ruespielers ring changes on each other's interpretations of the tribal mythos, thus did the same familiar figure in various incarnations play the perfect master hero, thus was Pater Pan both the inspiration and creature thereof.

Naturellement, the ruespielers also had access to the vast store of word crystals, books, tapes, computer chips, scrolls, und so weiter that our species has accumulated over several millennia of creating fictions, to which they resorted when all else failed, and even I could have had an instant repertoire by the simple expedient of plagiarizing the perfect masters of the past.

But this was an expedient which somehow never crossed my mind even before I saw how audiences would melt away when they recognized an oft-told tale, or rather, as I was to learn, when the Child of Fortune ruespieler wandered too far from his own mythos.

For on Great Edoku, where the most sophisticated maestros of every art and the greatest of mages gathered to do commerce, the only charm of the ruespieler was that her stories, like the mildly intoxicating dim sum of Dani or the wooden filigree jewelry of Ali, were volkchoses of our demimonde, expressions of the spirit which moved through us.

Whether this was a form of condescension or whether, as Pater and the ruespielers would contend, Children of Fortune, or at any rate Gypsy Jokers, were justly treasured by the Edojin for the wu of their true essence, je ne sais pas, for the inner beings of the citizens of Great Edoku remain unfathomable to me to this very day.

Be that as it may, if one wanted to secure ruegelt from the Edojin, one played the avatar of the Child of Fortune, and extolled the virtues of the tribe, which by his own admission had its highest expression in the living legend who walked among us.

While I was entirely innocent at the time of the art of literary criticism or the lore of human psychoethology, I did sense that Pater was right when he said that all of the stories were patches of the cloth of some whole, vraiment, that in keeping with his identity as the Gypsy King of the Jokers, his boldest lies were also a kind of truth, for from the point of view of the Edojin, at any rate, the Pater Pan who walked among us, the legend whose mantle he had assumed, had in some ultimate sense indeed ridden the long light years with the Arkies, liberated the wage slaves of the Pentagon, been an ancient Gypsy King, no matter whether the flesh in which the same was now contained had passed through all that history or not.

As to the ur-tale itself, the Void at the Axis of the Great Wheel about which all the specific stories revolved, this, alas, remained a central mystery, at least to my perceptions. Which is to say that while the shedding of my intellectual virginity was no less exhilarating than the shedding of my erotic virginity had been, I entered the boudoir of the former with far less craft and self-preparation than the latter, and as a consequence I was far more reluctant to be more than a voyeur.

Each day I resolved to essay my first ruespiel in the form of one of the tales I had heard, and each day I put off my debut to the next, until finally I perceived that I should be content to learn and listen until the spirit was ready to speak through me.

As to when and how my own song would finally be called forth, I had the volktales of our tribe to guide me and the embodiment thereof for a sometime lover, and what I had learned from both was that the Spirit of Fortune spoke through the vie of its Children, that one need first dance to the music before learning to sing the song.

And so there was a time for me that was Golden, a long summer's day of youthful awakening and carefree adventure of the spirit that need never end, or so at the time I thought.

Everything that I did was alive with meaning, for was I not a Child of Fortune in my heart of hearts, leading the life that the spirit thereof commanded, thereby contributing my small part to the mythos of the whole, and enhancing my own enjoyment thereof with the intoxicant of a noble raison d'être for same thereby?

While I spent more and more of my time trailing after ruespielers and absorbing their tales, I neglected not, or at least not entirely, the more pragmatic aspects of the vie of the Child of Fortune, which is to say that though my deepest attention was to the entirely nouvelle monde of the imagination and intellect which had opened up before me for the first time, I certainly retained a healthy enough loathing for fressen bars to continue to perform as a tantric artist and to hawk Ali's jewelry at least with enough diligence to keep such stuff from passing through my lips.

Nor did my dedication to my newfound role as student

131

impel me to or require a life of monkish celibacy. Indeed there was a certain enzyme of aphrodisia produced in a young brain whose cortices of imagination and intellect were aroused to the levels of excitation of the adolescent erotic backbrain.

Far more ruespielers than one were to benefit amorously from the kundalinic circuit established between my avidity for their tales and my pheromonic receptors. Upon listening to a reasonably attractive ruespieler declaim a tale to my liking, I would often develop a lusty desire to plumb its deeper meanings en boudoir, and indeed, after all his available erotic energies had been depleted, the fellow was then persuaded to discourse on his craft, if only to dissuade further challenges to his sated manhood. Moreover, once both my tantric puissance and sincere desire became general lore among the ruespielers, I was not without volunteers willing to trade instruction in their craft for demonstrations of mine.

Throughout this long golden summer's day, Pater Pan remained my friend and lover in equal measure, displaying naught but approving amusement at my self-appointed role as courtesan of the ruespielers, while demonstrating often enough that the embodiment of their collective oeuvre was also a natural man.

It seemed to me that my life had attained a plane of perfection, that I inhabited a golden dreamland designed for my own delectation, and if this was a street of dreams, I saw nothing beyond into which I ever need awake.

All that was required to raise this perfection to transcendence was the moment when I was finally moved to perform my own tale. Vraiment, there was a certain sweet tension in the contemplation of my debut as a ruespieler, not unlike the joys of contemplating one's first passage d'amour with a new object of desire, and as with such kundalinic energies, the pleasure of the charge lasts longer than the pleasure of release.

Mayhap the foregoing was the rationalization of a sluggardly soul content to drift along in a bliss without risk or change, and indeed I regarded standing alone in the street and declaiming with a certain trepidation. But in truth, since I had no tale to tell, I could hardly be faulted for lack of spiritual courage for failing to make a fool of myself by blathering in public for the sake of hearing my own empty words. Did not the true Child of Fortune wait for the spirit thereof to speak through her?

Be that as it may, all things pass, and even our days of Golden Summer must one day end as our minds do tell us, though the fact that the universe would seem to have imposed this stricture upon us will no doubt remain forever beyond the praise of the human heart.

10 Well do I remember the true moment when the carnival ended and the morning after began, though, in point of quotidian fact, the Gypsy Jokers dissolved into legend slowly and piecemeal, even as Pater Pan had intended. For the only truly thespic moment in this otherwise gently entropic process was the very first, the moment in which in more ways than one, the spirit left us and moved on. And that was a satori that none of us who were put through it are ever likely to forget.

The event began as a joyous extravaganza, indeed the peak experience of my time as a Gypsy Joker. Pater Pan arbitrarily declared the revival of the ancient Terrestrial festtag of Mardi Gras, in which the Children of Fortune of Woodstock had smoked their pipe of peace with the Great God Mammon in the form of a parade through the city during which all they sold during the rest of the year for profit was showered gratuit as a love offering on the populace. Pater had decided to revive this noble tradition to thank our friends, the Edojin, for their beneficence, and also because he needed a festive spectacle to celebrate the mysterious event he promised for a climax.

Who does not love a parade, nē, and most particularly, who would refrain from dancing in a joyous crowd through the streets and parklands, toxicated, celebrating, and in general encouraged to behave as extravagantly as possible, when given the license to do so, indeed when you are among those hosting this bacchanalia for the public good?

Who would be so mean-spirited as to drag her feet in the hedonic pursuit of such an enterprise, and who would expect the mystery promised for the esthetic cusp of same to be anything but lighthearted?

Not I, not anyone in the parade, and as for the Edojin, certainement they were at least amused by the spectacle of the Gypsy Jokers parading through their streets and parklands, around their public platzes, past their very dwellings, snaking through the vecino like an ancient Han Dragon Dance, its Captain and Pilot the King of the Gypsy Jokers in his Traje de Luces, and its random recomplicated course steered by the Jump of his whim.

We all marched behind our Piper in the Mardi Gras parade, for our encampment was empty, and all that was portable therein in the way of entertainment and cuisine perambulated through Edoku, offering itself to, indeed thrusting itself upon, the populace thereof. The length of our dragon was measured in terms of the intervals required to keep half a dozen musical troops from overlapping into total cacophony. Jugglers juggled, acrobats tumbled, dancers made their way dancing, singers ran up and down the parade to form ever-changing impromptu choruses. Most of the ruespielers remained mute, but a few were mad or toxicated enough to attempt to bellow tales, or at any rate disjointed fragments of same, over the general din.

Those of us who had no entertainments of our own to donate were given our entrée into the spirit of the Mardi Gras in the form of bulging sacks filled with finger food, packets of toxicants, little flasks of wine, and even some simple cheap jewelry, which we tossed to the Edojin along the route at our whim and pleasure. I myself had both a sack of Dani's dim sum spiced with a double dose of toxicants and a bag of Ali's jewelry to dispense. The latter, naturellement, was not painstakingly crafted in his usual mode, but consisted of simplified versions of his true art cast in their ersatz scores from molds.

The parade wound from our encampment up through the previously quiet lanes between the residences of the hills, out across the river and along its bank, then back in a course like the body's intestines through the vecino of strogats at the feet of the glass towers, emerging therefrom in clear sight of our empty camp once more, and then across the noonday desert to the great waterfall, along the line of buttes from which it descended, to a shallowly-sunken bowl of a meadow surrounded on three sides by miniature mountain peaks over which a sun was forever in the process of setting, casting a brilliant early-sunset glow over the final proceedings.

As we paraded through the various venues of the vecino, singing, making music and circus, and tossing little treats from our bags to passersby, we collected a certain number of amused Edojin who followed in train alongside, though since no parade route had been announced, indeed since the Pied Piper seemed not to know what turn he would take from one moment to the next, we never marched formally past static throngs. We were a random bolide of a parade, and fortune rather than planning was required to place anyone along our way.

So in truth, by the time we had all reached the parade's terminus in the amphitheater of bright sunset, there were more of our tribe present than Edojin auslanders, though we retained the curious interest of a goodly number of the latter.

For the span of perhaps two hours, the meadow became the venue of a general fete into which the parade devolved, indeed gathered there in that compass were all the Gypsy Jokers of the streets as well as all those who plied their trades in the caravanserei, and here in the meadow of sunset, one could view our tribe entire and all its divertissements, stripped down to its essence, shorn of its tents and concealments, and of any strictures of pecuniary cunning.

Food and toxicants were passed from hand to hand with no thought of recompense. Musicians played, singers sang, buskers entertained, ruespielers told their tales, and all refrained from accepting the donations that many of the Edojin present persisted in tossing. As for artists of the tantra, these performed al fresco tableaus in which all were invited to join, and in which none need pay a price for pleasure.

As for me, once I had emptied my cornucopia of dim sum and bijoux, I merged myself into the generality of the fete, partaking of food and toxicants thrust into my hand, wandering from entertainment to entertainment, ruespiel to ruespiel, unmotivated, for some reason, to join in the tantric performances or seek out a lone lover for a ménage à deux.

Vraiment, the only lover I would have sought out at the very midsummer's eve of the Gypsy Jokers was Pater Pan himself, and the domo of the fete was a quicksilver target whom only fortune could place in my arms. Over there, peeking up above the crowd around a ruespieler, disappearing from my sight for tens of minutes, then visible again in the distance in the act of draining a wine flagon, vanishing from view once more, Pater Pan was a mountain that must come to Mohammed, and I was a particle of random motion across a crowded stube.

And then, with the precision of a domo of the floating cultura who senses when the revelry is balanced on the razor-edge of fatigue, Pater Pan appeared as if by thespic magic, indeed in a cloud of sparks and smoke and thunderclaps, atop the rim of the natural amphitheater.

The effect was so preternaturally perfect as to verge precipitously on the comic. Pater had set off a fireworks display of some duration and complexity to attract the attention of all, and when the donner and blitzen ended and the smoke cleared, there he stood, radiant in his Suit of Many Colors, his golden mane of hair and beard transfigured into a boddhi's aura by the flaming actinic disc of the setting sun against which his noble visage was so exactly centered.

Standing there in a range of bonsai mountains and backlit by a sunset that sublimed his material corpus with the photosphere corona of legend, Pater Pan appeared a Titan, a haut turista from Olympus, even to eyes entirely cognizant of the art that went into the effect. You couldn't help but be awed, if only by the transcendental chutzpah.

"Hear me, oh my Children of Fortune!" he shouted with immense pomposity into the hush of his entrance. "Attend, all ye Gypsy Jokers! Behold the King of the Gypsies and the Prince of the Jokers in all his magnificent glory standing before you! See how the puissance of his grandeur dwarfs the very mountains and towers triumphant against the firmament!"

At this truly excessive braggadocio, many present, myself included, found heckling japes forming upon our lips. But none of them quite came forth. For the transcendent image etched upon our retinas gave sufficient pause to create a moment of stasis into which Pater Pan stepped with the timing of a perfect master.

Abruptly, he sat down, leaning his back up against one mountain and draping his arm over the peak of another, converting the cordillera into his somewhat lumpy chaise.

"Of course they're very *small* mountains," he said in a very different voice, to general laughter. "As for my magnificent glory, it owes a good deal to thespic lighting, and the firmament against which I tower triumphant is no more than the usual Edojin ersatz of the real thing. Sometimes I forget that. You forget it too."

He stood up again, but now the magic of light and perspective was permanently shattered, and he paced in little ellipses as he spoke, as if to prevent his image of glory from reforming.

"Lest we forget, the King of the Gypsies is only a Child of Fortune, and the Prince of the Jokers is a natural man," he declared with entirely uncharacteristic modesty. "The Child of Fortune remembers that no one should follow leaders, and the natural man knows that the only guru worthy of his students is he who knows when enough is enough." He adopted a somewhat hectoring stance as he declaimed the last, as if to chide us for succumbing to his own excessively puissant charms.

"Sure, and I hope you can still all remember that," he said more conversationally. "I hope I will leave behind Children of Fortune who hear the songs of their own spirits, rather than a ragged band of acolytes who hear only the blarney of *mine*. For Great Edoku is but a single patch of cloth on the fabric of our Second Starfaring Age, and our time here is but a single swatch of time in the millennial story of our kind. And this natural man who stands before you swore a mighty oath to see all and be all on all the worlds of men before his race was run. So swore I, and so should you all swear, for Pater Pan would be no true Child of Fortune if he abandoned his own Yellow Brick Road for the bothersome role of your perpetual patriarch."

He paused, and then, so it seemed, looked directly in my eyes and broke my heart, though others, I was to learn, also shared this privately poignant perception.

"I have sung the song and passed on the lore, I have known you as friends and lovers and named your tribe, and now I hand on the torch. *Enough* is *enough*. Ask no more of the King of the Gypsies. His day as domo of this fete is done. On the morrow, the Prince of the Jokers departs to continue his wandering ministry to the Children of Fortune of the far-flung worlds of men. The Gypsy King of Edoku is dead, long live the Joker Prince of the Yellow Brick Road!"

Naturellement, I need not describe the descent into general pandemonium generated by this announcement, nor the transformation of our fete into a ragtag babbling rabble filtering in small troops back through the arrondissement of towers to the Gypsy Joker encampment like a high tide receding from a rocky coast back into the sea.

But mayhap the general mood of our retreat bears some elucidation, for while the mal d'esprit that one would have expected was certainly in evidence, there was a complex overtone to it, for none could deny in her heart of hearts that Pater Pan had spoken truth.

Had we not elected his artfully self-graven image as the leader not merely of our tribe but of each of our spirits? And had we all not learned from Pater Pan himself at least enough to know that this was a violation of the very spirit which he had taught us? For is not the true Child of Fortune anyone who follows the lead of his own spirit and no other? Could we therefore deny that the King of the Gypsy Jokers must die lest we forget that Children of Fortune have no chairmen of the board or kings?

And as for me, who knew the natural man better than most, how could I deny the right of the man who had opened up a world for me and more to seek whatever delights he could find on whatever planets he chose?

Thus speaks the suddenly enlightened noble being in the immediate afterglow of a powerful satori, but the natural woman and soon-to-be-abandoned lover within had long since resurfaced by the time I returned to the encampment, and that Moussa was more than capable of quotidian jealousy, though the identity of the rival remained confusingly elusive.

The area in front of Pater's tent was a chaos of supplicants by the time I arrived, in no mood to meekly await my turn for an audience with the pontiff. Dozens of Gypsy Jokers of both genders were speaking to Pater and each other all at once, though most of them who had insinuated themselves closest to Pater were female and clearly had more on their minds than verbal discourse.

139

This observation did little to cool the ire of my impending abandonment and without thinking, I found myself activating the Touch, as if marshaling the only of my powers on which I believed I could rely in such extremis. A moment later, I found myself putting it to use that it shames me to recount, goosing my way through the crush in a series of yelps of astonishment and moans of mysterious ecstasy, until I stood before Pater in the full flush of my wrath.

But Pater Pan stepped into the moment with that preternatural timing of his, and turned away wrath with a brilliant smile at my appearance, and a gesture towards the open flap of his tent. "Moussa!" he cried. "Vamanos! We must talk!" And, taking me by the hand, he led me inside as his chosen favorite on his last night in Edoku before the eyes of the tribe and the outrage of my rivals.

On the one hand, I was filled with joy at this openhearted confirmation that I had been at least his first among many, but on the other hand, was this not to be a sad good-bye?

"Pater. . . ."

"Moussa. . . ."

We stood there beside the bed, which was the only piece of practical furniture, I not knowing whether to be touched or enraged, and he, from the look of him, for once caught without words.

"Why are you doing this, Pater?" I finally demanded.

"I made not my meaning plain?"

Snorting, I changed the configuration by flopping down on the bed. "Thus spake the King of the Gypsies and the Prince of Blarney spinning koans for the general enlightenment. I believe I have a right to know what's really in the heart of my departing lover."

"You demand to share the secrets of my soul?"

"I must at least assure myself that you have one."

Pater laughed, he shrugged, he sat down on the bed beside me, and regarded me with a fey expression. "The King of the Gypsies may be gone, but the Prince of the Jokers remains," he said. "So if I am required to jive you not, you must give proper value for value received."

"Have I ever even had the power to dissemble with you, Pater?"

"Have you not?" he accused. "Have *you* not jived *me* as to the true secret of your tantric powers? Have you not put me off with displays of wounded outrage at my failure to believe that it derives full-blown from the innocent essence of your spirit?"

"Bien, if you will speak now from the heart, my poor one and only secret will then be revealed," I said impulsively, for what did I have to lose by revealing all to a lover who was about to become lost? "The reasons of the perfect master who acts for the good of the body politic I believe I already comprehend, but I must know the personal selfish reasons of the natural man."

"You do see deeply, Moussa," he owned. "For while the altruistic role of guru and public benefactor has its own selfish rewards, he who imagines he has transcended the ego's desires in the service thereof is but a hollow shell. Vraiment, this natural man does indeed have his own arcane lust, his mad personal passion, beyond even playing the Pied Piper of Pan to the Children of Fortune of the worlds of men."

"And you do not speak of that passion inherent in our genital architecture. . . ."

He laughed. "That is neither arcane nor mad," he said. "Whereas the passion of which I speak for sure is both!"

"To wit. . . ?"

"Do you not wish to be immortal, Moussa?" he said.

"Who does not? But it is hardly a passion anyone save perhaps a mage of the healing arts has the means to even insanely pursue. . . ."

"Wrong!" Pater declared in deadly earnest. "After all, one may pursue and even achieve immortality of the spirit in the memory of posterity by doing great deeds or crafting deathless art. . . ."

"Or by becoming your *own* deathless work of art as some have done. . . ." I suggested dryly.

"For sure, as I have long since done," he owned. "But I pursue immortality of a more hedonic and entirely less selfless kind, the kind the Arkies knew. . . ."

"*The Arkies?*"

He nodded, and the strangest look came over him, a look which all but forced me to credit his tales of a birth beyond the dawn of the ancient Age of Space, for in that moment his eyes

141

appeared preternaturally old, as if brimming to overflowing with a million years of sights no mortal man could have lived to see.

"The Arkies passed their generations aboard the great slow arkologies that first brought men to the stars as all do know," he said. "But slow as they were by the standards of the Jump, on their longest voyages they approached within sufficient hailing distance of the speed of light to contract the timestream within. Thus, in a voyage that consumed mere decades of lifespan, might hundreds of light-years be crossed, and far more marvelously, *centuries of time.*

"*Why* would the Arkies choose to remain in perpetual motion between the stars? For sure not because the arkologies offered more adventures and delights within their hulls than a planet entire! No, the true dream, the inner heart of the Arkie Spark, was to *be there for the whole tale!* To weasel a consciousness which spanned *millennia* of the saga of our species out of the poor three hundred years of our bodies' time! Vraiment, to pursue the impossible goal of knowing the tale of our species' history entire before expiring into the unknowing void! To be, at any rate, as immortal as our kind itself, not as a legend, but in the flesh as a witness, and a natural man!"

"Madness!" I exclaimed. "Impossible! And at any rate, all that, like the Arkies themselves, passed with the First Starfaring Age...."

"So say those who call themselves mages of history!" Pater declared. "Towards the middle of the First Starfaring Age did it not become common for colonists to pass the long light-years in cryonic sleep, and was not lifespan thereby preserved from time and boredom? Arkies possessed of sufficient funds and daring took to freezing themselves for centuries, awakening for a few months to live another chapter of the long story and replenish their funds, and then jumping through time in the cold of sleep once more. Some were said to have done this scores of times and lived to see the Second Starfaring Age unfold!"

"You display an amazing erudition in the inner lore of the Arkies," I said dryly.

"Porqué no? I was there!"

"Is this all in the service of telling me that the man beside me is a fossil Arkie thawed from the glacier of time?"

"Have I not told you that before? Did you believe it then?

Do you believe it now? Believe that I saw the First Starfaring Age or not, believe at least that I mean to see the undreamed of wonders of the *Third* unfold, or nobly perish in the attempt!"

"Impossible!"

"For sure?" said Pater Pan, with the strangest haunted look stealing into his eyes. "Consider. No lifespan at all is lost in electrocoma passage on Void ships, and compared to the cryonics of the First Starfaring Age, successful awakening is so assured that we think nothing of risking it for the sake of mere economic convenience, nē."

"But . . . but Void Ships take mere days or weeks to voyage among the worlds of men, not centuries. . . ."

"Vraiment!" Pater exclaimed. "Therefore, the more you see of the worlds of men, the more you see of *time*! Moussa, Moussa, have you never yearned to walk the streets of future cities, to meet the citizens of a far future age, to be there when our species at long last greets fellow sapients from across the sea of suns? Have you never railed in your heart against the knowledge that the greatest chapters in our species' tale will surely unfold after you are dead and gone? The Arkies sought to cheat the hand of unjust mortality with a few long slow dangerous leaps, but in the Second Starfaring Age, I seek to do it as it must be done now. . . ."

Snap! Snap! Snap! went his fingers. "Like that! As the Edojin use the Rapide!"

"Just how many worlds *have* you seen . . ." I whispered in wondering awe, for certainement while the goal he pursued must surely remain forever beyond the reach of mortal man, the millennial quest therefor seemed not entirely beyond the realm of universal law, though the mind both reeled and soared at its contemplation.

"Quién sabe?" said Pater Pan in a voice much less grand. "At least a hundred, if memory serves. And I seek to see the rest before my body's time runs out."

He shrugged. He sighed. And for the first time since I had known him I glimpsed a dark and wistful sadness lurking in the blue depths of my Pied Piper's bright eyes. "In truth, I know that in the end, I must fail, vraiment, what a monster I would be if I truly hoped to succeed, for not even I have the ego to truly wish to see our species vanish from the stars. But if in the end I cannot

143

sanely or justly hope to experience all of human time, then by the spirit which brought me down from the trees and by the Yellow Brick Road which goes forever on, I mean to attempt to experience at any rate all the worlds of men in the pursuit thereof, to die as I have lived, and declare my life a limited victory in the final moment thereof!"

Pater touched my hand. He cocked his head and regarded me with eyes which in that moment seemed both gay and sad, heroic and futile, and in them I saw both the noblest and bravest spirit in all the worlds of men and the smallest of boys terrified of the greatest of darks. "*Now* do you understand why the natural man, no less than the King of the Gypsies and the Prince of the Jokers cannot stand in place too long?" he said softly.

"Vraiment!" I declared. How mad and sad and doomed and marvelous it all was! What a tale to live as the adventure of your life! "Take me with you!" I said. "I am more than ready to trip the life fantastic through the planets and down the centuries with you forever!"

"I could not do that, even if I wanted to," Pater said, regarding me with a warm and wistful tenderness in which, nevertheless, I could read no regret. "We may be two souls of the same spirit, you and I, but this path that I have chosen is for my steps alone. The natural man who loves you would not let your young soul tag along as consort of such a Fliegende Hollander for the same reason that the Pied Piper must move on when the Children of Fortune have learned the music of his song. Your Yellow Brick Road must be of your own choosing. If the destiny thereof should one day bring you once more to my side, then I will welcome you as an equal spirit. But *only* as an equal spirit, never a consort. Never as the girl that is, only as the woman you will become. Comprend?"

"Yes," I said in the tiniest of voices. "I like it not, but I do believe I do."

And then, as if to dull the edge of the knife, the spirit of the Joker emerged once more, and spoke in a tone of the most loving cynicism. "Besides, spiritual imperatives and financial considerations coincide. Since the funds I need to travel are paid for with time, I can't afford a free rider, now can I?" Somehow this entirely false mingyness, under the circumstances, was the tenderest mercy of all.

We stared into each other's eyes for a long silent moment, saying good-bye, or, I dared hope, auf wiedersehen, hugging each other's spirits; he long since centered on the acceptance of this as his self-chosen destiny, I not having the least notion as to what my future destiny might be.

Then, as the silent communion began to stretch into a poignant agony, Pater, with his perfect mastery of timing, laughed, shrugged, and screwed his face into the comic rendition of a mean-spirited little boy. "And speaking of value given for value received," he said in an ironic tone, "now that I have shared the deepest secret of my soul, *you* must reveal the secret of the magic in your touch."

"Well spoken!" I giggled, amazed to find such laughter bubbling up in my spirit as if at the Piper's bidding. "Indeed, far more well spoken for once than the speaker himself believes."

I removed the ring of Touch from my finger and ceremoniously placed it on the little finger of Pater's right hand.

"*This?*" he exclaimed. "This common piece of bazaar jewelry is the source of your power?"

"Designed without esthetic appeal or apparent economic value to discourage the attention of thieves," I told him. "Attends." So saying, I reached out, took his hand, thumbed on the ring, and before he knew what I was about, had draped his hand squarely upon his own lingam.

The look that came onto his face at once should have been captured in holo or oils by a master craftsman, for I have never, before or since, seen such a mélange of amazement, pleasure, befuddlement, and embarrassment appear in such a simultaneous manner on a human visage. He pawed at himself experimentally and stifled a moan. He stroked the inside of his own thigh. He stared at the ring in befuddled delight.

"Merde!" he exclaimed. "I would be the last to deny the esteem in which I hold my own person, but even *I* would never have believed I could so love myself!"

"My father made it," I told him. "He calls it the Touch."

"Your father? Cuanto cuesta? Surely you can prevail upon him to grant a discount to an amigo? With this and the already puissant prowess of the great Pater Pan, I could plow a course through the women of the worlds that would make Don Juan and Casanova seem like dour celibates!"

"No doubt," I said dryly. "But it is unobtainable at any price. In all the worlds of men, mine is the only one there is, and my father has sworn an oath that no more will be made until I give my leave."

"Pas problem! Only direct him to make a single exception. . . ."

"And loose what priapic demon on the innocent women of the worlds?"

"Vraiment," Pater said quite seriously, removing the ring and placing it in my hands. "If every lover in all the worlds of men wore such a ring, what would become of the tantric *art*? If all of us were perfect masters of pleasure, would we still recognize those moments when via the flesh two true spirits meet?"

"I have noticed no lack of such a communion of the spirit between *us*. . . ." I pointed out.

"I am not utterly convinced that such a device may not corrode the courage of love's spirit. . . ."

"I feel no corrosion of my lover's courage!" I insisted.

"Bien. Then you will not object to my suggestion that our last passage d'amour on Edoku be au naturel. Is it not now just that the natural woman now emerge from her magic fortress to bid a true lover bon voyage?"

"Well spoken," I impulsively declared, for the trepidation I felt at his words, bizarrely akin to that of a young virgin about to disrobe for the first time before her lover, only served to spur me on. For what is courage except in the face of fear, and what is love if not the baring of one's own naked and imperfect truth?

So saying, I unwound my Gypsy Joker's sash from about my waist, and began to undress. In truth did I experience something of the trepidatious joy of a virgin's premiere performance, though fortunately not the useless ignorance of same.

Then we were in each other's arms and the truth of it was that while the duration and sensual intensity of the artistic performance might have been less preternaturally sustained, the essence of the experience, stripped down to the essentials of lingam and yoni, was quite the same.

At first each of us strove to overmaster the other with pleasure, and if this loverly contest was now more equal, indeed if for once Pater did obtain the upper hand, the outcome of this almost jocular overture was as before—we proceeded on to the

146

next movement, in which the duality of giving and receiving pleasure was annihilated in the experience of pleasure itself, and two
spirits reached a single cusp.

Vraiment, for once it *was* but a single cusp, and for once,
neither of us felt the need to essay or offer more. Which is not so
much to say that we were sated as to say that in tantra, as in any
other art, we both realized with the wisdom of our flesh, one does
not mar a perfect miniature by attempting to blow it up into a
work of epic proportions.

"It would appear that yours is a lover's spirit capable of
surviving such power," Pater said at length when we had covered
ourselves and snuggled together in the dark. "Myself, I would not
trust. Who, I wonder, is the real Gypsy, and who the real Joker?"

"The two of us," I said, strangely content now to lie in the
arms of this man who would be leaving on the morrow.

"I will be gone when you awake," Pater said, as if reading
my thoughts. "Better to say auf wiedersehen now than in a tearful morning, nē. I will cut a patch from your tunic before I go
and leave you a patch of mine to sew into your sash, so that we
will each wear a patch of the other's karma in the fabric of our
destinies."

Touched, I kissed him lightly on the cheek. "Leave me
with one thing more," I asked him. "Moussa is a kindernom given
me by my parents in homage to the patron creature of an innocent childhood long since past. Give me then a true name for the
Child of Fortune of the road, and I in turn will promise not to
assume it until I am worthy, which is to say until I have earned
my first coin as a ruespieler. Thereafter, I will be the name you
have given me until we meet again or forever, whichever comes
first."

"A name for the ruespieler you will one day be. . . ?" Pater
said thoughtfully. "Bien, I dub thee Sunshine, light of the world
and Lucifer's daughter, a star among many but equal to all, and
the sacramental wafer of the Children of Fortune of the Age of
Space."

"Sunshine . . ." I muttered sleepily. "It seems rather an
extravagant name."

"Would I name you for anything less than glory? Sunshine
you will be when you are ready to shine forth in the dark."

Those are the last words I remember him speaking that

night, though no doubt there were less coherent endearments muttered in that hypnagogic limbo of lost memory occluded by the impending onset of sleep.

True to his word, when I awoke, the King of the Gypsies and the Prince of the Jokers had vanished from my world.

11

Our immediate general response as Gypsy Jokers on the morrow of Pater Pan's departure was to make a valiant effort to carry on in the spirit of the tribe, both in homage to his legend, and out of a certain twisted quest for exoneration in his eyes that was not without its aspect of psychic vengeance. Which is to say we developed the retrospective perception that our missing protector and patron had never really *worked* at any of the enterprises we had established save as founder and inspirational dilettante. Were we ourselves not true Children of Fortune, vraiment were we not *Gypsy Jokers*? Surely we could maintain the spirit and commerce of the carnival on our own!

Naturellement, in moments of reflection even at the time, I understood all too well that the wound which Pater's departure had inflicted on our spirits was designed to produce precisely this response. Nor could I deny the justice in the challenge. If we were unable to be Gypsy Jokers without Pater Pan, how could we have counted ourselves worthy of being Gypsy Jokers *with* him?

And indeed for a time, to our credit, we succeeded in mantaining our enterprises by our own efforts. Ruespielers, hawkers, and buskers ventured forth as before, the tents of our caravanserei continued to draw customers for tantric performances, games of chance, and entertainments, and craftsmen continued to produce their wares.

149

Vraiment, it appeared that Pater's departure had truly served to teach the lesson he had intended. Whether what happened next was another koan prepared for our rough-hewn edification by Pater Pan or whether it was a malfunction of his scenario is difficult to clarify even in retrospect, for it hinged upon the peculiarly Edojin creative ambiguity towards matters of legal philosophy.

As I have said, the erection of Child of Fortune favelas was supposedly proscribed on Edoku, or at least as proscribed as anything short of violence or outright rapine could get. Indeed as far as anyone knew, the encampment of the Gypsy Jokers was the sole exception to this mandate, and as to how Pater Pan had cozened the Edojin into granting it, this was as great a mystery among us as the means whereby the Edojin enforced their displeasure against potential encampments of other tribes.

For if I have failed in the course of this narrative to adequately describe or even mention the governing councils and law enforcement officials of Great Edoku, it is not out of oversight or sloth. From the perspective of the Child of Fortune, such councils and officials were entirely nonexistent, since one never perceived such personages or their policies in evidence. Enforcement of the civilized niceties simply *occurred;* the apprehension and punishment of thieves and pickpockets by impromptu posses which Pater had turned into a remunerative enterprise seemed to be the general model of how the body politic of Edoku dealt with miscreants.

As to how the encampment of the Gypsy Jokers had become selfed to the social immune system of the body politic of Edoku, the subtlety of Pater Pan's politicking only began to emerge into view as matters began to deteriorate in its absence.

Within a week of the Mardi Gras parade, the custom of the encampment, far from being augmented by the mythos of this event, began to measurably decline. This was most pronounced when it came to the products of the craftsmen, which all at once seemed to be out of favor. Even the jewelry of Ali went begging for customers at reduced prices at his stand in the encampment, and it soon began to seem pointless for me to try to peddle it in the streets and parks.

The quality and artistry of our crafts had not declined, but alas, they had never found favor on the basis of same in the first place. Rather they had been emblematic artifacts of the treasured quaintness and romantic spirit of the Child of Fortune, to whom one gave ruegelt as an act of fond remembrance to one's own wanderjahr.

Perhaps Pater had been too cunning for our own good, for his own mythos had been such a selling point of our mystique that when it abandoned that mystique in public, our quaintness lost its wu, we were once more perceived as scruffy urchins, and trinkets that had once been votive items in the cult of our spirit were now regarded by the Edojin as tawdry junk.

It was not long thereafter that our tantric tableaus began to play to empty tents, and even those inviting participation began to lose their trade. For once the spirit of the Child of Fortune lost its currency as a stylistic mode, the Child of Fortune was no longer a popular fantasy of the erotic imagination. And on Edoku, where every fantasy of the imagination was made manifest, we could hardly compete with the thousand-and-one delights on the basis of our artistry alone.

As for solo tantric performance, which when all was said and done had been my only reliable source of ruegelt, a night in a tent pretending you were once more a Child of Fortune or an al fresco adventure with same upon momentary whim in the nearest garden, once they were no longer considered wu, became acts of esthetic barbarity.

Well did I come during this devolution to understand the reticence of lordly tribesmen to be observed by denizens of the Public Service Stations partaking of fressen bars! The only of our enterprises that retained some vitality was the vending of finger food from trays, for even the Edojin developed instant cravings for a snack, and would weigh not heavily esthetic judgments if the smell of same reached a hungry palate.

Soon, therefore, our cooks were importuned by hordes of their indigent comrades and lovers, for there was hardly anyone in the encampment who did not have a claim of friendship with one cook or another as I did with Dani. How could he stand idly by and gain profit by peddling his dim sum to the Edojin while I was reduced to choking down fressen? How could he refuse similar alms to anyone else with the same moral claim? How could any true Gypsy Joker see another, and by extension his whole tribe, humiliated in the Public Service Stations when he had the means and the art to prevent his fellow tribesmen from descending to fressen?

And indeed, at first our noble artistes de cuisine could not. Instead of devoting their attentions to selling their fare for ruegelt, they volunteered their efforts to the feeding of their fellows without thought of gain. But alas, without the infusion of ruegelt into this closed economic ecology, there was no way to purchase the ingredients to produce free meals.

At length Dani and his fellow guildsmen saw that further such altruism would in any event be self-extinguishing in the form of bringing their ruin, and, rather than tell their friends and lovers that henceforth ye shall eat fressen and face their outrage, they slunk off in a body without the agonies of more formal farewells.

Now all that we Gypsy Jokers had to distinguish ourselves from the commonality of the Publics were our emblematic Cloth of Many Colors and a desolate village of empty tents. The fressen we were forced to eat was spiced as well with the bile of shame, for in order to secure supplies of the loathsome substance without suffering the jibes of the masses of the Publics, we removed our tribal colors and came and went incognito.

While in truth I for one certainly felt unjustly punished by fate for a shortcoming whose nature I could not fathom, indeed after eating enough fressen could even style myself the victim of Pater Pan's malice, I for one also sensed that there was a satori in all this that transcended such niceties of moral expectation. For while it was easy enough to rail at the malignity of fate, to what agent of injustice could the outraged finger point? To Pater Pan, who had done nothing more evil than impart his spirit and lore and then leave it to us to carry the torch thereof forward? To the Edojin, whose greatest offense was that they no longer seemed to find us charming?

Vraiment, once the moving finger began seeking out targets, only great feats of willful ignorance could prevent it from pointing within.

Certainement, we had all come to rely far too much on Pater Pan and far too little on ourselves for our initiative, and by the time the cooks had left the encampment, all of us who found ourselves forced to subsist on fressen when left to our own independent devices had quite absorbed this lesson.

For myself, this was not so much a lesson in humility as a lesson in my own lack of necessary hubris, which is to say chutzpah, for Pater had left me the name of Sunshine for my career as a ruespieler, and had told me aspects of his tale that were not at all current in the repertoires of others. Moreover, I had fairly well memorized the gists of a dozen or so tales, and one would have thought that someone reduced to fressen would have been a good deal less punctilious about originality.

Yet somehow I never summoned up the courage to stand on a crowded street and begin to declaim. I, who had blarneyed the King of the Gypsy Jokers out of one hundred coins of ruegelt, could not bring myself to address the Edojin in search of far pettier sums!

In truth I do now believe we were all somewhat overharsh in our self-judgments and became more so the longer we lingered in our spiritless encampment, for though at the time we could not quite perceive it, the true lesson that we were being taught was not so much that we were incompetent sloths as that we were still very new to the vie of the Child of Fortune. We had known nothing but the perfect befuddlement of the rube in a strange land, and then the first Golden Summer of our lives on the Yellow Brick Road, and what we were learning now was ultimately nothing more sinister than the final forced perception that all such Golden Summers eventually come to an end.

I finally achieved this satori the night the ruespielers decided to quit the camp. I say we were all overharsh in our self-judgments, and the truth of it is that I was perhaps overharsh in chiding myself for lacking the courage to begin spieling, for certainement in those days it took great chutzpah for even the most artful and experienced of our ruespielers to address their tales to the Edojin. Indeed, more and more of them had given up trying.

For if our crafts no longer had wu in their eyes, and our buskers no longer charmed, and even our tantric services were now considered nikulturni, how much less would the Edojin be inclined to donate ruegelt or even pause to listen to tales extolling a mythos whose trend had come and gone?

As an intimate of many of the ruespielers, and moreover, one known to diligently admire and aspire to practice their art, I was invited to the convocation that was eventually held in one of the now vacant tents—or at least my attendance was not discouraged once I got wind of it.

It was obvious at once that the generality of the meeting had been resolved before it began to quit the encampment and scatter to the winds while they still had a coin or two for the Rapide. Indeed, by this time, the cooks were not the only Gypsy Jokers who had departed. One by one, craftsmen, tantric artists, and street performers had drifted away to try their luck in other parts of Edoku where *any* Gypsy Joker was a legendary creature, so that by the time the ruespielers held their meeting, the tribe was down to half its number, and of these, the majority, like myself, were Children of Fortune without the marketable skills to believe that their prospects might be better elsewhere.

One by one, ruespielers arose to announce their intention to seek fortune elsewhere. After no more than a half hour of this testimony, further reiteration of the obvious was clearly redundant, and the meeting broke up into a farewell party full of toxicated conversations.

I bade farewell to Shane and Lance and other onetime lovers in something of a daze, yet a daze heightened and amplified by something more than social toxication. For I was bidding farewell to more than friends, lovers, and artists whose tales I admired; like it or not, I was also bidding farewell to all possibility of continuing the life which had so perfectly satisfied my spirit during the Golden Summer. Pater was gone, and the central magic of that time with him, I was no longer able to earn ruegelt as a tantric performer, and now, once the ruespielers were gone, I could no longer share that life of the intellect to which I had become fondly accustomed by dallying in their company.

Yet, strange to tell, as the evening progressed I felt less and less desolated by this loss and more and more possessed by a peculiar elation, an elation whose source, under the circumstances, was impossible to find.

Until, after several hours of aimless farewell fete, Shane Kol Barka became sufficiently inflamed by the moment and his own toxication to offer up as a valedictory yet another time-warped transmogrification of the tale of *The Spark of the Ark*, which it would seem, he extemporized on the spot for the occasion.

"As all do know, when the First Starfaring Age ended, the way of life which had sparked the Arkies time out of mind went

154

whirling down the onrushing black hole of the Second Starfaring Age as Void Ships began to speed between the worlds of men like the Rapide, ending the isolation of one planet from another and ending too any sane raison d'être for the great slow arkologies which were the Yellow Brick Road caravans of the Arkie generations. . . ."

He paused, inhaled more toxicant, and went on in an even more florid and hectoring tone. "Yet, think ye not that the Second Starfaring Age sprung full-blown from the brow of Jove nor that the Arkies folded their tents of an evening and gave up the ghost sans a certain rage against the dying of their light! For the great and now useless arkologies still existed, and with the scrap heap as the only other bidder, some Arkies were able to purchase for a song the arkologies in which they had once been happy coolies.

"Alas for the most part theirs were pitiful and maudlin tales which hardly bear repeating, tales of the pathetic and indigent curators of a once noble spirit futilely attempting to keep alive a way of life whose time was long since past, and for the first few centuries of the Second Starfaring Age, deteriorated hulks of arkologies would drift into solar systems like ancient rusted ghosts, with their denizens long since expired from cryogenic failure or starvation, or worse, bearing a generation of babblers whose very humanity had been sapped by the slow depletion of the oxygen supply to their brains.

"Yet as all here do know, the Spark of the Ark was *not* extinguished by the Second Starfaring Age. For it pleased Fortune that the King of the Gypsies was then an Arkie embarked on a slow voyage of exploration far beyond what was the furthest limits of the worlds of men when it began. For long centuries, he and a few comrades slumbered in cryogenic sleep while the arkology crept with its cargo of colonists towards the far virgin star that had been set as its goal by generations long dead, while unbeknowst and unseen all around them, the great Second Starfaring Age blossomed into full flower.

"So when at last the arkology reached its preordained destination, voilà, it found itself not in orbit about a virgin world far from the homes of men, but orbiting Novi Mir itself, a bustling hub of the Second Starfaring Age which had been well-

155

settled for centuries and which now lay well within the sphere of our species' domestication.

"Thus all aboard had been translated via space through time into a far future in which the Way they thought they would follow forever had long since passed into legend. Those Arkies who had been born and lived out their lives as the last generation of the arkology's timestream became but one more tribe of fossils living out the shell of a dead dream, the very last Arkies, wandering from world to world in their Fliegende Hollander until their line expired.

"But the King of the Gypsies, upon awakening like Barbarossa from what in his timestream was but a single night's sleep, saw with the eyes of the true spirit and spoke thusly unto those who had slumbered through the centuries with him. . . ."

Shane paused, and stared out across our company as if we were those ancient Arkies, and when he declaimed again, it was as that Gypsy King of old, and mayhap another.

"The days of our tribe are ended. Doomed are those fools who seek to live out a lost Golden Age, for by so doing they lose the very spirit which makes any age golden. Let us therefore not rail against the destiny that has flung us by our stiff necks beyond all hope of remaining what we once were. Rather let us embrace the unknown future with the spirit we embody, for the true Child of Fortune of whom our past personas were but one time-bound avatar knows that the Yellow Brick Road is a journey with no final destination."

Shane Kol Barka quaffed a draught of wine, and when he continued, he was the teller of the tale again, delivering his peroration.

"Thus spoke the Gypsy King of the Arkies, and by so saying became the Pied Piper of the new breed of Children of Fortune of our Second Starfaring Age. Thus spoke the King of the Gypsies and by so saying became the Prince of Jokers to our very own tribe, never truer to the spirit thereof than when he freed it from the maya we had clung to!"

Somewhat shakily, he finished in a much more conversational mode, leaning up against the chair from which he had risen and speaking not so much as a ruespieler but as a fellow Gypsy Joker.

"Thus speaks Shane Kol Barka, thus should we all speak

156

now, and by so saying, free ourselves from our Golden Age as Gypsy Jokers and go forth into the streets of Great Edoku as naked beings in homage not to the *maya* but to the *true spirit* thereof."

While a bit short on plot and a bit long on toxicated didacticism, Shane Kol Barka's tale spoke nonetheless to the mystery which had been confounding my heart. Why had my mourning for a perfect bliss now lost been slowly replaced by an excited expectation for the nameless? Why had this occurred upon learning that my days as a consort of the ruespielers were now perforce ended?

Naturellement, because now the difficult and arduous decision to venture forth from the camp of the Gypsy Jokers as a lone traveler on the Yellow Brick Road had been removed from the realm of my own efforts. All that I might have wished to cling to had been yanked out from under me. I was now a free spirit, for I could choose no other course.

Vraiment, like all satoris, this one in retrospect seems like a recitation of the obvious, for like all satoris, it only brought to full awareness in the moment of enlightenment those unfaced truths which were inherent in what one already knew.

And like all true satoris, it sent the spirit forward into its corollaries. For by observing how an impromptu tale somewhat toxicatedly declaimed had chanced to crystallize a moment of clarity out of my own foggy occlusions, I had a glimpse of the highest achievement to which a ruespieler might aspire.

It was enough to finally make me resolve that I would not linger in the nostalgia-haunted encampment of the Gypsy Jokers on the morrow when the ruespielers would be gone. Rather would I go forth into the streets of Edoku as a naked being and, come what may, summon up the courage to emulate my noble mentors.

And indeed I did so. Or at least I stuffed my few belongings into my pack, made my farewells, and sweet-talked Ali out of sufficient ruegelt as a bon voyage gesture to finance a single Rapide trip to nowhere in particular.

Indeed, rather than return to any venue on Edoku I had previously frequented, nowhere in particular was where I decided to go. Which is to say I simply ordered up the lengthy list of "Public Squares" on the screen of my Bubble, closed my eyes as the choices scrolled by, and chose the first destination to meet my eyes when I opened them. "Luzplatz," I told the Rapide, and was forthwith carried thither.

Immediately upon emerging from the Rapide station, which was hidden in plain sight as a strobing cube of blue brilliance, I was given cause to wonder what jape the trickster of random chance enjoyed at my expense, and given cause as well to realize to what extent I had forgotten that the vecino around the Gypsy Joker encampment was in no way any more typical of Great Edoku than any venue therein was typical of any other.

All unknowing, I had chosen to expend my funds on a one-way Rapide translation to perhaps the most outré and daunting vecino I had yet seen on the planet.

I was surrounded by tall buildings as stark in their rectilinearity and as pristine in their neutral surface texture as a forest of monoliths. Which is not to say that the buildings surrounding the Luzplatz were paragons of unadorned functionality, for every surface thereof was ablaze with a chaos of color to the point where at first glance they all appeared to be constructed not of matter but of energy. Some walls were simple glowing expanses of red or blue or hot yellow, others were covered with arabesque patterns, serpents, rivers of multicolored luminosity. Some displayed portraits of landscapes, or cities, or even people, done up in highly stylized modes with a palette of light. Some of these patterns and pictures remained static, some of them evolved slowly over time, and still others moved in realtime like a holocine. No building seemed illumined in a style designed to blend harmoniously with that of any other, and even one wall of a single building might display lighting effects of three or four different modes.

It was quite literally a dazzling spectacle, for the eye was hard-pressed to resolve this chaotic brilliance into coherent architectural modules; rather did it seem to me that I was surrounded by huge jagged curtains of light patched together out of assorted swatches of multicolored energy, not unlike the Cloth of Many Colors which I wore as a sash about my waist.

The Luzplatz itself was a wide circular strogat formed by the convergence of half a dozen radial avenues. The outer perimeter thereof was girdled round with boutiques, tavernas, restaurants, and the entrances to hotels, all illumined in the same riotous mélange of styles. In the center of this circular platz thronged with people was a pièce de resistance of a bonsaied landscape suitable to the extravagance of the vecino of which it formed the axis.

A moat of foaming water completely surrounded a heavily wooded island which rose to a mountain peak perhaps seventy meters tall. Everything was in perfect scale—tiny breakers lapping a fringe of white beach less than a meter wide, miniature trees as tall as my finger was long, barely visible rivulets of water tumbling down little canyons—yet the whole was dwarfed by the brazenly brilliant ersatz works of men surrounding it.

But the effect of the bonsaied island was in no way diminished by this reversal of scale between the urban and natural realms, for the central peak thereof was a mighty miniature volcano in the permanent full glory of eruption. Red-hot lava flowed down its sides to send clouds of hissing steam billowing into the air where it touched the water of the moat. The crater glowed like a cauldron of starstuff, and at regular intervals blasted fusillades of brilliant bolides high in the air. Above it towered a boiling pillar of smoke which rose beyond the tops of the buildings into the black, star-speckled sky and which glowed an evil deep orange cast by the furnace of magma seething beneath it.

Moreover, after my senses had to some extent adjusted to all this perpetual light and fire, I saw that, shrunken with distance, was another spectacle curiously congruent with the endless volcanic display of the Luzplatz.

The entire vecino lay under perpetually clear black starry night, all the better to set off its mad chaos of aggressively artificial illumination, and the surrounding geography was therefore veiled in darkness. The single exception was a full-scale snow-capped cone of a mountain shining in its own private blaze of noon in the far distance. The eye could tell at once that it was far off and huge rather than another nearby miniature, for on its somewhat flattened peak, suborbital rocket shuttles could be seen to take off and land on thin trails of fire, and so too did less flamboyant shuttles arrive and depart thereon to service Void Ships in orbit.

The tame bonsaied volcano, the brilliantly lit buildings towering over it, the gateway to the stars in turn dwarfed by the perspective of distance, it all seemed designed to make some elusive philosophical statement, whose inner esthetic, alas, seemed entirely ambiguous to any but the Edojin.

Suffice it to say that all at once I found myself a rube in Xanadu once more, a Child of Fortune ordinaire among many, a stranger once more in Great and unfathomable Edoku.

There were several Publics in the immediate vecino of the Luzplatz, and despite initial appearances, a short walk in any direction was sufficient to take me to any one of several different styles of parkland and garden in which to sleep. In this arrondissement, as elsewhere on Edoku, my simple animal needs presented no practical problems.

Indeed, had I wished, no doubt I could have satisfied less basic needs in the Publics of the Luzplatz, for during my brief forays therein, I soon enough learned that the organized tribes in this vecino were few and mainly devoted to the pickpocket's and pilferer's trades, while the mystique of the Gypsy Jokers was far from unknown. I had only to wear my Cloth of Many Colors to be immediately accounted an aristocrat in these circles, albeit a somewhat fallen one. On the other hand, knowledgeable as I had become in the various enterprises of the streets in comparison with these greeners, I could have concealed my tribal identity and no doubt speedily organized my own little tribe with myself as domo.

Nevertheless, I chose to do neither. Young I might have been, but never jejune enough to fantasize a return to the society of the Publics in which I had been a commoner as a petty little queen. Disbanded though the Gypsy Jokers might be, I was still too infused with the spirit thereof to wear the Cloth of Many Colors and eat fressen in Publics at the same time.

I therefore chose for a time the vie of the solitary, venturing into the Publics in anonymity when necessary but eschewing, for the most part, the social life, such as it was, to be had by lingering therein. For I had sworn an oath to myself that I would go forward along the Yellow Brick Road as a ruespieler, never backward into the society out of which I had evolved, and indeed, I knew on some inner level that by keeping to my own company, I would be forced to screw up my courage to declaim, if only to escape from ennui.

I spent my first few days in the vecino of the Luzplatz

160

haunting the stroget surrounding the volcano, assessing the ambiance, familiarizing myself with the ebb and flow of street traffic, sizing up the crowds, und so weiter, or so I told myself. In truth, of course, I was accomplishing nothing at all save procrastination, for the Luzplatz was thronged at all hours, the ebb and flow of the bustle resembled nothing so much as the randomness of brownian motion, and as for the ambiance, it was the very same mélange of purposeful commerce and hedonic extravagance to be found in any similar venue on Edoku, if energized to a somewhat higher pitch by the blazing displays of light and the perpetual eruption of the bonsaied volcano.

At length, this cowardly dissembling became all too evident as such even to the most superficial levels of my self-awareness, and there was nothing for it but to proceed into the heart of my fear.

There was a ring of stone benches circling the moat around the volcano, and, forcing any further thoughts from my mind, I took off my pack, jumped up on the nearest bench, spread my arms wide as I had watched many ruespielers do, and announced the title of my spiel in as loud a shout as I could muster, if in a voice not exactly without a tremulo: *"The—the Tale of the Spark of the Ark!"*

While I could see that I had caught the momentary attention of most of the passersby within range of my voice by the simple expedient of leaping into prominent visibility and assaulting their eardrums, the same effect could as easily have been produced by setting off an explosion, which is to say that heads turned at the sound of the noise, but as soon as the source thereof had been verified, all those whose attention had been attracted went on about their previous business and pleasures.

Far from undaunted, but by now thoroughly committed, I focused my eyes on the arabesque patterns of light swirling across the wall of a nearby building to shield myself from knowledge of the size of my audience or the utter lack thereof, and launched into my own recomplicated declamation of the version of the tale that Shane Kol Barka had told at the ruespielers' farewell fete, for this had been spontaneously declaimed in such rude style, yet with such effect, at least upon my own spirit, that I felt that even such as I might retell it with some improvement.

"Think not that the Second Starfaring Age sprang full-blown from the brow of We Who Have Gone Before when the Jump Drive was invented, nor that the Arkies of the First Starfaring Age meekly gave over a noble way of life that had endured for millennia when the Void Ships began to knit together the isolated island worlds of men! For the Spark of the Ark is with us today, attend my tale and learn how. . . ."

While I was attempting to avoid gazing upon the passing throng as I continued to declaim for fear of being entirely tongue-tied by what I might see, I could not avoid counting the house, as it were, out of the corner of my eye, and perceiving to my dismay that it was nil. Nowhere in all that bustle and movement could I detect a stationary person or a look of rapt attention.

". . . some Arkies were able to purchase the arkologies in which they had been . . . in which they had been willing coolies. . . ."

What a fool I felt! Standing there shouting into an entirely indifferent whirlwind! Yet strangely, the more foolish and futile I felt, the more I felt my courage grow, for as I grew to lose all hope of attracting an attentive audience, the acceptance of certain defeat by this measure caused me to redefine victory into something attainable, which is to say that I was seized by the angry determination that, come what may, I would not be silenced by indifference, I would tell my tale to the end, even if the only audience was my own spirit.

". . . for it pleased Fortune that the Piper of Pan followed the Arkies he had led on a long slow voyage of exploration beyond the furthest known limits of the worlds of men. . . ."

With hindsight's vision, and not without a certain affection for that foolishly brave girl tremulously declaiming her tale into a vacuum, do I now perceive what a strange, noble, and pathetic figure I cut, an urchin with a pack at her feet standing on a bench before the dwarfing spectacle of an erupting volcano, shouting at the indifferent milling throngs, first in hope, then in embarrassed terror, and finally with the full-throated voice of wounded outrage.

Yet, to my own inner credit, I persisted, and when I finally came to the end of the ordeal, my voice was firm, my body was trembling, my spirit was addressing persons unknown or at least unseen, and I fairly shouted my defiance, switching to Lance Della Imre's florid version of the peroration at the end of the tale.

"And where in our Second Starfaring Age is the Spark of the Ark to be found? Everywhere! Nowhere! On Great Edoku itself! In the very Children of Fortune that you scorn! Vraiment, in the teller of this tale! Even within the Arkie Sparkie hearts of all you poor quotidian Edojin who still retain within yourselves the nobility of spirit to honor at least the memory thereof within you by showering me with ruegelt!"

Alas, of course, nothing of the sort happened. Instead I stood there trembling, sweaty, sore of voice and empty of spirit, while throngs of Edojin went their lordly ways with no more than a shrug here, a moue of distaste there, a few passing heads nodding ironically to each other.

A single soul deigned, or mayhap merely chanced, to meet my eyes: a green-haired woman with space-black skin dressed in a flowing gown of golden cloth. She looked at me for a moment en passant, shook her head ruefully, smirked, shrugged, then airily tossed a single coin in my direction.

I know not what was in her heart, or rather I choose not to dwell upon my surmise, for whatever mélange of contempt, pity, or rueful admiration caused what to her was no doubt a casual gesture immediately forgotten, of all the coin I was to earn at the ruespieler's trade, none ever meant more to me in the moment of donation thereof than that very first.

Nor was I to earn very much more ruegelt in the Luzplatz until Fortune chose to smile on me in the unlikely person of Guy Vlad Boca.

Each day for a week I repaired to the Luzplatz, mounted my bench, and declaimed one tale or another of the repertoire I had learned from the ruespielers of the Gypsy Jokers. I found to my considerable satisfaction that once I had dared this for the first time and survived the indifference of the throngs who refused to become my audience, once I had conquered both the initial fear and subsequent embarrassment of failure, the act of spieling my tales in public held little further terror.

Alas, I also found to my considerable consternation that while repetition might work to ease my trepidation and improve my delivery, the results remained all too negligible. Now and again a few people might pause to listen to a portion of my tale before moving on, upon occasion a few isolated Edojin might

163

even stay for a full performance, but sad to say, the number of coins I accumulated in a week was exceeded by the number of days therein.

As to what part my rudeness in the performance of my art played in this paucity of donations, I am both too proud and too modest to attempt to assay, but certainement the mythos I was extolling seemed as much currently out of favor here in the Luzplatz as it had become in the vecino of the Gypsy Joker encampment. Shorn of the aura of charm in the eyes of the Edojin which seemed to have departed with Pater Pan, the figure of a Child of Fortune ruespieler celebrating the mythos of her kind had little power to hold an audience in the person of a somewhat bedraggled young girl seeking to draw approving attention to her own spectacle from that of an erupting volcano!

Vraiment, it was impossible to hide this perception from myself for very long, yet what else was I to do but persist? True, I might have used my handful of coins to take the Rapide to greener pastures, but I had no notion of where such a venue might be found, and it somehow seemed better to squander them on a single modest meal in a taverna to prove to myself that I had at least earned one day's respite from fressen.

The truth of the matter was that while I longed for escape from my current karma, indeed while I came to decide that I had had more than my fill of Edoku, no such avenue of escape was open, unless I was willing to surrender the life of a Child of Fortune and return to Glade. And having been the lover of Pater Pan, gained access to the Gypsy Jokers, learned the rudiments of the ruespieler's art, and even begun to practice it, if not exactly remuneratively, I was not about to slink home as a failure in my own eyes.

From this static karma, I was to be rescued by Guy Vlad Boca, my self-styled Merchant Prince, though when I first set eyes on him, he seemed anything but my savior.

Once again, I was standing on my bench before the ludicrously mighty backdrop of the Luzplatz's volcano, declaiming into a void with little hope of monetary reward. On this occasion, I was attempting for the first time Nuri John Barbrera's truly bizarre and historically highly inaccurate *The Name Tale of We Who Have Gone Before,* for while this might be one of the most difficult of all the tales I knew to tell, it had the twin virtues of enlivening the mythic panoply of the Child of Fortune cycle with the inclusion of both We Who Have Gone Before and the Void Pilot as additional elements.

In this tale, the Arkies of the arkology which first discovered the planet of the vanished sapients are the Child of Fortune figures, but rather than have the historical Alia Haste Moguchi and her mages toil for years to wrest the secret of the Jump Drive from the arcane artifacts thereon, she is transmogrified into the ur-scientist Faust, who straightaway scribes a pentagon of confinement around his computer, and summons up the departed spirit of We Who Have Gone Before with arcane incantations and puissant personality-modeling programs.

By the mating of this alien dybbuk's mythic phallus with the willing yoni of his own lover, she who will therefore become known to the dark fascination of our Second Starfaring Age as the Void Pilot, will he therefore be enabled to Jump in an augenblick of their cusp through long light years of the void between the stars.

Since the unknown nature and fate of We Who Have Gone Before is the central mystery of the Second Starfaring Age, and since the Void Pilot is our high priestess thereof, mayhap *this* at least would have more timeless appeal to the Edojin than further unvarnished celebrations of the Child of Fortune mystique, which, if truth be told, were beginning to wear a little thin even to my own ears.

Be such hopes as they may, matters went pretty much as before until I reached the point in the tale where Faust first peers within the pentagram to behold in dismay what his arcane powers have conjured.

"Faust's gorge rose and his disgust equaled his outrage as he beheld his Mephisto, for rather than appearing in the avatar of a lofty alien sage, the demon spirit of the vanished race of starfarers had incarnated itself in human archetype as the horny billy goat Pan, chortling lubriciously and stroking his mighty phallus—"

"And so are We Who Have Come Before!" I heard a loud and entirely boorish male voice shout to a sprinkling shower of laughter.

"But not even this could sway Faust's purpose," I persisted, imagining in that moment that I knew quite well how he must

165

have felt. "With cooing words and iron determination did he lead his reluctant Beauty to the mystic boudoir of the anything but reluctant Beast."

"Quelle chose! Let Beauty speak for feminine reluctance, but let the Faust of the species speak for our own priapic beast, bitte!"

My ears burned with another round of laughter, and my ire rose against this buffoon. It could hardly be said that I was such an object of public favor that the sanity of my spirit required a heckler to deflate my overweening confidence.

"Let such professions of masculine swinishness await their own good time," I snapped back, "for soon enough the fruits thereof shall certainement be revealed, männlein, as the lingam of We Who Have Gone Before penetrates the yoni of the Pilot to the priapic piping of Pan!"

That, at least, was an image of sufficient outrageous crudity to command at least an interval of silence from any audience, and vraiment, it could now be said that something in the way of an audience was indeed in evidence, for a small but definitely interested crowd had now formed before my bench.

"For voilà, as the unnatural lovers attain their Great and Only cusp, it is the Pilot and the Arkies who Go Before to carry the Arkie Spark forth from the transient world of history into the legendary now of our Second Starfaring Age, while Faust, poor Faust, is left behind to lust forever after tantric mysteries beyond his poor constipated ken."

"Alors, first you style Faust a fellow willing to procure his own inamorata to a goat, and then you accuse the very same unprincipled rogue of an excess of righteous anality!" said the voice from the crowd.

"It would not be the last time Circe transformed a perfect master of the masculine gender into a barnyard maquereau," I rejoined to modest titters. "And lest anyone doubt the ability of the femme fatale of our species to truly transform men into swine, voilà, observe the living example!"

At this there was quite a more satisfying round of laughter, for the source of all this disturbance was now striding boldly forward to this introduction, through the small knot of Edojin, who only too willingly parted to allow what by now they no doubt considered my foil to approach my rude stage.

166

In truth, he was quite a handsome young man, somewhat thespically accoutred all in black velvet to match his long flowing black hair, and somehow also appropriate to his pouting lips and languid carriage. He wore his skin au naturel, rather than tinted in the Edojin mode. All in all, even I in my anger had to own that this Prince of Swine presented a visual aspect entirely more pleasing than the boorishness of his manners.

"Hola, what a—*mythmash!*" the fellow exclaimed, giving me a conspiratorial wink whose meaning was then entirely beyond my comprehension, and then turning to face the little crowd with his arms folded across each other in a gesture of hauteur.

"Is it not enough that you have gifted Alia Haste Moguchi with a phallus and renamed her Faust? And proceeded to outfit him or her or it with the Goddess of Swine as consort? Vraiment, and styled the arcane spirit of We Who Have Gone Before as a slavering goat-creature with an enormous throbbing wong? Now would you have these good folk believe that the Jump Drive which propels our Void Ships from star to star consists of a goat copulating with the queen of the pig people? Who would have thought that such a fair young visage could mask a foul mind of such perversity!"

At this there was a bout of laughter at my expense which fairly singed my ears. "It takes one to know one, n'est-ce pas?" I said. "Vraiment, who but a low-minded maestro of perversity could hear the tale of the birth of our great age rendered in lofty metaphor and on the spot immediately translate it into the bestial imagery of his own poor excuse for a mind?"

"Was I the one who styled Alia Haste Moguchi a maquereau named Faust, We Who Have Gone Before a priapic billy goat, and the figure of the Pilot the queen of the pig people?"

"Vraiment, for like all who lack the art to tell a tale but conceive themselves gifted with the intellect to serve as critics of same, your snout is rooted in the quotidian muck of literality and your ears are deaf to the metaphorical music of the spheres. You are therefore a true brother-spirit to the Faust of my tale."

"*Moi?* Good folk, I swear a solemn oath that never have I served as matchmaker to the mating of a goat and a pig for my own amusement!"

"I stand corrected," I said, "for quite obviously rather than being the matchmaker, you are the progeny thereof!"

167

At this, I was rewarded by the cresting of the continuous undercurrent that had begun to serve as counterpoint to our exchange into a fine breaker of laughter. Indeed, by now I had begun to perceive what had degenerated into a contest of insults as a sporting event devoid of all real malice. Moreover, the coherence and thrust of my tale having been entirely destroyed thereby to the amusement of the first audience that had ever paid me heed, I decided to give over any further attempts to continue in an earnest vein and ride with the current flow of karma.

"And *you*, I surmise, fancy yourself the Pilot of the tale?" he rejoined when the laughter had subsided. "Or mayhap the horny goat-god? I confess to a certain confusion in these matters of gender, for as the teller thereof, you seem to have enough difficulty keeping the *species* of the participants in your orgy straight!"

"Whereas you when participating in *your* orgies no doubt have difficulty keeping . . . *other matters* straight!"

To the roar of ribald laughter which greeted this jape, he leapt onto the bench beside me, declaring: "Au contraire, I now must stand revealed as the great billy goat Pan himself, for I cannot fail to . . . *rise* to such a challenge!" And he rolled both his eyes and hips lubriciously.

"Well spoken!" I said. "In truth, we were all growing somewhat jaded with the . . . *limpness* of your responses! I much prefer the self-proclaimed libidinal billy goat to the impotent creature of the intellect."

"No doubt! For I surmised all along that your desire was to play Circe to my Pan!"

"Au contraire," I proclaimed, "for while I may lay claim to the tantric puissance to turn a man such as yourself into a swine, reversing the procedure is clearly an act of prestidigitation beyond the scope of any woman's art!"

So saying, I thumbed on my ring of Touch, and, out of sight of the laughing crowd, thrust my hand deep into the crack of his buttocks. What happened next seemed to owe as much to the quickness of his thespic instincts as to the sudden kundalinic shock which must have taken him completely by surprise, for he screwed up his face into an outrageous caricature of swinish rut, sank to his knees grunting and making to plant slobbering kisses at my feet, leaving his derriere high in the air with my hand planted therein for all the world to see.

Having achieved this apex, or rather nadir, of obscene comedy, there was nothing for it but to maintain this grotesque figure for a long moment, while the audience, which by the time of this climax had reached some several score, roared and groaned, and began to toss coins.

Upon being showered with the first few droplets of what became a substantial rain of ruegelt, as if by prearranged choreography, we disengaged from our ribald tableau, glanced back and forth at each other, and, holding hands, assumed bowing postures until coin no longer rained upon us and the impromptu audience dispersed.

"Allow me to make a somewhat more formal introduction," he said, as he aided me in scooping up the booty. "Guy Vlad Boca, servidor de usted."

Vraiment, in his outré manner, he *had* served me well, for there were some three score pieces of ruegelt by my immediate rude estimation. A few weeks of the same success at various venues and we might gain sufficient ruegelt to quit Edoku for other planets of our respective choosing.

"I somehow sense that you are no Edojin. . . ?" I asked hopefully.

"*Moi?*" he said with a little laugh. "Far from it, I am a simple Child of Fortune like yourself."

"Bon!" I declared, for this was precisely as I wished. "May I suggest we dine together at our mutual expense, for together we have certainly garnered enough funds to escape from the vileness of fressen, and together I believe we have affairs of mutual profit to discuss."

"I would be delighted to dine with you and I am sure I would find our discourse amusing at the very least," Guy said somewhat superciliously, or so it seemed. "May I in turn suggest the *Crystal Palace*, an emporium whose cuisine I have . . . ah, heard, is of high repute?"

"Porqué no?" I agreed, for I had no counterproposal to make.

"And whom shall I have the honor of dining with?" Guy asked.

"I am Moussa Shasta—" I paused, hefting the weight of

169

the ruegelt I had just earned by my own wits, if at the cost of my unremunerative dignity. "I am *Sunshine* Shasta Leonardo, Gypsy Joker and ruespieler extraordinaire," I told him. For had I not at long last also earned the right to style myself thusly?

purples, in which the only decor was the essences of the colors themselves.

As for the cuisine, which I gracefully allowed Guy to order up, we dined on a feast of some twenty tiny dishes presented in the rijsttafel mode, though in place of the traditional pot of steamed rice as the ground for the multiplicity of cuisinary miniatures, we were served a great mound of thin and highly saffroned pasta gently fried almost to the point of crispness in some pungent oil. With this repast, we drank a powerful clear wine, like an aromatic sake, which seemed to be laced with mildly psychotropic herbs.

Reposing there in a palace of romantic light liberally sprinkled with richly clad Edojin, daintily picking at artfully prepared dishes representing a good dozen different cuisinary modes, sipping at a wine which warmed my body with a fine sensual glow, I felt several light-years removed from the quotidian vie ordinaire I had so long endured on Edoku. Once more I had returned to the pampered haut monde which I had enjoyed as a favored daughter of the elite of Nouvelle Orlean, as a haut turista on Edoku itself who had airily gone through two months' worth of funds in the same number of weeks. While my time as a Gypsy Joker and lover of the great Pater Pan still shone in memory's afterglow, here I felt that I had returned to my proper station. And it was a grace from which I was determined not to fall again.

And Guy Vlad Boca, so it seemed to me, was the chip of credit, as it were, whereby such a style of life might be indefinitely sustained, if only I could bend his services to my purpose.

In the service of which, I therefore kept my ring of Touch activated, and continually contrived to chance to brush my hand against various portions of his anatomy as we ate, drank, and spoke—touching his hand or arm to emphasize points of my discourse, patting his thigh in innocent friendly appreciation, snuggling close to him, and in general exercising the usual seductive feminine wiles, greatly augmented by my secret electronic power.

Nor, if truth be told, was I myself entirely immune to the erotic aura which I spun around our intimate tête-à-tête, for certainement he was a handsome enough fellow, with a languid and loose-limbed air that bespoke an attractively sensual spirit, he had proven himself quick and clever enough, and the rosy atmospheric glow of the *Crystal Palace,* not to say that of the toxicants in the wine, suffused my own body with a pleasantly lustful warmth.

"I sense that our fortunes were intended by destiny to pleasantly intertwine, Guy," I told him, leaning quite close and regarding him coyly over the lip of my wineglass while smoothing his leg with my hand.

"Indeed," he said, his eyes warmed by a smoky sunset glow, "I would have little objection to some pleasant intertwining once our gustatory appetites have been properly sated."

"All in its own good time," I promised. "But I have in mind an enterprise even more intimate than a passage d'amour, indeed one which would spice the same with the piquancy of a deeper sharing, much as the psychotropics in this wine enhance its toxicating pleasures. . . ."

"Mmmmm. . . . ?" he purred dreamily.

"Our very presence here bespeaks our combined ability to profit together at the ruespieler's trade, nē. . . ."

"Ruespieler? *Moi?*" he said with a certain lack of focus, for my hand had slid further inward along his thigh.

"You have never been a ruespieler?" I said in some surprise. "I would have thought. . . ."

He beamed at me and moved his face closer to mine. "I have never told a tale in my life," he said. "Though I own to a quick wit verbal. . . ."

"Well then fear not, and leave matters of repertoire to me," I assured him somewhat hyperbolically. "In fact what I have in mind requires no learning in the ruespieler's art."

"What *I* have in mind requires no verbal skill at all," he cooed, clasping his hand upon mine as it held my glass. I withdrew my other hand from his thigh, the better to focus his flagging intellect on my words. He pursed his lips in a moue of minor pique.

"Be serious, Guy!" I chided him. "Attend! What I propose is that you and I repeat what we have to our profit so recently performed until we have secured enough funds to purchase electrocoma passage to some other world, and in the meantime to purchase pleasures such as this which Edoku affords. Within a month, we should be on our way."

"Hmmm. . . ." he said. "Would not such an entertainment soon jade the Edojin, whose fickleness is all too legendary?"

"We need not perform in the same venue twice," I told him. "Moreover, while continuing to play the same bantering duet, we might contrive to vary our japes from time to time for variety's sake." I replaced my stroking hand upon his thigh, moved it even closer to the kundalinic quick of him, and gazed romantically into his eyes. "Well what do you say, Guy? Partners and lovers in the grand adventure of the Yellow Brick Road to our mutual pleasure and enrichment. . . ?"

"Wandering troubadours of erotic comedy together?" he mused somewhat superciliously. "Guy Vlad Boca, Child of Fortune and ruespieler extraordinaire, with his lady by his side. . . ?"

"Vraiment! What do you think?"

"Je ne sais pas. . . ." he said in a bantering tone. "It might be drôle. . . . I can see some possibilities for amusement. . . ."

"Merde!" I exclaimed. "Drôle? Amusement? I offer you a partnership of love and profit and that is the best you have to say for yourself?"

Guy leaned even closer and leered at me slyly. "Guy Vlad Boca has never been one to pursue an enterprise for mere pecuniary gain," he said loftily. "As for love, such might convince me to agree, though it would take some art. At the very least, a demonstration thereof is in order, nē. . . ."

I tugged briefly and none too gently at the handle of his manhood as if to yank him thereby out of his supercilious mood and watched his eyes go wide and his full lips tremble. "If it is a demonstration you require," I said forcefully, staring deep into his eyes, "I shall provide one that will leave you shaking like jelly and panting to serve my yoni. . . ."

"Indeed?" he replied throatily. "In point of fact, that end, at any rate, you have achieved already. . . ."

In some haste, we guzzled down the last of our wine, and settled up the tab, which, alas, consumed most of the ruegelt we had earned together. But this minor catastrophe barely impinged upon my mood, for certainement there would be no lack of funds once I had worked my tantric puissance on Guy and won him to our enterprise.

The choice of cuisinary venue having been Guy's, the choice of boudoir was left to me, both to serve the balance of reciprocation, and for the reason that Guy, by now consumed by priapic lust,

174

seemed entirely unequipped to give that nicety or any other serious and judicious consideration. Lacking sufficient funds to rent a chamber in a hotel, and not wishing to perform our nuptials in the nearest secluded woodland or garden, I conducted us via Rapide to the garden atop the butte, where, what now seemed like half a lifetime's karma ago, Pater Pan had conducted *me* for our first passage d'amour.

Upon emerging from the lift tube which carried us from the base of the waterfall to the shallow bowl of gardens sunk into the clifftop, a not unpleasant feeling of sweet tristesse for that lover in this venue at that temporal nexus spiced my anticipation of what was to come, as hand in hand with Guy I beheld the little rolling green hills and dells, the crystal pools and burbling brooks, the blooming stands of trees planted along the hilltops as hedges of seclusion. I inhaled the warm perfumed breezes, bounced gaily in the low gravity gradient, removed my shoes and luxuriated in the strange furlike feel of the lawn beneath my bare feet, as I led Guy to a dell by a pool, not unlike the one in which I had first shared love with Pater.

At length, when we reposed on the velvety lawn beneath the cerulean sky, I looked inquiringly at Guy, seeking his approval of the wu of the venue I had chosen.

Guy slowly ran his gaze about the flowering trees on the hillcrest above us, the clear pool on whose shore we lay, the forest rimming the horizon, then regarded me as if sizing up my relation to this bucolic paradise.

"Well?" I finally demanded.

"Quaint," he said in that supercilious tone with which I was becoming quite familiar. "In fact, all in all, rather charming." Then, seeing that consternation upon my face which had been his jocular intent to evoke all along, he broke into goodnatured, albeit raucous, laughter.

"What a beast you are, Guy Vlad Boca!" I exclaimed in much the same spirit. "How in need you are of proper taming!"

So saying, I rolled over upon him, clasping my lips to his, and running my hands, both natural and electronically augmented, freely over the most intimate parts of his body.

How unlike the response of Pater Pan in this very venue upon a similar occasion Guy's was, indeed how unlike the response of any male within my experience! Far from returning my

175

challenge to the pouvoir of his manhood with attempts at over-mastery of his own, far from entering into a loverly contest of erotic wills aimed at contesting my mastery of him through pleasure with his own skill at the evoking of same, he immediately gave himself over to unbridled and entirely unconstrained enjoyment of my ministrations. He embraced me tenderly but with little force, he rained little soft kisses on the nape of my neck as I seized his lingam, he moaned and sighed, he fairly purred as I enveloped his body, his head rolling back and forth, eyes half closed, as he flowed softly beneath me like the waves of a tropical sea.

Strange to tell, this entirely frank self-absorption in his own pleasure, far from vexing me with its openly languid passivity, inflamed my lust to a fever pitch in some arcane manner. When we broke our embrace to disrobe, it was I who stripped off my tunic in graceless haste, and he who slowly and teasingly shed his clothing as if for my delectation, smiling slyly at me all the while.

When our nude bodies came together, vraiment, he assumed the superior position and thrust his manly lingam home with a rhythm that left nothing to be desired in terms of vigor, but there was nothing of the rutting animal or egoistic cocksman about it.

Instead, as I spurred him on with my Touch deep in the root of him, he gave himself over to a slow and smoky ecstasy, as if experiencing my pleasure as his own, and somehow turning back his own wanton enjoyment of my preternatural powers upon myself, so that the more I perceived his thoughtless and mindless appreciation of the moment-to-moment pleasure, the more I became inflamed with the lust to drive him to ever more wild heights of abandon.

Our passage d'amour went on and on in this vein for an endless, or at any rate measureless, time, and though we essayed tantric figures of some variety, the *inner* figure never changed. Vraiment, though I had had lovers of greater artistry and certainement of more sheer tantric power, never had I experienced such a total egoless surrender to ecstasy at my touch as that of Guy Vlad Boca, and never had a man therefore made me feel more potent as a mistress of the tantric arts. Mayhap this is what spurs a man on to feats of tantric heroism in the arms of a woman; je ne sais pas. Suffice it to say that when at length, verdad at what seemed like tantalizingly languid leisure, we eased seamlessly into one single mutual cusp, I felt entirely content, indeed overweeningly pleased with what I had wrought.

Guy, for his part, lay on his back with his hands clasped behind his head, his full lips parted in a sensuous smile of pleasure, his breath deep and slow, and his eyes shut to the world for a long while before he summoned up the composure to speak.

"Now *that,*" he finally said, "was *amusing.*"

"*Amusing!*" I shrieked. "Is that all *anything* is to you, Guy, *amusing?*"

Guy propped himself up against the slope of the dell and softened my anger with a little laugh. "Au contraire," he said. "It takes a great deal to truly amuse me. If you knew me better, you would know to what lengths I am willing to go to be amused, and that I have in fact paid you the highest compliment of which I am capable."

"Well, then," I said, somewhat mollified, "have I sufficiently *amused* you to convince you that my proposition that we ruespiel together as partners and lovers until we have accumulated sufficient funds to leave Edoku offers enough hope of further amusement for you to consent to give it a try?"

Guy laughed. He regarded me with the strangest unreadable expression. "Oh verdad!" he said. "I can think of no one else I would rather have as a traveling companion. However . . . I must confess that thusfar I have been traveling with you under somewhat false pretenses."

"False pretenses?"

"Hai! I fear I have thusfar withheld complete revelation of the full grandeur of my being."

At this modest confession, I was quite literally rendered speechless.

Guy, naturellement, suffered no such aphasia. "All we have told each other is our status as Children of Fortune and our names," he said. "Let us now therefore exchange the tales thereof and I promise you all will be gloriously revealed to your delight. Please begin, Sunshine, for I would not wish your name tale to come as a great anticlimax."

So bemused was I at all this mystery that I scarcely reacted to the implied insult in my haste to get to the bottom of it, which is to say I did as he asked, relating the tales of my maternom and

177

paternom without of course mentioning the Touch, and telling the tale of my nom de rue, Sunshine, and my career as a Gypsy Joker, without needlessly overemphasizing the degree and depth of my intimacy with Pater Pan.

"Drôle," Guy said when I had finished. "A true Child of Fortune of the spirit!" He rose to his feet and tied the arms of his black velvet blouson about his neck so as to accoutre himself with a swirling cloak, more for thespic effect than out of any modest impulse to clothe his nakedness.

"I am *Guy Vlad Boca*," he declaimed grandly, "and while I too am a true Child of Fortune of the spirit, I hardly need reduce myself to begging in the streets in order to travel from planet to planet as insensate cargo in electrocoma, danke, nor need anyone upon whom I choose to bestow my favor.

"My mother, Boca Morgana Khan, was born to parents of rather formidable wealth on Melloria, her father being Khan Norman Margo, magnate of fabriks on several worlds, and her mother Morgana Desirée Colin, a Void Ship domo of no little repute before meeting her father. Her freenom, Boca, she chose after a wanderjahr amusing herself in the floating cultura homage à La Boca Felicita, a legendary singer and thespian of the First Starfaring Age, for while she never followed that trade, or truth be told any other, she fancied that her great beauty, wit, and sweet voice would surely have served to gain her fortune thereat had not her patrimony felicitously removed the necessity.

"My father, Vlad Dominik Ella, was born into more modest circumstances on Novi Mir. His father, Dominik Ivan Dona, was the proprietor of a palace of pleasure, and his mother, Ella Dane Krasnaya, labored therein as an artiste ordinaire. His freenom, Vlad, he chose after a wanderjahr begun as a freeservant on Void Ships and concluded as an established gambler and tantric performer on same, homage à one Vlad the Impaler, a legendary monster of prehistory, famed, naturellement, for his numerous acts of impalement, though apparently not of the sort of which my father was boasting.

"My parents met aboard the *Celestial City*, and it was pheromonic congruence at first sight, or at any rate upon first impalement. Boca's parents, naturellement, were somewhat less than enthused when she returned to Melloria with such a swain, marking Vlad as a fortune hunter, which, in a certain sense, he was. In return for his acceptance of a probationary year, Khan Norman Margo gifted him with a substantial sum of credit, with the understanding that only if he returned with this wealth doubled would he be welcomed as a kinsman, expecting, no doubt, that that would be the last he would see of this rake.

"However, to the delight of all concerned, Vlad's instincts as a gambler, and perhaps his penchant for impalement as well, when combined with working capital, served him in good stead as a traveling merchant, trading among the worlds of men in whatever commodities might be bought cheap and sold dear, and when he returned to Melloria, his wealth had in fact quadrupled.

"Today, my father, Vlad Dominik Ella, is the owner and maestro of Interstellar Master Traders, and his wealth exceeds that of my mother's parents by an order of magnitude."

Having concluded his declamation of this extravagant name tale, Guy sat down beside me as if to reestablish our less formal relationship. "And so here you see before you Guy Vlad Boca, Child of Fortune on his wanderjahr vraiment, but no wandering minstrel I!" he said. "Rather I am the scion of Interstellar Master Traders, a Merchant Prince, as it were, traveling at leisure from world to world for my own amusement to be sure, but also absorbing the lore of my future trade."

He reached into a pocket of his blouson and withdrew a chip of credit which he held beneath my nose as if it were a priceless gem. "This little bauble draws without limit upon the coffers of Interstellar Master Traders, a well of plenty without bottom for all practical purposes," he declared. "I am commissioned to do as I will for a period of my own choosing, the only proviso being that I, like my father before me, may never return to Melloria to claim my full patrimony until I have achieved a balance of profit over expenditure in the ratio of two to one. At the rate things are going, this may take some time. But then I am in no particular hurry."

Entirely ignoble emotions coursed through me at the conclusion of all these revelations. Anger at Guy for not having used his magic chip at the *Crystal Palace*. Anger too at the mininess of my own parents in comparison to the bountiful largesse of Vlad Dominik Ella, which is also to say mean-spirited envy of Guy for his good fortune. Finally, and most painful, despair that my plan to earn ruegelt with his aid had now apparently come to naught.

"You were just . . . *amusing* yourself with me," I finally said in a tone of angry dejection. "You never had any intention of joining me in the ruespieler's trade. . . ."

"Indeed," said Guy, with an entirely incongruous grin. "And I must say I still find you most amusing, ma chère. Though of course I must reject your proposal."

But before I could vent my wrath, Guy stayed my words with a finger to my lips. "However, as a Merchant Prince in training, I am constrained to give fair value for value received," he said. "Since the commodity in question is amusement, let me counter with a proposal that I hope *you* will find amusing. Shortly I will be leaving Edoku for Belshazaar, a planet which I expect will be far more amusing and certainly more remunerative than this one. If *you* find the notion amusing, why not accompany me thither in the *Unicorn Garden,* at my expense, of course, or to be more precise, courtesy of Interstellar Master Traders?"

I could scarcely credit my ears. I could hardly believe in such good fortune. Indeed, considering the source, at first blush I was not quite certain that I could trust it. "*Belshazaar. . . ?*" I said guardedly. "I've never heard of Belshazaar. What is there to draw us thither?"

"On Belshazaar there is a forest known as the Bloomenwald," Guy told me. "It is reputed to be a veritable cornucopia of psychotropic perfumes, essences, saps, pheromones, und so weiter. While hundreds of them are already on the market, scores more are discovered each year, and a merchant who secures a droit of monopoly for a period in a few of the latest stands to gain a tidy fortune. At the very least, it should be the height of amusement to sample the full panoply of what is available."

My enthusiasm for quitting Great Edoku for such a venue was considerably less total than Guy's, but on the other hand, what were my prospects on Edoku without him save continued indigency and an endless banquet of fressen?

"Gratuit. . . ?" I asked carefully. "Why should you do such a thing for me?"

"Porqué no?" Guy said airily. "From each according to his ability, to each according to her need, as the ancient communards had it, nē. And when it comes to credit, my ability is bottomless, and your need is total. Besides, as I have declared, I find your company amusing."

"We would not travel in electrocoma. . . ?"

"Quelle chose!" Guy exclaimed in somewhat supercilious outrage. "Do you imagine Guy Vlad Boca would find it amusing to sleep through a voyage when the divertissements of the floating cultura lie readily at hand? Do you account me such a boor that I would offer such passage to a lover? Come, Sunshine, join me as an Honored Passenger in the Grand Palais of the *Unicorn Garden!*"

"I might be convinced to agree . . ." I owned in a tone of mock reluctance. Naturellement, in truth no further inducements were necessary, for it was precisely such access to the haut monde of the floating cultura for which I had so strenuously albeit unsuccessfully campaigned against my parents' refusal. And while Sunshine might have evolved beyond Moussa, she was hardly less determined to live the true vie of the Child of Fortune, which is to say she followed the Yellow Brick Road for sake of the adventure of the journey not the goal of the destination, and in this respect was not Guy Vlad Boca a kindred spirit and the Grand Palais of the floating cultura the true camino real?

"If love is that which would convince you to agree, a demonstration thereof would seem to be once more in order," Guy said. "And I do believe I am once more ready to rise to the occasion."

So he was. So it did.

13 And so, in the company of my Merchant Prince, I bade farewell to Great Edoku, my days with Pater Pan, my comrades in the Gypsy Jokers, and my burning ambition to pursue the career of a ruespieler with scarcely a look back once I had gained access to the Grand Palais module of the *Unicorn Garden.*

Call me fickle mayhap, but consider also that had my parents followed the entirely admirable example of Dominik Vlad Ella and provided me with sufficient largesse to begin my wanderjahr in the style to which I had wished to become accustomed, I would never have chosen Edoku, never suffered the indigency and fressen of the Publics, never met Pater, never become a Gypsy Joker or a would-be ruespieler, and therefore never have met Guy Vlad Boca, who would therefore never have needed to rescue me from penury in the first place.

Which is to say that once we were ushered aboard the *Unicorn Garden* and conducted to a sumptuous if not quite spacious stateroom by suitably deferential freeservants, once I beheld the departure fete taking place in the grand salon, I was immediately possessed of sufficient sophistic logic to convince myself that one way or the other it had always been my proper destiny to voyage between the worlds in this style.

For what a different style it was from my previous experience at starfaring!

No sooner had our belongings been properly ensconced in our stateroom than the ship's annuciators invited our presence at the departure fete now taking place in the grand salon. The Grand Palais module of the *Unicorn Garden* was divided into five decks; counting downward from the bow to the stern, which was how the gravity gradient was arranged, these were the vivarium, the grand salon, the cuisinary deck, the entertainment deck, and the deck of dream chambers. Of these, the grand salon was the chief venue of the fetes, or rather the continuous fete that went on throughout the nine-day voyage under one nom de jour or another.

Maria Magda Chan, Domo of the *Unicorn Garden,* had commissioned a grand salon done up in a style which I can only call organiform, which is not to say that any flora or fauna were in evidence. Upon entering from the spinal passageway of the ship, one stood upon a landing stage from which a semicircle of stairs descended, and from which vantage one could therefore view the grand salon as a work of art entire.

I was first struck by the fact that not a single hard surface, flat plane, angle, or indeed even any simple geometric form, was in evidence. Chaises, banquets, tables, vraiment even the lighting fixtures, were all done up as items of upholstery, stuffed with foam, or fluff, or water, or air, and covered with velvety, furry, or indeed skinlike fabrics. All forms flowed, bulged, and curved, reminiscent in an entirely abstract manner of breasts, derrieres, thighs, phalluses, und so weiter, though none of it descended to the crassly representational. Similarly were the hues thereof derived from the organic realm—subtle browns and greens, soft floral tints, human skin tones—though nowhere were colors matched to form in an obvious manner. Even the walls, floor, and ceiling were upholstered in patterns of the same style, and the lighting tended to pinks, roses, and ambers. The total effect was of an abstract sensuousity balanced precariously but successfully on the edge of obscenity.

"Fantastic!" I exclaimed in delight.

"Amusing," owned Guy. "Naturellement, I have seen better."

The occasion of this fete, or rather the initial excuse for the opening of the endless round of such festivities, was the celebra-

183

tion of our departure from the solar system of Edoku via Flinger. While we Honored Passengers sipped at wines, inhaled toxicants, and nibbled at dainties offered by circulating floaters, a holo of our Void Captain, Dennis Yassir Coleen, appeared in the center of the grand salon to offer his salutations from the bridge. After this formality was concluded, his image was replaced by that of the great cryowire filigree tube of the Flinger outlined against the stars, and then by the gaping mouth of the hundred-kilometer spiderweb cylinder, seen from the stern of the *Unicorn Garden* as our Void Ship was drawn backward down it.

When we had achieved Go position at the bottom of the Flinger, we were treated to a final fond farewell image of Great Edoku itself, floating like a brilliant multifaceted and multicolored jewel against the black velvet of space in its orbiting nebula of luz redefusers.

At this moment, I reflected upon the manner in which the style of the grand salon resembled that of an arrondissement on Edoku writ small, and how the Honored Passengers therein resembled and yet did not resemble a similar gathering of Edojin, for while the dress of the Honored Passengers was no less rich and flamboyant than that of the Edojin, there was something somehow less frantic in its general effect, less given over to pushing high style over the edge into the bizarre for the sake of outrage.

"Do not our fellow Honored Passengers resemble a somewhat subdued collection of Edojin?" I remarked idly to Guy.

"Au contraire," he sniffed. "It seems to me that Edoku is something of an attempt to ape the floating cultura by folk who do not quite possess the charming self-assurance that only bottomless wealth can confer. A Grand Palais for the masses, as it were."

Be such lordly judgments as they may, Great Edoku now disappeared into memory, replaced by a holo of my future's image, to wit the starry blackness of the void as seen from the prow of our ship. A moment later, we heard the Void Captain chant the word "Go!" and all at once this starscape dopplered into a smear of blue as the Flinger accelerated the *Unicorn Garden* to relativistic speed in a sudden surge of mighty energies. Then the ship's visual compensators cut in and we beheld the pointillist starscape of the deep void hurtling toward us.

Our journey had begun. Soon our Pilot would be circuited

into her module in the Jump Circuit and then platform orgasm and the arcane machineries derived from the science of We Who Have Gone Before would propel us several light-years toward Belshazaar in an augenblick.

There was a smattering of polite applause and a considerably more enthusiastic round of bon voyage toasting.

"Come," said Guy, "now that the formalities are concluded, let us peruse the amusements that the *Unicorn Garden* has to offer."

Naturellement, the *Unicorn Garden,* or rather the Grand Palais module thereof, had a profusion of amusements to offer, all of them designed, as I was to learn, to focus the attention of the Honored Passengers inward toward our ersatz little bubble of hedonic reality, rather than outward to confront the vast cold emptiness of the void through which we traveled.

The entertainment deck offered up holocines, games of chance, and a vast library of word crystals, as well as all manner of musical, thespic, and dance performances put on by artists hired expressly for the purpose, or by freeservants doing double duty. Many of the latter were also available at a fee for private tantric performances.

The vivarium of the *Unicorn Garden* I found reminiscent of some similar venue of Edoku, though of course the scale of this domed parkland was greatly reduced from even that of the bonsaied landscapes which abounded on the planet of the Edojin.

Here, under an impossible holoed sky crammed with rainbows, moons, ringed planets, comets, auroras, tornado clouds, and a plethora of other such fancies rendered in miniature, was a living garden which made no pretense whatever to mimicking the surface of any world trod by man. The vivarium, no more than an acre or two in area, was done up as a forest clearing, so that the walls of the ship, which would otherwise have formed a confining horizon, could disappear behind a thick screen of trees. No two trees in this "forest" appeared to be of the same species, and no species seemed to have escaped the gene-crafter's art. There were trees whose barks were red, silver, furred, even feathered. Golden apples, huge roses, immense flowers of every sort, indeed even giant jewels and glowing tapers sprouted surrealistically in their boughs. As for the clearing, while green grass indeed formed the quotidian background for the tapestry, more of the ground than not was overgrown with brilliantly hued mushrooms and fungi.

The centerpiece of this vivarium was the pond in the center of the forest clearing, around whose shore benches were scattered, upon whose surface blooming water plants of various sorts and colors floated, and in the middle of which, reachable by footbridge, was a tiny desert island with shining sapphire sands shaded by a single immense palm.

But it was in the design of the fauna that the gene-crafters seemed to have done their work in a toxicated state, for the vivarium abounded in living creatures of legend, all done up in miniature. Pterodactyls the size of my hand skittered through the treetops. Knee-high griffins gamboled in the wood. Tiny tyrannosaurs and winged dragons begged morsels from Honored Passengers. The pond was stocked with little sea monsters—serpents, cachalots, squid, icthyosaurs, und so weiter.

And of course the vivarium of the *Unicorn Garden* could hardly be complete without half a dozen of its namesakes, each of the purest white, each with a golden spiral horn, and each no more than half a meter high. As for virgins in whose laps they might lay their little heads, these were the only mythical beasts not in evidence.

When it came to the dream chambers of the nethermost deck, the serpentine corridors thereof contained at least a score of these exotic private boudoirs, hardly any of them owing even inspiration to the natural realm.

One might engage in erotic exercises floating upon viscous rainbow-hued and jasmine-scented oil, or drifting weightless within a spherical mirror, or sightless in perfect velvet blackness, or brachiating in zero gravity in a construction of golden rods, or reposing in a nest of azure fluff, or indeed in a chamber padded in what at least gave the illusion of being living human flesh.

Nowhere in the country of the Honored Passengers, however, was there a single port or tele whereby one might experience the vast star-speckled blackness just beyond the hull of the ship, and indeed not even artistic representations of same were in evidence.

And when I chanced to comment on this at table, it was

almost as if I had attempted to turn the discourse toward the fecal in terms of the general response I received.

Of the decks of the Grand Palais, the cuisinary deck was the most quotidian in terms of its decors, though this is not to say that the productions of the *Unicorn Garden*'s chef maestro, Mako Carlo Belisandra, were anything less than superb examples of the art.

There were three different salons de cuisine, each appropriate to a different gustatory mood. For those desiring merely a casual meal, there was a simple refectory, with plushly upholstered thronelike stools set in rows along tables of polished black stone, the whole set beneath a trellised canopy of vines. For small private soirées or intimate dining à deux, there was a chamber entirely divided up into secluded tented booths of various appropriate sizes, each richly embroidered, painted, or quilted in a different style, each romantically illumined by braziers, and each containing a low bronze table surrounded by nests of cushions.

Finally, there was the formal grand dining salon, large enough to accommodate the entire company of Honored Passengers for banquets presided over by our Domo, our Void Captain, or both. Here the walls were paneled in some rough-grained greenish-brown wood framed and embellished by rococo golden metalwork in floral designs, the floor was of black marble, as was the great fireplace, and each of the tables was illumined by a crystal chandelier depending from a ceiling painted to resemble a cerulean sky replete with a few fluffy white clouds. Each of the ten round tables could seat ten diners, and each consisted of a disc of bronze mirror glass supported by a heavy ebon pillar which matched the wood of the leather-upholstered chairs.

It was here that Guy and I chanced to draw seats at the Domo's table at the banquet marking the occasion of our first Jump. The Void Captain, naturellement, was occupied at the moment on the bridge, though he would join the fete later, and as for the Pilot circuited into the Jump Drive, she, of course, would never be seen throughout the voyage.

The other seven diners at our table represented a fair cross section of what I had already learned were the four main species of Honored Passengers making up the floating cultura, though of course they hardly eschewed interbreeding.

Kuklai Smith Veronika and Don Terri Wu were men of

mature years, and even more mature fortunes, who were more or less retired from pecuniary activities and who spent their lives constantly voyaging among the worlds of men, typical haut turistas seeking nothing but their own pleasure. Then there were those who gained access to the floating cultura by serving the pleasures of such patrons, whether as high courtesans such as the breathtakingly beautiful Cleopatra Kay Jone, or by the fascination of their discourse, such as the mage of astrophysic, Einstein Sergei Chu, or as thespic or musical artists. Thirdly there were those, of whom Mary Menda Hassan, on her leisurely way to serve a stint as professor of Terran prehistory on Dumbala, was a prime example, who traveled, either at their own expense or via the patronage of employers or institutes of learning, for serious purposes of commerce, science, or scholarship.

Last, and in terms of the esteem in which they were held by their fellow Honored Passengers, least, were richly endowed Children of Fortune like Guy, who passed their wanderjahrs in the floating cultura simply because their parents could afford it.

In addition to Guy, this social and intellectual proletariat was represented at our table by Imre Chanda Sumi and Raul Bella Pecava, two young men whom Guy had already judged "amusing," at least in terms of the pharmacopoeia of exotic toxicants they had brought aboard.

As for my station in this hierarchy, it seemed at best problematic, for I was not even an independently subsidized Child of Fortune, and while I never failed to wear my Cloth of Many Colors, the ensign of the Gypsy Jokers carried absolutely no cachet in this society.

Indeed the very discourse thereof did little to draw me into the stream of conversation until the occasion of the first Jump brought forth my grand gaffe.

Over the entré of terrine de fruits de mer, Kuklai Smith Veronika and Cleopatra Kay Jone wittily debated, at least by their own lights, the virtues or lack thereof of composers of whose work I was entirely ignorant. Einstein Sergei Chu held forth on the future stellar evolution of our galaxy over the saffroned fruit soup in terms far too mathematically arcane for me to follow even if the subject had held my interest.

While we dissected the Fire Crab in Black Pepper Aspic, our Domo led a discussion of the relative merits of Grand Palais presided over by a number of her colleagues, and since I was the only one present who had never traveled as an Honored Passenger before, any contribution of mine would hardly have been relevant.

Mary Menda Hassan's discourse on our hominid ancestors over the Goreng de Charcuterie might as well have been in the sprach of same for all I could make of it, and as for the discussion of psychotropics which Guy, Imre, and Raul insisted on inflicting on our enjoyment of the sashimi salad, this was a subject of which I was already beginning to have a surfeit.

The Tornedos de Vaco with Smoked Black Mushrooms in Madeira Sauce had just been served when a loud chime sounded. All present paused in midbite for a moment and then went on with the meal. This minor mystery was enough to call forth my first conversational gambit.

"What was that?" I asked.

I was treated to strange looks of distaste from all at the table. "The ship just Jumped," Guy told me matter-of-factly. "Now as I was—"

"Quelle chose!" I exclaimed. "We have just leapt several light-years through the Void and the moment is marked with no more ceremony than that?"

There was an uncomfortable silence during which my tablemates exchanged peculiar glances with everyone but myself. Entirely misreading the moment, or mayhap simply determined to press on now that I had raised a subject upon which I felt that I could at last discourse, I persisted.

"Indeed, why has it not been arranged for us to view this spectacle en holo? Vraiment, nowhere in the Grand Palais are we afforded a vision of the starry grandeur through which we voyage. Furthermore, have none of you noticed the bizarre absence of even motifs relating to same in the works of art and decor with which the Grand Palais is embellished? It puts me in mind of the esthetic of Edoku, wherein . . ."

I stopped in midsentence, for I had now become the object of that general air of distaste suitable to a miscreant who boorishly mentions fecal matters at table to which I have already alluded.

"I have said something untoward?" I inquired uneasily. "Would someone be so kind as to enlighten me as to the nature of my faux pas?"

Guy said nothing, and indeed seemed to be doing his best to pretend I was a stranger, a useless stratagem, for as my traveling companion, the sphere of opprobrium around me clearly extended to encompass him, and even Raul and Imre, as fellow Children of Fortune, squirmed in their seats under the disdainful regard of our lordly tablemates.

"This is your first voyage, kinde?" the Domo finally said.

"My first as an Honored Passenger," I told her. "Though I have previously traveled between Glade and Edoku in electrocoma."

The latter amendment hardly seemed to enhance my social status, eliciting instead a further curling of lips and nostrils.

"*Je comprends*," said Maria Magda Chan. "One may hardly expect punctilious observation of the niceties from such a novice . . . *Honored Passenger*."

"What niceties?" I demanded crossly. "If I have said something nikulturni, perhaps one of you worthies would inform me of the nature of my transgression so that I may avoid further injury to your delicate sensibilities?"

"Well spoken!" declared Imre, and was immediately subject to a round of scowls for his chivalry.

"Since you profess the admirable desire to avoid further offense, ma petite, as Domo it is indeed my duty to instruct you in the social graces," Maria Magda Chan said. "Which is to say it is indeed nikulturni to refer to such matters as the Jump or that through which we are constrained to travel at table or in other polite discourse."

"Which is also why starscape motifs, let alone tele views of the . . . ah, Void itself, are not quite in favor among the floating cultura," Kuklai Smith Veronika added in a somewhat kinder paternal tone.

"I stand corrected, and will endeavor to refrain from such offense in future," I said dryly. "But since I am admittedly such a naif in these matters, perhaps someone will explain *why* those who choose to voyage through the mighty grandeur of the firmament eschew the esthetic appreciation of same, vraiment, why is it nikulturni to wish to experience through the senses the marvel of the Jump upon which our entire civilization depends?"

"Merde!" muttered Cleopatra Kay Jone. Guy fetched me a kick in the shins under the table. Quite crossly, I replied in kind.

"Have we not heard enough of this?" Don Terri Wu snapped angrily.

But our mage of astrophysic, Einstein Sergei Chu, seemed to warm to the broaching of his own subject of expertise. "Well and courageously spoken, child," he declared. "Certainement a subject worthy of more consideration in these circles than it receives. As for the aversion of our floating cultura to visual confrontation with the medium through which our ship travels, consider, bitte, the true nature of the physical reality in question. For beyond this thin hull is a deadly vacuum of nearly absolute cold which, though mathematically bounded, is for all practical human purposes remorselessly infinite. Vraiment, we are all but microbes in a bubble of air, protected from instant death only by our own fragile machineries. Should our life support systems malfunction, should the Jump Drive—"

"Enough!" cried Don Terri Wu.

"Vraiment, more than enough!" agreed Maria Magda Hassan.

"Must we be subject to this vileness merely to satisfy the morbid curiosity of this . . . this unwashed urchin?" demanded Cleopatra Kay Jone.

Einstein Sergei Chu, however, seemed to take a certain malicious pleasure in the general discomfort. "And as for the Jump, meine kleine," he persisted, "though we have long since elucidated the physical nature of our universe and the laws thereof from the finest structures of the microcosm to the grandest productions of the macrocosm, of the true nature of the single most important phenomenon therein in terms of utility of which we know, we remain in abysmal ignorance. We are like primitives who know how to strike fire from flint but have not the foggiest notion of the chemistry or physics of flame. Like such primitives, we have learned enough of the lost lore of We Who Have Gone Before to build Jump Drives to serve the most essential purpose of our culture, but as to the mass-energy nature of the Jump itself, we are precisely like those savages who fear and worship the unknowable fire which serves them, and surround therefore both the subject and the High Priestess thereof with ignorant taboos of mystification."

"Outrageous!" exclaimed the Domo.

"Grossity!" declared Don Terri Wu.

"*Amusing,*" owned Guy, referring no doubt as much to the resulting contumely as to the sagacity of Einstein's discourse, and favoring me with a grin. Raul and Imre broke into callow giggles which even *I* found somewhat boorish.

At this strategic moment, Void Captain Dennis Yassir Coleen entered the dining salon. "I will have no more of this at my table in the presence of our Void Captain!" Maria Magda Chan hissed angrily. And, so saying, she rose to greet that worthy with a great show of affection and indeed lascivious attentions.

Such matters were discussed no more at the banquet, nor, indeed, were they to be touched on again for the duration of the voyage. Nor did the innocent instigator of the brouhaha summon up the courage to join in the table talk again for fear of igniting I knew not what.

Nor did any of those present ever again deign to engage myself or my fellow Children of Fortune in civilized discourse for as long as we were aboard. Indeed, whether by dint of the spreading of the tale of this contumely, or whether by long-established general custom, we were seldom included in the social pavane of the floating cultura at all.

"A somewhat subdued collection of Edojin," I had styled the floating cultura to Guy. "Possessed of the charming self-assurance that only bottomless wealth can confer," he had told me.

As for the bottomless wealth of the Honored Passengers, this was everywhere in evidence. But as to the charm of their self-assurance, this was a virtue I was hard-pressed to detect. Certainement, these maestros of manner and artifice chose not to honor us with the blessings thereof, and at least for my part, the feeling was mutual.

At the merciful conclusion of the banquet, Guy, Raul, Imre, and I repaired to our stateroom for another session of what was becoming something of a regular ritual, to wit the sampling of the impressive variety of psychochemicals with which Raul and Imre had provisioned themselves for the journey.

While I had fancied myself something of an adept of the lore of psychopharmacology courtesy of my séances with Cort, the sophistication of his smorgasbord thereof compared to what these well-subsidized Children of Fortune had accumulated in their travels as what I had imagined the sophistication of Nouvelle Orlean to be compared to that of Great Edoku.

Vraiment, memory will not serve to recall which toxicant, or indeed which mélange of toxicants, we imbibed on any particular occasion, for these sessions blur into a pixilated generality in hindsight, so that the memory of one outré psychic state can hardly be distinguished from that of another, nor, even at the time, did my indulgence therein exactly serve to sharpen my perception of linear temporality or grave particularly clear images upon the cells of my brain.

Suffice it to say that for the first half of the voyage I sampled several dozen substances gathered from any number of worlds, and productive of an impressive range of conscious, semiconscious, and entirely torpid states, though in truth all of them might easily enough have been classified under a limited number of taxonomic phyla.

Certain of these psychochemicals produced states of hilarity in which the most asinine japes were good for prolonged fits of raucous giggling. Others would have us staring mindlessly at the walls or each other for hours at a time. Some of them loosened our tongues and fortified our wit to the point where we were capable of endless elegant discourse, or at least what seemed like same at the time.

But a few were well-crafted psychic enhancers, under the influence of which we would wander the Grand Palais in a state of innocent wonder like haut turistas in Oz, delight to an overwhelming degree in the cuisinary art of Mako Carlo Belisandra, take in musical or thespic performances, or simply stroll about the vivarium enjoying the bizarre ambiance thereof with childlike glee.

Then too, some of these psychochemicals were aphrodisiacs, though congruence of effect upon the male and female of the species was by no means assured.

I might be consumed by the most torrid lust, whereas Guy wished only to discourse endlessly or contemplate the ineffable, or Guy would become a priapic hero, only to be confronted by a lover to whom tantric performance existed only as an abstract and entirely outré concept. But on those occasions when our chemically augmented desires coincided, vraiment, we would become two organisms with but a single tropism, and blissful indeed was the indulgence thereof! And when the spirit moved us, we would repair to the dream chambers and enhance our already chemically augmented pleasures with congress in these fantasy realms expressly designed for the enjoyment of same.

Finally there were those rarest and choicest of substances capable of producing a state of being wherein the realm of the senses was synergized with the realm of the mind to the point where maya's veil seemed to dissolve into a clarity of perception within which all truth seemed revealed. Paradoxically enough, it was within the thrall of one of these true psychedelics that I experienced the satori which caused me to eschew further experiments with same for the rest of the voyage of our bubble of ersatz reality through the Void between the worlds.

Soon after we all swallowed the little brown tablets, we began to feel the initial effects, namely a brightening of the senses, and a desire to be in motion. Raul suggested that we visit the vivarium, and we all readily agreed, for thusfar the psychic enhancer seemed to have produced a mutually congruent effect on the four of us that verged on the telepathic.

But this did not persist for very long. When we had reached the vivarium, Raul rather strenuously suggested that we repose together on the grass and attempt by silent meditation to achieve a satori which he felt lay within the reach of our collective grasp but whose ineffable nature was entirely beyond his powers of description.

As for me, it would have been difficult to conceive of an activity more productive of discomfort under the circumstances, for the vivarium, with its fanciful ersatz trees, even more ersatz sky full of contradictory meteorological and astronomical elements, and its pathetic collection of miniature mythical creatures, far from elevating the state of my spirit as its art intended, soon began to achieve the aspect of a willful veil of maya whose illusion grew more and more transparent with every passing moment, threatening to dissolve entirely to reveal a void of ennui the continued contemplation of which produced only a growing formless dread the full revelation of whose nature was the last satori in the universe I would have wished to attain.

Nor were Guy or Imre much interested in a contemplative inward journey in these environs.

"I wish to wander," Imre told Raul. "Rather than waste this

194

experience on singular contemplation, I would surfeit my senses to the point of overload."

"Perhaps the dream chambers would be the most interesting venue," Guy suggested.

I exchanged telepathic glances with him. The last thing I wanted was a ménage à trois with him and Imre, whom I found not the least bit attractive, nor was I in much of a mood for tantric exercises in general. Such was the puissance of the psychedelic that all this was conveyed in a twitch of the eyebrow and a curl of the lip as was Guy's confirmation of his understanding of same, or so at least it seemed.

"For there we may overload our perceptions with a rapid tour of any number of arcane realities," he said, to make the nonerotic nature of his proposal plain.

Not without a certain grumbling from Raul, we left him in the vivarium to seek nirvana, and repaired to the dream chamber deck, where, as far as I was concerned, Guy and Imre behaved in a manner entirely unsuitable to this concourse of private boudoirs, this venue designed for romance. Fortunately, the individual dream chambers sealed themselves against intrusion when they were occupied, so at least no erotic exercises were interrupted by their boisterous laughter and silly jabberings, but we were the object of more than enough outraged and offended glances on the part of loverly couples strolling hand in hand through the corridors to do considerable damage to the already low repute in which Children of Fortune were held by our fellow Honored Passengers.

My mood, au contraire, was anything but jocular as I trailed after these callow creatures while they capered through the corridors, bounced about in zero-gravity dream chambers, engaged in mock combat in the chamber filled with azure fluff, pulled faces within the spherical mirror, performed obscene pantomines in the chamber of ersatz human flesh, and in general treated the venues in which Guy and I had made love in a manner which cast little credit on the romantic spirit of the male of our species, at least in the eyes of this observer of the opposite gender.

Moreover, once the romantic ambiance of the dream chambers had been destroyed by this adolescent male desecration, I began to perceive what, at least under the influence of the psychotropic, seemed the less wholesome aspect of the very con-

195

cept of the dream chamber itself. For just as elaborate tantric tableaus that would ordinarily arouse the erotic imagination may come to seem mechanical and even disgustingly perverse to a viewer whose libidinal energies have for one reason or another been forced into dormancy, so did these dream chambers come to seem like the pathetic stratagems whereby jades might seek to arouse memories of the natural man or natural woman they had long since lost. Which is to say that once the chemical and the actions of my jejune companions had contrived to rob me of all possibility of enjoying the *effects* of the dream chambers, I could perceive nothing but the empty artifice of the means of their production.

In short, I fell into a cafard of spiritual angst which did little to enhance my present appreciation of Guy Vlad Boca. Under the influence of comrades such as Raul and Imre, and the chemical kiss of a surfeit of toxicants, my prince seemed to be turning into a frog.

For the first time since he had rescued me from penury and dashingly swept me up and away into the floating cultura, I began to make invidious comparisons between Pater Pan and his noble vision of the Yellow Brick Road and Guy Vlad Boca, whose self-declared highest vision was amusement, between the paucity of funds and wealth of spirit I had known as a Gypsy Joker and what I had begun to perceive as the wealth of funds and paucity of spirit of the floating cultura, my Merchant Prince lover, vraiment by this time myself for finding myself here.

But to his credit, and mayhap to the credit of the puissance of the psychedelic as well, Guy sensed my growing discomfort of spirit. As Imre wandered aimlessly up the corridor a few paces ahead of us, he caught my eye, read what was written therein, or at any rate scanned the general gist of it, favored me with one of those gay smiles of his, and nodded in conspiratorial agreement.

"Vraiment, these jejune frolics are no longer amusing," he said. "Come, let us repair to the grand salon and join the fete."

I nodded my agreement, then nodded once more in the direction of Imre, nuancing the gesture with but the slightest flare of my nostrils. This too Guy read quite fluently, shrugging with only the corners of his mouth.

And so, leaving Imre to his own devices, we departed the dream chamber deck and made our way to the grand salon, at last shed of what to me had become our unwelcome entourage, and for the moment at least, if with his luster slightly tarnished, Guy Vlad Boca had once more proven himself my prince.

In the grand salon, the fete was in full flower, which is to say this venue was, as it seemed to be at every hour, well-stocked with Honored Passengers; sipping elegantly at wines, nibbling at dainties, judiciously inhaling toxicants far less powerful than what we had become accustomed to in our private séances, and discoursing in little groups on subjects which, as always, seemed abstruse beyond either my ready comprehension or real interest, empty of any real passion, and possessed, therefore, of a level of civilized sophistication which I paradoxically envied, though of course I could not then admit it to myself.

As usual, none of these elder elegances were particularly eager to include jejune Children of Fortune such as ourselves in their conversations, and so Guy and I seated ourselves on a chaise in the midst of the fete yet also psychically distanced from it, all the more so on this occasion courtesy of our chemically enhanced perception thereof, which, at least for my part, was not exactly conducive to an empathetic appreciation of same.

So we secured tall fluted glasses of wine from a passing floater and sat there sipping languidly at them with our noses in the air in what at least to us was drôle parody of the manners of the Honored Passengers, though no doubt the humor thereof was lost on everyone but ourselves.

"In all veracity, Guy," I inquired in a supercilious tone not untinged with a certain envious contempt, "as a mage of the subject famed throughout the far-flung worlds of men, do you truly find our present company as perfectly amusing as they seem to find themselves?"

"In as much veracity as I am presently capable of mustering, ma chère liebchen," Guy replied more or less in kind, "I have never found *anything* as perfectly amusing as the floating cultura seems to find itself."

"Not even me?" I purred coyly.

"Vraiment," he said in a most peculiar tone, "not even myself!"

"An admission I never thought to hear from the lips of Guy Vlad Boca!" I declared lightly.

But Guy had suddenly become more somberly passionate

than I had ever seen him. "Do you imagine that one whose spirit had already attained the nirvanic perfection of total amusement would so avidly pursue the same in the imperfectly amusing realm of maya as do I?" he said quite solemnly. "As do Imre and Raul? As do this noble company of Honored Passengers? Vraiment, as do we all, yourself not excluded, if truth be told."

Perhaps it was the psychedelic acting upon my own perceptions, perhaps it was the same speaking through Guy, or more likely the single spirit induced thereby moving through the two of us; at any rate, his entire countenance seemed to alter before my very eyes, and what I now beheld seemed to be his naked spirit unveiled, a spirit whose surface gaiety masked some darker passion of the soul, a deeper Guy than I had previously known, and therefore suddenly a creature of some mystery.

"Who can deny that all human tales begin and end alike?" he said. "Beyond our birth is a nullity and beyond our death is a void, therefore all that we possess are the augenblicks between. Which in turn either amuse or do not. And so some seek wealth because it is more amusing than poverty, fame because it is more amusing than anonymity, power because it is more amusing than impotence, love because it is more amusing than loneliness, knowledge because it is more amusing than ignorance, sensual pleasure because it is more amusing than ennui, und so weiter. As for me, it is *the moment of perfect amusement itself* I seek no matter the means or consequence, for would not a single instant thereof transcend three quotidian centuries of anything less?"

"Surely," I said, "there must be more to life than that!"

"Vraiment? Then tell me what. . . ."

"The perfection of the spirit. . . ? The attainment of total clarity of consciousness. . . ?"

"La même chose!" Guy exclaimed. "Precisely the state of which I speak! Let destiny grant me only one eternal augenblick of such total clarity of consciousness! For would not such a nirvanic moment render all that follows and precedes entirely superfluous? For this single instant of perfect amusement, would I trade all and risk all, for to a being who has reached this ultima Thule, are not all other lesser amusements merely the snares of time-bound maya?"

But far from firing my spirit with his own murky and elusive passion, the confluence of Guy's words with the peaking of the psychotropic and the venue in which I found myself had all combined to tear away the illusions of intellect and emotion, artifice and spirit, vraiment of matter and energy themselves, to reveal not that nirvanic union with the atman of which the gurus of all schools do speak, but that which is revealed when the last layer of an onion is finally peeled away, to wit, absolute nothing, the cruel perfection of the Void. In that horrendous moment of entirely useless satori, I could perceive my own body as nothing more than a concatenation of cellular modules, and the cells as replications of molecular patterns, and the molecules as assemblages of atoms, and the atoms as clouds of particles, and the particles as mere waves of unlikely probability, and the probability as no more than momentary perturbations of a singular inevitability, and that inevitability was—was—was a nothingness whose concept the spirit dared not grasp.

From this perspective of unwholesome clarity, in which the grand salon and all within stood revealed as naught but illusion down to the finest subatomic particles, vraiment in which our very spirits seemed to conjure themselves improbably out of the Void, I suddenly understood all too well the nature of my faux pas at the Domo's table.

"Je comprends. . . ." I whispered.

"Vraiment," said Guy. "We must seek out that perfect moment when time stands still. . . ."

But I was hardly cognizant of even the music of his voice, let alone the import of his words, lost as I was in my own baleful vision, and the babblement thereof. "No wonder the floating cultura eschews all discourse, art, or vision which confronts . . . which confronts. . . ."

". . . that which the ancient sages called the Tao, and the Flower Children the Ego's Glorious Death. . . ."

". . . all the artifice, all the ersatz firmament and bonsaied mythical creatures of the vivarium. . . ."

". . . the mutual tantric cusp, the moment of mortal danger, the ultimate amplification of the biochemistry of consciousness. . . ."

It was all so horribly obvious. Just as the Void within that was now gobbling up my spirit was held back only by our usual heroic act of willful ignorance, so was the Great and Lonely Void beyond the hull of this ship held back only by the willful ignorance of the entirely artificial reality within.

Vraiment, was not the very vertiginous nausea which now gripped my spirit precisely what the entire floating cultura was designed to avoid?

"Vanity, vanity, it is as Einstein Sergei Chu declared, we are all benighted savages, without the courage to face the mystery at the dark heart of all our philosophies, whimpering and puling before the countenance of the Void!"

"And all the rest is useless boredom and maya's lies!"

"Quelle horror!"

"Must we be subjected to this display?"

"Return these addled creatures to the mental retreat from whence they came!"

All at once my consciousness was quite abruptly returned to the quotidian realm, where I perceived to my abashed chagrin that Guy and I had been sitting there hunched forward on our chaise, staring not at each other so much as through each other, babbling our mutually incomprehensible toxicated philosophies louder and louder, until we were fairly shouting, until, indeed, our unseemly public exhibition had at last provoked an equally strident public outcry against us.

Now we sat there like vile specimens, gazed upon by every disdainful and haughty eye, the objects of scores of curling lips and wrinkled noses, and subject to the lordly chastisement of a long loud silence.

I looked at Guy. Guy looked at me. Out of the corner of my eye, I stole a sidelong glance about the grand salon, where now, having stilled the unseemly tumult with their opprobrium, the Honored Passengers had once again turned their backs on the source thereof and resumed their rounds of assignations, imbibements, and rarefied discourse.

Vraiment, the horrid satori had passed. But not the memory trace thereof entire.

Guy shrugged. "Once more we would seem to have played the buffoons," he said with a fey little smile. "But alas, for this performance no ruegelt would seem to be forthcoming."

"We both seem prone, each in our way, to a tendency to declaim from on high when the spirit moves us without regard to social seemliness," I owned.

Guy peered into my eyes intently for a moment, rolled his own about as if regarding the precincts in which we found

200

ourselves, favored me with a little wink, and then became the old gay Guy once more. "Yet as the ancient wit had it, in vino veritas, nicht wahr!" he declared. "For who is social seemliness to say that seers and psychonauts such as ourselves babble not the truth?"

"Je ne sais pas, Guy," I admitted. "For who is to even say if we were proclaiming the same vision?"

Guy took my hand in his, lifted my chin with his hand, and kissed me lightly as he brought me to my feet. "Only you and I, nē?" he said. "Do we not in this very moment agree that this soirée has lost its power to amuse? Do not our two hearts now beat as one?"

I regarded once more the fete proceeding all around us, the great and glorious company of the floating cultura, the crème de la crème of our Second Starfaring Age, the haut monde to which a young daughter of Nouvelle Orlean had not so long ago avidly aspired and which regarded *me* and *mine* as callow and jejune.

"Vraiment it has," I said, making myself smile as I looked back at Guy, whose amorous interest was made quite frankly plain. "Mayhap they do."

Yet even as I clasped his hand and readily enough allowed him to lead me to our boudoir, I found myself fingering the sash I wore about my waist, and somehow the patchwork cloth thereof seemed nearer and dearer than it ever had before.

While the subsequent passage d'amour with Guy and a good ten hours of untrammeled sleep served to purge both the chemical from my metabolism and the metaphysical angst induced thereby from my spirit, in truth the divertissements of the voyage chez Grand Palais and those which Guy, Raul, and Imre continued to pursue together, cloyed from that moment on.

For while the chemically induced perception of the universe as a spiritually daunting void of nullity and ourselves as but illusory perturbations therein passed with the figurative dawn, the memory of the experience did not entirely fade.

In truth, as I knew even then, the weltanschauung which had so consumed my soul with dread under the influence of the psychotropic had been little more than the heightened subjective apprehension of the rudiments of quantum cosmology which we are all taught as children. Vraiment, our cells are composed of molecules, the molecules of atoms, the atoms of particles, and the particles of subparticles which diminish in mass, duration, and probability under dissection until one indeed discovers that the mass-energy cosmos is conjured into being out of theoretical ultimate particles of zero mass, zero duration, and zero probability.

But in the cold clear light of dawn, what of it? If all creation is but a cosmic ruespieler's tale whereby the characters conjure themselves out of their own imagination, then all that should concern the spirit is the art of the story or the lack thereof, nē.

Which is to say that it was the *style* of the tale the floating cultura chose to live out for itself which now cloyed in the light of my memory of the satoric revelation of the obvious. For had not I stared full-face into the countenance of what all this artifice was meant to deny, and escaped with nothing worse than a certain period of angst and terror? How could I therefore regard these Honored Passengers, who viewed *me* as callow, as the crown of creation they so obviously considered themselves? How could I regard the pavane from which I was barred by my lack of adult sophistication and urbanity as a vie to which I should aspire?

Or, as Guy would no doubt have put it, where was the *amusement* to be found therein for a true Child of the spirit's Fortune?

As for the amusements that Guy, Raul, and Imre continued to pursue for the rest of the voyage to Belshazaar, as far as I was concerned, this was more of the same.

The Honored Passengers surrounded themselves with an external environment of illusions crafted of matter and energy, while Guy, Raul, and Imre subsumed the reality of the Void beyond the hull and the Void within the spirit behind a series of illusions crafted of psychotropic alteration of the biochemical matrix containing the consciousness perceiving it. And woe unto that spirit should illusion misfire and reveal the very truth it was meant to deny!

No doubt much of the metaphysical cogency of the foregoing derives from the more mature perceptions of the teller of the tale, rather than from those of the young girl who eschewed further ingestion of psychotropic substances of any puissance for the duration of the voyage through the Void and who spent her time wandering aimlessly through the divertissements of the Grand Palais in a state of ennui.

I was surfeited with haute cuisine, bored with the passive consumption of art and performance, and certainement, I had had my fill of idle discourse, whether that of the elegant Honored Passengers or that of my so frequently toxicated companions. Only my desire for erotic dalliance with Guy was perforce enhanced, for of all the diversions offered up to pass the idle hours chez Grand Palais, this was the only one in which I might participate as an active agent.

In short, what life aboard the *Unicorn Garden,* what the vie of the floating cultura, lacked, as far as I was then concerned, was *adventure.* I did not want to be entertained, I wanted to *act.* I did not want to perceive, I wanted to *do.*

As to the nature of the adventure that I sought, as to what acts I imagined I wanted to perform, as to just what it was that I was consumed by the passion to do, this I knew not.

I only knew that I was more than ready to debark from the *Unicorn Garden* and stand on the real surface of an unknown world once more. And so I spent the remainder of the voyage looking forward to our arrival on Belshazaar, whatever the nature of that planet might be. Having arrived as an ignorant ingenue on Great Edoku, having gained access to the Gypsy Jokers by my own wit, having survived as a Child of Fortune on this most sophisticated of the worlds of men, having at last experienced the floating cultura itself and found it wanting, naturellement I assumed that experience had prepared me for anything.

Alas, once more I was to be proven a naif.

14 It may seem strange that I had given so little thought to what might await me on Belshazaar before I embarked on the journey thereto, and stranger still that I did not choose to fill my surfeit of idle hours aboard the *Unicorn Garden* with more diligent study of the planet which represented the light at the end of my tunnel of ennui.

In the first case, I had cared little about the goal of the journey because *my* goal was the journey itself, which is to say escape from the penury of Edoku into what I had always imagined to be the fascinating vie of the floating cultura. In a curious way, this state of mind was not unlike that of the instance of the second part, wherein my main passion was to escape the Grand Palais as I had escaped poverty, and that to which I was escaping seemed to matter a good deal less than the change of scene itself.

And of course, if truth be told, diligent study of *anything* had never struck me as an escape route from boredom at this stage in my evolution. Which is not to say that I was completely without curiosity about Belshazaar as each Jump took us closer to the reality thereof, only that I contented myself with a perusal of the entry therefor in the planetary ephemeris, at the conclusion of which I believed I had sufficiently prepared myself for our arrival.

Belshazaar, I learned from the ephemeris, was basically a

water world, with some 83% of its surface given over to ocean, and the bulk of its land area consisting of two widely separated major continents, Pallas and Bloomenwald. The former had been entirely defoliated centuries ago and redone in a human-optimized biosphere based chiefly, as such ersatz ecologies tend to be, on that of Earth. Here resided most of the population of a mere fifteen million, and the majority of that in the vecino of the main city, Ciudad Pallas.

Bloomenwald, the other continent, had been left in its native state, for here grew the mighty Bloomenwald itself, the economic raison d'être for the entire planetary economy.

Belshazaar's gravity was only .4 standards; this apparently allowed trees to grow to gigantic size. When humans first discovered Belshazaar, they found one relatively sparsely vegetated continent, Pallas, and another in a somewhat wetter and warmer clime covered with an enormous interlocked forest of equally enormous trees. Little grew on the forest floor beneath the dense canopy of branches nearly half a kilometer up, and in fact faunal evolution on Belshazaar had proceeded mainly on the endless rolling skyland of the treetops, known as the Bloomenveldt.

As Guy had told me and as the ephemeris confirmed, the Bloomenveldt was indeed a cornucopia of natural psychotropics. The perfumes, fruits, seeds, saps, and other natural products of the Bloomenveldt were apparently redolent with organic molecules that affected the nervous system, endocrine metabolism, and brain chemistry of our species. Hundreds of such products of the Bloomenveldt were already items of commerce, and the main industry of Belshazaar, and certainement its only contribution to interstellar commerce, was the gathering and synthesis of same.

This, the ephemeris pointed out somewhat peckishly, was the scientific and moral justification for the rude total defoliation of the native vegetation from Pallas; a human settlement surrounded by such a psychotropic flora would hardly be viable. What the ephemeris did not bother to dwell on, and what never occurred to me at the time, but what was later to prove the heart of the matter, was the question of how so many molecules produced by the flora of one world could possibly have so many direct and subtle effects upon the psychochemistry of a sapient species which evolved on another.

Nor did the ephemeris convey anything of the esthetic

wretchedness of Ciudad Pallas, surely the most peculiarly repulsive city that I in my modest travels had ever seen.

Assuming, quite erroneously as it turned out, that we would travel to what appeared to be Belshazaar's only real scenic attraction immediately upon debarking from the shuttle, I quite deliberately avoided viewing any holo of the Bloomenwald aboard the *Unicorn Garden* so that I might apprehend this natural wonder with virgin eyes. As the shuttle spiraled down to the surface of Belshazaar, the vision of the planet as seen from space entirely lacked the grandeur and bizarrité of the similar approach to Great Edoku. I beheld great featureless blue-green seas, a huge continent of almost equally uniform deep green fringed with rather narrow beaches and studded with a few bleak rocky massifs peeking up through the endless treetops, and then we were coming down toward the singularly unappetizing-looking continent of Pallas.

Seen from above, most of Pallas appeared to be a sere desert landscape of bleak grays and dull browns, for apparently those who had sterilized the native biosphere had not bothered to extend the benefits of the ersatz Earth-based biosphere much beyond the extended vecino of Ciudad Pallas. And even there, in the grossest possible contrast to Edoku, esthetic considerations seemed never to have crossed their minds.

Smeared across a wide plain roughly in the middle of the continent was a vast hodge-podge irregular checkerboard of autofarms, vast enough, I was later to learn, to supply the nutritive needs of the entire populace. These huge fields of yellow, dun brown, and subdued green were bordered, one from the other, by irrigation channels, along which grew only enough incongruous fir trees to serve as windbreaks.

In the center of this depressingly functional landscape was the even more depressing aerial vista of Ciudad Pallas, toward which we descended with merciful rapidity. This appeared as a predominantly gray and glassy silver sprawl of human habitation, smudged in the middle of the surrounding farmland like a great greasy thumbprint.

As for the vista which greeted my eyes when first I set foot on Belshazaar, this was enough to make me turn to Guy with a curled lip and wrinkled nose as we stood there on the grim black tarmac between the shuttle and the terminal. *"This,"* I sniffed, "is your notion of an amusing planet?"

The shuttleport was built atop a low hill and consisted of little more than a wide expanse of black tarmac, a large oblong terminal building of plain gray concrete and untinted glass, and a number of large warehouses done up in the same dismal mode. From this vantage, one could gain a general visual impression of the surrounding cityscape, such as it was.

This general visual impression was that of a gray urban wasteland sprawling to the horizon in all directions. Which is not to say that Ciudad Pallas appeared to be in a state of economic rot or physical decay; indeed some ruined buildings, verdigris, or even a fetid favela or two would have at least served to imbue the view with some kind of atmospheric ambiance, and the city itself with a feeling of human history. Au contraire, Ciudad Pallas looked as if it had been fabricated, one arrondissement at a time, by the same doggedly functional mentality which had defoliated the continent and replaced the native flora with nothing more than the hundreds of kilometers of esthetically bleak cropland which surrounded the city.

Judging from the regular rows of buildings, the streets of each arrondissement appeared for the most part to be laid out in relentlessly rectilinear gridworks. Each arrondissement seemed to be given over to a particular function, for the buildings of each were as similar as if they had been fabricated and planted at the same time, like the monocultural fields of the autofarms.

There were arrondissements of modest towers, arrondissements of geodesic domes, arrondissements of undisguised fabriks, arrondissements of low rambling structures which appeared to be residence blocks, und so weiter. As for the architectural styles offered up for the esthetic delectation of the eye, the less said the better, for there appeared to be no attempt at art at all. All forms were simple geometric shapes, the predominant colors were concrete gray, muted aluminial sheen, and pale vitreous green, adornments seemed nonexistent, and as for the art of the landscaper, this was nowhere in evidence. Nor, from this vantage, could I pick out parklands, grand public squares, or indeed anything emblematic of civic pride or public amenity.

The odor of the atmosphere I can only compare to the deadly chemical neutrality of the taste of distilled water. The

207

deepest of breaths could detect no floral perfumes, no aroma of parkland, no stench of decay, not even the subtle smell of urban bustle.

"Quelle chose!" I told Guy. "What a wretched city! When do we depart for Bloomenwald?"

"*Bloomenwald?*" he exclaimed as if that were the most outré suggestion in this world. "There's nothing there but a few research stations and a vast expanse of forest."

"And what is to be found here but an immense expanse of ugly buildings, if I may ask?" I demanded.

Guy smiled. "Appearances are often deceiving," he assured me. "Once we have secured lodgings, I will show you the manifold opportunities for amusement, not to say profit, concealed within the admittedly banal exteriors of Ciudad Pallas."

And so he did, if entirely to my dismay.

Intracity transport in Ciudad Pallas was accomplished mainly by floatcabs which followed guideways in the center of the streets. Like the Rapide, their data screens did double duty as municipal directories, but unlike the Rapide, prices were often quoted for various entries. Guy, therefore, chose the Hotel Pallas by the simple expedient of finding the most expensive hotel in the city, and in like manner rented the most expensive suite it had to offer.

Having said that the Hotel Pallas was the most expensive in the city and that our accommodations were among the most expensive therein, I am hard-pressed to sing its further praises. The building itself was a stark tower crafted mainly of glass and with no particular architectural distinction. Our suite consisted of a large bedchamber, a cuisinary salon connected by pneumo to the hotel kitchen, a toilet, a bath, and a huge sitting room. As for the decor, there was a great deal of thick carpeting, plush upholstery, wooden paneling, polished brasswork, black marble, and an equally great paucity of artful employment thereof. The pièce de résistance was an immense expanse of sitting-room window that offered a magnificent view of the full awfulness of Ciudad Pallas.

If a certain churlish ingratitude on my part toward Guy's admittedly unstinting largesse may be detected in the foregoing, vraiment I must confess that the tour through the city from the shuttle port to the hotel had only served to reinforce my initial distaste for this venue.

From ground level, Ciudad Pallas afforded a no less dismal ambiance than it did when viewed from the shuttleport. The arrondissements of the city were not without streets given over to restaurants, boutiques, markets, and the usual civilized necessities, but grand public squares, gardens, or parklands were nowhere in evidence, and indeed the sight of a few pathetic trees scattered here and there was rare enough so that each modest specimen became an event of esthetic significance. For the most part, the streets seemed designed as efficient conduits for floatcabs, private vehicles, and foot traffic, and that was the end of it.

As for the modest foot traffic visible from the floatcab, this seemed divided into two subspecies. On the one hand, there were purposeful and for the most part plainly dressed men and women perambulating rapidly from one building to another, and on the other hand there were any number of individuals in rather tacky garments and lacking something in the way of personal grooming who seemed to be drifting around in a befuddled daze.

What was totally lacking was the brightness and gaiety, the extravagance and ease, the very spirit of the life of the streets, which reached an apogee in Great Edoku and which was also always quite in evidence in Nouvelle Orlean. While my firsthand experience in municipal ambiance was admittedly limited, holos of other cities and word crystals describing the vie thereof led me to believe that few other cities in the worlds of men were as bereft of the joie de vivre of the streets as this one.

"Quelle horror!" I muttered sourly as I stood in our sitting room looking out over the cityscape I had already come to loathe. "What are we *doing* here, Guy?" I pouted. "What secret charms can this ghastly place contain to persuade you to dally here another hour?"

"Have I not told you that the main industry of Belshazaar is psychotropics?" he said. "Ciudad Pallas is admittedly somewhat indifferent to the esthetics of the *external* landscape precisely because attention to same is largely superfluous in a city where the full glories of the *internal* landscape are available to all in such extravagant measure."

I liked not the sound of it, I liked it not at all. "If the sole attraction of Ciudad Pallas is the ready availability of a wide vari-

209

ety of psychotropics, why subject one's enhanced perceptions to such dismal surroundings? Surely, with your chip of unlimited credit, you can purchase whatever psychic enhancers your heart desires and consume the same in some venue far more conducive to spiritual elevation. . . ."

"Ah, but here whatever psychotropics the heart desires are available *gratuit!*"

"*Gratuit?*"

"Indeed *better* than free!" Guy enthused. "Here in Ciudad Pallas, one may be *paid* to consume psychotropics! In this noble city, serving as a subject for psychochemical experimentation is an honored profession!"

"*What?*" I exclaimed and collapsed into the nearest chaise, for such a notion was not something I felt I could contemplate in an upright position.

"Vraiment!" Guy went on in the same grandly enthusiastic vein. "New substances are constantly discovered in the research domes, nē, and these must then be evaluated here under controlled conditions before the viable ones can be offered up on the market. Naturellement, each potential new product must be tested upon scores of human subjects, therefore many psychonauts, as it were, must be employed in the service of the advancement of scientific knowledge and pecuniary profit. Can you think of any career for which I am better suited? Do you know of anyone more likely to achieve success in this noble calling than Guy Vlad Boca?"

"Merde!" I snapped. "What need have you of further funds? You hardly need to serve as an experimental subject in order to earn your keep!"

"True," Guy admitted. "I have no need of further funds. But I always have need of further amusement."

Even knowing Guy as I did, the logic of all this still seemed elusive. "But I thought you had already chosen a career as a traveling merchant, as heir apparent and scion of Interstellar Master Traders," I pointed out.

"Indeed I have."

"Well then, if you *must* soak your brain in an ocean of assorted psychotropics, why not simply *purchase* them? Or if you have suddenly developed scruples against expending your father's fortune on your own amusement—which have never before been

210

in evidence—why not simply announce your identity to the local purveyors of psychotropics and request free samples of their goods for marketing evaluation?"

"Not a bad notion . . ." Guy mused. "But neither as amusing nor as potentially profitable as my own. True enough, as an announced agent of Interstellar Master Traders, I would be showered with free samples of whatever was already on the market. But the opportunity for greatest profit lies in learning of the best of the newest psychotropics *before* they are offered up to general commerce. Thus, by posing as a mere indigent Child of Fortune, as one of the thousands of paid experimental subjects in which the city abounds, I may learn of the best new products before any other merchants do. And by approaching the manufacturers thereof *before* they begin to solicit importers and offering a modest premium for exclusivity, I can score a series of commercial coups such as will do my father proud."

"Pfagh!" I snorted. "The truth of the matter is that you find the notion of being *paid* to sot yourself on arcane chemicals incognito more *amusing* than the idea of simply purchasing them or securing samples as a merchant!"

"Well spoken!" Guy exclaimed with an idiot grin. "In this matter, the maximization of amusement and the maximization of profit happily coincide. Moreover, I might point out that you too may enhance your consciousness at a pecuniary profit."

He took hold of my hand and fairly dragged me to my feet. "Come," he said, "let us begin our enterprise. A moment unamused is a moment lost forever, as a wise man once said."

And so our endless round of the laboratories and mental retreats of Ciudad Pallas began. Our first visit was to a modest laboratory occupying a single floor of a large tower, and the first sight to greet us therein, and one that would become all too commonplace in the days ahead, was that of an anteroom crowded with about a score applicants for the position of experimental subject.

A more unsavory collection of human specimens would be hard to imagine. Most of our fellow applicants of both genders were of the same general age as ourselves, the males frequently bearded with stubble, the females in a state of dishabille, and both sexes exuding an odor of stale perspiration contaminated with peculiar aromas of acetone and other acrid byproducts of

211

dysfunctional metabolisms. A few of these folk were of a more advanced age and had clearly been pursuing the "profession" of psychonaut longer than was prudent, for these were gaunt of frame, hollow of cheek, deeply shadowed around the eyes, and had a disconcerting tendency to stare fixedly at the walls or ceiling, muttering to themselves.

At length, a woman in a plain gray smock appeared through the doorway to the inner sanctum and announced that the fee offered for the day's experiment would be six units of credit. At this, three or four of the applicants departed with their noses in the air. The rest of us were subjected to a perfunctory examination with a metabolic monitor to weed out those whose bloodstreams or protoplasm might be contaminated with lingering byproducts from other such sessions which might skew the results of today's séance.

Only half a dozen passed this muster, among them, naturellement, Guy and I, who had yet to contaminate our metabolic purity as experimental subjects. We were ushered into a plain gray-walled room containing a series of tables. Before each table was a padded chair. Behind each table sat a gray-clad and bored-looking functionary. Upon each table was a rack of glass vials filled with fluids, powders, and gaseous essences, a word crystal recorder, and a metabolic monitor.

Guy and I were seated at adjacent workbenches. The sallow-skinned, blonde-haired woman seated across the table from me affixed electrodes to my temples, placed a probe under my tongue, inserted another into the pit of my right arm, and did not deign to speak until I was properly attached to her monitoring machineries.

"Bitte, you will spiel your subjective experiences as they occur, trying as best you are able to confine yourself to style of feeling, sparing us any flights of loquacity or philosophical musings, which in any case will be edited out of the transcript," she recited in a flat bored voice after these amenities had been concluded.

"Sniff," she commanded, opening a vial of clear fluid and thrusting it under my nostrils. I sniffed.

"Spiel."

This was easier said than done. A smoky-sweet odor went directly to the back of my brain, where it ignited a ravenous hunger for some specific food I had never encountered. "Total

212

hunger," I said. "For something quite specific that I've never encountered, it's quite difficult to try to explain. . . ."

"Superfluous also. . . . Inhale. . . . Spiel. . . ."

The next vial seemed to have no odor at all, but I was abruptly consumed by a raging lust, or more precisely a genital demand for sexual relief completely divorced from my psychic state, which could not have been less interested in such matters at the time.

And so it went. In order to have six units credited to my chip, I was required to sniff, inhale, quaff, or touch something like a dozen substances, and report as laconically as possible on the psychesomic effects thereof. These ranged from narcoleptic torpor to a state of nervous excitation that had me fairly vibrating in my seat, from a sudden loss of color vision to a state of visual perception in which everything glowed with its own inner light, from ravenous hunger, cellular thirst, and sexual lust to the absolute conviction that I had become a disembodied spirit.

At the conclusion of this first job of work as a psychonaut, I reeled out into the bleak streets of Ciudad Pallas in a state of some discombobulation, for though these outré psychic states had all been quite transitory, the memory traces of this dizzying succession of narrowly focused psychic states had loosened my moorings to quotidian consciousness to the point where it took some time to return to reality ordinaire.

Guy, however, assumed a critical air. "Trivial substances," he said loftily. "I found none of it more than passingly amusing, did you?"

"Not even that," I admitted quite truthfully.

He withdrew a sheet of paper from a pocket and studied whatever it was he had scrawled thereon. "While they were crediting your chip, I learned of several other laboratories seeking psychonauts today," he said. "Let us see if the next one offers better fare. . . ."

So saying, he fairly dragged me into the next unoccupied floatcab and we were off to another laboratory, if not exactly against my will, then certainement not with my avid approval either, for if truth be told, I was still in no condition to strongly approve or strongly protest anything.

*   *   *

213

To Guy's growing consternation, we were rejected as subjects by the other four laboratories we visited on that first day in Ciudad Pallas, for apparently the rapid succession of substances we had tested at the first had left sufficient aftereffects in our metabolisms to render us unfit as biochemical tabulae rasas at least until the next morning.

As far as Guy was concerned though, the time was not entirely wasted, for while we waited in the anterooms of the various laboratories with our fellow would-be psychonauts, he questioned the more experienced members of this profession, or at any rate those capable of coherent discourse, on the inner lore of the trade.

Apparently the laboratories were not considered the prime venues of employment. For one thing, most of them were given over to the initial screening of the latest psychotropics to emerge from the research domes, so that more often than not one's time was wasted on psychotropics of trivial effect. For another, they were rather mingy when it came to pay scales. Furthermore, for the modest wage they offered, one was usually subjected to a whole battery of substances, which wreaked sufficient confusion to the fine detail of the metabolism to make it rather unlikely that one would be accepted as a fit subject by more than one laboratory in the same day.

"The mental retreats are much to be preferred," Guy was told by one of the more experienced—which is to say gaunter, older, and more hollow-eyed—psychonauts. "Primero, they offer only one psychotropic per diem. Segundo, they perform molecular adjustments on the extracts, so that the experience is likely to be enhanced. Tercero, the pay is much better, due to the enhanced risk. Al fin, should . . . unexpected difficulties arise, they have the facilities and commitment to restore one's base consciousness to the extent possible, or at worst to care for those who are no longer fit to continue to follow the trade."

Naturellement, the competition for these choicest and most remunerative positions was somewhat severe, but, we were assured, the fact that we were relatively naive subjects would count heavily in our favor for several weeks, which is to say until that advantageous situation no longer obtained.

His mood considerably buoyed by this knowledge, Guy picked diffidently at the undistinguished dinner we consumed in

our suite before retiring, nor was his tantric performance anything more than perfunctory, for his attention was on the morrow throughout, and he kept up a nearly continuous babble on
the subject of mental retreats and psychotropics even as we lay in
each other's arms.

For my part, I had already had more than enough of Ciudad Pallas before I had even set foot on its unappetizing streets,
my initial experience as a psychonaut had done little to convince
me that I had found my true calling, and the society of the
laboratory waiting rooms had not exactly impressed me with its
sparkle and wit.

As for the effect this venue seemed to have on my lover,
this seemed to resemble that of the company of Raul and Imre
writ large, with the added disadvantage that Ciudad Pallas lacked
even the esthetic divertissements of the Grand Palais of the *Unicorn
Garden*.

And alas, my lover was also my benefactor, which is to say
my sole source of funds save what I might earn at the psychonaut's
trade, for the possibility of picking up my nascent career as a
ruespieler seemed entirely out of the question here, nor did I
imagine I could earn much ruegelt as a tantric performer in
Ciudad Pallas either. The unpleasant truth of the matter was that
I was trapped in this wretched city until Guy no longer found it
amusing or until I could secure enough funds of my own to
become an economic free agent. And in Ciudad Pallas, there
seemed to be only one way to accomplish that.

So I saw no alternative to accompanying Guy the next
morning to one of the mental retreats in which the city abounded.
And indeed my initial impression of this establishment did much
to raise my spirits, for, of course, that was precisely what the
design and decor thereof were artfully crafted to do.

The mental retreat was a dome atop a plain gray cube, and
from without, it presented no more a pleasing aspect than any
other building in Ciudad Pallas. Within, however, it was an entirely different matter. The dome was of transparent glass and it
enclosed a large central courtyard around which the dormitories,
offices, and laboratories of the mental retreat were constructed.
This central atrium put me in mind of the vivarium of the *Unicorn
Garden*, save that the natural sky was visible through the dome,

215

and the style of the garden it contained was quite simple, consisting merely of some ordinary trees of several terrestrial species, an expanse of lawn, beds of flowers, a modest fountain, and a sprinkling of wooden benches.

The interior hallways, the room in which we were interviewed, and the chamber in which the psychotropics were administered, were all paneled in rough-grained wood, ceilings were painted a deep blue, and forest-green carpeting abounded.

All in all, an ambiance of ease and tranquility had been successfully created within these cloistered walls, and, moreover, the functionaries of the mental retreat seemed to take care to dress in a congruent style, in flowing garments of either natural browns and greens or gay primary colors. As for those who, by their abstracted airs and lack of attention to personal grooming, appeared to be long-term habitués of the mental retreat, these were dressed in a similar style, and were permitted to roam the corridors and garden at leisure.

The only sour note was struck by the usual denizens of the waiting room, who appeared no different from their compatriots of the same venues in the laboratories.

After the usual metabolic screening process, Guy and I were accepted as subjects and offered twenty-five credit units apiece to test what was described as a single promising substance. This was indeed a far cry from the rates that seemed to prevail in the laboratories, and even I therefore agreed with some enthusiasm, tempered only by the fact that, as usual, we were kept in the dark about the experience we were about to undergo in order not to skew our reactions with expectations.

My trepidation increased however when Guy, myself, and the four other psychonauts who had been selected for the day's labor, were led away into separate private cubicles by our own individual functionaries.

Mine was good enough to ask my name and introduce himself as Doctor-Professor Sigisimund Farben Bruna, a nicety absent from the commerce of the laboratories, though the courtesies did not extend to an exchange of name tales. Electrodes were affixed to my temples, a probe inserted into a vein, and another into my vaginal cavity, but rather than leading to cumbersome stationary machineries, the wires therefrom lead to a cunning little portable unit fastened to my waist by a belt.

216

"You will be free to wander the grounds, Sunshine," the Doctor-Professor told me in a warm, somewhat syrupy voice, as if he were a thespian playing the part of himself. "I will accompany you, and we will converse freely."

"That is the entire process?" I asked somewhat dubiously.

He favored me with a friendly smile that also seemed to owe something to conscious craft, though perhaps it was merely his ice-blue eyes and somewhat overdignified visage combined with my own natural unease which created the impression of a kind of professional sincerity. "But of course changes in your physiology will also be monitored," he said, "so that your anecdotal reportage may be temporally correlated therewith. Thus, given enough subjects, do we develop a more or less precise profile of the psychic states generated by stepwise biochemical alterations caused by the substance in question."

"Which is?"

"A floral extract of some molecular complexity in which certain speculative modifications have been made," he said vaguely, producing a small vial of clear blue fluid. "We commence, ja?"

I shrugged somewhat fatalistically and quaffed the potion, which had a not unpleasant smoky-sweet savor, if somewhat contaminated by a tooth-tingling metallic aftertaste.

"And now. . . ?" I inquired.

"A stroll in the garden, ja?" suggested the Doctor-Professor. "We have reason to believe that perambulation expedites metabolic absorption."

And so we repaired to the garden, where other such functionaries, be they Doctor-Professors or not, were shepherding other psychonauts, Guy among them, taking pains, or so it seemed, to keep us all at a considerable distance from each other.

While awaiting I knew not what, I sought to engage the Doctor-Professor in discourse upon the subject of his professional interests, seeking thereby to gain some further knowledge of the true nature of the peculiar establishment in which I now found myself. "This place styles itself a mental retreat; are you therefore a Healer of malfunctioning psyches?"

He shrugged somewhat owlishly. "An obsolete concept, nicht wahr," he declared. "Here we delude ourselves not that there exists a singular gestalt of healthy human consciousness toward which all variant states need be bent by our art. Au contraire, our

217

aim is to develop a broad enough palette of psychotropics so that any given psychic state may be produced to order."

"Je ne sais pas. . . ."

"One client enters a mental retreat in a cafard of egoless fragmentation, ja, and we are commissioned to reattach his psyche to a unified perception of the quotidian realm. Aber ein anderer may enter with an excessive ego-grounding in the wheel of maya and commission us to produce a psychic state wherein that ego is dissolved into nirvanic union with the atman. Or indeed we may be commissioned to increase the availability of certain arcane psychic gestalts to serve economic and social necessities. . . ."

"Such as?"

"Most lucrative of all is the obvious need for a psychotropic which would reliably induce in neutral female subjects the rare psychic gestalt of the Void Pilot personality, for vraiment, that would usher in a golden era which might fairly be called the Third Starfaring Age," he enthused. "As things stand now, we must search the mental retreats and demimondes for *naturally occurring* anorexic addictive personalities of the required extremity, and so unfortunately rare is this syndrome that we never have more than two hundred or so in active service, ja, and this process is to the reliable scientific production of Void Pilots as ancient alchemy is to quantum chemistry, nicht wahr. . . ."

He brought himself up short and stared at me narrowly, as if suddenly realizing that he had wandered into regions of discourse best not broached to experimental subjects such as myself. And indeed such frankness did little to enhance his moral stature or that of the mental retreats of Ciudad Pallas in my eyes, nor did it exactly increase my confidence in his concern for the personal well-being of experimental subjects or patients.

There was something odious, or so it seemed to me, about the notion of producing any given state of consciousness to order, for the question then arose as to *whose* specifications were to be followed. And judging from his unwholesome enthusiasm for the ghastly conceit of artificially creating the miserable state of psychic dysfunction necessary to the calling of Void Pilot in order to facilitate interstellar commerce, not to say enhance his own, these specifications need not be at all conducive to the personal happiness of the subject . . . or victim.

Which is to say that the style of consciousness induced by his words in my own being was that of a certain dread. For what was about to happen to *me*?

Vraiment, this thought had no sooner taken form in my brain than I became aware that something *was* happening.

A strange hollow tingling sensation was slowly spreading up my back and then along my limbs from a point of focus which seemed to be located in the chakra at the base of my spine. Not so much a loss of sensation as a shift in my perception of the kinesthetic image of my own body, as if my spine, and then the bones of my limbs, and then the flesh encasing them, were effervescing into some clear ectoplasmic substance, transparent not so much to sight as to my body's internal kinesthetic senses. . . .

"The effects begin, ja?" the Doctor-Professor said, studying me intently. "Speak, schnell bitte, before the next stage commences!"

"Je ne sais pas. . . ." I stammered in no little trepidation. "I . . . I seem to be evaporating . . . my flesh is turning into air . . . into liquid crystal . . . into . . . into. . . ."

"Ach gut! Nominal thusfar!"

Nominal? The effect was spreading more rapidly every moment. My arms and legs, then my hands and feet, became ethereal unreality, as transparent to kinesthetic perception as clear glass is to light. Vraiment, I could stand, I could flex my feet, move my fingers, yet somehow, to some sense that was neither feeling nor sight, nor even volitional control, they were not there. . . .

"Spiel! Recite! Speak, bitte, we must have *data!*"

"I'm dissolving!" I cried in no little terror. "I'm fading away!" For now my entire body seemed to have ectoplasmated into nothingness from the point of view of the kinesthetic centers of my brain. Though I could see it, and move it, and even feel the pressure of the ground beneath the soles of my feet, in some elusive fashion, my consciousness had retreated up the column of my spine to the citadel of my brain, as if my spirit were dissociating itself from the corporeal matrix in which it arose. . . .

"More data! More data!" the Doctor-Professor demanded. "This is excellent thusfar!"

"The light! The light!" I cried in panic, and then in panic not unalloyed with a certain tremulous wonder, for as the dissolving of kinesthetic awareness began to engulf my head like some amoeboid creature spreading its protoplasm from the base of my neck, through my jaw, up my cheekbones, the green of the trees, the brown of their trunks, the reds and blues and yellows of the beds of flowers, the cerulean tint of the sky, vraiment even the sallow skin-tones of the Doctor-Professor, began to take on a luminous glow, seemed to pulse and shimmer, then to take on an independent substance, as I became little more than the impalpable sensorium against which they impinged. . . .

"Speak! Speak! Attempt coherence, bitte!"

"Oh! Oh! Oh! I can feel them!" I moaned. For indeed I—insofar as an "I" still remained—no longer sensed the brilliant colors as hues pertaining to the surfaces of trees, faces, flowers, or sky, but as independent entities of light magically transmuted into matter, as living organisms engulfing my nonexistent body, as a garment of Cloth of Many Colors, or rather Cloth of Many Touches, for somehow sight had transmuted itself into feeling, and feeling to caresses, and caresses to . . . to. . . .

"Speak! Speak! Schiess, why must it always be thusly at the most critical stage!"

But I could not speak. For there was no longer any "I." There was only a perfect clear emptiness where that "I" had been and a skin of exquisite multicolored flame surrounding it. Vraiment, a skin of kundalinic fire, for as light had become touch, so touch had become tantric ecstasy. All that now existed in the space where I had been was a living mantle of orgasmic substance, a transcendent being that was naught but an interface of orgasm, a flaming aura of static ecstasy burning through the very fabric of space and time.

How long did I remain in this egoless ecstatic state? While I was later to learn that the duration of the experiment was several hours, such measurements had no meaning whatsoever in the subjective realm thereof. For there was neither a timebound ego to measure the hours nor any interface between objective reality and the subjective perception thereof.

Suffice it to say that after some interval quotidian awareness returned to a Sunshine Shasta Leonardo who found herself supine upon a lawn under a blue domed sky, inhaling the effluvia of her own sweat as she breathed in ragged gasps and gazing with unfocused vision into the face of Doctor-Professor Sigisimund

Farben Bruna shaking his head in rueful dissatisfaction and appraising her with a coldly professional eye.

"I suppose you have earned your twenty-five credit units," this worthy owned grudgingly. "Though I would pay twice that amount for a subject capable of ingesting this substance and remaining coherent enough to tell the whole tale."

15 By my own adamant choice, my first venture as an experimental subject for the mages of the mental retreats of Ciudad Pallas was also my last, and no argument of Guy's to the contrary could sway my determination not to submit myself to what I can only call such *horrid* pleasures again. For while I could not deny his contention that this was a potentially lucrative occupation, I neither trusted in the good intentions of these Hippocratic mercenaries, nor wished to risk my sanity to serve the cause of their profit.

As for Guy, who had been dosed with the same substance and reported a similar sequence of experiences during the floatcab ride back to the Hotel Pallas, he, au contraire, had found it all quite amusing and was just as adamantly determined to continue his career as a psychonaut.

"I cannot comprehend your reluctance," he declared more in genuine amazement than pique. "How can you define the spirit's transcendence of the limitations of the body's sensory apparatus as anything but an enhancement, vraiment, how can you define a timeless and endless orgasmic cusp as anything but ultimate ecstasy?"

"One might say the same for what Void Pilots supposedly declare to be the true ultimate ecstasy of the Jump itself," I snapped. "Would you then have me famish myself into anorexia, rot my brain with a profusion of crude opiates, dally awhile with the Charge, and spend several years in a mental retreat so that I may then enjoy platform orgasm as a Pilot via congress with the Jump Circuit?"

The most unwholesome dreamy look insinuated itself onto Guy's face. "Indeed it is said that in the moment of the Jump the Pilot achieves far more than platform orgasm," he muttered speculatively, "that via union with the Great and Only Void out of which the dance of matter and energy arises, the spirit achieves ecstatic merger with the atman and transcends thereby the limitations of maya and temporality. . . ."

I could scarcely credit my ears. "Now you enthusiastically parrot the apocryphal mystical babble of the Void Pilot. . . ?"

"The Great and Only exists, and the Jump transcends the limitations of the quotidian realm of energy, matter, and time, as witness the fact that we ourselves have so recently traversed light-years in days via its instrumentality, nē," Guy told me. "Therefore may not the Void Pilots achieve the ultimate state of consciousness of which our species is capable?"

"Be that as it may," I pointed out, "the beneficiaries of this transcendent congress with the Void are rendered thereby incapable of enjoying the pleasures of a natural woman, unfit for social intercourse, and expire within a matter of years."

"Vraiment," Guy admitted, "but may not the bargain be worth it? May not that which we fleshly creatures seek in each other's arms be but a pale shadow of an ultimate bliss which our untimebound spirits remember? And indeed, are not matters of lifespan irrelevant to a spirit which experiences a single moment of transcendent time?"

"Next you will declare your intention to become a Void Pilot?" I snorted.

Guy shrugged. "Alas, as you know, that is a path to the ultimate transcendence of maya's realm which is open to the steps of your gender alone," he said with tendentious gravity. "Yet here, in the mental retreats of Ciudad Pallas, do they not seek an elixir which will create the biochemical matrix of a consciousness capable of experiencing same in ordinary female brains? May they not therefore at length concoct a potion which will grant such a cusp to the poor masculine likes of myself? Vraiment, is this not the ultimate of the amusement which I so avidly seek?

223

How can I therefore eschew the path spread before me by the mages of Ciudad Pallas out of cowardly trepidations for the state of my mere corpus?"

At this I was quite literally rendered speechless, nor would I rise to the bait of his babble for the rest of the evening. Nor, alas, would he give it over long enough for a proper passage d'amour before I lapsed into merciful sleep. And on the morrow, he was no more able to comprehend my refusal to accompany him to another mental retreat than I was capable of comprehending his refusal to simply purchase psychotropics of proven ability and effect if he was so set on devoting himself to the contemplation of his own spiritual navel.

"I seek not realms which others have known, for I know of no man who has yet attained the realm which I seek!" he insisted. "Vraiment," he said with a leavening trace of his old wry humor, "no doubt that is half the reason I seek it. But how can you style yourself a true Child of Fortune and not wish to avail yourself of spheres of consciousness never previously known to mortal man when a veritable smorgasbord of same is laid out for your delectation?"

"How can *you* style yourself a true Child of Fortune and waste your time, not to say risk your spirit, besotting yourself in this wretched city when all the worlds of men are laid out as a veritable smorgasbord of adventure for *your* delectation, courtesy of your father's bottomless largesse?"

"The worlds of men, the worlds of the spirit within this single man, la même chose, nē?"

"Phagh! Merde! Have you not noticed the denizens of the laboratories and mental retreats? Is that what you wish to become, Guy, a gaunt, hollow-eyed wretch staring vacantly at walls and muttering incomprehensible imprecations to yourself?"

"Ah, but who is to say what splendors of the spirit, what transcendent heights of amusement, are in fact contained within such seemingly decadent fleshly shells?"

"A maestro of sophistry?" I suggested archly.

Und so weiter. In the days to come, when Guy would return to our suite after a sojourn in the mental retreats, at times glassy-eyed and torpid, but more often than not vibrating with ill-focused energy and babbling of incomprehensible wonders,

224

this dialectic would go another round without approaching any closer to synthesis.

Nor, on the other hand, and to Guy's considerable moral credit, did he ever intrude pecuniary considerations into our fruitless discourse, though I would have been hard put to counter same. For while he was earning an average of some twenty-five units of credit a day in the mental retreats, I, a pauper dependent upon his largesse for my very bed and board, only occasionally visited a laboratory to earn a pittance, and then only under the pressure of a boredom that became more unbearable every day.

In the face of his undeniable magnanimity of spirit when it came to matters of finance, I could hardly summon up the meanness of soul to hector him on subjects where he in turn would have been most vulnerable: to wit, that firstly he was entirely responsible for my presence in this ghastly city, and secondly that his puissance as a lover was dwindling away to nullity as his libidinal energies were sucked down the black hole of his solipsistic psychotropic obsession.

Would I have left Guy Vlad Boca at this point had I possessed sufficient funds to escape Belshazaar on my own? Je ne sais pas, for no such choice was in fact open to my consideration. But mayhap, I still would not have abandoned Guy to the demimonde of the mental retreats, or so I would like to think.

Certainement, I had discovered to my dismay an unwholesome side to his spirit that was more and more coming to the fore. But it was a generous and open-hearted spirit too, and even his obsessive quest for psychotropic nirvana clearly emanated from a core of passionate if foolhardy courage which I would have had to have been a churl to deny.

Then too, the more simple fact of it was that Guy had rescued me from penury on Edoku and freely given whatever it was in his power to give. What sort of Child of Fortune, vraiment, what sort of human spirit, would I have been if I had left such a comrade to be pulled down by his demons without at least offering combat to the same to the limits of my power to do so?

Be such moral conjectures as they may, as karma would justly have it, I lacked the coward's resources to flee from the field of honor, and at length I was presented with both the dire necessity to act and the pragmatic means to do so.

While Guy was off pursuing his solipsistic pleasures, I was

left to my own devices, and these were limited indeed. I wandered the bleak streets aimlessly, or rather seeking divertissements that were not to be found therein, namely some analog of the society of the Gypsy Jokers, some promising venue in which to essay a ruespiel, or failing that, at least some opportunity to earn ruegelt as a tantric performer.

Alas, none of the Children of Fortune of Ciudad Pallas had interest in any enterprise save that of the mental retreats and laboratories, what passed for street crowds depressed me beyond any thought of standing up and spieling, and I had entirely lost the pluck to offer my services as a tantric performer to passing strangers, and certainly to passing strangers as unappetizing as these.

But on the tenth day, awash in ennui and self-pity, I was trudging with downcast eyes along a street given over to the usual unimaginative facades of shops and streets, when all at once I was confronted with a vision that jolted me out of my funk and set my spirit soaring.

The entire facade of a libraire had been given over to a holo display designed to entice custom within. As to whether the generality of the citizenry of Ciudad Pallas might be entranced by this sight, je ne sais pas, but as for me, I stood there dazzled.

For there on the grim gray streets of Ciudad Pallas was a window into another and grander reality: a holo view of the Bloomenveldt itself.

Under an azure sky fleeced with passing clouds, a vast meadow stretched away to the horizon, undulating gently in a breeze. Imagine a dense bank of clouds seen from above, soft billowing mounds, not of white or stormy gray, but of a deep and verdant green.

For what I beheld was the treetop canopy of the Bloomenwald, an aerial rootwork of great interlocking branches from which grew a magically solid veldt of huge leaves, solid enough so that I felt I might step off the street and walk away into wonderland, yet tossing and rolling like foam on the wind. Green and yet not entirely green, for the entire vista of undulating skyland was strewn with a profusion of flowers of every conceivable form and hue, as a desert may be seen to spring into riotous bloom after a day of rain. Flowers whose immense size was revealed by a troupe of

226

tawny-furred bipeds who were to be seen hopping in great soaring bounds among flowers which quite dwarfed them.

Ah, I could all but feel the "land" rocking beneath my feet, feel the sun on my skin and the wind streaming through my hair, I could almost smell gorgeous floral perfumes wafting to my nostrils upon it.

Merde, we were utterly demented to remain in this vile city for another instant when such an Enchanted Forest grew on this very planet! No wonder the citizens of Ciudad Pallas and the denizens of the laboratories and mental retreats seemed so unwholesome! No wonder Guy seemed to be fading into babblement before my eyes! For who but a crippled spirit would be content to experience such a natural reality second-hand in vials when the Bloomenwald itself was but a short flight away?

Surely even Guy would be roused from his psychotropic obsessions by this grand and glorious sight, surely he would be moved to travel forthwith thither, surely the means had been placed in my hands whereby I might save him from himself!

Without further thought, I entered the libraire and purchased a copy of the holo so that I might display it for Guy at once, utterly indifferent to the fact that this purchase consumed nearly all of the meager credit on my chip, leaving me with only enough to take a floatcab back to the hotel. This final expenditure I also freely made, unwilling to trade time for credits by returning afoot.

A small pamphlet concerning the Bloomenwald was included in the price of the holo, and this I avidly perused while the floatcab carried me through the streets of Ciudad Pallas, all too eager to ignore the tawdry reality through which I need pass in favor of immersion in the lore of the Enchanted Forest.

On Belshazaar, I learned, wormlike forms had evolved directly into vertebrates and thence into higher fauna, and insects had never arisen. The flowers of the Bloomenveldt being of such enormous size, the ecological niches occupied on other worlds by insectile forms were here taken over by mammalians of considerable size and cerebral development. As in the more common mode where insects filled these niches, the flowers exuded molecules in their perfumes, pollens, nectars, and fruits designed to effect the motivational metabolisms of their pollinators.

But since on Belshazaar these pollinators were mammalian

227

forms with developed cerebral cortices, the molecules the flowers evolved to modulate their behaviors also had their effects on man.

Thus was the economy of Belshazaar based upon the chance evolution of an ecosystem in which higher forms had been adapted to serve as the pollinators of the Enchanted Forest.

The pamphlet went on to elucidate a few of the finer details of the ecosystem of the treetops, but by the time I had reached this section of the simple dissertation, the floatcab had reached the Hotel Pallas, and I gave over my studies of same in favor of rushing to our suite to confront Guy with the holo.

I burst into the suite in the full flush of my enthusiasm, and, seeing that Guy reposed on a chaise in the sitting room gazing out over the dismal cityscape provided by the great window, I went directly to the viewer circuited thereto and inserted the holo. The wretched view of the vile city was forthwith replaced by the glorious vision of the Bloomenveldt, as if we were perched in a treehouse above the aerial meadow, looking out on what would soon become our garden of delights.

"Look, Guy, isn't it marvelous?" I burbled. "Ah, how—"

". . . so close, vraiment, beyond the dance, rising within me, it is as they say, as Jesu Christo had it, behold, psychonauts of the spirit, you too can walk on water, you must surrender all else to do it, but you can walk on water. . . ."

Only when he utterly failed to react to this glorious vision did I perceive the metal band around his head, and the wire leads depending therefrom, and the little console to which they were connected. Only then did I realize that he had been addressing himself in an eerie hollow voice at the moment of my arrival. Only then did comprehending rage replace my ignorant joy. For while I had discovered Xochimilco in the treetops, Guy had discovered the Charge.

I knew little about the Charge in those days save the general lore, and I would have expected Guy Vlad Boca to be far better versed in such matters than I, but what I did know was more than enough to outrage my spirit and send an adrenal tide boiling through my blood which balled my hands into fists.

The Charge is in essence the electronic amplification of the electrohologram of human consciousness without topological distortion, so that the Charge Addict seems to remain the same

228

personality only more so, an enhanced version of himself, if only in his own eyes. Of course, if as is all too likely, the Charge Addict is a skewed personality to begin with, amplification produces something a good deal less savory than a bodhisatva.

Worse still, while each increment of Charge achieves an increment of amplification of the electrohologram of consciousness, each increment of Charge also creates an increment of instability in the overall pattern, so that as higher and higher states of consciousness are supposedly achieved, the personality that reaches them grows vaguer and vaguer, until, at least in theory, perfect Enlightenment is reached by a perfect human cipher.

Without even pausing at the time to think these thoughts, I ripped the wires from the console, and flung the vile thing against the wall with all my strength, smashing it to pieces.

Guy Vlad Boca at last acknowledged my existence to the point of turning his face in my direction, his eyes blinking in perplexity in the sudden light of relative reason. "How could you do such a thing to yourself, Guy?" I screamed. "Is mental seppuku in slow motion your concept of the perfect amusement?"

"Mayhap not . . . *perfect* . . ." Guy babbled, staring off into inner space once more, "but mayhap as close as we can approach to the edge. . . ."

"Merde, this is more than I can countenance," I exclaimed, and without further rational consideration, I tore the electrode band from his head, and employed the ring of Touch in a manner which I had never before attempted, applying my hand to the base of his skull, and sending a jolt of energy to the centers of his backbrain which should have been sufficient to have a corpse up and turning cartwheels.

This at least was enough to return him to some semblance of natural awareness.

"By what right did you do that, who are you to judge another spirit's quest, I merely toyed with the edge . . ." he said, regarding me first in righteous anger, and then like a little boy whose mother has caught him with his hand in the pastry bin.

"What would you have had me do, sit patiently by and watch you slowly erase your consciousness?"

"*I* am no sordid Charge Addict, *I* would never have proceeded to the Up and Out," he said with a great false show of indignation belied by the queasy expression around the corners of his eyes. "I merely wished to *taste* the nirvanic joys which the Charge Addicts celebrate, never would such a master psychonaut as Guy Vlad Boca have had the weakness of will to fall victim to terminal addiction."

"Indeed? As you have not had the weakness of will to give yourself over to the far less puissant temptations of the mental retreats?"

"How can it be less than a noble calling to pursue profit and enhance consciousness while serving the cause of medical science at the same time?"

"Vraiment?" I said, hunkering down beside his chaise. "If your consciousness has become so puissantly enhanced, then why are you entirely oblivious to the glory before your very eyes!"

He regarded me with a befuddled expression.

Groaning with exasperation, I seized his jaw in my hand and directed his gaze by main force toward the holo image of the Bloomenveldt which had replaced the unwholesome vista of Ciudad Pallas beyond the window. His eyes widened in surprise and seemed to regain some modicum of their quotidian vitality.

"Yes, Guy," I cooed in as seductive a voice as I could muster under the circumstances, "not this wretched city of unnatural experiments and even more unnatural denizens, but the *Bloomenveldt* of which all herein is but a pale and tortured shadow. Vraiment, and this is but a holo. Ah, can you not imagine us standing there hand in hand in the Enchanted Forest of the treetops, with the warm sun on our skins, and a thousand rich perfumes intoxicating our senses, borne on the same breeze that ruffles our hair and whispers through the branches, and rocks the very ground we stroll upon like transcendent beings along the rolling surface of an arboreal sea. . . ."

Guy's reaction to this romantic extravagance was to shrug, and own: "Tres simpatico for the devotee of bucolic pleasures, but as for urbane and sophisticated spirits like ourselves, surely you jest?"

"How can you not be possessed of the passion to hie yourself there at once?" I said as evenly as I could, choking back my consternation at his obtuseness by pragmatic act of will.

"For what purpose? For all its grandeur, it is only a forest. . . ."

"*Only a forest!*"

"Surely the cities of man abound in more artful amusements and adventures of the spirit than anything that mere brute nature can provide."

"Including the present loathsome venue?" I said in a sneering tone.

"Most particularly Ciudad Pallas, here in the most advanced laboratories of the psychesomic sciences," said Guy, "for where else in the worlds of men are the most arcane states of consciousness to be experienced, and at a profit in the bargain?"

I choked back my disgust and anger in favor of guile, for at this point it was quite clear that there was no hope of persuading Guy to quit Ciudad Pallas for the Bloomenveldt by an honest appeal to esthetics.

"There, mon cher dumkopf, *there!*" I declared, pointing at the holo of the Bloomenveldt.

"There?"

"Naturellement, Guy," I purred in his ear. "Where else do you suppose all the psychotropics you have already sampled originate? If *profit* is what you seek based on a droit of monopoly on the latest substances to emerge from the research domes, how better to steal a march on all competition than by seeking them out at their very source? If what you seek is the attainment of a state of consciousness which has never before existed in a human brain, why piddle about with synthesized derivatives rather than experience directly the full organic complexity? Is anything the mental retreats have to offer, is foolish flirtation with the Charge, any more amusing than *that?*"

"Je ne sais pas. . . ." Guy muttered reflectively. "To be the first, to boldly go where no human spirit has gone before, and mayhap to enrich ourselves beyond measure in the process. . . ."

And all at once, he was positively beaming at me. "Well spoken, ruespieler, well spoken, ma chère Gypsy Joker," he declaimed floridly. "You shall have your heart's desire, y yo también, for vraiment, what higher adventure for we two free spirits of the upper air than that which you propose!"

Even then I do believe that I realized that I had ceased to be an ingenue when I applied this forthrightly self-serving strategem. For by no stretch of the imagination could I delude myself that I had appealed to the best that lay in Guy Vlad Boca.

231

But contrawise, did not the vie of Ciudad Pallas appeal to his worst weakness with deadly perfection?

No longer the innocent naif I, I had learned my first lesson in quantitative moral calculus, though at the time I had no concept of how bitter that lesson was to become.

16

There were no hotels on the continent of Bloomenwald, not even the rudest of inns; indeed the only human constructs were the research domes scattered up and down the eastern coast on the margin of beach between the great forest and the sea. As for accommodations within the Bloomenwald itself or atop the canopy thereof, these of course were nonexistent, for in the first instance the forest floor was a gloomy land of perpetual night choked with unwholesome saphrophytic fungi and infested with an assortment of ill-tempered poisonous reptiles, and the Bloomenveldt, while certainly a solid enough terrain to stroll upon, was hardly suitable as a base for architectural constructs.

Fortunately, auslander turistas did visit the Bloomenwald from time to time, though the natives of Belshazaar, aside from the workers in the research domes, entirely shunned the continent thereof, so a limited number of rooms were available in the domes, provided one was willing to pay the outrageous rent demanded.

As for equipping our little expedition, this we were advised to do before our departure. Since the climate of the Bloomenveldt was perpetually balmy, tents or heavy clothing were redundant, and should we be so foolishly venturesome as to stay away from the dome long enough to require nourishment, we would have to content ourselves with cold concentrates, for the notion of build-

233

ing a fire on the treetops would be, to say the least, ill-advised. Thus, aside from cold concentrates and canteens, our kits contained only three items of equipment: simple beacon receivers in the event we lost our way, filter masks which we were assured were an absolute necessity, and floatbelts to nullify gravity so that we could flit from branch to branch and not fall to the deadly forest floor in the event of a botched landing.

Guy, who had certainly never fancied himself a woodsman, expressed the usual trepidations of the confirmed urbanite during these preparations, but I, who had gone on many an expedition deep into the Bittersweet Jungle of Glade, assured him in all sincerity that I was a maestra of forest lore well versed in the skills of survival therein. So I truly believed, for was one forest not very much like another, even though the Bloomenwald was a forest writ large? Only the question of predators would have given me pause, and these, we were told, were nonexistent.

Within forty-eight hours, we had completed our preparations and boarded the suborbital shuttle, for once I had succeeded in altering the vector of Guy's enthusiasm, he threw his energies and argent into the project as totally as he had pursued his previous obsessions. There were no more sojourns at the mental retreats, the Charge was never mentioned again, and once more our passages d'amour had achieved a frequency and duration, not to say piquancy, appropriate to a natural man and a natural woman about to share a grand adventure.

Of the shuttle flight to the continent of Bloomenwald, there is little to tell. We arose from Ciudad Pallas' shuttleport as if emerging from a dream of ennui, arced up through a featureless blue sky above an equally featureless ocean, winked through a starry blackness on the edge of space, then descended through a fleecy cloud deck to land on a sandy promontory jutting out into the sea.

Of our first moment on the continent of Bloomenwald, au contraire, much might be said, for this seemed another world entire.

On the tip of the peninsula where we had landed perched a large geodesic dome, whose facets flashed and shimmered in the bright sunlight like the eye of an insect. Landward of our debarkation point, the peninsula joined a narrow strip of beach, and beyond the beach towered the Bloomenwald.

To the naive eye, the edge of the Bloomenwald, seen from the beach, would no doubt have seemed a seacliff palisade, and even I, knowing what I saw, had difficulty crediting the fact that this five-hundred-meter-high wall of brown and black and deep gray crowned with green was in fact the margin of a forest. As far as the eye could see in either direction, this cliff towered over the beach. As a geological formation it would have been impressive enough, but as an endless thicket of living trees, it was so out of scale with the comprehensible that even the educated eye took a good while to unravel the optical illusion.

For what appeared to be a solid cliff of loamy brown earth streaked with formations of gray and black rock was in fact nothing so substantial. The vertical columns of brown upon long second glance revealed themselves as the mighty trunks of enormous trees, and the formations of black and gray rock were nothing more than the deeply gloomed aisles of shadow between them.

"Amusing enough for you, Guy?" I finally managed to whisper.

"Daunting. . . ." he muttered. "I can certainly see why no one would be mad enough to venture within."

I shuddered at the very thought. For beneath the canopy of the Bloomenwald was an equally vast shadowland somehow deeper in the darkness than any true night could have been, and merely viewing the gigantic edge thereof was enough to set the spirit shivering. As for the unpleasant fauna reputed to lurk therein, one could only be struck with the certainty that whatever chose to dwell in such a place must be of a disposition inimical to the human spirit.

But then we were here to explore the bright sundrenched meadowland of the Bloomenveldt high above, and as to the metaphysics of this image of a land of light crowning the realm of darkness, I was more than content to leave this to the poets, as we turned our backs to the land and our faces to the sea and made our way to the research dome.

Domed though it was, the research station sported no central garden, nor did it offer any grand overlook on the edge of the forest. Rather was the interior entirely divided up into three floors of modular rooms given over to laboratories, office spaces, dormitories, und so weiter, and most of the windows looked out on the sea.

Our room, for all the outrageous rent, was no less spartan than the rest of the establishment. There was a bed, an armoire, two night tables, two uncomfortable chairs, toilet facilities, and that was the end of it. As for decor, this tended to unadorned walls in muted pastel colors, thin carpeting in the same pallid hues, and no interior plantings whatever. This was a *scientific station* given over to serious pursuits, not a resort, and despite the fact that we were paying through the nose, we were here on sufferance.

While the ambiance, or total lack thereof, of the research dome made this all too apparent, the director of the station, a tall silver-haired woman named Marlene Kona Mendes, was good enough to spell this out in words of one syllable on the occasion of a rather grim welcoming lunch in the refectory staged for our benefit.

"This is a research station engaged in serious studies, and you will therefore trouble not scientists on duty or intrude your presence into the laboratories, bitte," she said over a meal of bland cuisine little better than the concentrates we had purchased in Ciudad Pallas. "Further, if you are so foolish as to become lost on the Bloomenveldt, do not expect us to mount any rescue expeditions. We have a complement of only some two dozen, and none of us have any time to waste tracking down errant turistas. We assume no responsibility, legal or moral, for your safety, comprend?"

"The clarity of your exposition is quite admirable," Guy replied dryly.

Also present at this luncheon were two other turistas who had rented rooms at the station. Omar Ki Benjamin was an elegantly dressed fellow of perpetually ironic mien from Calabiria who styled himself a sufic poet and had been here a week gathering inspiration, or so he said. Sori Smit Jana was a taciturn woman with disconcertingly intense gray eyes who chose to cloak her planet of origin and mission on the Bloomenveldt in mystery.

"I will however give you the same advice I give all such dilettantes, though no doubt you too will ignore it," Marlene Kona Mendes continued with an expression of prim disapproval. "Firstly, I would advise you not to wander more than an hour or two's journey into the Bloomenveldt. Secondly, and even more advisable, never, at any time, remove your filter masks. Thirdly, if you are truly prudent, which I somehow surmise you are not, you will rent, at an additional daily fee, sealed atmosphere suits which will entirely protect you from the floral effluvia."

Guy and I glanced at each other in some bemusement. Sori remained enigmatic as always. Omar laughed.

"Vraiment," he said, "and when enjoying sexual congress, take care to avoid orgasm. When imbibing wine, stop short of intoxication."

Marlene Kona Mendes shot him a black look, but something about her expression told me that this was a ritual gesture oft repeated.

"It may amuse you to learn that the mages who so earnestly study the psychochemistry of the Bloomenveldt eschew all subjective experience of the object of their obsession," Omar said. "When constrained by practical need to venture forth into the treetops, they do so entirely encased in armor. As to whether they conducted their passages d'amour similarly accoutred, je ne sais pas, but certainement, it would be *prudent,* for as all do know, the human body is rife with microorganisms."

"This is so?" I asked the director in some amazement. *"That we are less than natural men and women?"*

"That you never venture forth naked to the natural elements, of course," I said.

"Indeed. We are scientists, not mystical libertines such as some present whom I might mention."

"Mea culpa!" declared Omar. "Mea maxima culpa! Insofar as I seek to experience the most extreme states of consciousness that the universe offers our species, I am a mystic. Insofar as I fear no risk in the pursuit thereof, I proudly unfurl the libertine's banner!"

"Well spoken!" Guy exclaimed. Naturellement.

"Vraiment?" said Marlene Kona Mendes dryly. "Then why do you return each night to our mean-spirited company? Why do you not join those who wander the Bloomenveldt in a fog? Why do you not apply for admission into the society of the Bloomenkinder?"

"I am a mystical libertine, not an imbecile!"

"You mean to say there are humans *living* on the Bloomenveldt?" I said.

"Indeed," said Sori, exhibiting loquacity for the first time, "there are those who wander up and down the coastal fringes between the domes for weeks at a time. As long as they keep the sea in sight, they can always find their way to the next, even unmasked. As for food and drink, the Bloomenveldt provides these in profusion."

"As to how many of the denizens of the Bloomenveldt may still be entitled to style themselves *human,* that is another matter," Marlene Kona Mendes said.

"She seeks to frighten you with the legend of the Bloomenkinder," said Omar.

"I speak of anyone foolish enough to go unmasked!"

"It would appear that we have much to learn," I said, growing somewhat discomfited in the role of ignorant audience to a debate that had been apparently going on for some time.

"The permanent human condition, nicht wahr?" declared Omar. "One would assume the two of you will be eager to begin on the morrow. I would be honored to be your guide."

And so, once the sun had risen the next morning, Guy and I set forth on our first visit to the Bloomenveldt in the company of Omar Ki Benjamin. "Despite my japes at the expense of our good director," he said as we made our way down the promontory toward the beach, "I would advise that you don your masks at least for the present. The initial impression is disorienting enough as it is."

Upon reaching the beach, we did so, strapping on the half-masks, which covered nose and mouth while leaving vision unobstructed. We already wore our floatbelts, and Omar instructed us in their use, which seemed simple enough. Indeed the only control was a knob whereby the range of gravity nullification might be adjusted along a continuous range between the Belshazaar-normal value of .4 standard g and the highest setting, which would provide a negative gravity of .1 standard, which is to say a gentle lift of the same value. For safety's sake, this would cut off after ten minutes so as to prevent a wearer who for some reason had lost consciousness from drifting upward beyond the life-sustaining envelope of the atmosphere.

238

Omar led us inward across the beach for a few score meters, "for best dramatic effect," or so he told us. From this vantage, the edge of the Bloomenwald no longer appeared as a solid palisade; rather did perspective reduce me to the size of an insect peering upward at a vegetal vastness which rose before it to blot out the sky. Indeed, I could gaze within the deeply shadowed aisles of monstrous tree trunks and dimly perceive the pale white shapes of unwholesome fungi festooning the loamy forest floor, and even hear, or so at least it seemed, the scrabblings and chitterings of unseen creatures within.

"Up, up, meine kinder!" Omar cried. "From the maya of the groundlings to the sublimity on high!"

So saying, he twisted the control knob of his floatbelt and began to rise, and a moment later Guy and I followed.

We drifted slowly upward along the shadowy facade of the forest edge like mites ascending to the sky before the mouth of a cave too enormous for their modest perceptive powers to grasp, or like birds spiraling upward before an onrushing front of evil black thunderheads. Then, none too soon for me, we reached the level where the treetop canopy began, and the dark and gloomy immensity of the nether reaches at last gave way to billows of green foliage brilliantly dappled throughout by the bright morning sunlight.

And then, all at once, we had finally overtopped the roof of the forest and rose like the sun in the east, like homeward bound angels, over Eden.

It had been one thing to view the Bloomenveldt en holo but quite another to experience it for the first time in its own true scale. Vraiment, it was immense, in toto and in detail, and yet it was an immensity that, far from daunting the spirit, filled it with delight.

The morning sun behind us illumined in sharp chiaroscuro the wrinkles and folds and hillocks of a green veldt as endless as the blue sky above it. From this perspective hovering scant meters above the surface, the huge flowers which grew in a riotous profusion of bright colors appeared as isolated blooms on the green backdrop in the foreground, but seemed to fairly cover the land as the eye moved toward the horizon. Each ellipsoid leaf was about the size of three or four beds, and they grew in thick bunches along gigantic twigs, which in turn sprouted from

239

unthinkably huge branches which appeared only as suggestive shapes beneath the almost seamless carpet of foliage.

And the whole rolling and undulating subtly in the gentle breeze with a sighing, rushing sound not unlike that of a mildly-tossing sea. This selfsame wind, caressing my sun-warmed skin and tousling my hair, seemed to serve as an organic connection between my body and the living, breathing landscape of the treetops, a breath I seemed to share in common with the Bloomenveldt, uniting its spirit with my own.

Naturellement, it was Omar who first broke the silence of that rapt moment. "Set your floatbelts to a tenth gravity and follow me, meine kinder!" he called out, and so saying, drifted downward to touch foot on a giant leaf. No sooner had his feet touched the surface, than, with a great whooping laugh, he bounded high into the air again in a fat lazy arc which carried him a good fifty meters away from us before he touched down once more, at which point, with an agile twisting spring, he propelled himself back in our direction in like manner, to alight like a hopping insect directly below us.

"Come, come, if an old mystic libertine like me can bound freely through the treetops, you youngsters should master the art in a twinkling!"

Guy and I exchanged glances, shrugged, grinned at each other, adjusted our floatbelts, and soon enough discovered that it was so. It was something like bouncing on a trampoline and something like zero gravity ballet. A great leap took virtually no effort at all at this low gravity setting, nor was a landing at all jarring to ankles or knees, and the stately interval of glide between seemed the esthetic equivalent of birdlike flight itself. It was not long before we were cutting aerobatic capers for the sheer delight of it, turning cartwheels and somersaults, executing abrupt changes of direction on the bounce, landing on our hands and vaulting backwards through the air to alight on our feet.

"I grow weary just watching two such natural Bloomenkinder," Omar called out at length. "Shall we proceed with the guided tour?"

And so we did for the next several hours, accustoming ourselves to the sights and sounds and feels of the Bloomenveldt, becoming one with the wonderland of the treetops under the aegis of our mystic libertine guide.

240

On the one hand, any one part of the Bloomenveldt seemed much like any other, but on the other hand no two venues thereon were quite the same. Here on this magical land built on air, there were no landmarks or geographical features, only an endless, rolling, tossing veldt of boughs and branches, as formless and fluid as the waves of a sea. That was the seamless sameness of the Bloomenveldt.

But this sea of green was afloat with an abundance of flowers, of which the only sameness was that of immensity of scale, for they seemed to grow in a bewildering variety of shapes and hues. Great yellow blooms the size of a banquet table with spikey black stamens like so many cast-iron spears. Bunches of violet bells, each the size of a man, depending from a central stem. Carmine cups filled with fluid and large enough to serve us as baths. A greater variety of huge blooms within sight of each moment's vision than memory will hold. Fruits there were as well in an equally bewildering variety, hidden under flowers, hanging between them from stems, or nestled in the crotches where leaf stems met twigs.

"How is it possible for such a profusion of different flowers to grow on trees which by their leaves would appear to be all of the same species?" I asked Omar at length.

"I am a poet, not a genetic botanist," he told me. "But as I have been given to understand, each tree, being immensely long-lived by our standards, produces flowers which are genetically heterogeneous, cross-pollinating itself in an onanistic manner, as it were, in order to keep pace with the more rapidly evolving fauna of the Bloomenveldt. Like certain terrestrial coelenterates, the trees of the Bloomenveldt are colonial organisms, at least in a genetic sense." He shrugged. "Alas, that is the extent of my knowledge of such esoteric lore."

As for the fauna of the Bloomenveldt, these creatures fled at our less than stealthy approach, and we were able to glimpse them only from afar or as quick flurries of motion fleeing from our disturbance.

I saw troupes of the tawny-furred bipeds I had seen in the holo clustered around blood-red blooms streaked with black. Small black-furred creatures scattered like a flock of birds on membranous gliding wings when we stumbled upon them as they sucked nectar from the depths of pale orange flowers with long tubular

241

tongues. Legless serpentine mammals with fur diamond-patterned in brown and green slithered away into the foliage as we approached a cluster of huge red puffballs.

There seemed to be some profusion of animal species, all of them mammalian, or at least mammalian-seeming, all of them quite shy of our approach, and all of them seeming to frequent no more than two or three different varieties of flower.

"Vriament, each type of flower exudes pheromonic essences specific to its own choice of pollinator, and laces its nectars and fruits with alkaloids evolved to please the palates of same," Omar told us. "Though at different seasons or different stages of rut, the same animal may be attracted to different flowers, even as we may be seized by pheromonic attractions to different sorts of mates depending upon our ages, state of intoxication, or even the phase of whatever moon there might be, for even in the chemical realm, variety is the spice of amorous life, nē."

"Speaking of which," said Guy, "now that we have mastered the art of perambulation in the treetops and visually acquainted ourselves with the flora and fauna thereof, is it not time we shed these filter masks and sampled the arcane perfumes for which the Bloomenveldt is famed?"

"Quelle chose!" Omar said with a grin. "You mean to say you intend to ignore the sober and prudent advice of science in favor of the reckless abandon of the mystic libertine?"

"When imbibing wine, Guy Vlad Boca is not known to stop short of intoxication," Guy informed him.

"And you, my lady fair?"

"When enjoying sexual congress, Sunshine Shasta Leonardo takes not care to avoid orgasm," I replied gamely, not to be outdone, though not without a certain trepidation either.

"Well spoken, my true Children of Fortune!" Omar declared. "And as a token of the esteem in which I hold such spirit, I will remain masked in order to serve as your ground control, as it were, for at least at first, it takes a bit of getting used to."

And so Guy and I doffed our masks, stowed them in our pockets, and, at the direction of Omar, the three of us leapt off the leaf on which we stood, and came down in the vecino of a bloom consisting of a wide circular veranda of velvety purple petals surrounding a tall tubular column coated with the most delicious crumbly pink pollen.

242

Delicious? Vraiment, utterly delectable, for my nose, indeed my backbrain, was filled, sotted, indeed transformed into a locus of pure desire by the most wondrous aroma—compounded of the crust of roasted meat, and the savor of rich brown chocolate, and a dozen more subtle undertones of gustatory lust—which informed my mouth with absolute chemical certainty that the grandest production of the premiere chef maestro in all the worlds of men was as fressen compared to this perfect pink ambrosia.

I had only to bury my face in the pollen mass, embrace it, shovel great handfuls into my gaping maw, and my tastebuds would explode in a veritable orgasm of gustatory ecstasy—

"Emphatically not recommended!" Omar shouted, restraining me by main force as I attempted to bury my face in the pollen, and yanking Guy away from a similar attempt with his other hand. "Jump, kinder, jump!" he commanded, and actually delivered a kick to my backside.

This was enough, vraiment, *only* this would have been enough, to make me leap off the petals of this wonderful flower, and as I did so, I observed Guy subject to similar prodding.

No sooner had I soared beyond the olfactory aura of the flower than what the moment before had seemed the most perfect, innocent, and natural desire in all the worlds was at once revealed as the most bizarre and ghastly of gustatory perversions.

The three of us came to rest on a leaf a prim and decent distance away from any of the surrounding flowers. Guy and I regarded each other in blushing embarrassment, as if each had caught the other in a sexual act too loathsome to contemplate.

"Take care to maintain a certain psychic distance from your chemical desires," Omar told us. "With a bit of practice, it is possible to enjoy the effects without succumbing entirely to the tropisms thereof. Perhaps we should next try something a bit more soporific. . . ."

Our next flower was a yellow bloom like a great carpet of downy moss overhung by tassels dripping a fine black powder. The aroma thereof was like a luxuriant tropical wind speaking to me of the passive pleasures of sweet and languid repose. I wanted nothing more than to lay myself down on its soft surface and stare mindlessly up into the azure depths of the sky. This I proceeded to do with Guy by my side. No sooner had my body contacted the yellow petals than I was showered by a dust-fine rain of black pollen which seemed to sparkle in the sunlight and caress my skin like a lover's soothing touch.

Minutes, hours, or an eternity of mindless perfection later, my nostrils were assailed by a stench the fecal fetor of which would have made the stink of rotten meat seem like jasmine, the soft down of the petals beneath my back all at once became a bed of itchy prickles, and I leapt unbidden into the air to come down, trembling and writhing, on a leaf beside Omar. A moment later, Guy arrived, brushing pollen off his body as if it were flecks of burning ash.

"As I warned you," Omar said, "it takes a bit of getting used to at first. But once you have become wise to the wiles of the various flowers, you may learn to use the effects to serve your own pleasures rather than the single-minded purposes thereof."

He pointed out a cluster of brilliant pink blooms perhaps a leap of thirty meters away. "Now *those* you should sample on your own," he said. "See if you don't find the effects thereof entirely pleasurable."

Not without a certain trepidation at least on my part, Guy and I bounded over to a leafy pink apron overhung by translucent canopies of petals through which sunlight streamed to envelop us in a lambent rosy glow.

Indeed this rosy ambiance extended beyond the visual realm to encompass smell, and taste, and touch, and senses previously beyond my ken, for no sooner had I entered the seductive sphere of this floral boudoir than my entire being became suffused by a veritable synesthesia of rosy fire. My eyes saw through rosy sheets of light, my nose was filled with rosy musk, my very ears were filled with an ethereal music which somehow hummed a rosy mantra, rose was the taste of the very tongue in my mouth, Guy's skin beneath my touch assumed a rosy aspect to my fingertips, and the sum total of all my senses was a burning rosy lust.

And so we coupled there in the rosy twilight, with the quick and smoky passion of mindless innocent animals, without art, without restraint, without mindfulness of Omar, without in truth even conscious awareness of the act itself.

After we had reached our mutual cusps, the spell seemed to vanish into the wind, leaving only a heavy rosy torpor out of which we smiled contentedly at each other before taking to the air once more to rejoin Omar, who had observed the proceedings from a discreet distance.

"Lust, hunger, torpor, thirst, und so weiter," he said. "It would seem that from the floral viewpoint, these simple tropisms are quite sufficient to comprise the only meaningful motivations of we mammalians who fancy ourselves the crown of creation. Which is to say that if one is a flower, one need only secrete substances sufficient to incite them, and one may lead such creatures by the backbrain to serve the single purpose for which they were quite obviously designed, to wit the distribution and consequent cross-fertilization of one's pollen."

He laughed. "However, if one is a mystic libertine, this simple floral reasoning may be made to serve entirely mammalian purposes."

Omar smiled at us indulgently. "So now that you have done your best for floral evolution, meine kinder, let us conclude our lesson by revisiting the very same blooms forewarned and therefore in full possession of that sapient critical consciousness which distinguishes us from the natural fauna of the Bloomenveldt."

And so, at his insistence, we did. We returned to the bloom of gustatory passion and reveled in the marvelous aroma of cuisinary nirvana but were able to resist the unseemly lust to gobble. Upon revisiting the yellow flower whose perfume urged languid repose, we stood before it inhaling the most wonderful peace and serenity of the spirit while resisting the urge to lie on its petals. As for our pink passion flower, once we were standing beneath its rosy canopy in full consciousness of the effects of its pheromonic suasions, and, moreover, erotically sated by our recent exercise, we were able to enjoy its aphrodisia of the senses from a more abstract connoisseur's perspective.

At length, the sun began to go down over the Bloomenveldt, casting deep green shadows over the brighter hues of the treetops, and we replaced our filter masks and proceeded in soaring bounds toward the deepening blue of the sea on the eastern horizon.

"Aha!" cried Omar as the three of us poised on a leaf for the next leap. "A wandering spirit approaches!"

Away to the north, where his pointing finger directed our gaze, I saw a dark shape which at first I took for one of the animals of the Bloomenveldt bounding over the treetops more or

245

less in our direction. Then I realized that its leaps were far too grand to be achieved without the aid of a floatbelt and perceived it as an approaching human.

"Let us tarry a moment and seek to engage him in discourse," Omar suggested. "If this proves possible, it may be of interest. If not, it will at least provide an object lesson."

A few minutes later, a rather bizarre figure alighted on a neighboring leaf: a tall, plumpish, dark-skinned man with a ragged mane of long blond hair, whose body seemed to be bursting out of a tattered tunic several sizes too small for him. Vraiment, he wore a floatbelt, but no filter mask was anywhere in evidence, nor did he carry any sort of pack. His eyes, though clear and healthy-looking from a physiological perspective, seemed not quite focused on quotidian reality.

"Greetings, wanderer," Omar called out. "I am Omar Ki Benjamin, and my companions are Sunshine Shasta Leonardo and Guy Vlad Boca. . . ."

The man stood there staring at us vapidly and blinking, as if trying to remember the import of such niceties of introduction.

"Come, come, whom do I have the honor of addressing?"

In response, the fellow's blinking only grew more rapid.

"Have you been on the Bloomenveldt long?" I essayed, though by the look of him, the question seemed entirely rhetorical.

"The rising of the sun . . . awakening . . . the summons of the flowers . . . eating . . . the setting of the sun . . . sleep . . ." the fellow said haltingly, as if this were some cosmic revelation. "The cycle repeats itself . . . the great wheel turns . . ."

"Indeed," said Omar, "I have observed the same myself. But from whence do you come and whither do you go?"

"The great wheel turns . . . the spirit follows its karma along the trail of the wind. . . ."

"No doubt," said Guy. "But might you be so good as to point out where the trail of the wind has brought you. . . ?"

The wanderer seemed to make a great effort at inward contemplation. At length, he pointed to the west, then hesitantly swung his finger in an arc from west, to northwest, to more or less due north up the coast.

"If I may essay a translation. . . ?" offered Omar. "You have come from a research dome somewhere up the coast, and you have swung inland on your journey?"

The fellow nodded with some enthusiasm and then spoke as if through veils of mental fog which had at least begun to clear somewhat. "Research dome ... oui ... several weeks ago ... psychoanthropologist yo ... Meade Ariel Kozuma ... is that not my name. ...?"

"You are a psychoanthropologist named Meade Ariel Kozuma," I said firmly, getting the hang of the technique. "You left a research dome up the coast a few weeks ago ... on a field trip? To study ... those who wander the Bloomenveldt?"

He shook his head. "Nein ... not wanderers ... *tribes*. ..." He pointed westward with some excitement.

"There are *tribes of humans* living in the interior of the Bloomenveldt?" I exclaimed.

He nodded. "Noble flowers ... higher forms ... tribes ... go unmasked ... one with the flowers ... principle of subjective research ..."

"Alors!" exclaimed Omar. "Just *how far west* did you go, man?"

Meade Ariel Kozuma managed a quite human shrug. "Where flowers are one with man ... evolutionary symbiosis ... not like here ..."

"Merde!" exclaimed Omar. "Next will you claim to have visited the Perfumed Garden of the Bloomenkinder?"

The former psychoanthropologist summoned up the ghost of what had once no doubt been a characteristic moue of professional skepticism. "Legend," he said. "Entirely anecdotal."

The sun was beginning to set in earnest now, the shadows were deepening, and a cool offshore wind had begun to rock the crowns of the great trees. "We had best be getting back to the dome now," Omar told us. He turned to regard Meade Ariel Kozuma. "Will you not let us escort you back to the worlds of men?" he offered.

The psychoanthropologist shook his head with some vigor. "The great wheel turns. ..." he chanted. "The summons of the flowers ... the sun sets. ..." Then with a sudden bound, he sprang off the leaf, and disappeared in great long slow leaps across the Bloomenveldt toward the sunset like a stone thrown by a skilled giant skipping across the surface of some unthinkably immense pond.

247

"Most of them are like that," Omar said conversationally. "Some a bit more coherent, some less."

"There are *many* such wandering the Bloomenveldt?" I asked.

Omar shrugged. "One encounters them from time to time."

Guy was staring westward at the sunset with a rather peculiar abstracted air. "Tribes in the interior . . ." he muttered softly. "Higher forms. . . ? Bloomenkinder. . . ? The Perfumed Garden. . . ?" He turned to Omar and spoke more sharply. "Do such things truly exist?"

"Some of it no doubt may be true, the rest volkchose," Omar replied. "Humans have been visiting the Bloomenveldt for centuries, nē, and some, no doubt, like our bemused friend, wander off never to be seen again. Given sufficient chance and time, one can credit that some survive to produce progeny, tribes of ersatz natives, as it were, Bloomenveldt born. One hears such reports from time to time, but you have observed how unreliable the bearers thereof become."

"These tribes, then, are the so-called Bloomenkinder?"

Omar laughed. "Nein," he said. "The Bloomenkinder are creatures of legend, and the legend thereof is related by the hypothetical tribes to bemused wanderers, who in turn babble to such as we. Mythical beings thrice removed, as it were. Denizens of the Perfumed Garden, a Xanadu deep in the interior where Enlightened Ones dwell in nirvanic perfection with the flowers."

"Do you suppose that such a place can in truth exist?" Guy breathed in a solemn half-whisper.

"Vraiment," said Omar, "as do Xanadu and Oz and Paradise itself." He tapped Guy playfully on the head. "In here!"

He gazed uneasily to the west, where the disc of the sun had already touched the horizon. "It will soon be dark," he said. "Let us not tarry here further discussing the ineffable." And he bounded off in the direction of the sea.

"We must delve deeper into this," Guy said sharply. "*Much* deeper."

"It's only a legend, Guy."

"Bloomenkinder and Perfumed Gardens mayhap," Guy said with a dreamy yet all-too-determined look in his eyes. "But the tribes of the interior may be real enough, and one may therefore consider what hold the Bloomenveldt has upon such humans to cause them to remain. . . ."

"How might folk who know not of the existence of the worlds of men even be tempted to return thereto?" I scoffed.

"Ah, but *Meade Ariel Kozuma* was a *mage* in the worlds of men and did he not eschew our offer of rescue? What does *he* find herein more amusing than all the sophisticated pleasures of our Second Starfaring Age?"

After all my weeks in Great and ersatz Edoku, after the inward-facing reality of the *Unicorn Garden,* and most particularly on the heels of our sojourn in vile Ciudad Pallas, I was more delighted than I could have imagined to find myself once more in a totally natural realm under an open sky, let alone free to soar like a bird about a venue as exotic and beautiful as the Bloomenveldt. During the next five days, Guy and I, at first in the company of Omar and later à deux, spent our daylight hours gamboling in the treetops, sampling the perfumes of the great flowers, and conducting frequent and for the most part highly enjoyable tantric exercises under the influence thereof.

But Guy, after sampling the variety of floral psychotropics in the vecino with his usual diligence in such matters, soon became jaded by the immediate amusements at hand, and began to toy with the notion of penetrating the deeper mysteries of the interior.

The first symptom of this obsession appeared as a quite uncharacteristic scholarly interest in the genetic ecology of the Bloomenveldt and the lore of the human tribes thereof, and endless interrogation of the scientists of the research domes on these subjects under the guise of the sincere amateur student.

When it came to the question of the tribes of the interior, these worthies were either ignorant or deliberately unforthcoming or both, as if there was something they were attempting to hide, mayhap even from themselves.

It was readily enough conceded that the Bloomenveldt abounded with fruits, nectars, and pollens quite sufficient to allow members of our species to live off the land, and not even Marlene Kona Mendes attempted to deny that over the centuries any number of fools had wandered off into the interior never to be seen by civilized eyes again. Nor was it denied that what might have been the descendants of same had been fleetingly sighted by suited research teams foraging into the deeper Bloomenveldt in search of biochemical specimens. But these reverted savages uniformly fled at civilized approach, and, like the fauna of the treetops with whom they no doubt by now had more in common than with civilized folk, they were quite adept at eluding capture on their own terrain.

"In short," the director declared brusquely in what was clearly designed to be her final word on the subject, "there can be no more than a scattered handful of such creatures, they are of minimal scientific interest and even more useless in terms of possible profit, and the effort and risk of scientific study of these curiosities entirely outweighs any benefits that might accrue therefrom."

When it came to the subjects of their own immediate research, however, the scientists were more than willing to offer up their wisdom at interminable length to eager young persons expressing a respectful interest or a guileful simulacrum of same.

It was a matter of some dispute among them as to whether the flowers were actual organs of the trees upon which they grew or whether they were in fact symbiotes of different species, though at length it began to seem to me that this question was a mere verbal nicety, for functionally speaking, they were neither and both.

The great trees of the Bloomenveldt were so long-lived as to be all but immortal from a human perspective, and the Bloomenwald entirely covered the continent upon which it was found; therefore arboreal reproduction was necessary, indeed possible, only on those rare occasions when disease or disaster created a gap in the seamless canopy. Experiments had shown that upon such occasions the flowers of neighboring trees in fact dropped seeds onto the forest floor which grew into saplings. True too that the flowers grew directly from the boughs of the trees and were nourished by their sap. Furthermore, trees and flowers were as genotypically identical as Guy and myself, which is to say they shared identical chromosome numbers and genetic hardware.

But each tree's flowers were as genetically varied in the software expression thereof as the citizens of a human city, and they crossbred with each other to produce a rapid profusion of

250

variations, generation by generation, as if they were independent organisms. Indeed, floral evolution on the Bloomenveldt proceeded by leaps and bounds, and that was why the forest remained a bottomless cornucopia of new psychotropics, for these evolved in response to the flowers' intimate relationship to their mammalian pollinators. Thus did the trees, who themselves reproduced rarely, nevertheless contrive to maintain a richly varied gene pool.

Of what real interest was such genetic arcana to Guy Vlad Boca, who had never in my presence evinced a scholarly interest in anything save the varieties of human amusement?

"You do not comprehend, Sunshine?" he said when I interrogated him on the subect of his sudden development of a passion for genetic botany en boudoir. "Either these people are forthrightly *lying* to us, or mayhap there is a truth which their crabbed spirits fear to consciously encompass."

"How so?" I demanded.

"The whole object of their research is to derive new psychotropics from the forest, is it not? And these, they readily admit, are produced by the flowers thereof in response to the evolution of their pollinators, nē?"

"This much is obvious, but—"

"Yet they profess complete indifference to the study of the human tribes of the interior! *Who live generation after generation in unmasked intimacy with the flowers!* Noble flowers . . . higher forms . . . Did not the wanderer babble of such wonders to be found in the interior?"

"Vraiment," I said dubiously, "but considering the source, must one not grant a certain discount for hyperbole?"

"No doubt," agreed Guy, "but considering the source and style of the tales' denial, which is to say sour spirits who dare not venture even to the edge of the Bloomenveldt without sealing their perceptions away in atmosphere suits, one must also grant a certain discount for spiritual constipation."

"Like the mages of the mental retreats and laboratories of Ciudad Pallas . . ." I muttered. "Vraiment, on this planet, science would seem to have devolved from its courageous spiritual quest for truth and technological enhancement in favor of a single-minded search for profit."

"Be that as it may, it is also quite clear that even the great-

251

est opportunity for pecuniary profit lies with sedulous study of the tribes of the interior. Since there would seem to be no baneful force restraining these Bloomenkinder from returning to the civilized realm, they must *choose* to remain in the depths of the forest because—"

"Because they find the Bloomenveldt more *amusing* than the worlds of men?"

"I could not have phrased it better myself," Guy said dryly. "And what do you imagine they find more amusing? Surely it is neither haute cuisine nor theatrical performances nor elevated discourse. . . ."

"More puissant psychotropics!"

Guy beamed at me idiotically. "Go to the head of the class, ma chère," he said with unholy gleefulness.

"But if this is so, then why do the mages of the research domes refrain from study of the flowers and tribes of the interior?"

"Why the sealed suits?" Guy said contemptuously. "Why defoliate the entire continent of Pallas? Because they are like eunuchs studying tantra! Because, as Omar so justly put it, they lack the spiritual courage of the mystic libertine! Do not all men fear confrontation with states of being which their spirits lack sufficient grandeur to encompass? Leaving a golden opportunity for true Children of Fortune such as ourselves who fear not unknown realms of the spirit but pursue the same with an open heart!"

"Guy, you are not suggesting that we—"

"I suggest nothing, I only follow your noble lead, liebchen," Guy insinuated. "For was it not *you*, cher Sunshine, who so rightly declared that in the Bloomenveldt we might have the grand destiny to achieve states of consciousness never known before to human brains? And enrich ourselves by marketing the substances which produce them!"

"But no one has ever returned from the depths of the Bloomenveldt, or so it is said."

"Indeed. Imagine therefore what is to be gained by mounting the first successful expedition to the heart of the matter and returning with the fruits thereof."

"Imagine what would be lost by failure!"

"Have you not told me often enough of your mastery of forest survival lore?" Guy said. And indeed, if truth be told, I may have styled myself as more of a Diana of the jungle than a few weekends in the quotidian forests of Glade warranted.

"When all is said and done are we not mystic libertines, you and I," Guy persisted. "True Children of Fortune, adventurers of the spirit, more than willing to risk all to gain all."

What was I to say to such a challenge? On the one hand, I could hardly deny the spirit within me which had insisted on braving Great Edoku, all my parents' sage and pragmatic advice to the contrary, which had sent me in pursuit of the Gypsy Jokers against all the wisdom of the Public Service Stations, which had won the heart of Pater Pan with blarney, and which had brought me hither with this brave and foolhardy lover to the edge of the very adventure he proposed.

On the other hand, there was the part of me that knew with the coolness of intellect divorced from passion that what he proposed was dangerous to the point of insanity.

"Vraiment, my spirit is willing, but my reason whispers that such a spirit is quite mad," I declared in all honesty.

But such dualistic ambiguity had certainly never been Guy's style, nor was he fazed by my indecision. "In such a pass, one must await a sign to synergize reason and spirit," he proclaimed grandly. "And from my present perspective I am cavalierly confident that the same will be forthcoming."

And so it was, two days later, of a late afternoon. We were lying on a leaf close by a great carnelian circle of petals surrounding a bright green pistil which branched at its pinnacle into an overhanging canopy of fine windblown filaments dripping a sticky resinous pollen, which is to say far enough from the flower to avoided being dusted, but close enough to lie within its perfumed aura.

The state of being induced by the heavy, languorous scent of this perfume seemed perfectly suited to our mood. The still-bright westering sun bathed our limbs with warmth as it cast ever-shifting and slowly lengthening dappled patterns of shadow over the wind-tossed crowns of the great trees. Our leafy pallet rocked us into hypnagogic somnolence like a great green cradle in the hands of some forest spirit, whose breath we could hear in the susurrus of the breeze passing through the boughs and leaves. Empty of mind and full of spirit, drifting on the edge of sleep

253

where vagrant thoughts transformed themselves into the surreal images of dreams, I gazed up into a clear blue sky which mirrored perfectly the blissful cerulean void of my spirit.

Vraiment, at length I surmised that I had in fact drifted off the exquisite edge of this hypnagogic state into the realm of sleep, for out of the languorous fog there coalesced a visage out of dreams. . . .

A human face such as is not often seen in our Second Starfaring Age: an old man's face, seamed, and lined, and crowned by a mantle of long, thin white hair. The face of a man in the last year or so of his life, when all at once the Healer's arts which have preserved life's vigor for three hundred years and more suddenly fail, and the mask of mortality appears to herald the imminence of death.

Yet strange to say it was the clear tranquility of the spirit and peace of the heart written in the calm set of the withered lips and the limpid brown eyes which convinced me I had left the waking realm.

Then the visage spoke and thereby shattered the illusion of dreamy sleep, though not the languorous drifting mood thereof.

"May I share your leaf a while, mes amis?"

An old man crouched on the leaf beside us, naked not merely of clothing, but of floatbelt and filter mask as well.

"Are you a Bloomenkind of the forest?" Guy asked in a voice wherein avid curiosity was bizarrely softened by the reasonless tranquility of the flower's perfume.

The old man laughed, a happy musical sound, or so it seemed. "Not yet," he said.

"You are not a naked tribesman recently emerged from the depths of the forest?" I said in a similar dreamy state.

"Au contraire," said the old man, "naked do I go to merge my spirit with the Bloomenveldt before it leaves this moribund corpus."

"You are a pilgrim come to the Bloomenveldt to die?"

Once more, the old man laughed sweetly without a trace of irony or angst. "Dying one may accomplish in any venue," he said, "it is only the *style* of one's passage from the mortal realm and the state of one's spirit in the moment thereof that one may choose. As for me, I choose to die in the Bloomenveldt, for here

254

one may expire not in a state of dread, but in a state of enlightenment, into the loving arms of this great forest."

"You know the Bloomenveldt well?" Guy said sharply, willing up the effort to free himself from his torpor. "You are versed
in the secrets of its inner heart?"

"A century ago, I came here to study the forest as a mage
in the research domes. But something moved my spirit to doff
my atmosphere suit, don filter mask and floatbelt, and trek deep
enough into the interior to know that here I would come when
my time came to die. As for the secrets of the Bloomenveldt's
heart, these will forever remain a mystery to those who fear to
become breath of its breath. And in those days, such a one was I."

"You traveled to the interior and survived to tell the tale?" I
asked just as sharply as Guy, for if this was so, what clearer sign
could destiny have given us?

The old one dismissed the grandeur of this feat with an
errant wave of his hand. "If one never truly leaves the worlds of
men behind, how can one help but return thereto?" he said.
"Which is to say there is nothing to hinder the masked traveler
from passing through the wonders and glories of the Bloomenveldt
untrammeled thereby. The well-equipped turista will encounter
neither physical danger nor spiritual enhancement. To brave either,
you must doff the filter mask of civilization, and give yourself
over to the flowers."

"But even masked you learned enough to know that your
spirit wished to make its final journey here . . ." said Guy.

"Indeed, my young friend," the old man said. "For while
there may be much for a young spirit to lose by surrendering
itself to the forest, for an old spirit about to be forced to vacate its
quotidian premises there is only an enlightened ending to be
gained."

"And what was it that you learned all those long decades
ago that convinced you to essay such a final journey?" I asked
softly.

"The Bloomenveldt is alive!"

"Hardly a revelation of astounding proportions," I could
not quite refrain from pointing out dryly.

"Alive as you or I, mein kind," the old man said. "Possessed
of a genetic intelligence, a sapient spirit which it has received as a
gift of man. For millions of years did the forest slumber as mind-

255

less trees produced substances to manipulate the mindless pollinators thereof. But then our species came to Belshazaar, and sapients over the centuries wandered off into the forest, and so since that time the forest has been evolving in symbiosis with man. Deeper within the Bloomenveldt in the land of the Bloomenkinder, the flowers have evolved pheromones and alkaloids designed not to attract insensate mammals but our own sapient spirit. As we have gifted the forest with the template of consciousness, so does the Bloomenveldt offer us psychotropics crafted by that very chemical sentience to reward us with the highest realms of consciousness it currently knows how to grant. True symbiosis, a just and profitable bargain between our two species."

"The Perfumed Garden . . ." breathed Guy. "Where humans and flowers have achieved symbiotic perfection. Where floral and human evolution have contrived to merge. Where nirvanic transcendence arises from the very chemistry of the brain."

"So it is said," declared the ancient one. "And so do I seek this realm of the spirit as the physical matrix thereof expires."

"May you find what you seek," I told him with an open heart.

"Y tú también."

And with that, he arose, and with a somewhat feeble though long-legged gait, departed into the depths of the Bloomenveldt, into the rosy mists of dusk, into the deeper mysteries thereof from which no man had returned to tell the tale.

When he had disappeared like a wraith, Guy and I left the flower of his apparition to discuss on a neutral leaf what we had learned within the realm of its perfume.

"Was that not a sign that spoke to both your mind and your spirit, Sunshine?" Guy asked me. "Is there now anything to hold us back from the journey within to the heart of the matter? Will you now not join me in the quest to gain all now that you have been reassured that we do not really risk all? And now that you have spoken with the spirit of all there is to gain?"

And indeed it was. And indeed there wasn't. And indeed I would.

"Let us be gone in the morning," I said gamely, "lest my resolve vanish in the cold clear light of day."

17 And so as Belshazaar's sun arose over the Bloomenveldt the next morning, so did we—equipped with
floatbelts, filter masks, beacon receivers, kits for
collecting floral essences, a full month's worth of
concentrates, the assurances of the previous afternoon's apparition, and a plan of action which would
seem to be foolproof.

We would proceed due westward into the interior for five
days. At the speed we could make bounding across the treetops,
this should be long enough to penetrate several hundred kilometers into the Bloomenveldt, so if we spied no humans after five
days of this procedure, it could fairly be said that the mystics,
libertine or otherwise, were wrong, and the scientists, crabbed of
spirit though they be, were right, and no significant human population was to be found.

At which point, we would simply return from whence we
came. Even without the beacon receivers, there would seem to be
no danger of losing our way, for toward sunrise was the coast,
and once the beach was attained, one could not follow it in either
direction for more than two or three days without reaching a
dome.

The only peril would seem to be that of the spirit, for we
knew all too well the state of discombobulation that could be
attained by wandering the Bloomenveldt unmasked, courtesy of

the object lesson of Meade Ariel Kozuma. Therefore, at my insistence, if not without some resistance, Guy acceded to a further procedural pact. We would both go masked as we traveled inward, and if we paused to sample the offerings of any flower along the way, we would never unmask together—when one of us played the role of psychonaut, the other would always be there to serve as ground control.

We did not inform Marlene Kona Mendes or her staff of our intentions, but simply gathered up our gear and left, for on the one hand we had already been informed in no uncertain terms that we could expect no rescue mission from that quarter in the event of difficulty, and on the other, Guy's professed goal, or at any rate his pecuniary rationalization for this adventure of the spirit, was to steal a grand commercial march on these self-same mages by returning from the deep interior with samples of psychotropics which would put their pathetic efforts to shame.

We did, however, bid a fond and secret farewell to Omar Ki Benjamin, for it is difficult to embark on such a grand adventure without a bit of boasting into a sympathetic and reassuring ear, and from the quarter of this self-styled mystic libertine, we knew we could count on a moral support entirely in contrast to the hectoring we no doubt would have been subject to had we broached our intentions to the gnomes of the research dome.

Nor were we disappointed by the spirit with which Omar greeted our announcement. "Ah!" he sighed grandly. "And *I* style myself the mystic libertine! Vraiment, I am tempted by the song of my spirit to join you. . . . But no, this is a venture for two young lovers, nē, a romance for a dyad, hardly suitable for the sort of ménage à trois we would form together. But know that Omar Ki Benjamin is with you in spirit, and as a bona fide thereof, the following oath: should you safely return, I will compose a paean to your triumph; if such should not be the case, your memory will be honored in a tragic ode. So from a certain perspective, you cannot fail, my brave kinder, for one way or the other, you will live forever as the heroic or tragic protagonists of high art!"

With this supportive if somewhat egoistic benediction, and the bright morning sun at our back, we set out westward across the endless green veldt of the treetops, proceeding quite literally by leaps and bounds toward our unknown destiny deep within the Bloomenveldt, though of just how deep into the mysteries at its heart we would penetrate, and of just how strange our divergent destinies therein would become, we were cruelly and mercifully ignorant.

We passed the first day of our journey in entirely locomotive pursuits, bounding in great soaring leaps across a treetop landscape that assumed a certain oceanic if lovely sameness as soon as we had lost sight of the actual sea. The great arboreal meadowland rolling and tossing in the breeze extended as far as the eye could see, and since the only geographical relief was that of the occasional tree crown which grew a few meters taller than the generality of the veldt, the eye could see in a great unobstructed circle from horizon to horizon.

While in a certain sense the ambiance of our passage was therefore not unlike what I had upon occasion experienced power-skiing on Glade's ocean beyond the sight of land, the endless vista of the Bloomenveldt induced none of the visual ennui of a featureless sea, for far from presenting a boundless surface of featureless green, the Bloomenveldt was a splendid carpet of more colors than the memory could count or the eye resolve into anything but a wild prismatic smear, for the flowers grew everywhere, and the hues and forms thereof seemed, if anything, more profusely diverse the further inward we traveled.

Then too it was possible to catch glimpses upon occasion from the apogees of our leaps of the denizens of the treetops gathered around their favored flowers, though these creatures never failed to scatter into the foliage upon any attempt at closer approach.

After countless hours of springing from leaf to leaf with my conscious attention all but subsumed in the repetitive if delightful mechanics thereof, engulfed in the endless green sameness and equally endless floral variety of this universe in the treetops, I began to feel like a natural creature of the Bloomenveldt myself. Guy and I, like the creatures of any forest, soon enough came to tell the passage of the hours by the movement of the sun across the sky, for only when the disc thereof began to slide down past the sharp green line of the western horizon, sending pale streamers of purple and orange across the blue of the heavens

259

and deepening shadows across the Bloomenveldt, did we feel any sense of fatigue.

And even this was not so much a soreness of muscles, which in fact might have easily enough pressed on far into the night given the feather-lightness provided to their burdens by our floatbelts, but a certain self-satisfied if somewhat tremulous psychic fatigue in the face of oncoming night.

Of our first night on the Bloomenveldt, there is little to relate in terms of outré visions, but much to relate in terms of unsettling sounds and the impingement thereof on our spirits.

As twilight began to come on in earnest, we sought out a leafy bed well beyond any floral sphere of influence, for our pact to the contrary notwithstanding, it would have been impossible to consume our meal of cold concentrates through a mask, nor did the prospect of remaining masked while the other ate have much appeal given the less than festive nature of the fare to begin with. Moreover, it had not occurred to me until I was faced with the actual practical reality that *sleeping* in a filter mask was hardly the sort of physical discomfort or psychic claustrophobia that I would wish to inflict on either Guy or myself alone in a strange forest in the blackest of nights.

By the time we had found a neutral enough leaf, there was just enough light left to unpack our rations by, and by the time we had gobbled down fare that differed little from fressen save in the addition of unconvincing ersatz flavorings of anonymous vegetables and meat, the Bloomenveldt lay in the full thrall of night.

Under a mighty canopy of coldly luminescent stars, the world of the treetops lay in convoluted blackness, illumined pallidly thereby only sufficient unto transforming the dark shapes of the tree crowns into enigmas which the eye might populate with an abundance of fantastic and mayhap frightening forms. These phantoms of the night were given voice by the wind brushing through the leaves, and the chitterings, scrapings, and rustlings of unseen creatures.

Then too, the vagrant breezes blew ghostly wisps of floral perfumes to our unmasked nostrils, so that faint traces of chemical imperatives teased and swirled just beyond the conscious apprehension of our brains. Tendrils of torpor, fading mists of pheromonic lust, vagrant dying traces of indefinable sublimities . . .

Guy and I huddled on our leaf in each other's arms. Little was said, for there was little to say and much to feel, as we lay there in the velvety darkness under the glory of the stars, rocked by the wind shaking the treetops, listening to the vague murmurings and chitterings, inhaling faint fragrances that moved our spirits to contemplative torpors, and at length to slow and languorous lovemaking that arose seamlessly from the vapors of the night, and subsided just as imperceptibly into a sleep informed by exotic unremembered dreams.

In the morning we arose, blinking and stretching in the all-too-brilliant actinic light of dawn. After a cold breakfast of concentrates and water from our canteens, we donned our filter masks and pressed on to the west.

The second day on the Bloomenveldt differed little from the first, save that by late morning clouds began to form, and by early afternoon they burst forth with a brief but drenching warm rain, which forced us to take cover until it had passed. Ah, but even as the storm subsided into a lingering mist, the sun burst through the dissipating clouds, and for perhaps fifteen minutes a great rainbow formed, overarching a Bloomenveldt whose every leaf and flower glistened with a diamond sheen of moisture.

More to the pragmatic point perhaps, every depression in every leaf filled itself up with water whose chemical purity approached distilled perfection, in contrast to the suspect fluids to be found in the cups of many flowers, allowing us to top off our canteens, drink our fill, and ablute ourselves before traveling on.

Nor did our second night on the Bloomenveldt differ in any significant aspect from the first, and on the morrow we were awoken once more by the first full light of day, breakfasted, and went on. Once more the sky clouded toward noon and rained its life-sustaining moisture on the Bloomenveldt in an early afternoon shower of some strength but little duration, though this time we were somewhat disappointed when no rainbow formed as the sun overcame the mists.

But whatever disappointment we may have felt at the failure of this meteorological grace note to appear was soon forgotten, for it could not have been more than an hour after the end of the rain when at last we spotted humans.

I had ended a leap half a bound ahead of Guy, and was

awaiting his landing before jumping off again when he came down beside me shaking his head and waving his arms. "Wait Sunshine!" he cried. "I do believe I've seen Bloomenkinder! Or at any rate, something human."

"Where?"

He pointed off to the southwest. "No more than four hundred meters," he said. "By a yellow flower streaked with red. Let us proceed cautiously, for they may be as shy as the animals of the forest."

And so we did, jumping from leaf to leaf in short shallow arcs, rather than bounding along bumptiously at the full stretch of our powers. Soon we could make out three human shapes, raggedly clothed, but clothed nonetheless, gathered about a large open yellow bloom with red-veined petals and a cluster of short, fat, black stamens.

"How should we proceed. . . ?" Guy mused.

I shrugged. "A sudden approach might startle, and stealth might signal treacherous intent, so let us simply come upon them at an easy walk in plain sight like the friendly innocents we are."

And so we stepped out from concealment and strolled boldly but deliberately across the leaves toward the yellow flower. Far from fleeing at the sight of us, or taking any umbrage at our approach, or contrawise calling out greetings, the three habitués thereof seemed to all but ignore us, even after we had made our way to the edge of their flower.

Two men and a woman, all of them sleek with fat, reposed supinely on the flower's petals, their backs resting against the black stamens from which they were languidly clawing handfuls of crumbly black pollen which they proceeded to stuff in their mouths with complete disregard for the niceties of table manners. The tatters of cloth clinging to random areas of their corpulent bodies gave clear evidence that they had once been citizens of civilized realms, but their vacantly dreamy eyes and slackly torpid grins did not exactly bespeak an urbane awareness.

"Greetings, Bloomenkinder," I finally said, for want of any more cunning conversational ploy. I was rewarded by a certain mildly interested focusing of dim attention in our direction, which is to say they deigned to look at us, and the woman plucked a handful of pollen from the stamen behind her and held it forth in a rather indifferent gesture of offering.

262

"Mangia. . . ." she suggested in a peculiar voice that seemed somehow befuddled at its own existence, as if this might have been the first word she had uttered in weeks.

"No, thank you," Guy said uneasily. "We've already dined."

The fatter of the two men stroked the surface of the petal beside him in a gesture that, under the circumstances, seemed quite obscene.

Guy and I glanced at each other, entirely taken aback by this unwholesome spectacle of human reversion. "Uh . . . have you dwelt here long. . . ?" Guy asked in an inanely conversational tone whose normality seemed utterly inappropriate to the situation. But then what manner of discourse *should* one adopt to extract information from such creatures?

"How . . . long . . ." the woman muttered in an uninflected monotone, as if unsuccessfully attempting to grasp a concept whose meaning had long since fled. The three of them exchanged slow, befuddled glances.

"Bitte, are there other humans in this area?" I essayed.

"Humans . . ."

In some exasperation, I pointed in turn to the three of them, Guy, and myself, then counted off five fingers. "*Human*," I explained. "Here. Five." I swung my other arm in a wide arc as if to encompass the nearby forest, wriggling the fingers of that hand speculatively. "More? More humans?"

At length, this seemed to penetrate the perfumed fog to some small extent. "Humans . . ." mused the less obese man. He held up a hand and stared at it stupidly for a moment. Then he began to wriggle his fingers. He raised his other hand and began to wriggle the fingers thereof as well. Soon all three of them were wriggling all available fingers, giggling, and chanting "Humans . . . humans . . . humans . . ."

"Around other flowers?"

They gave over their gesticulating and peered at me dimly, as if wriggling their fingers and pondering a second word was a bit more than they could manage at the same time.

"*Flower*," I said, pointing to the bloom which so obviously held them in thrall, then holding up a single finger. I held up my other hand and wriggled my fingers questioningly. "*More* flowers? With *more* humans?"

263

Once more the three of them began to wriggle all of their fingers. "Humans . . . flowers . . . humans . . . flowers . . ."

When after another bout of giggling they had exhausted their interest and lapsed into silence, the woman regarded me with what under the circumstances passed for an expression of some intensity and at length summoned up what was no doubt an impressive skein of words, given the source. "Humans . . . flowers . . ." she said, spreading her arms wide and wriggling all of her fingers. "Red . . . blue . . . white . . . purple . . ." Then she ceased this flurry, stroked the yellow petal on which she lay, and painted an expression of orgasmic ecstasy across her slack features. *"Yellow . . ."* she purred emphatically. "Yellow, yellow, yellow, ah! ah! ah!"

"Ah! Ah! Ah!"

The three of them commenced to moan softly in rough unison, lying flat out on the petals now as if exhausted by their mighty intellectual efforts, and evinced no further interest in our existence.

"Higher forms?" I sniffed contemptuously to Guy. *"Noble flowers? Merde!"*

Guy shrugged. "Mayhap unknown inner bliss lies within these seemingly decadent corpuses. . . ?" he suggested ironically.

"Bien," I told him. "Then perhaps you care to unmask and smell the pretty flower. . . ?"

Even Guy Vlad Boca blanched at this jocular invitation. "There *is* a bright side, however," he pointed out. "We have proven that there *are* humans in the deep Bloomenveldt. We have proven that the gnomes of the research domes know not whereof they speak."

"Have we? Or have we merely discovered the handful of poor pathetic wretches of *which* they speak?"

"Quièn sabe?" Guy admitted. "Far too soon to tell. Let us tarry awhile in these environs and see what further close exploration may discover."

Vraiment, further explorations in this area over the next two days did prove fruitful, if less than exalting, for we encountered upward of a dozen flowers attended by small groups of apparently formerly civilized human revertees, and, given the wide scattering of our discoveries, the random nature of our search,

264

and the profusion of flowers in the vecino, no doubt we failed to discover a good many more.

As for the Bloomenkinder tribes of which the tales told, these were nowhere in evidence, for nowhere did we encounter more than three or four humans in attendance at any bloom, and by the tattered rags still clinging to their bodies, it was evident that these were all folk who originated in civilized realms, rather than being the mythical offspring of generations of indigenous savages, noble or otherwise.

For the most part, they were no more verbal, and sometimes less, than the first group we had encountered, though the nature of their devotions varied with the flowers they chose to attend, or more aptly put perhaps, with the variety of flower that had captured their spirits.

As well as three more examples of the yellow flower with black stamens, we encountered acolytes of a certain puffy black bloom who exhibited a mild form of territorial behavior, locking hands to form a circle around the object of their affection at our approach, and devotees of a certain species of brilliant pinkish flower who, by pantomimed gestures, invited us to join them in the energetic if inartistic orgiastic figures which they seemed capable of sustaining indefinitely under the influence of this bloom of animal lust.

Not even Guy was tempted to personal experimentation with the psychotropics offered up by the flowers we encountered in those two days, for it seemed all too clear that these revertees had fallen under the thrall of molecules originally evolved to evoke the rude mammalian drives of the native fauna, so that the states of consciousness induced thereby could hardly be said to be elevated above the human norm.

Nor might any of these psychotropics be said to be marketable, save perhaps as less than subtle remedies for anorexia, sexual ennui, insomnia, or worse, as agents of unscrupulous behavioral control.

On the afternoon of the third day, however, we happened upon a new variety of flower which tempted us sorely indeed.

Making our way via a series of short shallow leaps, we rounded a hillock of a tree crown to find ourselves directly confronted with an overhanging bell-shaped bloom whose pale and translucent violet petals cast an all-but-ultraviolet glow over the

265

mossy green pollen bed beneath it. Upon which two human figures were languorously copulating side by side in a slow, steady rhythm.

Indeed, to call this copulation would seem to be unjust, for the gaunt rag-clad man and the equally gaunt woman, while anything but appetizing in our eyes, were manifestly perfect each to the other in their own. For in the face of their beatific smiles, their tender gazes, and the very rhythms they offered up to each other's delight, one would have had to have been an utter churl to deny that, beneath the violet canopy and under the pheromonic influence thereof, they were truly making love.

Vraiment, Guy and I found ourselves holding hands and speaking in hushed whispers as we stood before this somehow charming, not to say arousing, tantric figure.

"We can hardly intrude upon such dyadic bliss. . . ."

"Indeed, let us wait until they have reached their final cusps, nē. . . ."

As it turned out, the latter stratagem proved as fruitless as the former politesse proved superfluous, for their passage d'amour went on interminably, which is to say that the rhythm thereof seemed designed to prolong the tantric exercise into infinity by the eschewing of any climactic cusp.

At length, Guy's mounting impatience overcame his gallantry. "This could go on forever," he whispered, securing a vacuum vial from his pack. "I *must* have a sample of this psychotropic!"

So saying, and against my hushed protestations to the contrary, he stole close upon them, vial in hand.

Hola, it was as if he did not exist! Their passage d'amour continued unabated and untrammeled as he crawled around the flower gathering vapors, nor did they pay him any heed when, seeing this, he experimentally exposed himself to their full vision. Indeed, not even when I strode boldly up to Guy and tugged him away by the sleeve did our presence have any discernible effect.

Vraiment, not even when we forgot to hush our speech in our excitement did our existence intrude upon the perfect dyadic consciousness of the lovers on the flower.

"We must try this, you and I, nē!" Guy exclaimed.

"I long to experience such bliss as well," I agreed tremulously. "But if we do, will we not be lost?"

"To all save each other, mayhap . . ." he said dreamily.

266

"We must think on this before we lose all capacity for same," I told him sharply. "Though certainement it would appear we have found a hint of floral paradise out of which poetry and romantic legend might justly arise . . ."

Eschewing other objects of exploration, we discovered three more of the violet blooms d'amour during that afternoon and the next morning, and on each we found dyadic figures similarly enraptured in perfect tantric bliss, indeed a bliss which seemed quite indefatigable, for we had yet to encounter such lovers engaged in eating, repose, or any other activity save endless love.

Guy, for his part, grew more and more displeased with my refusal to unmask with him and share such preternatural pleasures, while I demurred under the guise of unwillingness to eject lovers from their flower by main force. In truth, however, while like any natural woman my spirit, not to say my flesh, grew more and more desirous of knowing such erotic ecstasies, my mind rang bells of warning, for if such was the puissance of this flower's pheromone of passion that in its thrall lovers eschewed all nutriment or rest, how long before such tantric demons expired in blissful famishment in each other's arms?

Inevitably, we finally discovered such a bloom unoccupied, a vacant boudoir bathed in violet light, awaiting only two wandering creatures such as we.

"A sign, nicht wahr?" Guy insisted. "A clear signal from destiny, nē?"

"Mayhap from fate . . ."

"Pah! When imbibing wine, do you stop short of intoxication? When engaged in sexual congress, do you take care to avoid orgasm?"

"To quote the same source, I am a mystic libertine, not an imbecile."

Guy regarded me with an expression somewhere between contemptuous anger and a sullen thwarted pout.

"Very well then," I declared. "I invoke our pact. Which is to say that one of us must at all times play ground control to the psychonaut. Therefore, let us repair to the flower of your desires, one of us unmasked, and when that personage has fully experienced the naked joys thereof, the functions shall be reversed."

"This is the meanness of spirit in which you propose to conduct a passage of transcendent amour?"

"No meanness of spirit is intended," I told him crossly, "in token of which, and in the absence of any masculine gallantry to the contrary, you may have the honor of removing your mask first."

To this open-hearted gesture, Guy could hardly make any further demur, and so he nodded in silent agreement and began to doff his clothes. I did likewise, and in not much more time than it takes to tell, we stood naked before each other, or rather adorned only by the filter masks covering our noses and mouths, a spectacle inducive of a good deal more mirth than lust.

But no sooner had Guy removed his mask than the ironic grin which this bizarre vision had smeared across his face vanished, to be replaced by a beatific smile of priapic though not untender lust, unmistakably counterpointed, as it were, by the all-but-instant erection of his insistent lingam.

In truth more bemused than aroused, I allowed him to seize my hand and lead me forthwith into the shaft of violet light beneath the translucent canopy of the flower. In this venue I thought not to activate my ring of Touch, for while Guy had never voiced wonder at my preternatural erotic puissance, putting it down, no doubt, to his own preternatural capacity for the enjoyment of pleasure, it seemed to me that chemical enhancement would be more than sufficient without resorting to the electronic.

From my point of view, there is little to report of this opening movement of our two-part duet save the seeming endlessness thereof, the mighty duration of Guy's phallic prowess, and the ironic fact that it was Sunshine, the ground control, who experienced cusp after cusp via the ministrations of her pheromonically-enhanced psychonaut. For once, it was Guy who was given over to the granting of pleasure without thought or rhythm designed to bring about his own orgasmic completion, and I who surrendered sweetly to the abundance of my own ecstasies.

Vraiment, to the superabundance thereof, for Guy went on and on and on in the same even rhythm, long after sweet ecstasies had given way to a surfeit of pleasure and delight had given way to fatigue, and even fatigue had given way to a boredom of orgasms, if such can be imagined.

When I could tolerate this tender and loving selfless performance no longer, I at last activated the Touch and, seizing him by the very root of his lingam, brought him to a moaning, shuddering, piercing conclusion, which I felt sure would leave the mightiest of lovers incapable of proceeding further.

But no, quelle chose, no sooner had he brought his ragged panting under some semblance of control, than his still triumphant phallus was at it again, determined to fill me with yet more unwanted pleasure.

There seemed to be only one thing for it, even though I was certain that no power in the worlds of men or elsewhere could now provoke me to further desire. I tore the filter mask from my face and affixed it over Guy's by main force.

How wrong I was!

No sooner had I taken my first unmasked breath than a pungent, sweet, musky aroma went straight from my nostrils to the very back reaches of my brain, from which it flowed like a living serpent of fire down my spine to ignite a veritable kundalinic explosion in my lower chakras. Vraiment, a rosy, languid explosion which billowed upward, outward, and inward from the base of my spine to fill my loins, and my limbs, and indeed my cerebrum, with roiling clouds of sensuous pink smoke, which in less time than it takes to tell had completely consumed all other aspects of my being.

It seemed to me, or at any rate to the extent that there remained a "me," that my body had become an ecstatic outline of passionate fire, like the fabled burning bush, aflame yet unconsumed.

I seized Guy in my arms, rolled over upon him, and impaled the quick of him in the rosy translucence of my flesh. Ah, oh, he was beautiful! The flesh of his body had the warm sleekness of silk before a bonfire. Each ecstatic tremor of his flesh sent crystal fragments of achingly tender joy down my nerve trunks, the sounds of his pleasures ignited sparkles in my heart, and his face was that of a veritable deity, a mask of tantric perfection auraed by the glow of his marvelous spirit.

There was nothing in the universe but the exquisite texture of satiny flesh and silken sighs, nought existed but the rose-colored breath of his flesh against mine.

How long this persisted, memory would not bind. There were cries, and moans, and tremors, and wordless shouts, and then a thin and agonized voice crying "Stop! Stop! Stop!"

Then the mindless creature of fire that I had become found itself being borne through the air like a weightless cloud, something vile and rubbery was forced onto my face . . .

And . . .

And the sentient human that I had been found herself seated on a leaf gazing wildly at Guy. Both of us were masked, both of us were panting with exhaustion, and both of us were redolent with passionate effluvia and sweat.

We stared at each other, blinking, for a long while before either of us managed to speak.

"Vraiment, you were right, unmasked together, we would have been lost forever," Guy finally breathed.

"It would almost have been worth it. . . ." I sighed.

But not even Guy Vlad Boca was ready to suggest that we repeat this experiment mutually unmasked, nor did the notion of enjoying such dangerous ecstasies again as alternating psychonauts and ground controls much appeal to either of us. For while in a certain sense it could be said that the ground control drew as much erotic benefit from the psychonaut's chemically augmented tantric puissance as he did, the sexual disjunction cut both ways as well. For under the influence of the flower, the masked lover would always be pleasured to the point of boredom or pain, while the lover in thrall to the flower quite literally could never be sated.

Clearly this flower was only for lovers to whom mutual erotic seppuku was an acceptable ultimate consummation, and expiration via terminal fatigue or famishment was an acceptable price to pay. For such samurai romantics, the perfume of the violet flower might be a great boon, and indeed, under controlled conditions it might be a sovereign remedy for impotence, libidinal ennui, and even conjugal fecklessness, or so Guy believed.

Certainement, here was a product that Interstellar Master Traders should have no trouble marketing at a considerable profit. As for the morality of such an enterprise, Guy declared, the nature of the psychotropic's effect should be forthrightly delineated to the purchaser, whose destiny thereby would be placed entirely in his own hands.

Be that as it may, what we had experienced had demonstrated that there could be more to the Bloomenveldt's blandishments than crude appeal to simple mammalian tropisms, for the violet flower, certainement, produced an intense state of erotic arousal in which the spiritual dimension was not absent, as if somehow there was indeed a floral intelligence at work on the Bloomenveldt whose biochemical sapience was capable of the subtlety necessary to touch the human heart.

Mayhap we would have been able to put it all down to chance conjunction between Belshazaar's floral biochemistry and a randomly evolved human congruence therewith in certain isolated cerebral centers had we not soon thereafter encountered another mode of human and floral chemical convergence which affected what one would have thought were entirely spiritual levels of human sapience.

Consciously or not, whether simply carrying forth our original plan or being drawn deeper into the Bloomenveldt by the natural order of things, we drifted slowly westward during the next two days. Here we continued to find small groups of humans in thrall to what we had bizarrely enough begun to dismiss as quotidian blooms, and here too dyads blissfully bewitched by the flower of violet passion were also in evidence.

But now for the first time we encountered solitary humans in psychotropic communion with their own flower.

The upright petals of the flower in question were always blue, though the tint thereof might vary, and the stamen consisted of a large flat mound covered with fist-sized grains of soft white pollen. Upon this pallet the human devotee sat motionless with nourishment ready at hand gazing wide-eyed not at the glories and wonders of the Bloomenveldt but at entirely subjective vistas within.

Male and female, they were all in those terminal years of their lifespan when the hair grays and thins, and the skin dries into parchment, and the vital energies may no longer be reignited by the Healers' arts. But if their bodies were dismaying reminders of ultimate mortality, the spirits which peered inward in their limpid empty eyes, were, if the same are truly mirrors of the soul as the poets contend, in blissful transcendence of the limits of temporal linearity, at least from their own point of view.

Even such callow mystic libertines as we could not summon up the crudeness to attempt to rouse such living buddhas to discourse by insistent hectorings, nor would such a stratagem

271

likely have succeeded, for all such hermits that we were to encounter in the next two days moved only their hands to convey the occasional pollen grain to their mouths, and otherwise might have been temple icons of stone for all the awareness of or interest in the external realm they betrayed.

Whether such buddhas were drawn to the lotus, or whether the flowers were capable of granting ultimate enlightenment to ordinary human dross, or whether for that matter, these living icons in fact contained the spirits of which they spoke at all, we could in truth know not, for total vegetative nonsentience for all I knew could produce the same visual effect as transcendence of maya's veil. And indeed certain cynical wits have been known to contend that the mental states themselves are much the same.

"It would seem there is only one method of discerning whether these ancients are enlightened beings whose spirits soar in realms of grandeur beyond maya's tawdry veils or whether their sapience has been extinguished leaving only vacuous protoplasmic shells behind," Guy opined the night of the second day among the babas of the Bloomenveldt.

"Namely?"

"Namely to inhale the lotus breath ourselves and learn whether we become bodhis or zombies. . . ."

"Guy! Surely not even *you* would lay such a wager!"

"Of course I spoke in jest," he said, laughing rather unconvincingly and hugging me to him. "Still, if one *knew* matters were what they seem, what reason would there be to dally with lesser amusements endlessly if the ultimate were truly available for a mere breath of perfume?"

"*This for one!*" I declared pettishly, thumbing on the Touch and pulling on his lingam, for while Guy's mood was hardly one which aroused me to erotic passion, I knew no other more immediately puissant means of changing this unwholesome subject.

But as it turned out, on the afternoon of the next day we came upon a baba of the Bloomenveldt who at last deigned to address us.

Bathed in a golden beam of sunlight streaming through a break in the foliage behind as if the whole scene had been deliberately lit with thespic intent, was a great fan of petals whose hue was a blue that was almost black, the hue of that region of a planetary atmosphere where sky becomes space, or of that celestial moment between sunset and night. Upon the flat stamen covered with white pollen sat a naked man with hair and beard of the same color, his legs folded under him in the classic lotus posture, his back to the floral halo like a figure out of primeval temple art, and his lips creased in a beatific smile.

But, far from being lost in internal vistas, his great brown eyes tracked us as we approached with a clarity and sentience impossible to deny.

Nor, it seemed, could our eyes break their lock on his, as, without consultation, Guy and I strode hand in hand toward this baba and seated ourselves before him like dutiful acolytes before their guru. Mayhap it was the ambiance which so compelled us, mayhap there was true power in this ancient's eyes, or mayhap we both had the same thought, namely that since *this* hermit so manifestly acknowledged our existence, such an approach might at last induce one of these sphinxes to speak.

"Speak to us, bitte, baba," I said in a firm but respectful voice, "and show us that someone at least is at home beyond that sage facade."

The smile broadened into something more like a grin. "I have never been more at home behind my eyes," said a calm, clear voice.

"You speak!"

"Why then do the other hermits remain silent?"

"Only they may tell you, kind, and they choose silence."

"But you *do* speak to us," I said. "Why are you different?"

"Are not all humans different, each from the other?" the baba said. "In the worlds of men, I was a dedicated pedagog, so mayhap before my final flower do I choose to speak to young spirits in the manner of a loquacious bodhisattva."

"If this is so, why do you sit passively awaiting death, rather than return to the worlds of men and go up and out doing noble deeds like a *true* bodhisattva?"

The old man's eyes widened, and his permanent smile strayed for a moment from beatitude to the mundanely specific, to wit that of his former pedagogical self happening suddenly on an unexpectedly sharp student.

"In the worlds of men, I would expire raging against the

dying of the light," he said. "Only within the celestial sphere of my perfect flower may I know my final moment in the Tao."

"Hola! Then this is indeed the perfect lotus of ultimate enlightenment!" Guy exclaimed, fingering his filter mask in a most unsettling manner.

"Many flowers grow on the Bloomenveldt. Here each of us may find the flower of their perfection."

"Mayhap this is mine . . ." Guy said breathlessly, and made to remove it.

But before I could move to stop him, the old man stayed him with a sudden instant upraising of his hand, a puissant gesture indeed in light of his previous utter immobility. And when he then spoke, the tranquil certitude of the bodhi was married to the authority of the teacher.

"Seek first your own full blossoming, young spirit, before you contemplate this final flower!"

"Well spoken, well spoken indeed!" I was moved to enthusiastically declare.

And at this, by signs so subtle as to be perceivable only en gestalt, the spirit animating the withering body evinced a preparation to withdraw from further worldly discourse.

"Wait!" said Guy. "At least tell me then how I am to *know* the flower of my own perfection!"

"Let the Perfume of Paradise come unto *thee*, Mohammed."

"Vraiment, of course, we can only find our way by losing it, nē?" Guy exclaimed. "We must breathe in the spirit of this enchanted forest, we must seek our destiny bravely unmasked, that is what he is telling us, Sunshine!"

"This koan affords me no such unequivocal satori," I told him sourly.

"Merde, tell this groundling in words she may comprehend, bitte!" he demanded quite boorishly of the silent bodhi.

But the old man quite ignored this unseemly cajolement. His spirit had long since departed to the untrammeled contemplation of regions within. No effort of ours could conjure it to speak again.

274

18

Guy, on the other hand, was far from being at a loss for words.

"Look at the Bloomenveldt, Sunshine!" he proclaimed after we had withdrawn a decent distance, and I humored him to the extent of staring out across the endless rolling vista of foliage and flowers. "Can your eyes tell one part of it from another? Regard the sounds of the Bloomenveldt! Can you discern anything more informative than the whispering of the wind through the treetops or the chittering of unseen fauna?"

"Bien, the cogency of your discourse has convinced me that it all looks and sounds the same. . . ." I said sourly.

"But we know it is *not* all the same, do we not? Is it not quite obvious?"

"Isn't *what* quite obvious?"

"Merde, that you cannot use your eyes and ears to track down the inner mysteries of the Bloomenveldt, of course!" Guy exclaimed as if addressing a dimwit. "You must use your nose to follow that which rides upon the wind! Surely you can see that?"

"I am not an imbecile, Guy!" I snapped back pettishly. "But can't *you* see that we would like as not lose our way therein if we attempted to doff our masks and follow a floral piper?"

"But you yourself have said we can always find the coast by following the sunrise," Guy pointed out slyly. "There will be little danger if we adhere to the terms of our traveling treaty. One of us to be the psychonaut, and the other the ground control. Remember! It was *your* idea, nē?"

"*My idea?* It was never my notion to *travel* unmasked, only to insure that one of us always retain reason if we paused now and again to sample the perfume of a flower!"

Guy stared angrily at me.

"What do you suggest then, that we give over our quest just when we have finally caught the scent of our quarry?"

I regarded him with no less pique, but when it came to formulating a cogent rejoinder, my wits failed me.

"Does the silence of the sphinx signal assent?" he persisted sarcastically. "Vraiment, enough, *I* take your silence for assent, whether that is your intent or not!" And so saying, before I could protest, he doffed his filter mask, took a deep breath, and regarded me triumphantly. "Voilà, the intrepid psychonaut!" he declared. "Come, Sunshine, surely by your own lights, you cannot allow me to proceed without a ground control?"

And with that, he bounded off to the west, leaving me no choice but to follow him, muttering futile imprecations under my breath.

For the rest of the afternoon, Guy never paused long enough for me to hector him, but led us on a ragged zig-zag course generally westward, which is to say the direction logic had been taking us in the first place, before he decided to allow the backbrain to follow where the nose might lead it. And while I found his puissance as a tracker less than overwhelming, and his cavalier unilateralism boorish in the extreme, at length I was forced to admit that I could discern no obvious sign of danger.

Guy would drift down onto a leaf and kick off in his next leap apparently without conscious thought, though the direction of our vector would almost always alter slightly. In this manner, with Guy at the helm, did we proceed westward, like a sailboat tacking across unfelt breezes.

As the afternoon wore on, my anger attenuated as my curiosity began to come to the fore. What arcane scent was my foolhardy psychonaut following? What visions were wafting through his brain on the pheromonic wind? Or were we tacking this way and that to no coherent purpose?

276

Vraiment, if truth be told, by the time night began to fall, and prudence constrained even Guy to seek out a leaf well clear of any floral influences, my curiosity had taken on a certain envious tinge, for while I was not an imbecile, had I not readily enough owned to being a mystic libertine? Which is to say that I had never been one to stop short of orgasm in the throes of tantric bliss, nor, even in Nouvelle Orlean, had I been much for allowing even the most venturesome of swains to boast that they could go where I dare not follow.

As soon as we had broken out our concentrates, therefore, I quite forgot the ireful tirade I had been rehearsing to myself during the hot-blooded afternoon's journey, in favor of satisfying the curiosity which had come on with the glorious soul-stirring colors of the Bloomenveldt sunset.

But Guy, alas, from this vantage beyond the olfactory visions of the flowers, was hard put to render the memories thereof in the sprach of the poor quotidian ground control.

"It was as if . . . It seemed as though . . ." He shrugged, bit off a mouthful of concentrate, and chewed it down slowly before he tried again, as if trying to masticate some coherent verbal juices out of it. "Dilute residues of numerous faint far-off psychotropics in a liter or two of fine white wine and sip steadily at it as you gambol freely in the gardens of paradise . . ." he declared extravagantly.

"While that may serve as an excellent recipe for achieving a simulation of the experience, it leaves something to be desired in the way of descriptive imagery," I complained.

Guy gave me a strange look then, a sad look, the look of someone struggling to regain the fading memory of a moment of satoric enlightenment.

"It cannot be described in imagery, no matter how puissant," he told me. "Vraiment, it would appear that the memory of what it was like cannot even attempt to express itself in the realm of maya, for now does it all seem like a wonderful dream, existing on a plane of consciousness one cannot even quite remember down here with the groundlings . . ."

"With the groundlings?" I exclaimed. "Who are these groundlings to whom you are referring? There are only Guy Vlad Boca and Sunshine Shasta Leonardo alone here in the forest."

If truth be told, I was doubly vexed, first at his arrogant

277

proclamations of visionary superiority, and worse, at the extent to which his characterization of my role as ground control cut at the truth.

"Is this the mystic libertine who now speaks?" Guy taunted challengingly. "Is this the true Child of Fortune's spirit? Will you now take your rightful turn as psychonaut on the morrow?"

"Certainement!" I declared without thinking, though not without wondering as soon as the words passed my lips whether I spoke with the true Spark or whether I was merely foolishly but inevitably rising to the bait of reckless masculine challenge.

Be that as it may, in the morning, after we breakfasted quickly and abluted ourselves with morning mist condensed in the cup of a nearby leaf, Guy donned the mask of ground control, and with a gallant little bow, invited me to assume the lead, and I took up the gauntlet.

As always, we had chosen our leaf for the night to be well clear of any strong floral effluvia, so that when I inhaled deeply in search of a sign, I sensed little more than the rich odor of abundant greenery, the dawning savor of mist evaporating in warm sunlight, and vague undertones of hidden complexity to the vintage well below the sphere of conscious apprehension.

For lack of any more promising course of action, I put the rising sun at my back, adjusted my floatbelt to .1 g, and took off in a soaring leap to the due west.

As I rose upward, the heavy background odor of the greenery fell away like the thick shielding layers of a planet's lower atmosphere, and I found myself sniffing the rarefied ions of the psychostratosphere. In truth the molecules thereof were so dispersed up here at the apogee of my leap as to make the air seem almost odorless in contrast to the leafy aroma of the Bloomenveldt's surface.

But on the other hand, up here every flower seemed to have contributed a bit of its perfume to an incredibly complex but attenuated brew in which no single tropism could dominate. This mélange of phantom odors seemed to go directly to the brain centers themselves, where it manifested itself as a faint psychic scent, the breath of the Bloomenveldt entire, like the whisperings of a million distant voices.

Vraiment, it *was* like a sip of well-diluted psychotropic wine, for there were exhilaration and unvoiced promises in the savor of the breath of the Enchanted Forest entire, though no pheromonic imperative stood out far enough to reach the conscious level of the mind, and none held sway long enough to be coherent even to the backbrain. Thus the spirit that chose to ride this most ethereal of breezes might be deflected this way and that by the molecule of the moment, like a monomer film riding the solar wind.

Which is to say that when I came down on a leaf, I twisted my body in a movement that would seem to have been derived from the ballistic inevitablity of the moment, but which I nevertheless found to be deflecting my previous vector when in the same motion I pushed off.

The movement felt right, is all that I can really say about it, it seemed an inevitable step in the dance of faint floral essences in my mind, and in the dance of my spirit through the forest of flowers.

As the day wore on, I felt more at ease following the perfumed wind streaming through the unbound hair of my mind, more in harmony with Guy as well, indeed thankful to him for daring me to follow his brave example, for now I found myself trusting the caring spirit of the Bloomenveldt.

What reason was there to mistrust the spirit of a vegetative sapience whose own self-interest led it to design essences contrived to entice our delight? Why would such a symbiote do its partners harm?

For in the complex perfume high above the Bloomenveldt one could sense the moral neutrality of the flowers. If, as the baba said, the Bloomenveldt eventually offered each spirit its perfect flower, then did it not also follow that one could not succumb to other than the bloom of one's own perfected destiny?

Thus did I flitter vaporously for untold golden summer hours through the treetops of the Bloomenveldt like a blithe butterfly dancing joyously among the great and noble flowers.

But as the sun began to slide down from its zenith, I came down from the apogee of my latest porpoise leap through the psychotropic clouds, suddenly seized by a compulsion that had me twisting my body in an attempt to alter my ballistic trajectory in midair, which is to say a powerful odor had all at once emerged from the background, a wonderful aroma that beckoned insistently to the back reaches of my brain with extravagant promises of both perfect peace and sexual ecstasy, as if this perfume were compounded of both lotus and forthrightly erotic musk.

I came down on the next leaf somewhat clumsily, for my attempt at midair course correction was less than totally successful, just as my awareness of what I was doing had not quite yet caught up with the act itself. I bounded off again, not for maximum distance, but on a shallow arc which I now comprehended would take me to the source of the perfume, though as to why I would want to do such a thing, this was a motivational nicety which at that moment I could not quite conceptualize.

I landed on an apron of leaves upon which grew three flowers of the same species, separated each from the other by some dozen meters. Each was a towering tubular bloom whose tall and partially folded petals were colored a vibrant rose streaked with markings of an equally vibrant royal blue. The pollen-heavy blue heads of stamens peered up through the pursed floral lips at the apexes of the flowers like buds in the mouths of tall elegant vases.

This botanic detail by way of considered hindsight, for I noticed hardly anything at the time save an overwhelming bouquet of belonging and the humans clustered around each flower.

There were more of them than we had yet seen together on the Bloomenveldt before, a least a dozen, four or five to a flower. More of them than not were still adorned by scraps of civilized rags and had the overstuffed look we had so frequently seen.

But there was a far more splendid breed of human among them, nude and lithely perfect examples of both genders of our species, who stood with a proud erectness and moved with an animal grace which made it quite clear that they had never known the clothes or malaises of civilization. Vraiment, they were like a brood of avid athletes innocently chiding a congress of sybaritic gourmands with their noble bodily perfection.

All this I perceived in a gestalted instant, along with the overwhelming longing to be one of their company. Fortunately, however, Guy had caught up with me, and before I could lope forward, he had me in an embrace as much of triumphant joy as of restraint.

"You've done it, Sunshine!" he exulted. "You've found the Bloomenkinder!"

So it would appear I had. As I stood there struggling against Guy's embrace which was preventing me from achieving my joyous floral destiny on the one hand, and grateful for same in the higher centers of my mind on the other, I was enabled thereby to both sense the reality with nostrils entirely under its pheromonic thrall, and view it from another perspective as a forcibly detached observer.

Two of the Bloomenkinder, if such they were, and two of the civilized revertees, sat around the base of one of the flowers gorging on clusters of large, purple, ovoid fruit, and my mouth watered its demand to gobble its succulence. A similarly integrated group seemed to be waiting at the base of the furthest flower for some unimaginable event. More of both styles of humans dozed hypnogogically around the base of the third flower, whose perfume spoke to me of the pleasures of dreamless slumber. Then all at once, or rather with a rapid but stately vegetative grace, the furthest flower peeled open to lay itself out into a luxurious carpeted mat before those humans who had apparently been awaiting just this occurrence. Forthwith, they laid themselves down on the floral carpet, and began copulating in varying figures with gay abandon, and while what reason remained found this performance a less than artful spectacle, my loins were possessed of an entirely more avid opinion.

Vraiment, my nostrils were assailed and enticed by a roil of conflicting imperatives, and mayhap it was only the concern now evident in Guy's eyes, or the power of his embrace, or some inner reservoir of resource which both gave me the moral will to possess, that enabled me to make my hands put on my mask.

I stood there hyperventilating for several moments as the perfumes cleared like a dense fog bank under a hot rising sun from the hollows and copses of my brain.

Then I saw that Guy, perhaps taking this as a sign that I merely wished to exchange functions, was about to remove his own filter mask.

"No!" I shouted, clawing his fingers away from the straps. "Under no circumstances! I was only barely able . . . I was about to . . ."

Confronted with the force and anguish of my determination,

281

Guy for once relented. "Are these not the fabled Bloomenkinder?" he said in a poutish puzzled voice. "Is this not the Perfumed Garden?"

"These may be the fabled Bloomenkinder," I told him with all the firmness I could muster, "but certainement this is not the Perfumed Garden! Far from being exalted or subtle, these flowers exude overwhelming perfumes which induce crude and basic desires no more enlightened than the fulfillment thereof which you now observe. Only if your notion of perfection is to spend the rest of your life cycling between gorging on the same fruit, torpid unconsciousness, and brute mindless copulation, should you breathe this unfiltered air!"

"But at least these may indeed be true Bloomenkinder!" Guy insisted. "At the very least, we must attempt to question them!"

This I could hardly deny, though I was a good deal less than sanguine about our ability to entice these tribespeople of the Bloomenveldt into coherent discourse.

At first, we took the path of least resistance, and attempted to rouse the sleepers from their torpor with halloos, and then shouts. But the most we could induce by these methods was the heavy peeling of an eyeball for a brief indifferent moment.

Since intruding upon an abandoned orgy for the purpose of prying away participants to willingly submit to interrogation seemed hardly practical, we repaired to the banquet of purple fruit in hopes of inducing some idle table talk.

Four tribespeople squatted on their haunches devouring great mouthfuls of fruit by the less than elegant procedure of holding the juicy ovoids up to their mouths with both hands, chomping off bites of the dripping fruit as large as their jaws could encompass, and wolfing them down with an energetic series of gobbles. Two of these were obese men still festooned with raggy tatters, whose manner of dining seemed slobbery and distasteful. Yet the other two, male and female Bloomenkinder, who by any ergonomic measure were performing precisely the same movements to precisely the same practical effect, seemed no more ill-bred in the act thereof than moussas methodically dealing with berries.

None of them reacted to our approach with startlement or flight or territorial outrage, nor, on the other hand, did any of them offer food or greeting. The long and short of it was that, despite the appearance of these bizarre auslanders in their midst, they all continued to eat in the same tranquilly obsessive manner.

"Any brilliant bon mots, Guy? I confess that I am at a loss for a suitable conversational entrée into these social circles."

Guy shrugged. "Manners, at any rate, would seem to be redundant." So saying, he fairly thrust his face upon one of the fat fellows and spoke loudly, insistently, and slowly, as one might address a very young child or a rather recalcitrant parrot. "The . . . Perfumed . . . Garden. . . . We . . . seek . . . the . . . Perfumed Garden. . . . Do . . . you . . . know . . . the . . . Perfumed . . . Garden?"

The man went so far as to raise his gaze from the fruit to meet Guy's, though this did not at all disturb the gulping rhythm of his feeding.

"The Perfumed Garden! The Perfumed Garden!" Guy chanted, hand-signaling me to join his efforts. "The Perfumed Garden! The Perfumed Garden!"

At length, indeed at considerable length, our chanting drew forth a tenuous echo, much as the same procedure might eventually provoke mimicry from a talking bird or enhance the vocabulary of an infant. "Perfumed *Garden*. . . . Perfumed *Garden*. . . ." But rather than seeming to acquire a new sound, the man, blinking rapidly and giving over his chewing for a moment, seemed to be struggling to regain the sound of a distant memory.

"The Perfumed *Garden*," I said syncopatedly, and then added two more beats to the rhythm. "*We* seek the Perfumed *Garden*. . . ."

"*We* . . . seek . . . the Perfumed *Garden*. . . . Seek . . . the . . . Perfumed Garden . . . *Seek* . . . the . . . Perfumed . . . Garden. . . . *Seek* . . . the . . . Perfumed . . . Garden. . . ."

Meaning seemed to slowly leach into his parroting of the syllables and a certain dim sapience seemed to return to his eyes. He had stopped eating now, and the dripping fruit lay limply in his hands. "Seek the Perfumed Garden," he seemed to say more decisively, nodding his head almost imperceptibly as if agreeing with the wisdom of this proposition.

Having given our venture this blessing, it would seem that he had dealt with the matter to his own satisfaction, for he forthwith returned to his single-minded devouring of the purple fruit.

"The Perfumed Garden!" Guy cried, shaking the fellow back into attention by the shoulders. "Where is it?"

The obese fellow seemed to exhibit no ill temper at this admittedly boorish behavior, nor did any of his tablemates pay the matter any more heed than they had our verbal hectoring. Indeed, the tribesman almost seemed to manage a sort of smile.

"*Bloomen*kinder . . . *Bloomen*kinder . . ." he chanted, directing our attention via a glance of his eyes to the nearby examples of same.

"Ask the Bloomenkinder?" Guy demanded. "Ask the Bloomenkinder? Is that your meaning, ask the Bloomenkinder?"

"*Ask* the *Bloomen*kinder! *Ask* the *Bloomen*kinder!" the tribesman chanted, and then, having delivered up this advice, if such it was, he returned to his fruit and could not be roused to speak again even by shouting and shaking.

Shrugging, I addressed the nearest of the Bloomenkinder, a lovely female creature with taut bronzed flesh, long streaming blonde hair, a beatific smile, and lambently vacant blue eyes. "We seek the Perfumed Garden," I said, feeling rather foolish. "Is it true that you know where it lies?"

The sound of my voice caused her to look up at me for a moment, but for all the sapient response I saw in that transcendently tranquil face, I might have been addressing one of the equally beautiful and equally vapid flowers.

Nor did the male of the species prove any more responsive, though no doubt had the petals of the flower at that moment opened and the perfume d'amour blown forth, it would have been an entirely different matter. And despite my intellectual repugnance for sexual congress with insensate creatures, I almost wished they would, for seldom had I seen such a specimen of obvious animal virility.

Be that as it may, the injunction to ask the Bloomenkinder seemed some kind of dim Bloomenveldt irony, for the true Bloomenkinder seemed totally beyond responding to any verbal interrogation.

By this time the sun was beginning to sink toward the horizon, and the deepening shadows of impending twilight were beginning to spread across the foliage, casting a definite waning westering perspective over the endless veldt, in which all the dappled shadowy paths led toward sunset.

"Ask the Bloomenkinder!" I declared. "One might as well ask a marble statue!"

But even as I spoke, even as the leafy glade and its three flowers were bathed in the slanting amber light of late afternoon, the petals of the flower of copulation began to slowly fold upwards as all tantric exercises ceased. The humans left their floral boudoir to stand before it in motionless silence. So too did those among whom we stood cease their masticating, let fall the remains of their fruit, and rise slowly to their feet.

A few moments later, all those who had come to the Enchanted Forest from the worlds of men moved measuredly toward the flower where five such folk were already sleeping and joined them in the land of nod in less time than it takes to tell.

But the Bloomenkinder! Ah, the Bloomenkinder!

Wherever they had been when the floral clock had rung down day's end, so did they stand there now, and so would they stand until the sun's disc had bisected the horizon. And all of them stood there like sunflowers, staring due west along precisely the same vector, transfixed by the sunset, or mayhap turning toward that Mecca whose direction we had indeed been told only the Bloomenkinder knew.

And when we too had found our own leafy nest for the Bloomenveldt night, Guy proclaimed his unshakable conviction that the Bloomenkinder had indeed answered our question.

"Certainement, these Bloomenkinder must be in spiritual rapport with some lost Eden of theirs to the west," he insisted.

"Mayhap their genes are merely coded with some kind of tropic memory. . . ." I suggested dubiously.

"La même chose, for the further into the Bloomenveldt we penetrate, the more highly evolved the floral forms in terms of their intimate involvement with the psyches of their humans, and since these Bloomenkinder are clearly more perfectly attuned to the spirit of the forest than any other folk we have yet encountered, they must therefore derive from lands to the west. At any rate, we must certainly proceed in the direction they commend to our attention, for if such as the Perfumed Garden exists, who but the Bloomenkinder can possibly show us the way?"

"No doubt," I said, "but the way to *what?*"

"To what?" exclaimed Guy. "To the most puissant psycho-

285

tropics the Bloomenveldt has evolved from contact with our species! To the Perfumed Garden!"

"If such in fact exists," I replied, not by now sure whether I wished to attain this ultima Thule of his or feared that we would.

"Well then at least to the heart of the matter," Guy said, finally seeing that my enthusiasm in no way matched his own, though in no way giving it over for an instant. "In any event, it is *my* turn to be the psychonaut when we travel on tomorrow."

Thus did we indeed journey onward in the morning, with myself masked and following Guy, and Guy following whatever it was that came to him on the wind.

Until some time past noon, he bounded from leaf to leaf with long, high, straight leaps calculated to cover as much distance as rapidly as possible, and we proceeded in this manner due west with no tacking at all, as if by act of will he had determined to steer this steady course through the vapors.

Then, in the early afternoon, his leaps began to shorten, and the path we followed became more erratic. Several times he would leap directly upward, hang inhaling deeply at the top of his arc, and come down not a dozen meters from his point of departure. At length, his leaps became shorter but surer, and now we were running over the leaves like explorers loping over the low-gravity surface of an asteroid, zigging and zagging this way and that without any logical consideration, as if Guy were following some invisible trail like a hound on a scent.

Then all at once he slowed, and then stopped, and then stood there on a leaf peering motionlessly at something obscured from my vision by a dip in the terrain as I came up beside him.

And beheld the village, if so such a thing may be styled, of the Bloomenkinder.

Within the shallow dell of great branches immediately below us, an entire subbranch supporting as many as a hundred leaves had burst into bloom. There were at least a dozen flowers growing within meters of each other, so that the effect was almost that of a flower bed planted in an overgrown lawn. And there were several species of flower intermingling in this Bloomenveldt garden. There were brilliant pink cups like enormous open mouths whose petals were streaked with black, and flowers which were

286

the inverse color image of same. There were flowers that consisted mostly of conelike mounds of yellow pollen, and flowers that were mostly tall white petals. There were hanging clusters of lavender bells, and puffballs bursting with a profusion of rainbow hues.

And there were Bloomenkinder moving amongst the flowers, perhaps two score of them, engaged in what at least from a distance seemed almost like the varied quotidian tasks of typical village life.

Guy stood there with an utterly tranquil bliss painted across his face. "Beautiful. . . ." he sighed. "Perfect. . . ." I caught him by the hand as he began to drift forward.

"Guy! Guy! What's happening to you?"

Guy seemed to struggle with his words, even as he struggled against my restraint.

"Can't you feel it, Sunshine?" he burbled ecstatically. "The rightness of all creation . . . The great wheel slowly turning in harmony with the music of the spheres . . ."

He paused, blinking. He turned to favor me with the most radiant smile. "Fear not, ma chère," he said softly and with utterly tranquil certainty, "no harm can come to us in this Garden of Perfection."

Never had I seen Guy Vlad Boca so seemingly at peace with his own spirit, vraiment such was the calm clarity he fairly exuded, and such was the undeniable visual beauty of the village of the Bloomenkinder, that I allowed him to lead me forward among the flowers, among the perfect Bloomenkinder, with their clear and empty eyes, their magnificent unveiled physiques, and their innocent animal grace.

The Bloomenkinder moved about from flower to flower slowly and gracefully, never seeming to impede each other's movements, yet never seeming to need to step aside to avoid doing so, as if moving as parts of a single organism, or more aptly perhaps as if following a carefully crafted choreography in their waltz among the flowers.

Their eyes betrayed awareness of us just as they betrayed a certain positional awareness of each other. They seemed to regard us as natural obstacles, to be adroitly avoided with calm adjustments of their dance, but paid us no further heed. Vraiment, I too believed now that no harm could come to us here, for it was

287

as if I were walking down a street in a dream, wrapped in a voyeuristic cloak of invisibility, incapable of being harmed on the one hand, and incapable of social intercourse with the citizens of this land of nod on the other.

But certainement, never in my dreams had I ever wandered through such a venue as this.

Here, as in our previous experience, there were flowers where tantric exercises were taking place, flowers serving as refectories and floral dream chambers, and a pheromonic clockwork could easily enough be perceived circulating the Bloomenkinder between the phases of the cycle.

But here the flowers were so many and the species thereof so varied, and the resultant complexity they evoked in the behavior of their humans so recomplicated that one could not be entirely certain that the dance of the Bloomenkinder was not informed by sapience.

Three different fruits and at least two nectars were offered up by the flowers of this garden. Clusters of head-sized black berries grew at the base of the lavender bells. Both the pink cups and their black negative images grew amidst shaggy white melons, and both were filled with syrupy fluid. Long tubular fruit grew from the base of the tall white flowers. Some of these same flowers were exuding perfumes of lazy repose, so that Bloomenkinder dozed amidst the fruit, and some of them were the venues of abandoned yet somehow stately tantric tableaus, figures of considerable complexity being enacted without crushing so much as a single berry.

Moreover, the floral sequences seemed to cycle with balanced regularity, as if, like conscientious parents, the flowers sought to discourage bouts of obsessive excess. Rather than gorge themselves to torpor on a single fruit or nectar, the Bloomenkinder would wander from that flower to this, sampling the various courses and sipping at the vintages, like diners at a buffet.

Even in the sexual realm, variations were in evidence which at least raised the question of sapient style. There were short, intense, recomplicated figures involving any number of participants in frenetic multiplex interpenetrations, which sustained themselves for only a few minutes. There were smaller and more stable groupings which might go on at some length, and even dyads of conventional lovers.

"One might almost believe that these are revelers at some abandoned fete circulating between the smorgasbord and the boudoir," I whispered to Guy as we wandered wonderingly through this Bloomenkinder garden.

"Well spoken!" Guy declared grandly. "For do we not behold that very paradise of which the bodhis speak, where perfect innocents enjoy an endless soirée of tantric and sensual delights and strife and toil are forever banished?"

"The bodhis speak of a *spiritual* parameter to nirvana as well," I reminded him. "For surely there is more to it than endless toxicated carnival."

"Vraiment," Guy said. "Can you not smell the state of perfect spiritual harmony in which these fortunate people exist, the animal grace of every move, their beatific visages. Is this not the ultimate state all men seek?"

"Je ne sais pas. . . ." I said. "I see harmony and grace, vraiment, but I have no wish to become a member of this perfected company."

"Nor I, alas," Guy said quite regretfully, "for since we can never be innocently perfect Bloomenkinder, these cannot be *our* perfect flowers." His visage brightened. "But does it not promise a Garden of more sapient Perfection for such as we further on in the psychic interior? Ah, Sunshine, I can smell it on the wind. . . ."

Vraiment even I could at least dimly perceive the allure of this promise, for who could deny that I indeed beheld the possibility of a certain sort of human perfection?

For the Bloomenkinder, if one granted them awareness at all, must indeed exist in a state of perpetual bliss. Had not their desires been reduced to sex, food, drink, and repose, were these not met with immediate gratification as soon as they were aroused by the perfumes of the proprietors? Did they not sleep and eat and make love with the perfect wu of zen archers?

Which is to say that even masked I could feel the beneficence of the Bloomenveldt, the care it seemed to take for the animal happiness of its charges. Who was to say that somewhere deeper in its heart that puissant concern did not extend to the sapient spirit, for had we not already encountered flowers which would seem to have gifted the dying babas with the vision of enlightenment to illumine their final hours?

So did I slide into a dreamy state myself, so was I almost

tempted to remove my filter mask and breathe the perfume of this fairyland garden, so did I consider asking now for my own turn as psychonaut, so was I all but seduced by the forest spirit.

Until at length we happened to pass close by one of the great rainbow-hued puffballs.

Upon close inspection, this flower proved to be compounded of thousands of tiny blooms of red, blue, green, yellow, or mixed tints thereof, gathered together to form a round fluffy hedge atop a short thick stalk surrounded by an apron of thick, mossy, yellow pollen.

Upon this floral blanket crawled two chubby, torpid, naked human infants, entirely unattended, which struck me as the height of parental irresponsibility and hardly indicative of enlightened beings.

But when I examined the stalk of the puffball more closely, I saw the ultimate extent to which the Bloomenkinder had surrendered their spirits to the flowers.

Around the circumference of the stalk grew a ring of bright pink mounded protuberances which dimpled out at their centers into tiny tubular carmine teats. And teats they were in more than metaphor, for suckling on three of them, eyes closed in gurgling pleasure and squirming slowly in delighted contentment, were three more human infants.

Upon confronting this ghastly example of vegetative motherhood, I fairly dragged Guy away from the flower. "Put on your mask!" I hissed. "We must talk at once in the cold clear light of day."

"I have no wish to put on my mask," Guy said airily.

"That is exactly the problem," I snapped, in no mood to take no for an answer, and I reinforced my words with tugs and kicks and frowns and gesticulations, as I shepherded Guy out of the village of the Bloomenkinder, and if he had not been persuaded by the agitated determination of my will, I might very well have essayed a resort to brute force.

"Mask yourself!" I demanded when I had gotten him to a leaf well clear of floral influences. "I do believe this has gone more than far enough!"

"Certainly not!" Guy replied in a tone of infuriating tranquility. "Indeed, why do you not toss aside your own forthwith,

290

for upon so doing, you will never wish to filter out the perfumes of paradise again. . . ."

"Merde, Guy, just listen to yourself!" I fairly snarled. "Proof enough that it's time we gave over this mad quest and returned eastward to the coast!"

"Quelle chose!" he exclaimed. "Return to the coast? Give over our quest? When we are *this close* to attaining the ultimate object thereof!"

"To attaining *what*?" I snapped. "Surely not even *you* wish to become an empty Bloomenkind of the forest, blissfully content to mindlessly copulate, eat fruit, and sleep, while your sentience is given over to the pheromonic massage of your backbrain, and your offspring suckle at vegetative teats!"

"Of course not," Guy said airily. "Here I smell only perfect flowers for perfect Bloomenkinder. The Perfumed Garden of *our* perfection must surely lie deeper within."

"Phagh!" I snorted. "How much *more* such perfection do you require? Do not these Bloomenkinder satisfy your criteria of perfect symbiotic union with their flowers? They eat, sleep, and copulate at the behest of their floral overseers in a state of blissful surrender thereto, and rather than drink the milk of imperfect human sentience, they are weaned on the sap of the lotus!"

"Vraiment, the flowers lovingly husband the welfare of their humans. . . ."

"At the price of their human spirits, a pact known to be a devilish bargain since our ancestors climbed down from their trees!"

"Devilish bargain?" scoffed Guy. "Have we not seen flowers who offer molecules of enlightenment to dying humans in their hour of need? How much more proof of the Bloomenveldt's love for our species can you require?"

"Merde!" I exclaimed, having long since had enough of this futile dialectic. "Will you not return to the coast with me now?" I said, knowing full well the answer, for all too clearly his vaporous whim was set in iron.

"Will you now refuse to go forward with me into the glorious promise of the Bloomenveldt's heart?"

We stood there alone in the Enchanted Forest, each attempting to stare the other down at this fateful karmic nexus.

"If I *insist* on turning back, will you go on alone?" I at length demanded in a fury.

291

"If *I* insist on going forward, will you *return* alone?" Guy rejoined in a smug tone of tranquil sweetness.

"Will you not at least don your mask?" I pleaded despairingly.

"Will you not now doff yours so that as comrades, lovers, and true Children of Fortune, we may breathe the perfumes of paradise as a single perfect spirit?"

"Hijo de caga, nom de merde!" I snarled, admitting with as perfect a vacuum of good grace as I could muster that he had won.

For while Guy may have been bluffing, while *he* might in the end have followed *me* had I turned my back and strode eastward boldly, I knew full well that *I* could not fail to follow *him* if he turned *his* back on *me*. For not only did my cowardly aspect dread the thought of lone travel on the Bloomenveldt, but my more heroic nature could not abandon a comrade spirit in the jungle whether or not that spirit would have been ready to abandon me to follow his star, and no matter how much ire I now felt against him.

And to turn the screw of my frustrated fury a notch tighter, I knew full well that Guy had been able to win this contest of wills precisely because he knew this too.

And so I found myself following Guy ever deeper into the Bloomenveldt, or rather being dragged along like a small girl leashed to a large hound hot upon a scent.

For the rest of the day, Guy bounded along in great leaps to the west, pausing only to take his high hanging jumps from time to time to sniff at the air, like just such a hound following a pheromonic trail through a realm of perception wherein the bold relief of the olfactory topography belied the apparently featureless plain of the eye's vision.

By the time we stopped for the night, I was in a foul and sullen humor indeed and hardly in any mood for discourse with the likes of him, mystic or otherwise.

But Guy Vlad Boca read nothing of this in either my mein or my silence. Vraiment, he hardly gave over his blissful babblement even while eating and drinking, he noticed not the perfect one-sidedness of the conversation, indeed I could not be entirely sure that he even noticed my existence, so toxicated was he with the glories of the perfumed visions with which his brain was so thoroughly besotted.

". . . I *know* it is there now, for I can taste it calling to me on the wind, faint but surging with power, as one may sense the life-giving waters of a mighty river flowing unseen and unheard not so far away in the forest, the great river of the Bloomenveldt spirit flowing around me and through me, carrying me away in the loving embrace of its clear blue waters. . . ."

Und so endless weiter. Indeed by the time we had finished our meal and I could look forward to the nighttime surcease of consciousness, it was hard to be sure who or what spoke, for Guy by now was not even looking at me as he declaimed, rather did his eyes abruptly shift randomly from focus to focus like those of a nervous rodent, or worse, like the eyes of a man in the throes of some arcane possession. So too did his voice take on a deep and almost syrupy timbre which I had never heard before, and the pronoun of the first person had vanished from the repertoire of his Lingo.

". . . home to the spirit's safe harbor in the ancestral forest, back to the long-lost garden, forward into the perfume of perfect bliss, when you were Bloomenkinder of the Earth in the innocent spirit's grace, the great wheel turns, and the rain returns to the sea, and the many return to the one from whence they came and that moment is forever. . . ."

There I lay in the darkness longing for sleep while Guy, or whatever dybbuk of the wood spoke through him, assailed me and the night with these visions in a hypnogogic voice which at length had me finding myself hearkening to them, hearing in them the whispered blandishments of some long lost lover.

Vraiment, I found myself erotically aroused, as if about to be enthralled by some incubus.

Alors, when I became aware of this state, my present distaste for the person of Guy Vlad Boca was overcome by both endocrine imperative and the need to do whatever had to be done to still that insinuating voice.

Which is to say, I thumbed on my ring of Touch and forthrightly applied it to the handle of the natural man.

But the same would not rise to the occasion, my own best efforts and the puissant craft of Leonardo to the contrary! For all my efforts, I might have been massaging a carrot. Indeed such a tuber would in fact have been an improvement when it came to firmness of form.

But when at limply endless length I had succeeded in falling into a frustrated, fearful, and petulant sleep, I was rudely awoken by Guy, who had already set to work with a virile vigor and not so much as a by-your-leave.

Never had Guy Vlad Boca been such a puissant lover, never had he taken unto himself such a machismo of command, for he persisted silently and remorselessly against my outrage, which was soon somewhat diminished in conviction by my hours of sexual constriction and the entirely uncharacteristic tantric mastery of his assault.

Vraiment it was an overweening assumption of the most primitive masculine prerogative, but under the circumstances, it became rather difficult to maintain the proper feminine outrage in the face of an endless succession of mighty ecstatic cusps, each one a greater relief than the last, each one propelling me further down the merciful black velvet path of sweet oblivion, until I expired into the arms of sleep and my demon Bloomenveldt lover.

The morning after, naturellement, it was quite another matter. "What got into you last night, Guy Vlad Boca?" I shouted at him upon awakening and disentangling myself from his embrace with a vigor that entirely disregarded the sanctity of his slumber. "How dare you force yourself upon me against all my protests to the contrary!"

Guy, upon awakening to this loud indignation, favored me with a smile of radiant innocence.

"Alors," I said angrily, but not without a certain ambiguous embarrassment, "now you will grin at me like a simian and tell me how much I enjoyed it!"

"Enjoyed what?" Guy said, regarding me with the same shining visage of innocent ignorance.

Could it be that this ignorance of all unchivalrous behavior was not feigned? Vraiment, did Guy Vlad Boca have this perfect power to artlessly dissemble under even the best of circumstances?

"It's really true, Guy?" I said, studying him closely for any sign of irony. "You remember nothing?"

Guy slowly rose to a sitting position. Still smiling the same bodhi smile, he turned his face from me to look westward across the endless ethereal Bloomenveldt, pastelled to ghostly luminescence as the rising sun only began to burn away the morning mist.

"I remember what the Bloomenkinder know," he said in that same strange basso profundo as he clumsily scrabbled to his feet, still gazing fixedly to the west like a Bloomenkind at sunset.

Entirely distractedly, he began cramming his effects into his pack, not for a moment giving up his visionary fixation.

In a panic, I stuffed my own pack as best I was able, for Guy was already hoisting his in less time than it takes to tell, and poising for a great leap westward.

Then off he went without so much as another word, and I was reduced to catching up as best I could, bounding along in Guy's train once more as he sniffed and snuffled across the Bloomenveldt. Vraiment, and in the canine manner, he seemed to grow ever more excited as he bayed along the trails of scent.

By midafternoon, he began to veer off to the southwest in a jerky series of tacks. And then, two or three hours later, his behavior grew even more frenetic, like that of a hound brought the first full whiff of the scent of his quarry on a change in the wind.

He came down from one of his leaps with a rigid, narrow-eyed alertness, and stood quite frozen like that on a leaf, as if to await my arrival. But as it turned out, a sudden return of his lost gallantry had nothing to do with it, for when I arrived at his side he entirely ignored my presence and continued to stare fixedly along the vector of his own nose. No doubt had he been equipped with a tail, it would have pointed out straight behind him.

"What is it, Guy?" I demanded. "I see nought but the usual endless leaves and flowers." For indeed that was all there was to be seen, not even a Bloomenkinder garden was in evidence.

"A grand and mighty spirit summoning its true children home," said that dybbuk voice through Guy Vlad Boca's lips. "The spirit of once and future flowers."

"Quelle chose, Guy, before you succumb to such a puissant tropism as you describe, put your mask on at—"

But without another word, he was off in a great leap directly along the point of his fixed vision, and I was constrained to follow at once or risk losing sight of him entirely.

Nor did I have much space for thought for the next hour, for all my efforts were of necessity dedicated to negotiating leaps

295

of sufficient force and rapidity to keep Guy in sight as he bounded across the Bloomenveldt at the greatest speed of which his efforts were capable. Nor did he seem to have any further doubts as to the precise vector of his destiny, for his course now had the geometric inevitability of a ballistic trajectory.

And then, at the apogee of one of my own leaps, I thought I spied an anomaly on the horizon exactly on the compass point toward which Guy was heading, no more than the first hint of land that one perceives after a voyage on an open ocean.

I made my next leap shorter and higher, trying to gain as lofty a vantage as possible without being left behind. Vraiment, there *was* something there, just on the line of the horizon, a splash of colors and shapes.

But I had no time to pause for thought when I alighted from this crow's nest in the air, for Guy was pulling away from me already, and I had had to maximize my speed to catch up to him, indeed to merely keep him in sight. So I paused not for another clear view of whatever it was we were approaching by leaps and bounds until after quite a chase across the treetops, and indeed I only managed to catch up with him at all when he was brought up short by a sight that transfixed us both.

We stood together on a tall hillock of foliage looking out over a long shallow dip in the Bloomenveldt. The center of this plain in the treetops rose gently into another highland formed by the elevated crown of a single great tree.

In an overwhelming display of floral exuberance, the entire great treecrown had burst into flower, like a proud peacock displaying his full brilliant glory among the quotidian arboreal fowl.

"Behold, oh ye true children of the Enchanted Forest," said a voice that in that moment seemed to speak for both my by-now-long-lost lover and that which had claimed him. "Behold the Perfumed Garden."

19

We both stood there for a long silent moment, beholding the celestial city on the hill, for the dense profusion of great flowers seemed to grow in organized groves, color by color, form by form, so that the huge garden seemed for all the world to be divided up into arrondissements, like a true city of men.

Indeed, I was put in mind of my first sight of Great Edoku seen from space, for while the Perfumed Garden was bathed all over by the same bright afternoon sunlight, the districts thereof were a mosaic of brilliantly contrasting facets of color, so that the whole took on the aspect of an impossible gem shimmering in all the hues of the rainbow, a vision of breathtakingly chaotic color, in which, nevertheless, an elusive order seemed to be implied, just below the level of conscious apprehension.

As for Bloomenkinder, while these could hardly have been individually visible from this far vantage, their presence seemed to reveal itself in a seething motion overlaid on the vision, a wavering of the whole image like that of an overcomplicated mandala one has stared at in a toxicated state for too long.

So too could I hear the collective human mantra of the unseen and yet seen denizens thereof, for the air hummed with a faint celestial vibration, an ethereal wordless song emanating from unknown hundreds of distant human voices all harmonizing on the same single note, a note which sent my spirit soaring, a siren Om of paradise, which had my feet inching forward, and my hands beginning to move toward my mask.

Guy stood there beside me with his head bent back, and his nose in the air, and a beatific smile beaming from his face, and his eyes squeezed shut to better savor the perfumes, like a small boy inhaling the aroma of the most wonderful bakery.

Alors, if *my* spirit had all but been captured from afar by sight and sound alone, what must *he* be feeling now?

"Guy. . . ? Guy. . . ? Talk to me, Guy, tell me what it is that you smell on the wind!"

His eyelids peeled open, and he half-turned his head to face me. But his eyes seemed as clear and vacant as those of a Bloomenkind, and his nostrils continued to flare around long, deep draughts of perfumed air.

"The Perfumed Garden. . . ." said that eerie dybbuk voice. "*My* Perfumed Garden," said Guy Vlad Boca, albeit in a voice that seemed to speak as an echo, as a memory he had already let go, dopplering away to extinction down the corridors of time. Logic should have filled me with terror, but Guy had taken my hand in his, and his voice, in perfect tonal harmony with the distant hum of the Perfumed Garden's mantra, insisted that there was nothing here for us to fear, that we were only going home.

"Come . . . come . . . come home. . . ." Guy chanted, as if he, or some forest spirit, or vraiment both, had read my thoughts, or indeed as if his thoughts, and mine, and the voice of that spirit, were but notes of the same transcendent mantric chord.

And then without further rational thought, I found myself bounding hand in hand with Guy in great leaps toward the Perfumed Garden, like moths to a flame, like motes of dust rising up a great shaft of golden light to greet the sun.

Nor did we pause for a moment until we stood as groundling insects at the base of that mighty floral metropolis.

Groves and hedges of brilliantly colored flowers rose up the gentle slope of the great treecrown before me to fill the world. And I beheld multitudes of my own kind buzzing and dancing about them like an ecstatic swarm of bees on a midsummer's mother lode of floral beneficence.

A vast multitude of Bloomenkinder, a golden citizenry of

naked and physically splendid humans, enlivened the avenues and groves of this city of the flowers with their recomplicated and utterly graceful pavane. They dined at great floral banquets, they slumbered in municipal parks, they engaged in arcane civic activity impossible to fathom at this remove, they sauntered in streams along the avenues between the flowers like gay boulevardiers, and all with a choreographed perfection of motion and timing which would have done any maestro of the dance proud.

But while the resemblance to the buzzings and scurryings of bees was given the lie by the way the Bloomenkinder made art of every motion with all the style and grace appropriate to our mammalian species and then some, when it came to the collective mantra of a beehive, the metaphor was far closer to the sensual and spiritual reality.

For the mighty wordless human song that filled the world, like the buzzing of a million bees, was indeed a collective mantric chorus that vibrated to the spiritual and genetic wavelength of its own species. Mayhap this soul-stirring thrum of human joy might have been a mere drone of monotony to an apiary ear, just as in the buzz of the bees *we* hear nothing but the dead hiss of insectoid static. But just as the buzzing bees must hear the song of their spirit in the voices of their fellows, so did this mighty mantra of the collective human spirit draw my singularity toward union with the chorus of the whole.

Indeed I found myself humming that mantra under my breath from somewhere deep in the depths of my throat, and it seemed as if my very bones were vibrating to its harmony, and I became aware that Guy was singing it as well, his mouth wide open in a radiant smile, the sound pouring up through him in a single mighty tone, that selfsame tone which had resonated in the voice which had first spoken through him the day before, and which now seemed to speak to my own soul.

"Ah ... ah ... ah ... om ... ah ... ah ... ah ... home. ..."

I turned to Guy with my own blissful smile. Slowly, his face turned itself toward me, so that I could see upon it the mirror of my own joy. I squeezed his hand. "Oh Guy," I said softly, "I just didn't know. ..."

Guy seemed to look into my eyes for a long moment, and it seemed as if several spirits were regarding me from the endless

299

depths of his. The gay Child of Fortune whose wit had won me on the streets of Great Edoku, the Merchant Prince who had lavishly rescued me from penury, the deeper and darker Guy who had emerged psychotropically on the *Unicorn Garden*, the nascent Charge Addict, the obsessed and intrepid psychonaut of the Bloomenveldt, the creature who had made love to me last night in the forest, they were all there behind his eyes, they were all at peace with each other, they were all one, and in that moment, vraiment, did I find it in my heart to love them all.

And so hand in hand, two hearts beating as one, two spirits humming the same glorious mantra, or so at the time it seemed, did two no longer lost children of man enter their Perfumed Garden.

We walked in dazzlement down the aisles of great flowers, through a living kaleidoscope of brilliant colors and achingly lovely pastel shadows, for the very air within the Perfumed Garden was suffused and romanced by the bright sunlight streaming through thousands upon thousands of translucent petals, and at first I could only bathe myself in the rainbow radiance and laugh in delight.

But soon enough I perceived that we promenaded among throngs of stately Bloomenkinder like grimy ducklings among serene and impassive snow-white swans gliding in a recomplicated pavane about the surface of an untrammeled pond. Everywhere I looked, I saw perfected exemplars of my own species moving with the balletic fluidity of creatures whose movements are governed entirely by the natural imperatives of the laws of motion, following their destined trajectories with innocently perfect grace.

Was not Guy the wiser spirit after all? For was not my every sense filled with overwhelming beauty save that which tasted the air? And if I dared doff my mask and partake of that deepest communion, might I not too learn that here I had found my perfect flower? Of what use were struggle and travail and sapient dissatisfaction when with but a sigh of surrender one might transcend the maya thereof to a garden of perfect bliss?

Vraiment, mayhap I would have torn off my mask to inhale the timeless perfume of floral paradise without further moral struggle in the throes of this blissful satori, had I not then felt the insistent tug of Guy's hand in mine, and come out of my reverie to realize that he was already leading me toward a grove of blue and green speckled flowers.

Here a veritable horde of Bloomenkinder was consuming the yellow fruit, half again as large as a human head, which grew in profusion about the stalks. This they accomplished by deftly splitting the soft spheres in half with the sides of their hands and scooping the purple gelatinous pulp into their mouths with their cupped fingers. Without a word or a sign, Guy let go my hand and marched straight to the banquet of huge messy fruit.

He sank to his haunches forthwith and set to work in the manner of the surrounding swarm, with all their avidity for the luscious purple slime, but with little of their genetically perfected precision. When he struck the huge fruit to cleave it open, he mashed it into a disaster. The gelatinous pulp dribbled and spurted from his fingers as he then sought to shovel the remains into his mouth with both hands, and he seemed utterly indifferent to the fact that he was plastering the vile-looking purple goo all over his face and into the crown of his hair in the process. From both the esthetic and psychic viewpoints, it was truly a jolting and revolting spectacle.

Certainement it was more than enough to dissuade me from any temptation to breathe the seductive aroma of this vile succulence and be constrained to emulate the same thereby!

I hunkered down beside him and fairly shouted in his ear. "Guy! Guy! You're fressing like a swine! You're gobbling goo like a demented animal!"

He did not so much raise his eyes from his fruit to acknowledge my existence and continued to scoop dripping handfuls of pulp into his slobbering mouth without even breaking rhythm, spattering me with gobbets of same in the process.

"Merde!" I snarled. "This is more than I can countenance!" I kicked the dripping mess of fruit from his hands. This at last penetrated the sphere of his attention. He slowly turned his head to peruse the source of this disturbance with vacantly blissful eyes, then turned away again, smashed open the nearest yellow fruit, and returned to his feeding ritual.

"Guy! Guy!" I shouted. "It's Sunshine! Don't you know me? Don't you even know I'm here?"

At this, he paused in his devouring devotions, and for a moment it seemed as if he were indeed aware of my presence, for

301

as his head slowly looked upward from his meal, and he let the fruit fall from his fingers, it seemed for an augenblick that he was responding to my words. But no, alas, his eyes looked straight past me, and his nose went high in the air, and he arose to follow it without looking back.

Only now, unwilling as I yet was to essay the use of force, and constrained thereby to trail after a Guy who utterly ignored me on his grand tour of the Perfumed Garden, did the generality of perfection begin to resolve itself into some inspection of detail which hinted at the unseen Serpent therein.

Dozens of different species of flowers offered up a bewildering variety of fruits, pollens and nectars, not at isolated kiosks, but in whole groves thronged with avid Bloomenkinder gobbling up the produce like flocks of birds descending upon orchards.

Whole precincts of flowers were given over to slumber. Great naked shoals of Bloomenkinder lay sprawled all over the acres of velveteen petals provided, dreaming I knew not what in the bright clear light of day, and appearing for all the world like the exhausted yet tranquil morning after some mighty communal orgy.

And then Guy's trajectory chanced to bring us past the nursery.

Here clusters of human infants hung from the vegetal teats of a huge stand of rainbow-hued puffballs like so many berries, and others crawled about their leafy playpen within a ring of silent female Bloomenkinder who moved only when necessary to keep the toddlers from straying.

While a single Bloomenkind lay supine and utterly silent on a leaf near the edge of the grove in the act of giving birth.

She seemed entranced into a semiconscious state of dreamy ecstasy, wherein her protoplasmic mechanisms were nevertheless performing their functions in an exemplary manner that would have done the best of Healers proud. Her breaths were deep and regular in the approved rhythm and every muscle in her body was perfectly attuned to maximize the efficacy of her contractions. When after a short and entirely silent labor, the infant emerged, the mother started its breath with her own, bit off the umbilical cord at the navel, methodically licked the baby clean, and then straightway affixed its tiny mouth to the nearest free floral nipple.

She then began to devour the afterbirth, a process which at last forced me to avert my eyes.

Now I truly beheld the Serpent lurking in the Garden, the price one paid for hearkening to its sweet promises of symbiotic perfection.

For if this was a paradise designed for man by the flowers, it was a version crafted by the indifferent, cold hand of the Bloomenveldt, not the warm-blooded mammalian spirit, which is to say it was a *floral* vision of the perfected pollinator known elsewhere to himself as man.

Not even the love of a mother for her newborn babe was permitted to mar this floral vision of paradise, for from the point of view of the flowers, the highest form of pollinator society, naturellement, was not a perfect commonwealth of sapiently enlightened human hearts, but the pheromonically predictable perfection of a human hive.

"Merde, Guy, we must quit this place forthwith!" I shouted, and once more I was tantalized by the illusion that I had reached what was left of the natural man, for, without demur, he took a deep breath, smiled at me in blissful harmony, and straightaway seemed to march off on a purposeful new vector.

But rather than the nearest egress from this vile venue, he made straight for an extensive orchard of tall blue flowers, where whole congregations of Bloomenkinder sat, each to their own flower, like a great swarm of buddhas in a forest of bo trees. There they sat like idols, staring fixedly up into the cerulean void, and chanting the booming mantra that was both the incarnated voice of the Bloomenveldt manifested in human throats and the Bloomenkinder's paean of homage to the perfect and mindless spirit thereof.

Certainement this song which called to the very protoplasm from which my psyche arose was the most horrid floral simulacrum of all, for this noble mantra of the human spirit was now revealed as no more than the chorus of the genes, no more than the empty-minded buzzing of mammalian bees.

And Guy Vlad Boca let fall my hand, in thrall to that Bloomenkinder chorus, gracefully seating himself in the lotus position under the nearest unoccupied flower and proceeding to gaze into the clear blue nothingness of the Bloomenveldt sky as

303

he merged his lonely and precious singularity into the nirvanic voice of the All.

At the time, I could imagine no more terminal straits than this, I had no further belief that any unaided words of mine could summon his sapience forth. I had no further recourse but to main force, and certainement this was no time to eschew the most puissant power at my command.

Which is to say the only possible path to the spirit within this beatified corpus was via the route of the natural man. I therefore activated the Touch and applied it where it was likely to do the most good.

When it came to the flesh, the art of Leonardo produced the limpest of results, for no doubt the hormonal matrix of erotic interest must exist before the kundalinic serpent can be aroused to uncoil via electronic stimulation of the software of manhood.

But if pheromonic imperatives controlled the biochemistry of his brain to the point where tantric arousal was out of the question, the nerve trunk that led from the phallus to the centers of most primal awareness was at least still connected to what was left of the élan humain of Guy Vlad Boca.

Which is to say that, while that which I grasped remained flaccid, Guy's face began to surface the evidence of some ambiguity between chemical and electronic stimuli as he regarded me now. His eyes struggled toward recognition. His lips began to move tentatively around the single mantric syllable they were mouthing.

"Yes, Guy, yes, say something, say something," I fairly begged, tugging imploringly at his phallus, "tell me at least that you are still there."

And then as he sat there motionless among all those Bloomenkinder bodhis, his head turned almost imperceptibly, and he seemed to be smiling straight at me, and his eyes met mine, and his mouth fashioned that continuous stream of monotone arising through it into the single word that could allow in that moment the singular sprach of Guy Vlad Boca to speak from within the mantric Lingo of the eternal empty All.

"Ah . . . ah . . . ah . . . amused. . . ."

I all but burst into tears to hear this, tears of both sorrow and fond remembrance, for here I beheld both my lover and my lost comrade, the gay spirit I had met on the streets of Edoku and the psychotropically-obsessed creature of Ciudad Pallas, the mystic libertine and the Bloomenkind he had become, at the end point of the vector all those avatars had been so avidly pursuing, speaking to me in the voice of the forest of the final joy that now filled his heart.

Yet the tears came not, for at least I had roused some poor semblance of the natural man, mayhap all was not yet lost.

"What amuses you, Guy?" I said, cooing softly in his ear, kneading his flaccid lingam in a pulsing rhythm, as if to pump cleansing kundalinic energies up from the deepest root of his manhood to do battle with the chemical minions of the Bloomenveldt spirit investing his brain.

His eyes gazed directly into mine now, and there was no mistaking that someone or something knew that I was there. Vraiment I could feel some vague stirrings in his phallus now, as if the manly serpent were beginning to uncoil in its sleep.

"I . . . we . . . amused. . . ." he said in a quavering voice, as if more than one animating spirit were attempting to use the same lips.

"Speak to me, Guy Vlad Boca," I demanded softly, redoubling my electronically-enhanced ministrations. "Let the natural man once more arise!"

"Sunshine . . ." he said quite clearly. "My mystic libertine . . . sip steadily at it as you gambol through your perfect flower. . . ."

"Guy, Guy, it *is* you!" I cried.

"Never before or since have I known such perfect bliss. . . . Seek the Perfumed Garden. . . . Let the mountain come to thee Mohammed. . . ."

Was it indeed no more than fragmented memory speaking? Certainement, his phallus began to slowly fill with the life juices of manhood, certainement, he had given over his mantric chanting, certainement, our eyes were locked in unwavering rapport, which is to say that whatever now spoke through those random syllables, be it a true lover waving his last good-bye or a dybbuk of the Enchanted Forest, tell me not that it did not speak for me.

"Guy, listen to me, Guy, come with me," I said as seductively as I could under the circumstances, drawing him slowly and gently to his feet by the handle of his manhood. Vraiment, I met with anything but resistance, for his eyes gazed into mine with a

305

meaning whose frank intent would seem to be made quite firmly plain by his now quite thoroughly aroused lingam.

Mayhap I could lead him from the Perfumed Garden by this lever, for certainly it would not be the first time masculine obstinacy had been overcome in this manner. And once I had gotten him to a leafy venue well away from floral influences, mayhap the natural union of lingam and yoni would bring the natural man to his senses.

"Ah . . . ah . . . ah . . . amuse. . . ." he moaned in a deep hollow voice, at once the Bloomenveldt's floral mantra and the frankest profession of entirely mammalian joy, for his eyes closed in ecstasy, and his lungs inhaled in long priapic pants, and he moved his throbbing phallus back and forth in an unmistakable rhythm within the embrace of my hand.

"Oh yes, Guy," I babbled rapidly, "let us quit this place for a secluded venue and we will show each other the amusements proper to a natural man and woman and then some, this I promise you. . . ."

Und so weiter, just to keep his ears filled constantly with the sound of human Lingo, as I managed to lead him in this obscene manner from the greater obscenity of the mantric grove.

But once we had cleared the immediate pheromonic influences thereof and entered the dance of the Bloomenkinder down the floral avenue, Guy, or that to which his spirit moved, sought out his own vector, breathing in great silent draughts of perfumed air now, rolling his eyes in ecstasy, and now it was I who was constrained to follow the course set by his lingam, which all but threatened to writhe like an impatient serpent out of my hand.

Since in truth I had no idea where I was at the time, one direction would be as efficacious as any other, so if Guy wished to lead me to a boudoir of his own choosing, I could see nothing for it but to follow the path of least resistance. Vraiment, when I let Guy proceed along his chosen path, he readily enough allowed me to clasp an arm around his waist in proper loverly style the better to keep hold of his lingam, and my female sensibility did not exactly have to be tuned to a fever pitch to know it had hold of the natural man.

"Where are we going, Guy? And what do you intend to do

when we get there?" I asked him, summoning up an incongruous air of erotic playfulness with a mighty act of will.

He paused, he turned to me, he favored me with a smile of blindingly radiant lust. And then his hand found my yoni, fondling it with a frank avidity that set my heart and hopes soaring, and I let go of his lingam so that I might throw both arms around his neck and plant a joyous kiss on his lips.

But Guy, forcefully eschewing this attempt at loverly embrace, brushed my arms aside, and, gazing fixedly over my shoulder, pulled me to him, and attempted to thrust his lingam into my yoni through the intervening cloth.

I whirled myself out of this animalistic embrace, and then it was that I saw that without my knowing it, we had reached the venue of his intent.

The Perfumed Garden path which we had been following had debouched into a grotesque floral amphitheater where low mounded Bloomenveldt hillsides almost entirely surrounded a vast central grove. All around the hillsides grew bed after bed of tall blue flowers. Under the flowers, swarm after swarm of Bloomenkinder bodhis sat, humming the eternal booming mantra of the Enchanted Forest, hundreds upon hundreds of mammalian bees in a nirvanic paean of glory to the blissful nothingness of the hive.

The flowers of the vast central grove were the rosy pink color of a lover's naked body by firelight, and their fat velvety petals lolled out on the surrounding leaves like a carpet of tongues.

Upon these fleshy cushions a vast seraglio of copulations was taking place, hundreds of interlocked bodies coupled and recoupled in tantric figures of such lithe sinuosity and perfect ecstatic abandon as to have put a temple frieze of fabled Hind to shame. It was almost more than the eye could credit or the ear comprehend. Yonis, lingams, indeed every conceivable erotic orifice and protuberance, united and recombined in a vast and sinuous collective motion, spurred on in their extravagant copulations by continuous sighing breakers of orgasm cresting and rising on the surface of the fleshly sea.

But rather than stirring my passions, such a spectacle doused my kundalinic fires with an icy hand round my heart.

Certainement, as a tantric tableau, there was nothing lacking in the way of artistic perfection. Each and every performer

307

was a paragon of the human body's form, and the recomplicated figures were done with a flawless grace and egoless sincerity beyond that which even after years of study perfect masters of the art attain.

But I would have been more aroused by the sight of the breeding season in a primate preserve. For at least at a primate preserve I would have been observing creatures copulating in the style appropriate to their kind. Here, au contraire, I beheld the intimate communion of the tantra reduced to mindless tropism. Here were my ears filled with the buzz of the human hive melded in solipsistic harmony with the moans and sighs of an eternal tantric cusp.

Thus might it have been in our ancestral Eden, but so too will it become should sapience expire from our far-flung worlds, leaving only the indifferent nothingness from whence we came behind to sing its empty and triumphant song.

But Guy Vlad Boca had long since become incapable of such distinctions between form and spirit, between pheromonic imperatives and the human heart. He was flinging off his pack and tearing off his clothing, ripping the straps of his filter mask from around his neck and tossing his last sapient hope aside, and then he was upon me, thrusting his insistent lingam against my yoni, attempting to breach my citadel and prod me with it toward the venue of pheromonic rut at the same time.

I pushed him away with a mighty shove, he stumbled a few steps backward, and then righted himself, at which point he paid me no further heed, dashing around me as if I were a natural obstacle, and flinging himself into the midst of the breeding ground.

Whereupon he forthwith seized up the nearest female in his embrace, who avidly impaled herself on his throbbing phallus, even as another impaled her from the rear, and then he was tumbling and rolling away from me into the vile melee, lending his own voice to the moans and the cries, enveloped in an arabesque sinuosity of torsos and limbs.

Needless to say, this was more than any fear or rational consideration could constrain me to condone! Snarling with outrage, I reached out for Guy with my hand of Touch, and succeeded in grabbing the nether root of his lingam, seeking to remove it from the Bloomenkinde's yoni and Guy from his madness.

But instead of yanking Guy back into human reality by his manhood as I had intended, I only succeeded in sending a shockwave of tantric amplification heterodyning across the cross-connected erotic figure. Ecstatic cries rose into a shrill and insistent chorus, and bodies writhed and spasmed in spreading chain-reactions of orgasm. And dozens of hands were dragging me deeper into the fray. I stumbled and fell, and Guy was torn from my grasp, and I was battered and pulled this way and that, while phalluses prodded at every part of my body, and it took all of my strength just to keep from being drawn under by a riptide of flesh.

I lost sight of Guy entirely, indeed all thought of him left my mind as, in the midst of this rape most foul, I struck out in rage and terror, attempting for the first time if without much skill in the martial art thereof to use the Touch as a weapon.

I had never before been in a physical conflict in my life, and now I found myself fighting off a riotous obscenity of mass sexual overload which I myself had unknowingly triggered. But for every blow that I managed to land in the region of a painful plexus, another always seemed to strike a tantric chakra, so that all my efforts to defend myself further exacerbated the endless legions of my attackers.

Then I felt my pack being torn from my back, and hands at my floatbelt, and fearing that this would go next, I did the only thing I could, turned it up to .1 g lift, and attempted to free myself from my tormenters long enough to leap clear.

I succeeded in jumping clear of the ground, but my upward progress was impeded in midair by the press of bodies and the scrabblings of hands.

Then I felt myself being drawn back down into the mire of bodies, and fingers were tearing randomly at my filter mask, and suddenly it was ripped away, and phalluses thrust forward from every direction toward every orifice, and I felt myself reaching for them with my hands and my yoni and my mouth as a knee-shaking tsunami of blind animal lust surged through my body—

As I felt my consciousness subliming into a blood-red mist of egoless libido, I had the last combat-born and adrenaline-charged presence of mind to perform two valedictory acts of sapience before I passed over to the flowers.

309

I exhaled from the bottom of my lungs, and then stopped my breathing.

I struck out with vicious and electronically augmented karate blows, and kicked off some unknown portion of some unseen body with both of my feet.

As I soared free of the melee, something hit me in the stomach with wind-killing force, and I was constrained to suck in a great charge of pheromone-saturated air, and then something else smashed into my temple as I broke clear—

—and I had one last moment of roaring red consciousness, scrabbling to reach the lingams and bodies receding beneath my ravenous grasp before even that lapsed into darkness.

20

I awoke to the gentlest of thumps as I floated down supinely onto a leaf, nudged back the last increment into consciousness by this most tender breaking of a most languid fall.

The Perfumed Garden was nowhere in evidence, which is to say that my eyes opened and focused on naught but the endless flower-strewn green plain of the Bloomenveldt, nor had I chanced to descend near a Bloomenkinder village or even within the overpowering chemical aura of any flower.

Bonne chance indeed! Now I remembered leaping upward with my floatbelt turned up to .1 g, thrust out of a vile unspeakability whose details I was not ready to call up from beyond the veil of my present dreamy vagueness. There had been a wonderful surge of roaring lust, and a blow on the head. . . .

Slowly, my consciousness firmed up to the point where I began to understand what must have happened.

I had been rendered unconscious as the gentle lift of the floatbelt bore me aloft, and I must have drifted up higher and higher until the floatbelt's safety mechanism had automatically turned down the lift to prevent me from drifting up beyond the life-sustaining level of Belshazaar's atmosphere and then deposited me randomly on this leaf.

I must therefore have risen quite far, through several atmo-

311

spheric streams, which must have blown me this way and that for unknowable distances, which is to say I had been thoroughly shaken by the cupped hands of fate and then tossed like a die back onto the gaming board of life.

And then I began to perceive that while the Perfumed Garden was nowhere in sight, it could not be said that its influence was completely absent from my sensorium. For as my memory regained the clarity of my restored vision, I remembered the frenzied tangle of naked limbs and torsos, the forest of clutching and groping hands, the thrusting clusters of phalluses, with a sad and longing nostalgia, knowing I had been an utter fool to abandon such an eternal ecstasy of perfect sexual delight.

Yet at the same time, higher portions of my mind remembered all too well that the real-time emotions encoded with these experiences had been those of outraged disgust and terrified anger.

Out of this disjunction between the true memory of the event and my present perception of same through a rosy haze of diffuse sexual arousal, arose yet a third aspect of my immediate consciousness, namely a detached observer who could readily comprehend that the difference must be the result of something borne on the wind.

Vraiment, as I sat up and began to size up the full extent of my dilemma, I knew that I could easily enough find my way back to paradise by surrendering my spirit to the rosy waves of this lustful tide, which, though fainter than the night breeze wafting the aroma of the Bittersweet Jungle down to the porch of my parents' manse in Nouvelle Orlean, would surely nevertheless carry a soul cast into its gentle undertow back home to floral nirvana.

As I fought against this dreamy desire, my awareness was sharpened by the adrenal surge of the struggle, and I began to fully comprehend the peril, not to say hopelessness, of my position.

My filter mask was gone and so was my pack. I had supplies of neither food nor water. I had lost my homing beacon. I was at an unknown locus deep in the interior of the Bloomenveldt, hundreds, or for all I knew, thousands of kilometers from the coast, at any rate a journey of weeks even at maximum speed along an unerringly perfect vector.

But in comparison to the peril that faced my spirit, the physical magnitude of such a trek faded into insignificance, for in order to survive, let alone escape from the land of the Bloomen-kinder, I had no choice but to eat of the fruits and nectars and pollens of the Bloomenveldt, for no other sustenance was available. I would have sold my soul for a sack of fressen bars, for that might very well be the price extracted for the gustatory largesse of the flowers.

Worse still, unimaginably worse, I would have to journey for weeks across the Bloomenveldt with my lungs and my spirit naked to every pheromonic tropism wafted my way on its per-fumed breezes.

Nor did my moral senses provide an unambiguous direction, for did not love and honor demand that I make all possible ef-forts to rescue Guy? Could I fairly call myself human if I fled to save my own spirit and left a fellow sapient being in mindless thrall to floral fascism?

Besides, would it not be easier and infinitely more pleasant, since surrender to the Bloomenveldt was in any case inevitable, to do so by returning to the Perfumed Garden and at least live in mindless bliss with my lover rather than as a lone lost Bloomenkind of the forest. . . ?

But I knew full well from whence this thought arose, and not even the perfumed whispers of the Bloomenveldt could per-suade me that I had any hope of extracting Guy from its bosom unaided.

I had only two real choices, both of them bleak. I could make for the coast by myself or I could return to the Perfumed Garden and attempt to rescue Guy. In the latter case, I would expend my last moments of sapient consciousness in a futile at-tempt to do the impossible, and the last thing I would know would be my joyous surrender to the enemy of my spirit. In the former case, on the other hand, would I not meet the same end? For no one had ever returned to the worlds of men from the land of the true Bloomenkinder, and no one was in a better position to appreciate why than myself.

As I pondered this perfect synergy of pragmatic impasse and moral dilemma, the sun had sunk far past the zenith, and the light was subtly deepening to golden, and the shadows of nearby flowers and distant hillocks of foliage were definitely pointing the way to the west, to the sunset to which the beautiful and empty faces of unknown thousands of Bloomenkinder would soon be turning in vegetative homage.

Somehow vision perceived in this clearly polarized afternoon landscape what logic and morality could not. I could, like the Bloomenkinder, turn my face to the sunset of the spirit, or I could, like the true Child of Fortune, follow the rising sun into the sapient perils of the unknown future.

The choice was as clear as the difference between karma and destiny. Guy had surrendered to the inevitability of the former, but a true Child of Fortune could only seek to be the master of the latter and follow that Yellow Brick Road toward self-made dawn which had thusfar taken our species from the trees to the stars.

I found myself in that moment fingering my sash of Cloth of Many Colors. I found myself remembering the Moussa who had won it, and the Sunshine who had worn it proudly when she finally dared to stand up and spiel in the Luzplatz. I remembered he who had given it to me and named me a true Gypsy Joker, and how I had successfully pursued him against all odds. I remembered the girl who had been expelled from the Yggdrasil without even the wit to find a toilet. I remembered how I had arrived in Great and incomprehensible Edoku to wander its chaotic reality in a befuddled daze.

There was only one thing for it. Only a massive expedition could hope to rescue Guy, and only I might lead it to the Perfumed Garden. If I surrendered to karma now, the Perfumed Garden would remain an invidious legend of nirvana.

I rose up. I adjusted my floatbelt to .1 g. I turned my back to the west in defiance of the way of the Bloomenkinder, vraiment, in defiance of the very Bloomenveldt itself, and fixed my eyes on that point on the eastern horizon from which the light of a new dawn must inevitably arise after even the darkest of nights.

No one, it was said, had ever returned to the worlds of men from the land of the Bloomenkinder.

I sprang off my leaf in a mighty bound toward whatever lay between me and the coastline. No one, I told myself grandly, has ever returned to the worlds of men from the land of the Bloomenkinder *before*.

* * *

I gave no thought to rest until the sun's disc sinking past the horizon had painted the sky with the gauzy rose and purple banners of oncoming night, and the first faint stars had begun to shine in the blackening blue above the rim of the eastern horizon.

Vraiment, my spirit had risen up from despair to the outskirts of hope as the golden afternoon wore on, for I had naturally fallen into the pattern I had adopted as a psychonaut in less perilous precincts to the east, or rather my will had succeeded in enforcing its mirror image.

There I had allowed the subtle currents of diluted psychotropic wine wafting through my nostrils to freely move my spirit and my body like a kite upon a gentle breeze. Here, where the pheromonic weather was a good deal stronger, did I apply the compass of the ascetic's code: tacking against any perfume which aroused my desire. When the promise of gustatory delight without measure drew me to the left, I made a wide swing to the right, and I fled from any lustful impulses like the perfect celibate monk. Thus did I avoid landing in precincts from which I might find myself lacking the will to depart.

So did sapience triumph over the biochemical imperatives of the Bloomenveldt, or so I told myself, for had I not turned the very power of the enemy into the servant of my own pathfinding?

Now, however, it was becoming night, and in the lonely blindness of the dark, with things unseen scrabbling and scurrying through the leaves and branches, and all the breezes reeking of sleep, I had a good deal less confidence in the power of the light of reason over the shadowy phantoms of the presentient cortex.

Certainement, I should have felt hunger with some keenness as I huddled on a leaf in the blackness watching the stars come out. Certainement, considering my peril and the night sounds of this most alien of forests whispering around me, fear should have robbed me of any rest. At the very least, my brain should have been aswirl with the memories of the day's events, and trepidations concerning the events of the morrow.

But in these environs, or so it would seem, the Bloomenveldt, after its own self-interested fashion, took care to assure that none of its charges stumbled to the forest floor in the middle of the night or failed to receive the measure of sleep that their metabolisms required. Uncounted thousands of flowers altered their daytime profusion of pheromonic imperatives to fill the entire

Bloomenveldt with the peacefully leaden perfume of a single purpose.

Not hunger, not fear, mayhap not even outright terror, could have long kept any mammal awake in this overwhelming perfumed fog of sleep. Not even this sapient Child of Fortune alone with her thoughts could deprive herself of the Bloomenveldt's gift of deep and uninterrupted slumber.

When I awoke in the bleak early moments of sunrise, however, it was an entirely different matter. The sun peeked up through a cool gray mist dimming the greens and floral hues of the Bloomenveldt to ghostly pastels. Certainement, I had not been awoken by either the bright light of dawn or the natural clock of my own metabolism at this repulsive hour. No, it was a ravenous hunger which had been sufficiently powerful to break my sleep; my stomach seemed plastered like an aching membrane against my backbone, my head ached with hollow emptiness, and my consciousness could contain naught but the thought of luscious fruits.

The faint odors of which seemed as pervasive as the mist slowly beginning to burn off the Bloomenveldt. The trace aromas of fruits I had never seen evoked sharp memories of wonderful savors I had never tasted.

Since it had been nearly a day since I had last eaten, my hunger of the morning seemed far less unnatural than the absence of same last night. Yet the phantom flavors teasing across my palate on the breeze alerted me to the fact that there were external agencies at work. No doubt, just as the nighttime perfumes masked all hunger behind an impenetrable urge to sleep, so had the conclusion of these secretions with the dawn abruptly allowed it to surface redoubled by time.

But while it may have been the flowers that were filling my nostrils and caressing my tastebuds with promises of gustatory delight, my ringing head and aching stomach were clear evidence of true famishment on a metabolic level. Which is to say that no matter what powerful psychotropics the food behind such pheromonic blandishments was likely to contain, not even the mightiest ascetic heroism was going to prevent me from having to eat sooner or later.

Still, mayhap I could apply the same contrarian strategy

316

which had served me well thusfar and avoid eating any fruits to which I was drawn by the perfumes and consume only those which the Bloomenveldt appeared to have laid out for other species. By so doing, I might at least avoid ingesting psychotropics evolved by the cunning of the flowers as specific snares for our own.

Thus resolved, I drank water from the abundant supplies thereof condensed in the hollows of nearby leaves, and then set off to the east in a series of short, high, hanging hops, ignoring all blandishments of aromas by act of will, and seeking to spy out an untenanted flower by vision alone.

As chance would have it, I had not proceeded in this manner for very long when I spotted a small grove of flowers of several different species not two hundred meters to the north. Not only were no human figures in evidence, there seemed to be no aromas leading my backbrain by the nose toward it.

What I saw when I arrived at this grove's margin, however, was a good deal less than an appetizing spectacle. Half a dozen species of flowers had arranged themselves in widely separated stands of two or three blooms, and with the exception of those of one species with which I was all too familiar, these all seemed to be somewhat immature specimens, nor was any fruit in evidence, as if the Perfumed Garden had recently sent out a colonial expedition which had not yet matured to the point of attracting its own Bloomenkinder.

But when I approached one of the stands of rainbow puffballs which seemed to be the only fully mature flowers in the garden, I saw that this surmise was both florally correct and humanly wrong in a peculiarly horrifying manner.

For here in the deep Bloomenveldt with no adult humans anywhere in evidence, clusters of human infants were nevertheless hanging from the vegetative teats of the flowers. Somehow, the flowers had either chemically commanded the mothers thereof to deposit their offspring in this venue, or worse still, exuded pheromones which drew hundreds of toddlers wriggling across the Bloomenveldt to improve the species by utterly ruthless natural selection.

Either way, this juvenile offspring of the Perfumed Garden was growing its own first generation of human pollinators.

While the gorge and outrage that such a sight called forth would be difficult to exaggerate, some logical circuits in my mind

317

remained capable of making a cold calculation. No doubt the reason that this grove did not exude perfumes attractive to adult humans was that it had not matured to the point where it was ready to serve as a proper host to same. Since the sap secreted by the teats was clearly sufficient to sustain these infant Bloomenkinder in robust health, might it not do the same for me? And since the *perfumes* of the grove lacked molecules with puissant effect upon the adult human metabolism, might not the *milk* thereof be equally lacking in danger?

Putting aside all esthetic considerations, gustatory or social, I sought out a stem as free from babes as possible, lay down on the leaf before it, applied my mouth to one of the pinkly rounded breasts thereof, and gave suck to the hard red teat.

A thick, tepid, somewhat sweet syrup oozed into my mouth, its simple savor not designed to appeal to mature tastebuds, so that the esthetic experience was like drinking liquified and sweetened fressen. But as the syrup slowly poured down my throat, my stomach welcomed it as the plants of a desert welcome rain after a long parching drought, and the very cells of my body seemed to sigh in relief. Avidly, I sucked at the floral teat with unrestrained enthusiasm, until I had established a steady flow with much unseemly smacking and gurgling.

I could not have been at it for more than a few minutes when, in almost less time than it takes to tell, a bubble of nausea suddenly exploded in my gut, a spasm of utter rejection that had my whole body trembling, and a series of retches wracked me down to the limbs.

I spat out the teat and managed to roll up onto my haunches clutching my stomach as I vomited charge after charge of thick green liquid over the edge of the leaf.

Fortunately, rather than expiring in a series of dry heaves, the episode ended as soon as the last of the sap had been expelled, and aside from a certain soreness of the ribs and a painful sharpening of the demanding emptiness in my stomach, I was no more the worse for wear, as if the flower had merely sought to provide a harmless lesson.

Vraiment, that lesson had been well taught! What the Bloomenveldt provided for the young of our species was crafted to be intolerable to the adult metabolism thereof.

Having no further business to conduct in this noxious

nursery, I fled the vecino thereof in a random series of short leaps, thinking for the moment of nothing more than putting it well behind me. It did not take long, however, for my ravenous hunger to reassert its demands, and for the perfumed promises of succulence to clutch at my backbrain with ever greater strength.

I knew full well that if I did not find safer fare soon, I would reach a state where I could no longer resist these siren calls to ease my famishment at the first Bloomenkinder larder my nose could find. With my remaining will, I resolved therefore to seek out lone flowers whose perfumes promised nothing and sample the fruits thereof, even though my confidence in this strategy was now severely eroded.

Nor, alas, did my pessimism prove unfounded. Discovering flowers indifferent to the attendance of my species was easy enough, but none of the fare offered up thereby was at all palatable.

Some of these fruits repelled by the perfect loathsomeness of their flavors: there were fruits whose taste filled the backbrain with a rank fecal odor, fruits that tasted like ancient overripe cheese, fruits which to my palate seemed redolent of urine. But the greater part of the fruits I forced myself to sample caused such powerful retching the moment their pulp touched my mouth that I was spared the full horror of the flavors thereof.

The message could not have been clearer had it been graven in monumental letters of stone. In these deep precincts, at any rate, humans could eat only the fruits to which the perfumes drew them, and these, no doubt, were therefore liberally laced with molecules designed to perfect their behavior as pollinators. It was a closed circle which seemed to allow no space whatsoever for sapient will.

In utter despair leavened only by an equally powerful outrage, with my stomach pounding in agony, my ears ringing with faintness, my legs beginning to go wobbly, and my nostrils constantly assailed by promises of swift and delicious surcease from this entirely self-inflicted torture, I set off for want of any other course of action into the warming blaze of the rising sun which had long since burned away the mist of morning.

Even then I must have known that I was only postponing the inevitable. For as the day wore on past noon, the pains in my stomach grew stronger, I was becoming too weak with hunger to even completely control the trajectories of my ever-more-feeble leaps, I was becoming increasingly dizzy to the point where consciousness was beginning to wink on and off, and, contrawise, the smells of delicious fruits mine for the taking had come to dominate my sensorium to the point where there was room in my mind for no other thought save the by-now-equally-tropistic self-command to follow the direction of sunrise which I had programmed what was left of my sapient spirit to follow.

But inevitably my body weakened to the point where it could no longer maintain a sapient spirit to follow its own song, and the perfumed breath of the flowers seized the remnants of my consciousness, which is to say that, with a great sigh of animal relief, I finally allowed myself to follow the summons to the nearest floral banquet.

There were some score flowers in this garden: lavender bells, yellow cups filled with nectar, pink flowers of passion, crumbly black cones of pollen circled by small white aprons of petals, mayhap other types as well, for my sensorium was skewed entirely away from sight and sound into a sphere where smell and taste merged to dominate my perceptions and within which hunger and the glorious satisfaction of same had become the sum total of my being.

I buried my face in the thick clear nectar pooling in the nearest of the yellow cups, unmindful of the two Bloomenkinder doing likewise beside me, and slobbered mouthful after mouthful down my throat, all but groaning in ecstasy.

For the smoky-sweet savor thereof was the perfect fulfillment of that which was promised by the aroma of sugar-glazed and crisply roasted meat which filled the nether reaches of my brain. As for the effect upon the famished cells of my body, this can only be likened to a million sparkling pinpoints of gustatory orgasm.

When I had sucked up my fill, or rather, no doubt, when the pheromonic winds changed to fill my being with something like the odor of steaming chocolated cinnamon pastries fresh and redolent from the oven, I abandoned the nectar cup forthwith and quite literally without a conscious thought repaired straightaway to one of the great black mounds surrounded by white petals, where I immediately proceeded to stuff great handfuls of crumbly black pollen into my mouth, trembling with delight as I chewed the sticky and crunchy grains which savored of spiced nutmeats enrobed in velvety chocolate creme.

As well do I remember huge black berries that drew me with the aroma of fine brandy and tasted like minted wine, long red fruit redolent of jasmine and black mushrooms and savoring of fruits baked in meaty caramel.

I existed in a state of perfect bliss, for the sum total of my consciousness consisted of the tantalizing aromas of gustatory lust and the all-but-immediate orgasmic satisfaction thereof. As to how long this cycle of feasting endured, je ne sais pas, for certainement there was no sapience of a sufficient level of intellect present to count the minutes or hours, or even to encompass the very concept of time.

Nor did I pay the least heed to the Bloomenkinder in whose midst I dined, any more than they found an apparition such as myself sufficient to arouse table talk or eye contact or the slightest momentary diversion from the single-minded task of fressing. We walked from flower to flower and we ate. That was the sum total of our blissful existence.

Until, that is, a flower decreed otherwise.

I was hunkered on the soft fat petals of a great open pink blossom devouring large blue ovoids with several other mindless Bloomenkinder, when the winds of desire changed and with them the very nature of my being.

A blood-warm rosy perfume seemed to pour straight through me, dissolving my gustatory obsession the moment the first molecules thereof had soaked into the volitional cells of my backbrain, and all at once, smell, taste, and the pleasures of gluttony faded away to faint abstractions which could scarcely be said to exist.

For now it was touch and feeling that had become the sensory crowns of my creation. My skin had become an interface of palpitating nerve-ends crying out to be caressed, my mouth ached to fill itself with warm velvety flesh, and my loins burned with a lustful fire that had the immediacy and urgent impact of completely dehydrated thirst.

Nor was I alone in my sudden transmutation into a fiery creature of polymorphous lust. In less time than it would have taken to consider had sapient consideration entered into the matter at all, I had thrown myself on the nearest male body, ripped

321

the necessary entrée in the fabric of my trousers, and impaled the circle of fire of my yoni upon a lingam.

Nor did this at all suffice. Sucking and grasping, I wrapped my lips around the first phallic fruit I could seize up and drew it in to the root. Vraiment, my nether orifice was forthwith breached as well to my avid satisfaction, and I felt mouths at my nipples, hands and tongues at the small of my back and thighs, and then naught existed but a carmine fog of all my senses, and an endless series of multiplex cusps that went on and on and on.

Vraiment, more than propriety or shame prevents me from detailing the variety, scope, and duration of the ever-changing interlocked tantric figures in which I took an actively enthusiastic part, for the truth of it is that I was lost in a timeless and mindless realm wherein even the distinction between the flesh and the gratification thereof had been completely annihilated.

Suffice it to say that this state endured and then ended with the same suddenness with which it had begun. A cool pheromonic wind blew through me, like the cold, crystalline clarity of the void between the stars, and all at once sensation evaporated from the surface of my skin and the kundalinic crannies of my erotic spaces, and all that existed was a disembodied spirit that sought the complete and blissful nothingness thereof.

This spirit found itself being transported atop a numb fleshly automaton and deposited supinely on a leaf beneath a lavender bell, where four other Bloomenkinder already lay staring motionlessly up into the clear cloudless sky.

Time stopped. Sound ceased. Smell, taste, and kinesthetic awareness of the contours of my own body faded away. I was naught but an empty volume of space-time gazing up fixedly into an equally perfect and featureless cerulean mandala of tranquil nullity. I was one with the Bloomenveldt. I had achieved the mindless perfection of the clear blue void.

21

Blue, blue, blue, blue . . . An endless, measureless, timeless perfection of blue . . .

And yet, at length, if duration could be said to exist in such a state at all, something became aware of a perturbation in the clear blue nothingness of its being.

Yellow . . . Was there not a yellowness moving all but imperceptibly across the blue . . . ?

It began to assume a substance and a form. . . . A fiery circle of yellow, haloed by streamers of the same hue . . . like a face surrounded by a corona of glowing golden hair . . . like the circular entrance to a long tunnel of light . . . at the end of which . . . at the end of which . . .

A spirit seemed to slowly come into being, which is to say that, just as the clear blue emptiness had been disturbed by the golden circle of light, so was the perfection of nonbeing now trammeled by a desire, a tropism, a formless urge to follow the yellow out of the blue to . . . to . . .

But then the golden circle began to deepen toward orange as it drifted downward through the blue void, and the cerulean hue thereof began to darken toward purple, and I found myself rising slowly to my feet, dimly aware of others like myself, standing motionless and staring into the sunset as the orange disc cracked the geometric precision of the horizon and fractured the purple perfection of the vaulted sky with rays of umber and somber red.

Yet as the sun was swallowed up into the black lake of oncoming night, some dying ember of independent intellect seemed to struggle up painfully from the depths of perfect mindless bliss to blink torpidly at the tiny pinpoints of silver that had begun to pierce the blackness of the sky.

For a few moments, as one by one the stars began to come out, mayhap there was a spirit that recognized those silvery speckles as such, for if fragmented memory plays me not false, that spirit viewed them through a veil of liquid gauze, as if weeping for the loss of something it could no longer fathom, as if someone still knew that each of them was a mighty sun, that up there in the heavens high above the Bloomenveldt, circling round the stars, were the far-flung worlds of men.

Just as memory marks not the divided hours of that first seamless perfect day as a Bloomenkind, so too in the track of my memory does it seem but one long day that I passed before the chance coincidence of sunrise and the turn of the floral cycle came together to rouse me from the reasonless creature of the forest that I had become.

The time came round at last when I awoke at dawn, was moved to breakfast on nectar, and was then transported by what blew me on the wind not to eat of fruit or engage in copulations, but to repose under a lavender bell in empty-minded meditation upon the cerulean void.

But chance, or mayhap what we style fortune, placed my venue of repose so that, rather than fixing my gaze upon the featureless perfection of the clear blue sky, I laid myself down with my face to the east, to the rising sun, which at this hour lay just above the eastern horizon bathing the Bloomenveldt in golden brilliance.

And as I lay there staring at the rising sun as it slowly began its ascent to the zenith, so did the angle of my gaze imperceptibly rise with it, for my vision had been totally captured by this single slow event in the timeless and featureless void of blue.

Mayhap the power of the flower was less total over one who had once enjoyed sapience and then lost it than over born and bred Bloomenkinder suckled at the very teats of the forest in

324

whom sapience had never arisen. Mayhap my previous conscious determination to follow the rising sun to the east had so percolated down to the nether reaches of my brain that it had attained, or from another viewpoint degenerated, to a simple tropism to rise up to follow the yellow, even as many plants will keep their leaves and flowers turned to a sun as it travels across the sky of day.

Be that as it may, some dim sort of vegetative awareness began to slowly seep into the percept sphere of the creature who lay on that leaf staring mindlessly at the golden sun rising toward its apogee, painting the greenery of the Bloomenveldt with a bright gloss of light that, rather than emanating from the yellow face of glory, seemed to be ascending eastward and skyward toward it.

Which is not to say that anything resembling human sapience had returned, for this faint urge to rise up to the golden face of the sunrise was no doubt no less a visual tropism than those of the senses of smell and taste which had come to command my hours.

Yet, dim and mindless though it be, *this* tropism was not a command of the Bloomenveldt. Rather, I do now believe, had the remnant of my sapient spirit succeeded in condensing all that had once been me into this single simple tropism to follow the yellow face of the sun upward into the sky, for it was a puissant compendium indeed from the point of view of the consciousness trapped beneath the surface of my presently mindless brain.

For was that consciousness not named Sunshine, and had that name not been given by a spirit whose face was haloed by golden hair? Vraiment, had not I once consciously chosen that selfsame golden rising sun as the ensign and guidepost of my determination to attain once more the worlds of men?

Destiny had therefore chosen to place within my sphere of vision in a state of florally induced hypnogogia an object of precisely that color most likely to rouse my spirit from its cerulean trance.

Slowly and without conscious thought, my right hand freed itself from the nirvanic catatonia in which my body lay, and like the heroine of a romance struggling under the crushing gravity of a cruelly massive planet, it crawled agonizingly across my waist and turned the knob of my floatbelt as far clockwise as it would

325

go. Then, as if exhausted by this effort, it fell limply to the surface of the leaf by my side.

Which slowly fell away.

For, supine, still gazing fixedly at the object of my tropic desire, propelled by the .1 g upward thrust of my floatbelt, I had indeed begun to rise to meet the sun.

As my body slowly rose up through the levels and breezes of the atmosphere, so too did my awareness rise slowly up out of the depths of its nonbeing toward the golden light of sapient consciousness. I can no more sharply define the moment when my spirit could fairly have been said to have returned to full sovereignty than one may the morning after remember the precise moment the night before when the same passed over the line into sleep.

Suffice it to say that after some time I quite literally found myself drifting slowly on the ever-changing breezes above the Bloomenveldt, with my clothing in tatters, my face caked and smeared with a vile crust of dried fruit pulps and saps, and the vague but horrifying memories of what I had been forced to become.

My first act of will, taken even before my consciousness had fully cohered, was to turn down my floatbelt to .1 g positive, and spy out a leaf as I came drifting down from which I might establish a firm trajectory for my next leap to the east.

Indeed, I hardly knew what I was doing or why until I had kicked off that leaf on a mighty bound toward that single smiling golden face in all this endless world of hostile green. Then I shouted for the sheer need to hear a sapient human voice. "Follow the sun, follow the yellow, follow the sun, follow the yellow!"

For several more leaps, I continued to shout thusly until the repetition fell into the rhythm of a chant, not really aware then of what I was doing or why. But at length this mantric return to verbality of a sort also served to restore the coherence of same to the stream of my thoughts, which is to say I became more shrewdly cognizant of the method of what no doubt would have appeared to an observing ear as my madness.

For in truth only then did I come to dimly comprehend the means whereby some buried level of my mind had rescued my sapient spirit from its dreamless slumber. Which is to say I had recovered the wit necessary to realize that I had in fact been following a self-imprinted visual tropism, which I had now instinctively augmented with a verbal mantra acting upon somewhat higher centers of my brain.

And rather than give over this mantra in the bright yellow light of relative reason, I instead reduced its volume to a less shrill level designed to preserve my voice for the long haul, and crafted the words into a monotonous singsong rhythm designed to drone it as deeply into the biologic levels of my being as I could manage without being a perfect master of the meditative arts. "Follow the *sun,* follow the *yellow,* follow the *sun,* follow the *yellow.* . . ."

So too did I then expand modestly upon the lyric with a final phrase which spoke of and to the higher purpose thereof. "Follow the *sun,* follow the *yellow,* follow the Yellow Brick Road. . . ."

This simple song did I chant endlessly and softly to myself as I bounded across the Bloomenveldt. And far from distracting my higher thoughts from pragmatic considerations, the perpetual chanting of this mantra served to calm and focus them, for now I was all too cognizant of the true nature of my predicament, and conscious as well of the only possible escape therefrom of which I could conceive.

For the brute fact was that I could not reach the coast without food, and the pit of nonbeing from whence I had barely managed to rouse myself to follow the rising sun was the only source thereof for hundreds of kilometers.

Which is to say I had no choice but to risk this death of the spirit not once more, but again, and again, and again, or die an even more final death of the body through starvation. Indeed, as I had already learned far too well, given a sufficient level of fatigue and famishment, I would sooner or later no longer retain the biologic energy to support a conscious will, and be drawn by the perfumes to the fruit like a moth to the flame.

Therefore, since I could count on no continuity of sapient will to carry me through, indeed since all that was certain was that I must suffer repeated loss of same in order to maintain my body's vitality, my only course was to accomplish with what I hoped was the greater puissance of conscious craft what I had already once barely managed to achieve by accident of fate.

Which was to use these periods of conscious lucidity to

327

engrave a mantric tropism upon the presentient levels of my mind with perpetual chanting repetition and diligent meditation, so that even when reason and conscious will had once more fled, my Bloomenkind self would, during periods of enforced floral nirvana, be programmed to follow the yellow, to follow the sun that sooner or later must rise during a cycle of such meditations into its percept sphere.

"Follow the sun, follow the yellow, follow the Yellow Brick Road. . . ."

Of the days, or mayhap weeks, that I spent trekking eastward across the Bloomenveldt in this manner from one meal of fruit to the next, there is little to be said that is not entirely contained within the endless repetition of the mantra I had given myself.

"Follow the sun, follow the yellow, follow the Yellow Brick Road. . . ."

For this became the sole content of my periods of sapient consciousness as well as the faint background music of the timeless intervals I was constrained to pass as a Bloomenkind.

"Follow the sun, follow the yellow, follow the Yellow Brick Road. . . ."

Though at the time I knew no more of the science of mantric imprinting or the art of autohypnosis than the simple techniques we are all taught in the early years of schooling, some years later, upon delving deeper into the subject, I was to learn just how puissant the mantric technique I had naively cobbled together out of bits and pieces of knowledge and coincidence really was.

"Follow the sun, follow the yellow, follow the Yellow Brick Road. . . ."

For what I had in fact done was crafted what the masters of the art call a synergetic mantra, wherein a conventional mantric rhythm keyed to the biorhythms of the consciousness in question is linked to a simple verbal metaphor of deep meaning thereto. A visual mandala is then provided which is the imagistic cognate thereof, so that the two most sovereign senses are merged into receptors for a single synergetic image of sight and sound, which, by becoming the content of the sensorium entire, focuses consciousness down to a single imperative.

Under proper conditions and the direction of a true perfect master of the art, an appropriate incense is also provided, as well as a psychotropic selected to induce the desired kinesthetic percept-state, so that no sensory data not linked to the synergetic mantra may intrude. Though I knew it not at the time, I had happened upon a technique oft times applied by adepts of the martial arts, Healers, and perfect masters of the meditative sciences.

And while I was constrained to serve as my own perfect master as best I could, chance, necessity, the perfume of the lavender bells, and what little art I possessed had conspired to create a synergetic mantra of which the greatest of such mages could be proud.

"Follow the sun, follow the yellow, follow the Yellow Brick Road. . . ."

The visual component thereof had been pared to the simplest possible mandalic formulation: a yellow circle, archetype of a life-giving sun. Nor could a perfect master have done much better with the drone of similar syllables contained within the mantra.

So no matter how often hunger drove me to the fruits and perfumes of a Bloomenkinder garden, and no matter how many cycles I passed in utter thrall thereto, the inevitable precessing of these selfsame cycles of eating, copulation, and hypnogogic repose must sooner or later place me beneath a meditative flower in an early morning hour beneath the rising sun.

Whereupon that visual mandala would inevitably call forth the chanting of the mantra synesthetically linked thereto. . . . "Follow the sun, follow the yellow, follow the Yellow Brick Road. . . ."

And this in turn would generate the stylized motion of my hand turning the control knob of my floatbelt, and I would rise slowly up into the air high above the Bloomenveldt until some semblance of sapience returned, like a mystic bodhi levitating out of maya by sheer force of will.

"Follow the sun, follow the yellow, follow the Yellow Brick Road. . . ."

Only by virtue of my possession of this single nonfloral tropism might I have been said to in any way distinguish myself as a self-motivated creature from the Bloomenkinder of the forest.

For just as the mantra had become the sole content of my

being when I was constrained to sojourn among the Bloomenkinder, so was my mind incapable of encompassing any other thought as I bounded eastward across the Bloomenveldt. So if the foregoing description of this stage of my journey across the Bloomenveldt may seem to lack something in terms of its recounting of the linear skein of events, the truth of the matter is that the human personality of the teller of this tale was for all practical purposes absent as a memory-binding witness from the corpus moving through them.

Just as the voice and speech patterns of a person long dead may be encoded into an electronic matrix and cunningly manipulated to produce an artificial personality with which one may even discourse, my body followed a program impressed upon it by a vacated spirit, but in truth no one was at home.

Nor would anything that might fairly be called true sapience return until the mantric cycle was perforce broken by a decided turn for the worse, and even then the teller of the tale would have been hard-put to recognize the same in the babbling apparition resulting therefrom had I chanced to encounter her on some civilized street.

"Follow the sun, follow the yellow, follow the Yellow Brick Road. . . ."

Guided by the shadows cast before me by a sun sinking well past its zenith, I was drifting gently downward toward the next in an endless succession of leafy springboards when—

—All at once, the rhythm of chanting, soaring, landing, and kicking off again was abruptly shattered by a sudden plunge from about ten meters up that had me slamming into a leaf with such unexpected force that my knees buckled, and I staggered forward into a half-roll, and then fell on my chest skidding across the surface toward the brink of a five hundred meter fall to the forest floor.

Sheer animal reflex reached out with both hands to grip the edge of the leaf as the front half of my body slid out into vertiginous space, and I hung there supported by my arms and the suddenly considerable weight of my lower torso in a state of absolute adrenal terror before summoning up sufficient awareness to haul myself back to safety.

No doubt nothing less could have shocked back a return to

even such sapient consciousness as I now enjoyed. Which is to say that in the backflush of adrenal arousal, an ego reappeared to the extent that I was aware of just how close I had come to sudden and horrible death. As well, with the breath knocked out of my body, I had for the moment given over my chanting.

But that was about the extent of it. By now my throat and lips were no longer needed to keep the mantra vibrating in my brain, and as for the sun, as for the yellow, as for the Yellow Brick Road, the tropism to press onward to the east had in no way diminished.

I scrambled to my feet and bent my legs to kick off into the next leap, and then it was that something even more primal than the imperative of tropism, some kinesthetic animal instinct, intervened. Rather than leap with all my power in the direction of the eastern horizon, which under the circumstances might very well have meant my death, I essayed a tentative jump straight upward, with no more intelligence behind it than that of a wounded animal testing its strength.

Instead of soaring on high, I went up about a meter and came down hard.

Then it was that some semblance of true consciousness returned to inform my cerebral centers of what my body's instincts had already known.

My weight had returned to Belshazaar normal.

The power core of my floatbelt had expired.

Although I was incapable of such technological appraisal at the time, the obvious truth of the matter was that I had overtaxed the energy reserves of my floatbelt by employing it in a manner for which it had never been intended, to wit, repeated and overly prolonged use at full upward thrust.

But the import of the catastrophe was all too clear even to the dim creature who stood there on a leaf, dwarfed now to an even greater degree by the green immensity of the Bloomenveldt, and who now tremulously resumed her mantric chant in a new minor note of despair.

"Follow the sun . . . follow the yellow . . . follow the Yellow Brick Road. . . ."

Vraiment, the yellow sun still shone in the sky behind me casting lengthening shadows toward the eastern horizon, and the Yellow Brick Road still lay before me, nor was the compulsion to

22 Traversing the Bloomenveldt as a groundling was a far cry from bounding across it in great soaring leaps as a relatively blithe creature of the air. Not only did it take half a day and more to cover the same distance that I had previously traversed in a few long leaps, now I could rely only on my own care and agility to save me from a terminal fall to the forest floor.

Thus the transitional step from one leaf to another had become a matter of some significance and forethought, and what had once seemed the minor rises and dips of the surface now assumed strategic significance, for without a usable floatbelt, I could only spy out the lay of the land before me by ascending the relative heights of the taller tree crowns.

And while the passage of the sun across the sky and the direction of the shadows it cast were sufficient to keep me following the yellow, the lay of the land ahead assumed dire significance when it came to keeping my spirit on the Yellow Brick Road. For now if I stumbled unaware into the pheromonic influence of a grove of flowers, or even of a single sufficiently cunning bloom, there would be little hope that I would ever set foot on that road to sapience again.

As for the consciousness animating the creature gingerly picking her way from leaf to leaf and pausing three or four times an hour to scout ahead and plan out a safe path between the flowers, this began to evolve further toward sapience under the evolutionary pressure of the more complex behavior that brute survival now required, just as our species had long ago evolved out of presentience when it began its long march from the mindless Eden of the trees.

For I was forced to consider every footfall, I was forced to scout ahead, I was forced to memorize a safe path through the future landscape and achieve a level of cognitive abstraction sufficient to follow this mental map of the landscape through the moment-to-moment existence of the realtime present.

Indeed, such a sophisticated perception of the relationship between space and time might very well be said to be the minimal definition of sapience itself.

So by the time the sun had begun to sink behind the western horizon, it might be fairly said that some semblance of the "I" who tells the tale had returned to inhabit the brain of the protagonist thereof.

I knew that soon I must select a leaf of relative safety upon which to spend the night, for it would not be long before every flower of the Bloomenveldt would begin to exude the irresistible perfume of sleep. And upon selecting same and settling down on it, I had achieved a level of consciousness all-too-able to reflect upon its plight.

I had no concept of how long I had been traveling, how far I had come, or how much more Bloomenveldt lay between me and the succor of the coast. I had only the dimmest notion of how long the human body might continue to function without food, mayhap a matter of weeks for a perfect master of the yogic arts, but certainement a matter of mere days for such as myself. But I knew with only too much certainty that, without my floatbelt to extract me toward the sunrise, to eat of the fruit of the Bloomenveldt, or even approach within smelling distance of the flowers thereof, would mean my sapient doom.

I, who to say the least had never been a devotee of the ascetic disciplines, would have to essay a fast of heroic proportions. Moreover, in order to do so, I must never for a moment allow my conscious will to once more lose sovereignty over the imperatives of the flesh, for the time would inevitably come when my very cells would cry out for nourishment, and if no "I" was present to provide restraint, no "I" would ever return from the mindless realm of the Bloomenkinder.

And while the mantra continued to vibrate in my brain even when my lips were sealed, and the golden face of the sun continued to shine in my mind's eye even as the first stars of night began to appear in the blackening sky, I knew full well that mere tropism would not be sufficient to maintain the conscious awareness which now swore an oath to itself that the body in which it arose would expire before the human spirit therein gave up the ghost.

"Follow the sun, follow the yellow, follow the Yellow Brick Road. . . ."

As I sat there on my leaf, determined that if I must die in this uncaring vastness it would at least be as a sapient being who deserved to call herself human even to the end, the mantra ringing in my brain and the golden mandala filling my mind's eye began to take on new complexities of meaning, or rather the message I had left for myself in the simple tropism which had brought a mindless creature through hundreds of kilometers of Bloomenveldt began to exfoliate its layers of meaning in the re-emergent mind of the human spirit who had coded it into her backbrain in the first place.

"Before the singer was the song, which has carried our kind from the trees to the stars," Pater Pan had often enough declaimed, and vraiment, where was I now but cast back into the treetops of presentience from whence long ago our species had begun its gallant march to sapience and the stars?

And what was the Yellow Brick Road I now sought to travel but the recapitulation of our species' phylogeny via my own personal ontogeny? Vraiment, as the most ancient lore of our species has it, in the beginning was the Word, the tale we told ourselves as we wandered from apes into men, the tale the Piper told still.

Tattered, begrimed and besmeared with the juices and pulps of the fruits of forgetfulness and the sweats and stains of literally unspeakable acts, the Cloth of Many Colors still tied about my waist seemed the banner of all that remained of who I had been and who I must now struggle to once more become—Sunshine Shasta Leonardo, Child of Fortune, Gypsy Joker, *ruespieler*.

For was it not the Word which had created our humanity

335

in the first place? Might it therefore not carry me back from the forest of unreason once more along the Yellow Brick Road that led homeward to the sapient worlds of men? Out here on the Bloomenveldt there might be no one to hear my tales but myself, but there was something far more precious than ruegelt to be won or lost.

And so there in the treetops, I summoned up my courage as once I had in the Luzplatz in Great Edoku, and into the darkness, into the loneliness, into an utter insensate indifference far deeper and more terrible than that of any audience of Edojin, I raised up my voice and began to spiel for the survival of my soul.

"The Spark of the Ark!" I declared to myself, and launched into a bizarre version indeed of Lance Della Imre's favorite tale, in which my clouded memory and my present concerns combined to rewrite it into a song of myself.

"Say not that the Arkies of the First Starfaring Age meekly gave up the ghost to the flowers when a way of life that had existed since the first Child of Fortune dared climb down from the trees was lost on the Bloomenveldt! For the Spark of the Ark which led us along the Yellow Brick Road out of the forest of unreason when we were wage slaves of the Pentagon is with us today in the Arkie Sparkie heart of the teller of this tale. . . ."

Short on art, mayhap, and certainement shorter on verbal coherence, it all rolled out in a glorious hebephrenia, as after aeons of naught but the same mantric drone, I reveled in the sound of a sapient human voice spieling the story of my own soul. Never has any ruespieler had a less critical or more appreciative audience than I was for myself!

Nor did the audience jade or the ruespieler tire until the nighttime perfumes of the Bloomenveldt rang down the curtain of sleep on the performance.

In the morning, I arose spieling still, declaiming mélanges of every tale I knew to myself, and transmogrifying them into my own singular song of the Yellow Brick Road.

"Follow the sun, follow the yellow, follow the Piper of the Yellow Brick Road, who was born when first I climbed down from our ancestral flowers, and who from that day unto this has taken us leaf by leaf along our Mardi Gras parade to the dawn of

336

the Second Starfaring Age in the long slow centuries between here and the coast. . . ."

Babbling thusly, I set first one halting step on the Yellow Brick Road eastward, and then another and another, following the command of my own tale.

No doubt any Healer in attendance at this stage of my journey would have judged me mad, for it cannot be denied that what he would have observed was a gaunt and starveling creature exhibiting clear symptoms of hebephrenic cafard.

For hour by hour, day by day, the longer I walked, the more famished I became, and the more I filled my ears with bits and pieces of half-remembered ruespielers' tales, the more the parts of the many became an infinitely recomplicated mantra of the one, of the only tale there presently was to tell.

Indeed if psychosis, as the Healers do claim, is a disjunction between the events of the external realm and the images thereof presented by the sensorium to the brain, if a dissolution of the interface between the journey across the wilderness of the treetops and my spirit's journey via my tale was mere psychic dysfunction, then by such an objective definition, vraiment, I was quite insane.

But those same Healers could not deny that such a malaise may only arise in a sapient brain. Which is to say I was at least still capable of human sanity or its equally human converse. Whereas those whom science could only judge perfectly adapted to the external reality of the Bloomenveldt were the mindless Bloomenkinder thereof.

From the point of view of objective scientific reportage, there would be nothing of concrete substance to relate but an endless repetition of the round of any given day.

I arise already spieling. My stomach screams its starvation, and the hollow throbbing of my head sends sparkles of static confetti across my visual sphere. I fill my belly with water collected from the hollow of a leaf.

I turn my face to the golden visage of the rising sun, and I walk, babbling to myself. I walk until the sun has passed its zenith, and I walk until it has set in the west. I walk through the gathering darkness until I am inching along by feel alone. I walk until the perfumes of night slide me into dreamless sleep.

*   *   *

Time, the mages have long told us against the evidence of the senses, is not a regularly spaced absolute along which events are strung linearly like beads. Rather it is a relationship among points in a four-dimensional space-time matrix, so that when events vary we perceive an interval of time between them. But within a crystal lattice of space-time wherein events are identical, we perceive them as a simultaneous one.

As without, so within, for the mages tell us too that dreams that seem to last for eternities in the consciousness of the dreamer occur within literal augenblicks when the duration of their electrical discharge is measured by instruments.

So too have gurus, shamans, mystics, sufis, and masters perfect or otherwise, alluded time out of mind, if with less scientific precision, to a state of being in which events are perceived with the transtemporal logic of dreams and quantum cosmology, called variously the Tao, the Ein-Sof, the Einsteinian universe, the Great and Only, the Dreamtime.

The ancient tribe who sought by just such famishment and mantric declaiming as I now employed to take their willed Walkabouts through the Dreamtime named it best for this teller of the tale attempting to recall her passage through it.

For any ordinary Healer will tell you that the consciousness arising in the brain of a starving body will sooner or later begin to blur across the line separating waking awareness from sleep, so that as the flesh begins to expire, the spirit begins its Walkabout through its final time of dreams.

As to when I could have been said to have passed over into the Dreamtime, je ne sais pas, for we never remember the crossing over from the waking realm into dream, still less so when we continue to set one foot down after the other long afterward, dreaming our Walkabout on our feet.

Certainement, the golden face of the sun in the blue sky above the Bloomenveldt that I perceived would have registered on any astronomical instrument. Certainement, I was not dreaming that I began to direct my spiel toward this solar audience.

But when the corona of light haloing the sun began to coalesce into a nimbus of golden hair, when it seemed to me that there was a pattern of human features on the face thereof,

338

.

vraiment, when it started to speak, then surely had I long since passed over into the Dreamtime.

Was this hallucination, dream, or true translation into the Great and Only Tao? Who is to say which? Indeed, how is one to even make such distinctions? For are not hallucinations, dreams, and arcane mystic visions all the tales that the spirit somehow contrives to tell to itself?

So if the Pater Pan who spoke to me out of the face of the sun was a conjuration of my dreaming brain, and the words that he spoke were only part of my own tale, had not the song that I sang to myself been learned from the very man who now spoke in the dream? Thus might I have been dreaming it all, but thus too did the true spirit of a lover contrive to frustrate the constraints of space and time to be with me in my hour of need on the Bloomenveldt.

"Follow the Piper of the Yellow Brick Road, follow the Pied Piper of the Bloomenkinder back from our ancestral flowers, muchacha," Pater Pan said as we sat together naked by a crystal pool in a pleasure garden high on a plateau in Great Edoku, even as I was walking across the surface of one more leaf.

For the landscape through which I journeyed had now taken on a nondualistic logic precisely like that of a lucid dream. For while I could perceive a yellow sun shining above an endless green plain with sufficient awareness to maintain an eastward vector, like a lucid dream, the tale I was telling myself had the power to at the same time conjure up an overlay of visions in the Dreamtime.

"Once we were all Bloomenkinder in the Perfumed Garden of Eden, Sunshine," Pater told me as he swirled his Cloth of Many Colors around his shoulders and declaimed his name tale. "Now I will lead you to the Gold Mountain even as I led you out of the city of the Pentagon to the long slow centuries between the stars."

And now, even as some part of me knew that my body was still trudging across the Bloomenveldt in a state rapidly approaching total famishment, in the Dreamtime I was wandering the streets of Great Edoku, alone, out of funds, with my bladder demanding protoplasmic relief exactly as my stomach cried out for food in the treetops.

"Remember?" said Pater's voice in my ear. "Remember when

339

you became a free creature living by your wits in the streets of Great Edoku?"

While I threaded my way among the great leaves of the treetops, I was tracking two Gypsy Jokers through the streets and parklands in search of their carnival, and when I stared at the golden face of Belshazaar's sun, it was my first eye to eye meeting with Pater Pan outside our shower stalls.

"It has taken us millennia of diligent tale-telling to create the ultimate triumph of the ruespieler's art, our own magnificent sapient selves," Pater said as we stood there admiring each other. "Have you not noticed your gift of gab?" he said as we lay on the bed in his tent.

"So keep telling the tale of the Pied Piper of the Bloomenveldt, muchacha," he said as he concluded his farewell to the Gypsy Jokers reclining on bonsaied mountains.

At last I found my own voice in the Dreamtime. "What *is* the tale of the Pied Piper of the Bloomenveldt?" I heard myself say.

And at the sound of my own words, I was transported to the most arcane Dreamtime of all. I was walking across the Bloomenveldt now even in my dream, and I was following Belshazaar's sun toward the coast, and the only disjunction between the observable reality and the Dreamtime of my spirit was that in the Dreamtime Pater Pan walked beside me.

"The only tale there is to tell," he said with a strange smile.

"How does this tale end?" I demanded.

"This tale never ends, ruespieler."

As I heard myself discoursing with this animus within a Dreamtime landscape identical to that of the waking realm, the spell of the Walkabout began to unravel, as within any dream, one may upon occasion talk oneself awake, or as an event of sufficient import transmogrifying itself into Dreamtime imagery may rouse the sleepwalker back into the dream of life.

"When will I awake from it?" I said as Pater Pan's image began to fade like a Bloomenveldt mist burning off into the rising sun.

"When the Pied Piper leads the Bloomenkinder of Hamelin back to the far-flung worlds of men," said the face of the sun as I trudged across the foliage.

"Then don't leave me out here without your song!" I shouted as the vision began to fade.

"Pas problem, lady fair," said a disembodied voice. "For now you know who the Pied Piper of the Bloomenveldt is, do you not, ruespieler. . . ?"

"Anyone who tells the tale!"

And I emerged from the Dreamtime with the words ringing from my lips across the Bloomenveldt. I was now once more confronted with a sea of wind-tossed green under a hot yellow sun, and there was no Pater Pan at my side, nor the sound of any voice save my own and that of the breezes murmuring through the branches. I was faint and light-headed from a hunger pushed deep down beneath stomach pains into cellular famishment, indeed I was a teetering crouched figure whose very metabolism was about to collapse.

But I was not alone.

For whether the Piper who had brought me thither was a figment out of the tale I was telling myself in the Dreamtime or whether some quantum vapor of a lover's spirit had somehow succored me therein, or whether these are indeed the same in a manner which no waking consciousness may comprehend, my Walkabout through the Dreamtime with that spirit guide had in any event brought me to this single purple flower.

Four human figures sat on its velvety petals avidly devouring round yellow fruit. The corpulence of their frames and the tattered bits of cloth still clinging to them gave unmistakable evidence that these had once been sapient citizens of the worlds of men.

During my passage through the Dreamtime, I had put the land of the Bloomenkinder behind me. Only the borderland region of lost civilized souls lay between me and the coast.

23

I had emerged from the land of the true Bloomen-kinder with the peroration of the Tale of the Pied Piper of the Bloomenveldt upon my lips and I emerged from the Dreamtime with the tale I had learned, or been given, or had told myself therein springing forth from them still, nor did I give over my spieling as I staggered forward toward the purple flower.

"Once you and I were Bloomenkinder in the Perfumed Garden of Eden," I quite redundantly informed the two men and two women who continued to focus their perfect attention on their fruit even as this bizarre apparition approached. "Now the Pied Piper of the Bloomenveldt bids us follow our Arkie Sparkie hearts from our ancestral flowers to the far-flung worlds of men. . . ."

Mayhap in a certain sense I was in the Dreamtime still, for while a part of me was there advancing slowly on the purple flower and its devotees, another part of me stood before the Luzplatz volcano seeking to persuade the bustling throngs of Edojin therein to hearken to my ruespiel. For indeed, to the conscious-ness then paused at the edge of the flower's pheromonic aura, they were much the same thing.

I could taste a faint perfume of sweet and sour succulence, and the very cells of my body gibbered their demand for me to fall upon the yellow fruit. On the Bloomenveldt, I knew that here

342

on the coastal fringes of the forest, floral evolution and human devolution had not yet progressed to produce the perfect symbiosis between flowers and Bloomenkinder. These corpulent fressing creatures were not Bloomenkinder but once-sapient beings who had chanced to fall under the sway of far cruder pheromones crafted not to snare men but to control the more primitive brains of the native mammals of the forest. Here a strong enough will might prevail against these less puissant molecules.

In the Edoku of my Dreamtime, I knew that I must earn the ruegelt of survival by the power of the Word alone, though now my tale need please no other ears than my own. For as long as I continued to tell my tale, as long as I could hear my own voice singing my song, as long as I remained Sunshine the ruespieler, so long would I remain on the Yellow Brick Road, for there was only one camino real of sapience through the forest of unreality, the way of the Word, and I was on it now.

"Remember when you were Children of Fortune. . . . Remember when you were free and sapient creatures living by your wits in the streets of Great Edoku. . . ."

As I spieled, I slowly resumed my approach to the purple flower, deeper into its sphere of olfactory influence, testing the puissance of the Word against the pouvoir of the perfume, as for so long I had pitted my naked will against far more powerful versions of same in the combat of the fast.

"Remember how the Pied Piper of Pan led you out of the Perfumed Garden and into the Gold Mountain across the long slow centuries between the stars. . . ."

My trepidation began to lessen as I remembered my passage via the Dreamtime from the Perfumed Garden to this borderland of the sapient spirit, as my sovereign will kept me moving forward in a deliberately measured pace against all the blandishments of the perfume and all the outraged impatience of my body.

Mayhap the shorter and darker of the two male creatures, mayhap the *man* hunkered there on the flower remembered a time when he was a free creature of the Word too, for his eyes raised themselves from his meal in a certain blinking and pathetic befuddlement, even as he continued to bite chunks of firm green pulp out of his yellow fruit.

"And where has the Pied Piper of the Bloomenveldt gone

343

now that you sit there like a bestial wage slave of the Pentagon eating the fruit of forgetfulness with your spirits Gone Before?"

I was within reaching distance of the fruit now, still spieling, my spirit still in sovereign command of the tropisms and hunger of my body.

"Nowhere, everywhere, here in the teller of the tale, vraiment within the last Arkie Spark of your own human heart!" I shouted the last into the face of the man who squatted before me, who, having now given over his fressing entirely, met my eyes with what I imagined might be the struggling ghost of a sapient glimmer.

"There!" I cried, pointing at the late morning sun. "Follow that Arkie Spark within you, follow the sun, follow the yellow, follow once more the Yellow Brick Road. . . ."

And as the rag-clad fellow fixed his gaze upon the golden-maned face of the Pied Piper rising in glory above the maya of the Bloomenveldt, I snatched up a fruit with my other hand, tucked it under my arm, and, obeying the moral of my own tale, turned my back to the flower and my face to the sun, and retreated to the east with as much flank speed as my weakened body could muster. Nor did it even occur to me to cease my spiel now that the fruit thereof was mine.

"Follow the sun, follow the yellow, follow the Pied Piper of the Bloomenveldt who has led us from apes into men. . . ."

I did not eat of the fruit until I had stopped loping, and I did not stop till I was far beyond the pheromonic aura of the flower. Even as I tore open the yellow fruit with my overgrown nails, even as I gobbled down great chunks and felt the cells of my body cry out in orgasmic release from their nutritive celibacy, I continued to babble ever-mutating versions of the only tale I had to tell where there was no ear to hear it but my own, or so I believed. For only the Pied Piper of the Bloomenveldt could keep this Child of Fortune on her Yellow Brick Road, and the Piper would be with me only so long as anyone told his tale.

Upon finishing my meal, I rose up at once, turned toward the sunrise, and set forth, spieling still. I must not have chanced to look back for several hours.

But when I did, I saw, staggering and sweating with the protests of long unused muscles not fifty meters behind me, the man whose eyes had risen for a moment from their nonbeing to meet mine at the purple flower.

He must have been soaking up the words of my tale for hours, aroused from the perfect thrall of his flower by the sheer enchantment of the novel sound of a human voice, mesmerized thereby to follow the music, or mayhap, in some dim manner, hearkening as well to the words of the song.

All during that day he followed me at some distance, struggling to keep up with the sound of my voice, for as far as I was concerned, the tale I was telling was a song I sang only for myself, and I had neither ambition to attain guruhood nor the patience to slow my pace for his benefit. That night we slumbered on leaves a good twenty meters apart. For I had no desire for discourse with someone sunk so deep in the pit of nonsentience out of which I had thusfar so painfully crawled, and he was content to listen to my tale from a distance, as if somehow mindful himself of the gulf that separated our spirits.

Mayhap the foregoing is merely the post facto dissembling of self-justification, for I can make no claim that I had then attained that sublime level of enlightenment wherein the bodhi is content to shine without grasping at worldly consequences. Suffice it to say that while he may have chosen to follow, I chose not to lead, for if I had then addressed him it would have been only to tell him that a true Child of Fortune has no chairmen of the board or kings. If this be judged callous indifference by the moral philosophers, I can only declare that moral responsibility or its converse were concepts my spirit did not contain at the time, and throw myself on the mercy of the court.

On the following morning when my spirit rose to the sun, feeling all the stronger for the previous day's triumph, I straightaway sought out another flower without a thought for the creature my words had placed in my charge, nor, on the other hand, did I eschew enticing him further with the declaiming of my endless tale to myself.

Soon enough I came upon an orange bloom where three gaunt women were munching on fibrous blue fruit of a tuberous shape. I strode boldly up to them this time, in the full verbal tide of my spiel, and one of the women seemed to listen out of the corner of her ears with a certain indifferent attention, which had me stand there and reach a proper conclusion like a true ruespieler of the Gypsy Jokers rather than immediately grab for the fruit like the same forced to snatch fressen incognito from under the noses of denizens of the Publics.

"And who is the Pied Piper of the Bloomenveldt who will lead you back into the Spark of the Ark?" I declaimed as I approached the end of the cycle. "The Child of Fortune within us all who is the teller of the tale, and in the honor of whose spirit within yourself you will now shower this ruespieler with ruegelt!"

The exiled Edojin in rags blinked at me strangely for a moment, and the logic of the Dreamtime and the logic of the quotidian moment came to coincide. "Fruit, bitte," I told my audience. "Give . . . me . . . fruit. . . ."

Then, as if a key had been turned in the lock of some long-forgotten reflex of etiquette, she handed me one of the blue tubers with a grotesquely patronly flourish, as long ago she might have tossed a coin to a busker on a civilized street.

To the extent that I was able to be moved to such complex emotion, this was no doubt the crowning achievement of a ruespieler's career, but to the extent that I could still be said to retain a sense of revulsion, I was quite horrified by this engramatic ghost of a human response.

On the next morning, still trailed by my disregarded acolyte, I repaired directly to a flower to spiel for my breakfast again, and so my feeding cycle evolved. No longer famished, no longer fearing the power of the floral perfumes, I must on some level have known that now I could easily enough have marched up to any flower and snatched up a surfeit of fruit with my own hands.

Yet in the Dreamtime, I was a Gypsy Joker ruespieler earning her survival by the power of the Word, and so, striding boldly into the pheromonic winds behind my verbal shield, I stalked like the very Princess of ruespielers straight up to a yellow flower where three Bloomenkinder sat devouring purple fruit and forthwith brought my continuous tale around to the hat-passing phase with the cavalier mendicancy of a Gypsy Joker Queen.

"Long has the tale of the Pied Piper of the Bloomenveldt been told along the primrose path of our long march from the trees to the Luzplatz, and now the Piper must be paid, which is to say the teller thereof must be honored with fruit! Fruit! Fruit! *Give me fruit!*"

Since the verbality of these revertees was to say the least limited, and since the actual tale I retold endlessly was a mythmash of personal imagery no doubt all but incomprehensible to an audience other than myself, no doubt the two fat men and the even fatter woman responded more to the sheer presence of a volcano of gushing verbality in their midst than to any apprehension of the content of the tale. Yet in another sense, every syllable of human Lingo I declaimed *was* the essential haiku version of the tale, for sapient speech itself was the protagonist thereof.

Thus I moved the grotesquely fat woman to forthwith hand me her fruit by the mere act of demanding same in the manner of a ruespieler, even though I could hardly have been said to have fairly earned this ruegelt by a proper and complete telling of my tale. Nor, having once achieved my aim in the manner I had chosen, did I have any intention of regaling these three lost Children of the yellow flower with an extended version consciously designed to rouse their spirits.

Nevertheless, as I turned to leave with my booty, the refugee who had been following me for two cycles now caught up with me at the yellow flower. Rather than attempt to emulate my impossible example, he simply snatched up a fruit and trailed after me as I retreated, blathering still, to resume my journey toward the Pied Piper of the sun.

Mayhap it was the sight of my first follower marching off behind his Piper into the sunrise, mayhap it was indeed the power of the Word itself to rouse some dormant spirit within; certainement it was no act of will of mine or power which I consciously sought to wield.

Be that as it may, there were now *two* lost children of the forest following the Pied Piper of the Bloomenveldt toward the dawning light. She who had paid me my ruegelt in fruit had now joined the Gypsy Jokers' Mardi Gras Parade.

And there would be others.

Some would follow for a day and then be ensnared by the flower of the next morning's breakfast, others would join the tribe for a few days and then revert, but none of the lost children of the forest who first began the journey were to emerge once more in the worlds of men.

For while the tribe of the Pied Piper of the Bloomenveldt was to maintain a permanent population of some half dozen, more or less, as the collectivity thereof marched eastward across the Bloomenveldt, children of the forest came, tarried awhile, departed into the darkness from whence they came, and were replaced by others, even as the immortal spirit of our species itself has been carried forth from the trees to the stars via billions of transient mortal avatars.

From hindsight's pristine moral stance, even I must own that my callous indifference to the karmic responsibilities I had acquired when I cast my net of words into the sea of what once were men was a good deal less than proof of my complete return to the true spirit of humanity. Which is to say that to my own retrospective shame, I no more sought heroically to regain the allegiance of followers who strayed back into the forest of unreason than I had braved a futile return to the Perfumed Garden to seek to rescue Guy. And if the latter had been forgone at the expense of much pain to my spirit, the former was a matter of perfect innocent oblivion. For in the tale of the Dreamtime I was living, I was no chairman of the board or king, no guru avid for followers, no Pied Piper of Pan, but just Sunshine the Gypsy Joker ruespieler, alone and singing for her sustenance, the anyone who told the tale.

At length however, I wandered into precincts where dyadic couples were sometimes to be encountered, engaged in tantric unions of such terminal intensity, and at any rate about flowers totally lacking in edibles, that any attempt at approaching them would be pragmatically futile, gauche from any minimally civilized perspective, and, moreover, as events quickly proved, it would have been perilous indeed to assume that the power of the Word could retain sovereignty over the garden perfume of the kundalinic serpent.

For upon the very first such occasion, as I myself gave the passion flower the widest of berths and continued onward, I chanced to look back and see that the two nethermost of my followers, a spindly scrawny fellow who had joined the parade only a cycle ago, and a grossly fat woman who had been waddling distantly in my wake for some days now, had paired off and were

348

making for the flower, groping each other grotesquely as they shambled toward it in their unseemly libidinal haste.

Then it was, I do believe, that the awareness of the possibility of karmic debt and human caritas intruded into the perfect moral void of my spirit, for now at any rate, upon losing two of same to the flowers in this starkly graphic manner, I began to perceive that there were indeed *human beings* in my van whom I had somehow managed, without consciousness of trying, to lead a certain distance along the road from darkness to sapient light.

And while from the viewpoint of cosmic equity, it was *they* who owed *me* a debt of gratitude for what I had so freely given, from the point of view of evolutionary responsibility, it was *I* who had cast my net of words into the sea of the Bloomenveldt without regard for the plight of those lungfish brought up out of the floral deeps struggling and gasping to breathe sapient air.

Which is to say that while extinguishing my own consciousness in a futile attempt to rescue Guy might have been a useless act of suttee, that consciousness was in no current danger of imminent extinction, and mayhap I owed it to whatever spirit that had saved me to have a like regard for the lost sapient spirits that fate and my own unknowing efforts had chanced to place in my charge.

Vraiment, in practical terms there was not much more for me to do but continue my endless spieling trek eastward, avoiding even distant approach to the flowers of lust as best as I was able, make some minimal concessions to not letting my charges fall too far behind, and hector those who began to stray off the Yellow Brick Road with imprecations they could not understand and kicks and shoves which were somewhat more efficacious.

Which is not to say I achieved any perfection as a shepherd then, moral or otherwise, for when it came to approaching a passion flower after two of my lost children had stolen away thereto, there I drew the line, for I would not endanger my own survival to attempt to save such doomed spirits, nor would I allow any event to long delay the march to the coast. In this was self-preservation of this individual in harmony with the preservation of the collectivity of the tribe, for if there was no longer anyone to tell the tale, the days of our tribe would be forthwith ended.

Indeed, if truth be told, I was no shepherd diligently herding sheep, for I was primarily conscious of my charges as an imposition, like a hiker who finds herself adopted by a pride of lost kittens and cannot fail to accept a certain tender regard for their safety or consign them to the wilderness without regret, but who would just as soon not have to assume a position of guardianship over them.

So, vraiment, I proceeded more slowly and cautiously now, reluctantly mindful that I was somehow responsible for a collectivity of other spirits as well as my own. And now, trailed by some four acolytes emphatically not of my choosing, a new level of consciousness reappeared, a being I would contend had at last earned the right to once more be called fully human.

For while the subject of my sanity at any stage of the tale and the sequence in which my consciousness reevolved was to be a matter of endless learned debate by Healers and mages far better versed in the scientific lore than I, in the entirely amateur opinion of the subject in question, my full *humanity* was restored when I accepted responsibility, however reluctantly, for preserving the humanity of others.

At the time that I encountered the bodhi in the wood, there were four members in the Pied Piper's tribe, the four final members as it would turn out, for we attracted no new Children of Fortune this close to the coast, nor was I to brook the loss of another of my charges to the forest again, not now with my moral awareness renascent, and the flowers of lust behind us.

Three of them were men: a thin blond fellow whom I inventoried under Goldenrod, an obese man who became Rollo, and a balding man I thought of as Dome. For while it could hardly be said that these lost creatures of the forest exhibited what could be styled a human personality, it seemed both just and convenient to grant them the nominal dignity I certainly would have given to the aforementioned lost kittens.

The woman was the most human-looking specimen of the lot, which is to say her physique was neither gaunt nor obese, and her eyes upon occasion seemed to assume a questioning look. She I dubbed Moussa, for in her I dared hope I saw a spark of myself, a kindred though mute spirit, whose life I now held in the cupped palms of my hand.

Of the four that I was to lead out of the Bloomenveldt, she was the only one who after arduous efforts was to reclaim her full sapient citizenship in the worlds of men. And Moussa did she take for her freenom years later upon her release from mental retreat in hommage to she who named and told her wanderjahr's tale.

These were my companions when I happened upon the bodhi in the wood, as I came to style him in the nomenclature of memory. We came upon him suddenly. I rounded a hillock of tree crown and emerged right into a bowered dell on the other side, where a man sat in the posture of the lotus before a flower whose petals fanned out behind him to enhalo his existence in a lambent blue aura.

This was no moribund sage in his final years of life meditating into eternity by the look of him. He was a taut and golden-skinned man whose naked body gave every evidence of excellent health. Sleek black hair hung down to his shoulders. He seemed almost fit enough to pass for a Bloomenkind.

But his clear green eyes seemed not to be the vacant orbs of a Bloomenkind gazing mindlessly into a blue void, rather did I somehow sense the presence of a fully sapient spirit contemplating limpid inner depths. Or at any rate a visage of sufficient novelty under the circumstances to give my ceaseless babble the first moment of pause it could remember.

As if tuned to the very frequency of my thoughts, the bodhi's attention seemed to rise up from those inner depths to regard me with a sudden keenness, though, in hindsight's vision, my little tribe and I must have presented a vision of even more striking novelty to him than he had to me.

"Who are you?" he said in a strong tranquil voice. "Where have you come from?"

Simple and logical enough questions one might suppose, but ones which at the time I was not exactly psychically equipped to answer succinctly. "We are the Children of Fortune of the Bloomenveldt following the song that draws us thither as apes from our ancestral flowers to the far-flung worlds of men," I declaimed, in the only mode of discourse of which I was presently capable.

"You are the mystical Bloomenkinder of the forest?" the bodhi exclaimed, maintaining the immobile perfection of his yogic posture, but verbally allowing a rather unsagelike astonishment to

351

betray its presence in his voice. "Vraiment, it would seem you have indeed come a long march from your ancestral flowers!"

"It has taken millions of years of diligent study to produce the ultimate triumph of the ruespieler's art, our own magnificent sapient selves," I readily enough agreed.

At this his eyes widened, becoming somehow more humanly focused and more inwardly distant at the same time, as if *I* were a creature of some Dreamtime to *him*. "From how far into the forest have you come, Bloomenkind?" he asked me expectantly, as if hanging on some hoped-for answer. "You speak as one who has found her perfect flower."

"I speak as one who was a perfect Bloomenkind of the Perfumed Garden before there was anyone to tell the tale," I told him rather crossly, for such unwholesome obtuseness was enough to rouse a certain ire, and ire reevolved my consciousness to yet a more recomplicated level. "You speak as one who seeks a Perfumed Garden of perfection for your spirit."

At this a positively fawning expression came onto his face which cloyed my palate like treacle. "Can it be that my exercises are now at last to be rewarded?" he said breathlessly. "Are you a vision sent to me by destiny? Are you to be my guide to the Perfumed Garden?"

"Follow the sun, follow the yellow, follow the tale of the Pied Piper of the Bloomenveldt, to which we have marched for the long slow centuries from the trees to the stars," I told him, struggling to regain the power to craft the stream of my logorrhea into a more precise verbal instrument. "Follow not the flowers of the Bloomenveldt into the dim mists before the singer became the song. Seek not to become a perfect Bloomenkind in your Perfumed Garden, but follow the Yellow Brick Road."

"You have truly seen the Perfumed Garden?" the bodhi persisted, as if I had not at all succeeded in conveying even the vaporous spirit of my meaning, or as if his spirit simply refused to hear.

"Vraiment, once I was a Bloomenkind in the Perfumed Garden of our ancestral Eden, before I heard the Piper's song," I said, since this seemed to be the only thing he was willing to hear.

He stared at me in wonder. "And like a bodhisattva you then chose to return to the worlds of men?" he exclaimed.

"Enlighten me, spirit of the forest, show me the way to your Perfumed Garden of perfection."

My aforementioned ire had been rising throughout the latter part of this discourse, and while the logical rationale for it was beyond my comprehension at the time, and the inner psychic dynamics were only to be elucidated later in the Clear Light Mental Retreat, at that moment, it seemed to me that I was once more hectoring the spirit of Guy Vlad Boca, wearing the vile crown of the Charge in the Hotel Pallas, seated in just such a lotus position under his flower smiling just such a smile of vapid bliss.

"In the Perfumed Garden, there is no one there to tell the tale, and the Pied Piper of Pan never plays his song," I told him, my eyes misting with outrage, or sadness, or mayhap somehow both. "Join the Mardi Gras Parade and follow the only tale there is to tell to the encampment of the Gypsy Jokers in the Gold Mountain, for true Children of Fortune have no chairmen of the board or Perfumed Gardens of perfect flowers."

"You have been to the Perfumed Garden and of your own free will returned to the worlds of men?" the bodhi said incredulously. "You are this Pied Piper of the Bloomenveldt and these Bloomenkinder of the forest follow the song of your voice?"

"I am a simple ruespieler on the streets of Great Edoku," I told him. "I am anyone who tells the tale."

The bodhi of the wood began to draw back into the depths of himself at this, as if retreating from a surfeit of unwelcome satori, or mayhap in order to avoid suffering same. "Mayhap you are the sister of the Prince of Liars, storyteller, for you cannot be speaking truth," he said as he seemed to will his gaze inward. "*No one* has ever returned to the worlds of men from the land of the Bloomenkinder."

Thus had a terrified and lonely girl spoken to her own heart when she awoke on a leaf in the very darkest heart of the land of the Bloomenkinder with neither filter mask nor food. This doom of the spirit had that girl sworn an oath to overcome or die in the attempt.

I regarded the bodhi of the woods who now had completely resumed his gaze into the featureless emptiness of his self-chosen void, and I regarded Goldenrod, Rollo, Dome, and Moussa, my four dim creatures who had patiently stood there all the while, mesmerized by the sound of human discourse, struggling however unsuccessfully to escape from the very nullity he sought to embrace. Somehow, it seemed to me that in some strange Dreamtime of the human heart, their poor little spirits were more truly human than he.

And it was the Sunshine Shasta Leonardo who had sworn that oath who now looked on her charges with a more tender regard, and addressed *them*, not the immobile icon of spiritual perfection, with the very words that had begun the tale of the Pied Piper of the Bloomenveldt and which now served admirably as the summation thereof.

"No one," I said, "has ever returned to the worlds of men from the land of the Bloomenkinder *before*."

After this confrontation with the bodhi of the wood, I no longer stalked impatiently ahead of my lost children of the forest, but walked among them, addressing my spiel to an audience other than myself. And while nothing could yet quite emerge from my lips that was not cobbled together out of swatches of the only tale I had to tell, I grew self-conscious of the fact that I was practicing the ruespieler's art, if for a commodity of far more absolute importance than ruegelt. And when one of my charges threatened to stray, or showed reluctance to leave a flower of our feeding, I hectored the same as harshly and insistently as was needful in tones and cadences one would apply to an unruly toddler who had yet to learn the lyric of the human song.

Thus did we proceed eastward toward the worlds of men, and thus did I sow all unbeknownst the seed of the Word in this long-fallow ground.

The same was to sprout at a carmine flower at which we had been feeding in the company of two nearly terminally torpid human creatures who had long since gorged themselves to impressive obesity on the strangely meatlike pulp of the sweet blue fruit.

Rollo, it seemed, had encountered a flower whose fruit chanced to contain molecules too puissantly congruent with the ideals of his metabolism. With unwholesome and unsettling avidity did he rip chunks of the tough chewy pulp out of the fruit and gobble them down, and when it came time to depart, he was entirely deaf to my entreaties.

"Arise, Rollo, to follow the yellow, for the sun calls you

down from your ancestral trees to follow the Yellow Brick Road!"
I fairly shouted in his face at length, and when this too he ignored,
I shook him by the shoulders, and then turned his vision sunward
by main force.

"Follow the sun, follow the yellow, follow the sun, follow
the yellow. . . ." I began to chant over and over again, for this
indeed was the most primal version of the tale, the synergetic
mantra which had roused me from just this condition, vraiment,
from worse.

I continued to chant, pointing to the sun with one hand,
and keeping his face turned toward it with the other. When all at
once, I noticed a bizarre change in my own voice, for on certain
syllables the single note of my vocal cords seemed to be accompanied by a harmonic chord on another instrument.

Some moments later it dawned on me that this was more
or less the case.

While my efforts to fix Rollo's attention on our song of the
road and the rising sun thereof had thusfar been ineffective,
Dome and Goldenrod had out of traditional tribal custom fixed
their gaze thereon as soon as they had heard a few turns of the
traveling mantra.

So too had Moussa.

But, ah, Moussa, Moussa my appointed namesake, raggedly,
atonally, blinking with the effort, had begun to chant.

"Yellow . . . follow . . . yellow . . . follow . . ."

A moronic sprach mayhap, but certainement a sprach in
the Lingo of man.

Seizing upon this amazing event, I fitted my own voice to
this simple drone, waving my arms like an orchestral conductor at
Dome and Goldenrod, up and down with the beat.

"Follow . . . yellow . . . follow . . . yellow . . ."

At length, Dome joined in, and once there were three of
us, Goldenrod soon enough followed. And finally, roused at last
by the communal efforts of his tribal siblings, Rollo gave over his
eating, rose to his feet, set his eyes upon the sun, and began
forming flaccid and silent simulacra of the syllables with his own
pulp-smeared lips.

While the utility of applying this monotonous two-note chant
whenever one of my charges began to fall behind or threatened

355

to be captured by a flower proved admirably efficacious, the esthetic excruciation of it from the point of view of the ruespieler hardly rendered it suitable for a permanent song of the road, and so I continued to spiel the tale to them whenever I could, rather than make the sacrificial effort to keep them chanting.

For this I was to be chided more than once by certain mages in the Clear Light who informed me that I should have been much more diligent in my efforts to restore their powers of speech. I would counter now as I did then, which is to say that in spite of my laxity and indifference to the approved therapeutic methods, they began to speak anyway.

If true speech it may be styled, a point of some dispute in scientific circles even today. Certainement, the sounds that Rollo, Dome, Goldenrod, and Moussa began to make as I spieled them through those last days on the Bloomenveldt were undeniably in the form of words, and at the end, the tribal vocabulary contained nearly a dozen of these, though only Moussa was master of them all.

"Follow . . . yellow . . . sun . . . road . . . Piper . . . fortune . . . Bloomenkinder . . . children . . . far-flung-words-of-men . . ."

That was about the extent of it, and certain authorities were to claim that this vocabulary consisted of precisely those sounds which the teller of the tale repeated most frequently and with rhythmic emphasis, which is to say that much the same effect could be achieved with a tribe of parrots. Indeed I was once told that one of these worthies actually produced a cageful of aviary babel with just the same vocabulary to prove his point.

But when at length we finally reached the coastline, unlike parrots, my Children of Fortune were quite able to use their few poor words to make their feelings plain, or so in my heart did it seem to me.

Sunset had come the night before upon a Bloomenveldt lying under a thin cloak of fog, so that the sharp line of the horizon had disappeared into vague green mists for several hours before darkness. Morning awoke me with the wan yellow light of dawn, just as the rim of the sun was beginning to peer over the line of the eastern horizon. The fog had long since gone, the pale sky was brilliantly clear, and one by one my fellow creatures were beginning to arise from the perfumed sleep of the Bloomenveldt.

Then, as the true blaze of sunrise arose above the last

356

vestiges of night, a brilliant mirrored sheen fairly exploded into existence as the sun emerged from it in a visual paean to glory. For halfway to the horizon, the leafy green plain abruptly ended, and a sea of rippling silvered flashes began.

"Yellow . . . sun . . . Piper . . . fortune . . ."

Rollo, Dome, Goldenrod, and Moussa stood beside me as we watched the sun of our fortune arise at last over the eastern ocean.

Did they truly perceive it as I did? Did their minds contain some dim memory that the line between the Bloomenveldt and the sea was the visual dividing line between the forest of the flowers and the sapient worlds of men? Je ne sais pas, but tell me not that they could not entirely perceive that the tale of the Pied Piper of the Bloomenveldt had led them to a vantage from whence they could see the promised land where the Bloomenveldt of the spirit ended.

"Follow fortune, follow yellow!"

"Piper of the Bloomenkinder!"

"Far-flung-worlds-of-men!"

"Fortune Children follow yellow!"

Was it in truth only my sapient imagination overlaying random parroting with the exultation of my own spirit that spoke to me as I watched them babble their excitement at the sight of the ocean? In truth, as some would say, might a cock have also greeted the sunrise thusly, and with the same degree of sincere enthusiasm?

My spirit tells me not, nor did my eyes fail to see mouths rippling in what might have been attempts at smiles, nor was I deaf to gurgling sounds which might have been their happy laughter.

Certainement there was more than the spiritual vacuum behind the speech of a parrot in their eyes as one by one they came to look directly into my own.

"Piper!"

"Yellow!"

"Fortune!"

"Follow!"

"Vraiment, follow the yellow, my Children of Fortune," I told them, "for we lost children of the forest have now found ourselves."

"Follow the sun, follow the yellow!"

"Children found!"

"Follow Yellow Brick Road!"

They were more than human parrots; at the very least they were eager puppies, yipping and dancing to reach the end of the trail. And so did we set out for the last time into the Bloomenveldt sunrise toward the worlds of men.

Within a few hours, the interlocking foliage of the Bloomenveldt thinned out into a treacherous webwork of branches and long falls to the forest floor which we dared not approach. This was as far eastward as we could go. From this vantage, there was no seacliff plunge of perspective, nor any beach in view to mark the melding of land into sea. Some thousand meters before us, the irregular green sameness of the flower-speckled Bloomenveldt gave way to the shimmering clarity of an ocean under a cloudless sky with the clean sharpness of Occam's razor-edge.

And along this razor-sharp interface, all roads led to Rome.

For a few moments, my tribe milled about in confusion, for they knew not where next to go.

"Fear not, for you are no longer lost children of the forest, my Gypsy Jokers," I told them as I turned to the south and began the final march. "Follow the Pied Piper of the Bloomenveldt!"

"Follow yellow, follow *Piper!*" Moussa began to chant as she fell in step beside me, as if acknowledging to the both of us that the Word of the Piper superceded the mute vector of the sun.

"Follow yellow, follow *Piper!*" the others chimed in, tentatively at first, and then, as if achieving a level of abstraction sufficient unto resolving the conflict of tropisms by bestowing the yellowness of the sun and all that it implied upon the voice that they followed, with more certain enthusiasm.

"Follow yellow, follow Piper, follow yellow, follow Piper!"

Thus did our Mardi Gras parade begin, thus did the Pied Piper of the Bloomenveldt lead her Children of Fortune, thus did a raving, grimy, rag-clad girl lead four chanting creatures struggling to be human out of the forest of flowers to dance triumphant through the streets of the worlds of men.

24

But little did I know that, long before the sun had begun to slide down the sky, the gnomes of the research domes would suddenly bring the worlds of men to us.

Vraiment, though such a perception would never have occurred to me at the time, no doubt the research team that suddenly dropped in on us out of the sky were no more prepared for the bizarre sight we presented than our little tribe was for them!

It happened with just such mutually discombobulating unexpectedness. Four silvery human figures came floating down from the sky to land on a cluster of leaves not ten meters away.

They stood there gesticulating and making incomprehensible sounds to each other, and while it might be safely assumed that they were staring as intently at us as we were at them, this was impossible to verify, for they were sealed in full atmosphere suits—form-fitting coveralls and hoods of silvery fabric, filter masks, and impenetrable mirrored visors above them.

Moussa, Rollo, Goldenrod, and Dome had fallen silent. They stood there gaping vacantly, incapable of terror, mayhap rediscovering the emotion of surprise.

I myself, naturellement, had seen scientists in atmosphere suits often enough during my sojourn in the research dome to decode the import of these silver beings after a few moments of pure thoughtless shock. I too had once bounded in great weightless leaps across the Bloomenveldt, and while I had never sheathed my body in such alienating armor, certainement, I retained memories of what the Bloomenveldt was like from the other side of a filter mask.

But long before I could formulate any course of action, the research team went into purposeful motion. Two of them skipped with light gingerly steps to the leaf upon which we stood while the other two remained in place and aimed the lenses and antennae of various devices in our direction.

"Sprechen sie Lingo? Are you verbal?"

"In the beginning was the Word, and before the singer was the song," I replied, "which has carried us from our ancestral flowers to the far-flung worlds of men."

"Carramba!" exclaimed a voice from behind the left-hand mirrored visor. "She speaks, she declaims poetry no less, and you will observe no filter mask in evidence, nicht wahr! Ah, many theories will now be in need of revision! Certainement, this is a major find!"

"Who are you, kind, do you remember your name, how long have you been out here on the Bloomenveldt?"

"The Pied Piper of the Bloomenkinder has taken many millennia of diligent study to create that ultimate triumph of the ruespieler's art, our own magnificent sapient selves," I told him.

"What? Qué? Was ist los?"

"*Bloomenkinder!* Wahrlich! Observe these creatures, see their vacant expressions! It's true, we have found ourselves a tribe of the mythical Bloomenkinder!"

Now the two scientists gave over their attempts at discourse with me to peer and prod at my Gypsy Jokers. These, possessed of no sapient mode of reaction to such scientific scrutiny, stood indifferently motionless and mute throughout.

"Indeed! These folk are possessed of neither filter masks, floatbelts, nor full human consciousness. *Bloomenkinder!* What a treasure house their metabolisms must be! Our fortunes are made!"

"Once we were Bloomenkinder in the Perfumed Garden, but now we are sapient spirits of the Arkie Spark," I told them, for while the full sapience of my charges might be arguable, certainement they were no flower-suckled Bloomenkinder of the

Bloomenveldt depths, nor, after all we had gone through to reach this place, was I about to let us be so styled.

"Now you declare these are *not* Bloomenkinder?" one of the abstract silvery figures said to me quite pettishly. "When a moment ago you declared yourself the Pied Piper thereof?"

"This is hardly a scientific question of such triviality that we can expect to decide it on the basis of anecdotal interrogation in the field!" said the other. "We must forthwith remove these specimens to our facilities for proper study."

"Ja," said his colleague, and then addressed himself to the recording team. "Summon a hover. Have them prepare quarters suitable to feral humans. And apply for a droit of custodianship forthwith."

A scant half hour later, during which the scientists engaged in wild theorizing and even more enthusiastic financial speculation with little apparent regard for the objects thereof, a dull-steel-colored and vaguely ovoid craft came skimming in over the ocean, level with the canopy of the Bloomenveldt.

The ungainly cargo hover slowed to walking speed as it reached the edge of the Bloomenveldt and slowly inched its way toward us about half a meter above the foliage, until it had reached a more or less stationary position above the wind-tossed treetops no more than a few meters from where we all stood. Bivalve doors in the prow of the hover then opened like the maw of some great cetacean inviting entry.

As for me, I regarded this proposition with a good deal less trepidation than had Jonah or Pinocchio, and started forth across the intervening leaves with as much dispatch as the two recording scientists, who were now disappearing inside with their equipment.

When it came to what the scientists styled "Bloomenkinder," however, these remained entirely unresponsive to their urgings and proddings, and the other two were constrained, with something a bit less than good humor, to draw me back and enlist my aid.

"You will be so good as to herd your Bloomenkinder aboard so that we may depart, bitte," said the one.

"Wait!" cried the other. "The method thereof must be recorded, for it may be of some scientific value." Via a transceiver behind his filter mask, he summoned the others to the lip of the entrance to the hover's cargo bay, where they once more set up a

361

variety of instruments and aimed their lenses and antennae in my direction.

"Sehr gut!" said the fellow who seemed to be in charge, when he had gotten the word from the recording team. "Commence, bitte!"

While under more ordinary conditions I would have remonstrated with a good deal of pettishness at being ordered about in this cavalier manner, and indeed, as my career as a subject of scientific inquiry progressed, was to dig in my heels more than once at such rude behavior, at the time I wanted nothing more than to be gone from the Bloomenveldt, and was many weeks away from such consideration of the social niceties.

I therefore did as I was bade, which is to say I confronted Moussa, Rollo, Goldenrod, and Dome, and began to chant. "Follow Piper, follow yellow, follow Piper, follow yellow. . . ."

In a minute or two, I had them all chanting along with me again, and once this was achieved, the Pied Piper had little trouble leading her Children of Fortune across the last few leafy meters of the Bloomenveldt, if not exactly into the Gold Mountain, then certainement into the eager mouth of scientific scrutiny.

"Follow Piper! Follow yellow! Follow Piper! Follow yellow!"

"Fantastic! Wunderbar!"

"Nothing like it in the literature!"

The two mages brought up the rear, shaking their heads and muttering to each other. Then we were all inside the stark and bare gray-walled cargo bay, the doors snapped shut on this rich meal of unique specimens, and the Bloomenveldt disappeared from my sight forever.

The next two days were a disorienting mélange of periods of boredom and periods of frenetic activity of which I was an entirely passive object.

Upon reaching the research dome, we were all forthwith stripped of our rags, unceremoniously hosed down outside like so many domestic animals, and reclothed in plain and ill-fitting white smocks, though I adamantly refused to give over my sash of Cloth of Many Colors, which I belted around my waist.

We were then ushered into a large storeroom where crates and canisters had been piled high against the walls to make room for rude cots. We were fed an indifferent meal of overbroiled and unidentifiable cutlets with a soggy assortment of steamed vegetables and then left alone to our own devices.

While my former charges were content to lie on their cots and stare placidly at the harsh lighting fixtures set in the ceiling, I straightaway went to the door and discovered, with little surprise though not without a certain consternation, that it had been locked behind me.

I spent the next several hours alternately pacing about the storeroom and fidgeting on my cot, attempting all the while to marshal my psychic resources to meet the new reality.

Certainement, confinement within this grim bare chamber was a far cry from either the open expanses of the Bloomenveldt or the vision of triumphant return to the far-flung worlds of men that had kept me trekking onward thereon for what seemed like the better part of my young lifetime. I was avid to travel onward, though to where, and how, I no longer quite knew.

Indeed though I soon enough resolved to demand my freedom at the earliest opportunity, when at length a party of scientists entered the storeroom laden with a bewildering profusion of instruments, equipment, and recording devices, I found that I had no form within which to frame such a demand.

For while freedom *from* the present situation was a concept I could readily enough grasp, the question of freedom to do *what* seemed entirely unanswerable at the time. Freedom to wander aimlessly around the research dome? Freedom to return to a vie of endlessly wandering the Bloomenveldt? When it came to resuming my life's journey, I had no more concept of how to proceed or what to demand than did Moussa, Rollo, Dome, and Goldenrod.

Therefore, for want of any active goal to pursue or coherent demand to present, there seemed to be nothing for it but to passively submit to the samplings, measurements, and poking about of the scientists, who, au contraire, seemed to lack nothing in the way of purposeful motivation. Electrodes were affixed to various portions of my anatomy, instruments prodded and glided over every centimeter of my body, syringes withdrew blood, urine was demanded and delivered up, even samples of my tears, sweat, nasal mucus, saliva, and vaginal juices found their way into vials.

When these exercises were finally concluded, we were fed another indifferent meal, and then left alone once more. For what must have been several more hours, no event of significance occurred save those taking place within my own skull, and even these were of little note, for the inescapable passivity of my position cloaked my consciousness in a pall of ennui. What was I to do? What was I to even wish to do? Indeed, now that the tale of the Pied Piper of the Bloomenveldt had reached what should have been its triumphant conclusion, who in fact was I?

After some immeasurable period, the storeroom lights were extinguished, and I lay there on the unfamiliar cot in the darkness longing for an escape into sleep that was a long time in coming, for here the irresistible perfume thereof was of course absent, and my metabolism, long-accustomed to the nightly cycle of same, kept me awake and tossing until—

—I was rudely shocked into full wakefulness by a sudden blaze of light that had me leaping off the cot and halfway across the room to follow the sun, follow the yellow, before the sight of the bare gray walls and ceiling, the piles of crates and canisters, and the three men who had entered with breakfast, brought me back with a psychic thump to this most unpleasantly quotidian of all the worlds of men.

As far as I was concerned, the second day in the storeroom was no different from the first, though no doubt, from the point of view of science, much novel data must have been accumulated by the new rounds of intimate explorations.

Be such valuable research as it may, from the point of view of the subject thereof, nothing of significance could be said to have happened. I ate, I suffered examination, I lay torpidly on my cot, was fed another meal, was subject to further scientific ministrations, and once more was plunged into the darkness of an ersatz night.

But the next morning, shortly after a breakfast of toasted grains and nuts mixed with dried fruits, a new assortment of mages began to parade in and out of the storeroom. Which is to say that though the traffic of the past few days had been perceived as nothing more coherent than a blur of bodies, apparatus, and faces, I perceived that these were new visitors, for, if nothing else, their actions were quite different.

There were no more samplings of body fluids, no more pokings, proddings, and arcane measurements of protoplasmic

364

functions, for these assorted newcomers were laden with no instruments or apparatus at all.

Rather, like a tribe of Wayfaring Strangers divvying up their loot, one by one, and not without a certain haggling among themselves, but entirely without regard for any wishes of the objects thereof, they began making off with my lost children of the forest.

Rollo was the first to go, allowing himself to be dragged off passively by two dour-looking women. "Wait!" I cried, but they quite ignored me, and when I essayed a physical intervention, I was restrained by a veritable wall of mages. In like manner were Dome and Goldenrod removed from the storeroom against my incoherent protestations. Nor would any of the mages deign to enlighten me as to the nature of these occurences.

Indeed, neither Rollo, Dome, nor Goldenrod themselves either made any move to protest events or so much as bade farewell to their onetime savior. Only Moussa dug in her heels for a moment as two men dragged her off, and seemed to gaze inquiringly into my eyes. "Follow. . . ?" she seemed almost to ask. "Follow Piper. . . ? Follow. . . ? Follow. . . ?"

This was more than I could bear, and had I had my full wits about me, no doubt I would have activated the Touch and employed it in a manner that would not at all have been to the liking of these mages. "Where are you taking my Gypsy Jokers?" I demanded at the top of my lungs while three of them held me back by main force. "Are you mute Bloomenkinder? Speak—"

At length one of the men bearing off Moussa deigned to pay me verbal heed. "The Bloomenkinder have been assigned to various mental retreats where they will be well treated, kind," he told me. "Mayhap we will succeed in restoring them to full sapience. In any event, rest assured that your friends will have the best of care, and will have abundant opportunity to serve the cause of science."

And with that, Moussa too was gone. I was never to see any of them again, and, upon exhaustive inquiry years later, learned as I have said, that only Moussa was ever returned to full sapient sovereignty. Poor Rollo lived only a few more years, whereas Dome and Goldenrod still dwell in mental retreats on Belshazaar even to this day. Dome has never learned to truly speak, whereas Goldenrod eventually attained the verbal level of a small child.

To those who would now say that, given these results, I might have done better to leave the four of them to their blissful union with the flowers, myself at times, if truth be told, among them, *I* would say that the return of Moussa to full citizenship in the human species, vraiment, mayhap Goldenrod's eventual transformation into an innocent child at least equipped for some true human congress, justifies my actions when the karmic accounts are debited and credited.

Be all that as it may, I had no prescient foreknowledge of their future fates when they followed me across the Bloomenveldt, nor, once they were removed from my care forever, did I have any alternate course of action to suggest, even if the same would have been heeded. I only knew that I was now quite alone in the storeroom of the research dome wondering what fate *I* was now to suffer in the service of science.

But I was given little opportunity to brood on this, for almost as soon as Moussa had been removed, a tall, somewhat portly man with short iron-gray hair and a kindly if somewhat over-proper demeanor, entered the storeroom alone, ignored all his colleagues, and made straight for me.

"Guten tag," he said quite pleasantly. "Ich bin Urso Moldavia Rashid, servidor de usted. Bitte, I would discuss with you a proposition of mutual benefit." So saying, he executed a little bow, and gestured with perfect politesse for me to follow.

After all those weeks on the Bloomenveldt sans even the sound of coherent discourse and these two days during which I had been treated with less courtesy than that due a household pet, I was utterly charmed by this sudden display of civilized manners toward my person, and went along without even thought of demur. Urso ushered me out of the storeroom, down a hallway, and into a small chamber which might have been someone's office commandeered for the occasion, equipped as it was with desk, terminal, racks of word crystals, arcane charts, and chairs. He seated me on a chair directly before the desk and took his place behind it, for all the worlds as if this were to be some sort of interview for a position of importance.

"You are said to be quite verbal," he began, "so now that I have introduced myself, bitte favor me likewise, though a formal exchange of name tales can await another occasion."

I struggled to marshal my thoughts sufficiently to reply in

quotidian kind, for it was the niceties of civilized discourse which then seemed to me arcane, and the spieling of my endless tale the mode ordinaire of my verbality. "I am the only tale there is to tell which has taken us from the ancestral flowers to. . . ." I blinked. I paused. With a great effort, I made myself go on in a long-unaccustomed vein. "I am Moussa . . . I am Sunshine Shasta Leonardo, Gypsy Joker, Child of Fortune, ruespieler," I managed to say, and I was quite pleased with the results of my efforts.

Urso smiled warmly. "Gut," he said approvingly. "And I am Urso Moldavia Rashid, Healer, mage of psychic therapy, domo of the Clear Light Mental Retreat, in which capacity I tender my invitation."

"Invitation?"

"Invitation, proposal d'affaires, offer of succor, la même chose, nicht wahr, to wit, I offer you residence in the Clear Light on terms to be agreed upon."

"Incarceration in a mental retreat like my fellows?" I exclaimed in alarm and dismay.

"Nein, nein, nein!" Urso declared as if he found this notion as heinous as I did. "While I was forced to purchase droit of guardianship from these scoundrels in order to be allowed to make this offer, and while your mental competence may be a matter of some dispute, I hereby waive, as a token of good faith, any right of involuntary custodianship. The terms that I offer do not include involuntary incarceration. You will be provided with a decent enough private chamber, three meals per diem, a modest though civilized wardrobe, use of our therapeutic services gratuit, and within reasonable limits you may come and go at your own pleasure. All that your end of the bargain requires is your aid in our researches."

"Never will I agree to partake of the psychotropics of the Bloomenveldt and become a Bloomenkind of the mental retreats!" I told him with growing coherence, for I was beginning to remember all too well what sort of researches were carried on therein.

Urso laughed and brushed this objection aside with a wave of his hand. "Fear not," he said, "for in any case your prolonged exposure to the psychotropics of the Bloomenveldt renders you quite unfit as a subject for psychopharmacological research, nicht wahr. But you style yourself a 'ruespieler,' so-called, nē? And this,

I have been given to understand is one who earns her keep by the telling of tales. . . . ?"

I nodded my assent.

"Well, then consider my offer one of employment in your professional capacity."

"Ruespieler in a mental retreat?" I said in perfect befuddlement.

"As it were," declared Urso. "For if the statements of the scientists of this dome are to be credited, you own to, among other things, having penetrated to the realm of the so-called Perfumed Garden, having been a Bloomenkind of the deep forest, and, as evidenced by my own eyes, to have returned with the tale thereof to tell. Wahrlich? C'est vrai?"

Once more I nodded. "I have followed the tale of the Pied Piper of the Bloomenveldt from our ancestral flowers back to the far-flung worlds of men," I agreed.

"Well then surely you perceive that such an adventure of the spirit holds considerable interest for the sciences of the mind," Urso said. "So what is required of you is several hours per diem during which you will spiel us your tale thereof and your answers to whatever elucidatory questions we may pose to assist our inquiries into the scientific facts thereof. And while I freely admit that our primary aim may be the advancement of science, in the process thereof you will certainly gain sufficient renewed clarity to once more rejoin the body politic of the worlds of men as an independent agent. You will accept, nicht wahr?"

"And if I do not?"

Urso shrugged. "As a man of honor who has sworn the oath of Hippocrates, I am constrained to eschew all coercion in these matters," he said, not entirely convincingly. "As my bona fides thereof, I offer sufficient alternative largesse to pay your passage back to Ciudad Pallas should you refuse. . . ."

"And how am I to survive on the streets of Ciudad Pallas?" I asked, for I now remembered all too well the vile bleakness thereof, and the fact that the only employment available to a Child of Fortune therein was as an experimental subject.

Urso threw up his hands in an admission of ignorance and favored me with a smile that was a bit too smugly self-assured for my taste.

Nor did I have any rejoinder to make to this eloquent silent reply. Indeed, now that consideration of the practicalities of survival had been thrust upon me, even in my present state, I knew all too well that I was being offered a good deal less than a free choice.

For I was confronted with an alternative of impotent indigence even more perfect than what I had faced when I had been expelled from the Hotel Yggdrasil. At least Edoku had provided fressen and Public Service Stations for the indigent. As for returning to Glade with my tail between my legs, the chip of credit which would have allowed me to do so was now lost with my pack in the depths of the Bloomenveldt. And while my father would no doubt have supplied me with a duplicate, it would take weeks to apply for same by Void Ship mail and more weeks for it to arrive, during which I would expire of starvation.

Surely Urso Moldavia Rashid was hardly ignorant of this situation, which is to say that while *he* may have sworn an oath against coercion, fate had paid no heed to such niceties, and as he must have known quite well, I must accept his offer or perish.

25 And so, after a short shuttle flight to Ciudad Pallas and a quick floatcab ride through the unappealing streets thereof in the company of Urso Moldavia Rashid, I took up residence in the Clear Light Mental Retreat.

By the esthetic standards of Ciudad Pallas, this no doubt might have passed as a triumph of the architect's art. A sprawling, single-story, crescent-shaped structure, windowless from the vantage of the street upon which it was sited, its inner curve embraced about two hundred degrees of a large circular garden, the circumferential boundaries of which were completed by a high concrete wall cunningly hidden from the easy perception of those within by a closely planted screen of even taller fir trees. The garden itself was mostly green lawn, dotted randomly with oaks and veined with winding flagstone paths that went nowhere in particular. Here and there small beds of flowers had been planted, wooden benches set out, and little shaded gazebos erected.

My room, like those of all the other residents, faced this interior garden with an entire wall of glass which slid aside to allow egress directly thereto, and which could be opaqued at my pleasure. There was a bed, an armoire, several chests, and a chaise, all crafted of reddish rough-hewn wood, and the usual toilet facilities done up in grainy gray stone. The walls were a cheery yellow, the ceiling cerulean blue, and the carpet a tawny concoction of shaggy ersatz fur.

All in all, an environment crafted to tranquilify the mind and brighten the spirit, though to my eyes the enclosed garden with its cleverly concealed wall soon seemed rather reminiscent of the vivarium of the *Unicorn Garden,* which had similarly masked the reality of confinement behind a screen of trees.

Nor were the other terms of residency less than as promised. I was supplied with a small wardrobe of tunics, skirts, and trousers, and three meals were indeed provided daily in the refectory. And if these left a good deal to be desired in the way of culinary artistry by the standards of a Grand Palais, a proper Edojin restaurant, or even the finger food of the Gypsy Jokers, at least it could be said that the fare of the Clear Light was an improvement over that of the research dome storeroom, let alone the monotonous raw produce of the Bloomenveldt.

As for the promise of freedom to wander the streets of Ciudad Pallas when my presence was not required by the mages of the mental retreat, this was a privilege of which I sought not to avail myself for quite some time, for on the one hand my rapidly returning memories thereof were entirely depressing and uninviting in comparison to the bucolic ambiance of the Clear Light's garden, and on the other, I hardly felt myself yet ready to sally forth into the long-unfamiliar milieu of urban thoroughfares.

Nor was the vie of the mental retreat one of boredom or ennui, at least at first.

After weeks of spieling my endless tale to no other truly sapient ears than my own, indeed for that matter after perfect lack of avid audiences as a ruespieler in Great Edoku, it was quite exhilarating to find myself encouraged to babble on daily at great length to rapt audiences of Healers and mages, no less, and to observe that my least mutterings were duly recorded on word crystal for posterity.

This is not to say that I was set behind a podium in an auditorium like a learned lecturer. Rather did I spend four hours a day and more in a small windowless room in the bowels of the mental retreat seated across a table from two to half a dozen people at a time, with Urso usually presiding during this stage of the process.

As for my audiences, a different combination seemed to

371

appear daily, apparently drawn from a pool that must have numbered several dozen scientists; how many of these were on the staff of the Clear Light itself I was never to learn.

At first, I was simply encouraged to retell the Tale of the Pied Piper of the Bloomenveldt over and over and over again sans interruption or interrogation and was not even properly introduced to the audiences for same, exactly as if I were indeed a ruespieler declaiming before random anonymous throngs, though alas no ruegelt was forthcoming at the conclusion of the performance.

During these first two weeks or so, such recitations seemed to be the sole form of my therapy, and I would be an ingrate if I dismissed the benefits thereof as accidental byproducts of entirely self-interested scientific inquiry. For I was allowed, indeed encouraged, to tell my tale in all its endlessly mutating versions long after the variety thereof must have been thoroughly exhausted from the point of view of my listeners, indeed beyond the point where it began to seem like so much repetitious babblement even to myself.

This, it would seem, was precisely the nature of the therapy.

First the endless retelling of the tale began to converge toward a consistent version, much as the odes of the preliterate bards must have converged toward the memorized consensuses that were to be eventually transcribed into those written versions which have passed down to us today.

Then I began to attain a certain self-consciousness of this very process, at which point craft entered the picture as I struggled to compose my verbal gushings into a coherent spiel capable of being reproduced for the understanding and delectation of the worlds at large. Which is to say I developed during this period the spiel which I was later to declaim for ruegelt in the uninspiring streets of Ciudad Pallas.

Finally, I began to perceive that the endlessly recurring motifs of the Piper, the sun, the Yellow Brick Road, ancestral trees, und so weiter, far from being venues, personages, or objects in an actual skein of events, were in fact *images* encapsulating complex gestalts of meaning beyond my entirely conscious apprehension strung together in a sequence that was somehow both literally false and spiritually true.

To those who would declare that the independent rediscovery of the hoary concept of literary metaphor was not exactly overwhelming evidence of intellectual puissance, I would point out that from the point of view of a singer who had long been entirely subsumed within the song, this satori, if no great and original contribution to the evolution of the literary art, was a powerful enlightenment indeed when it came to my therapeutic rediscovery of my own true self.

Indeed, if she who had roused herself from floral nonbeing to follow the synergetic mantra of the sun, the yellow, the Yellow Brick Road, across the forest canopy and into the Tale of the Pied Piper of the Bloomenveldt might have been said to have been in a state of schizoid cafard, then this reemergence of a self-conscious teller as a being distinct from the metaphorical creature of the tale might be said to mark sanity's full return.

Which is to say that upon gaining such insight, I had indeed finally followed the Tale of the Pied Piper of the Bloomenveldt all the way back from the ancestral flowers of mindless tropism to full sapient citizenship in the self-crafted worlds of men.

Nor were the mages and Healers unmindful of the success of this therapy, for not long after my discourse had attained the coherence of a ruespieler self-consciously crafting her tale, the nature of our séances together changed.

Having allowed a quotidian personality capable of rational discourse to reconstruct herself out of this babble of metaphor, having cozened the teller to prise herself a sufficient distance from the protagonist of her tale, they gave over any further interest in the metaphorical version thereof and began to question me quite sharply on the objective events in question from the points of view of their various disciplines. Which is to say they became openly eager, indeed often owlishly impatient, to pin down with scientific precision the phenomenological realities behind the Tale of the Pied Piper of the Bloomenveldt.

Urso Moldavia Rashid for the most part presided over, not to say refereed, these interrogations, for interrogations rather than therapy sessions they had certainly become, and ofttimes it became necessary for Urso to mediate among the mages present to prevent the proceedings from turning into an unseemly learned brawl.

If I neglect to properly transcribe herein their endless questions, my perpetually inadequate replies to same, their sometimes acrimonious disputations among themselves, and what at length seemed to become their fruitless reframing of the same interrogatories, the truth of the matter is that I remember precious little of the details, save that most of their efforts seemed aimed not so much at advancing theoretical knowledge as at extracting data which might aid them in advancing the pecuniary fortunes of Belshazaar's main industry, the development and marketing of psychotropics derived from the Bloomenveldt, an enterprise which had a good deal less than my enthusiastic support.

As far as I was concerned, the whole process was disjointed, mendacious, productive first of mental fatigue generated by my sincere if inadequate efforts to answer fully, then of indifferent boredom as I felt myself reduced to the role of a repetitious parrot, and finally of a sullen irked pettishness verging on rebellion. No doubt a full account of these sessions would be of genuine interest to those equally obsessed with the same subjects, and these I refer to the scientific annals thereof which they may peruse for decades without exhaustion, for it would be only slightly hyperbolic to declare that whole rooms full of word crystals on these sessions were dutifully recorded.

After a good many weeks of this, I was quite convinced that there were no more therapeutic benefits to be had by remaining in the Clear Light Mental Retreat as far as I was concerned, which is to say I had now come to view the establishment not as a place of succor but as a venue of confinement from which I must summon up the courage and resource to escape.

Once I had been a daughter of Nouvelle Orlean, once I had been an indigent naif on the streets of Edoku, once I had been a mindless creature reposing on the petals of a flower, once I had been the Pied Piper of the Bloomenveldt, and while certainement I was none of these things now, I knew just as surely that if my tale was not to end as tragicomic farce, the terminus of my Yellow Brick Road could not be my room in a mental retreat.

Vraiment, had not Pater Pan himself long ago declared that my road must be of my own choosing, and that if the destiny thereof should bring me to his side, he would greet me as an equal spirit? Certainement, as a patient in a mental retreat, as a scientific specimen, as a prisoner of penury once again, I could hardly style myself the equal of such a free spirit who tripped the life fantastic out among the stars. Mayhap Pater Pan was the Piper of my spirit's journey still, for whether or not destiny would ever place me once more at his side, I heard the song he had sung to that spirit calling me forth to resume my wanderjahr on the Yellow Brick Road as clearly now as ever I had upon the Bloomenveldt. I yearned to be the true ruespieler I had never really yet become, telling my tale not for room and board in a mental retreat, but in the streets of great cities for electrocoma passage among the far-flung worlds of men.

But *how?*

In terms of the financial realities, my situation was precisely what it had been when I had been forced to accept Urso's offer. Vraiment, I could quit the Clear Light whenever I chose, but I had neither funds to assure my survival, means of earning same in Ciudad Pallas, nor any way that I could see of removing myself to a more promising planet where I might at least have some real chance of surviving by the practice of my art.

I was caught, or so it seemed, in an economic trap whose confinement, though no more readily visible than the walls of the Clear Light hidden behind their screen of trees, were also no less concrete.

Before the desperate determination to escape this velvet prison had taken hold of my spirit, my vie in the mental retreat had been both ritualized and solitary, a recapitulation in some psychic sense of my days on the Bloomenveldt, for, truth be told, if I could fairly be said to have regained my own full interior sapient sanity, I had yet to gain true re-entry into the social complexities of the exterior realm.

I slept, I ate, I took occasional strolls about the garden, but now that the interrogatory sessions had reached the stage where their profitability was strictly one-sided, they kept me at it for most of my waking hours, as if to deliver up the botanical and psychotropic details I was incapable of revealing by a torture of ennui.

Nor had I even regained sufficient social consciousness to feel keenly the lack of tantric exercise, for when the natural

375

kundalinic energies intruded into the centers in which erotic imagery arises, what arose unbidden was my last sexual experience on the Bloomenveldt, to wit a combat for my very spirit against a vile floral version of eros.

And if this was not enough to keep my kundalinic serpent torpidly cold and coiled, the only social circle whose possibilities lay open to me was that of my fellow inmates, and when at length I began to feel the lack of congress with kindred spirits to the point where I attempted to engage them in discourse, I only learned what my instincts had already known.

This dispirited and pathetic lot were no spirits I would care to claim as kindred. The Children of Fortune of Ciudad Pallas, as I had long since known, eschewed the arts, crafts, entertainments, and shady enterprises whereby the tribes of Edoku had traded pleasure for ruegelt in favor of earning their way as psychonauts in the mental retreats and laboratories, where funds were to be acquired by indulging in what they otherwise would have paid to enjoy when they could afford it.

Which is to say that even the generality of this single-minded tribe had little to discourse upon but the psychic effects of arcane chemicals and which laboratories and mental retreats were presently paying the highest wage.

The inmates of the Clear Light were drawn from these unwholesome ranks to begin with, and most of them had been deposited here as the result of the inevitable unfortunate experiment that must be suffered by anyone who followed the psychonaut's trade long enough in Ciudad Pallas. Which is to say when at length they dutifully quaffed a potion which translated their psyche into a schizoid realm of sufficient extremity to prevent even the mighty and puissant sciences of the mind from extracting it.

Thus the garden of the mental retreat was frequented by two species of inmates: hebephrenic babblers whose mutterings and sputterings were entirely incomprehensible to anyone but themselves though of manifest cosmic import thereto, and those who had lapsed into stony catatonia and sat on the lawn or on benches gaping into some private void.

As for me, at the moment I could happily count myself among neither, but the more I attempted to converse with creatures who were no more verbal than so many Bloomenkinder on the one hand, or who responded to any conversational gambit with a stream of hebephrenic gabble in their own secret sprach on the other, the more fearful I became that I must sooner or later end my days as one or the other unless I contrived to escape from the mental retreat.

Finally, early one afternoon when I had been given a brief respite from my service to science, as I was walking aimlessly in the garden with the yellow sun shining out of a cerulean sky down upon me, I was put in mind of my days as the Pied Piper of the Bloomenveldt, and resolved out of ennui, pique, or desperation to strike back at the ambiance of the mental retreat with sheer devilment.

I decided upon a quixotic gesture which was not only to throw the place into the desired uproar, but which in the end was to lead to my escape from the situation. Mayhap my prescient spirit in the act thereof was wiser than my intellect knew, or mayhap the final movement of my therapy at the Clear Light Mental Retreat was designed to accomplish my voluntary egress. Mayhap both Urso and I had our own way in the end.

Be such retrospective speculations as they may, I selected a venue within easy earshot of some dozen or more inmates sitting on the lawn in various states of torpor or babblement, much as I had once sought out promising platzes or corners when I was a street peddler in Great Edoku. Here a wooden bench had been conveniently set out under the shade of a large oak. This I mounted even as I had once stood upon a similar bench before the ersatz Luzplatz volcano, summoned up sufficient courage to overcome my sense of the ludicrous, took a deep breath, and began to declaim in as loud a stentorian roar as I could muster.

"Merde! Caga! Chingada! Once you were Children of Fortune following the Yellow Brick Road of your wanderjahrs out among the stars to seek bright destiny and your own true names! See what in this Bloomenveldt of the spirit you have become! Dispirited wretches! Human legumes! *Bloomenkinder!*"

The sheer volume and shock of this novel verbal assault was sufficient to cause several of the babblers to lapse into momentary silence and gaze woodenly in my direction. Even two or three of the catatonics managed to focus their eyes more or less upon me, or so at least it seemed. Pathetic though this response might be by any objective standards, it served well enough to

377

goad me on, for even this was more rapt attention than I could be said to have achieved when first I dared to essay the ruespieler's art in the Luzplatz.

"I too left the planet of my birth to follow the camino réal that has led us from our ancestral trees to the far-flung worlds of men!" I screamed as loudly as I was able, for when it came to attracting and holding the attention of *this* audience, volume was no doubt a good deal more critical than a well-crafted tale told with erudition.

"Vraiment, I too fell into the nethermost psychotropic bowels of this loathsome planet! Indeed I found myself besotted with perfumes and pheromones which make the psychotropics of the laboratories of Ciudad Pallas seem like the cold crystal air of a mountain!"

Whether I had touched at last upon the only subject sufficient to rouse the interest of these zombies, or whether it was only the volume, the rapid rolling cadence, the sheer passion with which I sought to imbue every shouted syllable, every eye now paid me rapt attention. Some of the inmates even rose slowly to their feet and shambled closer to my bench.

"You have become inmates of a mental retreat, but I became a perfectly mindless Bloomenkind, without so much as a spirit to call my own," I shouted most abusively in their faces. "Yet my spirit roused itself to follow once more the song of the Piper that we all once followed from apes into men and so must you all rouse your spirits now!" I bellowed at them, quite enjoying my own tirade by now. But what I craved now was some *response*.

"Behold the sun which forever arises above the Bloomenveldt of your spirits, my pauvres Bloomenkinder!" I shouted more craftily now. "Behold the face of the Pied Piper which we have followed from the depths of the forest of unreason!"

Vraiment, I was raving with the best of the teppichfressers now, and yet another part of me observed the proceedings with calculating clarity and no little wry satisfaction and knew quite well what I was going to do next.

"Follow the sun, follow the yellow, follow the Piper, follow the Yellow Brick Road!"

I began to chant.

"Follow the sun, follow the yellow, follow the Piper, follow the Yellow Brick Road. . . ."

Most of the inmates in my vecino were on their feet now, and in the middle distance I could see more of them shambling across the lawn to the hubbub.

They began to sway to the rhythm of my words. Like a musical maestra, I began to move my arms to the beat, palms upward, enticing them to join in.

As for the erstwhile catatonics, these were never roused to more than a bobbing of their heads, but those who a few minutes before had been locked into their own hebephrenic sprachs of babble were easily enough cozened by my efforts and the communal reinforcement thereof to take up the chant.

"Follow the sun, follow the yellow, follow the Piper, follow the Yellow Brick Road!"

At length, when I had whipped up a veritable frenzy of chanting, there seemed nothing for it but to lead my Gypsy Jokers on a Mardi Gras parade about the garden. As to what in truth had moved me to carry this unholy prank to such an extreme, or indeed how far I was prepared to take it, je ne sais pas, for I had no sooner leapt from the bench and danced forward a few steps still chanting, when Urso, with at least half a dozen other functionaries of the mental retreat in train, came puffing and running across the lawn toward me.

"Cease this outrage at once!" he shouted at me, as red-faced with ire as with exertion. "Schnell, schnell, schnell, remove them all to their rooms!" he ordered his minions, gesticulating wildly with one hand, and dragging me away toward the main building with the other. Nor did he address me again until he had succeeded in removing my person well away from the tumult where my baneful influence could no longer make itself felt.

"And who do you suppose you are?" he demanded angrily. "What do you suppose you are doing?"

I pulled away somewhat haughtily from his grasp. I smiled a superior smile at him, filled with self-satisfied contentment, for the answer to his question was wonderfully clear and plain.

"I am Sunshine Shasta Leonardo, ruespieler," I told him with the voice of sweet reason. "Naturellement, I must practice my art."

A most peculiar change came over Urso Moldavia Rashid,

379

for while on the surface his anger appeared unabated, beneath it I sensed some unknown satisfaction which sapped it of a certain credibility. "The Clear Light no public platz ist!" he snapped back with somewhat unconvincing spontaneity. "As perhaps you will notice, bitte, this is a mental retreat! We can hardly permit you to agitate our unfortunate patients in such an unseemly manner!"

"What do you suggest?" I demanded. "That I continue along as I have as an object of endless futile interrogation until I am indistinguishable from the poor wretches you seek to prevent me from addressing?"

"You are free to leave the Clear Light at any time," Urso pointed out fatuously. "And indeed if such an event occurs again, you will be expelled!"

"You would have me expire of starvation?"

We had reached the entrance to the building now, and Urso's demeanor abruptly altered. "You mistake my meaning and my spirit," he said in an almost apologetic tone. "I have only your best interests at heart."

"Well then what *are* you suggesting, Urso?" I demanded.

"That certainement your therapy has reached a stage where you must direct some thought and effort to your future life, for as you yourself have just so nobly declared, you certainly have no wish to remain an inmate in a mental retreat forever."

I looked at him with new eyes. Mayhap I had mistaken his spirit, for whatever else Urso Moldavia Rashid may have been before or after, in that moment he was a true psychic Healer, for he had spoken the truth that was in my own heart.

"I could not agree more wholeheartedly, Urso," I told him with unconstrained sincerity. "But what am I to *do*?"

"I may have some wisdom to offer in the practical realm as well," Urso said. "Let us make ourselves comfortable in my office and I will donate the time to elucidate at proper length."

To this I could find no reason to demur, and so what had begun as the hectoring and physical removal of a miscreant became a friendly tête-à-tête, or so at least it seemed.

"Neither of us wishes our arrangement to continue indefinitely, nicht wahr," Urso said when he had made ourselves comfortable in his cushioned lair of an office. "So while I am willing to grant you shelter and sustenance in exchange for your

380

continued cooperation in our inquiries for a transitional period, I suggest that you avail yourself of your freedom to come and go and seek out means of gainful employment."

What a roil of emotion arose in me at these words! For while I wanted nothing so much as to regain my liberty, when it came to the economic means of securing same, my mind was utterly vacant. Which is to say that while I could hardly deny the wisdom and veracity of Urso's injunction, the emotions that they summoned up, alas, were frustration, anger, and dread.

"Gainful employment. . . ?" I muttered unhappily. "I am versed in no marketable skill or lore, and as for earning a wage as a subject for psychotropic experiments, my experiences on the Bloomenveldt have left me entirely unemployable as a psychonaut, even were I mad enough to resort to same."

"Indeed," purred Urso, and now the insinuating tone of his voice became quite evident, "but you are, as you have declared, Sunshine Shasta Leonardo, ruespieler, nicht wahr. Who has also righteously announced the necessity of practicing her art. . . ."

"*In Ciudad Pallas?*" I exclaimed. "You may indeed be a maestro of your own art, Urso, but it is evident you know nothing of that of the ruespieler! This wretched city is entirely devoid of the life of the streets! There are no suitable venues, the citizens thereof—"

"—however unpromising, are certainly more promising in terms of both artistic appreciation and financial largesse than the indigent inmates of a mental retreat, nicht wahr?"

Once more Urso seemed to have earned his keep as a true psychic Healer, for I could hardly deny that it would take little more courage to declaim to the denizens of Ciudad Pallas than it had to stand up for myself in the Luzplatz and seek to entice the lordly attention of the indifferent Edojin.

Urso smiled at me. "What have you to lose by trying?" he said.

"Well spoken, Urso, well spoken indeed!" I declared, smiling back at him for the first time since this discussion had begun.

Would not the old spiels which had worn out their welcome in Edoku nevertheless be novel tales from a greater metropole to the bumpkins of this most culturally provincial of planetary capitals? Indeed did I not now have a grand tale to tell which was entirely my own and mayhap one of piquant local relevance to the inhabitants of this planet? Vraiment, had I not now prevailed by the power of the Word in the very Bloomenveldt itself? Had I not been willing to hector the very dregs of psychic disaster swept up from those selfsame unpromising streets as they vegetated in a mental retreat? Did I have anything further to fear in the way of stage fright? Did I have any better alternative?

I shrugged. "Nothing ventured, nothing gained, n'est-ce pas?" I said almost gaily.

"Gut!" exclaimed Urso heartily. "And if you will forgive my anticipation of the decision I knew you would come to in the end, I make practical recompense in the form of this necessary gift."

From his desk he withdrew a portable chip transcriber such as are employed in private games of chance.

"Having researched the subject but scantily, I nevertheless believe I am correct in believing ruespielers, so-called, are traditionally paid in so-called ruegelt, actual physical tokens each representing a unit of credit. . . ."

My spirits suddenly sank. "I had forgotten that the very concept of ruegelt is unknown in Ciudad Pallas," I groaned. "How may I therefore command the citizens thereof to shower me with coin when none such exists?"

"With this device I have taken the liberty of providing for your use," Urso said. "The donor inserts a chip in one slot, the recipient in another, the amount of the transfer is selected, and the transaction is accomplished."

"It seems a rather unwieldy procedure in comparison to the simple tossing of some coins," I said uncertainly, though of course this was the normal mode of commerce throughout the worlds of men, and ruegelt only a concession to the demimonde on the more sophisticated planets thereof.

"Come, come, this is mere grumbling, is it not?" Urso chided in an avuncular tone. "To those whose spirits hold back from every venture, a less than perfect universe provides abundant excuses for sloth, nicht wahr?"

Once more I could not escape entirely from the feeling that he was serving his own self-interest no less than he was justly advising mine.

"Touché," I agreed nevertheless, for whatever else Urso might be, however I might have been manipulated to get me

382

here, and at whatever profit to whom, Urso Moldavia Rashid, by means fair or foul, had guided me back to my Yellow Brick Road.

And so, the next afternoon, under an overcast sky, with my Cloth of Many Colors tied about my neck as a scarf and the chip transcriber in my pocket, I set forth.

Not having set foot on urban streets for months, I found those of Ciudad Pallas both daunting and strangely reassuring. For while I now found myself moving among more people than I had seen in one place for many weeks, and while the regular gridwork of streets, the geometrically rigid forms and unadorned facades of the palisades of buildings, indeed the very gray substance of the concrete beneath my feet, seemed grim, lifeless, and ersatz, wandering in this venue was a far cry from the psychic perils of the Bloomenveldt, and Ciudad Pallas certainly seemed modest and quotidian enough in comparison to my memories of Great Edoku.

And while I might have been tempted to regard myself as a bumpkin fresh from the wilderness, or worse, as an inmate of a mental retreat taking her first tremulous steps out into the worlds at large, my perception of the citizens of Ciudad Pallas soon enough disabused me of any excessive humility.

For I saw no throngs of extravagantly clad and tinted Edojin promenading with the lordly and languid grace of folk who considered themselves the sophisticated crown of creation, nor even such haughty urchins as the Gypsy Jokers who had once seemed so daunting when I was a naif of the Public Service Stations.

Rather was I in the midst of modestly clad folk scurrying through the streets with, for the most part, the blank expressions that befitted this pallid venue. The majority of them seemed sober and industrious-minded citizens intent on affairs of business, while others, by the unlaundered look of their clothing and the dishevelment of their persons, could readily enough be identified as what passed in Ciudad Pallas for Children of Fortune, to wit the denizens of the waiting rooms of the laboratories and mental retreats with whom I had become all too familiar on my previous sojourn in the city.

Vraiment, I felt myself to be more connected to the spirit of Belshazaar, such as it was, than any of these natives and longtime residents thereof. For did not the life of its chief city revolve

383

entirely about the psychotropics derived from the flowers of a continent upon whose treetop canopy most of these folk had never dared venture? Indeed was it not true that even the most adventurous natives of Belshazaar, the mages of the research domes, experienced the true reality of their own planet only within the alienating carapaces of their atmosphere suits? Was it not true that even the Children of Fortune of Ciudad Pallas, who imagined themselves psychonauts of the spirit, imbibed the essences thereof only second- or thirdhand in ampoules and vials?

Of all the humans who clung to the surface of this benighted orb, there was only one who had penetrated the central mystery of the dark soul thereof and returned with the tale to tell, and that was I, Sunshine Shasta Leonardo, true Child of Fortune, ruespieler, erstwhile Pied Piper of the Bloomenveldt.

What a tale I had to tell to the denizens of this city! For though they might have by unconscious act of will actively eschewed knowledge of the true nature of that upon which their world was founded, the Tale of the Pied Piper of the Bloomenveldt was their own true story, if only they had the courage to listen, if only I could summon up the art to touch their cramped spirits!

As for a proper venue within which to tell the tale, this, alas, was another matter, for one street was very much like the next, one indifferent knot of citizens much like every other. As far as I could tell, Ciudad Pallas was quite devoid of parks or civic centers or platzes where streets converged to provide a proper public forum.

At length, I gave over my futile search for such a venue, ceased my wanderings at the intersection of two streets much like a hundred others, stood before a towering building of glass and steel of no particular distinction, took in a deep breath, screwed up my courage, and began to spiel.

"The Tale of the Pied Piper of the Bloomenveldt!" I announced at the top of my lungs, and as I began the spiel itself, I found some inner craft modifying it away from the cryptic haiku form in which it had evolved as I lived it, away from the coherently crafted summation thereof which had emerged from the endless repetitions under interrogation, and toward an extreme condensation of the full version which years later I was to encode onto word crystal in this very histoire.

"Vraiment, all present here do surely know that the spirit

of Belshazaar, the raison d'être for your own presence on this planet, resides not in this grim gray city of lifeless glass and stone, but across the sea atop the mighty Bloomenwald where the great flowers exude the psychotropic substances upon which your economic vie depends and which is the sole fame of Belshazaar among the far-flung worlds of men!"

A few passersby had paused for a moment, if only to peruse this novel event, for never before had the streets of this city seen a ruespieler explode from anonymous silence into full-blown declamation. Half a dozen or so of these had remained when they heard me begin to speak of that subject surely dearest to any audience's heart, to wit the spirit and economic welfare of their very own selves. This in turn created a small eddy in the stream of street traffic, so that all must slow down a bit as they passed the spiel.

"I stand before you as one who has wandered deeper into the Bloomenveldt than any human spirit may safely go, who has walked among the fabled Bloomenkinder, seen the legendary Perfumed Garden of floral perfection, lost my élan humain to the puissant flowers, been rescued therefrom by the Pied Piper of the Bloomenveldt, and returned to this very corner upon which I now stand to regale you, good citizens of Ciudad Pallas, with this mighty tale!"

My audience had grown to more than a dozen now, and even some of those who had paused out of curiosity and then moved on seemed to do so with a certain reluctance, as if they indeed wished to hear more but were unfortunately required elsewhere.

"Hearken therefore to the Tale of the Pied Piper of the Bloomenveldt! Learn of the wonders and terrors and the true nature of the forest of unreason upon which the very life of this city depends! Hear of the bodhis of the Bloomenveldt! Cringe at the depths to which the human spirit may descend! Glory at the power of the Word to bring that selfsame spirit back from the ancestral flowers to full sapient awareness! Listen to the Tale of the Pied Piper of the Bloomenveldt, which is my own, and yours as well, the only true tale there is to tell, the one which we all have followed from apes of the trees to lordly citizens of the far-flung worlds of men, and in the process thereof become once more true Children of our species' Fortune on the Yellow Brick

385

Road from tropism and determinism to sovereign captaincy of the great arkologies and gallant Void Ships which have made us the masters of the stars!"

I had attracted almost two score expectant listeners by the time I had finished this florid and extravagant preamble to my tale, a good many of them sober burghers of Ciudad Pallas, but more of them than not lost Children of Fortune of the laboratories and mental retreats, who no doubt heard more keenly in my words the song that had once been in their own hearts.

As for me, I was toxicated with my own spiel myself, though it was that state of clear and lucid toxication of which such as the sufis do speak, wherein the fiery passion of the spirit and the cool clarity of the intellect are revealed as one.

Which is to say that as I began to recount the story of my trek with Guy Vlad Boca into the floral heart of darkness, as I observed my descriptions thereof emerging spontaneously from the mysterious center of my own inner void, vraiment even as my body trembled with an arcane energy I had never felt before, there was a cool calm part of me that stood outside both the teller and the tale and knew with certainty that this was the very first time I had *truly* practiced the ruespieler's art.

This, all unknowing, was what I had sought to become when first I had listened to the ruespielers of the Gypsy Jokers and longed in my unformed ignorance to walk the path of their vie. *This* was what had been missing from my poor efforts in the Luzplatz as I parroted the oft-told tales of others before I knew a tale to tell that was my spirit's own.

And while the Tale of the Pied Piper of the Bloomenveldt with which I had heroically babbled my way across the forest canopy had certainly arisen from the depths of my own heart, when it came to the coherent craft which must carry even the most puissant of stories from the spirit of the teller to those of the audience, I had never been the master thereof until now.

And so, as I launched into the story of my escape from the Perfumed Garden, the beginning of my unmasked journey across the Bloomenveldt, even my description of how my insensate spirit had roused itself from the lotus of forgetfulness to follow the sun, follow the yellow, follow the Yellow Brick Road, I found myself able, for the first time, to tell my own true tale with a coherence and accessibility to ears other than my own of which I had never before been capable.

For now it could justly be said that I was at last what I had so grandly to Urso Moldavia Rashid proclaimed: Sunshine Shasta Leonardo, ruespieler, in the act of truly practicing her art.

And now in the living process thereof, at least while the telling of the tale continued, I cared not that I was an indigent forced to survive by dwelling in a mental retreat, nor that I addressed a bare handful of people on the unpromising streets of an unwholesome city on a world which I wanted nothing more than to leave.

For as I spoke of the Pied Piper of the Children of Fortune whom we had all followed along the camino réal from the ancestral trees to the stars, as I spoke of the Pied Piper of the Bloomenveldt leading her charges out of the forest, as I spoke of Pater Pan, and Sunshine Shasta Leonardo, and all the true Children of Fortune who carried forth the Spark of the Ark, like all true tellers of all true tales, my own spirit was the most avid audience, to whom I addressed my spiel in my heart of hearts.

Be that as it may, when at length I came to the conclusion of my tale, I remained true to the quotidian necessities of the calling which I had now found, which is to say that while my spirit may have been filled with amour propre for the ding an sich, this did not prevent my more pragmatic side from seeking remuneration therefor.

At least a score of people remained attentively before me as I reached the finale, drawing forth my chip transcriber and waving it invitingly under their noses with a proper mendicant's flourish.

"And so this is my story, and this is our song, and if the Tale of the Pied Piper of the Bloomenveldt has touched your spirits, if you too style yourself a true Child of Fortune, then cast aside all mean-spirited minginess, bitte, insert your chips herein, and give what magnanimity requires so that the teller thereof may carry it forth among the far-flung worlds of men!"

Alas, while the telling of the tale had pleased these worthies' fancies as evidenced by the rapt attention which they had remained throughout to bestow, when the Piper sought her pay, their enthusiasm was a good deal more restrained.

387

Which is to say that one by one they turned up their noses at my entreaties and swiftly began to melt away.

Only one fellow remained, a disheveled young man, or more properly put, mayhap, an aging boy, quite obviously one whose funds were secured as a subject in the laboratories, who stood there uncertainly, blinking rheumy and clearly worshipful eyes in my direction, and fingering something concealed in the pocket of his trousers.

"Come, come," I wheedled, "are we not true Children of Fortune, you and I, kindred spirits of the Yellow Brick Road? Will you not show the miserly folk of this city that we care for our own? Together, let us put these Bloomenkinder of the spirit to shame! A single untl of credit will do the deed if that is all your fortune can spare. . . ."

Strange to say it was a quite uncharacteristic modesty rather than a certain guilty shame which I felt as I observed this poor urchin mooning at me as once I must have gazed at the Gypsy Joker ruespielers when I was a waif such as he. How much older I felt as he smiled shyly at me, withdrew his chip of credit, and inserted it into my transcriber.

"Two credits for the Pied Piper of the Bloomenveldt," he said. "Someday I too would wish for such a tale to tell!"

I was moved to plant a kiss on his cheek when this transaction was concluded. "May the Yellow Brick Road rise up to greet you," I told him. "And may you summon up the means to follow it to a far better world than *this*!"

"Tu también . . ." he muttered, blushing, and then he was gone.

26

Thus in this most unlikely of venues did I at last become the true ruespieler I had never succeeded in being in the far more lucrative streets of Great Edoku.

Which is far from saying that I was ever able to earn sufficient funds at the trade in Ciudad Pallas to quit my room and board at the Clear Light Mental Retreat. Indeed, even had the slim proceeds of my efforts been enough to secure a room in some modest hotel and enough nourishment to insure my survival, still I would not have given over Urso Moldavia Rashid's gratuit provision thereof, for when it came to the retention of my modest funds, I became a miser with the best of them.

Nor was this the result of a newfound meanness of spirit; au contraire, having fairly discovered my own true calling, having set my spirit if not quite my feet back on the Yellow Brick Road, all my efforts, energies, and funds were husbanded toward the purpose of escaping from Belshazaar and resuming my wanderjahr's journey on better worlds than this.

For even though my earnings as Ciudad Pallas's sole ruespieler were paltry indeed—twenty-one credits in the best week I enjoyed—I was confident that this was more the fault of the city's karma than my own. There were no proper platzes or parks where I might draw a decent crowd, what small audiences I did address were largely unacquainted with the traditions of my trade, the burghers of the city had little enthusiasm for street performance, and the dispirited Children of Fortune of the laboratories and mental retreats who were the most generous of spirit were alas only slightly less indigent than myself.

Yet by my own lights, I seemed sufficiently advanced in my craft to meet with financial as well as artistic success, if only I could secure the funds to remove myself to some planet where the streets were alive with gay-spirited throngs and the joie de vivre so absent from Ciudad Pallas had reached a reasonably full flower.

For did I not possess not only a considerable repertoire of tales acquired from the Gypsy Joker ruespielers of Edoku but a unique tale as well that was entirely my own? And was not even my modest success against all odds here on Belshazaar proof that I had the wit and craft to properly tell them?

It was only a function of effort over time, or so I told myself during these weeks. Slim though my daily earnings were, every credit thereof was retained against the day when I had accumulated sufficient funds to purchase electrocoma passage in a Void Ship leaving Belshazaar for greener pastures. Sooner or later, though alas more likely the latter than the former, I would have enough credit on my chip to travel on.

And as far as I was concerned, it mattered little as to where, for the journey itself was what I now sought to resume. Once I had enough funds to travel to *anywhere* else, I would take myself forthwith thither, and on that new planet would I ply the ruespieler's trade until I had earned enough to pay my way to the next, and the next, and the next, worlds without end, tripping the life fantastic like Pater Pan, from star to star, following the Yellow Brick Road of the wandering ruespieler, vraiment startripping through the centuries even as he, mayhap even to meet him once more before my body's time ran out.

Was it a man I sought to follow, or the Pied Piper of a tale? Did I truly dream of regaining the companionship of a lost lover or was this merely an ultima Thule my spirit placed like the rising sun above a road that had no ending?

La même chose, nê, for Pater Pan the natural man was a wandering spirit, and Pater Pan the Pied Piper of the Yellow

Brick Road was the spirit of wandering, and to Sunshine the ruespieler, were they not one and the same?

Be that as it may, in the end my tale was to take a different turning, indeed as I spieled for pittances in the streets of Ciudad Pallas, the wheel had already turned, though I was to be the last to know. Far sooner than I could have dreamt, I was telling my last tale for the citizens of Ciudad Pallas, though at the time I knew it not, for my chip still held less than half the credit I needed to purchase passage to the nearest world.

The tale I was telling at the time was, appropriately enough, *Spark of the Ark,* the venue was an undistinguished Ciudad Pallas street like all the others, and the audience consisted of some half-dozen burghers, four Children of Fortune, and a handsome dark-haired woman whose form-fitting suit of iridescent gold and silver feathers seemed to mark her as a turista from some more sophisticated sphere.

"And where did he go when the Jump Drive rang down the final curtain on the great slow centuries of the First Starfaring Age?" I declaimed, segueing into my climactic appeal for funds. "Everywhere! Nowhere! Into the space between which lies within our human hearts! Here within the teller who brings you the tale, vraiment even within the Arkie Sparkie hearts of you, my poor lost Bloomenkinder, which is to say all of you who still retain the nobility of spirit to insert your chips into my transcriber and donate your funds to she whose life is the singing of the song!"

So saying, I waved my transcriber in the customary manner before them, and in their customary manner most of them chose to fade away, though two of the Children of Fortune were good enough to honor my efforts with a single credit apiece before departing.

Now only the dark-haired woman in the suit of feathers remained, neither fleeing at my mendicant's appeal nor making any move to loose the strings of what surely must have been an overflowing purse. Instead she stood there regarding me quite strangely, with a wry yet somehow warm smile on her lips, and a peculiar look of nostalgic merriment in her wide blue eyes.

"Quelle chose!" I demanded, forthrightly confronting her. "From your haute couture it is evident that you are a woman of

391

wealth and grace! Surely you will not be so mean-spirited therefore as to deny the Piper her pay?"

She laughed good-naturedly, withdrew a chip from the
folds of her garment, inserted it into my transcriber, and watched
my eyes widen in delight and no little astonishment as she transferred a full hundred units of credit to my own.

"I too once practiced the ruespieler's trade long ago and
far away," she said. "Hola, in a certain sense it might be said that
I follow it still. At any event, I do believe that it is you I have
journeyed to this tiresome planet to meet."

"*Me?*" I exclaimed.

"You are Sunshine Shasta Leonardo, are you not? Of whom
the case histories speak? The Lady of the Ode?"

"*Ode?*"

"Vraiment, Omar's ode, *Our Lady of the Bloomenkinder,*
naturellement."

"*Omar Ki Benjamin?* He really wrote the ode he promised?"

She laughed. "Of course. The old roué is a man of his
word. The problem has always been getting him to give it."

"You are a friend of Omar's?"

She shrugged. "A subtle question, liebchen. We have been
lovers from time to time for decades, yet I am still not quite sure.
But then we know how such men are, nē?"

"*We do?*"

"We had better!" she declared. Then, sensing my complete
befuddlement, which no doubt would have been evident to the
coarsest oaf, she took me by the hand. "Come, kindelein," she
said. "It would seem that I have much to tell you, though of
course not half so much as you have to tell me."

"Where are we going?" I managed to inquire.

She made a moue of distaste. "Alas, my suite at the Hotel
Pallas," she said. "One cut above a rude bordello, as far as I'm
concerned, but the best Belshazaar has to offer, I was given to
understand."

I nodded. "I dwelt there once," I told her.

"Well, then, you know what I mean!"

And so, hardly knowing how I had gotten there or why, I
found myself ensconced with this bizarre yet somehow immediately simpatica woman in a suite in the Hotel Pallas much like the

one Guy and I had once shared, all thick blue carpeting, brown plush upholstery, tawny wood paneling, polished brasswork, and dominated by a huge window that presented a grandiose and repulsive vista of this city of charmless gray and ugly expanses of glass.

"Feh!" my hostess agreed when she saw me gazing distastefully thereon. "You will be as happy to be quit of this place as I, nē? But come, be seated, have some of this wretched wine that they dare to charge such an outrageous price for, and hear my name tale, for naturellement, I already know yours."

She ushered me to a couch, sat down beside me, uncorked a bottle of wine, filled two goblets, wrinkled her nose, and gulped down a draught. The wine, when I tasted it, was nowhere near as vile as I had been led to expect.

"Bien," my new friend declared, for so I had already begun to consider her, though I did not quite know why.

"My name is Wendi Sha Rumi. My father, Rumi Mitsu Cala, was, or rather still is, a composer and performer of musique et lumière native to no planet in particular, for he was conceived and raised to manhood aboard a succession of Void Ships, his mother, Cala Abdu Etroy, having been a freeservant thereon, and his father, Mitsu Bryan Chiri, being a Void Captain of same. His freenom, Rumi, he chose for the premiere of his first composition in homage to the legendary sufic poet of old.

"My mother, Sha Smith Gotha, alas deceased, was a Void Ship Domo. Her father, Smith Willa Carlyle, was an artisan of bijoux to the floating cultura, and her mother, Gotha Lee Kotar, was, to be frank, a courtesan thereof, of great beauty and tantric skill, or so it is said. Her freenom, Sha, she chose upon becoming a Domo hommage à Sha Lao Hari, one of the earliest to follow that art, and the first to fit out her Grand Palais with a vivarium, or so the legend goes.

"My parents met when the courses of their endless voyages intersected aboard the *Pegasus D'or,* and one of the results of this union, naturellement, was myself, also raised entirely en passage, as it were. Thus I am a third generation native of the floating cultura, which no doubt does much to explain my distaste for planetary surfaces, let alone for such a pismire world as this.

"Eschewing parental largesse out of some ill-conceived rebellious pride and wishing to wallow in all that the worlds and the men thereof might have to offer, I passed my wanderjahr, and a long and wild one it was, ma petite, as a nouvelle indigent Child of Fortune making her way from world to world by the usual means, which is to say courtesy of wealthy lovers, via tantric performance, as a freeservant, by strategems amounting to little more than theft, and finally as an itinerant ruespieler with a plethora of dark and spicy tales to tell, my dear.

"At length, vraiment at great length, it slowly began to dawn on me that there were far more lucrative markets for same than streets and platzes, which is to say I began to record my romances and stories on word crystal, an alteration of medium which I commend to your attention, liebchen, for the sale thereof now allows me to live in the style to which all civilized folk should wish to become accustomed.

"My freenom, Wendi, I chose as a suitable nom de plume for the publication of my first word crystal, homage à the collector of lost boys in the tale of *Peter Pan,* for certainement I had collected enough of the same during my wanderjahr, and the gentlemen of the priapic gender were the audience I sought to capture for my libidinal romances—"

"*Pater Pan!*" I exclaimed. "The tale of *Pater Pan?*"

"*Peter* Pan," Wendi corrected. "Though it is arcane indeed that you should hear the other, for in fact long ago I briefly knew a man who styled himself thusly, and what a fellow he was too, liebchen, with a great golden mane of hair, the most outrageous blarney, and a suit you would not believe. . . ."

She smiled at me broadly as I sat there with my mouth gaping open. "Then again you might," she said archly, "seeing as how it was sewn together of a patchwork of assorted swatches not unlike the very scarf you wear!"

I gaped. I gargled. I gulped down a great swallow of wine. Wendi patted me on the knee and laughed uproariously.

"Pardon, ma pauvre petite, of course I was enjoying a small jest at your expense," she said. "Naturellement, your connection to the fellow, being recorded in the copious annals of your case history, was known to me from the start. Which is not to say that he and I were not lovers too, long ago and far away. Verdad. C'est vrai. I tell you true."

At last I found my tongue. "Annals? Case history? Pater

Pan?" I stammered. "I know not what to say. I am filled with questions I cannot frame."

Wendi raised an admonitory finger. "All in good time," she said, pouring me another goblet of wine. "But I have been babbling on at endless length and I have not come all this distance to hear the sound of my own voice, pleasing though it may be to my ears. It is your turn to speak, ruespieler. I would hear the tale of the Pied Piper of the Bloomenveldt from the lips of same, for the dry monographs which the proprietors of the Clear Light Mental Retreat have thusfar licensed for publication obviously omit the most spicy and piquant details. I would learn why Our Lady of the Bloomenkinder is presently reduced to spieling for pittances on these mean streets. Drink up, then speak! I swear a solemn oath that I will seek not to gain profit by stealing your tale. And when you have enlightened my ignorance, then I will surely enlighten yours, at least to the extent that my poor powers command. Drink! Speak! Favor me with the telling of your own true tale!"

And so, my loquacity along the way well lubricated by more goblets of wine than I could count, I related to Wendi Sha Rumi a greatly condensed summary of the events I have thusfar recounted in this very histoire, omitting only those matters which cast less than glory upon my own person, some of the more intimate details, and of course whatever mature retrospective analysis I have attempted herein, which was beyond my intellectual powers at the time.

"Ah, I knew we would be friends when first I perused Omar's ode!" Wendi declared when I had more or less concluded. "For surely you are a sister of the spirit to the girl that I once was, and with good fortune, I am surely a sister of the spirit to the woman you will one day become." She frowned. "But despite your natural talent as a teller of tales, there remain matters I do not entirely comprehend. . . ."

"That *you* do not comprehend!" I exclaimed. "Vraiment, there is little of your presence on Belshazaar or my presence in this very room that I comprehend at all!"

"Well, then, let us take turns as interlocutor and respondee, my dear," Wendi said. "The first question may be yours. . . ."

"What are you *doing* here, Wendi?" I asked. "What do you want from me?"

"Do you wish me to frame my reply in terms of spirit, art, or commerce, liebchen?"

"Surely," I told her dryly, "as an author of romances, you are capable of combining all three. . . ?"

"Well spoken!" Wendi declared with a little laugh. "In terms of spirit, as I have said, I knew you were a time-warped sister of my own heart when first I encountered Omar's ode. In terms of art, when I then perused the dry details of your adventure in the annals, I recognized an uncompleted tale of great promise that I wished to hear from the heroine herself in order to enrich my own mastery of the art, for as you will learn, a serious practitioner thereof must never give over studying the work of colleagues. As for commerce, I have secured a modest commission to assist you in preparing a proper version of your adventure on the Bloomen-veldt for inclusion in the Matrix."

"Matrix? Commission? Annals? Qué pasa?"

"One moment, liebchen!" Wendi chided. "For speaking of commerce, it is your turn to answer *me*. To wit, why in all the worlds do I find Our Lady of the Bloomenkinder, the heroine and author of the Tale of the Pied Piper of the Bloomenveldt, the subject of so much learned if far from artful publication, begging for pittances on these wretched streets?"

"In order to secure funds, naturellement!" I told her. "Why else? So that I may purchase my escape from what you have so justly styled this wretched place!"

Wendi regarded me with astonishment. "You are in fact declaring your *indigence,* child?"

"I do possess some two hundred and sixty units of credit on my chip. . . ." I said in a somewhat pitiful voice.

"Two hundred and sixty!" Wendi exclaimed. "With that you might purchase two nights' lodging in this despicable hotel! I do not at all comprehend."

"I do not comprehend what it is you do not comprehend."

"Caga!" Wendi fairly exploded. "Nom de merde! The Clear Light Mental Retreat has licensed the publication of any number of learned and fatuous monographs dissecting your exploits, and while admittedly these are certainly less than popular fare, several thousand copies of each must surely have been purchased by institutes of learning. What wretched rate of royalty have they cozened you into accepting? One colleague to another, how mingy *was* the advance?"

"Royalty? Advance?" The more she spoke, the less I seemed to understand. "I am supplied with a decent enough room, three dull meals daily, and several changes of clothing, and that is the long and short of it," I told her. "You are saying I should receive something more?"

"WHAT?" Wendi shouted, bolting from the couch. She began pacing in small circles before me, fairly bellowing her outrage. "Chingada, what a naif! And to think *I* once had the temerity to style myself a proper thief! Child, while you have been spending all these weeks answering their stupid questions and begging alms in the street, the mages of the Clear Light Mental Retreat have been churning out monographs by the roomful on the data you have been so naively donating gratuit, at considerable profit to themselves!"

"They have. . . ?"

"Of course they have!" Wendi exclaimed. "Unlike you, my little ingenue, they were not exactly born the day before yesterday!"

Slowly, she subsided from her wrath, sat down beside me, and laid a friendly hand on my knee. "Fear not, Sunshine," she said in a much calmer voice, but one that was nevertheless edged with burnished steel. "I will aid you in dealing with these mountebanks forthwith. *Healers* they style themselves even as they rob innocent children!"

So saying, she grabbed me by the hand and fairly yanked me to my feet. "Andale!" she said. "We will have it out with this Urso fellow at once!"

"But . . . the Matrix . . . your commission . . . what is happening. . . ? You haven't told me *anything*. . ." I stammered as she dragged me toward the door.

"In the floatcab, liebchen, I will elucidate as best I can, though, hola, it would seem you have more to learn than even I can teach!"

Night had fully fallen by now, and as the floatcab followed its guiderail through the largely empty streets of Ciudad Pallas toward the Clear Light Mental Retreat, Wendi Sha Rumi told me of things that were at length to open up worlds.

"Consider, Sunshine," she said, "that since the Gyptians

started carving graffiti on the walls of their tombs, or at any rate since Gutenberg printed his first book, our species has been churning out mountains of paper, tapes, cines, holos, word crystals, und so weiter on every conceivable subject and then some. And since some centuries before the Age of Space, these have all been replicated thousandsfold, to the point that to our Second Starfaring Age almost none of this knowledge and art has been lost. We now number hundreds of billions on nearly three hundred worlds, and still this process continues apace."

She shook her head in wonder and amazement. "The imagination boggles, nē. Paradoxically enough, there is so much knowledge that if some sense were not made of it, it might as well be lost. Thus the Matrix, wherein the sum total of human knowledge is stored in subatomic coding that makes word crystal seem as crude and coarse as tablets of baked clay. Or rather the Matrices, for each Void Ship contains a copy to be continually updated as their paths cross."

"Each Void Ship contains all of human knowledge?" I exclaimed in utter wonderment.

"Nein, nein, nein!" Wendi said. "What an impossible useless mess *that* would be! The *sum* total of all human knowledge, child, the *edited* sum total. For example, Omar's ode is in the Matrix, but most of the learned babble churned out by the mages of the Clear Light on the subject of your adventure is merely noted in the bibliographical index. And even with stringent editing, it requires years of study to learn how to properly extract what one desires from the chaos of the Matrix."

She turned to me and smiled. "Which brings us to our business at hand," she said. "It has been decided by those who decide such things, which is to say the inner circle of the floating cultura, as it were, that your sojourn upon the Bloomenveldt is of sufficient interest to posterity so that a short and definitive version is deemed worthy of storage in the Matrix. Thus I have been commissioned to journey to Belshazaar on the *Mistral Falcon,* which waits in orbit even now, to assist you in the preparation of same, along with certain mages who have come along for the ride. Your fee will be two thousand units, admittedly a mere token sum, but I assure you that inclusion of a summary in the Matrix will in no way reduce the sale of the full and glorious romance you will no

398

doubt some day publish, indeed the cachet thereof will no doubt enhance—"

She cut herself off in midsentence, for our floatcab had now pulled up outside the Clear Light. "Speaking of credit units," she said, "I see we have reached our destination. So let us conclude this tawdry business as expeditiously as possible, so that we may swiftly flee this loathsome planet and begin our collaboration aboard the *Mistral Falcon, nē!*"

Thus, with my head reeling from this rapid-fire round of wonders and revelations to the point where I could scarcely think, I found myself being drawn down the hallways of the Clear Light by Wendi Sha Rumi, who shouted out to all and sundry for Urso Moldavia Rashid to be summoned to his office at once, and who refused to give over her strident demands until the whole mental retreat was in an uproar, and Urso at last appeared therein where we awaited him, scowling darkly, and muttering imprecations under his breath.

"What outrage is this?" he demanded angrily. "How dare you throw this mental retreat into a tumult and summon me from table like—"

"Like a thief caught in the act?" Wendi suggested in a cold, hard voice. "As for the nature of the outrage, that is for me to inquire and you to reply, Urso Moldavia Rashid! To wit, have you robbed this child of her droit of authorship out of mere pig-thick ignorance or deliberate guileful malice?"

"Who *is* this woman?" Urso shouted at me. "Speak at once, lest I expel you out upon the streets forthwith!"

"How dare you hector this innocent thusly?" Wendi bellowed. "As for expelling her from this establishment, I assure you that soon enough she will be gone. Which is to say as soon as you have rendered up some five thousand credit units, a modest enough estimate of the amount you have embezzled."

"Embezzled? *Moi?*" Urso said, shifting over at once from bellicose outrage to a tone of wounded innocence which would have seemed utterly sincere had not the transformation occurred with such rapidity. He sank down into the chair behind his desk and demurred not when I seated myself before him. Wendi, for her part, remained standing with one hand on her hip and the other pointing a finger of admonishment.

"Embezzled, *you!*" she declared. "For many long weeks has Sunshine been the subject of your learned interrogations, and many have been the monographs published thereon, to the great benefit of this institution's scholarly repute and to the pecuniary enrichment of all concerned save the font thereof herself."

"For those selfsame many weeks, she has enjoyed the benefits of our therapeutic ministrations," Urso pointed out defensively. "You know only the Sunshine Shasta Leonardo whom *we* have returned to full sapient sanity. Had you met the babbling creature who first emerged from the Bloomenveldt, you would not value our services to her so lightly."

"Well spoken!" I was moved to declare, for I could not deny the justice in his words.

Wendi, however, fetched my ankle a kick and shot me a look which further served to admonish me to silence.

"I do not undervalue the worth of your therapeutic efforts at all," she told Urso. "This I have already credited to your karmic and financial accounts. Otherwise, I would surely have demanded three times as much for the droits."

"The arrangement between us was freely entered into," Urso said in a rather whining tone, turning to me for support. "Will you deny this, Sunshine?"

Before I could begin to answer, Wendi held up her hand for silence. *"Freely entered into?"* she fairly snorted. "First you declare that your craft is entirely responsible for her present sanity, which is to say that she was quite barbled when you grabbed hold of her, and then you declare that the poor demented creature was capable of entering a business arrangement freely, and while in a state of perfect indigence to boot?"

Urso drummed his fingers on the surface of his desk. He shrugged. He sighed. His face took on an almost obsequious mien. "I am a Healer, not an author or an advocat," he said quite meekly. "I know nothing of these matters. Mayhap I have unknowingly violated some nicety thereof, but I am innocent of all guile or willful wrongdoing. . . ."

"Well spoken," Wendi said in a tone of poisonous sweetness. "Then you will no doubt be more than willing to rectify the innocent results of your ignorant actions, nē?"

Urso studied her narrowly. "In the interests of harmony

and justice, I suppose I might bring myself to part with two thousand credit units. . . ." he said speculatively.

"Four thousand," said Wendi. "Seeing as how we have now established what you are, would it not be unseemly to haggle over the price?"

"Three thousand," Urso countered immediately.

"Three thousand five hundred. After all, just as the Clear Light Mental Retreat has gained a certain scholarly renown among the worlds of men courtesy of my young friend, so might it gain a certain odor of ill repute should the content of this conversation penetrate beyond these walls. . . ."

"Done," moaned Urso. "You drive a hard bargain, certainement."

"Au contraire," drawled Wendi Sha Rumi. "I am known throughout the worlds of men as a high-minded esthete hardly able to properly attend to the grubby details of commerce."

Urso fairly choked.

Wendi laughed.

After Urso had transferred the funds in question, Wendi accompanied me to my erstwhile room, where I began to stuff the meager wardrobe with which I had been provided into my pack. She fingered one of the tunics distastefully. ·

"It is hardly worth the effort to pack this rubbish, liebchen," she said. "Hardly suitable for the society you are about to enter." She eyed me speculatively. "We are not that different in general measurement," she said. "It will be simple enough to alter some of my attire so that you may be properly dressed. Obviously there is no point in attempting to seek out haute couture in *this* nikulturni burg!"

With enough credit on my chip to purchase three or four electrocoma passages, I at last began to catch my psychic breath, which is to say I determined to seize control of my own destiny from the admittedly beneficent hands of my friend and would-be mentor, who had scarcely even given me time to ponder my own desires since we had met.

"I cannot thank you enough for your aid, Wendi," I told her. "But I have my own road to follow, and, thanks to you, I now have the funds to embark thereon."

"Your own road to follow?" Wendi said slowly, as if she had

been presented with something of a novel notion. "Vraiment, we must all follow our own star, ma chère," she agreed forthrightly. "The fact that I have come all this distance to meet you should in no way be taken into account. But what, may I ask, is this destiny which in your heart supersedes telling your tale to the posterity of the Matrix? Never have I heard anyone eschew this honor before. . . ."

"To follow the path of the wandering ruespieler and see the worlds of men," I told her.

"If that were all, why do you object to traveling at least the first leg of your journey in proper style?" she said, eyeing me narrowly.

"The worlds of men are many, and lifespan's duration is limited," I told her. "I care not to waste weeks of mine voyaging as an Honored Passenger, for I wish to make the attempt to see them all, to trip through the centuries in the sleep of electrocoma in the process and experience thereby as much of our species' tale as I can manage before I must die."

Wendi smiled a strange little smile. "It seems to me," she said, "that I have heard these words before. . . ."

I stared back at her. "You really *did* know Pater Pan," I said.

"Indeed," Wendi said. "And it would seem he told us both the same story of his millennial heart's desire." She regarded me sharply. "Do you seek to emulate his example or are you still smitten by his charms?"

"Je ne sais pas," I told her in all honesty. "Mayhap they are one and the same. I seek to travel the road of the spirit that we share certainement. . . ."

"And at the end of it, if fortune is kind, to find the natural man?"

"Mayhap . . ." I muttered. "Indeed, since I left Guy Vlad Boca in the Perfumed Garden I have been moved to seek the embrace of *no other* natural man. . . ."

"This is a confession of prolonged celibacy?" Wendi exclaimed.

"I suppose it is. . . ." I muttered. "Though somehow I have never thought of it that way before."

"De nada, liebchen, de nada!" Wendi exclaimed, perceiving my discomfort at this admission. "Men being what they are, it happens to us all from time to time, let me tell you. It will pass, it will happen again, it will pass once more."

"You do not think me a silly naif for being so smitten that I suffer sexual dysfunction, for seeking to live out a Gypsy Joker's tale. . . ?"

"As for the former, I may be no Healer, ma chère, but the natural woman's wisdom tells me that one whose most recent rounds of tantric exercise consisted of mass ravishment by spiritless male animals is presently not withdrawn from the arena out of mooning longings for a lover light-years gone," Wendi assured me. "As for seeking to live out the tale, this *does* impinge upon my area of professional expertise, for whether you know it or not, what you are truly seeking is a fitting ending to your wanderjahr's story."

"I am?"

"Vraiment, and justly so! For we must always end one tale truly before another can be fairly begun with a clear spirit, in life, as in the literary arts."

She shook her head and smiled to herself in a self-congratulatory manner. "I *knew* that I must hear your tale from your own lips or miss its essence!" she declared. "But I knew not why."

"And now you do?"

"Vraiment," Wendi said. "Omar's ode ended with your escape from the Bloomenveldt and the scientific literature considers your return to sapient sanity the proper climax, but while the tale of the Pied Piper of the Bloomenveldt is history, the tale of the wanderjahr of Sunshine Shasta Leonardo has not yet reached its proper esthetically satisfying conclusion, for you have not yet lived through its telling yet. Whether for reasons of the heart or by puissant unconscious literary instinct, you seek the right conclusion, liebchen, which is to say a proper conclusion to this romance requires a moment of triumphant reunion with your long-lost lover. Bon! Let us be gone! This must be accomplished in the interests of both kismet and art!"

I had finished packing while we spoke, and Wendi now grabbed up my pack and fairly shooed me out the sliding glass door into the garden. "Wait!" I found myself crying to her yet again. "Where are we going?"

Wendi paused in the doorway. "To the *Mistral Falcon*, where else?" she said.

"But you yourself have just agreed that I should seek out Pater Pan among the stars. . . . ?"

"And how do you intend to do that, my dear?" she asked indulgently.

I shrugged. "By traveling among the worlds of men as rapidly as possible so as to maximize the probability of random encounter," I said. "Beyond that it is in the hands of fortune, is it not?"

Wendi shook her head ruefully. "I can see that your knowledge of mathematics is even more deficient than my own," she said, leading me by the hand out into the garden, where thousands of stars shone in the clear dark night. "Look up there, and see how the worlds of men are scattered among the stars," she told me. "I am not sure of the equations, but the approximate odds against such a random encounter occurring may be imagined by multiplying the count of the worlds of men by the mean distance between them."

"But . . . but my path need not be entirely random. . . . I would of course seek out information along the way. . . ."

"Nevertheless, such a quest would consume your entire lifetime without reaching its proper climax."

"I don't understand you, Wendi," I complained pettishly. "First you tell me it is artistically right and proper that I seek out a reunion with Pater Pan, and then you tell me that success is all but impossible!"

"Impossible?" Wendi exclaimed. "When have you ever heard me declare that anything is impossible? Via the Matrix on the *Mistral Falcon* we shall winkle the fellow out soon enough."

"Via the Matrix?"

"Naturellement, how else do you imagine one keeps track of people in our Second Starfaring Age? While Pater Pan is hardly a figure of sufficient historical interest to have a running account of his wanderings recorded in the Matrix, certainement he has left a strong enough spoor of tales, legends, and little tribes in the process thereof for a maestra of the Matrix to construct a tracking program that will locate a recent locus in the data banks."

"How is such a thing possible?" I exclaimed.

Wendi shrugged. "Such mathematical legerdemain is entirely beyond my comprehension," she said. "But one need not trouble one's head with the same in order to employ it any more

404

than one need be a mage of cosmological physics to travel by Void Ship."

Wendi began striding across the silent and empty garden to the main exit of the mental retreat, but I still hung back.

"What is it now, child?" she demanded impatiently.

"I cannot go with you," I told her. "For surely the three thousand five hundred credit units I possess, plus the two thousand unit fee you allude to, will at best cover the expense of a journey as an Honored Passenger to one nearby planet. And where will I be then? An immobile indigent cursing my own extravagance again!"

Wendi's irritation evaporated. "I see you have exchanged a quantum of innocence for a packet of practicality!" she said approvingly. "No longer the high-minded artiste incapable of attending to the grubby details of commerce!"

She stood there in the garden for a moment, pondering, then she rubbed her hands together in glee. "Bien!" she said. "Now I will instruct you in a bit of the lore of same. As she who has a commission to oversee the preparation of your Matrix entry, I do declare that the same cannot be properly finished without an esthetically satisfying conclusion, who can deny this, nē? And in my expert literary opinion, this requires a climactic confrontation with Pater Pan. So much for the art of it, ma chère."

She waved a finger in my face and assumed an owlish air. "Now attend to the means whereby we artists gain our pecuniary vengeance for the depredations of the merchants, who are forever seeking to take advantage of our high-minded innocence," she chortled, obviously enjoying herself immensely. "Since we are both agreed that a reunion scene with Pater Pan is essential to a properly crafted Matrix entry, expenses incurred to achieve the same may legitimately be charged to the cost of scholarly research."

"Are you suggesting what I believe you are suggesting?" I said, slightly aghast in a moral sense mayhap, but taking a certain delighted amusement in a ploy that would certainly do any Gypsy Joker proud.

Wendi hugged me proudly. "Indeed I am!" she declared. "By this accounting, we will travel in proper style until our quarry is found, and if this may take some time, why that is fortune's gift to circumstance, for we travel gratuit, liebchen, as is only our right as free spirits of the arts!"

Yet still something held me back.

"Merde, what ails you now, child?" Wendi said, for no doubt my final trepidation was writ clearly upon my face.

"In truth, the floating cultura pleases me not," I blurted rather sullenly. "I have passed that way before, and I have no wish to have such idle empty folk look down their excessively elegant noses at me again!"

"Am I an idle, empty person?" Wendi said gently. "Have you observed me peering down at you from heights of aristocratic haughtiness?"

"Of course not . . . I didn't mean. . . ."

She took my hand and squeezed it as she led me inside the Clear Light and through the corridor to the streetside egress.

"Je comprend, liebchen, truly I do," she said. "The truth of it is that while you voyaged within a Grand Palais, you never voyaged within the floating cultura, you were never an *Honored Passenger* therein. You were treated as a mere fortunate urchin, and so you felt like a ragamuffin intruding into the fete, nē. . . ."

"One might I suppose style it thusly. . . ." I admitted grudgingly.

"Ah, but this will be another matter, Sunshine," Wendi said as we reached the street. "For you are that urchin no longer! For now you will travel by the invitation, hola, by the *largesse* of the floating cultura, not by purchasing intrusion therein."

With a little bow, she bade me enter a waiting floatcab. "For now you are no longer a ragged little Child of Fortune, but the heroine of an ode, a personage whose words are deemed worthy of the Matrix, with none other than Wendi Sha Rumi as your collaborator, friend, and patron! Surely she who trekked unaided across the Bloomenveldt lacks not the courage to brave as a darling daughter thereof the haut monde of our Second Starfaring Age?"

I laughed. I sighed. I shrugged. I entered the floatcab. "By now I should know better than to attempt to argue with Wendi Sha Rumi," I said as it bore us away.

"So say you now," said Wendi Sha Rumi. "But by the time our voyage together is over, we shall no doubt have disabused you of such unseemly humility. Then we will *truly* be sisters of the spirit, you and I!"

27

And so, I found myself once more entering the grand salon of a Grand Palais module to attend a departure fete, as Belshazaar's Flinger accelerated the *Mistral Falcon* toward the moment of its first Jump.

While the *Mistral Falcon* differed not from the *Unicorn Garden* when it came to configuration and function, when it came to the style of the Grand Palais module, which is to say the ambiance within which the experience of the voyage was to take place, this, naturellement, was as different from my previous experience as one might expect from any two works by maestras of the same art.

The dream chambers of the nethermost deck did not vary greatly from those which I had experienced on the *Unicorn Garden*, nor did the range of divertissements offered up on the entertainment deck, but when it came to the cuisinary deck, here the personal style of Su Jon Donova, Domo of the *Mistral Falcon*, had scope for proper assertation.

The walls, ceiling, and floor of the formal dining room were transparent screens upon which slowly evolving patterns of color and shape were projected which altered from course to course like the accompanying wines. More often than not, these were abstractions, but upon occasion representational landscapes, faces, famous paintings, und so weiter, would emerge from the

407

sinuous and stately dance of color and light only to melt away once more. In keeping with this style, the tables and chairs were airy filigrees of golden wire, appearing for all the worlds as if they had been woven to order by enchanted spiders.

The refectory, in contrast, was paneled in bluish rough-hewn wood, and the long tables and benches thereof were carved out of the same substance with rude adze marks left deliberately in evidence, the floor was carpeted with dust of the selfsame wood, and the ceiling was hidden by a veritable Bloomenveldt of hanging greenery.

The third salon was done up in what to my untutored eyes seemed a perfect replica of the classical Eihonjin mode—plain walls and ceiling of white paper framed by tawny wood, a floor covered by straw matting, black- and red-lacquered low tables, upholstered cushions with backrests, and an abundance of free-standing screens that could be arranged and rearranged to produce any desired dining configuration.

Su Jon Donova's concept for her vivarium was in stark contrast to the baroque hodgepodge with which Maria Magda Chan had provided the *Unicorn Garden*, and much more to my liking.

Under the dome atop the Grand Palais, a sere silvery sea of low desert dunes seem to extend to the horizon in all directions, melding into a circle of pure shimmering mirage where the sand met the sky. Above, a surreally brilliant starscape such as might be seen from the surface of a planet at the galactic center lit up what otherwise would have been the blackest of nights, mightily aided in this luminescent endeavor by a huge golden three-quarter moon perpetually at the zenith, so that the uncanny effect was that of a midnight brighter than the day.

The floor of the vivarium itself was ringed by small dunes of actual sand emerging seamlessly from the holoed landscape to enclose the oasis of the garden, a wide expanse of lawn over-topped with green palms, gnarled succulents, and enormous cacti. In the center of the oasis, naturellement, was a clear pool, about which were pitched tented awnings, replete with cushions and campfires in brass braziers.

All in all, this vivarium seemed somehow both a cunning statement of the reality through which the Void Ship moved and a fair escape therefrom. For indeed was not the *Mistral Falcon* truly bearing our caravan across just such a starry desert night, and on the other hand, was not the ship, vraiment the very vivarium itself, our little oasis of life in the vast and dead immensity thereof?

As for the grand salon, here the predominant motif, in piquant contrast to the vivarium above, was water.

Sheets of the same lit from behind in subtle aqua, rose, umber, and royal blue foamed down walls of black rock, white marble, rough-cut quartz, to enclose the grand salon in quietly rushing waterfalls. From the ceiling depended an immense chandelier of water blazing golden from within, an arcane inverted fountain whose sprays and plumes, gravity-controlled against all quotidian physics and visual expectation, spumed downward from the center and rose upward at the circumference to create a magical arabesqued canopy of watery delight.

As Su Jon Donova had so rightly, at least to my taste, surmised, such an envelope of liquid magic quite sufficed for wonderment, and so the grand salon was done up in rather homey furnishings, albeit furnishings suitable to the home of a pasha or magnate: a profusion of couches, chaises, and chairs, all substantial and cozy items of abstractly carved woods, upholstered in velvets, leathers, and the furry hides of animals, or at least the ersatzes of same. Freestanding fireplaces of brass standing before each wall of waterfall, carved in mythic representations of the avatars of the wind's four quarters, were the only real notes of baroque extravagance.

I had been decked out for my debut by Wendi in a simply cut formfitting black gown brilliantly embellished with floral designs done in multicolored jewels lit from within by pinlights. "Fitting raiment for Our Lady of the Bloomenkinder!" she had declared when she saw me in it, and she herself wore a gauzy creation of multilayered veils of dozens of pastel hues which drifted and tumbled with every movement, so that she seemed enrobed in a sunset cloud. All her entreaties to the contrary notwithstanding, I had wrapped my Cloth of Many Colors about my head in a turban, for I was determined to retain some grace note of identity that was entirely my own.

Thusly accoutred, and fortified by the knowledge that I was no less extravagantly clad than the generality of the Honored Passengers who already thronged the grand salon when we arrived,

I embarked on a round of introductions under the guidance and patronage of my mentor, who seemed to be on terms of easy intimacy with every lordly creature in the room.

"Ah Kort, ça va, and this is Sunshine Shasta Leonardo, she who traversed the Bloomenveldt armed with no more than a tale. Kort Jaime Mustapha, liebchen, is a poet even as our Omar, indeed some say better, including yourself Kort, nicht wahr?"

"Our Lady of the Bloomenkinder, is it then? Enchanté, muchacha, one does not often meet the mythical protagonist of an ode, except of course of the autobiographical variety, to which many of us are alas addicted."

"Sunshine Shasta Leonardo, meet the Domo of our fete," Wendi declared, seizing upon a short dark woman wearing an arcane articulated suit which seemed to be fashioned out of the iridescent red carapaces of thousands of insects.

"I am given to understand that you have been honored by an invitation to enshrine yourself in the Matrix," Su Jon Donova said. "Bitte, how does such an august personage regard my own poor art, if I may make so bold?"

"Without demur or hesitation, I can truthfully declare that never in my entire experience of same have I encountered a Grand Palais which pleased me more," I drawled.

Wendi hid her face with her hand to conceal a grin which she revealed to me as soon as we made to go on. "Well spoken, ruespieler," she whispered in my ear. "Certainement, you have the proper instincts to swim in these waters, liebchen!"

Mayhap this was so, or at any rate, viewed from within by one with a proper entrée to the dance, the pavane of the floating cultura seemed genteel enough to lose its power to daunt, and the rules thereof simple enough to comprehend in comparison, for example, with the vie of the Edojin, the niceties and complexities of which I have never been able to truly fathom even to this day.

Such as Wendi might freely banter with mild jests at her interlocutor's expense but must goodnaturedly accept the same in return and leaven her discourse from time to time with equally trivial self-deprecations. Younger and less mature fish such as I, however, should keep to the more respectful manners appropriate to somewhat junior status, flatter a bit but not to fawning excess, and in return could expect a certain more formal politesse toward their tenderer persons from their seniors.

"Here is my protégée, Sunshine Shasta Leonardo. Sunshine, this is Dalta Evan Evangeline, a literary archeologist who will aid us in the imagistic formulation of your Matrix entry, for there are few such in the worlds of men more adept at rummaging through the dustheap of old mythic bones than she!"

"Indeed? I am avid to discuss such matters with you at length, for I am but a ruespieler with, I would hope, some talent, but little learning when it comes to the age-old lore of the craft. . . ."

"Au contraire, to be frank, it is I who seek enlightenment from you, for while I may be knowledgeable in the lore of the tale-teller's art, it is the true creators thereof who are the masters, perfect or not, of the same, whereas I, alas, can only analyze as a learned eunuch might seek to encompass the mysteries of the tantric arts. . . ."

Und so weiter.

The truth of it was, as in my maturity I was to learn was the truth of such matters generally, is that one's regard for any given social realm is quite strongly the product of one's perception of the regard in which oneself is held therein. When I traveled in the *Unicorn Garden* as a parvenu whose only entrée into the society thereof was a physical presence purchased by the largesse of Guy Vlad Boca, I held the floating cultura in a lofty disdain which nicely mirrored the position of grudging sufferance I unhappily occupied. But now, as the protégée of Wendi Sha Rumi, and as a personage whose deeds and mythos were held in some respectful regard, naturellement I found that the Honored Passengers were not quite as empty and obnoxiously arrogant as I had once supposed.

Which is to say that when, exhausted and gently toxicated by the refreshments and the company, I was ready to quit the fete for my bed, I was closer to considering myself a princess of the floating cultura than an intruder into a realm beyond her proper station.

Naturellement, as is true for all save the highest and lowest of our species, the reality lay in the vast ambiguous region between.

If I have thusfar failed to mention the *Mistral Falcon*'s sequence of destinations, I gave such matters even less regard at

411

the time, for the fact that the ship would journey to Winthrope, Novi Mir, Flor del Cielo, Lebenswelt, und so weiter, was of absolutely no consequence to me, for I had no plans to sojourn on any of these worlds, nor did I even have an ultimate destination in mind save that presently unknown world upon which Pater Pan at length might be found.

Thus, in contrast to my voyage from Edoku to Belshazaar, I had in fact, all unknowingly, boarded the *Mistral Falcon* as a psychic citizen of the floating cultura already, which is to say as a voyager for whom the journey itself, rather than any immediate destination, was the goal.

Indeed, via this karmically induced fusion with the weltanshauung of the floating cultura, I too found myself paying little attention to matters outside the universe of the Grand Palais, and vraiment, the first Jump occurred, as it turned out, entirely outside my sphere of apprehension, for at the time I was in the process of making my first acquaintance with the Matrix, the raison d'être of my presence aboard the *Mistral Falcon* in more ways than one.

For such a puissant artifact, the appearance of the Matrix was quotidian enough, indeed deceptively archaic. One corner of the ship's library was given over to a rather bulky oblong console a good three meters long and two meters high, decked out with telescreen, holo projector, word crystal transcriber, flimsy printer, microphone, speaker, and even a large keyboard whereby letters and numbers might be inputted by hand, so that the whole thing gave the appearance of some ancient computer out of a holocine drama set in the Age of Space. Or as if some sculptor had set out to recapitulate the entire history of our species' data storage technology in a single composite piece of artwork.

Small wonder I had never noticed such a device aboard the *Unicorn Garden*, for I had not exactly haunted the library in the first place, and without knowing what wonders of knowledge were in fact contained therein, I no doubt would have taken it for just such a piece of sculpture, nothing more than a quaint object of decor.

Willa Embri Janos had already arrived when Wendi and I made our entry. A fair-haired, somewhat squat woman, she had been introduced at the departure fete as a data retriever of some renown, which is to say an adept of the not inconsiderable art of inducing the Matrix to cough up what was desired, a matter of no little complexity, as I was about to learn.

"As I have told you, we are seeking the most recent locus of a fellow known as Pater Pan," Wendi told her.

Willa nodded, and spoke the name to the Matrix. At once, an endless procession of words and numbers began to scroll across the tele. "Cancel," Willa ordered, and the tele went blank. "As one would have expected, there is no main entry, but there is a superabundance of minor cross-references under all manner of headings and bibliographical notations referring to quite a few obscure monographs not in the Matrix. We will need as many correlatives as possible in order for me to construct an algorithm to extract what we need from secondary and tertiary sources."

She turned to regard me. "Bitte, muchacha, begin. . . ."

"Begin *what?*" I asked in some befuddlement. "Alas, I fear that I have hardly understood a word you have said. . . ."

At this, Willa Embri Janos' eyes widened, and she shook her head in a minor gesture of reproof. "We must have a list of other possible cross-references to this Pater Pan—places, names, activities, und so weiter. Proper nouns only, por favor, or I will be fairly buried in random data. Into the microphone, if you please. . . ."

"Gypsy Jokers . . . Child of Fortune . . . Piper of Pan. . . ?" I began uncertainly. "Is this what you require?"

Willa nodded. "Just so," she said. "But please to avoid such massive generalities as 'Child of Fortune' or we will be drowned in a tsunami of references. . . ."

Shrugging, I went on with this bizarre babble. "King of the Gypsies . . . Spark of the Ark . . . Yellow Brick Road . . . Hippies . . . Arkies . . . Ronin. . . ." Und so weiter, ad infinitum, or so it seemed, though in truth I could not have gone on for more than five minutes before my string of words wore out. There was something rather distasteful to me about this attempt to reduce the essence of Pater Pan to a finite list of proper nouns, for I could not help but realize that the same reductionist process could as easily be applied to my own identity, and with a list of words not one half as long.

"I believe I am finished," I said at last. "What occurs next?"

"It would take you some months of diligent study to comprehend the mathematics of the processes I must now apply, though

413

certainement well worth the effort," Willa told me. "First I must construct a program to induce the Matrix to winnow through all these reference points so that all data bearing upon the central subject are released, then I must induce it to establish a sequence along a temporal axis, then trajectories must be hypothesized and compared to the data field. . . ."

She shrugged. "Suffice it to say that all this will take days if we are fortunate and weeks if we are not. . . ."

I found the whole arcane and lengthy process quite daunting to contemplate, especially in light of the fact that I myself was now expected to contribute to this massive chaos of data. "Am I going to have to learn all that in order to record my own entry?" I asked in no little dismay.

Willa laughed. "Anyone can *add* knowledge to the Matrix by the simple expedient of playing an ordinary word crystal into it," she said. "It is *extracting* specific knowledge which requires learning and art!"

She regarded Wendi somewhat owlishly. "There is a lesson in this for you, Wendi Sha Rumi," she said. "Which is that promiscuous babble does not necessarily contribute to wisdom as it adds to the total store of data. Therefore have a care that you aid our young friend in producing a suitable entry, which is to say one that is short, concise, shorn of excess generalities and verbiage, and as objectively accurate as possible."

"I have prepared entries for the Matrix before, Willa," Wendi pointed out dryly.

"Indeed. In profusion. But do remember that as a guardian of the Matrix's coherence, I must pass upon the suitability of what you present."

"Has my work ever failed to pass your muster?"

"Not in a long while," Willa admitted. "But you *do* tend to prolixity, so have a care you do not infect our young friend's style with your own vice."

Wendi laughed. "In addition to her skill as a data retriever, Willa fancies herself a literary critique manqué," she told me. "When it comes to the former, I bow to her expertise, but as for the latter, she is an amateur at best."

"Be that as it may," Willa rejoined, "it is the taste of we *amateurs* that you authors of romances must please in order to earn your wage, nē?"

414

At Wendi's suggestion, vraiment at her insistence, we took a light lunch of sushi and sake together in the refectory, for, she declared, the evening meal was to be a formal banquet at which many courses would be consumed, and at which I would be required to have my wits about me, for she had arranged for us to be seated at table with those who were to aid in the refinement of my Matrix entry, and Void Captain Dana Gluck Sara as well, who had expressed some interest in hearing the Tale of the Pied Piper of the Bloomenveldt from the lips of the heroine thereof.

After lunch we repaired to her stateroom, where she explained the procedure we would follow in our collaboration.

First, I would freely record my tale onto word crystal in my own style, indeed before we were done, I would no doubt record several versions, for the point at this stage was to exhaust the possibilities of my own spontaneous declamation thereof.

Then we would vet this raw material together with various mages so that the imagistic vagaries of my descriptions of events, flora, psychic effects, und so weiter, might be sharpened and when necessary replaced by terms of scientific precision and accuracy, so that the entry would be comprehensible and informative to any hypothetical person who might call it up from the Matrix several centuries from now.

When I protested that such a procedure seemed to me to insure the death of art, she only laughed.

"Indeed, as an author of romances, no one is more in sympathy with such a plaint than I, liebchen," she told me. "But we are charged to produce a *Matrix entry*, not the romance which you may create when the spirit moves you and which will no doubt earn you fame and fortune. As for the pain of reducing art to dry didacticism, the final stage of our work will be more painful still, for then we must go over every word and syllable with a cold and ruthless heart. For while Willa Embri Janos may be something of a philistine when it comes to literary style, she knows whereof she speaks when it comes to the utter concision required to produce what the Matrix must have."

She patted my knee. "I hope we will still be friends at the conclusion of this unpleasant task," she said.

"We will always be friends, Wendi, come what may!" I declared with an open heart.

415

Wendi laughed again. "Say that when we have engaged in mortal combat over every word of your own precious prose, liebchen!" she said.

"You will find that those of us who honor the floating cultura with our presence and not the other way around will be interested in your unique adventure," Wendi told me sotto voce as we entered the formal dining room. "It is fair entrée into serious circles, ma petite, just do not assume that it will yet make you the center of the universe."

The inner wisdom of this caveat eluded me at the time, but by the time the banquet was over I was to be taught this lesson quite well.

There were six other diners at the table Wendi had put together: Void Captain Dana Gluck Sara; Willa Embri Janos, Lazaro Melinda Kuhn, and Dalta Evan Evangeline, all of whom I had already been introduced to; Timothy Ben Bella, psychopharmacologist and yogic adept; and Linda Yee Lech, who was styled one of the foremost mages of evolutionary psychesomics in all the worlds of men.

Which is to say a heady and learned company indeed, and one which Wendi had quite obviously assembled around the subject of my young self. This knowledge was something less than reassuring to the same, for on the one hand it put me in mind of the endless interrogation sessions at the Clear Light, and on the other it made me trepidatious concerning my ability to hold my own at this exalted level of discourse.

Fortunately, as I was soon to learn, the manners of these worthies were a far cry from what I had experienced from the mages at the mental retreat. The first course served was a crepe of fruits de mer enrobed in a thick saffron sauce and accompanied by a rather sweet white wine, after which came a fiery curried vegetable consommé with tiny bits of pickled fish and a powerful anise-flavored vodka. Then came smoked black mushrooms stuffed with pungent forcemeat and served with a bone-dry red vintage.

During these preliminaries, Wendi favored me with an introduction to the Honored Passengers whom I had not yet met, and the table talk concerned the art of our chef maestro, Escoffier Tai Bondi. For my part, I took the opportunity to say little and im-

416

bibe a respectful amount, so that by the time we were served Vaco Filets Bordelais, garnished with fried maize noodles and accompanied by a wine so deeply red that it appeared almost black, my trepidations had been entirely dissolved, my tongue was lubricated to a fine loquacity, and I was more than ready to render up my spiel at Wendi's request.

For the next twenty minutes or so, I held this audience of mages and puissant intellects spellbound with a rather extravagant telling of the Tale of the Pied Piper of the Bloomenveldt, a version not unlike that which I had developed on the streets of Ciudad Pallas, if somewhat augmented by the noble vintages I had consumed.

I seem to remember that during this spiel we were served a barbecue of assorted vegetables accompanied by a cunningly spiced white wine as well as a goreng embellished with several varieties of charcuterie washed down with a dark-brown beer, though my memory of this stage of the meal was somewhat clouded by both beverages and the exhilarating sight of seven pairs of keenly bright eyes approvingly turned upon my person and seven pairs of intellectually avid ears hanging on my every word, or so it seemed to me.

Suffice it to say that by the time I had concluded over a salad of fruits steeped in a crème of smoked nuts, I felt like the queen of all the worlds.

But just as this sweet course did not prove to be the conclusion to the banquet that I had supposed, so did the conclusion of my declamation lead to two more intellectual courses of which I was to prove something less than the chef maestra. Out came a cold red fruit soup liberally laced with kirschwasser and garnished with tiny croutons of nut flour stuffed with cinnamon jam, and with it the questioning commenced.

"You are *quite* certain that these true Bloomenkinder were entirely devoid of sapience?" demanded Linda Yee Lech. "Which set of parameters did you apply, the Menzies-Rademacher criteria, which have been around for centuries, or ahem, my own more recent construct?"

"I'm afraid that the differences between the two are presently rather vague in my mind," I bluffed, for of course I had no idea what she was talking about. "S'il vous plaît, if you would be so good as to refresh my memory. . . ."

"The Menzies-Rademacher criteria hinge on the question of whether meaning is carried in a grammatical sequence or whether each cry is an isolate," Linda Yee Lech reminded me. "Whereas my construct, which relies upon a systems analysis of the absence or presence of social interactions, is far less of a blunt instrument."

"As I have said, the Bloomenkinder are perfectly mute," I told her. "As for social interactions, these may have appeared complexly patterned, but no more so than the doings of a beehive."

"You were able to inventory a sufficient number of interactions so that this was confirmed by analysis to a probability of better than fifty percent?" Linda Yee Lech asked sharply.

"I'm afraid not," I admitted. "But if you had seen, as I did, human infants suckling at floral teats, there would have been no—"

"Con su permiso," Timothy Ben Bella interrupted politely. "If I may, I believe the question Linda is trying to approach is whether we are dealing with innocent animals in which sentience never arises or sapient humans whose higher centers are severed from volitional expression by the exudations of the flowers. . . ."

"Or indeed whether *the Bloomenwald itself* may not be deemed sentient," Lazaro Melinda Kuhn declared. "And if so, did such sentience evolve in symbiosis with the devolution of its human pollinators, or was this Perfumed Garden phenomenon preexistent? Did you observe a progression of intermediate floral forms? Did any of the native mammals exhibit such florally coordinated behaviors on a somewhat less complex level?"

"As for a progression of intermediate floral organization from isolated flowers to the complexity of the Perfumed Garden, vraiment, one would have had to have been blind not to observe this," I said. "But as for observing the intimate behaviors·of the native mammals, it was entirely impossible to approach them even closely enough to see them very clearly. But surely the suckling of human infants at vegetative teats indicates that the latter must have evolved to service the former, nē?"

"A probable deduction. . . ." Lazaro admitted. "But did you observe the young of any native species engaged in the same behavior? The presence of same would obviate your puissant logic, kind. . . ."

"Je ne sais pas," I admitted lamely. "I never thought to inquire at the time. . . ."

"And what of the vapors you have styled 'pheromones' and 'perfumes'?" asked Timothy Ben Bella. "Is this mere literary license or did you obtain samples for analysis?"

"Vraiment, we obtained samples, but alas they were lost with our packs."

"Merde! Quelle catastrophe!"

"Mayhap all is not lost, Timothy," Lazaro said. "For certainement we know enough of the general botany of Belshazaar to deduce the general biochemical class of its exudates by the morphology of the specific organs secreting same. Describe for us then, bitte, Sunshine, the various floral structures responsible for the vapors producing the several specific psychotropic effects you encountered. . . ."

"I'm afraid that in my psychic state I was hardly capable of noticing. . . ."

"But surely you were at least able to differentiate among the substances exuded by stamens, pistils, and perhaps specialized scent organs?"

I could only shrug my admission of perfect ignorance.

"Give over hectoring the poor child on these matters, Lazaro," said Linda Yee Lech. "It is hardly a moral flaw not to be a trained botanical observer! However when it comes to psychic experiences, these at least we all observe with ultimate intimacy. So tell us, Sunshine, in less anecdotal terms than you have thusfar employed, when you were in your deepest thrall to the flowers, was your sapience entirely absent, or merely suppressed by a biochemical overlay? Which is to say, did your higher centers bear witness to their own volitional impotence or was, as it were, no one at home?"

"There appears to be no temporal discontinuity in my memory-track, if that is what you mean. . . ."

"Hmmm. . . ." mused Dalta Evan Evangeline. "To come at it from a possibly more fruitful angle, would you say that the stimulus of the rising sun which first roused you from this state had sapient mythic meaning to you from the outset, or was it a phylogenically primitive tropism upon which the later more complex structure was retrospectively erected?"

"Qué?"

419

"Ho, ho, sehr gut, Dalta!" exclaimed Linda Yee Lech in forthright admiration. "Indeed it must have been the former, for the revertees who once possessed human consciousness responded to her verbal cues, whereas the Bloomenkinder never did!"

"True," said Lazaro, "but on the other hand if she *was* responding to a mere visual tropism, then they could just as easily have been responding to a mere auditory tropism."

"But if so, then why did *the Bloomenkinder* not respond to it?"

"Because it is exactly this lack of response which proves that they lack sapient human consciousness!"

"Phah! What a tautology!"

"Round and round you go," Wendi finally broke in after her long and quite uncharacteristic silence. "Yet you miss the true point entirely!"

"Which is, if I may make so bold?" drawled Lazaro.

"That there were three entirely different responses by members of our own species to the very same chemicals, naturellement!" Wendi declared.

"Well taken!" exclaimed Linda Yee Lech. "Vraiment it is clearly the imprinting of the collective unconscious that the Bloomenkinder lack! Hola, this may indeed settle one of the hoariest disputes of psychesomics!"

"How so?" inquired Dalta Evan Evangeline.

"It would seem to prove quite conclusively that what we style the collective unconscious is culturally and verbally transmitted, rather than being species genetic coding!"

"Rubbish!" scoffed Lazaro. "If that were so, then how could you account for the cross-cultural and transtemporal universality of same?"

"Oh so? Then how would *you* account for its absence in the Bloomenkinder if it is inscribed in the genes of our species?"

"If one grants the Bloomenwald some sort of vegetative sentience, then the genes wherein the collective unconsciousness is encoded may have been deliberately extinguished by selective breeding even as we have altered the genetically determined behaviors of domestic animals."

"Anthropocentric projection!"

Und so weiter.

By the time we were into a green salad dressed with peppered oil and sweet and sour vinegar, the discourse had proceeded into esoteric realms of biology, genetics, psychesomics, esthetics, and evolutionary ecology whose general outlines I could only struggle to dimly comprehend, and to which I could hardly coherently contribute. Over yet another dessert, of chocolate pastry filled with rose-flavored custard, I sat there quietly listening to intense and occasionally acrimonious debates on the psychopharmacology of the Bloomenveldt, the theoretical parameters of vegetative sentience, the essential definition of the élan humain, the ethics of continental sterilization, et cetera, in terms whose firm meanings I strained my brain to comprehend, for I understood enough to know that my own simple tale was the central subject of all this commentary.

It was exhilarating to have my adventures taken so seriously by such manifestly serious intellects, but it was also daunting to realize how much wider and deeper knowledge and insight went on any conceivable subject than I had ever imagined, particularly when the callowness of my own intellect was being so amply demonstrated using the subject matter of my own personal experience.

"I never dreamed there was so much to learn even about the events of my own existence," I moaned to Wendi when we departed at the banquet's end, with my mind as torpid with elusive discourse as my stomach was with haute cuisine. "How are we ever going to incorporate it all in my simple tale?"

Wendi laughed. "One thing at a time, liebchen, one thing at a time," she assured me blithely. "Now you must sleep well, Sunshine, for tomorrow our work begins in earnest."

And so it did. For three days, I declaimed my tale in numerous versions onto word crystal to the point where I began to loathe the sound of my own voice, and then for three more days we worked to combine them into a version suitable for submission to our panel of mages. By the time this process was completed to Wendi's satisfaction, my brain was reeling with intellectual fatigue, and I wanted nothing more than to be finished with the whole task. The truth of it is that never in my young life had I ever engaged in such strenuous intellectual labors; indeed, if truth be told, prior to that time, I had been a virgin when it came to any real work at all.

421

Throughout all human history, the young of our species have been subject to endless rubrics on the joys of labor, the ennui that is the inevitable result of indolence, and the psychic satisfaction to be gained by absorption in some mighty work, the more demanding the better. Be such homilies as they may, the pleasures thereof remained beyond my comprehension until the next stage of the process began.

"One thing at a time," Wendi had promised, and so it was done, which is to say rather than being subject to whole batteries of learned interrogators at once, the mages were given word crystals of the draft version of the Matrix entry to peruse, and then I went at it with them one at a time, over lunch or dinner, in the vivarium, or in their staterooms, more often than not with Wendi at my side.

Now the situation was in a certain sense reversed, for while my teachers certainement never lost interest in what they might extract in the course of such discourse for their own intellectual use, teachers they indeed were, resources placed at my disposal, and what puissant teachers they were!

In the stateroom of Lazaro Melinda Kuhn, I learned the dark and ambiguous answer to a question that had never trammeled my mind until, at length, after a surfeit of his gentle but rueful complaints at my less than scientifically lucid descriptions of the flora and fauna of the Bloomenveldt, it suddenly intruded into my awareness.

"Why then depend on the anecdotes of such as myself?" I demanded. "Why in all the centuries that men have dwelt on Belshazaar has not a proper scientific expedition been mounted to the interior of the Bloomenveldt. . . ?"

I was suddenly brought up short by my own words, which is to say by the shameful mortification induced thereby. For had I not once promised to myself that if I escaped to the worlds of men I would one day return with just such an expedition to rescue Guy Vlad Boca? And what had I done to accomplish same? Precisely nothing!

"Vraiment, why is one not mounted now?" I demanded with guilt-driven stridency. "Indeed, why does not a fleet of hovers descend upon the depths of the forest canopy to rescue our human comrades from such vile floral facism?"

Lazaro's demeanor darkened. "I wondered when you would

422

ask that," he said with a sigh. "I had hoped it would not fall to me to be confronted with the question, for the answer, I fear, does not exactly reflect honor on our species."

"What do you mean by that?" I said defensively, for, thinking as I was of my abandonment of Guy, I assumed that the lack of honor he alluded to was my own.

"The psychotropics derived from the Bloomenveldt are a source of great profit, nē," Lazaro said. "Indeed they are the entire economic base of that unwholesome planet. The fact is, that if you inspect the literature, you will find quite a few cryptic mentions of the apocryphal Bloomenkinder. The unpleasant truth is that the existence of same has been suspected for centuries."

"Then why—"

"Think, my innocent young friend, and with greed in your heart! If proof of such a state of affairs was secured and laid before the worlds of men, what would be the result?"

"What else but a hue and cry and a demand on the part of men and women of good will for the rescue of—" I cut myself short. I stared at Lazaro. He gave me a strange little shrug. "You don't mean. . . ?"

"But alas I do, my young friend," Lazaro said uncomfortably. "Not only would the citizens of Belshazaar find themselves morally required to rescue the Bloomenkinder, there would no doubt be many who would demand the extermination of the Bloomenwald as a proper vengeance for the outrage. And even if the voice of science could prevent such floral genocide, it would appear that the presence of Bloomenkinder is necessary to induce the flowers to evolve the very psychotropics which enrich the planet. An unwholesome symbiosis mayhap, but a true one, which is to say one which indeed benefits both species—the one with more efficient pollinators, and the other with huge pecuniary profit."

"They *know?*" I exclaimed in horror and outrage. "They know and still they do nothing?"

Lazaro shrugged. "They know, they don't know, certainement they have no wish to know that they know."

"Merde, I always sensed a vileness of spirit throughout Ciudad Pallas, but I put it down to lack of esthetics!" I muttered. "Never did I imagine creatures that styled themselves human could thusly abandon the spirits of their fellows in such a cowardly manner for mere profit!"

423

Nor could I think of anything else when I departed to keep my luncheon appointment with Linda Yee Lech. "Something must be done!" I declared angrily, after hectoring her on the subject at considerable length. "We must force these mercenary miscreants to rescue the Bloomenkinder!"

"Are you so certain of your moral rectitude in this regard?" she asked me evenly. "Remove the Bloomenkinder from the forest and what have you accomplished? At the cost of wrecking a planetary economy and impeding the progress of psychopharmacology, you will have rescued them from the ecological niche in which they evolved in favor of incarceration as an exhibit in a zoological garden. Even feral humans raised by other mammals do not develop sentient consciousness, still less will the symbiotes of the Bloomenveldt ever be anything but mammals in human form sans the élan humain, nē."

"But their progeny—"

"You would breed them in captivity?"

"No, certainly not, but—"

"Then you would commit genocide against the Bloomenkinder as well as against the Bloomenveldt?"

"Genocide? *I* am not the monster!"

Linda Yee Lech smiled and softened her expression. "Thus speak all humans, and truly so," she said. "Vraiment, this is a question which must trouble the spirit. For who is the monster here? Those who merely profit by a pre-existing condition while careful avoiding conscious recognition of the same? The innocent Bloomenkinder? Those who, like your Guy, have willingly surrendered their spirits to the flowers? The flowers of the Bloomenveldt, who merely follow their own natural evolutionary vector, mayhap to sentience?"

"Be questions of guilt or monsterhood as they may, I am talking about pragmatic action, not the niceties of moral calculus!" I declared pettishly.

"La même chose, in this case," Linda said flatly. "For here on the one hand we have a species in human form whose consciousness has long since diverged from our own and which will expire into extinction if it is removed from its floral symbiote, and on the other hand, a floral symbiote which may be evolving toward a sentience it can only achieve courtesy of its human

424

pollinators. We may expunge either or both from the universe, but we will never restore the Bloomenkinder to sapient citizenship in the human race. Do we therefore have the moral right to commit double genocide when there would not even be a beneficiary of such a scientific and karmic outrage? Are you really willing to take such matters into your own hands?"

"Put thusly, je ne sais pas. . . ." I was forced to admit. "But what of those sapient humans who wandered into the thrall of the flowers? What about such as Guy?"

"What about those who quite rationally chose to die in the arms of floral nirvana?" Linda Yee Lech pointed out relentlessly. "Would they wish to be rescued? Vraiment, would your Guy thank you if you rescued him from his perfect flower to spend the rest of his days in a mental retreat? If we were to impose our will upon such spirits according to our own concepts of righteousness, how would we be any less fascist than the flowers, who at least would seem to eschew the practice of continental sterilization?"

"Once more, what once seemed clear is now occluded by an excess of wisdom," I could only declare.

Linda Yee Lech smiled. "Unfortunately there are all too many instances when all that wisdom teaches us is that the ability to act is only the power to make things worse," she said.

Other enlightenments, fortunately, were a good deal less grim, and more relevant to my evolution as a tale-teller than to the jaundicing of my opinion of the moral stature of my own species. In particular, Dalta Evan Evangeline, the literary archeologist, did much to both open up my awareness to the abundance of nuance attached to most every image and figure I employed by several thousand years of human history and art, and lead me to a far deeper understanding of certain aspects of my own tale and those I had learned from the Gypsy Joker ruespielers as well.

This odyssey began innocently enough when she presented me with a copy of the tale of *Peter Pan* and suggested that perusal thereof might be of some relevant interest to the task at hand. Since I had been meaning to delve into this matter ever since I had been apprised of this work's existence, I readily enough agreed.

But after I finished the tale, I knew only confusion. Surely the freenom Pater Pan must be a somewhat less than perfectly erudite homage to the *Peter* Pan of the tale, and just as surely I could see a good deal of Pater in the domo of the tribe of lost boys. Yet the ending of the tale contradicted the spirit of the Yellow Brick Road entirely, which is to say I could hardly imagine my Pater approving of the moral imposed by fiat when the lost children forsake their vie for the quotidian realm of adults, nor did the Wendy of the tale have more than a passing resemblance to the Wendi that I knew who had chosen this freenom.

When I broached these matters at a lunch of pasta with sautéed vegetables and grated cheeses with Wendi and Dalta, the latter's interest seemed piqued as if I had presented her with new food for thought, and the former shook her head in ironic amusement.

"These matters of names, images, and their millennial transmogrifications are even deeper and more arcane than you are beginning to suppose, Sunshine," Dalta said. "The name 'Pater Pan' alone might be the subject of a lengthy monograph. . . ." She paused, fingering her chin. "Indeed, I do believe that I will compose it!"

"Mayhap you would care to elucidate at less than exhaustive length?" Wendi inquired dryly. "For I too once knew the gallant in question. . . ."

"Well, if you are content with a mere skimming of the surface," Dalta said in a similar vein. " 'Pater,' for example, has the meaning of 'father' in a long-disused sprach of Lingo. 'Pan' was the priapic goat-god of libido in a certain ancient mythos, and also refers to 'Pan-theism,' the concept that the Atman is equally distributed throughout the world of maya. The reference to '*Peter* Pan' you have already mentioned, and 'Peter,' paradoxically enough, refers to both the first pontifex of a religion opposed to the doctrine of Pan-theism, and the phallus. Moreover, in yet another ancient image-system, the 'Peter Pan Complex' denotes, as in the tale, a personality which eschews maturity in favor of permanent neoteny. . . ."

"Hola!" exclaimed Wendi. "Then the full translation of the name would be. . . . Pope Lingam of the Libidinal Atman Goat, a fine epithet for the master cocksman we both knew indeed!"

Wendi and I both burst into laughter. "Do you suppose the tales the fellow we both knew told were informed by such scholarly erudition?" she asked me.

426

"Somehow I doubt it," I said. "Yet who can deny that he nevertheless chose a literarily puissant freenom?"

"As did you when you wove the same nuances into your tale and then some," Dalta said quite solemnly, for she had not joined in our mirth any more than she had shared our intimate knowledge of the object thereof.

"Indeed. . . ?" I said, out of politesse more than avid interest.

"Oh, vraiment," Dalta said. "The god Pan played seductive music on his pipes, which is to say he was the Piper of the libido. But when he becomes the *Pied* Piper we are also in another mythos. The Gypsies were an early avatar of the Children of Fortune, and the Joker refers to a transmutational card of the Tarot, the court jester of the ancient kings, and the god of holy mischief in more than once cycle. The *Gypsy Jokers,* however, were a tribe of wandering motorized barbarians like the Angels of Hell, the Slaves of Satan, and the Golden Horde. The rising sun is the ensign of the ancient Emperors of Nippon, hence of the virtues of bushido, but is also a punning reference to the Risen Christ, as well as to Prometheus, who brought the light of knowledge to our species, and who is also known as Lucifer the Light Bringer, who somehow also contrives to metamorphose into Satan, Prince of Darkness. . . ."

"Quelle chose!" I japed. "I am overwhelmed to learn of the depths of my own unsuspected erudition! Alas, it would seem impossible in our Second Starfaring Age to tell a simple tale without summoning up all unawares a whole pantheon of hidden spirits! How then am I to become a maestra of the Word when each mot of my Lingo has a secret sprach all its own?"

"It will take years of diligent study naturellement," Dalta said enthusiastically. "If you wish, I will have the Matrix prepare a bibliographical sequence for you to follow. . . ."

"Study the bones if you like, I suppose that can do no harm," Wendi said archly. "Just do not take such learning too seriously. It is magic of a sort we work with our spells of words and it is better that we do not feel we must pin down every last nuance of reference thereof lest we find ourselves suffering from creative constipation!"

At that even Dalta was constrained to join in the laughter at her expense.

427

*   *   *

Nevertheless, as the *Mistral Falcon* reached Winthrope and then Novi Mir, and as the work progressed toward the stage when there was nothing left to do save wait for Willa Embri Janos to locate Pater Pan and put what we had into final form via the 'mortal combat over each word of my own deathless prose' that Wendi had promised, I found myself digging ever deeper into such lore utilizing both Dalta's personal expertise and monographs that she suggested, and hola, by the time this editing process had begun, I did indeed find myself haggling over each subtraction or alteration of a word that Wendi suggested.

Strange to say, or mayhap under the circumstances, not so strange, I had no interest in erotic intrigues, or in the numerous arts and entertainments offered up by the Grand Palais, and my palate began to grow indifferent to the splendors of the haute cuisine and noble vintages I consumed as so much functional fressen. For all of those pleasures at the time seemed but pale shadows of that mighty passion which all unawares had seduced me into the innermost vie and raison d'être of the floating cultura, the lust for knowledge.

Not so much for any particular item of knowledge—though certainement there was much I wished I had known earlier—but the growing glorious perception of how much knowledge truly existed in the worlds of men after all these thousands of years of science, art, and history. And not only did I marvel at how extensive and inexhaustible all this knowledge was, but how much true wisdom had been encoded with the mere data, how much of an interconnected whole it all was, what puissant intellectual forces our Second Starfaring Age could muster even on a subject as ultimately trivial in the cosmic scheme of things as the tale of my own wanderjahr as a Child of Fortune.

And yet, refracted and focused through the events of my own life, knowledge seemed to become something even more vital than itself, just as the events of my own life amplified by knowledge became something much more than a simple tale.

Thus, without a clear perception of ever having crossed the karmic threshold, I found myself perceiving my karmic position not as that of a Child of Fortune approaching the climax of her life's tale, but as that of a woman yet unknown confronting the immensity of her future becoming.

428

In short, I had my first precognitive perception of myself in my own version of the adult of the species, and the first inkling that this was a beginning, not an end. In some dim way, I knew that at some point in my voyage aboard the *Mistral Falcon*, I had met the me I wanted to grow up to be.

28 Thus I was somewhat psychically unprepared when, five days out of Flor del Cielo, Wendi and I were summoned from our all-but-completed labors to the library, where Willa Embri Janos announced: "I have at last found our quarry. Pater Pan is on Alpa, or at least he was there two months ago."

She handed me a flimsy upon which was transcribed a formidable list of planets, several score at least, dated in chronological order from top to bottom, with the earliest entry some seven centuries old.

"As to his hyperbolic claims of being a relic of the First Starfaring Age or even beyond, je ne sais pas," she said. "But certainement, he has gotten around quite well and for a mighty span indeed in our own era!"

"Well done!" exclaimed Wendi. "How did you manage such a feat?"

"Not without difficulty," Willa told her. "For the legends the fellow pretends to embody generalize into greater and greater vagueness the further back you go, to the point where it sometimes seemed that whole armies had their turns in playing the part. At length, however, I hit upon the notion of sifting this mass of confusion through a net constructed out of verified records of Child of Fortune tribes fitting the general parameters of the Gypsy Jokers as described. Thus, by cross-referencing these tribal histories with the legends, I was able to compile the list you now have, in raw form. Then it was merely a matter of establishing the sequence, extrapolating the trajectory, and verifying that such a phenomenon indeed has recently come into being on the planet to which the arrow thereof pointed, to wit Alpa, to a probability of at least seventy percent."

"Formidable!" I exclaimed, with an enthusiasm that seemed somewhat strained even to my own ears. "Some day I must learn this most puissant craft!"

But in truth, my spirit had been thrown into some turmoil, for it had been days, or even weeks, since I had given any thought to what had once seemed to be the raison d'être of my presence on the *Mistral Falcon* in the first place. For in a sense, the girl who had followed her Pied Piper across the Bloomenveldt, into the streets of Ciudad Pallas, and thence out among the starways in this very ship, was no more. For in the process thereof, believing all the while that I had been seeking to regain a Golden Summer out of my past, I had instead found a vector toward my unknown but enticing future. Vraiment, I still sought to follow the spirit of my Yellow Brick Road, but the nature thereof had changed, for now the Yellow Brick Road I sought to travel was a version appropriate to the adult of my kind, the path of knowledge, and vraiment, frank artistic ambition, a road upon which I had not known my feet were so firmly planted until this very moment.

Thus, rather than greeting Willa's announcement with the unbridled joy I would have thought it should have brought, I felt instead a certain ill-defined sense of loss. For now the end of this voyage was in sight, and truth be told, I found to my own surprise that I liked it not.

Wendi Sha Rumi seemed to have some inkling of what was passing through my soul. "Alpa . . ." she said to Willa Embri Janos. "How many transfers will it require to get there from our next planet of call?"

"We shall soon see," Willa said. She addressed the Matrix console. "Flor del Cielo to Alpa. Void Ship connection between."

A moment later words and numbers appeared on the telescreen.

"Buena suerte indeed!" she exclaimed, pointing to the tele. "Observe! The *Arrow of Time* even now approaches Flor del Cielo. From there to Heimat is its course, and thence to Alpa itself."

My spirit sank, nor, despite my protests against its meanness to the contrary, would it rise. Now my feelings must surely be written plain upon my face, for Wendi eyed me with a certain knowing concern.

"It pleases you not, liebchen, nē?" she said. "Je comprend." She took my hand. "Con su permiso, Willa. Come, Sunshine, we must talk."

We repaired forthwith to the vivarium, where, strolling around the oasis pool under the brilliant ersatz sky of the desert night, I searched out the words to render up my feelings to my mentor and friend, and thus to clarify them to myself.

"Je ne sais pas. . . . It is as if I had begun another tale . . . and all at once I find myself thrust back in time into the previous one . . . or rather . . . The truth of it is, I suppose, that I have found a new path toward what I wish to become, and mayhap should continue thereon rather than . . ." I threw up my hands in frustration.

Wendi laughed. "Mayhap the matter is not quite so arcane as you suppose," she said. "Simply that having found your future calling as a teller of tales for an audience of the worlds at large rather than as an itinerant ruespieler, you are avid to embark on your new career without digression or delay. . . ?"

I nodded. "Just so," I said. "Or rather, all at once, I have now learned that I have *already* embarked thereon."

"Well spoken!" Wendi declared. "Only do not suppose you have already learned all the necessary lore."

"Oh indeed not!" I exclaimed. "Vraiment, I have learned more on this voyage than in all of my previous life, yet what I have learned best is how much there is to learn before I may truly style myself a maestra of the literary art! Scientific knowledge sufficient to accurately describe arcane events and venues, the annals of the art itself, lest I find myself repeating the stories of others innocently unaware, the millennial history of our species in order to sift truth from hyperbole, the inner meanings of words and images, the ability to use the Matrix as Willa does to properly apprise myself of the foregoing . . ."

We sat down beneath one of the tented awnings beside the pool, and I gazed off at the ersatz horizon where the illusory sands merged in a shimmering zone of mirage with the equally illusory sky. And found to my satoric astonishment that it *pleased* me now—the vivarium, the Grand Palais, the company I had found, the vie of the floating cultura itself, all that had once seemed arrogant vanity and empty illusion to the Gypsy Joker ruespieler.

"Hola, Wendi, you spoke truly at the time, but I could not credit it!" I exclaimed. "For never would I have thought to hear myself say these words. I do believe I *love* the true inner vie of the floating cultura that you have shown me! Certainement, I have no wish to leave it now!"

Wendi laughed. "How much you remind me of myself!" she said. "But you too must learn, as I did, that there is more to learn of the tale-teller's art than is contained in all the Matrix's annals and philosophies, Sunshine. You must learn the hard truths of the inner lore."

"The inner lore?"

"Vraiment. First you must learn that if you wish to be a teller of the spirit's true tales, ma petite, you must seek knowledge of the worlds of men, naturellement, but beyond that you musk seek the inner knowledge of your own spirit. Patience is required, hola, a commodity always in short supply, but the courage of ruthless honesty as well."

"In this you find me lacking?" I said pettishly.

"Certainly not thusfar, ruespieler!" Wendi declared. "But the author of true lies must be willing to swear the oath of the lodge, which is that come what may, at any cost to the natural woman or even to the spirit itself, the first allegiance of the teller must be to the tale."

"Je ne comprend pas. . . ."

"Take the tale in question, liebchen, for this is the lesson you must learn before our work is done," Wendi said. "Is not the Matrix entry we are commissioned to finish your own name tale, my dear, at the proper conclusion of which, the Child of Fortune that was chooses a freenom for the woman she has become? And were what we have transcribed thusfar a romance rather than the story of your own life, would you not fling the word crystal across the room in outrage if it ended without the proper note of closure? Does not *the story*, to which you must swear total allegiance, require a closing chapter on Alpa with Pater Pan?"

"Perhaps you are right. . . ." I was forced to own.

433

"*Perhaps* I am right?" Wendi exclaimed rather archly. "Child, have you not known me long enough now to know that I am *always* right, and no perhaps about it?"

"And modest to a fault as well."

We both laughed, but Wendi soon enough became even more earnest. "On the one hand, you wish not to delay your pursuit of career and muse for a moment, and on the other hand, you fear that the first sight of this most puissant of your lovers will forthwith subsume your newfound intellectual passions under a tsunami of amour and cause you to give it all over in favor of clinging as a consort to his side, nē."

"Quelle chose!" I protested. "Do you take me for a mooning romantic ready to throw my life away for love?"

Wendi cocked her head, shrugged, and regarded me more as an equal sister now, or so it seemed. "Quién sabe?" she said almost gaily. "Who of us knows the answer to that until the moment of truth comes? But certainement, the tale of your wanderjahr is not over until it does, nor is *The Tale of the Pied Piper of the Bloomenveldt* going to be concluded in a manner suitable to inclusion in the Matrix without its climactic scene."

Wendi patted me on the knee and spoke gently. "The former I tell you as woman to woman, my dear. Come what may, you can never be content until you learn what is in your own heart. What is there to fear, after all? Either you will enjoy a romantic reunion for a sweet interlude, free yourself of your erotic indifference thereby, and then resume your own path, or you will find the eternal mate of your soul and alter your vector through life in freely given joy."

Wendi sat back at a greater distance and spoke somewhat more distantly. "But the latter I tell you in my editorial capacity, and it is she who was commissioned to assure that your story is put into proper form for the Matrix who speaks now. We must end our account with your reunion on Alpa with Pater Pan, even should it mean that you run off with him forever, are jilted within a year, never tell a tale again, and end up as a tantric performer on some rude frontier world. That is what it means to swear the oath of our lodge, ma chère. Your life and happiness come second, ruespieler; your first allegiance must be to the tale."

I looked away from her for a moment to gaze up at the ersatz stars of the vivarium sky, beyond which lay the true reality, the deep Void through which all our lives journeyed, and scattered among all that daunting firmament, the oases of our spirit in the desert of the night, the far-flung worlds of men. Was it not a tale which we had followed out across the stars from our ancestral trees? Were we not both the teller and protagonist thereof? Was not the Yellow Brick Road the same as the tale-teller's path? Had not both Pater Pan and Wendi Sha Rumi justly declared that before the singer comes the song?

"Vraiment, Wendi, you are right," I told her at length. "We must find the true ending of one tale before we can properly begin another, nē. In the spirit of our calling, there is no other choice."

"In this case even more well spoken than you comprehend, Sunshine," Wendi said somewhat owlishly. "For speaking now finally as one colleague to another, we have enjoyed a long voyage at the expense of public benefaction on the grounds that reuniting you with Pater Pan was a legitimate requirement of our collaboration, and as even the most extreme of ivory tower artistes must sooner or later discover, we Pipers are not the only ones capable of demanding our pay."

Strange to say, once having resolved thusly to following the Pied Piper of my wanderjahr to the conclusion of this tale, my spirits lifted, and indeed it soon enough seemed to me that I had been foolishly jousting with shadows.

For what was there to fear? Did I really believe that upon seeing Pater Pan again the Child of Fortune that I had been would fling herself into his arms and give over entirely the new path that the woman I sought to become had found? Or that that woman could not countenance perceiving the domo of her Golden Summer as a Child of Fortune as just another natural man?

Mayhap that had been the source of my trepidations, for I could conceive no other. The floating cultura would await my return from Alpa, as would the vie of the teller of tales, which had existed as long as sapient speech and would persist as long as humankind. The only things I had to fear, certainement, were within my heart, and neither ruespieler nor author of word crystals could remain on the Yellow Brick Road by refusing to learn the secrets of her own soul.

And so I threw myself into completing our work as best I

presently could and brooded not over the missing climactic scene until even Wendi finally declared that every word and syllable of what we had on word crystal was as perfect as it could become.

"Indeed," she declared as we ate a late supper of barbecued fruits de mer in the refectory after what was to be the last of these lapidary sessions, "there is a point beyond which further revisions only cause one's prose to devolve. Hola, in my editorial capacity, I do declare we have certainly reached that point now. C'est fini! There is no more useful work to be done until we reach Alpa. Avail yourself of the divertissements the Grand Palais has to offer, take a lover, have several, besot yourself with toxicants, celebrate a justly earned holiday in the best traditions of our craft."

I shook my head. "Now that I have resolved to properly end the tale, and now that there is nothing to be done but await its conclusion, I fear I will be able to do nothing but rattle fecklessly about this Grand Palais and then that of the *Arrow of Time*, wanting only for the endless days to pass. . . ."

"Well then, why bother?" Wendi said airily.

"Why bother?"

"Were this a romance I was creating, I would simply make a time-jump to the next meaningful scene rather than bore my audience with a detailed description of a period of prolonged ennui," Wendi said. "Why not grant yourself the same mercy? We will reach Flor del Cielo in a day or two, and when we do, why do you not simply proceed to Alpa in the dormodule of the *Arrow of Time*? While you sleep the dreamless sleep, I will voyage in the Grand Palais thereof and do some work of my own that I have been neglecting, and by the time you awake, I should have found Pater Pan's encampment thereon for you."

I snapped my fingers, once, twice, thrice. "Like the Rapide!"

And so once more I found myself climbing a metal ladder in the long central corridor of a dormodule stacked from floor to ceiling with glass cubicles and taking my place among the less-than-Honored Passengers sleeplessly dreaming around me.

But now I felt no fear as I laid myself down on the padded pallet with the spiderwork helmet behind my head. Nor claustrophobic dread when the cubicle door slid shut behind me. So much had come to pass since I had trepidatiously essayed my first such journey from Glade to Edoku. I had left the world of my birth, braved Great Edoku itself, survived the perils of the Bloomenveldt, voyaged as a true Honored Passenger, found my life's calling, and soon, vraiment in the next augenblick of my waking existence, I would reach the planet where the tale of my wanderjahr was to end. And had not Pater Pan's own words, confirmed by the Matrix itself, told me that he had survived this selfsame process scores or mayhap even hundreds of times?

Vraiment, did not esthetic justice require that I journey to him thusly?

And so I felt only peace as hidden machineries began to hum, and my head was touched by a cool, calm, mechanical caress that promised an instant translation to the triumphant conclusion of my wanderjahr's tale. Snap! Snap! Snap! Like the—

—Rapide!

The door to my cubicle slid open as I awoke, and, rubbing sleep from my eyes with a casual gesture as if arising from a short nap, I rolled off the pallet, and climbed down the ladder, expecting to find myself in the midst of the sort of debarkation bustle and excitement which had greeted me when I had similarly awoken in the dormodule of the *Bird of Night* upon my arrival at Edoku.

Instead I found myself alone in the dormodule corridor save for Wendi Sha Rumi and the Med Crew Maestro of the *Arrow of Time*. There were no fellow passengers climbing down from their cubicles, no floaters bearing luggage, no announcements by the ship's annunciator, no electricity in the air—only Wendi, the Med Crew Maestro, and myself amidst stacks and rows of silent sleepers.

And if this was not a rude enough awakening, there was Wendi's demeanor to contend with. Never had I seen her so somber, so trepidatious. Indeed, she seemed to be avoiding direct contact with my eyes.

"What's wrong?" I demanded.

"There have been no anomalies in the revival procedure, I assure you," the Med Crew Maestro burbled. "I am merely present in the ordinary line of—"

"Why have none of the other passengers been awakened? Has there been some dreadful malfunction in—"

437

"Certainly not!" the Med Crew Maestro snapped indignantly. "Rather ask this personage here why proper procedure has been interfered with to awake *you* a day earlier by special dispensation, for we are yet a good twenty-four hours or more out of Alpa!"

"This is so?" I asked Wendi. She only nodded. *"Why?"*

"Because you have a difficult choice to make, Sunshine," she said with uncharacteristic lack of energy. "We must have time to discuss . . ." She cast nervous sidelong glances at the rows of sleeping voyagers which walled us in, at the sour demeanor of the Med Crew Maestro. "But certainement, not in *here!*"

To this I could readily enough agree despite my anxious curiosity, for the ambiance of the dormodule was one to impose hushed silence, the Med Crew Maestro was quite impatient for us to be gone, Wendi's mood was more than enough to fill me with dread, and I could hardly imagine a venue less suited to the absorption of dark tidings. I therefore held my tongue and allowed her to lead me out of the dormodule, along the ship's spinal corridor, and into her stateroom, all in silence.

Once the door was closed behind us and we were seated side by side on the bed, Wendi laid a hand on my knee, and, still not quite meeting my gaze squarely, she spoke.

"True to my word, I have located Pater Pan," she said. "He resides in the resort town of Florida on the Côte Grande of the equatorial continent of Solaria, where he is the domo of a Child of Fortune tribe of sorts."

"But that's marvelous!" I exclaimed. "But why then the long face? Why—"

Wendi held up her hand for silence, and at last she met my gaze directly, albeit with troubled eyes. "I must now make what I know all too well will be a futile gesture," she said. "In my editorial capacity, I am ready to declare that your entry is suitable for the Matrix in its present form, and that a trip to Florida would be worse than superfluous now."

"What? But you were the one who insisted—"

"Woman to woman, friend to friend, I must attempt to advise you to accept this boon at face value, and quit Alpa as soon as we arrive in orbit, on the first Void Ship to anywhere else," Wendi said without any real conviction, or so it seemed to me.

"What are you talking about, Wendi?" I demanded. "Such crypticism has hardly been your style!"

438

"In both my editorial capacity and as the friend of your heart, I must tell you that what you would find in Florida would be anything but an esthetically satisfying denouement for your wanderjahr's tale."

"Merde, Wendi, spit this unwholesome morsel out no matter how vile it may be," I told her angrily. "Do you imagine that either the teller of tales or the natural woman could allow you to prevent her from seeking the true ending to her wanderjahr's tale? Was it not you who made me swear our tribal oath that our first allegiance must be to the tale?"

"Vraiment," Wendi said with a little shrug, "but I can find no way to construe what you wish now to learn as anything but a violation of the spirit thereof."

"Cease this mystification!" I fairly shouted. "Do you expect me to contain my curiosity on a matter so dear to both my spirit and my art on the grounds that ignorance would be relative bliss?"

Wendi's demeanor altered entirely. "I said that a futile gesture was required, liebchen," she said in quite a harder tone of voice, "for what a beast you would have thought me if I had not at least made it, after you hear what you must hear now. So think me not a beast also when I say that, colleague to colleague, I would have thought the less of you if I had succeeded."

"Wendi—"

"—Pater Pan has become a Charge Addict, that is the long and short of it, my pauvre petite, he follows the path of the Up and Out."

I must have shouted wordlessly, but all I remember of that moment is slumping there on the bed in a sudden daze as if my psyche had been rung by a mallet.

Images out of memory, rather than words, poured in a foaming tide through my brain. Pater Pan's gaily smiling face haloed by his golden mane of sunshine. The brilliant orb of the rising sun above the Bloomenveldt. The sight of the ocean on my triumphant return to the worlds of men. Guy Vlad Boca smiling at me lustfully across our rijsttafel in the Crystal Palace as we happily played at guile and assignation. Guy's slack and vacant visage beneath the band of the Charge console in the Hotel Pallas. Guy beaming at me beatifically on his lotus in perfect Bloomenkind bliss. But of the visage of that against which all my white-hot anger and darkest despair might seek its proper vengeance, as to whatever adversary now sought to claim the spirit of Pater Pan as in the Perfumed Garden it had finally claimed Guy, here there was only the featureless face of the Void.

"Sunshine! Sunshine!" Wendi was shaking me by the shoulders. "Are you all right?"

I blinked. I shuddered. Something grew coldly determined inside of me. At length I made to answer this most foolish of questions. "I have my senses about me if that is what you mean," I found myself saying. "Of course we both realize that I must go to Florida the moment this ship reaches Alpa."

Emotions recomplicated in the backwash of the shock into a complexity I could scarcely comprehend. Once had I rescued Guy from the Charge's vile embrace by force of will and arms, and yet all my efforts failed to rescue him from his perfect flower, and I was forced to abandon the spirit of a true friend and lover in order to save my own. Now he whose spirit had warped space and time to be at my side in the Dreamtime in my hour of need on the Bloomenveldt stood in the same peril from which I had once rescued Guy. Surely the survival of my own spirit was hardly in question this time! Surely I could not once more abandon a friend and lover to pitiless fate, to whatever demon of his own spirit had impelled him to this seppuku of the soul!

All this came out through my lips in that statement of cold unshakable determination, and all of it Wendi seemed to apprehend therein. "Of course you must, my poor liebchen," she said with sympathetic softness. "Were I you, I would shame myself if I did less than the same. . . ."

She hugged me for a moment and then released me. "I would accompany you to Florida if you wish," she said, "but this offer is only another futile gesture in the interests of friendship, nē. . . ."

"Indeed, Wendi," I told her softly. "But understand that I refuse it in the same tender spirit with which it was extended."

"Well spoken, friend and colleague," she said. "I will tarry in Lorienne, which passes for Alpa's main metropole, and await your arrival, for now my previous offer in my editorial capacity is canceled, and we must end the Tale of the Pied Piper of the Bloomenveldt with whatever happens in Florida."

"I can promise you nothing, Wendi," I told her in all honesty, "not even that we will ever see each other again."

"Hola, but I can promise you *two* things in compensation, liebchen," Wendi Sha Rumi told me. "First, that the tale will end as they all do and another begin, though there is no way your heart can believe it now, and second that if you can find a way to make *this* ending of your tale sing sweetly to the spirit, I will freely acknowledge you as a more perfect master of our mutual art than I."

I passed the hours between my awakening to this bitter news and the arrival of the *Arrow of Time* at Alpa learning all I could about the Charge, for I was no longer the naive young girl who had ventured out upon the perils of the Bloomenveldt foolishly and blissfully unprepared by study of the dangers of the psychic terrain. But what I learned in the perusal of this lore, alas, did little but daunt my spirit.

The Charge, as I had already known, amplified the electrohologram of human consciousness without distorting the topology thereof, so that what Charge Addicts claimed to experience was an enhancement of subjective consciousness without relative distortion of the pre-existing personality.

But since each increment of Charge achieves an increment of amplification at the expense of the stability of the overall pattern, the "personality" of the Charge Addict grows less and less defined, much as the resolution of a visual holo image, while not distorted by the destruction of areas of the recording medium, becomes vaguer and vaguer, until the terminal phase is reached in the Up and Out.

While all the monographs I perused remained in accord up to this point, like the personality of the Charge Addict itself, that which was said to be known about the nature of what emerges in the Up and Out grew vaguer, more fragmented, and more nebulous the further the mages sought to delve into this arcane realm.

Some called it a series of "pseudopersonalities" generated by the random firing of neurons in cerebral memory banks from which the individuality of the previous occupant had been erased. Others contended that species genetic coding kicked up into the vacated electrohologramic level, and that it was the archetypes supposedly stored as the collective unconscious in our gene pool which manifested themselves.

As for what spoke toward the very end, upon this subject, only the devotees of the Charge themselves would speculate, and as one might expect, they were uniformly of the opinion that the Atman itself merged with their spirits in the actual moment of the Up and Out.

Small wonder then that there were those who still sought Delphic pronouncements from the lips of such oracles, for alors, were not all the religions of primitive man but the willed belief that by following their precepts, practices, and esoteric rituals, such a living nirvana might be achieved this side of death? Vraiment, have not such psychonauts of thanatopsis always been our shamans?

And are such shamans, or at any rate pretenders to their throne, really absent in our sophisticated and enlightened Second Starfaring Age? Was not Cort, my psychonaut lover in Nouvelle Orlean, such a one? And Raul? And Imre? And the dying babas of the Bloomenveldt? And most of all, Guy Vlad Boca, who had found the perfect amusement of his short lifelong quest in the Perfumed Garden of his perfect flower.

But *Pater Pan?* No amount of exhaustive research could cause me to even imagine how the King of the Gypsies and the Prince of the Jokers could fall victim to the thanatotic seduction of the Charge. Not the Pied Piper of Pan, for whom the goal had always been a journey with no final destination, not he who had sworn to see all the worlds of men and the whole of our species tale or nobly expire in the futile attempt. How could such a man have chosen to end his tale in vicious farce, as a Charge Addict expiring in a small city on a planet of no particular renown?

I knew not. I understood it not. Yet soon enough I would confront the inescapable reality thereof. Nor would all the powers of my spirit or the desires of my heart in the end prevail against it.

29 Florida was a small city built between a wide crescent of beach along a tropical bay and a low range of wooded maritime alps, mere hills if truth be told, which neatly defined its inland boundaries, though as one would expect, many of the most extravagant manses were sited along the haute corniche which ran just below the crestline on the seaside slope. The bay was blue, the sands quite a striking rose, and the foliage of the hillsides tended to pastel tones of reddish-green. The sky was a brilliant azure, and the waters of the bay were sprinkled with a score or more small sandy islands upon which grew no more than sparse clumps of some purplish salt grass.

Amusement piers and covered pavilions jutted out into the bay here and there and the waters themselves sported all manner of pleasure craft, though sails seemed to be favored, and blue, rose, and white were the dominant tints thereof.

Indeed to style Florida a small city might be going too far, for in truth it was more of a large town decorating the bay with a fringe of low and deliberately unobtrusive buildings whose precincts could be covered from end to end on a balmy afternoon's stroll. By unstated agreement, mayhap by legislative fiat, no structure rose more than four stories, and most were done up in white, rose, or blue, so as to harmonize with the color scheme of the landscape. As for fabriks, these were nowhere in evidence, and those edifices given over to commerce were confined to small inns, restaurants, boutiques, tavernas, and the like. Some small open floatcabs were available, but for the most part the populace seemed to favor traveling afoot.

In short, upon debarking at seaside from the hover which had borne me from Lorienne, I found myself in a scene of bucolic tranquility and benign isolation from the hurly-burly of the centers of the civilized worlds, a venue for vacationers and sportsvolk or for those who preferred a vie of mellow retreat from urban complexities. Strange to say, the ambiance thereof put me in mind of Nouvelle Orlean somehow, after so many weeks of treetop wilderness on the one hand, and the flagrantly ersatz environments of Edoku, Ciudad Pallas, and Void Ships on the other, though certainement Florida was Nouvelle Orlean writ quite small and modest.

As for locating the venue where Pater Pan was most likely to be found, this was simplicity itself, for even from the beach I could readily enough spy out a sprinkling of varicolored tents set on a shelf of land about three quarters of the way up the slope of an overlooking hillside.

Eschewing floatcabs, I forthwith set out inland afoot through the streets of the town toward the hillside in question. These were paved, or rather strewn, with a particolored gravel made up of tiny marine shells and the fragments of larger ones which crunched pleasantly enough underfoot as one trod upon them.

The denizens of the town seemed divided up into two distinct species: somewhat pallid urbanites obviously on holiday, and well-bronzed natives who were clearly in the minority. Breechclouts, shorts, halters, und so weiter were the favored attire, nor were nude bodies lacking, though naturellement the esthetic effect of all this bare flesh was a good deal more pleasing when it came to the handsome natives than when it came to the turistas. Peculiarly enough, though there was a plethora of youth in evidence, and though such a resort community would seem to be ideal for such enterprises, there seemed to be no organized troupes of buskers, hawkers, ruespielers, und so weiter on these promising streets.

Nevertheless, the sun shone brightly, the town presented a pleasing aspect, the balmy air was redolent with vegetative sweetness and salty sea-tang, and my spirits soared against all knowledgeable trepidations, for it was difficult indeed to credit such a setting as the venue for such dark and urban horrors as Charge Addiction.

Nor was my mood anything but lightened when, puffing a bit and lightly filmed with sweat, I reached the shelf upon which the caravanserei was situated. While this encampment had nothing of the size and grandeur of that which the Gypsy Jokers had established in Great Edoku, the sight of it filled my heart with a rosy nostalgic glow for the Golden Summer I had enjoyed as a newborn Child of Fortune therein. And though this encampment boasted no more than a score or two tents of various sizes, shapes, and colors, the view therefrom put what I had known in Edoku to shame. From the outskirts of the caravanserei, I looked out over the shaggy shoulders of the hillside, down across the tiny houses of the town and the shining rose-colored beach to a shining azure sea upon which minuscule sails of blue and white and rose drifted in the breezes like a swarm of brightly-colored sea-midges.

Only when I entered the encampment itself did the spell of peaceful and perfect beauty begin to unravel.

For one thing, there was a preponderance of scarcely-pubescent Alpans in evidence, obviously hardly of an age to be Children of Fortune of other worlds embarked upon their wanderjahrs, and while some of these wore the Cloth of Many Colors, their scarves and sashes were patched together out of swatches of new cloth rather than being the fairly-won emblems of a wandering vie.

Moreover, and more disturbing still, there was almost nothing in the way of crafts or finger food or street theater troupes or musicians or even tantric performers to be seen, as if, as I soon found out to be true, this encampment was living primarily on the largesse of not-too-distant parents. The few true Children of Fortune that I spied seemed a rather unwholesome lot, too long in the tooth for the vie, mayhap predators gathered to prey upon the energies, not to say the parental subsidies, of the young Alpans.

As for the activities which were taking place, these were hardly calculated to cast credit on the mythos. Many young folk were lying about in an obvious state of red-eyed stupefaction. Others could be seen gulping down great drafts of wine or imbibing various toxicants, and what commerce I noted was mainly in these commodities. Here and there couples and groups were en-

445

gaged in rather feckless tantric exercises of little or no artistry and not much more energy. Scraps of food were scattered everywhere as well as empty flagons attended by small yellow insects, and the general aroma, if not quite overpowering, reeked more of decaying organic matter and unwashed bodies than of perfumed incenses and cuisinary savors.

I loathed the ambiance I experienced as I wandered the camp under the indifferent gazes of its inhabitants, which is to say I dreaded what I would discover at its center, for I knew only too well who and what that would be. Nor was I long in seeking out the locus thereof, for near the center of the encampment was the largest tent of all, a closed pavilion sewn together out of Cloth of Many Colors.

I was accosted at the flap which concealed the interior of the tent by a rather scruffy and bleary-eyed fellow perhaps five years my senior who barred my way and thrust a chip transcriber under my nose. "Four credit units for an audience with the Oracle," he told me.

"What? Quelle chose? What is this outrage?"

"A small price to pay for the true voice of the Up and Out," he said with lofty diffidence. "Try to obtain the same elsewhere on Alpa at more modest cost if you wish, and see how far it will get you."

"Merde!" I muttered angrily, but I handed over my chip rather than haggle over such a pittance with this churl for another moment. After the required credit was transferred, he held open the tent flap and admitted me to the unwholesome inner sanctum.

The interior of the tent was strewn with dusty and threadbare cushions. Upon these some dozen acolytes sat, reclined, or indeed dozed, in varying degrees of stupefaction, swilling wines and beers, sniffing at toxicants, and focusing various states of befuddled attention upon the figure propped up in a large nest of pillows in the center of the tent like some pathetic pasha.

Vraiment, it was Pater Pan.

But alas, not the Pater Pan I had known.

His Traje de Luces hung in loose folds about his gaunt frame. His golden hair and beard were unkempt and scraggly and streaked with gray. His skin was seamed and sallow, and there were hollows in his cheeks and dark baggy wrinkles under his eyes. His eyes. . . .

His wonderful blue eyes seemed larger and brighter than before, set off now in deep shadowed sockets, yet vague, and fragile somehow, like balls of shattered blue marble. About his brow was the metallic band of the Charge, wired to a console all but hidden within his throne of pillows.

A young girl stood before him intently as if receiving wisdom. And Pater Pan was indeed speaking, albeit with eyes that seemed focused on some middle distance, and in a hollow declamatory tone that seemed addressed to no one or everyone in particular.

"Tarry not in the mean streets of Hamelin town, but follow me into the Magic Mountain . . ."

"Does that mean that I should now commence my wanderjahr?"

"Fear not the Gypsy King, gajo, for we must all one day be stolen from our parents' houses, and run away to join the circus. . . ."

"But now you say I must await a sign?"

"As a ronin, I know no master but honor . . ."

"But—"

"Enough!" said an older girl squatting at the feet of Pater Pan. "You have already had fair value for your four credits!"

Eagerly, a boy arose from the front ranks and elbowed her aside. "How am I to gain the affection of Krista, Pater Pan?" he demanded.

"Be not a swinish wage slave of the Pentagon, but embark in the Gold Mountain on the long slow centuries between the stars, and follow the Arkie Spark within you. . . ."

I stood there in the back of the tent for many minutes, appalled, disgusted, transfixed, and despairing, as one by one paying customers were ushered in and out of the presence to hector Pater Pan with their picayune questions and receive in turn this Delphic babble.

I had sufficiently steeped myself in the scientific lore to know that what I beheld was a man who had long since gone beyond the point of no return on the path to the Up and Out.

"The King of the Gypsies is no more, long live the Prince of the Jokers, though of course they are very *small* mountains. . . ."

For while the cadences and music of this flow of words had

447

a certain hypnagogic fascination that drew the mind's ear down into its murky depths, in truth, I knew, these were isolated and fragmented memory-quanta being released in the absence of a sovereign pattern. No Charge Addict who had progressed to this stage had ever returned as a sapient spirit to the worlds of men, for the integrated personality by now was not merely suppressed but erased forever, or so the mages declared, leaving only disconnected cerebral data banks firing off their memories at random.

"Before the singer, I was the song, which we followed along the Yellow Brick Road from the ancestral trees to trip the life fantastic out among the stars. . . ."

The Pater Pan whom I had known and loved was gone forever, or so science insisted, and were I to now rip the band from his head against all the efforts of these wretched acolytes to the contrary, all that I would succeed in rescuing would be a halfling creature such as I now beheld who would linger a few years thusly in the care of the Healers of some mental retreat.

I was too late. That faceless force which had claimed Guy Vlad Boca had somehow indeed contrived to claim even the noble Pater Pan, as if to avenge itself upon me for my singular triumph over it as the Pied Piper of the Bloomenveldt in the most ghastly manner at its disposal.

Yet if I could truly do nothing, neither could I let it be, for as Wendi would have had it, and as I now understood in a state of rage that transcended reason, now was the time for a futile gesture.

I strode boldly and forcefully to the front of the tent, superseding those waiting their turn at their oracle before me without demur, for the energy of my passage brooked none such in this company.

"Pater! It's Sunshine!" I cried.

"In the Summer of Love in the city by the bay, we all wore flowers in our hair. . . ."

His preternaturally bright yet entirely empty eyes seemed to stare right through me, and his babble, for all I could tell, was for the benefit of these callow creatures who hung on every word of it as much as for myself.

"Merde!" I shouted, fairly trembling with fury. "You are Pater Pan, and I am Sunshine Shasta Leonardo, and once we were friends and lovers in Great Edoku! Do you remember nothing of our time together?"

448

"The caravans of the Gypsies and the Tinkers singing the only tale there is to tell in the black forest of the night. . . ."

"Merde! Caga! Speak to me, Pater, as a natural man, and not as the voice from a cerebral whirlwind!"

"Cease addressing the master thusly!"

"You've had your four units' worth!"

"Give someone else their turn!"

I whirled on the clamor that had arisen behind me, feeling almost as much true personal puissance in this company as that which I thespically injected into my voice. *"Silence, churls!"* I commanded, "I am Sunshine Shasta Leonardo, the Pied Piper of the Bloomenveldt, and I would discourse with my old comrade and lover with no further unseemly interruption from the likes of you!"

While the chance that any of those present had the slightest notion of who or what the Pied Piper of the Bloomenveldt might be was vanishingly slim, so spiritless were these sorry excuses for Children of Fortune that my words, my demeanor, and the force behind them were quite sufficient to cow them. Far from mitigating my ire, the respectful attitudes of obeisance which they then all assumed, even down to the oracle's timekeeper, only served to arouse my utter contempt, for no true Child of Fortune of my acquaintance would have bowed so meekly to the mere assertion of authority.

"Remember, Pater, please remember," I cajoled Pater Pan, imploringly now, seeking to feel with my words for the smallest purchase with which to pry open this shell and reach the natural man within. "Remember when you were the King of the Gypsies and the Prince of the Joker? Remember? Do you not remember a time in a garden atop a waterfall? Do you not remember how I seized hold of your lingam in a shower stall? Do you not remember the Sunshine that you named? Do you not remember the night you told me what was in your heart of hearts?"

Pater Pan's face at last slowly turned in my direction like a leaf following the sun, but still his gaze seemed to stare right through me. "Remember. . . ?" he said. "Remember. . . ? Remember. . . ?"

"Yes, Pater, *remember*! Remember Sunshine, oh please, bitte, kudasai, liebchen, *remember me*!"

"Remember Sunshine. . . . I remember Sunshine beneath

the towering red trees of the great forest. . . . I remember a Sunshine in my arms as we made love on the wing in the long slow centuries between the stars. . . . I remember a Sunshine on Novi Mir. . . . I remember a Sunshine on Edoku. . . . I remember a Sunshine on Elysium. . . . Remember the Sunshine of my life along the Yellow Brick Road. . . ."

This at last was far more than I could countenance! If the spell that I must counter was that of the electronic mastery of the Charge over the higher centers of his brain, if the power of the Word now failed me, then I must resort to the employment of electronic powers of my own. I must use the ring whose puissance I had not sought to employ for pleasure or gain since it had worse than failed me in the Perfumed Garden. I must resume my erotic career at once, any lack of piquant or quotidian desire to the contrary, for I could see nothing for it but to seize him by that kundalinic root which customarily overrides all cogitative imperatives when gripped by feminine force.

To wit, I thumbed on my ring of Touch, and to the oohs and gasps of the voyeurs in the tent, grabbed hold through the fabric of his trousers of his flaccid phallus. "If you remember nothing else, mon ami, mayhap you will remember *this!*"

Did his glassy eyes widen? Did some human light return thereto? Certainement, though with unseemly slowness, I felt the sap of manhood rise within my grasp. Strange indeed it was to feel the serpent stirring in a lingam once more after my long celibacy in a venue and a moment such as this! Stranger still, and somehow unwholesome, to feel the kundalinic knots uncoil within my own loins in such a pass, to find my natural woman once more via this most unnatural of tantric acts.

For long moments I stood there holding on for dear life to the handle of his phallus. For long moments did I gaze unwaveringly into his eyes, and for long moments did I imagine his true spirit looking back at me. Was it an extravagant fancy, or did I truly sense the hum and crackle of electronic combat between the dark power of the Charge and the kundalinic force at my command?

Be that as it may, at length his lips began to move again, and when they did, another spirit spoke, or so to me it seemed.

"The Sunshine of the magic touch . . . She who out-joked the Joker . . . On Edoku somewhere under the rainbow . . ."

His voice grew firmer, as did his lingam in my hand, though the former still seemed to speak from very far away, and the latter only pulsed motionlessly in my grasp. "I remember a pool in a garden. . . . I remember a hand beneath a shower stall. . . . I remember a sister of the same spirit. . . ."

"Yes, Pater, yes!" I cried, squeezing the quick of him.

"I remember Great Edoku and I remember the ruins of We Who Have Gone Before and Babylon and Tyre I remember the summer of love and the night of the generals and I remember clambering from the trees to gaze in newborn wonder upon the sapient sunrise above the plain. . . ."

Merde, he was drifting away again, or mayhap he had never truly been there! Had it been only a chance concatenation of neurons firing in a burning brain which had seemed to speak for a moment as the natural man? Be that as it may, it was that natural man I had come here to hear; not the oracle of these worshipful urchins, but he who had chosen for reasons unknown to give his spirits over to the mercies, tender or otherwise, of the Charge, nor would I be content until I had summoned *that* Pater Pan forth and demanded why.

"No more of this Delphic babble!" I cried, yanking at his phallus as if I might extract by brute force alone that natural man. "Speak from the heart! How could you of all men have surrendered your spirit to the vileness of the Charge? Speak in the name of the spirit we once shared!"

Did I imagine now that a pale ghost of the old spark had returned to his eyes? Was that a rueful smile upon his lips?

"Moussa . . ." he said. "My teller of tales has come to say good-bye. . . ."

"Why must you say good-bye, Pater? Why must this horrid thing be?"

"Je ne sais pas, muchacha," Pater Pan said, and now I was certain it was in some sense he. "All our Yellow Brick Roads must have an ending, though no one has ever told us why. . . ."

"Is this the man who once swore to experience all the far-flung worlds of men and bear witness to our species' tale entire?" I demanded behind tear-filled eyes.

"C'est moi, muchacha, he who rode the Arkie Spark through the long slow centuries in dreamless sleep, and who now has lost his race against time, which in the end not even I could win."

With a dreadful new understanding, I regarded his sunken frame, his fraying hair well-streaked with gray, his seamed and leathery skin. Thus had the dying babas of the Bloomenveldt appeared as they sat before their final flowers. The body's time had caught up to the spirit of the eternal Gypsy Joker at last, the hand of death lay on his shoulder.

"I remember all that I've ever been, muchacha, and even more that I haven't, and I remember all I said good-bye to before you summoned me forth," Pater Pan said, in a pained and mournful voice that had me fighting back sobs. "Only now I have to remember what we all spend our lives seeking to forget."

"Oh Pater, *why*?" I said tearfully. "If all our lives must end, must the noble tale of yours end like this?"

"The Inuit walks tranquilly out upon the ice to sit for one last eternal night under the frozen time of the stars. In Han of old at the end of our days we gave ourselves over to the poppy's lotus breath when the time came to let go our place upon the wheel. The Arkie freezes his Spark in the long slow centuries between the stars. The sage quaffs his psychotropic hemlock. The Prince of the Jokers travels, snap! snap! snap! like the Rapide into the Up and Out."

In my mind's eye, I saw the babas of the Bloomenveldt at peace with themselves beneath their final flowers, a peace quite literally beyond the understanding of one whose spirit and body could look forward to centuries of youth rather than weeks of terminal decay. Yet in my heart, I saw Guy Vlad Boca, a spirit who had chosen this selfsame mode of passage from sapient human consciousness in the full flower of adventurous youth.

"Weep not for me, girl," Pater Pan said. "The me you knew is already gone, and you are speaking with a Joker dybbuk he left behind to say good-bye. But I'm real enough to feel sad to leave the worlds all over again, and if you are still a sister of my spirit, you will let me go."

"I can truly do no other?" I asked from the depths of my spirit. For in that moment I was once more addressing myself to Guy as well as I turned my back on him in the depths of the Bloomenveldt and sought the lonely path of my own salvation. I had told myself then that I could do no other, nor in all the time between had I ever reconstructed a more fruitful course of action, but I had never really believed I had acted honorably in my heart of hearts until this very moment.

"You can only keep a mortal spirit in mortal torment," Pater Pan said, "after he who was at home has long since fled into unknown realms. I was happy when I went, for rather than expire in regretful agony, I chose to take one last journey down the Yellow Brick Road and see whatever there is to see in the final mystery of the Up and Out."

"May that road rise up to meet you, mi amor," I said, bursting into tears as I released my hold on the handle of the kundalinic machineries which had summoned forth this echo of the natural man.

Long had I chided myself for failing to risk the all of my own sapient spirit in a berserker effort to rescue Guy from his ultimate and terminal amusement. There in the depths of the Bloomenveldt I had turned my back and let the spirit of a friend and lover go, informed by no greater wisdom than the moral calculus of survival. Therefore had I secretly owned myself a coward in my heart of hearts.

Now, in this Tent of Many Colors, did the bitterest lesson of all yet grant me self-forgiveness, for now I knew to my dismay that greater love and courage of the spirit could sometimes be required to stand aside with an aching and uncomprehending heart and let be what must be.

Teary-eyed, shaking, not knowing what I felt, or even what I should properly feel, I turned to quit this place for the nearest venue of solitude, to find myself confronted with some dozen pair of mooningly worshipful eyes.

They were all staring at me as once they had stared at Pater Pan, as if I had annointed myself pythoness of their noxious cult, and established myself as the consort of their master. Thus had I ironically achieved what once I had so avidly sought, to preside over a Child of Fortune carnival at the Gypsy King's side! All the more did this perception enhance the distaste which I felt at being the focus of the miasma of fawning subservience which fairly exuded from these lost Children of Fortune like a cloying mist of vaporous treacle. Never had even Rollo, Dome, Goldenrod, and my Moussa regarded their Pied Piper thusly in the depths of the Bloomenveldt.

"What do you imagine you are staring at like that?" I demanded angrily.

"The Pied Piper of the Bloomenveldt . . ."

"Conjurer of mighty spirits . . ."

"Pater Pan's true lady . . ."

"Bah!" I snarled. "You call yourselves Children of Fortune? Conjure only with that spirit which moves through your own hearts, and give over your lust for all other gurus and deities, feckless urchins!"

So saying, I brushed aside, at least for the moment, their vapid attentions, and stormed like a whirlwind out of the thanatotic shadows of the tent into the bright clean glare of day.

But naturellement, I could not leave the encampment with the final chapter of Pater Pan's tale yet untold, nor for that matter could I snatch many moments of solitude from the entirely unwelcome solicitations of its inhabitants with which I was all-but-constantly surrounded from the moment I left the tent.

No sooner had I emerged into daylight than I found myself the center of a ragged little mob of acolytes who thrust food and wine and toxicants upon me and who trailed after me like pathetic puppies wherever I went. The former I waved away with impatient gestures, but as for my train of would-be followers, even shouts and imprecations would only drive them off a certain distance, a score meters or so, from which vantage they kept me under constant observation, tracking my movements en masse from a respectful distance, even when I was constrained to visit the encampment's foul and reeking latrine.

All that first afternoon this went on, while I wandered aimlessly about the camp, seeing and hearing nothing, only seeking to marshal my psychic resources to see this tale through to its final end. Vraiment, in pragmatic terms, there was nothing to prevent me from turning on my heel, fleeing from this unwholesome and sorrowful venue, leaving Alpa, and taking up my new life as a student of the tale-teller's art with never a backward glance. The natural man who had been my Pater Pan had said his good-bye and vanished into that final Void from which there is no rescue, and there was nothing I could accomplish by remaining here save bear witness to the final passage of what remained in that Tent of Many Colors into the Up and Out.

But of course in the end this proved quite sufficient to require the teller of tales to endure this story to the bitter end, for I knew all too well that if I abandoned it now my spirit would never know a moment's peace. For while the Child of Fortune that I had been had achieved the sad wisdom to let the spirit of the lover of her Golden Summer go to follow the unknown final path he had chosen, the woman I sought to become, she who had sworn the lodge-oath of the tale-teller, must be true to the first allegiance of the craft, and could not truly begin another tale until *this* one was completed in a manner that could satisfy the heart.

For was this not my wanderjahr's name tale, and if I ended it now with no spiritually satisfying conclusion, who was I to become, what fitting freenom could I choose, in homage to whom or what could I draw an esthetic moral therefrom? No, if I was to become anyone, it must be the teller who now approaches the end of this tale, and who therefore in that very moment of inevitable decision became the woman who transcribes these words now.

And so, by the time Alpa's sun had begun its slide down the sky, I had resolved to remain in this encampment for as long as the corpus of Pater Pan lived, and if the mages spoke true, if the genes themselves, or the collective unconscious of the species, or vraiment the Atman itself, as the Charge Addicts had it, found voice in the terminus of that brain's amplified passage, then this echo, or urgeist, or mere random discharge pattern, would I hector in search of that peace of the spirit which no mere human wisdom could grant me now.

Having so resolved, I allowed one of the boldest of the Children of Fortune to approach me, a handsome golden-haired and bronze-skinned boy at least two years younger than I, who eyed me with the collective worshipfulness to be sure, but whose eyes were enlivened by a certain speculation that led me to believe that the same had not entirely overridden the more wholesome and individualistic regard of his nascent natural man.

"Since I would seem to have been nominated as pontifex entirely against my will," I told him, "I may as well avail myself of the minimal prerogatives thereof. To wit, a tent where I may enjoy at least enough privacy to sleep without the presence of an audience, and a meal to consume therein."

455

"Pas problem, o Pied Piper of the Bloomenveldt," the boy said. "My tent and my bed are yours."

"Indeed?" I said dryly, both outraged and charmed by his frank and callow boldness.

He seemed to writhe in embarrassment, though there seemed to be something thespically feigned about it. "I will of course seek other temporary lodgings," he said quickly. "If that is what you prefer. I am called Kim, you may rely on me, noble maestra, I will be happy to cater to your every need." Now his feigned embarrassment seemed to be replaced by the genuine article, through which he nevertheless spoke with a certain charmingly boyish manliness. "Even those needs which you may not feel now."

Indifferent to the thrall in which I seemed to hold this boy save for the practical means to which I could put it, but preferring the relative spunk of his company to the cloying worshipfulness of his unwholesome fellows, I allowed Kim to enter my service, which is to say I was grateful to let him lend me his plain little tent, see to my food and drink, and contrive to keep the others well away from his prize.

I ate a wretched meal of heavily fried fruits de mer and vegetables washed down with a large quantity of raw green wine, and, rendered empty of thought by the force of the day's events, drowsy by the wine, and torpid by the leaden and greasy repast, I soon enough lapsed into merciful unconsciousness on Kim's pneumatic pallet.

The sun was high in the sky when I awoke the next morning, but Kim appeared in the tent as soon as I had risen with a breakfast of fresh fruits and well-sogged grains in milk which gave evidence that he must have been waiting patiently outside with it for hours.

He sat there watching my movements as I ate in silence, and did not speak until I had gotten it all down, which, despite my lack of real appetite, I felt morally constrained to do.

"Pater Pan has fallen silent, and there is much despair among us," he said. "But I have told them, o mi maestra, that surely the Pied Piper of the Bloomenveldt who is his consort and sister of his soul will summon his spirit forth to speak."

"You have no right to make such promises for others!" I told him crossly.

"I did wrong?" he exclaimed with guileful innocence. "I spoke not truth? Your plan is to linger here and do nothing? You remain here for some reason other than to discourse with the spirit of your great lover?" He cocked an ironic eyebrow at me. "Can it be that you tarry here only because you have been smitten by the charms of some lesser being?"

"Merde!" I snarled, if only to suppress a laughter that would have been entirely unseemly to these dreadful circumstances. "Very well then, Kim," I told him, "I will attempt to fulfill your public prophecy, if only because there is nothing else for it to escape from your outrageous amorous intentions." Though in truth I had to own to myself that he had seen my inevitable intention quite clearly and could hardly be chided too severely for seeking to enhance his repute among his fellows by grandly predicting the same.

A contretemps was taking place in the Tent of Many Colors when I arrived. A good two dozen persons were crowded together within its fabric walls, babbling and contending, and, directly in front of the throne of pillows upon which Pater Pan sat like a tranquil bodhi, three young men and an even younger girl were demanding refunds from the keeper of the oracle's time.

"Four credit units for silence!"

"Return my funds forthwith!"

"Fraud!"

"Nom de merde!"

The odor of too many less-than-fastidiously-laved bodies, the raucous din, the image of petty moneychangers in a temple which rose unbidden to my mind, all served to overcome my indifference to the tribal matters of these miscreants with righteous ire.

"Return the funds you have appropriated from these rubes at once!" I forthrightly commanded as I strode to the front of the tent. "True Children of Fortune do not pick each other's purses, nor is it seemly to gain profit at all from the passage of a noble spirit from the mortal realm. There will be no more trafficking in such ghoulish enterprises while I remain in this camp!"

There was stunned silence at this. She who had been measuring Pater Pan's time in credit units and her confederate with the

457

chip transcriber at the door were the first who dared raise their voices in protest.

"So says who?"

"What right have you to restrict our freedom of enterprise?"

"My name is Sunshine," I told them and the generality. "I style myself thusly as a Child of Fortune among my fellows. I command no one but myself. And myself I will command to leave this encampment rather than submit my eyes to such a sight again."

I gazed about the tent, and now I was the ruespieler, working the crowd with my eyes and voice. "But if you wish to style me the Pied Piper of the Bloomenveldt, if you persist in regarding my words as those of your perfect master, that is your affair, urchins, not mine. So hear me as whom you will, I tell you that neither Sunshine the Child of Fortune, nor whatever arcane personage's mantle you choose to drape around my indifferent shoulders, will remain among you if this vile practice does not cease."

"And at any rate as long as the Pied Piper of the Bloomenveldt does not by her arcanely puissant powers call forth the voice of the oracle, we can hardly expect to continue a profitable commerce in the wisdom of same," Kim piped up brightly.

"Thus speaks the voice of astute practicality," I said dryly.

"And now that we have agreed to your condition, mi maestra, you will call forth the spirit of the great Pater Pan for us, nē?" Kim announced slyly.

"Thus speaks the voice of a true Gypsy Joker," I muttered under my breath, for while I could not but admire his guileful way with words, I was not about to encourage more of it with praise.

And so I seated myself on a cushion before the pillow throne for the long haul, attempted to erase the perceptions of my unwholesome surroundings from the forefront of my sensorium, gazed into the empty blue eyes of the frail corpus thereon, and attempted to conjure with the ectoplasmic spirits of the Up and Out.

As to the true psychesomic nature of what I sought to summon forth from this burning electronically amplified brain, je ne sais pas even now, nor have any of the manifold theories proposed by mages of many persuasions ever satisfied me entirely.

Certainement, there is abundant evidence that the genes of nonsapient animals store more than structural templates, for we observe the expression of their data in behaviors as complicated as those of a beehive and in natural sprachs as complex as the species songs of birds. Who is therefore to say what genetic messages may be encoded in the gene pool of our species, to be released, mayhap, only when the higher cerebral centers of the individual consciousness surrender up their sapient sovereignty?

Or contrawise, may not a new electrohologram at length cohere out of the electronically amplified fragments of memories fused together by scientific pouvoir in the vacated brain? For while two long starfaring ages in the Void have long since given the lie to the hoary notion that nature abhors a vacuum of matter and energy, the quantum forces would certainly seem to abhor a vacuum of *structure*, so that it might be inevitable that whatever psychic fragments remain in a Charge Addict's brain must under sufficient increment of Charge relate to each other once more in a hologrammic pattern of the whole.

Was it in some sense Pater Pan that at length I succeeded in summoning forth? Was it the collective unconscious coded into the genes of his body, at last permitted to speak through the verbal centers of his brain by the power of the Charge? Was it only fragmented memories cohering in a new pattern about a void? A spirit, or only an ersatz electronic simulacrum of same?

Vraiment, it may be justly said that science has banished the deities and demons, the ghosties and ghoulies, of our primeval superstitious past into the realm of metaphor where all such mythical creatures belong, but hola, in our Second Starfaring Age, only to create new and even more arcane ghosts in the civilized machineries, whereby doppelgängers of the spirit arise out of matter and energy themselves!

I sat there for the better part of an hour in silence, feeling entirely the fool. And yet the more the fool I felt myself, the more it seemed to me that the way of the Fool was my only course of action. To wit, I must play the pythoness, and simply say what was in my heart.

"Speak to me as you did in the Dreamtime on the Bloomenveldt, Pater Pan," I said at last. "For if you were a figment out of my Dreamtime then, then I must be a figment of your Dreamtime now."

459

There was a susurrus of murmurs at this breaking of the hushed silence behind me, but the figure on the pillow throne remained perfectly still and mute.

"Sing me the song of Yellow Brick Road, tell me a tale that will let my spirit leave this place in peace, even as I let go of your own rather than hold it to me in torment."

For what must have been hours, I babbled on thusly, without the mediation of intellect between feeling and words, and for what must have been hours, I might as well have been addressing my increasingly bathetic entreaties to a statue of stone.

"Merde, why have you chosen to end the tale of your noble life as a vegetative hulk in thrall to the Charge, and why have you cursed me with the telling thereof, and why should I not give over attendance at this lugubrious epilogue and flee as far from here as my fortune will take me?" I fairly raged at last. "If there is any geist present in your poor corpus, speak now, or you must forever hold your peace!"

I rose, and made to depart, moving with a thespic slowness, quite unsure, if truth be told, whether or not I would indeed carry through with this bluff.

Be the sincerity thereof what it may, Pater Pan's lips began to move as if something within him were struggling up toward speech, and then a voice spoke with the apparatus of his throat.

"Remember me," it said quite plain.

I froze there in my tracks, and an absolute silence fell in the tent.

"Vraiment, I am here for no other purpose," I whispered at the apparition before me, speaking through an old man's flesh with the voice of he who had departed, and yet, somehow not with the voice of Pater Pan, for though the tones and the rhythms of the music were the same, another spirit was singing the song.

"Remember exploding from nothingness into a trillion fragmentary motes," this voice, whatever it was, began to declaim, even as the eyes of Pater Pan's withered face remained as lifeless as two blue marbles. "Remember coalescing into numberless suns out of less than mists. Remember spheres of rock in the everlasting night. . . ."

Who or what spoke? Je ne sais pas. The Atman that had witnessed the universe's explosion into existence from a point of nonbeing? A tale the natural man had once told or heard? The genetic memory of the species?

But be that as it may, whatever spoke now could not be taken for what had spoken in random babblement before, for *this* dybbuk of the Up and Out compelled my attention as fully as the previous oracular avatar had mesmerized its feckless acolytes.

Vraiment, I was hardly aware of sinking back down on my cushion before it, taking my place at its feet with the rest.

"Remember drifting in the sea in long helices of life. . . . Remember crawling out gasping on the land. . . . Remember descending from our ancestral trees to gaze at the sunrise above the plain. . . . Remember your first footsteps on Luna. . . . Remember your long slow centuries between the stars. . . . Remember the mysteries of the Jump that has spread your kind among the far-flung worlds of men. . . . Remember you. . . . Remember me."

"I am here to remember," I seem to recall myself saying, but I seemed to have been transported once more into the Dreamtime, for once more a spirit that in quotidian terms could not be said to be present had nevertheless contrived to appear before me, even as the Pied Piper of my Golden Summer had been with me in my hour of need on the Bloomenveldt, even as we may readily enough discourse with departed spirits and archetypal images in the realms of quotidian sleep.

"Remember this moment of remembering," Pater Pan said, and now it almost seemed as if it were truly he, for his eyes were turned upon me, and I could not deny that it was a Sunshine that he remembered to whom he now spoke.

"Remember Moussa. . . . Remember Sunshine. . . . Remember that you came to tell the tale. . . ."

"Vraiment, I cannot deny that this task would seem to have fallen on me," I admitted. "But tell me then how I am supposed to make this story sing? Shall I be constrained to declare that I could honor your spirit with nothing better than a denouement of tragic farce? How can I honorably end this tale thusly?"

But the answer was silence, and whatever had spoken would speak to me no more that day.

Nor for the next three days could I summon forth so much as a syllable. I allowed Kim to tend to the animal requirements of

461

my existence, and I spent my waking hours speaking to the silent sphinx within the tent.

What did I say to Pater Pan during all these endless hours of one-sided babblement? Vraiment everything that was in my heart and spirit and more and in every conceivable mode of address, from rage to cajolement, from tearful sobbings to dark gravehouse jests, from the tale of my travels across the Bloomenveldt to the tale of *The Spark of the Ark* and everything and anything between.

All of which availed me nothing. Pater Pan had given up taking nourishment days before my arrival, and now even my attempts to force-feed him nutritive liquids were rejected by his body, as if what remained of the protoplasmic will of the same had determined upon a terminal fast unto death. Day by day, indeed hour by hour, I found myself constrained to watch his body grown gaunter, the webwork seaming his skin withering it to dusty parchment, his golden hair thinning out to a mange of gray straw no longer quite covering the pallid skin of his pate.

This nascent corpse did I find myself hectoring futilely, until at length I had come to loathe the sound of my own foolish voice.

As Kim ushered me into the Tent of Many Colors on the morning of the fourth day, I found I could bear to question the sphinx no longer, nor could I bear any longer the sight of the King of the Gypsies and the Prince of the Jokers expiring thusly, enclosed from the worlds he had so joyfully wandered, and surrounded by this feckless and indolent travesty of the Gypsy Jokers which gave the lie to the true song of both the natural man and the Pied Piper whose spirit was now passing from the worlds.

And if no words of mine could cause the sphinx to speak, then at least let it not be said that I allowed his mortal remains to decay into death in this malodorous tent suffocating with heat and thanatotic vapors.

"Enough of this!" I cried. "Roll up these walls of Cloth of Many Colors and let in the light of morning. Schnell, schnell, schnell, let us breathe more natural air!"

"Come, come," Kim cajoled, "let us break down the walls and let the sunshine in!" So saying, he straightaway began undoing one of the flaps from its stakes, and within a few minutes, enough of the tribe had followed his example to transform the spiritually and odorously stifling tent into an open-roofed pavilion looking out through the encampment on the golden sun rising high above the brilliant mirror of the azure sea.

Upon the newfound breeze wafted the subtle sweetness of the wooded hillsides, and the more insistent tang of the sea, and the organic overripeness of the untidy encampment, and subtle pheromones of holiday essences from the streets of the town far below, and the effluvia of human bodies borne away by the breeze and sublimated by the heat of the tropical sun.

Mayhap all of these random molecules combined to form a new perfume as puissant to the biochemical perception of Pater Pan's corpus as it was to the nostrils of my own spirit, for certainement both the mages of science and my own experience in the depths of the Bloomenveldt would tell us that it is the olfactory senses which most directly connect the stimuli of the exterior realm to the tropic responses of the deep backbrain.

For his nostrils seemed to widen almost imperceptibly upon his first few breaths of this new atmosphere, and it seemed that his eyes looked out over the ocean, and with determination, I could imagine the faintest of smiles on his lips, when he once again, after his long silence, spoke.

"I remember . . ." said that preternatural voice which had so captured my attention when last it spoke. "I remember a day like this long ago with the sun shining over San Francisco Bay. . . . I remember hills in Great Edoku where it was always morning when I was the King of the Gypsies and the Prince of the Jokers. . . . I remember awakening from a century's sleep to see the sun rise on a new world and breathe once more the living atmosphere of another planet. . . ."

Quelle chose, what new arcana of the Charge was *this*? For while the first words were spoken in that strangely impersonal voice which alluded in its identity to the genetic spirit of our species' collective genes, the following remembrances were uttered in three successively different voices, that of the Pater Pan I had known and loved and two unknown personas. Yet while each of these voices seemed as humanly specific as the memory-images they rendered up, the total effect was of some singularity of spirit attempting to speak through a multitude.

"I remember the arkology *Gold Mountain* and the day we pooled our fortunes to purchase our destiny. . . . I remember Fat

Tuesday on the sun-drenched levee. . . . I remember a Mardi Gras parade. . . ."

Images continued to pour from the mouth of the old man staring out over the hills at the sunrise above the bay of Florida, each one with the voice of a different fleshly avatar, or so it seemed, each one singing sweetly of a fond memory of the eternal Yellow Brick Road.

Yet somehow all these fragments of different sprachs seemed avatars as well of a single Lingo, as if some spirit deep below the crown of the cortex were firing off far-from-randomly-chosen quanta of memory in an attempt to semaphore its meaning into the realm of conscious speech.

Vraiment, it might just as well be said, as the mages would no doubt contend, that far from being the collective urgeist of the genes speaking through patterns of memory release, what we all in fact perceived was the order our subjectivities persisted in imposing upon the voice of random chaos babbling through a sapiently vacated brain.

Indeed who is to say that these are not one and the same, for certainement, we observe such order arising full-blown from the quantum chaos at the deepest level of existence, and so too was the macrocosm created by the spontaneous explosion of being and order into the perfect nothingness of a dimensionless void. Who is to say that chaos itself is not the ultimate principle upon which all order is recomplicated?

In the absence of scientific certitude along this interface between the quantum reality and such metaphysic, let me then simply say that I perceived that something, call it what you will, was attempting to speak through the selection of images gushing forth from the amplified and dissociated memory banks of Pater Pan's dying brain.

As to whether the Children of Fortune gathered there under the awning of the pavilion were of the same perception, or whether any utterance at all from their silent oracle would have been equally sufficient to command their awe and attention, je ne sais pas. Be that as it may, while those already at the scene of this advent forthwith lapsed into marveling silence, some sort of entirely nonverbal semaphore seemed to communicate the tidings thereof to the rest of the encampment. Mayhap the opening up of the tent of oracular secrets to the clear gratuit view of all would

464

at any rate have been sufficient to assemble a crowd. At any rate, within short minutes, several score of this pathetic tribe were lying about the area, fortifying their perceptions with wine and toxicants as they hung on every word.

As for me, I sat there silently too for a time, listening to that profusion of voices sing a paean of nostalgic glory to a succession of golden moments of summer along an endless Yellow Brick Road. How sweetly they sang of the ancient remembered youth of our species, where all of them and all of us are forever wandering the free path of our spirits, where all summer's days are golden, and love and laughter rule the stars. Personas rose to remember Edoku and Novi Mir, Hind and Elysium, arkologies and gypsy caravans, places and times Pater Pan could have lived through, and those which might exist only in the Dreamtime extravaganzas with which he had embellished his name tale.

Were the verses of this song merely the memories of tales? Or were they truly sung by a chorus of onetime fleshly avatars of some deeper spirit?

An end to such futile speculations, for the singer matters not when the song touches the heart as this one touched mine.

And as soon as I truly penetrated to the simple truth of this self-evident perception, the same found its voice, for whether I was addressing a random crackle of neurons or not, I must make it hear me, for if this was indeed once more the Dreamtime, I must once more conjure survival wisdom from its spirits.

"O I hear your song of remembrance, Pater Pan, if it is indeed you who are the singer thereof," I told him. "I hear the Piper of Pan calling us down from our ancestral trees, and I hear the tale that I followed from the depths of the Bloomenveldt back to the far-flung worlds of men. I hear a noble lover's laughter, and the blarney of a Gypsy King. I hear the Pied Piper of the Yellow Brick Road telling his tale truly even from beyond its ending. . . .

"Now hear me, whoever or whatever you are, or even if you are nothing," I all but bellowed as I rose to my feet. "It is Moussa the waif and Sunshine your Gypsy Joker and the Pied Piper of the Bloomenveldt who bids you answer in the very spirit of which you sing! How can I hear that spirit singing its own true song to the end with a sweet puissance which breaks my heart

465

and yet see with uncomprehending eyes that now it draws naught but the indolent and the lame?"

Indeed so just was my characterization of Pater Pan's final tribe that the indolent and the lame in question, who lolled about in various states and degrees of toxication marveling at this very discourse, lacked even the collective spirit to raise so much as a single voice of protest when I styled them to their object of worship thusly.

But as for he who sat on the pillow throne, something in my words must have vibrated to the frequency of an appropriate cerebral center, or mayhap all current scientific theory to the contrary, some true spirit is implied in any verbal sequence.

Certainement, it was not my subjective imposition of order on random chaos when he turned his eyes from the sun to gaze into mine. As to whether anything but a doppelgänger was there to regard me through them, je ne sais pas, but cerebral echo or no, it knew me well enough to speak my name.

"Sunshine . . . Sing your own song, ruespieler, tell your own tale. . . ."

"This is the only tale I have to tell, and I am doing my best," I told this apparition plaintively, quite as if he were my old lover and friend, for if this was the Dreamtime, then the logic thereof allowed such intimacies. "But I cannot end it thusly!"

"This tale never ends, muchacha," Pater Pan reminded me in the Dreamtime. "Before the singer was the song, so when the singer is gone, will the song remain. As long as there is anyone to tell the true tale."

"How can I relate in the true spirit of the Yellow Brick Road that the Pied Piper thereof, after calling us down from the forest of unreason and leading our Mardi Gras parade out among the stars, expired pitifully at last, leaving behind only these poor lost Bloomenkinder of Alpa, this unwholesome travesty of the spirit we shared as Gypsy Jokers?"

"Were we not all Bloomenkinder of the forest of unreason before we heard the song that we followed from the trees to the stars?" Pater Pan said, and while the voice was his, the words he threw back at me, if memory serves, were my own. "Wherever in the worlds of men that there are Bloomenkinder of the spirit, there you will find lost Children of Fortune awaiting their own Piper."

"And you were mine before I even met you!" I cried. "You saved my spirit from destruction on the Bloomenveldt in a Dreamtime such as this!"

"And who will be mine now save she who tells our tale?"

"*Me? Yo?*"

"Who is the Pied Piper of the Bloomenveldt?" Pater Pan said, speaking so plainly now in my own oft-repeated sprach that I could all but see my own ironic self mocking me from within his eyes.

"Merde," I sighed in this moment of dizzying satori, "anyone who tells the tale!"

"Will you not let this torch pass to you, ruespieler?" Pater Pan said. "For who else is there to take it up from the failing hands of this loving ghost who only stayed behind to pass it on? Auf wiedersehen, mi vida, hail and farewell."

I could feel a spirit's passage then, another standing wave of Pater Pan's consciousness propelled by the Charge Up through his speech centers and Out into the void. I need not question the body now staring out blindly to sea again further to know of a certainty that this avatar would not speak through it again.

For with this spirit's passage passed the Dreamtime too, and I came tumbling back out of it into the quotidian realm, knowing not with whom or what my spirit had communed therein, but knowing full well what I had to do.

I rounded on the great gathering of scruffy and toxicated urchins who fairly surrounded the pavilion now, and what a sorry audience they were to bear witness to such a spirit's passage!

"You have heard, have you not?" I declaimed at them. "From the very lips of he upon whose dying words you so fatuously and uncomprehendingly hang! For want of the proper spirit on your part, the torch thereof devolves on me. Nor when the time comes will I let *you* leave it in the muck!"

For all my eloquent invective, I might as well have been addressing my lost children of the forest, for they looked upon me like the deity of all lost children, wanting only to be saved from the adventure of their own devices, and waiting for me to tell them whatever it was they imagined they wanted to hear. Even Kim seemed not to have understood a word of my true meaning.

"Who here can sing a tune?" I demanded. "Who here can play a pipe or strum a string? Who can carve in wood or work

467

wire into bijoux? Who knows how to steam dim sum or juggle balls or practice some semblance of the acrobatic arts?"

They gaped at me uncomprehendingly as if I too had now started speaking in parable.

"Merde!" I cried. "Is there none among you who knows a single tale? Hola, is there not even one among you who would boast of adeption in the tantric arts?"

"Ah, mi maestra, I knew you would come to the question of my own natural talent sooner or later!" Kim declared to a cleansing burst of laughter. "Let me proudly be the first volunteer in whatever enterprise you care to have me serve!"

Once this obscene levity had loosened their mood, other voices began to pipe up.

"It might be said I play the pipes, if none too well. . . ."

"When I was a child, I fashioned animals out of clay. . . ."

"I think I know how to bake tarts of meat or fruit. . . ."

"I know a tale called *The Wandering Dutchman* that I used to tell in school. . . ."

"All these things and more you shall begin doing now as true Children of Fortune," I told them. "While I am something less than a maestra of cuisine, or a musician, or an adept of any craft, and would starve to death if I had to sing for my ruegelt, I have many a tale which I will readily donate, nor am I exactly a naif when it comes to commerce in the tantric arts. So then, let us learn to become Gypsy Jokers once more together, and gather our ruegelt where we may."

"Who would purchase our primitive goods?"

"Why would anyone pay to hear our songs?"

"Florida abounds with entertainers far more amusing than we. . . ."

"We must compete with palaces of haute cuisine. . . ."

". . . and tantric artists all the way from Lorienne."

"Thus be it ever!" Kim exclaimed with quite another energy. "I would rather forage my fortune in the streets than say I never tried!"

"Well spoken, indeed, Gypsy Joker!" I declared pridefully. "Speak not of the daunting haut monde of this little resort village to one who was an indigent Child of Fortune without even your bountiful parental largesse in Great Edoku! Surely it has always been thus on every world. Yet on every world, if Children

468

of Fortune do not exactly wax wealthy, still do we prevail. For the true patron of our custom is never the jaded connoisseur, but the memory of one's own wanderjahr in every human heart. Fear not, my Gypsy Jokers, that is a largesse the true spirit may always obtain."

I pointed down the shoulder of our little mountain at the tiny blue and white and rose buildings of the town below, at the minuscule figures on the beach, and the bright sails of boats flitting across the bay.

"Below us lies Florida, a town given over entirely to holiday and frolic," I told them. "I swear to you on my honor as a Gypsy Joker, meine kinder, that no true Child of Fortune could hope for an easier field to gather ruegelt from than such a seaside resort!"

And so did my wanderjahr come full circle round as, with tears in my eyes but not without the true song in my heart, I found myself constrained to become the Pied Piper thereof, the Wendi Shasta Leonardo who transcribes these words, but certainement not the Wendy whose spirit I found so cloying in the *Tale of Peter Pan.*

For far from seeking to shepherd these lost children back into the parental embrace of the quotidian realm of maya and earnest toil, the spirit of *this* Wendi sought rather to set their feet upon that Yellow Brick Road which goes ever on, in final homage to the Golden Summer of my own life that once the truest of friends and noblest of lovers had given unto me.

30

Florida was no Great Edoku, the urchins of our encampment were far from being Gypsy Jokers, and certainement I possessed not a tenth part of the survival lore of the Yellow Brick Road of such as Pater Pan.

Still, while skill, craft, and artistry might be severely lacking, the spirit was now there, and as I had learned on Edoku, it was tribute to this spirit of one's own fondly remembered days as a Child of Fortune which provoked largesse, rather than informed critical admiration for the crudely manifested artifacts thereof.

So, under my direction and prodding, amusement tents arose, offering tantric tableaus and private performances, as well as rude musical entertainments, and even certain rather brief and clumsy theatrical events. Several craftsmen's stalls were erected, offering naive sculptures, wooden jewelry, wire bijoux, and most lucratively, various pouches on thongs, belts, or even headbands, which soon proved quite popular in such a seaside resort given over to nudity or minimal clothing.

Finger foods of several sorts were prepared in the encampment: baked tarts, steamed dim sum, cuchifritos, and most novel of all, a kind of vegetable lo mein stuffed into a savory baked tuber, which could be eaten without fork or chopsticks as one strolled along. So too did nascent musicians and jongleurs gambol about the encampment, greatly enhancing the carnival ambiance, if not exactly elevating the artistic atmosphere.

And, as I had learned from Pater Pan, hawkers and buskers were sent forth into the town below to peddle trinkets, finger food, beverages, and pouches, and to perform on the streets and beaches, thus garnering ruegelt while attracting patronage to the camp.

In particular, the beaches proved to be a lucrative venue, for while the streets of the town abounded with restaurants and tavernas, swimmers and sunbathers were naturally pleased to be offered drinks and tidbits on the spot, and their critical faculties were necessarily loosened by having unsought entertainments brought to them.

The guileful and enterprising Kim even somehow scraped together enough capital to rent a canoe, from which he peddled food and drink prepared by others directly to the pleasure craft sailing about the bay.

As for ruespielers, at first there were none with the courage and brass required to ply this trade in the streets, or even in the encampment. But Kim soon enough began hectoring me to teach him some tales, at first, so it seemed, so as to retain my company for as many hours as possible, for the purpose of continuing his frankly amorous advances which had long since become the butt of good-natured banter between us, but later as a more or less serious student of same, whose manifest gift of gab needed only some proper material to find itself rewarded with ruegelt.

Indeed, when I secretly overlooked his premiere performance, a telling of *The Spark of the Ark* to an audience of loungers at beachside, I found myself warmed by something more than pedagogical pride, and vraiment, had it not been for the presence of my dying lover's corpus in the center of the encampment and the unseemliness of even such thoughts under the circumstances, I do believe I would have been happily ready to reward his pluck at the conclusion thereof with the fulfillment of his so avidly expressed priapic desires.

In short, within ten days the enterprises and spirit of the Children of Fortune had come to Florida. Vacationers wandered around our caravanserei sampling this and that, if not exactly amounting to a great throng or inundating us with funds, and our hawkers and buskers became quaint and familiar figures on the streets and beaches of the town.

As for Pater Pan, no spirit spoke through him again, nor did I seek to summon forth same, and indeed, once our young tribespeople had found proper enterprising focus for their youthful energies, few of them even tarried long before the skeletal figure in the open pavilion.

During the daytime, we kept the Tent of Many Colors open to the warmth and the shaded sun and the breezes, rolling the flaps down only at night when the air grew cooler. But while Pater Pan remained in free and easy sight of the inner vie of the encampment, by unspoken agreement, we communally contrived, by one subtle means or another, to keep the turistas well clear of our central mystery.

And despite the continued silence of the figure on the pillow throne as it proceeded to ride the Charge Up and Out into its final hours, a mystery indeed remained. For even as the flesh melted away from Pater Pan's gaunter and gaunter figure to the point where I marveled that he could yet sit upright, even as the hair fell from his skull like deep autumn's leaves in some less benign clime, even as his visage sharpened to the bony icon of mortality, his eyes seemed to grow larger and more brilliant in their deepening sockets, one could almost perceive them glowing from within with the blue light of a brain that would now seem to be burning itself out in ecstasy.

What a strange deathwatch it was, in the midst of a newborn carnival, with the eyes of the object thereof all but glowing like wan blue suns, and a smile that came to be fixed on his lips of such beatific contentment as must have graced the visage of Buddha under his bo tree!

Only his flesh gave the lie to this aura of bliss that he fairly exuded, and yet the weaker and frailer the body became, the broader grew his smile, and the stronger grew the inner light that seemed to be burning behind those eyes that grew larger and larger the deeper they receded into their sockets.

Vraiment, this was a sight not even I could bear for long, for on the one hand the manifest presence of imminent death dragging out the body's terminal agonies to amazing extremis is no fit object for youthful contemplation, and on the other hand what would seem to be manifesting itself within whispered in my

472

ear that upon witnessing the passage into the Up and Out, I too could do no less than seek the same manner of my inevitable final journey.

But as fate or cosmic justice would have it, while I never tarried long in Pater Pan's presence, I was there in the final moments.

It was the luncheon hour of high noon, and I was passing close by the Tent of Many Colors on my way from teaching Kim a new tale to a kiosk purveying dim sum. It was a warm bright day in the Child of Fortune encampment, and the flaps of the tent were open, and to naive eyes, it no doubt would have seemed that the skeletal figure on the pillow throne with its beaming smile of contentment was looking out in well-earned contentment on the fruits of his endeavors.

My eyes filled with tears as I stopped for a moment to regard him, and yet I do not believe that what I felt was sorrow. There my Pater Pan sat, looking out over the brow of the hill at the tiny buildings of the town below, where even now the Children of his spirit plied the trades he had taught us, and beyond which he could contemplate, if he so chose, the clear crystal sea, and the bright golden sun above it.

Vraiment, if such a spirit must pass from the worlds, how better than this, in a Gypsy Joker encampment, alive with noise and laughter, redolent with the smells of cooking foods, embraced by the eternal carnival that had been his spirit's song, with a warm sea breeze ruffling the remnants of his hair?

And then, as if the final quanta of spirit which yet remained in that skull case had waited for only this moment to arrive, the moment when the teller thereof at last knew that she could make his tale sing sweetly, the final arcana of the Up and Out began.

On this much at least do the mages and the devotees of the Charge agree: that in the terminal moments of the Up and Out, a phenomenon occurs which can occur in no other. When a sufficient number of neurons have been burned away by electronic amplification, the next increment of Charge triggers a kind of psychesomic chain reaction. Every remaining memory trace is simultaneously activated, every cerebral center still functioning is flashed into electronically amplified excitation at once, and the remaining energy left in the corpus is sucked up through the brain as it is burned away entirely by the overload.

Be the extravagances of the Charge Addicts as they may, the mages of psychesomics readily enough own that this is the theoretical limit of human consciousness, a state of total cerebral activation that can be attained only in the few moments before the brain expires as the inevitable price of its existence.

Could ironic fate have prepared a darker jape for us than this? Only in the moment of death itself may the psychonaut of our spirit attain its perfect flower.

Vraiment, to have studied the scientific annals, even to have come to peace with this inevitable ending of the tale, is one thing, but to observe the Up and Out itself was quite another.

Tremors all at once began to ripple randomly through the stringy musculature of Pater Pan's body. His arms and then his legs began to twitch and jerk as if some volitional force within him were reaching for control. And his face. . . .

His facial muscles too began to dance, but here at far from random, for somehow they began to rearrange themselves into a series of coherent yet sequentially different visages, as if wavefronts of personality patterns were flashing through them. Yet the eyes that looked out on the worlds for the last time through all of these masks of humanity seemed to be windows into a singular spirit, quite at home in each momentary avatar, yet preternaturally bright and unchanging just the same.

For indeed while the last mask of the King of the Gypsies and the Prince of the Jokers wore the faces of all the natural men he had been or boasted of being, each one his own vision of unutterable bliss, the eyes of the inner being that shone through them bespoke a singular ecstasy.

It all transpired too rapidly for a crowd to form, for there were less than a dozen folk within eyeshot at the time, and when Pater Pan suddenly stood up, it was with the vigor and force of his full manly flower.

Vraiment, the Healers will tell you, there is nothing arcane about such sudden appearance of hysterical strength in terminal patients, and there were ancient warrior cults capable of summoning these powers forth by primitive psychesomic rituals. The spirit can command otherwise impossible feats of strength from the body when the further survival thereof is no longer an issue.

474

Be that as it may, the actual sight of such a triumph of vital energy over terminal fleshly decrepitude was something neither I nor anyone present had ever witnessed, and none of us were capable of movement as Pater Pan strode boldly past us, out from under the tented awning, and into the brilliant golden warmth of noon.

He moved with apparent volitional purpose through the encampment, walking with long but measured strides, beaming at the manifold enterprises thereof with the ecstatic smiles of all his successive memories of all such carnivals that he had walked through, and as he made his way through the aisles of tents toward the edge of the camp overlooking the town and the sea, there he was one final time, leading a Mardi Gras parade of Children of Fortune along the Yellow Brick Road.

Tell me not that this was a foul travesty of that gay parade in Great Edoku, as some cramped souls might own, do not tell me that we did not dance to the inner music thereof as we said our final farewell to all that was left of Pater Pan.

He walked to the lip of a steep canyon cliff, and then he turned to face us. The musculature of his body sagged into slumped immobility as if it had nobly completed its final worldly task and had given up the ghost. Nor did any more avatars pass through the mask of his face.

That face, withered though it was, seemed ageless now, for the musculature thereof had ceased all its exertions, so that all that remained was a tabula rasa of perfect relaxation, upon which a radiant bliss was inscribed by those burning inner eyes.

I looked into those eyes for the last time, though in another sense, I will always see them still, I gazed at his face for a final good-bye, and saw not the skull all but bursting from beneath the flesh, but the face of the spirit that would always be with me favoring me with a final Gypsy Joker smile. Nor did it matter that all there present were later to declare that he smiled his last smile just for them.

Then a final contraction tightened the muscles of his body, and he coiled into himself as if to spring. He spread his arms wide as if for the last time to embrace the eternal carnival, as if to spread his spirit's wings and soar into flight.

Then indeed he began a mighty leap upward, but rather than his body leaving the earth, his spirit seemed to soar Up and

475

Out of his body at the apogee with a final ecstatic sigh, and before his body could collapse behind him, he was gone, onto the wind, into the lambent sunshine, into the arms of that spirit which would never die as long as there were Children of Fortune to pass through it on the far-flung worlds of men.

How long I stood there before I became aware of time's movement once more, je ne sais pas, for my vision was not transfixed by the pathetic and timebound sight of Pater Pan's fallen corpus but rather by the timeless mandala of an eternal sun in a brilliant blue sky.

As once I had seen his face blazoned upon Belshazaar's sun via pheromones and famishment in the Dreamtime of the Bloomenveldt, so did I seek by fully conscious act of will to see him smiling down upon me with the golden face of Alpa's sun now.

Vraiment, and if in *this* Dreamtime, I knew full well that what I saw was no more than the mirror of the spirit that lived on only within my own heart, neither could that spirit be said to have vanished from our mortal realm while I honored it therein.

At length, I found myself drawn back into the stream of time, not by any sound which shattered the crystalline eternity of the moment, but by the pressure of the unnatural perfect absence of same which seemed to have draped itself around my shoulders like a leaden cloak.

Slowly, reluctantly, I rounded on those gathered behind me, knowing all too well what I would now confront.

All those who had been in the encampment to witness Pater Pan's final passage now stood there before me between the caravanserei and the edge of the cliff. In all their eyes, I saw what they must have seen in my own, and this warmed my heart.

For were these newborn Children of Fortune not the true progeny of the union of our spirits? If it had been the Pied Piper of Pan who had brought them together, had it not been the Pied Piper of the Bloomenveldt who had set them dancing down the Yellow Brick Road? Were these true Children of Fortune's spirit not the posterity I had given my lover and were they not as well the sweet ending to my tale that he had left for me?

But in those eyes I saw as well the worshipful obeisance against which I had railed and guarded myself since first I had found it fawningly directed toward my person in that stiflingly thanatotic tent, and this, to say the least, pleased me not, for it would seem that the Gypsy Joker's last laugh was on me.

For had he not in their presence passed the torch of his spirit into my reluctant hands? And had I not wrapped his mantle around me in ire, in order to rouse those lost Children of Fortune from their thanatotic mooning so that I would never again see in their eyes that feckless longing for a perfect master which I saw there now?

Vraiment, I had told them often enough that Children of Fortune have no chairmen of the board or kings! Yet had I not been constrained by karmic justice to lead them back to the Yellow Brick Road even as the Pied Piper of the Bloomenveldt had been constrained to spiel her unsought charges back to the worlds of men?

Indeed, here I stood like Antony over fallen Caesar, like Liberty holding aloft her torch, and there my huddled masses stood hanging on my first words, which grew ever more pregnant with portent the longer I gazed upon them before I spoke.

Yet how could I chide them for regarding me thusly now? For these were not the feckless urchins I had first found but Gypsy Jokers of the true spirit whom I however reluctantly had led to that becoming, which is to say that I had indeed succeeded in carrying the torch of Pater Pan's spirit from that moment until this.

But now if I was to be true to that spirit, if that spirit was to live on in their hearts, I must find the words to pass that torch along, not to some papal successor, but into the hands of each of them, into the hands of the republic of the spirit, where at least according to this teller of the tale, it has naturellement always belonged.

One last time I sought communion with my Pied Piper, and one last time he contrived to speak to me in the Dreamtime from beyond the temporal veil, as if even the Prince of the Jokers could not lie easy until I had solved his ultimate koan.

For all at once Pater Pan was there before me at the end of my Golden Summer's Mardi Gras Parade, outlined by sunset glory against the bonsaied mountains of Edoku, and saying the necessary good-bye that broke all our hearts. While at the same time, in a strange duality of perspective, I had *become* that avatar, for it was *I* who stood before our tribe in that valedictory moment now.

Vraiment, my wanderjahr had come full circle round, for certainement this was indeed the end of my Golden Summer's Mardi Gras Parade.

Then it was that my eyes sought out Kim, or mayhap his eyes in that moment had the puissance to draw me to them. He stood near the front ranks, from which vantage, and having caught my eye, his face could speak to me plainly enough. And upon that visage I seemed to see what I sought, a kindred child of the same spirit, ready to carry forth its torch as his own Piper, though as yet he knew it not.

Vraiment, this was not the end of day, for the sun shone brightly in the clear blue sky, before me the gay tents of our caravanserei still flapped like proud banners above the Yellow Brick Road, and the Pied Piper of the Bloomenveldt was not the Gypsy Joker King, which is to say that it was *I* who told the tale, nor was it in my heart to call down the sunset on anyone's Mardi Gras parade.

"What would you have me say to you?" I asked them gently. "Before death, there are none but vapid words of wisdom, and before life, we have only the wisdom of our own hearts."

A low murmuring rumbled through the little throng. "What shall we do now?" someone called out.

"Why ask me?" I demanded without ire. "Who am I but one of you?"

"You're the Pied Piper of the Bloomenveldt!"

"You're Pater Pan's true love!"

"You're the Gypsy Joker Queen!"

At this last, I felt the words bubbling forth from my lips as they emerged from the void into my brain, and the song which has carried our species to the far-flung worlds of men from our ancestral trees seemed to be singing itself through me even as I spoke from my own heart.

"Children of Fortune *have* no chairmen of the board or queens!" I fairly shouted at them. "Have I not told you that often enough? Have I not freely imparted my meager knowledge of the lore and craft of our immortal tribe? When it comes to the spirit thereof, this each of us must find in our own hearts. So the only words I can speak in homage to the spirit of Pater Pan are those

478

which come from mine now, and those I have already spoken. True Children of Fortune have no chairmen of the board or kings. True Children of Fortune seek not after chairmen of the board or kings. Certainement, no true Child of Fortune would *wish to be* a chairman of the board or king!"

And I turned my back and slowly began to walk away.

For a long moment, I heard only silence, and then the faint far-off music of one of our musical troupes piping its way back to the carnival from the streets of the town far below.

And then I heard subdued stirrings and murmurings, as the song of the Yellow Brick Road once more reached their ears. As the music played its way closer, up piped the unmistakable voice of Kim.

"Come, let us remove this sad reminder of a joyful spirit to a more seemly venue, nē, and then what is there for it but to carry on with our enterprises, for while Children of Fortune have no chairmen of the board or kings, when it comes to ruegelt, neither can we expect to be showered with corporate or royal largesse!"

At this, there was laughter, and the scurrying of feet soon thereafter, so that I had no need to look back out of fear that I had let the torch that Pater Pan had entrusted to my care fall through unready hands. Rather did I join his spirit in one last private smile between us, in the knowledge that under the constraints with which our universe confronts us, I had found the true ending to the only tale there is to tell, the one which allows we Gypsy Jokers to have the last laugh.

I did not stop walking until I had reached the pinnacle of the hill above the encampment, where I sat alone staring out to sea until twilight began to gather, and Alpa's sun came down in sheets of brilliant purple and umber light painted across the sky and sheening on the tropic ocean. One by one, the stars began to come out as, one by one, the lights of the town below began to enliven the gathering night.

Not far below me, the camp of the Children of Fortune greeted the evening with music and laughter and the sounds of gay young voices, and this was as it should be, for the King of the Gypsies and the Prince of the Jokers should be toasted with his own sacraments, and not lugubriously mourned.

I could not but smile at the music of the carnival as it wafted up toward me on the onshore breeze. Yet, as I sat there, I found myself staring up at the stars beckoning bravely and bright to me up there in the universal night, each a mighty sun, and scattered like a handful of seed among them, the far-flung worlds of men.

And I knew that the tale of the wanderjahr of Sunshine Shasta Leonardo had come to its end.

Once I was the little Moussa, the wide-eyed waif who had wandered into the beginning of her story, once I was Sunshine the ruespieler seeking only her own Yellow Brick Road, once I had been the Pied Piper of the Bloomenveldt who had learned to care for the spirits of her unwanted charges, and at last had I not become the true teller thereof when I passed along the torch?

As I sat there in the gathering darkness reflecting thusly, Kim came puffing up the hillside to join me, and I found myself welcoming his company, welcoming what I was pleased to see in him of the Child of Fortune that I had been.

"You are looking at the stars, mi maestra?" he said, hunkering down beside me. "Soon you will be out among them, nē?"

I regarded him with some amazement. "I had not realized your varied talents included the reading of minds!"

Kim beamed his pleasure at my approval, but shrugged off taking credit for this mental feat. "Why would you tarry long on Alpa?" he declared rhetorically. "You have no true lover to keep you here, and he who would gladly have served as same will himself soon enough be gone."

"You plan to leave Alpa, Kim?" I exclaimed in some surprise.

"Did you not leave the planet of your own birth to follow the path of the Child of Fortune on grander worlds? Vraiment, have you not taught me the ruespieler's craft, and have I not a certain skill when it comes to commercial enterprise? Florida is a pleasant enough little town for the enfants of Alpa to play at being Children of Fortune in, but once I have earned my passage therein, I will be off on my true wanderjahr out among the stars!"

"You seek my approval for this venture?" I said, for he smiled at me with hopeful expectation.

"Surely you will not deny me the same!" he declared. "Surely you will not now seek to claim me with a profession of undying carnal love?"

480

I burst out laughing and could not help but hug him to me, nor could I help but feel pleasure at the touch of his frankly delighted flesh, nor could I help but be charmed by the rising of his young manhood against me.

I pulled a distance away from him but kept my arms on his shoulders as I stared into his lustful eyes. "Now, it is *you* who are rejecting *my* advances?" I said, toying my lips with my tongue, and grinning at his newfound and entirely becoming shyness.

"Do I take your meaning right, mi maestra?" he asked in quite a smaller voice.

"Seeing as how we are both soon to depart from this planet, mayhap never to meet again, and seeing as how I see in you a brother spirit, you need only summon the courage to give over showering me with honorifics and address me lover to lover as Sunshine like a proper natural man, and you shall forthwith have your heart's desire in this romantic venue, out here above the ocean and beneath the stars," I told him, setting my hands on my hips.

"Sunshine, Sunshine, Sunshine!" he yipped like a happy puppy, and then like puppies indeed, we were tumbling each other in the grass, as he sought to apprise himself of my intimate possibilities with more eager avidity than manly grace and skill.

Indeed even doffing our clothing was a matter of some confusion as Kim sought to undress us both at once while continuing to attempt to fondle me at every moment with both hands.

As for me, while my body was enjoying the sheer lustful avidity of this callow lover, my spirit took pleasure as well in the very charming naïveté thereof, which both gave the lie to Kim's boasts of tantric expertise, and made me appreciate the chutzpah thereof with all the more delight.

When after a good deal of this erotic tussle and groping, we had at last revealed our nakedness to each other, Kim hesitated, propped up on his elbows atop me, regarding me with some trepidation, even as the pride of his lingam sought to enter my yoni with a will of its own.

"Quelle problem, männlein?" I asked him as lightly as I could.

"Ah ... oh ... the truth of it is that I am given to hyperbole!" he stammered. "No doubt you will be entirely appalled to learn that I may not be quite the adept of the tantra that I sometimes pretend . . ."

I laughed, and pulled him to me, and rolled myself over onto him. "In this moment, no other declaration could so inflame my passions, liebchen," I told him, and became the director of our tantric figure, taking matters firmly into my own hand until they became firmer still, and proceeding to give him a series of lessons in the art I would hope he would not soon forget.

Yet though I sought to apprise him of the variety of possible tantric figures in some detail and at great length, I eschewed the employment of my ring of Touch, for on the one hand I had no desire to leave him pining away for the memory of an impossible magic moment of ecstasy which the natural favors of no other woman could ever match, and on the other hand, I would have been a villainess to overmaster such manfully admitted innocence with secret electronic powers.

Indeed, it was as we lay in each other's arms there, after he at length had absorbed sufficient schooling to overmaster my natural woman with phallic prowess that brought me to a single soul-satisfying cusp, that in my heart I relegated the Touch to my father's commerce. Let it be used to treat dysfunction or rouse the jaded energies of the erotically feckless, in the service of whom it would no doubt be a great boon. But as for this natural woman, never more would I intrude such unnatural machineries into open-hearted intimacy with the natural man.

After a time we dressed, and stood there together for a few last moments, looking out across the nearby lights of the encampment, and the more distant lights of the town, and the lights in the sky above the ocean, brighter and more distant still.

"Mayhap our paths will cross again out there sometime," Kim said. He laughed gaily. "And if they do not, rest assured I will remember this night with you always."

"And indeed you certainly should, my little Gypsy Joker!" I declared. We laughed together, and with that we parted, for certainement there is no better loverly farewell than that.

I watched Kim descending the hillside toward the Gypsy Joker encampment, toward his true wanderjahr, toward the Yellow Brick Road upon which I had first set foot a Child of Fortune's lifetime ago, until he had entirely disappeared from my sight into the carnival where his borning spirit belonged.

Then I began descending the other side of the mountain toward the town below and my future life in the worlds of men beyond. There was a spring in my step and no regret in my heart.

For it was in that moment that I chose to name myself Wendi Shasta Leonardo, in homage to my friend and mentor and to my own new version of the heroine of the ancient mythos, but in homage as well to this very future self who now half a lifetime later looks back on her Golden Summer as a Child of Fortune, and in the spirit thereof, transcribes these, the last words of her tale.